PANTECH TRILOGY

YA DYSTOPIAN

F. LOCKHAVEN
M.A. OWENS

Editors
André MacLean
Katie Siciak
Marcus Bender
Grace Lockhaven

TWISTED KEY
publishing
2023

First Printing: 2023

ISBN 978-1-63911-085-8

Twisted Key Publishing, LLC
www.twistedkeypublishing.com

Ordering Information:
Special discounts are available on quantity purchases by corporations, associations, educators, and others. For details, contact the publisher at the above listed address.

U.S. trade bookstores and wholesalers: Please contact Twisted Key Publishing, LLC by email twistedkeypublishing@gmail.com.

TABLE OF CONTENTS

PANTECH CHRONICLES
SHADOWFALCON
BOOK 1

PANTECH CHRONICLES
INSURRECTION
BOOK 2

PANTECH CHRONICLES
PANDEMIC
BOOK 3

In Memory Of
Dr. Linda Joyce Taylor
June 22, 1948 - October 30, 2021

Dr. Taylor, in addition to being a great vet, was a wonderful human being by any measure. She was a fierce advocate for animals and inspired the very protagonists you'll find in this novel. She was also the veterinarian who took care of the real animals that make up the cast of the Detective Trigger series, including Trigger himself. Whenever I brought him into her office for a checkup, she would announce that "The Detective" was there to see her. Her passing has left an empty space in many hearts that we'll never quite fill.

Thanks for everything, Dr. Taylor. You were awesome.

M.A. Owens

PANTECH CHRONICLES

SHADOWFALCON

BOOK 1

CHAPTER 1

I began to open my eyes reluctantly before changing my mind and tightening them shut again. Normally, I'd leap from my bed the moment consciousness became mine, but last night, unlike most nights, my dream had been something pleasant. When this happened, I liked to lie still and hope to fall back into it again, picking up where I left off. Not an exciting, action-packed adventure, or a romantic getaway with my dream guy, or counting my limitless wealth. No. In this dream, I was in a world alone. I rested on the baking hot sands outside my village, no bloodthirsty insects swarming my body to shower me in stings and bites, no shouts to take me from—

"Taylor, what are you doing? Get up. Your brother is already packed and ready!" The shout echoed both inside and outside of my mind. My beautiful mother stood over me when I wrenched apart my eyelids to look up at her. Well, beautiful on the outside at least, with her jet-black hair, narrow brown eyes, and skin far too pale to be suited for the desert. Her hair and her heart matched, I think, but I dare not say so.

"I'm up. It's the first time I've overslept in months, so cut me a break, huh?" I protested, though realizing I'd used up pointless oxygen in doing so no sooner than I'd finished the sentence.

"You haven't slept in. Your brother's just up early since he cares about making a good impression on others. You know that our guests are due any day now." She shoved her hand in my hair, her fingers getting stuck after just a few inches of brushing through. "You've been gifted with beauty, the best of both your father and I, and you can't even be bothered to take care of your hair." She pushed my head away roughly.

"Right, gotta look pretty for digging up terror ants and stitching up wounded pets. Thanks, Mother."

She frowned a deep, harsh frown that made her forehead wrinkle. "You never know who will walk by, or whose eye you'll catch when you return, or whose pet you're treating. If you fail your exam and get stuck here, your first goal should be to marry well."

I tensed. I'd gotten to hear this lecture several times a week for the past few years, and since I'd turned seventeen, almost every day. To say I was sick of it would be an understatement. At seventeen, I was already our village's veterinarian. I'd become an apprentice at fourteen and should've studied for ten years, but my teacher died suddenly of a stroke a few months ago, leaving me to take over and the apprentice who'd started a year later than me, Cara, to become my apprentice. I could take care of myself.

At one time, my father had been a renowned inventor and teacher, but our…'guests,' as Mother liked to call them, had put a stop to that. His inventions interfered with our village's adversity rating because they made everyone's lives easier, and he was warned that if he continued, they would have to raise the threshold for passing the exams, something our 'guests' came by to administer yearly and allowed every eighteen-year-old the opportunity to be selected for service by PanTech, and leave the adversity zone. Father became more and more bitter. It was hard to be around him nowadays. Even the most minor accident would send him into a tirade of expletives and combinations of expletives. Sometimes new ones, as though he was determined to at least be able to continue inventing something.

"Okay," I said to my mother, taking a deep breath. "I'll comb my hair. Now, could I have some privacy? I'd like to get dressed, so my dear brother doesn't have to keep waiting." I felt a tinge of guilt hit me the moment I finished the sentence. It was meant to be a sarcastic remark to irritate Mother, but my brother had always been good to me. Better than anyone else had, at least, even though he was a fool and a coward without equal. Well, except for maybe Mother, with her 'guests', and 'we should be thankful' and all of her phrases that made Father's face contort into shapes that might resemble a volcano if it were trying desperately not to erupt despite desperately wanting to…if volcanos were human, I guess.

"Good. Maybe try speaking a bit more lady-like too. I know you think you're above it because you've been lucky in life, but if you are fortunate enough to experience greater adversity, your beauty and your manners may be all you have. Sharpen them while you can."

I rubbed my forehead, wondering if my face was taking on the strange, furious, involuntary shapes my father's did when she said things like this to him. I hoped I had better self-control than he did in that respect. "You're right, of course. Thank you for your advice." I opened the door, encouraging her to leave as politely but as quickly as I thought she'd let me away with. Thankfully, it worked. She sighed, nodded to me, and stepped quickly through the door, which I promptly closed behind her, calling up every ounce of my will not to slam it so hard it exploded into ten thousand splinters. At least, that's what I imagined it would do if I could manage to convert my irritation directly into physical strength.

Closing the door left me staring into the mirror that hung from it, cracked, from the times I hadn't been able to summon that willpower. Maybe I'd inherited my temperament from my father, the way my brother did from our mother. I'd inherited his dark skin as well, but unfortunately not his hair and eyes. Every time I looked into this mirror, I saw a darker-skinned version of Mother, looking back at me and judging me for being such a disappointment. I'm not sure why I cared. Would Mother really be happy if I put on makeup, spent an hour brushing my hair, and walked around town pretending to struggle with carrying some tiny something until a handsome, rich boy tore it from my hands, steadied me on my feet, and kissed me deeply before promising I'd never want for anything ever again? My cheeks warmed a little at the thought, but I snapped back into reality, scolding myself for getting caught up in the scene that played out in my mind. Stupid imaginary handsome stranger and his perfect kissing technique, muscled arms, and long wavy hair blowing in the desert wind. Grrr! I'll punch him in the face if I ever see him…maybe. I shook my head violently and slammed my open hands into my cheeks. *Pull it together, Taylor.*

I threw open my closet doors. My tiny wardrobe of highly practical and very unladylike outfits filled the tiny space, including the very unpretty one I designed to slow down a terror ant attack in the case that my latest technique of harvesting their hives didn't work or didn't work well enough. It was more of a psychological trick I played on myself than anything else. After all, it only took a few terror ant bites to leave you hunched over a bucket for days heaving out your guts and wishing your mother had never given birth to you in the first place, or that you could at least swap pains with her in the process. There was nothing quite like a terror ant bite. I was tempted to describe it as a hot nail being driven into the skin, but that would stop hurting after a few moments, whereas the terror ant's bite didn't for days. The tingling and numbness lasted weeks, sometimes months, in older bite victims. The lucky ones, that is. More than a few bites would land you in the grave. Your hollow bones, at least. They made quick work of everything else. I had to give my brother credit for being willing to go out and do this with me. Bravery and stupidity are siblings, my father used to say. It ended up being an ironic statement in his case.

I threw on the outfit and flung open my door before realizing I had forgotten to comb my hair. I quickly closed it again and spent the next few seconds brushing my comb through my hair painfully, completely disregarding the 'proper' technique my mother showed me. I didn't have all morning, after all. Correction, the morning was all I had. Once it became light out, the terror ants were more active, and this would be suicide. It could be regardless, but we could at least take the proper precautions to put the odds in our favor. A terror ant hive was such a delicacy to PanTech's proper citizens that it could supply my clinic and feed my family for weeks. Apparently, you could only find them here, or so I guessed. It's not like we knew anything about the other adversity zones. Or how many there were. We assume that there must be several, considering we didn't recognize any of the employees who came by to check in our cozy little village to ensure our adversity level was still optimal. For our own good, of course.

My second attempt to leave my room worked out better. Just outside my door, rounding the corner, was the common room where my mother was preparing food. My brother was sitting at the table, a small piece of meat on his plate. He'd remembered my instructions, at least. If you ate a full meal while trying to wear these clothes, things would get unbearably tight very quickly. The longest I'd ever been able to wear it when testing it was a few hours, and by then, you're up against prolonged restricted breathing or a heat stroke, both of which were preferred death to terror ant bites. "Thanks for being ready," I offered. "We'd better get going."

My father's attention was held by a mess of papers on the large wooden table, glancing over them while finishing a long puff on his smoking pipe. Preparing the upcoming school year's curriculum in something, I suppose. He was brilliant, so it could've been anything. But, aside from my brother and I, he didn't have the heart to teach anymore. "I still think you're crazy for doing this, Tay, and even crazier for dragging your poor brother along.

When you get back, I'll need you to deliver these to the school. I'm nearly done now, so I expect I'll be done with them by then." He never looked up at us or took his eyes off his papers. He only took another long pull from his pipe and blew out a cloud of smoke that filled the air with a pleasant cactus berry aroma. Father was clever with language. It was frowned upon to offer your children too many kind or encouraging words. It would affect their adversity, after all, to have parents who were too kind. But, in that one simple phrase, implying he expected us to be back soon, what he'd really said was, *You're brave. I believe in you. You'll succeed, and I'll see you soon.*

"Sure, I'll drop them off on my way to the clinic," I said. "Ferris, are you ready?"

"Born ready. Born ready to get this suit off as soon as possible, at least," Ferris replied, wiggling uncomfortably in his chair.

I sighed. "If you're going to start complaining this early, you're going to really love it when we start walking around in them. Or when you have to put the mask on. Or when the first terror ant crawls—"

"Okay! I get it. Try not to be too grateful. You'll hurt yourself." His tone said he meant it as an insult, but his smile said the opposite. Only I saw the smile.

"Alright, you two need to leave. I have work to do," Father said. "You said you needed the cooler morning air before the sunrise for this to be safest, so you better get going." *Good luck,* he was most likely thinking.

I took a deep breath, or at least what would have to substitute for a deep breath, grabbed my rucksack with the supplies I needed next to the door, and lit our lantern. I stopped just before opening the door and took a long look around. I was probably crazy for doing this, and who knew what my brother was thinking. The two of us looked at each other. I placed my hand on the door handle for a long moment, my way of offering him one last chance to change his mind. He didn't.

We flung open the door and ventured out into the dark, open desert to tempt fate for profit.

CHAPTER 2

"Did we really have to cover ourselves in that nasty-smelling meat grease?" Ferris whispered behind me.

"No. I mean, you didn't have to. It would take you all day to get the suit on, and your sweat would attract the ants. Be my guest and try something different next time," I replied at my normal volume, making no effort to mask my irritation at even being asked such a stupid question.

"Alright, sheesh. You're the expert. I'm just making conversation." He whispered, as though he couldn't help himself but be polite, even in the dark when no one else was likely to hear him.

"Well…," I started, "you could try asking useful questions. Like maybe ask me why I chose to use the grease instead of any one of the many more pleasant oils Mother keeps around the house. You could also ask me why the sugar water line in the sand works to draw them from their nest. You could ask—"

"You're scared, aren't you? Me too," he offered, whispering even more quietly this time, his tone softening. He was the only person who could make me angry and remind me why I loved him in the span of a few seconds. Well, aside from Father, when he had one of his verbal tirades. It was hard to tell at a glance that we were brother and sister. His hair was rough, like Father's, and he kept it tied in a tight ponytail. His skin was a softer brown, much closer to Mother's, and he had Father's emerald green eyes. He also had Father's natural affinity for language. If he said the wrong thing, he knew the right thing to say to instantly make it better, no matter who he was speaking to. He hadn't lost his temper and started shouting foul language for all the village to hear. At least, not yet. Maybe that would happen when he got older like they say it did with Father.

"You…," I started to say, in my usual snappy tone I often took with him, that he rarely deserved. I took a breath and started again. "You're right…I'm sorry. I'm a little on edge. And yeah, I'm a little scared. Have you ever seen a body swarmed by terror ants?"

"Unfortunately…yeah, I have."

"And you still came?" I laughed nervously.

"I know *you* have, and you're still going."

We both went quiet and continued to walk through our dark village by the dim lantern light. We could see not a single toy or a sign that children existed. They were carefully hidden away indoors. I'd heard of some parents going as far as hiding them in the walls or under the floor's stone. Mother forbade them in our house, but Father always found a way to sneak things to us that *technically* weren't toys. I remembered the first doll he made for me. Anatomy reference, as he called it. You're never too young to study the human body, especially if you may have a future in medicine. Of course, it turned out that I would be interested in medicine, but the doll I just played with in my room. After he'd given me another, I made them talk to each other quietly. I still remember the day Mother caught me by listening through my door and meant to throw them into the fire. Father managed to stop her. He told her it was an exercise he'd given me to simulate human interaction in the role of a physician trying to diagnose a patient. There was no point in facing adversity as a child if you were too uneducated to be of use to PanTech.

That was when he still pretended, of course. When he was still trying to appease Mother. Now, he rarely did. He'd call PanTech every name in the book and say he didn't care if they executed him, before he'd finally calm down and return to his work as though nothing ever happened.

I shook my head vigorously, flinging the thoughts from my mind. The last thing I needed was for my head to be in the clouds. "I use the grease from rotten meat because the stench slows down the ants. They like sweat and sweet smells. Sweat is how they target their prey. They aren't scavengers, so if you smell rotten, they think twice before swarming you. It buys you a little time if you rile them up. Not long. A few seconds at best before they do…whatever it is they do to determine you are, in fact, alive and swarm you anyway. I've tested this with animal carcasses. Sometimes they hesitate as long as five seconds. And, of course, these suits are too tight to get into otherwise."

"Ah, right, that makes sense. That explains the sugar water too," Ferris said, in his normal voice, I assume accidentally. He snapped his head around quickly to make sure no one had heard him and might be upset that he'd disturbed them. This is something I did not like about my brother. He was good at making everyone like him, but he cared far too much about whether or not they did.

"See, you're getting it. Now we just have to not die. I saw a hive not far from here, just out of sight of the village that needed to be dealt with anyway. Do you remember how to put the rest on?"

He started to twist to see inside his pack but realized he wouldn't easily be able to and just swung the pack around in front of him instead. He pilfered through it a moment. "Gloves, mask, wraps to cover the gaps. We're going to roast in these, Taylor."

I nodded. "Yep, if we drag our feet," I said, slowing my pace. "It should be around here somewhere. We have to be careful not to get too close. We need to stop just at the edge of the lantern light."

I wished now that I'd practiced more with spotting these in the dark by dim light. If we accidentally stepped on a hive, we'd be dead by the time we realized the ants bit us. Figures I'd overlook a detail *that* important....

"We have to be getting close," I said. Now I was the one whispering. "We're taking baby steps from here on out. Help me look for them. There's usually one or two nearby, even at night." I squinted and looked side to side as I walked, mere inches with each step. "I don't see anything yet." Suddenly, Ferris grabbed my arm hard. I turned to see what had alarmed him, but he didn't speak. He only pointed. I followed his finger's direction and saw one of the little demons crawling just at the edge of the light. "We'll put our hat and gloves on. You go first. I'll watch it. They never spend more than a few minutes out of the hive before switching guard with a new ant."

"Got it." He opened his pack, pulled out the gloves, and began working them on, taping them up at the small overlap at the wrist, before struggling several minutes with the hat. "Nice thinking with the mesh hood. I'm not sure how we could get bit through this thick leather either."

"Don't be so sure...," I said. "Keep an eye on it." Once I completed my suit, I took one more look up to the sky. Good, still pitch dark.

"Over there," he said, pointing a few feet from where I'd last seen the ant. "I saw it crawl into the hive over there, after another crawled out."

I dropped my pack on the ground, pulling out two small clay bowls and a large bottle filled with sugar water. "Stay here," I whispered. "I have to isolate that one, quickly. Get the shovel ready. Remember, right along the lines of the water. Hard, just along the edge, then throw it aside. Three good times should do it, then run like your life depends on it. It does."

He nodded, bent down, and started connecting the two parts of his shovel. I began to drag my feet toward the ant hive in even, smooth motions. In my previous experiments, I'd found that stepping alerted them the quickest. The vibrations underground set them off. Things sliding along the surface of the sand alerted them much more slowly. I stopped a foot or so away from the ant, swallowed hard, and brought the bowl down as quickly as I could, trapping the ant beneath. I dragged the bowl a few feet further from the nest, pushed it down into the sand, and let go. After a few tense moments of watching the nest open, I pulled the top from the bottle and began pouring the water in a narrow line a few inches from the nest's opening, on the side opposite Ferris and I. I went back and forth for a moment until the bottle was finally emptied. I threw it back toward Ferris, and he caught it, tossing my second bowl toward me, which I also caught. I slid my feet back a few steps and waited for the second ant to cycle out. What was taking so long?

I glanced back to Ferris, who shrugged his shoulders. I held up my hand, signaling for him to wait or be calm, but maybe I was projecting my own nervousness. They usually didn't take this long to come out. Did something go wrong with the water? Too much sugar? Not enough?

On top of everything else, I'd begun sweating profusely, which just added to my anxiety. Finally, an ant popped out and was immediately distracted by the sugary water pooled on top of the sand. Again, I did the same thing, capturing it under my bowl and pulling it over next to the other. I stood next to them for a moment, watching the opening. I held up my hand, ready to signal Ferris. Counting in my head.

Nineteen, eighteen, seventeen, sixteen.

I slid my feet back, slowly making my way back toward Ferris.

Fifteen, fourteen, thirteen, twelve.

I held up my hand, looking at him over my shoulder. He gripped the shovel tightly and nodded.

Eleven, ten, nine, eight.

I bent down, sliding my bottle back into my pack.

Seven, six, five, four.

I picked up my pack with my free hand, sliding it off one shoulder.

Three, two, one.

I brought my hand down in a sharp motion, and Ferris sprinted toward the nest, burying the shovel into the ground, then turning out the sand beside him. One down. He plunged the shovel down a second time. The angle was too sharp. No!

Ants swarmed out of the hive in all different directions.

"Drop it and run!" I screamed.

He tossed the sand aside and plunged the shovel down a third time.

"I said drop it, idiot! Forget it!"

The third shovel went in smoothly, and he turned up the hive, roughly the size of a human head. Ants were already swarming onto the shovel from the nest and would be all over him soon after.

"Drop it and run!" I shouted to the very limits of my voice, even though he was just a few feet away from me. This time, at least, he listened. He threw the shovel aside and bolted in my direction. I grabbed his pack from the ground and tossed it toward him before turning myself. We wouldn't have to sprint far. Just enough to get out of their range. We'd still be able to see the hive, but terror ants lost interest quickly beyond a certain distance.

After a few seconds of running, I stopped and looked over my shoulder. They'd stopped following us and instead swarmed around the nest with all the fury that comes with having your home unearthed when you were one of the most dangerous insects in the desert. They wanted something to pay.

"They'll swarm around for the morning, but they'll abandon the hive by noon," I said in my calmest voice before turning and punching him with everything I had in his shoulder.

"Ouch, what was that for?" he shouted, jumping back.

"Stupid! Stupid!" I screamed, punching him again, and drew back to hit him again before freezing in place. "Oh no…don't move. Don't even breathe."

He knew what that meant, and he became a statue. There was an ant on his shoulder…and another on his leg. I drew back my open hand and smashed the one on his shoulder.

He shrieked a full second later. At first, I thought I'd hit him too hard, but then I realized….

"Stay calm. Don't move!" I said, circling him to get a better angle on the ant on his leg. It bit through the leather!

"Get it! Get it!" He was trembling now, and his voice gave away the tears. Fear, or pain, both of which were understandable. I dropped to my knees and quickly swatted it before it could bite again.

"Let me check the rest of you. You stupid, stupid idiot!"

"It burns. Oh, man. I'm going to die." His trembling intensified.

I didn't want to think about it, but there had been villagers who died from a single bite, but none of them as big as my brother.

"You're not going to die," I said, still looking him over. "Okay. Okay…I think that's it. Next time when I say to drop the shovel, drop it!" I yelled, suppressing the urge to punch him again.

"I…," he began speaking but didn't continue, starting to sway. His head lowered.

"Ferris?"

His head snapped back up again. "I don't think I can walk with my leg. I can't feel it. Go get help."

I eyed the rising sun. As much as I loved the sun, I hated the sight of it now. I dropped my pack and ripped off my hat and gloves. "There's no time. Between the bite and the heat, you'll be dead before I make it back. Drop your pack. We have to beat the sunlight. Climb on my back."

"No, Tay. It's too far. That'll kill you too. Just go."

"Now!" I shouted, punching him again in the shoulder, though I held back a little this time.

He winced, though I knew it wasn't from me. I ripped off his hat and turned my back to him, kneeling.

"Ferris, hurry."

We stood there like that a moment in a stalemate of stubbornness, but he finally gave in, collapsing onto my back. Could I actually carry him all the way back? I could barely stand up with him. He was so much bigger than me. No. No, I would have to. I'd have to find a way.

I stared into the distance toward our village, not even in sight, my body already feeling like it was roasting beneath the breaking dawn. I wrapped my arms behind his knees and cried out as I shrugged to my feet. I gritted my teeth, closed off my mind from the heat and the pain, and took my first steps.

CHAPTER 3

I had the same dream again, lying on the hot desert sands, not a sound other than the light breeze passing over me. I stretched my limbs, grabbing handfuls of sand and letting it fall between my fingers. I was startled this time when I looked up and saw Ferris there. He was standing there, smiling, the wind blowing through his hair. I smiled back and tried to speak to him, but no sound escaped my mouth.

"You did this," he said, still smiling.

I tried to answer, but again, I couldn't speak.

"You did this," he repeated.

I panicked, grabbing my throat. I tried to stand but couldn't sit up. Ants swarmed up around me, but they passed over me, climbing up Ferris's legs, then his torso.

"You did this," he said again.

No, I wanted to scream. *I'm sorry,* is what I should have tried to say.

The ants bit at him ferociously, tearing his skin, but still, he smiled at me.

"You did this."

I opened my mouth to scream, but there was nothing. Finally, my voice came to me, as well as my strength. I bound up from the desert floor with a shriek, but something grabbed me—something I couldn't see.

"Tay…," the voice was distant. Muffled.

I fought again to get free, screaming for Ferris to run.

"Tay!" The voice was closer this time. Father?

"Tay! Calm down. I'm here. You're alright," came his voice, like sunbeams piercing a deep dark abyss. The desert faded around me.

"Father? I'm sorry…I thought I…Where's Ferris?" I shouted.

"Try to calm yourself. You're delirious from the heat. You must take water. Sit, please," my father pleaded as he offered me an open canteen.

I sat back onto my bed and took the water from him, drinking it with a thirst I hadn't felt in as long as I could remember. I finished the entire thing in less than half the time it should have taken. "Ferris. Is he okay?" I said more calmly this time.

"He is. He's not as tough as you, but he's tougher than you realize. He woke up about an hour ago, much in the way you did, raving about his sister." He laughed at this, for some reason. "Gather yourself, and go see him. I'm sure he already heard your screaming and knows you're awake."

I nodded. I'm sure he did. I was so unbelievably embarrassed for screaming in front of Father like that. I lowered my head and smelled my arm, then pulled my hair in and inhaled deeply, looking up at him with my eyebrows narrowed.

"Your mother," he said, pulling the unspoken question from my mind. I wasn't sure whether I should be thankful or angry. My hair was expertly combed and shampooed with the same fragrances Mother always used. My hands were soft with scented lotions, and I had a sinking feeling she'd put makeup on me, but when I leaned to the side so that I could see the mirror on my door, I was relieved to see that she at least hadn't gone that far.

I touched my face and sighed.

Father gave me a firm slap on the shoulder. "For once, I agreed with your mother. We could smell you coming before we saw you," he said with a broad smile. "Come. You seem to be feeling well enough." He gave me his hand and helped me stand. I still felt sick from the heat, and my memory was still a haze.

I looked down and sighed again. "Such a beautiful dress Mother has put me in," I said sarcastically.

"It is," he agreed, but without a hint of sarcasm, before motioning for me to follow him. I did.

Around the corner from my room was Ferris's. As Father pushed open the door, I saw Mother and our village doctor applying a salve to his wound.

"Knock, next time," the giant man growled. If you had any number of guesses as to what Doc Norman's profession was, solely based on appearance, you certainly wouldn't guess that he was a doctor. His beard was larger and thicker than Father's but just as white. Father wasn't a small man, but Doc Norman stood a full head taller, with broader shoulders and a barrel chest.

"Sorry, Doc," I said in my most ladylike voice I could muster. I didn't want my father flying off the handle and getting into an argument with Doc while tending to Ferris. "Thank you for tending to Ferris." Father raised a brow, but Mother looked as though she would explode with pride. This surprised me. I couldn't remember

Mother ever looking at me that way, and it hurt. It also made me regret that I'd spoken that way just to save Father's blood pressure. Then again, maybe that's what she was impressed with. She'd been telling me more lately that I needed to use my feminine gifts to persuade and stop behaving like I was her second son. Remembering that, the warm feeling that was there for only a moment quickly faded.

"Sorry indeed," Doc grumbled. "You should be caned for dragging your brother out there so—"

"I dragged him back too, didn't I?" I interrupted in my regular tone.

"Yes. So you nearly got Ferris killed, but you also saved his life. I hope you don't show that same kindness to my wife's spike-head lizard when she brings him to see you tomorrow."

"Your wife's spike-head lizard will probably follow my instructions better."

He looked down at Ferris and grunted. Or it could've been a laugh. Just about everything sounded like a grunt with Doc. "That I can believe." He looked to my mother, holding up the canister he'd scooped the salve from. "Twice a day for pain. I can do nothing for the healing, but that will happen on its own. He's young and strong."

She bowed her head. "Thank you, Doctor."

"Yes, thank you," Father added.

We stood silently for a moment before Father jabbed me with his elbow and cleared his throat.

I bowed my head. "Thank you, and please send my regards to your wife," I said, in my sweeter voice again. I could practically feel Mother beaming from where she sat on my brother's bed.

Suddenly, Ferris's arm shot up from the bed, pointing at me. "What has that feminine creature done to my sister?"

I gritted my teeth. "Shut up," I shouted. "I should've left you out there to feed the ants!" I turned quickly, outpacing my father's arm that had reached out to grab for me, and slammed the door behind me. I ran to my room and slammed that door, too, causing the mirror to fall off and shatter onto the floor before I could catch it. I put my hands over my mouth, sat on my bed, and started sobbing quietly. Why did I react that way? I hated when I lost my temper that way. He was clearly joking, and I knew he had to be in so much pain, even with Doc's salve. He was trying to make me laugh. It was Mother I was angry with, not him. But…I wasn't sure she deserved it either.

A knock came. "Tay." Father's voice.

"Just a minute."

"Come to the table when you're ready. I need to speak with you."

I didn't answer, just wiped my face with my sleeves and sniffed before climbing onto the floor and picking up the pieces of glass. I had intended to come in here and change, but now that I'd calmed down, I thought better of it. I had doubled my appointments yesterday so I could retrieve the hive today without a limit on time.

Time.

Time?

Time!

It was already past noon, surely. It would spoil if it stayed out any longer. I dropped the glass onto the table beside my bed and rushed from the room toward the front door.

"Tay," Father said firmly.

I stopped short of the door. "I'm sorry. I'll be back. I have to get the hive before it spoils!" I reached out and grabbed the handle.

"Stop!" he shouted.

"I said I'm sorry. I'll be back soon."

"It's late in the day. It would've been too late," he said.

"Oh no! Wait…*would've* been?"

He smiled and reached under the table, pulling out a large sphere wrapped in cloth.

I clapped my hands together and ran over to him, hugging his neck tightly.

He chuckled with surprise. "Aren't you glad I was so nosey when you explained all of this to your brother?"

"You're the best," I said genuinely.

"Me? Who said anything about me?" He raised his brow.

"You don't mean…," I said, my eyes widening.

"Don't you think you should—"

"Apologize? Probably…."

He narrowed his eyes at me.

I sighed. "Absolutely. Definitely. Big time."

I stood up straight when Doc walked up to us, and he stood in front of me, grabbing my head roughly, taking the other hand to pull up one of my eyelids. He placed the back of his hand on my cheek, then grabbed my hand and looked at my fingernails.

"Light sweating. Normal skin. Fingernails are showing signs of dehydration," I said.

Doc grunted. "You may behave like an animal sometimes, Taylor, but you're a human, or so your parents keep insisting. I'm the human doctor." He patted me on the head. "Get some rest, and drink as much water as you can keep down. Don't exert yourself anymore today."

He stepped out the door without another word.

I looked to Father. "Unwrap it," I said.

"The hive?"

"Yes. Can you think of a grander apology?"

"Guess not, but the chieftain pays by weight, doesn't he?"

I nodded. "It's alright. It'll just be a thin slice. Just enough for a taste."

He unfolded the cloth with a noticeable reluctance. I pulled a knife from a nearby drawer and slowly, very carefully, took a thin slice off the top. It was bright yellow and spongy, making a crackling noise as the knife slid back and forth. As I sliced, Father grabbed two plates.

"Four," I said, correcting him. "You better believe we're getting a taste too."

He went back and fetched two more plates, setting them close to the hive on the table.

"PanTech soldiers call this cake the 'Miracle of the Desert,'" I said to him as I finished the slice, balancing it carefully on the knife.

"Hmph!" He shrugged his shoulders. "I hope they eat an ant."

"The ants leave it," I said before pausing. "But, we can hope."

Placing the slice on one plate, I split it into four and divided it amongst the plates, picking up two of them.

"Grab the other two," I said before heading toward my brother's room and flinging open the door.

"Tay, I just wanted to say—" Ferris started.

"Sorry," I said, both cutting him off and, I realized, finishing his sentence. "I should be able to take a joke. Here, I thought we should have a taste before I take it to the chieftain." I handed a plate to him and Mother, then turned and took one from Father.

Ferris was the first to take a bite. "Woah! Totally worth getting bit by a terror ant. How can those evil things make something that tastes like this?"

Mother brought her piece to her lips, sliding it gently into her mouth.

"Well, I've found they like sweet things. I think they somehow refine it inside their body and condense the sugars over and over before regurgitating it into their nest material. Creates a flavor even PanTech hasn't been able to reproduce, apparently."

For a moment, I thought Mother would gag. She paused, but placing manners above all else, quickly resumed chewing before smiling. "Amazing. It's no wonder our guests love this so much."

Father winced, and I was afraid he was about to lose his temper, but he looked at me, grabbed the piece from his plate, and tossed it into his mouth. "It's good. Too good for them," he said.

Mother shook her finger at him. "Please don't say things like that. I've told you. What if someone hears you?"

"Let them hear me!" he shouted. "What more can they take from me? They already took my life's work."

"Your family. Your children's futures. We should be grateful to them. Living in adversity makes us better. It makes us strong."

He threw up his arms in frustration. "This again?"

I sighed, taking the piece from my plate, biting off half of it and chewing it slowly. I'd put all that work into scavenging for these in the past before I developed the extraction method, but not once had I tasted one. It was heavenly. It was like a cake, but a thousand times sweeter. The flavor seemed to melt into my tongue and didn't diminish as I held it there. I wondered for a moment how long a human could go without swallowing, but several shouts from outside our home startled me and I swallowed hard.

"They're here!" one said.

"Go and get changed. You'll want to look your best," another shouted.

Mother smiled. "Best you run as quickly as you can to get the rest of this to the chieftain so that he can present it to our guests."

I had been dreading this day for weeks.

CHAPTER 4

I quickly rewrapped the hive on the table and made for the door, barely slowing to turn the handle and spill out into the open world. Or at least what we were allowed to experience of the open world. PanTech decided just how open it was allowed to be. A wall encircled the entire area, several miles out from the village. I'd walked along its edges many times. It wasn't a wall that could be destroyed, or scaled, or even seen. Markers jutted from the sand to show where the invisible wall ran. Anything that wasn't human could pass through it, but if a human tried, they were pushed back and paralyzed temporarily. Father said that when he was younger, a boy had actually managed to run through it, so they modified it. Now, the effect started much sooner and became so strong that you would be completely incapacitated or dead long before you could sprint through it. "We knew that," he had said, "because a few still tried."

People like my mother didn't seem to understand that. I didn't care if adversity made me a better person. Maybe it did, but shouldn't I decide? Was I really expected to appreciate soldiers, our so-called 'guests,' to come by and make sure we didn't have too much food, or that people like Father hadn't found a way to make our lives easier, or people like me hadn't—

I shook my head, discarding the thought. I wasn't aware of any way they had of reading minds, but they had ways of knowing things that we often couldn't figure out. I focused my mind on what was in front of me.

Our home was almost on the other side of the village from the chieftain, so I would have to ignore the urge to vomit I had building in my stomach. I should have taken water with me, but in my haste, I'd forgotten. As I jogged through the village, most people outside moved in the opposite direction toward the village. I dodged and weaved through dead eyes and barely-beating hearts. They couldn't wait to see their masters and get their pat on the head. I was nearly knocked down by an elderly woman who rounded a corner at the same time as me as I finally made it in sight of the chieftain's home. She fell onto her back, dropping the basket of clothes she was carrying.

"Oh no! I'm sorry. Here, let me help you." I wrapped one arm under hers and helped her to her feet. I expected to get an earful, but she only chuckled.

"My, I guess my granddaughter was right about something exciting happening in the village."

"Aren't you going to go and see them?" I asked.

"Why? Are they going to help me with my laundry?"

"Never know. They might. They only seem to care about making your life harder if you're under eighteen or if you're making the life of someone under eighteen easier."

"Well then," she said, chuckling again. "It looks like they'll be glad I stepped out in front of you and almost made you fall. Don't worry about me, dear. Worry about yourself. You speak far too freely for a girl your age. You'll be safer keeping thoughts like that to yourself."

She was right, of course.

"I really have to be going. I'm sorry for running into you."

She waved her hand dismissively and gave me a push from behind. I bowed slightly, then ran the rest of the way to the chieftain's house, where he was waiting outside.

The chieftain was one of the only overweight men in the village, and I was convinced that PanTech had selected him specifically because they knew he would do a lousy job. In fact, that was almost a given, considering they punished adults for improving the youth's lives in any way. It was rare for him to be willing to pay for something like this, but he knew how much the soldiers loved their 'Miracle of the Desert,' and he leaped at the chance to kiss their feet.

He frowned at me when he noticed me arrive. "I thought you were coming earlier. Well, that will surely reduce your price-uh," he said, without giving me time to answer, turning to walk around behind his very nice house where he kept his scale, waving for me to follow.

The way he spoke annoyed me far more than anything about the way he looked like he was trying to change his accent deliberately so he wouldn't sound like the rest of us. The premise, of which, was so idiotic it was hard to be believed. The village is isolated. Where else exactly could he have come from? Aside from that, he was the son of the last village chieftain, so there really was no doubt. If you got him flustered enough, he'd revert to his usual way of speaking, but otherwise, he'll add this strange 'uh' sound to the end of a lot of his words. I also didn't like how he looked at the other girls in the village or me. At all. I found myself wishing I'd taken the time to change into my more practical clothes after all.

I handed him the hive carefully, and he placed it on the scale. "So, we're down from three hundred marks per pound to two hundred fifty," he said, shaking his head, as though he was disappointed in having to rip me off.

"Uh-huh," I said, still hoping to salvage the situation in some diplomatic way. What I'd rather do is pull out my knife and stick it in his neck, but as I have been told repeatedly lately, I was a lady now, and that would be very unladylike behavior.

"What would you say this paper weighs-uh…several ounces I'd imagine-uh."

"Not even an ounce," I said, crossing my arms.

"Right. Five ounces from the look of it-uh."

He peeled back the paper. "What's this? Did you take a slice-uh from it?"

I cocked my head. "What difference would that make? But no," I lied. "I did no such thing. It was like that when I pulled it from the sands."

"I see-uh. Remind me, how did you tell me you extracted it?"

"I didn't."

We were quiet for the next few moments. I hoped he was just as worried about me as I was about him. Even at two hundred fifty marks per pound, that would still keep the clinic and my home going for weeks if I really stretched it.

"Mmm, I don't believe you-uh. Two hundred marks per pound. It is both late and…damaged-uh." He wrinkled his nose and sniffed, then coughed without covering his mouth.

"With all due respect, sir, you won't be ready in time if we take much longer. I'd heard that our guests were making their way straight here first," I lied again.

I noticed that he'd taken his hand that had been down at his side and placed it on the table, curling his fingers under the bowl of the scale, lifting it ever so slightly to remove several ounces from the weight. "Right-uh. Let's see then. It looks like…umm…."

I rolled my eyes. "Sir, it looks like you accidentally moved up against the scale. You'd better take a step back while it settles on a number; otherwise it may add extra weight. I wouldn't want you to overpay."

He curled his lip. "Right-uh...," he backed a step away. We watched the number for a moment, and when the hand of the scale stopped moving, he turned and started dropping the small copper marks into a small sack, with his back facing me...of course. After a minute of clinging and clanging into the sack, he tied a string around it tightly, no doubt to discourage me from counting. The chieftain had plenty of money to spare. He no longer had to worry about his own adversity, and as long as someone was as self-centered as he was, PanTech couldn't care less. He certainly wasn't doing anything to make anyone's life more comfortable around here. You couldn't make him want to do that if you held a knife to his throat.

I took the sack from him. "Thanks. By the way, I spent weeks finding this one. They're getting to be rare. Probably going to need at least four hundred per pound next time."

"Four hun—" he shouted before stopping himself and lowering his voice again. "Four hundred per pound. Are you out of your mind?"

"No, and it was a lot of work carrying all of the gear out there and back, preparing it for transport, and getting it to you in time to present it to our guests. I also had to close my clinic today. I'm thinking about adding a delivery fee." I scratched my chin. "But you're a much more experienced businessman than I am. What do you think?"

He took a deep breath that sounded more like a wheeze. "Girl, I have ways of making sure your life here gets a lot harder, so you may not want to play that game with me."

He wasn't lying. He could, and PanTech would pat him on the back for it. *More adversity will make her better. You've done well,* they'd say.

I held up the sack. "I know you mean what you say. So do I. Good day to you, sir."

I bowed my head, turned, and left a little quicker than is customary, but I didn't want to give him time to think of whatever kind of sick thing he probably wanted to say. I hoped he wouldn't even ask me to get another hive for him. I'd improve the clinic going some other way. If Mother were here, she'd have been disappointed in me for disrespecting the chieftain that way and being so impulsive…why did I even care?

I made it almost back to our house when I bumped into someone again, my mind still in the clouds, worried the chieftain might retaliate.

"Hello," the voice said simply.

I'd stumbled backward and taken a moment to gather myself and look up. Standing before me was one of the PanTech soldiers. A handsome one, too, maybe a few years older than me. Shoulder-length blonde hair with bright blue eyes, and pale skin. Even more so than Mother's.

"I'm…," I choked on my words. Is he angry? You don't usually say hello that way to people you're mad at. Is it a test? Oh no, I should apologize quickly. "Sorry," I said finally. "I've been saying that a lot today."

"Hard day? Glad to see you're keeping it together."

"Umm…yeah! Really hard day," I said, scratching the back of my head and looking away.

I knew we weren't supposed to act like we were afraid of them because some of them found it insulting, but that was a tall order.

They wore armor that gleamed in the sun, with large rifles slung over their shoulder, a shorter sidearm on their hips. The armor made them look much larger than they were. One of the soldiers had told Mother about it one day when she was ogling his suit. It's filled with water, which some kind of portable power keeps cool. It's also harder than steel and a hundred times lighter. They wore helmets sometimes that I wasn't sure how they saw through. Some kind of equally advanced technology, I'm sure.

"I'll be going now. I'm sorry." I turned quickly to walk away, to take another route home.

He grabbed me by the arm as I turned, and my stomach felt like it would twist into a dozen knots all at once. I'd never been grabbed by one of them before. Usually, I managed to avoid them altogether.

"You'll need to come with me," he said.

CHAPTER 5

He led me by the arm, more like dragged me, for several minutes without a word.

"Hey," I said. "Do you know you're hurting my arm?"

He let go abruptly and turned to me. "Oh…right. The suit. Sorry, it enhances my strength. This is the first time I've worn one. Oh, I'm not supposed to apologize to citizens." He shook his head as if reprimanding himself inside his mind. "I'm Linus, by the way." He made a fist and sighed. "Not supposed to do that either. Mind if we just forget this whole exchange?"

I couldn't help but laugh. "Taylor."

"Nah, soldier, actually. Oh…you meant…wow, I'm really bad at this." He looked away, scratching the back of his head, his cheeks flush. Was he actually embarrassed?

I laughed again, resenting myself a bit for doing so. It must've been his first day. I'm sure after a few more, he'll be just as cruel and rude as most of the others once he'd received better training.

"Taylor. Nice meeting you. I was told to find any stragglers and lead them to the front of the village. Commander wants to give everyone a speech. No idea why, but it seemed important."

I nodded, hoping he'd trip over himself again and offer more bits of information, but he'd composed himself.

"Follow me, please," he said. Pausing for a moment, he corrected himself. "Follow me."

I obeyed. As much as this soldier seemed different from the others, I had to be on my guard. I found him almost hard not to like, but maybe that was a trick. Maybe acting nice to me and then taking me behind an unoccupied house and punching my face was some sick strategy to enhance my adversity. No, Father hated them for a good reason. I was right to, as well. I needed to keep on doing it.

We finally made it back to the front of the village, where he left me in the gathered crowd and took his place behind the commander.

"Just one?" she asked, looking at Linus as he approached.

"One, ma'am," he answered, his tone curt while still being professional. Clearly he hadn't forgotten the proper way to speak to his commander.

She placed her hands behind her, one hand gripping her wrist, resting on the small of her back. Her back was straight, and her head was slightly leaning back. She had red hair, freckled cheeks, and bright green eyes that were similar to Father's. Her suit fit her body shape, except larger. I always found it looked funny on women. All slender and shapely, with a tinier head sticking out of the top. Come to think of it, it looked funny on the men too, to a lesser extent.

Another soldier returned, empty-handed, nodding to his commander before taking his place behind her. This happened a few more times over the next few minutes, with most of the soldiers returning empty-handed, except for one leading two people behind him, one of which was the elderly lady I'd ran into earlier. It irked me that she was being handled so roughly. He had paler skin than Linus, and freckles covered his face. The lady slowed for a moment, and he shoved her, making her stumble forward, nearly falling.

"Move it!" he shouted.

I took a step toward him, but Linus grabbed my arm, pulling me back. I looked up at him, intent on arguing. He offered only a subtle shake of his head as a warning, but the disgust on his face gave away his personal feelings on the matter. Before I could open my mouth, the commander spoke.

"Everyone. Listen carefully to the words I have for you, a gift far kinder than you can imagine, given the circumstances. Indeed, I am putting my own safety at risk by giving you these words." The beautiful flame-haired tyrant droned on, and I mustered up every ounce of will I had to keep from slamming my palm into my forehead if her *kindness* didn't kill me first.

"We have always been kind to all of you, and the adversity we deliver to your young ones is from a place of love and hope for a better future, not just for your people, but for all people." She paced back and forth in front of the crowd, gesturing with her hands as she spoke. It was clear that she was going for the gentle motherly approach, but something in this woman's face gave away her hardness. There was a darkness in her features that I couldn't put into clear thoughts. Almost as though she was eager to get to the next part. The bad part. The threat, and probably a violent one.

"So you can imagine my disappointment," she continued, her tone hardening, "to learn that there are some among you that fail to appreciate our kindness and our dedication to building the character of our next generation. You must be wondering now why I'm standing before you talking about this when it would be so easy for us to remove this cancer with surgical precision."

She smiled, a poor attempt to once again appear kind. "This is the gift I alluded to. We have decided to allow you to deal with this problem yourselves rather than intervene. We've decided to allow your village to retain as much independence as possible, so long as you continue to earn it. Of course, I'm not permitted to speak of the other adversity zones, but let me assure you that some of them do not enjoy nearly the autonomy that your village does. You see, like the cancer I mentioned, it will spread if not cut out early. So the more it spreads, the grander the action required from us to halt it. Against the judgment of our experts, we will give you one opportunity to deal with the offenders. In the meantime, we will station outside the village and monitor the situation. Your chieftain will communicate with us regularly. We've communicated with him in advance, so he is prepared."

How had they managed to do this, I wondered. Spies? Informants? A long-range communication device? Yes, probably that one. After all, I'd seen the soldiers communicate this way before, touching their ears and speaking to no one there to hear them. Actually, it was probably all three. Our blubbering idiot of a chieftain in action, doing what he probably does best. Why should I be surprised?

Linus shot a glance at me but was quick to look away when our eyes met. Was there something he wanted to tell me? Didn't matter. Not like he'd have the chance to say it, even if he wanted to. More likely, he was toying with me in some cruel way. Send the handsome warrior to fetch the seventeen-year-old, nearly eighteen-year-old girl with rebellious thoughts. Paranoid? Maybe, but I wouldn't put it past them.

"And now, I'll step aside for your chieftain," she said finally.

Gods, no. I'd almost rather they unsling their rifles and start shooting.

He revealed himself from inside the crowd and stepped forward. "I have only a few things to say-uh."

Thank goodness.

He cleared his throat with the gurgling, slimy sound that was unique to him. "I only want to assure our guests that this matter will be resolved with diligence-uh, to show the appreciation that the overwhelming majority of us have for their kindness over the years-uh. We will try peace first, but failing that, we will step aside, and our guests will step in and deal with the traitors. That's all-uh."

He nodded to the commander, who motioned for the rest of her soldiers to follow her. I caught Linus glancing at me again, his expression grim. What was on his mind? I felt my cheeks grow warmer. Maybe I was on his mind. Come on, Taylor, pull yourself together. Now's not the time to have fantasies about handsome warriors coming to sweep you off your feet. Stupid. Grr.

He was trying to tell me something, though. I was almost sure of it. What was it?

They departed, and the rest of us were left to stand around, looking at one another in confusion. Some gullible villagers were no doubt sniffing about for the guilty party, hoping to sell out their own people to win favor from PanTech that would never come. Ever. I didn't want to be the first to leave, but as soon as the crowd started to move, I eagerly moved with it, making my way to my house, hoping no one else would speak to me along the way. Thankfully, no one did.

I stepped through the front door. Father and Mother were already sitting at the table talking. They stopped when they saw me.

"Catch the big speech?" I said, trying to sound apathetic.

"We didn't have a choice," my father grumbled. "They came and knocked on the door and didn't exactly ask."

"At least they knocked," my mother chimed in. "They don't have to, you know. They could have smashed the door down and dragged us out."

"Let them try it. I'd love to—"

The floor started rumbling and furniture shook. At first, just the empty chairs, but soon everything was shaking. A moment later, it stopped, and then a scream. Outside, somewhere. Had they found the rebels?

"Taylor, stay in—"

I bolted out of the door before Mother could finish her sentence.

I looked around, but couldn't spot anything out of the ordinary, and then the scream came again.

"Someone help me!" A woman's voice shrieked again, and a commotion followed. I ran toward it, my head spinning, both from nausea and excitement. The closer I got, the tighter the crowd was, but I forced my way through. I knew this woman! I came to see her animals every week to take care of them. She lived on the edge of the village and owned several pigs. She was crouched over a pig on the ground, breathing heavily and bleeding from some kind of large gash. There had been complaints about her pigs before due to the smell and noise. Had someone taken advantage of the commotion today to kill this one?

"Taylor, thank goodness. Help!"

I ran over as fast as I could, dropping to my knees. "Towel! Rags, something! We have to stop the bleeding."

A man stepped over and yanked off his shirt, tossing it to me. I looked at the wound briefly before covering it. What in the world? It was enormous and looked deep. He wasn't going to survive this....

"I'll do what I can," I lied, trying to comfort her. "What did this to him?"

She sobbed into her apron. "I don't know. I heard him squealing, and I ran out. It was right after the ground shook."

"Did anyone see what happened?" I scanned the crowd, looking at everyone. At first, no one would answer. Finally, a small boy who looked no older than five stepped forward.

"I...I did," he said nervously.

I continued holding the shirt over the pig's wound, but he'd gone still. Nothing could survive a wound that large.

I nodded to the boy before returning my attention to the woman. "I'm sorry. He's gone."

She took a deep breath and sighed, rubbing her face with her sleeve. "You did what you could, dear." She looked to the boy, expectantly, as did I.

"What was it? What did you see?" I asked.

He shook his head. "You won't believe me," he said.

I put my hand on his shoulder. "It's alright. Please, tell us."

He took a deep breath and looked as though he was going to cry. "It was a monster."

CHAPTER 6

I kept my hand on his shoulder and held my expression like stone. Several others crowded around couldn't help themselves but cackle in laughter. Others probably wanted to but chose not to out of consideration for the poor woman who'd lost a valuable member of her livestock. Me? I felt sick, sicker than I already was—what a day. My sickness came from deeper down. It was a dread that told me I'd already expected him to say something like that. I knew and didn't want to believe it. It would take a spear larger than any man could carry to make that wound.

"A monster?" I asked, my tone as even as I could make it. "What kind of monster?"

"A giant snake." He choked on his words as if fighting the tears that had become too much for the small child to bear.

"A giant snake…" I said. I'd meant it as a question, but it had come out as a statement. "From the ground? It came from a hole, didn't it?"

"You saw it too?" he asked, his tears temporarily halted by the hope that at least one other person in the village had seen what he'd seen.

"No. Will you please take me to the hole? Can you?" I asked, speaking quietly now.

He nodded.

I turned to the lady. "Please have your pig transported to my clinic. If you do, I'll pay you a fair market price for him. I want to study that wound more. The sooner, the better, please."

"You really think…" she trailed off.

"The sooner, the better," I repeated before turning my attention back to the boy. "Lead on."

We didn't have to go far; just around the corner of the woman's home was an overturned cart, filled with various tools, all spilled onto the ground. Behind it, there was an enormous hole, sand piled high around it. The hole had to be as wide as my arms outstretched, fingertips to fingertips. If this was what I thought it was, it would be a thing of nightmares, and this would be just the beginning. You'd venture into your nightmares to escape it if you had the choice.

"Brown, like the sand. Speckled gray. Fangs stick out of its mouth, wide in the front but narrow in the back. A head much thicker than the body."

"You did see it!" He hugged my leg.

Oh, how I dreaded that reaction. Gods. A giant Desert Burrower. They made this thing and transported it here. They let it go outside the village, and it was already applying its skill. A skill I'd seen used so many times on small animals outside the gates and sometimes inside. They were fast, had senses like almost nothing else. Maybe the mythical Shadowfalcon topped it, but that was assuming they were real. Father insisted they were, but I assigned mistaken identification to every sighting until I saw one myself. I'd personally seen the Burrower in action. It was one of those experiences that gave you the specific thought that you should let go of a deep breath, relieved that they are one of the smallest snakes and carry no venom due to the unique shape of their fangs. Miniature shovels on both sides, half circle around the front, hollow and open in the back so they can spin under the sand and propel themselves rapidly beneath terrain. The vibration would give it away at least, just before it surfaced, but ironically made it even more terrifying.

"No…but I think I know what it is. Thank you."

I reached into the pouch I'd been carrying in the side pocket of my dress, pulling out the sack of marks the chieftain handed to me earlier. I took one out and gave it to him.

"For me?" he said, his eyebrows furrowed. I didn't blame him. Children learned early to be skeptical of strangers' kindness, seeing that it was so highly frowned upon. If someone from PanTech saw me do this, I'd likely be reprimanded. At this moment, I couldn't care less what PanTech thought. I was more concerned with what they'd done.

"For you," I said and nodded in the affirmative. "Let's keep the payment our little secret. Say you found it in the sand."

He nodded vigorously, his eyes flashing with the useless knickknacks he could use this mark to purchase and, for just a moment, seeming to forget the horrific creature he'd seen.

"Run along, and maybe play inside for the next few days."

He ran but turned briefly to wave at me as he did. It was useless to ask him to keep that to himself. He practically broadcasted his appreciation to the whole world, with just the look on the face and the newfound bounce in his step. It very well could have been the first time anything like that had happened to him. Both things that had happened to him…

I hated PanTech so much. So much that, if there were some way for them to read minds, I'd be setting off every alarm at the moment. I couldn't tell the village to prepare. I couldn't offer my theory on where this creature came from. PanTech would deny it, as they always did with their tricks. They'd pretend to help. I'd have requested the one rifle the village was allowed to use, that every villager is allowed to fire ten times on his or her sixteenth birthday. Enough to become familiar with the function of the weapon. The trigger, the sights, the recoil, the noise. But not enough to become proficient. I had a knack for it, though. Enough that after the fifth and sixth round high bullseye, that I intentionally missed the last four shots almost completely.

Besides, I needed the authorization of a PanTech soldier to take it out on loan.

Wait…

Linus! What if he did have an eye for me? I could use that. I certainly couldn't threaten him or beat up another soldier and take their rifle. I wouldn't know how to use it anyway. It looked almost completely different from the old wood, metal, and smoke relic that exploded projectiles from brass-cased rounds and held ten magazine shots. I felt gross at the thought. What if Linus really was a nice man, and I took advantage of his feelings? What if I got him punished or even killed?

No…this was PanTech. I couldn't allow for such soft emotions. The sick feeling reminded me of the pig and put me back in the moment. I needed to have a look at it. Hopefully, they had it over at the clinic already. This snake shouldn't have venom, but I didn't put anything past PanTech. If they'd managed to create a giant one, maybe this one had venom or even shoots the venom from its fangs. Perhaps it could see in the dark. Maybe its scales were as hard as steel. I shook my head. Definitely not the thoughts I needed to be having if I wanted to be in the moment.

I jogged back toward the clinic, finding that four men had just dropped the pig onto one of my wooden examination tables under an open canopy. My first thought was that I hadn't cleaned it yet before I realized it didn't matter. I thanked them and began my examination. It was too bad I'd given Cara the day off today. I really could have used her help to take notes. It would all have to be in my head today. After another moment of consideration, I decided that was indeed for the best. A written record of my findings probably wouldn't be great for my health or the health of those around me.

I unlocked a box behind me and pulled out a long wooden rod. I inserted it into the wound, pushing it gently as far as I could, marking the depth with my fingers, and making a mental note of the length. Large enough to have easily swallowed the pig and dragged him down his tunnel. Easily. So, why didn't it?

Assuming they are like the normal burrower, they rarely fail to retrieve the prey they've bitten, unless they're young and inexperienced. Oh no…What if it's a baby? It would grow enormous. Even all of the animals outside the village couldn't sustain it. It would hunt us too, and we'd be easier targets. It would wipe us out before it became fully grown.

I took a deep breath and composed myself. Inexperienced. That was the critical part. If PanTech brought it here, it was probably grown and cared for in some kind of special environment. A big expensive lab, where they'd feed it on a cycle, and it would never have to hunt. It's new to hunting. That's why it bit the pig but didn't pull it back through the tunnel. Maybe the kid spooked it, but as soon as it realizes that we're no more dangerous than the pig, that won't last long. It's possible that if it came from PanTech, it would be somewhat tame to humans…unless they took precautions against that somehow. In either scenario, this meant that we need to kill the snake quickly. The more time it took, the more it would adapt to the environment around it. The more experienced it would be with hunting, and if it kills a human, it'll come back. None of its other prey will be as tightly packed as we are. This was a disaster….

I rubbed my forehead with my forearm. Right, I didn't even look for venom on the rod. There was no guarantee I'd see it, especially if it was unique to this animal and something I'd never seen before. I examined the tissue around the wound. There were no signs along the edge of venom that often spilled from the initial wound. Pig's tongue was normal, and eyes appeared normal. I breathed a sigh of relief. It seemed to be a mostly identical version of the normal burrower, but I wondered what difference that really made. The wound was too deep to even tell how deep it was. All I could tell was that it was huge but not quite huge enough to go through the other side. Even that wasn't a certainty because it could have failed to get a complete bite. Still, the estimate I could make seemed consistent with the size of the hole it burrowed.

We could plug the holes we find with poison and hope that it came back through and accidentally ingests it. Cross our fingers that would do the trick. Not likely. They rarely use the same holes twice unless they come back immediately to chase wounded prey. Once they retreat, the burrowed tunnel collapses quickly beneath the unstable sand.

I couldn't tell Mother and Father. If I got caught, they'd be implicated, assuming they don't end up being implicated anyway. At least if they genuinely didn't know what I'd intended, maybe they'd let them off. Ferris couldn't join me, even if he wanted to. He was going to be useless for at least a week, or more. If I went and simply asked the chieftain for the rifle, he'd report me for doing it unauthorized. I was fairly certain he knew already. Who could help me?

I stood there, racking my brain for a long while, and finally accepted the reality. No one. No one could help me. Even if I could manipulate Linus into authorizing my use of the rifle for some other reason, I had to hunt and kill this monster on my own...somehow. Fantastic.

CHAPTER 7

I considered what I might do with the pig's carcass or if there was anything I really could do with it. I entertained the thought of using it for bait but remembered that wasn't how Burrowers hunted. They felt the vibrations on the sand, ripped out of their tunnel, and stole their prey away. The pig wouldn't do much good for that. There was always eating the pig. After all, I would be paying for it, but I didn't want to risk that PanTech may have found a way to make the venom undetectable through normal means. In the end, the very inconvenient course of action I found to be best was to roll the thing out of the village and dump it far away so the carrion and scavengers that roamed the desert would eat it. Vultures would make short work of it.

Once I'd done that, the daylight was spent, and so was I. The snake needed dealing with, but there was nothing I could do about it for now, and I certainly couldn't tell anyone what I was planning. My father was waiting for me when I came through the door. A candle was burning on the table in front of him, and he was reading a book.

"Did you find out what caused that quake earlier?" he said, not looking up from his book.

So much for sneaking to my room without him talking to me. I should've known that would never happen. I considered for a moment what kind of lie I would tell. Should I lie? If I told him the truth, what would happen? Lying to Father felt about as wrong as wrong can be, and in the end, I couldn't do it. Not entirely, at least. A half-truth would have to do—a compromise to ease my conscience.

"A snake bit a pig, actually."

"And…that caused a quake?" he looked up at me as I sat at the table across from him, tilting his head.

I shrugged my shoulders. "Seems so."

He chuckled, and sat the book on the table, face-down, leaning back more comfortably in his chair. "Please."

"Please, what?" I asked.

"Please explain that to me. I'm not sure I understand how a snake biting a pig causes a quake. Must've been a pretty big snake or pig."

"How's Ferris?" I asked, trying my odds at changing the subject.

He sighed, narrowing his eyes at me. His eyes said *I want you to know that I know what you're doing, but I can see you're exhausted so, I'll play along.*

"Your brother has been in much pain. You can see it on his face, but he won't admit it, of course. The wound has worsened, as terror ant bites tend to do. It will likely worsen more over the next few days before it begins to heal." He paused, as if he'd just remembered something else. "Please don't blame yourself for it, Tay."

I shook my head. "Right. You were in the room when I had that nightmare. It's…I'm alright. I'm just glad he made it out with just the one bite, as terrible as one bite is. The ants were devouring him in my dream, but that could have easily been real. In the dream, he blamed me, but I know he wouldn't really. He…I bet he put you up to talk to me about it, am I right?"

He smiled and nodded once.

"I knew it. Brave in all the wrong ways."

I wished I could take the words back the moment they left my lips. Partly because it was unfair to my brother, and partly because Father was going to ask me.

"Why do you say that?" he asked, in perfect sync with my thoughts.

"I don't know. I guess I just hate to see him so brainwashed by PanTech. Everyone worships them like they're some kind of savior doing us a favor. They make our life better by making our lives worse? How messed up is that?"

"You'll get no argument from me about PanTech, but as frustrated as I get with the people of the village for not seeing them for who they are, they are both the oppressor and the savior for anyone looking to move from citizen to employee. Your own test will be coming up soon. Your brother will be testing with you, since he was barely too young for the last one. Or, have you chosen to stay in the village?"

In truth, while I hadn't really thought about it, I couldn't see myself leaving the village. Sure, Cara could take over as the vet. After all, she has almost as much training as me, but I just didn't feel ambitious, and I certainly did *not* want to help PanTech.

"They say that they have a veterinary laboratory beyond our comprehension. Imagine what you could study there if you were assigned to that section."

I grinned. "So, why didn't you go? Didn't you have one of the highest test scores ever recorded from this village?"

"Haven't I told you before? I get your point. I wanted to stay in the village so I could continue developing some of my inventions here. I wanted to make everyone's life here better. It was foolish of me not to expect what came next. Of course, as soon as I'd given up my chance at a high-level position at their technology institute, they sent soldiers here to destroy my inventions, and they forbade me from recreating them, further developing them, or creating new ones. They told me that it interfered with the adversity experienced by young villagers. They gave me a choice, you know, before they destroyed them. I could continue working on the inventions, but they'd have to offset their benefit with more artificially-imposed challenges to the village. More confiscated food. Introduction of new illnesses. Modifying native animal species to make them more dangerous."

I blurted out before I could stop myself. "Wait, they've done that before?"

Of course, Father picked up on the meaning behind what I'd said immediately. "Before? You mean…they've done it again? Tay, is that what you meant by the snake biting a pig caused the quake?"

Stupid. Stupid Taylor. I'd gotten him entirely off the topic. He wasn't even thinking about that anymore, then I go and sabotage myself.

"I'm not sure."

"I don't know, that sounded sure to me. They've somehow created a snake that's able to cause quakes? Why didn't I hear about such a thing passing through the village?"

I rubbed my forehead. I must've been close to collapsing from exhaustion. Today must've been the longest day of my life to this point.

"That's because it didn't pass through the village," I said. "It burrowed beneath, emerged, bit the pig, and escaped through its tunnel."

"A burrower, then. But that doesn't explain the quake. How do you know the snake was responsible?"

I stared at him blankly for a moment. I was quickly losing the energy to explain anything, and I knew it would come to him.

"Oh no…really?"

I nodded. "Yes."

"It's that big?"

"Enormous," I confirmed.

"Because of the rebels they've discovered…."

"That was my suspicion, too. Keep this between us, please. I don't want the whole town panicking, and they'll target us when they realize it came from me."

"You examined the pig, didn't you?" he asked.

I nodded. "I've been considering how I might deal with it, but I need more time to come up with something. I think tomorrow I'll visit the PanTech camp outside the village."

He furrowed his brow but said nothing.

"I'm going to go see a boy there. I think he's just a little older than me. Actually, I think he likes me. We ran into each other in town before the big speech, and he introduced himself to me. Pretty unusual for a soldier."

"Please be careful, Tay. I'm not sure it's a good idea to approach them directly like that."

"He's pretty handsome, too," I added.

"Tay…," his tone darkened, and the hint of sadness in his voice gave me a twinge of guilt. I'd only meant to tease him.

"I mean it. He wasn't like the other soldiers. Maybe he could tell me something about it. I don't think he'd hurt me if that's what you're worried about."

"Never trust PanTech," he said.

"I trust my instincts. They're all I have."

He pondered this for a moment before grunting slightly and nodding.

"Good night."

I stood up and stepped around the table, hugging him tightly around the neck.

"Good night," he said, not looking up at me again, already falling deep into his own thoughts. Maybe he was also considering ways to deal with the monster, but I'd get to it first. I didn't tell him that the real reason I was going to see Linus was to convince him to authorize my loan of the rifle and some ammunition. He'd have probably tried to lock me in my room if I'd told him that.

Thinking of my room, I wasn't sure I'd ever been so happy to see it when I finally went through its door. The bed, most of all. I frowned when I noticed the pile of broken glass still sitting on the table next to my bed, yet another reminder of how terrible this day had been. I picked up the largest piece and took a few moments to study my appearance. I wished that I looked more like my father instead of my mother. My reflection was almost like looking into her eyes, only with darker skin. She would always say that made me even more beautiful than her. Mother, of course, was not one for modesty. Then again, perhaps it was Mother I should seek advice from before seeing Linus tomorrow. I'm sure she'd have a lot to say about how I could manipulate boys into doing whatever I wanted. She'd say I was an exotic beauty to him, and I should wear my finest cultural dress.

Just the thought made me angry, no matter how right she was. I wanted to study and make new discoveries like Father had when he was young, not have some man take care of me while I experimented with scented oils and skin moisturizers.

I laid out my work clothing, almost to spite her in my mind. Maybe Linus would appreciate a woman who could perform a pig autopsy in the desert heat or bury her arm elbow-deep in a camel. Perhaps he'd appreciate my mind more than my body. Maybe….

What was I thinking? All I needed to do was to get him to agree to authorize my use of the rifle. I didn't need him to ask me to marry him. *Come on, Taylor. Pull it together.*

I collapsed onto my bed, burying my face into the pillow. I wanted to scream into it, but I was afraid someone would somehow hear me. It didn't matter anyway because I was asleep before I could even finish the thought.

CHAPTER 8

As I dreamed, I found myself again lying on the hot desert sand. My muscles loose and relaxed. The sun was wrapping me in a reassuring glow. A gentle breeze softened the heat enough to shift it from uncomfortable to comforting. My eyes were closed, allowing only a soft light into my vision.

I felt a hand gently touch my shoulder, but I wasn't startled. I opened my eyes and realized it was Linus, dressed in our cultural clothing. He was smiling at me, and his blue eyes felt so real, matching the sky so well that it was as though they were transparent as he leaned above me. I smiled back, and he leaned down slowly and met my lips with a soft kiss. I wrapped my arms around his neck, pulling him closer, meeting his kiss more deeply.

As I kissed him, he was yanked from my arms with a scream. I saw him being pulled away from me, toward the sky, and as he was pulled further away, I saw the snake that had appeared behind him. It pierced his body with its enormous fangs, pouring blood onto the desert floor. He punched and kicked at the snake's head with futility. As he hung from its jaws, it looked at me, silent and still, hovering above me like a serpent god, demonstrating his power.

Finally, Linus stopped struggling, and I knew that he'd died. His body became limp, his limbs dangling, his head wobbling slightly in the breeze as the snake continued to threaten me with his stare. He seemed to carry neither good nor evil intent with it— just a god indulging his hunger with insignificant beings.

Linus turned his head slowly toward me, his gentle smile returning, but with tears falling from his eyes onto the sand below.

"You did this," he whispered.

No. No, no, no, no, I sobbed, shouting the words in my mind, but I couldn't speak.

"You did this," he said again, his voice rising to a shout this time.

I filled with rage. I wanted to leap to my feet and tear off the snake's head with my bare hands. I wanted to smash him with the sun itself. I wanted to rip his fangs from his jaws and gouge out his eyes with them. My sadness gave way to a fury I rarely allowed myself to feel, a fury that threatened to swallow me whole.

And then, I was awake, sitting up in my bed so quickly it's a wonder I hadn't toppled onto the floor. My skin was wet with cold sweat, and I breathed as though I'd been running for hours. What did that dream mean? Did it mean anything?

A feeling of guilt suddenly gripped me. What if Linus was really as kind as he seemed? What if he did like me? What if he's not like most of the other soldiers, and I get him in trouble, or worse?

I rubbed the small tears away from my eyes. What a pointless thing to worry about. What was I supposed to do, let the snake kill everyone in the whole village? What if it was my father who was snatched by it next, or my brother, or mother, or Cara, or the kind old lady I met yesterday? Even if he was the kindest PanTech soldier ever to live, this is something I had to do. Sacrifices had to be made, even if what I had to sacrifice was a part of myself.

I rubbed my eyes again and stood up, getting dressed in my tattered work clothing, not unlike what all the village men and women wore when planning a day of labor. As I reached the door, I thought of Mother and sat back onto my bed, reaching into the drawer of the table beside my bed, pulling out the comb she'd given me. I spent the next several minutes combing my hair before tying it into a loose ponytail.

After I left my room, I stepped into the common area, hoping to avoid a conversation. Luckily, aside from Mother, I was the first one up. Her back was to me, cooking. I did my best to sneak quietly to the door, but, as expected, she heard me and turned around before I could reach it.

"Good morning. My, your hair is beautiful."

I inhaled deeply, putting on a smile that was somewhere between false and genuine. "Thank you. I finally took your advice, I suppose."

She looked down at my clothes, and I waited for her to criticize them, but she didn't. Her smile never weakened.

"I'm sure Father told you, but I'm going to head out to the camp today and see a boy named Linus I met yesterday. I may not be back until later, so don't worry about lunch." I reached for the door, resting my hand on the handle before she stopped me again.

"Yes, your father told me. I can only assume that you're going to see him because there's something you need from him."

"It's not like…," I started to protest, but wasn't it true?

"Sorry, dear, I didn't mean to make that sound like an insult. It wasn't. It was only an observation. I know you haven't had any interest in boys. I also know you don't particularly enjoy hearing my advice, but I would suggest you start considering it. It is a hard world, and there is a reason some women would kill to have your naturally beautiful appearance. You could see it as an insult to them to take it for granted, as though you weren't fortunate."

I sighed, clenching my teeth. "Mother…."

She chuckled, which surprised me. "Maybe work on your charm a bit, though. That's a skill that can be learned, regardless of your fortune at birth. Here, I made something for you." She pulled two small sacks from the counter and held them out for me.

I eyed them suspiciously, my anxiety building for what sort of contents these bags may have in them. "What are those?"

"Your lunch," she said. Then she added a wink. "And his. Salt-cured ham and bread I baked early this morning. Oh, and this." She reached behind her and fetched a bottle, handing it to me.

"Is that…cactus wine?" I asked.

"For you, only a few sips. For him, as much as he'll drink as long as he behaves."

My cheeks had already started burning. Should I thank my mother? Be furious with her? I wasn't sure anymore, but if it got me that rifle….

I grasped the bottle of wine.

"Small cups are in the sacks. Be careful, and remember that it's better to make someone your pawn than to become one." She reached out and moved a wisp of hair aside that had drifted onto my face.

"Thank you," I finally decided to say. "Really. Thanks."

She smiled, reaching down and opening the door for me, gently squeezing my arm.

Well, that was awkward, but Mother's coming-of-age conversations that had become more frequent in the last year were always awkward. I wasn't sure if that was her or me. Considering how enchanted everyone had always been with Mother, including my father, I could only assume it was me. *Guest*, I reminded myself. Not *soldier*. Not *invader*. Not *oppressor*. Not *enemy*. I couldn't let my words betray my thoughts.

I stopped by the clinic and gave Cara what she would no doubt find to be bad news.

She was only a year younger than me but petite. One might've guessed she was fourteen by looking at her and would've felt even more confident when they heard her small voice that matched her appearance perfectly.

"Hey there. It's going to be a busy day, with us being closed yesterday. You excited?" she asked, her fist pump making me believe there was no sarcasm in the question.

"Ah, uh, well…," I started.

She jutted out her bottom lip and crossed her arms. "Oh no, please don't tell me you're going out again today."

I scratched the back of my head. "I'm sorry, Cara. I really owe you one."

She slapped her cheeks and pulled her hands down her face, stretching her eyes and mouth toward her chest. "Ugh!" she groaned. "I'll do my best."

"I know you will," I said, smiling. I did know. Cara was one of the most reliable people in the village, and we'd become good friends since we started working together at the clinic. Even though I barely had more training than her, she never once complained about being my assistant. In fact, I think she was relieved. She might've run screaming if the clinic was suddenly handed over to her. "Good luck," she added.

"You too. Thanks."

I made my way to the gate, then through it into the desert before realizing I had no idea where this camp would be set up. What if I'd misunderstood, and they'd set up camp beyond the barrier? No, if the chieftain was sending messengers, they'd have to be inside the barrier, but that still could be anywhere within a several-mile radius of the village.

I stopped and looked around. It made sense that they wouldn't circle halfway around the village before going off to their camp. Odds were it was a straight shot from the gate if I was careful.

So, following that logic, I walked for several minutes in the straightest line I could manage. After a while, I found myself just short of the barrier, stopping next to one of the markers staked deeply into the sand. I looked around in all directions but didn't see anything at all. No smoke was rising. No raucous yelling. No visible tracks from their vehicles. I sat down in the sand, looking down at my feet.

Way to go, Taylor. Step one of your big plan is such a great success. It's surely a great omen of what's to come. I was…embarrassed, to put it lightly, so I wasn't about to show my face to Cara or my mother again so soon. Where could they be? Is it possible they lied about being nearby to intimidate the rebels into behaving? A bluff? I placed my hands on top of my head, racking my brain.

After an hour of this, I'd finally accepted defeat. Maybe if I got back early enough, I could think of a way to pry the information from the chieftain. Maybe I could tell him I had information about the rebels and wanted to go personally?

No. It could work, but more than likely, he'd insist on sending his own messengers, or he'd demand I tell him first and then…what? I'd have to make something up or be punished myself. Going to see the chieftain was riskier than just walking into the PanTech camp. Maybe I could just ask around and see if any of the villagers saw them while out hunting or saw what direction they went in when they left. Maybe, maybe, maybe. I could really go for a "definitely" right now.

I only made it about ten steps back in the direction of the village when a gust of wind came bearing a gift. Now, that was an odd smell. A good smell. A PanTech breakfast, no doubt, or what was left of it. I turned and traveled in the direction it came from and did not make it far before a tent came into sight. As I got even closer, I could hear talking.

When I got within shouting distance, I heard a chirping sound, and the talking ceased. A moment later, five soldiers were stepping out of the camp to meet me. Each one had their rifle pointed at me, their expressions unreadable at this distance, but I'm sure well within range to kill me.

"Umm…," I said, before clearing my throat, and raising my voice to a shout to be sure they heard me. "Our welcome guests," I continued. "I'm here to see Linus if that's alright." I offered the biggest, friendliest smile a seventeen-year-old girl could offer with five rifles aimed at her head.

CHAPTER 9

The five soldiers kept their rifles pointed directly at me, saying nothing and making no movement, indicating that they'd heard me in the first place.

I took a deep breath. "Hello! I'd like to see Linus, please!" I shouted much louder than the last time. Surely they'd heard me the first time.

After a few moments longer, one lowered his rifle and looked to the others. "Wow, did she say 'Linus'?"

Another shrugged. "Leave it to that idiot to tell the first pretty face he sees where the camp's located."

A third soldier spoke. "It's not like it's hidden. We've had two citizens stumble in here by accident already. It's not like we're on a management mission." He was promptly elbowed. I suppose I wasn't supposed to hear about management missions. It wasn't as if I knew what they were, but I could venture a few guesses.

The first to lower his rifle looked up at me. "Stay right there. One more step, and we'll shoot. Understand?"

I clenched my teeth. What was I supposed to do? Run in there and knife everyone before they could turn me into a red mist with their rifles? "Yeah, okay. I'll just…sit here." I sat on the sand. Maybe that would be less threatening.

After a moment, another soldier walked up to them, looked out to me, and removed his helmet. Thankfully, it was Linus, hopefully here to tell them I wasn't a threat to five armed PanTech super soldiers. He squinted and held his hand above his brow to shield his eyes from the sun.

"Taylor? Is that you?"

"You remembered me!" I shouted, pretending to be surprised, except part of me genuinely was surprised.

"You remembered *me*!" His smile reached his eyes. He stepped forward, then turned back to the other soldiers. "Tell the commander I'm taking some of my downtime outside the camp."

I wished they didn't have those helmets on. It was impossible to read their expressions or even be sure they were human. Sometimes I wondered anyway, with or without the helmet.

The soldiers didn't answer. Just turned and walked back into the camp as Linus strolled out to meet me, holding his helmet to his side, his rifle slung across his back.

"I was just starting to get used to the idea that I'd probably never see you again, but I'm glad I was wrong. I haven't been able to get you out of my mind since I saw you yesterday," he said, far more candidly than I expected. Just as I felt my cheeks flush with heat, it was countered by a low ache in my heart.

Please don't be the man you seem to be, said my heart, at the thought of hurting him if it were true. *But, that would be ideal for the plan*, said my brain, ever so slightly louder.

"I've…thought about you a lot too. I…um…." *Come on, Taylor.* "Will you have lunch with me? It would've been breakfast, but I got a little lost."

"Sure. I'd love to. Truth be told, until I'm called for a mission, I've got all kinds of time. I save it up and cash it out, usually because I don't get along so well with the other soldiers." He stopped a moment, looking away and scratching his chin. "Sorry, wrong way to say it. I get along with them fine. We're just not good friends. We don't spend time together off the clock. I mean…," his face began to turn red. "I'm talking too much," he finally said, with a big sigh.

I giggled involuntarily. I hated that I seemed to do that with him before I could realize it and stop myself. "It's alright. I probably know less about your world than you do about mine, so I enjoy hearing it, really. But, let's talk over lunch. There's a couple of big rocks a little ways from here that make some shade this time of day. Hope you like salt-cured ham."

He didn't answer. Not with words anyway. His smile said enough as it got just a little bit brighter.

We walked away from the camp and finally arrived at the rocks. I spread out a blanket on the sand and sat, pulling items out of the sacks my mother had given me.

"Wow, you made all of this?"

"I wish," I said with a weak laugh. "My mother made these."

Should have lied, Taylor.

His expression darkened. "That's one of those things a lot of people miss when they leave. You'll never see or hear from your parents again. My old man wasn't a good man. Got killed when I was just a boy over a game of cards. My mom was the only person

I ever met that was meaner than *he* was. She was pretty sick when I left. Guessing she's dead by now."

I stared at him blankly for a moment, trying to think of something comforting to say, but all I could manage to do was frown awkwardly for an uncomfortably long time.

"I…sorry to hear that. I'm guessing that made you a good candidate for PanTech though, with all your troubles?"

Wow. Couldn't have said something more stupid than that if you tried.

He laughed at that. "Sure, I suppose. I was pretty good with guns too. Joined up with a posse and caused a lot of trouble. Mostly robbed. Got into the occasional gunfight. Earned myself the nickname 'Blue-Eyed Devil' after one real nasty incident."

Strange. The more he talked about this, the more his speaking and accent seemed to change.

"Your voice," I said. "You sound a little different."

He scratched the back of his head. "Oh, right. Sorry. Seems that's one of my bigger problems. Despite being a pretty smart guy, I never seem to learn. When you arrive, they work to assimilate you into PanTech culture. You'll learn how you should be dressing, and speaking, how to hide your accent, and things like that."

With a smile, I handed him a slice of ham and bread. I was starting to understand why he found himself at odds with authority. "I bet you haven't tried cactus wine before."

He grinned. "You'd be right. Pour the cup full, if you don't mind. We're not allowed to have alcohol in the camp."

I did as he asked and handed it over to him. He took a big drink, then another, and another until the cup was completely empty. He passed it back to me with an even bigger grin than before.

"Thank you, Taylor. That really hit the spot." He bit into his ham, never taking his eyes off me as he chewed.

We ate silently for a few minutes without speaking, and he finally let his smile rest. Not for long, though.

He grinned, looking me in the eyes. "Let the two of us be frank with one another," he said.

"Umm…about what? You want to hear about my life in the village?" I asked, hoping that's what he meant. It wasn't.

"I think you know what I mean," he said, taking another bite of his ham.

I did know what he meant, but I wasn't about to blow my cover just yet, no matter how poorly thought out and lousy it was.

"Sure. I'm not a big fan of the cactus wine."

He tried not to laugh because his mouth was full now, but he failed, and part of it escaped his mouth before he threw his hand up to his face to stop it.

"What do you do for a living?" he quickly asked, his embarrassment—over losing part of his food in front of me—taking his confident talk down a notch.

"I'm a veterinarian."

He raised his eyebrow and let out a whistle. "You don't say?" He looked around. "Camels, and livestock, I reckon?"

"You what? Reckon?"

He rubbed his chin. "Sorry. I mean to say, do you take care of the livestock around here? This is my first time here, but I saw pigs and camels."

"I do. And pets, of course."

"Pets?" He looked at me as though he didn't believe what I was saying.

"Right, sorry. Some people keep lizards; we have mice out here, and of course, snakes."

He flinched a bit at the mention of snakes, and I didn't miss it.

"What about you? Do you have any pets?"

"No, I don't. I think I want something a little different, but nothing's ever really connected with me. Besides, I see plenty of other people's pets."

He nodded. "I had a horse once, before I left for PanTech. Had a dog when I was younger, but my pop shot him after he bit him. Was a good dog."

He seemed more distant all of a sudden as if the memory was dragging him back in.

"What's a…dog?"

He grinned. "You should try to pass your test and become an employee. You'll discover all kinds of new things. A lot more than dogs, assuming you think that life can be for you."

"Is it for you?" I asked, genuinely curious.

"No. I thought it would be. I thought I'd get there, and everything would be perfect. Finally, no more robbing or shooting people who didn't deserve to be shot, but it's the same thing, just with bigger guns and a bigger gang."

"They'll kill you if they hear you say that," I said coldly.

"Nah, it's not that bad. I've said worse," he admitted. "Now, about this plan of yours?"

Ah, I'd expected him to be duller than this, but it seems I just caught him in an awkward moment yesterday. He still seemed to really like me, though, so maybe....

"I need you to vouch for me to use the village's rifle."

He frowned, then sighed, but returned to his smile almost as quickly, as though he knew the answer before he'd asked.

"What do you need the rifle for? A lady like you shouldn't be doing the kind of dangerous things I'm betting you're about to do. You should let a man handle it."

"I'm *not* a *lady* like apparently where you're from, and I can handle myself fine, thank you!" I threw the contents of my glass of wine into his face and leaned forward, snatching up the blanket and stuffing it back into my pack. "I'll find another way."

I started to turn away, but I felt his hand grab my arm, firmly, but much more gently than yesterday. I whipped around and socked him in the jaw, sending him stumbling back a step, which probably surprised me more than it did him. He released my arm.

"Okay, I get it. I was wrong, and that was a stupid thing to say. Forgive me?" He rubbed his jaw. "Oh, and nice punch. You as good with that rifle as you are with your fist?"

"Better," I said, still feeling a wave of anger. Directed at the wrong person, as usual. I was lucky he didn't slap my head off with his super armor hand. Instead, he was already smiling again. It was almost intoxicating, the way he answered everything with a smile.

"In that case, I'll do it on one condition."

"You want a kiss?"

His face contorted. "What? Uh, no, I mean…do you want to?" He slapped himself in the forehead and pulled his hand slowly down his face. "Sorry, I mean…," he took a deep breath and exhaled, his face turning red. "That was a joke. You made a joke. Sorry."

I smiled. Suddenly, I wanted to tell him it wasn't a joke, in a way I hadn't expected I would, but I had to hide that. For now, at least.

"Just that you seem like a lot of fun, and I'm owed the downtime to do whatever I want with. It beats playing cards with a bunch of boring 'yes sirs' and 'no sirs.' I want to join you to hunt the snake."

"But I never said—" I started, but he cut me off.

"You didn't have to say. I never liked the idea of bringing that thing here in the first place, and I had a feeling that's what this was all about. Don't look at it as help. Look at it as doing me a favor in exchange. An equal trade between gunslingers. Deal?" He held out his hand.

I looked down at it a moment. I must be completely insane. Beyond all hope insane. This is probably the single worst thing I could possibly do, for him, and for me. I was going to regret this, and I knew it. I didn't know when or how much. Only that I would.

"Deal," I said, gripping his hand tightly in a handshake.

CHAPTER 10

Linus and I made our way back to town, garnering our share of ogling as we entered the gate. It was rare for a lone PanTech soldier to enter the town, especially walking side-by-side with a citizen, and the other villagers couldn't have made that any more obvious. No one dared to say anything aloud, but I guessed that most didn't approve of our being together. If I had to distill it down even further, it was probably my arrogance of walking next to him. I should be following, head bowed, eyes averted, in complete awe. My mother would have approved of that. At least, I think she would have. It was becoming harder and harder to tell anymore.

Since everyone was afraid to talk to me with my new companion, it wasn't long before we made it to the chieftain's home. I knocked on the door, and waited, and waited, and waited. Eventually he came to the door, and one of the village girls, about my age, ran out as he opened it. She didn't look up at me. Just hurried away like she was escaping a burning house.

The chieftain looked at me, waggled his eyebrows, and laughed. Linus had stood off to the side, looking at some of the items stacked outside the chieftain's house to pass the time, so no one noticed him yet.

I stared at him for a moment, my blood boiling, calling upon the divine power I needed not to put my hands around his throat.

"Well-uh?"

I didn't answer. I couldn't, yet. I was still cooling my rage. It didn't take long for him to become impatient, just watching me glare at him. "Listen here-uh, you stupid girl. How about I knock out some of those pretty teeth of yours-uh? Will that give your tongue more room to talk-uh?"

Linus had already started walking over. He stood in front of me and locked eyes with him.

"Good afternoon, Chieftain. I'm here to authorize the loan of your village's rifle to this girl. One-hundred rounds of ammunition."

Their eyes remained locked.

"Heh…uh…the rule states ten rounds-uh."

Linus grinned, shrugged his shoulders, raised his hands in mock defeat, then turned to look at me. "Sorry, looks like your chieftain is going to try to override me on this one. Maybe he thinks I'm too stupid to count." He turned to look back to the chieftain. "Right? Am I too stupid to count?"

The chieftain didn't answer, sweat beading on his bloated cheeks.

"No? Too stupid to know the rules, then? That must be it. Too stupid to know the rules." He turned back to me, smiling, before offering that smile back to the chieftain, then breaking out into laughter.

The chieftain looked nervously between Linus and me several times before chuckling himself.

Suddenly, Linus grabbed him by the collar of the shirt and flung him back into his house, sending him toppling over a table and knocking over two chairs that had been pushed beneath it.

I was frightened for a moment. I hadn't seen that coming, and it was violence I hadn't yet seen from him. He'd been nothing but gentle and kind with me. For a moment, my stomach twisted at the memory of throwing the wine into his face earlier. I guess he did like me after all. Thank goodness.

The chieftain struggled to his feet, his eyes wide. "My…my…uh…," he swallowed hard. "My apologies. I was only joking."

Linus kept his gaze cold and even, not even a hint of softness in his eyes. "When you come back around the corner, you better make sure that rifle isn't pointing my way, or I'll show you what a real joke looks like. Except I'll be the only one laughing. Now go!"

The chieftain scrambled toward a different part of his home, tripping over one of the chairs he'd knocked over, before returning to his feet and running out of our sight.

Linus looked down at me, smiled, and gave me a thumbs-up. "How'd I do?" he whispered.

My eyes were still wide, and I just slowly shook my head from side-to-side.

"Oh no. Did I overdo it? I overdid it, didn't I? Wow, PanTech really is nicer to you guys than they are to other places. This is how they all acted in my zone."

All I could manage was a weak, "I'm sorry."

He tilted his head, hoping for more of an explanation.

"I'm sorry," I continued, "You shouldn't be, though. He's not a good man. He deserved that and worse."

This seemed to relieve him a bit, but the implication that it was all an act wasn't something I bought. It didn't look rehearsed; it looked practiced. Linus hadn't been exaggerating when he talked about his past. Still, you didn't get far in this world by being soft. I wished that weren't the truth, but it was, and I knew that. I didn't need the help of a poet or musician. I didn't want any help at all, but if it was going to be forced on me, an experienced gunslinger with a mean streak certainly wasn't the worst thing that could be thrown my way. A hypnotically handsome gunslinger with a mean streak, wavy blonde hair, deep blue eyes, and seemed to like me was even better for some reason.

The chieftain came back around the corner, sweat now dripping freely from his chin onto his soaked shirt. He was carrying what I assumed was the rifle, wrapped in cloth, tied tightly with a string in several places, and a lidded metal bucket. He started to hand the rifle to Linus, but Linus instead nodded to me, who he passed it to instead.

"I'm not going to find any problems with this rifle, am I? It's your duty to maintain it, as we taught you."

"No. Of course not. It's well-maintained. This, I promise you."

"Will I find myself short on ammunition?"

He shook his head. "No. No. One-hundred rounds, as you requested."

"Thank you. Oh, and just one more thing." Linus smiled and took a step toward the chieftain, who recoiled reflexively.

"Y-yes?"

"That girl who left here when we arrived. Did you think I didn't notice?"

"Wha…what?"

Linus punched the wall next to the door, burying his fist into it, sending the chieftain cowering with his hands held above his head as if his entire house was about to collapse on him. "You going to imply I'm stupid again? We speak the same language. If you say 'what' one more time, I'll break your fingers."

"Linus!" I grabbed his arm, but he pushed me back, sending me stumbling backward and falling onto the ground. Several villagers had gathered around now, mumbling amongst themselves, no one daring to speak loud enough for Linus or the chieftain to hear them.

"I…uh…I've no doubt you noticed. She's nobody. What do you care about her?"

Linus reached over, grabbed his hand, and with a sickening crack, broke his finger. I put both of my hands over my mouth and gasped. What had I done by agreeing to bring him here? What if he treated everyone this way and was only kind to me because we were still within sight of his colleagues? What if he hurt more people?

"I heard a 'what.'" Linus still held his hand, the chieftain on his knees now, gasping in pain. "I saw her face when she ran out. If you bring any of the village girls in here again, I'm going to be back, and next time, I'll make sure there are no ladies present to remind me of my manners. Do you understand?"

The chieftain looked at him, his cheeks vibrating as he shook but turned his head away.

Linus moved to the next finger, slowly bending it back.

"Yes!" the chieftain shrieked. "I'm sorry. I'll never do it again. Please." He looked out to everyone in the crowd. "I promise. I won't lay a hand on anyone ever again. I swear!"

Linus smiled and let go of his hand. "That wasn't so hard, was it? Now we can all go back to being friends again." He pulled the chieftain to his feet, and dusted him off, then turned to me. I stood quickly.

"Shall we?" He reached for my arm, but I jumped back, unable to look at him. I tightly hugged the rifle, turned, and began walking away.

He followed behind me but didn't say anything for several minutes as we made our way back through the village. When we were finally alone, I stopped and turned to face him.

"Why did you do that?" I asked, my hands still trembling.

He noticed, and his smile faded. "I've met men like that before. Quite a few, where I'm from. I'm sorry you had to see that, but men like that only speak one language, and that's a threat of violence bigger than their own. Do you understand?"

I did understand. I wanted to do something like that myself almost every time I met the man. Every time his hand brushed against my arm or his gaze lingered on me for too long, and I felt sick to my stomach. I always had my knife with me if I needed it, and I would've taken great pleasure in burying it into his neck. So, why was I such a hypocrite with Linus? Why did I recoil from his touch like he was just as awful as the chieftain? I knew why.

"I'm sorry. I…I just didn't expect that from you. I thought you were so gentle that I wouldn't see you hurt someone like that. It scared me."

"Gentle and wouldn't hurt anyone, eh? I wish it were so. Maybe in another life, Taylor, but that's not the world you and I live in. The fact that I'm standing here before you now is all the proof you need that I'm not always a gentleman, that I'm a very different man when I need to be."

I felt like a fool. He was right, of course. It felt so obvious when he said it aloud. Had I used him to get the rifle? Had I cared about what might happen to him if he was caught helping me? Wasn't I ready to break his heart, and worse, if it meant rescuing the village from the snake? Could I do it still?

"I'm sorry." I ran over and hugged him around the neck with one arm, cradling the rifle in the other. I held on for a moment longer than I meant to before jerking away my arm and stepping back. "Thank you for standing up for that girl…and me."

His smile returned to his face. "Don't be so quick to thank me yet. I'm legendary for turning everything I touch into a mess." He looked up to the sky. "Well, that took longer than expected. Mind offering me a place to stay tonight?" His face reddened. "I mean…I don't mean…What I'm saying is *any* place. *Not* with you. I didn't mean you…necessarily."

"I'm sure my parents won't mind if you share a room with my brother, assuming you can handle him talking your ear off."

He rubbed his face, regaining his composure. "Do you think your mother could treat me to some of her lovely cooking and more of that cactus wine?"

"I'll put in a good word for you. Just…don't mention the snake, alright?"

"Didn't plan on it. No need." He pointed to the rifle cradled in my arm and held up the canister of ammunition in his other hand. "The beast's as good as dead already."

CHAPTER 11

Despite Mother's incessant worship of PanTech, she seemed genuinely surprised, almost uncomfortable, to see Linus walk through the door behind me. For once, Father actually looked up from his papers, holding his pipe in his right hand, raising one brow, but saying nothing. After a moment of uncomfortable silence and a gentle nudge from Linus, I cleared my throat.

"Everyone, this is Linus, the man I told you I was going to see today. He'll be joining us for dinner, and sharing a room with Ferris tonight if that's alright."

Mother smiled. "Of course. I'm just starting on dinner, so it's no trouble to make extra. We're so honored to have you join us, Linus."

"Ma'am," Linus said, nodding.

Father turned his pipe around and pointed the stem in the direction of the rifle I was still cradling in my arms. I met his eyes, and I think he already knew what I was holding.

"This?" I asked rhetorically. "Linus was quite a hunter in his zone and asked if I'd join him for some hunting tomorrow. Never hurts to have more meat, right?"

Linus never wavered in his smile and just nodded along.

"Well, you're probably going to be disappointed, young man. PanTech thinned our deer population several years ago. It was too plentiful a source of food to satisfy them that our children were sufficiently underfed. Adversity creates character, and PanTech does love its half-starved children."

An uncomfortable silence filled the room once again, for even longer this time. Mother shot Father a look that would have knocked him out if it were a punch, or at least sent him flying from his chair.

Linus scratched the back of his head. "Yeah…we went through the same thing when I was young. I'll not apologize for PanTech, but for what it's worth, I'm sorry myself."

Mother nearly tripped over herself, running over and grabbing his hand. "Oh no. Please forgive my husband. His tongue is so sharp it cuts right out of his mouth sometimes when his lips can't hold it back."

Linus only laughed. "I have the opposite problem. I can't find the right words at the right time. It made me rely on my hands a time or two too many. Anyway, the man speaks the honest truth. I'm taking my personal time right now, so I'm not representing PanTech. Just myself." He pointed to Father's pipe. "And, is that an honest to goodness smoking pipe in your hand? I haven't seen one of those in years."

Father's glare at Linus only hardened, but then he looked at me, and something in his eyes softened instantly, and he actually smiled. "I bet you haven't tried anything like this before. I have a second pipe if you'd care to join me while my wife makes dinner. My son never cared for it, so it'll be nice to have someone to smoke with."

I shook my finger at him. "That's because Mother wouldn't ever let me try it. I think it smells wonderful."

Mother let go of Linus and shook her own finger at me. "Ladies don't partake in such hobbies, Taylor."

I started to argue with her, but Linus's laughing drowned me out. "Yes, ma'am," he finally said.

I elbowed him in the ribs, but quickly pulled my arm back, rubbing it. Should've remembered the armor.

This only set Linus to laughing again, and he had to brace himself against the wall. It seemed even *he* had his limit to laughs and smiles, but when our eyes met, what I saw looked more like pain than happiness.

Father chuckled and stood to his feet. "What can I do, Tay, being so outnumbered?" He shrugged and disappeared around the corner, presumedly to retrieve the pipe and smoke weed jars.

My brother appeared around the corner, using the wall for support, his face covered in sweat. Mother rushed over to him, helping to hold him up.

"You shouldn't be up," she said. "The doctor said you needed at least a few more days of bed rest. Go on back to your room, and I'll bring you your dinner soon."

"Come on, Mother, you'll embarrass me in front of our guest here. You honestly expect me to sit in there when you guys are having all the fun out here? I can be in pain out here just as easily as I can in there, but with more conversation. The doctor's just being overly cautious. Just help me to my chair, if you don't mind."

She started to protest but realized how pointless that would be and helped him into his chair as he'd asked. He took a deep breath and let it out in a slow and exaggerated exhale. "Linus, was it? I'm Taylor's brother, Ferris. It's a good thing you picked Taylor. Otherwise, we'd be rivals for all the other pretty girls in the village, and I don't like your chances."

I felt my cheeks burning. I should've expected this from Ferris. Of course, he wouldn't let a little pain get in the way of embarrassing me. "Ferris!"

Linus broke out into laughter again before he'd fully recovered and had to stumble over and sit in one of the chairs at the table. "Since I did you such a big favor, maybe you could do one for me and put in a good word with your sister for me?"

Ferris grinned. "Not a chance."

Father returned with the extra pipe, already filled with smoke weed, handing it to Linus.

"Use the candle to light it. Just make a circle and puff it slowly. Careful, it may catch you off guard at first."

Linus eyed him incredulously and took two deep puffs as he moved the candle but dropped the candle before simultaneously picking it back up and nearly choking to death. He coughed and wheezed for several seconds while Father just grinned, and Mother looked absolutely petrified in horror.

At last, he caught his breath. "Wow!" he shouted. "This isn't tobacco!"

"Tobacco?" Father asked. "I wouldn't know. Is that what it was called in your zone?"

"That's what we smoked, but definitely not the same stuff," Linus said, still fighting off the remaining small coughs. He tried again, but much more slowly this time, finally getting a good light on his pipe. He puffed it cautiously, nodding to my father. "Some of the boys back home would get a real kick out of this stuff. They thought ours was strong."

Father only smiled and nodded, puffing his own, leaning back in his chair. "What was it like, in your zone? We seldom hear about the others."

Almost never? Try just never. Perhaps Father didn't want to deter him by saying we'd never heard anything beyond rumors of the other zones or overheard short conversations between soldiers.

Linus looked up at the ceiling like he was trying to recall something that happened a hundred years ago. "Well…I guess not too much different from this place, really. They tell us not to talk about it because it's a life we're supposed to leave behind completely. For most of PanTech's employees, this isn't too hard. Who would miss an adversity zone when you never have to worry about adversity again? Food of every kind you can imagine, medicine like you wouldn't believe, technology…," he trailed off, stopped, then took a puff of his pipe. "Sorry, that's not what you asked."

Linus paused again, taking a deep breath. "I lived in the desert too. Technology, I think, was probably on a similar level to your zone. We had horses. Big animals we rode on, like your camels, but shorter hair, and a lot more of them. Just about all of us had guns, like the one Taylor brought in. We even had smaller ones you could hold in one hand, with a revolving cylinder that held the rounds. That was my gun of choice. Something like the sidearm I'm carrying now, but not nearly as advanced." He patted the holster on his side that held the smaller gun soldiers always carried.

Ferris had been sitting quietly, for once, listening with his full attention. "You think all of the adversity zones are like ours? Do you know how many there are?"

Linus shook his head. "No idea how many there are, but there are quite a few. PanTech has the resources to manage a lot of them if they wanted to. One soldier told me that his zone was a city, where they spoke through something attached to a wire, and another person could hear them a long way away. They could have a box sitting on a table, and singing voices would come out, or PanTech would sometimes make announcements through them. I've seen things a lot more advanced since PanTech employed me, but I haven't been to any of their military facility much over the past year. Of course, the stuff I'm wearing is the most advanced thing I've seen yet, but I'm told that doesn't hold a candle to the things they have at the universities." He shot me a glance before lowering his head, slipping back into deep thought again.

Is that where the snake came from? One of PanTech's advanced universities, made in some lab with advanced technology and used to prey upon an adversity zone. I couldn't even begin to imagine all the good that could be accomplished from such a place. My father only had supplies and our lesser technology, and he'd invented things to improve our lives here before they stopped him. What's the point of having all of this technology and food if all you're going to use it for is to make everyone's life worse? None of this new information really changed anything. It just reinforced what we'd already suspected. PanTech is as sinister as they come.

"That sounds wonderful," Mother said, looking between Ferris and me. "Don't you want to pass your exam and be placed at one of them? You could study animal medicine, Taylor. Imagine all of the things you could do for humanity."

"Sure," I said. "I bet I could come up with new ways to starve people. I could take an animal that they depend on to eat and make its flesh poisonous. Or, maybe I could take a small animal they keep for pets and mess with their head, so they sneak into homes and kill babies. Imagine the endless possibility."

"Your disrespect really has no limit, I—"

"Mmm, what's that smell?" Linus interrupted. "Smells even better than the bread I had earlier."

"Oh, that's because it's much better fresh," she said. "It's actually the same bread. I'll bet it's done." She turned around, opened the door of the oven, and pulled out the pan. She sat it carefully onto the counter and sliced off equal portions for all of us, placing them on plates and setting them in front of us.

Ferris knocked a knuckle against Linus's armor. "You want to change out of that stuff? You could borrow some of my clothes. Can't be comfortable."

He grinned. "Quite the opposite. The whole thing's designed for comfort and cleans itself on the inside. It has to be drained and refilled about once a week, but it keeps us cool out here. All that, and it could still take a direct hit from your village's rifle, no problem."

Ferris just scrunched up his chin and nodded several times before taking a bite of his bread. It was nothing special to us, but clearly, Linus enjoyed it since he very reluctantly asked for seconds.

Once we'd all finished and spent a bit more time talking, we all retired to our rooms for the night. I could hear Ferris and Linus talking on and off into the deep hours of the night.

Tomorrow, we'd begin our hunt.

CHAPTER 12

Linus and I were up early the next morning, before anyone else. I guess neither of us got much sleep. When I stepped into the common area, he was sitting at the table alone, his mind off in another place. Something about him looked sad and distant. He was so absorbed in whatever he was thinking about that he didn't even notice me until I pulled the chair to sit down at the table, and he jumped a bit.

"Well, good morning, Sunshine," he said in a low voice.

"You're the one with the golden hair. Shouldn't you be Sunshine?" I retorted.

He tapped his chin, mulling this over. "I see your point, but I don't think it suits me. Kind of a feminine nickname. Some of the boys I rode with used to call each other that to try to goad a reaction."

"Well, you have golden hair, blue eyes, and you're always smiling and laughing, so I think it's a fitting description."

He smiled, almost on cue. "Okay, you got me, but I'd still prefer it if you didn't call me that."

I held up my hands in surrender. "If you insist."

He continued smiling, and just stared at me for a moment. I waited because it looked as though he wanted to say something. "I think those clothes suit you. Do you mind if I say that?"

If he hadn't asked if it was okay for him to say it…and after he'd already said it, I might've blushed. Instead, I laughed and pressed my hand over my mouth to keep from waking everyone else. "No, you can't say it. How will you take it back?"

His smile faded, and he frowned slightly. "Oh. Umm…," he looked away. "Sorry. You're just so beautiful, and I just said it without thinking and oh…man, I just did it again. Sorry."

This time, I did blush. Hard. "Oh, I was only kidding. I don't mind if you say it. I…uh…."

He scratched his head and stood up. "Well, are you ready to—"

"I think you are too," I blurted. I was so focused on finishing the sentence that I talked right over him. I expected him to get all flustered again, but he didn't. Instead, for just a moment, he looked as sad and distant as he did when I'd first stepped over to the table, as though he was remembering the death of a friend. Perhaps he was. "And, yes. I'm ready."

He pushed in his chair and signaled for me to walk over to the door, which he opened and held for me. I stared at him blankly for a moment.

"Oh…," he started. "This is a custom where I'm from. A man often holds the door for women. It's…hmm…a show of respect."

"Oh," I said, raising a brow. "Sounds…kind of strange. Can the women not open doors where you're from because of some kind of rule?"

He laughed. "No, Taylor. You know what," he said, stepping back from the door and letting it close. "I think you can handle this door."

I grinned but immediately wished I'd just humored him and walked out the door. Now he looked embarrassed again. I liked this Linus more than the one who felt like he had to hurt people, and I think he liked this part of himself too. The one that smiled and got rosy cheeks when he complimented me and got flustered when he tripped up on his words. And, in that moment, I hated the world that forced a man like him into a life of violence. PanTech's world.

I picked up my pack, and struggled for a moment to fit it on my back, then slung the rifle over my shoulder. It took some trial and error, but I finally remembered how to load the magazine last night, so all I had to do was chamber the round with the bolt, and I'd be ready to go.

I pointed to the goggles on my head and the mask hanging around my neck. "Does your helmet protect you from the sand if the wind picks up today?"

He nodded. "Sure does. Don't worry about me. I'll keep it strapped on my waist until I need it, though. I hate that thing."

I smiled and pushed open the door but was startled by two PanTech soldiers standing just a few feet outside of it. I stumbled back and was caught by Linus, who didn't seem surprised at all.

The soldier on the left was taller and bigger than Linus and looked several years his senior. His skin was reddish-brown, and his hair was dark and long, resting even with his shoulders. The soldier on the right was pale, with red hair. I recognized him as the jerk who bullied the elderly woman before the commander gave her speech. I'd give anything to dump a bucket of angry terror ants on his head.

He was the first to speak.

"You didn't return to the camp last night, Linus," he said.

I stepped to the side so that I wouldn't be between them and so I could watch all of them.

Linus grinned. "I think you're right. As usual, you're a master of the obvious. Pretty sure I didn't have to."

"I'm pretty sure the rules state—"

"Oh, go choke on the rules, Peter, but I doubt it'll make the commander like you any better."

Peter reached for his sidearm, but the bigger man put his hand on his arm, stopping him.

"Better thank Oscar here for stopping you. I'd have blown you away before you got it out of the holster," Linus said, grinning, resting his own hand on his sidearm, tapping his finger on it a few times, but not taking his eyes off Peter.

Oscar took a step forward and put himself between the two of them. "Cut it out, Linus. You know we're just doing our job. The commander sent us to check up on you is all, and that's all we're doing. You know she has a short fuse, though, so please stop pushing everyone. Every commanding officer has had enhancements performed, and you know that, so if you pull the same thing with her again like you enjoy doing with everyone else, she could shoot you five times before you drew your gun, even if you were the fastest human ever to live. Take it from someone with a few years of experience on you. Let that rebellious spark of yours burn out while you still can."

Linus gritted his teeth. It was the first time he actually looked angry since I met him. Even when he was dealing with the chieftain, he was smiling. He wasn't now.

"Noted, but I didn't ask to be a soldier."

Oscar sighed. "No, but you were *allowed* to be one. Don't forget that. You're on your last strike." He nodded to Peter before Linus could answer, and the two of them walked out of the village.

Linus still stood there, his jaw tight over clenched teeth.

"Are you okay? And what did they mean by you being on your last strike?" I asked, hugging his arm. "Are you going to get in trouble just for being here overnight?"

He finally managed to force a smile back onto his face. "You don't need to concern yourself with that, so please don't ask about it again. That's some personal business of mine I'd rather not get into…and no, I'm not going to get in trouble just for being here overnight. That rule is in place because usually, a soldier doesn't have as much downtime saved up as I do. It's never enforced. Peter just used it to take a jab at me. Don't worry." He took a deep breath and sighed. "Ready to hunt?"

I let go of his arm, not really buying his explanation, but thinking it'd be better not to push the conversation further. "I'm ready."

I wondered if they'd go back and tell their commander about the rifle I had. Everyone employed by PanTech, even the soldiers, was much more intelligent than the average person. They all had to pass the exam to be selected. Would they put everything together and realize I was hunting the snake and that Linus was helping me? Surely, he was forbidden from something like that, wasn't he?

"Good, I need to take out some frustration on something. May as well be a giant snake with super armored scales."

My eyes went wide. "Super arm—" I shook my head. "Did you just say it had super armored scales?" I asked, unable to override my urge to shout.

He put his finger over his lips to shush me and looked around, making sure no one had heard me. Thankfully, we were alone.

"Yeah, I might have failed to mention that part, huh? Relax. I'm pretty sure that rifle will still penetrate it, but a sword or spear probably won't."

I furrowed my brow, glaring at him. "Any other superpowers you'd like to tell me about before we're standing out there trying to kill the thing?"

"Well…," he started. "I don't actually know. I only overheard the scales part. I'm not even sure that's accurate, but it didn't sound like a joke when I heard it." He smiled again, reaching down to tap his sidearm. "Even if your rifle doesn't do it, my blaster will take care of it. But, if the blaster fails, my rifle could take down any living thing anywhere on Earth. But, you can also hear the thing being fired almost anywhere on Earth, and even though my helmet protects my hearing, you may go deaf if I shoot the thing while you're standing next to me."

And, they'll come to see why you fired, I finished for him inside my head.

"Fine. I trust you. Let's get out of the village before we talk about it anymore."

I should've known I'd lose my nerve. Not about the snake. I was ready for anything with the snake, but not with Linus. Before, I was prepared to sacrifice him to take care of the snake and save the village. Why did it suddenly weigh so heavily on me that he might get in serious trouble? Didn't I know from the beginning that he would? Hadn't I expected it?

We had only made it about a hundred yards out of the village and were still within sight when I took a deep breath and let it out. "Stop," I said firmly.

He wheeled around, looking in both of our side directions rapidly. "What, did you see something?" he asked, putting his hand on his blaster's grip.

"Uh…no! Sorry…," I trailed off. "I just…you don't have to do this, you know."

He narrowed his eyes at me. "Yeah, I know. And?"

"Well, it's just…," I looked down, trying to hide the tears starting to well in my eyes. *Really? Now you're going to get all emotional, Taylor? Face it. You're falling hard for this guy. Give me a break.* "Those soldiers sounded serious. What if they figure out that you're out here hunting that snake with me? You're going to get in trouble. Just…go back to your camp. You said yourself that this rifle should do the job."

"Yeah, I said it *should* do the job. Also, this is my door, Taylor."

I tilted my head at him. "Your…door?"

He nodded. "You know how you said earlier that holding open the door for women didn't make sense because they can open doors too? Well, I'm perfectly capable of deciding whether or not I want to go on this hunt with you. I know the risks far better than you do, so just banish those thoughts from your mind. They're silly, and you'll just blame yourself if something happens. I'm out here hunting it with you because it's something *I* want to do. I'll decide what's good for me, and PanTech can go shove it where the sun don't shine if they've got a problem with that. Got it?"

I furrowed my brow, hating to ruin the serious moment, but he'd lost me. "Shove what? Where the sun doesn't shine…you mean, like in the shade?"

He exploded into laughter and laughed so hard that he collapsed onto his hands and knees. Finally, he looked up at me, his lips pressed into a forced smile in order to hold back the laughter still trying to escape. He struggled to his feet, dusting the sand off his armor. "I'm not about to explain that one to you. Now, come on. We've got a giant, armored snake to kill."

CHAPTER 13

We'd continued walking for a while until we were out of sight of the village and in the opposite direction of the PanTech camp.

"It's entirely possible this thing has moved on. Do you think we could be that lucky?" I asked.

"It hasn't moved on," he replied, a little too quickly.

I stopped, looking at him. "How are you so certain of that?"

"I helped bring it here, remember? We were all briefed on what to expect and how to…guide the thing, in a way."

He continued walking, and I had no choice but to continue walking with him.

"What do you mean by 'guide' it?"

He looked up at the sun briefly before rubbing sweat from his forehead. "It's hot enough to melt steel out here."

"Linus."

"Yeah?" He said, finally stopping to look at me.

"What do you mean by controlling it?"

"I didn't say control. I said guide," he grinned.

I punched him in the arm. Ouch. "Come on. You're going this far. Why keep anything from me at this point?"

He sighed, pointing at a rock where we could catch a bit of shade. We walked over to it, and he sat down, patting the sand beside him. I sat next to him.

"It's not that…well…not that I'm *keeping* things from you, exactly. I'm just a little embarrassed, is all."

I chuckled, shaking my head. "I can't tell from one minute to the next what's going to embarrass you, make you angry, or make you laugh."

He smiled, running his fingers through his now sweaty hair. "Am I really that unpredictable?"

"Not really," I conceded. "I just need to get to know you better, or maybe I'm just making an excuse to get to know you better."

He put his arm around my shoulders and pulled me closer to him. "I'll take it, then."

We sat silently for a few minutes, less awkwardly than I'd expected.

"So, 'guide' how?"

He sighed, hanging his head. "PanTech set it up so that it can't escape. It has implants. One of which won't let it outside of a certain radius, within a sort of triangle-shaped area of the camp, where the camp is the point of that triangle."

"So that's why they're set up at the edge of the boundary…," I added.

He nodded. "Yep. You got it. And, as you probably already guessed, that range extends to just about the edge of the opposite boundary."

"Has it been trained to hunt humans?" I asked, bracing myself against the answer.

"Yeah…," he said, still not looking up.

"How…did they accomplish that?"

"Don't know, but I'm afraid to let my imagination fill in the blanks. Would caution you against the same thing," he said.

"Are they that cruel or that advanced?"

He raised his head and tapped his chin, genuinely considering this for a moment. "I'd say advanced. Based on my experience, they really do think they're doing the right thing and what's best for everyone."

"What about you?" I asked.

"You're kidding…," he frowned, looking genuinely wounded by the question.

"Sorry, dumb question, considering you're out here," I conceded.

He shook his head. "I guess I couldn't disagree completely that having a harder life makes us better people, but I think I'd rather be free and happy than 'better,' whatever that means. There was my dad, then my mom, and then a brief period of time where I wanted freedom so bad that I chose the freedom to do bad things. It's a little sad, I think, that I look back on those memories as my best. I thought with PanTech it would be different. I gave in and took their test, scored well, got accepted to an engineering school. Still, almost immediately, they considered me problematic. I argued with everything, snooped around in places I wasn't supposed to, and got on the bad side of every instructor I had. Ended up being sent off to the military division to learn discipline, but I didn't do a lot better there. Got into a fight my first day I was over there and got assigned to what they call 'low-tech' zones. No offense, but that's where they send their bottom-of-the-barrel people. Expectations are low, and this group is reduced to bullying people with sticks and rocks, maybe the occasional sword. Not that it makes any difference. Wrong is wrong no matter how hard it is to bully a zone successfully."

I kept quiet, just nodding as he ranted, not expecting the sudden openness.

"I'm no fan of PanTech, but my brother always felt like we could help change it from the inside if we passed our exam."

He shrugged. "Maybe, but that's not for me. I don't have that kind of patience or care for the world."

Now I regretted asking him about this in the first place. This conversation obviously wasn't good for his state of mind.

"So, about the super-armored snake...."

He perked up. "Yeah? What are you thinking?"

I scratched my neck and looked around. "I was actually wanting to ask what *you* were thinking. I have no idea how to bait one this huge without leading out big game. We can't afford to sacrifice any more livestock or camels. Also, since it travels underground, it could be anywhere within that triangle you mentioned."

He grinned. "Why, Taylor, I'm disappointed in you. You dragged me all the way out here without a plan?"

I lightly punched him in the arm. "*You* dragged *yourself* out here, remember? You keep saying so."

His grin stretched even wider. "Well, I hope this doesn't surprise you, but I actually *do* have a plan."

As much as I wanted to tease him, I wasn't surprised at all.

"Care to enlighten me?" I asked.

"PanTech needs to have a way to direct this creature where they want it, besides holding it within the radius I already mentioned. If they want to guide it to a specific spot in the village, say a secret meeting house for rebels, they wanted a way to summon it there. Otherwise, it wouldn't be much of a weapon."

"Let me guess," I said. "Special bait that brings the beast in quickly. I'm guessing something to make it extra hungry and extra violent."

He nodded several times. "Wow, Taylor. I knew you'd guess the first part, but not the second."

"Wait...I was right?" I glared at him. "It makes it extra hungry and violent..., and we *actually* want to use that to bring the snake here? Isn't it going to be hard enough to kill already without it going berserk? I was hoping we could sneak up on it and kill it while it was eating, the way you can with the small ones."

"Look," he said before sighing. "I get where you're coming from, but otherwise, we'll have to wander around aimlessly and wait for the thing to strike again. It won't be a pig next time, Taylor. It'll be a villager. It could be your parents. It could be your friend. It could be a child. If that's not bad enough, I'll run out of my personal time soon. I'm afraid if we don't do this now, you'll have to fight it alone. I do not want to risk that. I'd rather die killing it than to let you do this on your own."

My eyes went wide, and I felt myself blushing again.

"I'm not going to let it kill you, either, Mr. Hero. This rifle isn't for show."

He nodded. "Yeah, it's not. Alright, partner, are you ready to get this party started?"

"Ready as I'll ever be," I said.

He pulled a small box from his pack and stood to his feet.

He started to open it but just rested his hand on top, looking back at me. "I suspect Peter and Oscar, the two soldiers who paid me a visit this morning, realized one of these was missing and was hoping to catch me with it. That's why I went out of my way to make sure Peter lost his cool, and Oscar would have to back him off. They're not going to give up easily, but by the time they realize I really do have it, it'll be too late. Just avoid them, or play as stupid as possible, no matter what. Don't be fooled into cooperating with them, no matter what. Especially Oscar. He always seems to know the right thing to say to pull confessions out of people. Don't trust Oscar, no matter what he says. No matter what he offers you."

I nodded. "Alright, I'll remember that."

"Promise me," he said, his voice becoming harder than before.

"Okay, I promise," I said reluctantly. I wanted to ask him why I had to promise, but I knew I wouldn't get anything more out of him right now. "I'm ready when you are."

He closed his eyes and took a deep breath, looking up to the sky. Then, he smiled, opened the box, and reached inside. What he pulled out wasn't anything spectacular. I'm not sure what I was expecting. Maybe a machine that produces sound, or an insect with a pheromone that the snake was attracted to. This was nothing but a small pellet, and it looked like some of the compressed feed we used for some of our livestock. He placed it back into the box without closing the lid. He pulled out his canteen, opened the lid, and offered it to me.

"Drink?" he asked.

I took it from his hand and indulged in a small drink before handing it back to him. "Kind of small…isn't it?"

He looked at me and grinned before turning his attention to the box and pellet. "I was hoping you'd say that." He held his open canteen over the box and began tilting it before stopping and looking at me, his smile wide. "You might want to take a few steps back."

I did, and he began pouring water into the box, then tossed it quite a way away from us. It sizzled, then a foam shot out of it, covering the large area around it before soaking into the sand.

"Now?" I asked.

"Now, we wait. How long depends on how far it is away from us right now, but when it shows up, be prepared to give it all you have."

I unwrapped my rifle, pulled the bolt back toward me, and then pushed it forward again to ready a round into the chamber. I used my left hand to pull the goggles down over my eyes and stretched the scarf over my mouth.

"Aren't you going to put your helmet on?" I asked.

"Nope."

"Nope? Nope, why?"

"Because if I secure it on the suit, they'll be able to monitor what I say. No thanks. I'm used to the desert too, remember? I'll be fine. This foam will keep it from stirring up too much dust when it emerges."

I pulled down my scarf. "You're not big on giving information up front, are you?"

"You like me anyway, right?" he winked.

"I think I do unless there's something else you'd like to tell me that you've been holding back on?"

"Well, I wouldn't mind…," he began, then shook his head. "No, never mind."

He reached down and unholstered his sidearm, kneeling down and putting his hand on the sand. He stayed like this for several minutes, neither of us wanting to speak.

"Maybe…it didn't work?" I asked.

He just kept staring down, his hand pressed firmly into the sand. "Yeah, maybe I was supposed to take it out of the box first, or maybe I put too much—"

His thoughts were interrupted by a slow rumble. At first, subtle enough that I wasn't sure if I'd felt it correctly. He bent down further, pressing his ear to the ground, holding up one finger.

"False alarm?" I whispered.

He waited a few more minutes before letting out a big sigh of relief. "Looks like it's going to be a—"

He was interrupted again, and this time there was no mistake. The ground quaked beneath us, and I stumbled to my knees, holding the rifle with my right hand and steadying myself with my left. Linus leapt to his feet, pressing in some kind of mechanism on his sidearm, and it let out a low hum.

"It's about to emerge. Get ready!" he shouted before I noticed the smile return to his face. He wasn't dreading this at all or terrified like I was. He was looking forward to it. He was excited.

With a muffled thud and a splattering of the foam covering the ground, the demon emerged into the open air.

CHAPTER 14

Nothing I could have done, no thought that could have entered my mind, and no amount of preparation or training could have made me ready for this moment. Seeing this creature now, in its massive size and power, made me freeze in place. I could only stare, my mouth agape, my legs being sapped of their strength to hold me up. I wanted to run, to hide or to lock myself away in the safety of my home.

"Taylor!" Linus shouted.

I barely heard him and didn't register what he was saying. I could only watch the snake slowly move around us, ten times the size I imagined it. How could PanTech do this to us? This would have killed everyone. It's going to kill us....

"Taylor! Listen to me," Linus pleaded. "You've got to snap out of it. If you don't, you're dead. It had blood. It bleeds, and anything that bleeds, dies. You're going to make it die, and I'm going to help you. Lift your rifle, aim, and fire before it makes it all the way out. I'll cover you while you reload."

I snapped my attention back to reality, but my hands shook like a sheet of paper in the wind. I gasped and pulled in the deepest breath I could, then let it out. I did it again and again until, at last, I could open and close my hands and ignore the tears streaming down my face. I raised my rifle and fired the first few shots. The first two missed, but the third hit. I could tell it hadn't penetrated deeply. It took me a moment to realize I still had seven rounds in the magazine. It coiled close around me and fixated on my position. I shot the last seven shots in rapid succession, only about half hitting.

"It's going to kill me!" I screamed.

"No, it won't," Linus said, as calmly as he could. "I'll hit it as it strikes. It'll pull back. Reload. Now. This sidearm isn't rapid fire."

I dropped to my knees and pulled out a loaded magazine with ten fresh rounds, dropped the other magazine before throwing it into my pack, and slammed the bolt forward. As I did, the snake struck toward me with blinding speed. Still true to his word, Linus fired his blaster and hit the side of its head, sending it recoiling back and facing its attention toward him now. Blood was oozing from the much larger wound on the side of its head. I could tell from looking at it that it wasn't even close to being dead. We'd made a huge mistake. We were going to die here, and it was all my fault.

I raised my rifle and, more calmly this time, fired another ten rounds into its neck, opposite the side Linus had shot. It turned its attention to me again.

Now Linus looked panicked. "Come on. Come on, come on, come on!" The low hum came from his blaster. It needed time. I would have to load the rounds one at a time into an empty magazine now, and we were helpless in this moment. "Sling the rifle, grab some ammo, and reload as you run around it. We need to make it harder for it to zero in on one of us. I'll go the opposite way. Move!"

His last command was jarring in its harshness, and I did as he instructed. I released the magazine and slung the rifle, grabbed a handful of the ammunition, and struggled over the snake's back to make my circle around. Linus did the same but punched it as he did, making sure it paid the most attention to him. Just as he made it over the snake's back, it struck at him blindingly fast, and Linus dashed forward with equally impressive speed, narrowly escaping the strike. It was beyond human, and only the armor could have explained it. I pulled my attention away from him, and frantically tried to load rounds into the magazine while running, which was harder than I would have ever expected it to be. I dropped the first several before I finally got the hang of it. I'd managed to load in seven. The rest were lost in the sand.

I stopped, took a deep breath, and held the rifle up steady to my shoulder, pressing my cheek into it. I held my breath, and fired all seven shots. Slower, this time. I took the time to aim more carefully, even as the snake snapped its head around and repositioned its body to face me fully. I was calmer, slower, more careful. More precise. All seven shots hit the target and all in the neck near the others.

Linus punched it several times, trying to get its attention, but it didn't work this time. The snake shot toward me, and all I had time to do was hold up the rifle vertically so it couldn't close its powerful jaws and use its fangs to pull me into its stomach. I could feel the hot breath as it closed down on the rifle. It flung its head about frantically, trying to dislodge the rifle, knocking me through the air and landing hard on the ground, forcing all of the air to leave my lungs. My first gasp was filled with sand, which only made things worse. It was stirring up more and more sand now as it thrashed about. Finally, the rifle went sailing into a different direction. Fortunately, I saw where it landed, and pulled my scarf over my mouth and my goggles over my eyes. Linus would have a hard time now.

It came back for another attempt, but this time Linus was there between us, and fired the shot from his blaster at the last possible moment, doing the most possible damage. This time, a large chunk of its face was exposed, and one of its eyes was completely useless. This shot would have killed most mammals, but reptiles are more resilient creatures. They can take far more damage.

It flung itself backward and slammed onto the ground several times, sending Linus to his hands and knees from the small quake it had created.

We were especially vulnerable now. It took nearly a minute to charge that shot, and I didn't have any ammunition nor a rifle to load it in.

"You have to get up. Get your rifle back, and load another magazine. I have an idea, but you have to trust me. Go!" Linus shouted, before coughing on the sand that was coating his throat. His blaster hummed as it recharged again, a steady stream of smoke rising from it now. Was it overheating?

I jumped to my feet and made a run for the rifle. Linus ran with me this time, instead of in the opposite direction. I didn't understand why until we made it to the rifle. I knew it was here…somewhere, but I couldn't see it anymore. The sand must have covered it. I dropped to my hands and knees and started digging for it.

"I don't see it!" I screamed. "I can't find it. I can't see it," I said, losing my nerve again, feeling myself crying.

"Take a deep breath. It's there. Don't worry about anything except finding it," he said, positioning himself between the snake and me.

It raised its head again, and steadied itself, then struck at Linus. He grabbed onto one of the fangs with his left arm and stomped his foot into the bottom of its mouth. At first, I thought he would have the strength to rip its jaw apart, but he couldn't spread it open that far. He tried twisting the fang, but it had little effect beyond making the snake sway a bit. It hissed loudly and strained to collapse its jaws onto Linus. The power armor wasn't enough to match the snake's strength, and he slowly began to bend with the snake's effort, the point of the opposite fang resting on his shoulder. Though, he held firmly to his blaster with his right hand, refusing to abandon it.

None of this helped me to calm myself, but after a moment of digging, I finally managed to find the gun beneath the sand. I picked it up and ran toward my bag where the ammunition was, released the magazine, and began reloading, despite my hands trembling even more than before. I looked over my shoulder to see Linus clenching his jaw and growling in pain. The snake's fang had cracked through the shoulder of his armor, and the clear fluid that filled it was pouring out, tinged with red blood.

I slammed the bolt forward and ran back to him, stopping and firing ten more shots into the snake's neck, hoping against all hope that it would be enough to kill it once and for all.

It wasn't.

Blood poured from its many wounds, but it didn't seem to weaken it in the slightest, only angering it more. It picked up Linus and began thrashing around again. His blaster should have been charged by now, but it wasn't. Something must be wrong with it. Smoke billowed from it now, as if it were about to explode, but Linus held a death grip on it nonetheless. The snake weakened enough that it wasn't able to keep him up in the air anymore. I tried to release the magazine, but it was stuck. I tried as hard as I could to yank it out, but it wouldn't budge. I threw down the rifle and pulled out my knife, running and leaping onto the snake's head, stabbing into the already wounded areas, knowing the knife couldn't penetrate the undamaged scales. It did well enough in sabotaging the existing wounds.

It flung its head to the side, sending me flying through the air again.

The hum coming from the blaster was high-pitched now, and it shook violently in his hand. "Get back, Taylor! Run!" He shouted while slamming the gun into his bent knee, activating the charging mechanism again. He'd done this three times now, without firing it. Was he overloading it? I scrambled to my feet, barely able to keep my balance, and began to scoot myself back through the sand, further away. Linus threw the gun into the snake's throat, freeing his right hand to grasp the other fang. He roared and forced its mouth open with all his strength, but it wasn't enough. He couldn't pull the fang the final few inches from his armor. Ignoring his pleas, I ran back to the snake again, jamming my knife deep into its eye. It opened its mouth reflexively, and Linus was finally able to free himself from the fang completely.

He grabbed me in his arms and ran a few steps before falling, sending both of us collapsing to the ground. The snake raised its head again, readying for another strike. Linus rolled on top of me, shielding my body with his. As the snake twitched to move forward, I could hear an explosion, and a flash of light came from its mouth. Pieces of its flesh flew in all directions, as well as fragments of the blaster, like bullets thudding against the sand.

The snake fell to the ground with a thud. Its body coiled tightly for a moment, then went limp.

Linus pushed himself up off me and gave me a smile before rolling off to the side, onto his back.

"Have fun?" he asked, holding his shoulder and grimacing.

I raised my goggles and pulled down my mask, wiping my face. "I'm snotting everywhere, and my goggles are all fogged up from crying like a scared little girl. I thought I could be brave, but when it came right down to it, I was so scared I almost ran away."

He laughed but abruptly stopped and winced. "I think I'd call that normal. Don't sweat it. Oh, and thanks for saving me back there. Good thing you didn't run, or I'd be dead meat."

"Save…save you?" I said, more angry than surprised. "Linus, you are the worst liar of all the men I've ever met."

He managed something like a half-grin while gritting his teeth. "Guess maybe I'm not your type after all, then."

I smiled and threw my arms around his neck, kissing him deeply. He relaxed at first, pushing his lips into mine. He made a few grunting noises while tapping my shoulder before I realized my elbow was directly over his wound, pressing my full weight into it.

"Oh…sorry!" I said, feeling as though my skin was going to melt off my face. I can't believe I did that. But, wow. Just wow.

"Of all the things in the world a person should apologize for, *that* should go at the bottom of the list. Come on. Let's get you back home."

CHAPTER 15

It was only about midday when we made it back to the village. At first, I thought we'd be able to make it back to my house before the gawkers gathered around, but I was wrong. Some were well-meaning, offering to help us. One man took Linus's other arm over his shoulder and helped me support him as we walked. Others, I think, were just enjoying the novelty of an injured PanTech soldier, but there was a little more than that. There were still others, unless I was mistaken, who almost looked excited by it. Not that I could blame them, with everything PanTech represented.

I wished I had the time to stop and explain to each and every one of them how Linus was different. How he was heroic, and wanted to help people and make their lives better. How he stood up for others and for himself. How he liked those who valued freedom and how he'd risked harsh punishment and his own life just to experience what little of it he could. I wanted to tell them how I hated PanTech too, and how Linus was on our side…but I didn't know how much of that was true, and almost nothing is that black and white. Here he was, having joined them, wearing full PanTech battle armor, visiting adversity zones to make sure things were hard enough for us to become *better* than we'd be without them. *Better* than we'd be if we had enough to eat, enough medicine, and safety. No. It would be wasted words, and I had a feeling Linus didn't particularly care.

When we arrived at my house, I thanked the stranger for helping us but thought it better to send him away. Once inside, I sat Linus down at the table in the common room. Only after he'd sat down did I realize how much he was bleeding. The wound must have been deeper than I'd thought and that he'd let on.

"Please tell me that snake wasn't venomous," I said.

"Not that I know of." He tried to shrug, but could only manage it with one shoulder, immediately showing his regret for trying with a sharp wince.

"We need to get that armor off…right?" I asked, completely unsure of what to do. I'd never seen damaged PanTech armor, much less a soldier not wearing it. All I'd seen was most of them without a helmet, but that was common. With all the liquid shooting out and an open wound, this was something completely different.

He chuckled, what little he could manage. "I wish I'd paid more attention when they told us how to handle this. Give me a minute to think about it."

Just then, my mother walked in and screamed. Ferris came limping into the room as well and put his hands on my mother's shoulders.

"What did you do, Taylor?" Mother shouted.

"What's that supposed—" I started, but Linus cut me off.

"I didn't listen to her and ended up falling onto a rock. A…uh…sharp rock that pierced my armor," he tried, as poor a liar as he was. But, no one questioned a PanTech soldier. Even though it was perhaps the least convincing lie of all time, and Linus probably knew it, my mother shut her mouth and didn't push the matter.

"Get my sewing kit, Mother. It's in my room, near the closet. The thread is thick, but it'll have to do."

She shook her head. "No. I have one with a more suitable thread for a wound. I'll go and fetch it."

Ferris limped over to us, obviously still in pain himself. "There were two PanTech soldiers who came by earlier looking for you, Linus. They said they'd be back later."

Linus only smiled and nodded.

"So, the armor?" I asked. I was sure those soldiers checking in on him again was an important detail but probably less important than say…staying alive.

"Right. Well, it's not as simple as just removing it. It's…," he stopped, scratching his chin. "It's attached. Pretty deeply, and anchored in. The wires are thin, so they could either break when we pull them, or they could be stubborn. I'm getting lightheaded, so I think I've lost too much blood already. You're going to have to remove the torso, at least."

I just blinked at him. This was a lot to take in. I could tell by the look on Ferris's face that he was thinking along the same lines.

"That does *not* sound very reassuring," I said.

He attempted another shrug with the same result. "Ouch…anyway, sorry, what do you want me to do? Bleed out? There are covers that overlay with the armor. If you lift them far enough, you'll find brackets that you'll be able to pull up on the end where the lip faces up a bit. I don't know how else to describe it, Taylor, and I don't mean to be pushy, but you're probably going to want to do this sooner than later, or I'm going to be unconscious."

Ferris didn't hesitate, pulling up the flaps where the arms connected with the torso, fiddling a moment, and producing a loud snapping sound that shook the armor. I followed his lead with the opposite side, and after a moment, we'd removed the arms.

Linus's arms were smaller than expected, probably because of the sheer bulk of the suit. They were lean and muscular and extremely pale, contrasting from his tanned face. He must've been in this thing for a while. He did mention that they didn't really take it off. Just changed out the fluid inside.

"Alright. Good work. Now you'll have to go up along each side doing the same thing. When both sides are unbuckled, you'll have to do a line around my waist. Then, you'll both have to grab the bottom near the waist and the top near my neck to pull the pieces away from one another…I think," he said.

Mother came back into the room but stood silently in the doorway, her face wracked with worry.

It took Ferris and I several minutes, but we managed to undo the buckles. We pulled the two pieces in opposite directions, but they didn't budge.

"You have to lift up on the front armor. Slide up, then out," Mother said. "I have the thread ready. I'll take care of his wound once the armor is off."

Ferris turned and looked at her for a moment, the confusion clear on his face, but she didn't offer anything to alleviate it.

"Ferris," I said, getting his attention back on the task at hand. "Ready?"

He nodded, and we pulled the pieces apart. The remaining fluid in the armor's torso spilled onto the floor, but it was completely red this time, compared to the mostly clear fluid I'd seen spill out earlier.

I dropped the armor's chest portion and moved to get a closer look at his wound. It wasn't wide, but it must've been deeper than we thought. It couldn't have gone as far as his lung, based on his breathing, but it could've been almost that far.

Mother stepped forward and began unraveling thread, but I snatched it from her hand.

"I'll do it," I said, as firmly as I could.

"He's not a camel, Taylor. He—"

"I trust Taylor with my life," Linus interrupted. "And then some." He scratched the back of his head. "But…would you mind too terribly rustling me up some grub?"

"Some…grub?" she asked, and this set him into a laughing fit, which continued for a minute despite the obvious pain it caused him.

"Food, ma'am. Sorry. Anything is good, but some of that wine would really hit the spot."

She stepped around us and began preparing a meal for him, as he'd asked.

I didn't waste any more time. The wound was still oozing blood, and his hunger was probably partly because of the blood he'd lost already. I sewed quickly and efficiently, but not gently. Linus barely batted an eye. I felt his muscle flinch under the needle a couple of times, but he never protested or made a sound. He'd experienced this before. Maybe many times before. Realizing this made me sad. Was it pity?

No, not pity. Not exactly. It was realizing that he'd been through so much more than he'd let on, and he didn't have anyone to share his pain with him. Maybe I really did have it easy. Linus wasn't much older than me, but…looking at all of the scars that covered his torso, he'd seen so much more hardship than I had. Yet, he'd managed to hold onto some part of his soul and found a way to be kind. He never complained or made light of my troubles. His hardships had made him strong, resourceful, appreciative, and sometimes kind, but they'd also robbed him of love and happiness. PanTech didn't understand that.

He had deserved to be happy and to have food in his stomach and a warmth in his heart. He deserved to be loved, and I'd decided without a doubt that I wanted to give him my love in all the ways I could. Maybe he could retire to the village at the end of his service, or I could pass my exam and ask to be assigned to the same group as him, or….

Realization slammed into me, like closing a romantic book midway through, that PanTech would never allow this to happen. But, maybe…just maybe, I could continue to visit him while he was here. They visited at least once a month. If he saved up his personal time, and used it to spend time with me, just like he did today, then maybe—

"Taylor?" Linus asked, tilting his head and leaning down to look at my face. "You alright?"

I nodded, leaning in to look at the wounds along his sides. Several small wounds went up along his ribs, matching on both sides, where the wires embedded in his flesh had pulled out.

"I'm fine…but—"

"Mind if I borrow some of your clothes, Ferris? You're a little bigger than me, but baggy is good. Oh, and a poncho, like what you'd wear if you had to go out in the rain. And uh…a hat. May as well go all out. Widest brimmed hat you have."

Ferris nodded. "I usually just wear a wrap…but Father has some hats. I'm sure if he was willing to share a pipe, he won't mind if you borrow one of his hats."

"Where is Father?" I asked, irritated with myself that I'd only just now realized he wasn't home.

"He went out to deliver the lesson plans he'd been working on. Remember? He'll be going over them for a while. He won't be home for a few more hours, at least."

"Your rifle," Linus said, suddenly.

"What?" I asked, staring at him.

"Hand it to me. I'll need to fix the jam. We don't want to return a defective rifle, do we?" he smiled.

"Sure, but that can wait," I urged. "You can do it later, right?"

"Now," he said, holding out his arm with his hand open.

I handed him the rifle, and he pressed the magazine release, taking a couple of quick pulls before giving up. This wasn't good for his wound. At all.

"Linus, you can do this later. Please."

He ignored me and put the butt of the rifle stock down on the floor, pointing it up straight at the ceiling. He raised his leg and kicked the bolt. When it didn't move, he kicked it a second time, a little harder this time. A bullet ejected and flew across the room. He sat the rifle back in his lap, and this time the magazine fell out freely. He smiled and breathed a huge sigh of relief. Was he really that concerned with disappointing the chieftain? Or, maybe, he just didn't want to leave the village without a working rifle.

Ferris returned with the clothes, and Linus dressed quickly. He put on the long coat over his shirt, despite the weather. Didn't he say the suit kept him cool? Surely he was burning up with all of this on. Usually, when it rained, the weather was cooler. He fit the wide-brimmed hat on his head. He took it off again and just stared at it for a moment, before smiling.

"Not exactly what I'm used to wearing, but close enough," he said, putting it back on his head, and standing to his feet.

"Hey, what are you doing?" I asked.

Again, he ignored me. He placed the rifle inside his coat and leaned over, looking himself up and down, before nodding.

"Good enough."

Mother stepped over and sat a plate of meat and a cup of wine down in front of Linus, both of which he made short work of.

Linus stepped toward me and put his arm around me, holding the rifle beneath his coat with his other arm. He kissed me while Mother and Ferris competed for whose jaw would hit the floor first. He took a step back and gripped my shoulder.

"This is goodbye. Please don't say anything. Don't make this any harder for me than it has to be. I'm going to go meet the others before they have a chance to come here. Thank you, Taylor. When I finish whatever punishment they have for me, I'll come back to see you again."

I could tell. I could see in his eyes that he was lying to me. Of all the things for him to lie about, this is the one that I couldn't take. I couldn't just say nothing as he'd asked.

As I opened my mouth to speak, a knock came at the door.

CHAPTER 16

We were all startled by the knock because it came at the most inopportune time a knock could possibly come.

"It's probably Father," Ferris said, rising to his feet.

Linus extended his arm out in front of him, blocking Ferris's way to the door. They made eye contact, and Linus just shook his head, making his way to the door instead.

When he opened it, Peter and Oscar were standing there.

"Wow, you've settled in quickly," Peter said, his tone filled with venom.

"Going to need the armor repaired. Stuff's junk. You trip on a rock and next thing you know it's flying apart," Linus said, laughing.

Oscar shook his head. "Enough. You need to come with us. Will you do it quietly?"

Linus just nodded, taking a step toward the door, but Peter put his hand on his chest and shoved him back a step. "She's coming too," he said, pointing at me.

"Why? I thought you just needed me to come. Is this an arrest or a party? Should we just go invite the whole village?" Linus asked, his tone coming across more desperate than mocking.

"Come on. You expect us to believe you'll behave? You will if she's with you, I'll bet."

Linus looked to Oscar but found no support from the quieter man either. "He has a point."

Linus glared at them both, looking between the two of them and me several times. He was trying to modify whatever plan he had on the fly, but it didn't look like he was coming up with anything. His breathing became deeper, and his jaw clenched. Now, he was only looking at the two of them.

"It's time to go, Linus," Oscar finally said. He stood aside, nodding for Linus to step through the door, then to me to follow them.

Ferris took a step forward, but Mother grabbed him by the arm, shaking her head. She looked just as worried and upset as him, but it was probably for the best that she stopped him. If Linus thought it was wise not to contradict them, it would have been an even worse idea for Ferris to try something.

When I stepped outside, Peter grabbed me roughly by the arm. "No running off, girl. Understand?"

I gritted my teeth and pulled against him, which I doubt he even realized.

Linus spoke for me. "She understands. Since you're making me do things this way, can we at least stop by Taylor's clinic so I can say goodbye?"

Peter and Oscar looked at one another, before Oscar nodded.

We walked for a few minutes in silence before finally arriving at the clinic and being greeted by Cara.

"Oh, hello, Taylor. I didn't think I'd see you today. Is…everything okay?" Her voice softened as she noticed Peter's hand holding my arm.

Linus walked over to our large animal cage and peered inside. The door was raised, and the lock was hanging loose. "What happened here? I thought you had a camel in here yesterday. Does it look like someone tried to cut the bars in the back to you?"

We all tilted our heads almost simultaneously, and I started to step toward it to see what he was talking about, but Peter still held my arm.

"Do you mind?" I asked him, with a bit of bite in my voice.

He released his grip, and I leaned into the cage after Linus stepped back to let me through. I looked closely at the bars and didn't see anything out of the ordinary.

"Doesn't look like it to me. Not sure why someone would try to—" I felt a foot shove into my rear end, sending me falling into the cage. From my hands and knees, I spun my head around to see. It was Linus. He slammed the door of the cage down and fastened the lock. He took the key and handed it to Cara. "I'll kill you if you let her out before I'm gone. Understand, girl?"

Cara looked to me, then to Linus, clenching her fists and taking a step back. "I won't. I promise," she said, as she took the key with trembling hands.

"Linus, what are you doing?" I shouted.

"Things my way, Taylor. Not going to let them set the terms and use you some way to get to me."

"We weren't going—" Oscar started before Linus cut him off.

"Shut your mouth. You're a bigger snake than the one we just left dead in the desert."

"What snake? We don't know anything about—" Peter tried to speak, but Linus cut him off too.

"With all the noise we made? All of you know about it. Cut the crap. Let's go get it over with."

He walked away toward the gate only a couple of hundred feet from my clinic and stopped short of it, turning around and facing the two of them again. The three of them now had their sides facing me and barely within range of hearing.

"Why'd you stop?" Oscar asked. "I thought we were leaving."

"Saw Peter's hand hit the silent charge on his blaster. If you're that excited to kill me, at least look me in the eye when you do it. I didn't even think Peter was yellow enough to shoot an unarmed man in the back."

Peter rested his hand on his blaster. "Oh, come on, Oscar! He already knows we were sent here to kill him. Let's stop playing around. Whether the villagers know it or not doesn't make any difference."

"The commander didn't want us inciting the rebels…," Oscar said, his voice still calm and even.

"That doesn't even make sense. They'll be glad to see us killing one of our own. You can even stay out of it. We'll have us one of those high noon showdowns, and I'll show Linus here he's not the hot stuff he thinks he is."

"Peter…stop. She specifically asked you not to make a show of it. You're going to be reprimanded yourself at this rate."

"Let him," Linus said, tipping his hat toward Peter, then moving his poncho to the side to show the rifle.

"No! Please!" I pleaded, gripping the bars of the cage. "It was my fault. I asked him to come with me. I'm the one who should be punished!"

"It was within your rights as a villager to use the rifle assigned to your village to hunt the snake," Oscar said. "Linus, on the other hand, was forbidden to harm it, and this is just one of his many offenses. He's been given chance after chance. It was never going to end any other way."

I looked to Cara. "Cara, let me out, or I'll never forgive you!"

She hung her head. I hadn't noticed it, but she was crying, holding the key tight to her chest.

"Ready when you are," Linus said, nodding to Peter. "Better take a few steps to the side, Oscar."

"I won't. This isn't a game. Accept this with some dignity, Linus."

In a flash, Peter ripped his blaster from his holster but fired it before he could bring it up to aim properly, his head rocking back. His blaster let loose the shot that landed just in front of Linus, sending a spray of sand into his face. Peter fell backward onto the ground with a thud, causing a small cloud of dust to rise where he'd fallen. Dead before he hit the sand.

Oscar was only distracted a moment, his eyes wide as he looked down at his partner, but his hand was flying toward his own blaster even before he'd fully turned back to face Linus.

Linus had dropped to one knee, yanking the bolt back, slamming it forward to chamber a new round. Oscar drew his blaster and fired in the exact same moment, Linus fired his second shot. The blast had struck him in the side, sending him spinning and falling onto the ground. Oscar dropped his blaster and grabbed his neck with both hands, blood poured from between his fingers.

He dropped to his knees, choking out his final words. "You could've been a good soldier. You threw it all…away…," his last words came out garbled and quiet as he fell forward onto the ground. Linus dropped his rifle and tried to stand, blood pouring from the massive wound in his side. He took one step toward us but fell down onto his hands and knees. He rolled onto his back, coughing.

"Cara! Please!" I cried out, shaking the cage, tears pouring from my eyes.

She hesitated for a moment, then ran over and unlocked the cage. I ran as quickly as I could, stumbling and falling twice before I made it to where he was lying on the ground, holding his hand over his side.

"I'll take care of it! Let me see the wound," I demanded. "Cara, bring my medical bag. Hurry!" I shouted to her over my shoulder. She scrambled into the tent to retrieve it.

He just shook his head, refusing to move his hands. "Sorry, Taylor. I should've waited until we were out of the city and let them shoot me in the back, but I wanted to go on my own terms."

"Shut up. You're not *going* anywhere. After this, they're going to decide you're too good of a soldier to lose. They're going to punish you and make you go through some kind of training, and you'll be reassigned before you know it. *Move* your *hand*!"

Reluctantly, he agreed. When I saw it, I put both of my hands over my mouth, and all I could manage to do was tremble as I sobbed. I couldn't help him. No one could.

"H…hey," he said, his voice barely having any strength behind it now. "I was wrong."

"What do you mean? What were you wrong about?" I asked.

"Didn't think I'd ever be happy another day after I was recruited, but…you…being with you the last…," he paused, unable to continue speaking, taking a few deep breaths to try again. "Thank you, Taylor."

I grabbed his hand and held it tightly as I could. I wanted to say something in return. I knew I should, but I couldn't. I felt like I would choke if I tried to speak, and no words would come out. I lost myself again in my sobbing. I wanted to shout to the gathering crowd to help me, but I knew they couldn't. I wanted to scream at Peter and Oscar for what they'd done, but they were dead.

For a minute, Linus squeezed my hand in return, but his grip slowly loosened until soon there was no grip left at all. His eyes were open, gazing at the sky, but he wasn't there anymore. He was…gone.

I couldn't feel anything but the urge to scream. I wanted to beg him not to leave me.

A hand gripped my shoulder, and I didn't even wait to see who it was. I turned around and tackled them, landing blow after blow on their face, screaming with all the fury I'd been holding back.

It was Cara. She tried to shield her face. After a moment, I realized she just kept repeating the same thing over and over. "I'm sorry. I'm sorry. I'm sorry."

I jumped to my feet, shocked at the realization that I'd just attacked my friend. She was bleeding from her lip and nose and was still crying, making no effort to get up off the ground.

"Cara…I…," I clenched both my fists together in front of me, only now noticing they were both covered in blood, and screamed as loud as I could until I ran out of breath, and then I did it again. When I couldn't scream anymore, I grabbed the rifle, and I ran all the way out of the village as hard as I could, giving no thought to my direction or destination. I just wanted to run forever, until time ended, or until I couldn't feel the pain anymore, whichever came first, if either even came at all.

CHAPTER 17

I ran until I realized where I'd been running and stopped when I arrived. I'd gone back to the snake, and I wasn't sure why. Maybe it was because it was the last place we'd gone to. Maybe it was guilt. Or, maybe, there was another reason.

I reached down to my side, relieved that I'd brought my canteen of water along. I drank everything that was left, which wasn't much, and fastened the empty canteen back to my belt. I sat on the sand and took in my surroundings. It was starting to get dark, but tonight would be a full moon—the only night where it was possible to see anything ten steps in front of you. Tonight, in particular, was looking to be a bright one. Just as visible as a cloudy day. It was still suicide to be out here this late, as that was when the most unkind inhabitants of the desert went out to hunt and scavenge, and I was sitting at an enormous dinner table with more than enough to eat for all.

Maybe I'd die out here, and they could have me too. I'd always cared deeply about the animals here, ever since I was a small child. I wouldn't blame them. After all, the unkindest animal of all was us, humans. No other animal would kill their own just for craving freedom. Suddenly, without the fear of death, I found myself craving the idea of going out with a bang myself, in a way. What fascinating animals might be drawn to the corpse of this snake? The biggest and strongest of the desert? For once, they wouldn't have to fight over their food, but they probably would anyway.

The vultures were the first to arrive. A few had even arrived ahead of me, but within an hour, there were more than I'd ever seen in one place. They paid me no mind as they crowded next to one another, eating their fill, but in such a hurry that one might wonder if they had somewhere they needed to be. Like some kind of family appointment that had been long planned and couldn't be missed and they were too afraid to pass up this once-in-a-lifetime opportunity. And, so, they ate as quickly as they could. I soon learned what all the hurry was about.

A group of boars moved in on the opposite side, but not before some of them charged the vultures, who had probably seen them nearby as they swooped in earlier. Guess I'd have eaten in a hurry too. The boar alone wasn't the most menacing thing in the desert, but the fact they traveled in groups and attacked anything that sought to compete with them made them a force to be reckoned with. Being that they only came out at night, like most animals of the desert, I'd only seen a few in my lifetime. In the wild, at least, not counting the domesticated ones in the village. I readied the rifle, just in case.

The next animal to arrive was an iron fox, but most villagers called them the gray fox. Their soft, gray fur and fluffy, white-tipped tails made them one of the most beautiful animals you could ever hope to lay eyes on in this inhospitable place. She approached cautiously, crouched low, moving only a few steps at a time, watching as the other animals ate aggressively. They paid no attention to her, and she intended to avoid them. One hit from a boar's long tusk, and she'd be dead, but that could be said of most animals. She settled in next to a small piece that had detached itself…well…that had been forcibly detached from the rest of the snake, away from all the other animals. She took small bites, and while she slowly chewed, she held up her head to survey.

It reminded me to stop watching them so closely and take a look around myself. The sands of the desert glittered in the moonlight since this light was far less overwhelming than the sun. I slowly laid flat onto the sand, looking up at the moon and stars. For the first time, I could finally feel some calmness returning to my body. I couldn't process everything that had happened today right now, even if I'd wanted to, and I didn't. I felt as though if I allowed all of the hurt to absorb into my mind at once, I would die or go mad. No one had come to be with me out here, and while I wanted to use that as yet another reason to hate, I knew that there was no way to follow me all this way. Why should anyone risk almost certain death to hunt down someone who clearly wanted to be alone?

A shadow passed in front of the moon and came as a welcomed distraction from my dark thoughts. But, what was it? Vultures didn't fly that high, certainly not that quickly, and no other birds that I knew of flew at night. Before I could spend too much time thinking about it, another distraction came. Just as fascinating.

A small herd of deer appeared over a dune and made their way over to the snake. The first to arrive bent down and pulled off a piece. I couldn't believe my eyes. Deer were previously herbivores, but ever since PanTech *sabotaged* our plant life, most of the deer had died and we couldn't afford to hunt them anymore. If we did, they might go extinct with no hope of ever returning. The ones that survived must have adapted to scavenge in addition to grazing on what little plant life remained. I had seen some eating cacti, but *this,* I hadn't expected. I caught myself desperately wishing Father were here. I wanted him to see this.

Father…what must he be going through right now? What if he was trying to fight through the crowd to get to me just before I ran away. I wanted so much to hug him and cry in his arms. I wanted to hear him tell me that I would be okay and that he and Mother loved me, and they would help me through it. But, Father wasn't here, and he hadn't been there either. It was a selfish thought anyway. Why would I wish that sight on anyone? Father had genuinely liked Linus, and already despised PanTech far more than I did. He might have tried to help him and gotten himself killed in the process…just as I'd wanted to do.

Linus knew. He knew that I would intervene to help him, and he'd taken us by the clinic because he'd remembered seeing the cage before. PanTech knew he cared for me, and they *used* me to hurt him. To catch him off guard and make him vulnerable, and to stop him from getting the jump on them. He knew exactly what would happen to him if he helped me hunt the snake. He knew why they were there. He helped me anyway, and I led him to his death. I may as well have shot him myself. Oh, Linus….

I curled up and began to sob again. Holding my hand over my mouth, trying not to be loud and disturb the animals nearby, but the fox had noticed me anyway. It stopped eating and was watching me curiously. It snapped its head around suddenly and bit something. A shadow passed over it, stopped for a moment, then attempted to fly away, but crash-landed a few feet away. The fox looked toward it and collapsed instantly…dead? Not a sound had been made. What was happening?

I changed my position to bending down on one knee, holding the rifle in my hand. Had I gone mad? It was like a ghost made of shadow. If the fox hadn't bitten down on it, or if I hadn't been watching her at the very moment it happened, I'd have never known for sure that what I was seeing was real. I still wasn't sure.

Could she be sick? I crouched down as I walked slowly toward the fox. She was definitely dead if she let me get this close.

No…something was off. I leaned in closer, only to find that the fox was still breathing and breathing even harder as I got closer. Something moved again out of the corner of my eye, but by the time I focused on the spot, it was gone…if it had been anything. I gripped my rifle tightly. A small cluster of clouds was passing over now, making shadows jump and dance everywhere. One of the boars had started running in our direction, but before it could get too close, it fell flat onto the sand, collapsing midcharge. Was the flesh of the snake poisonous? Was it affecting the minds and bodies of these creatures to make them sick?

As the clouds cleared and the scenery was still again, illuminated by the full glory of the moonlight, I finally spotted something near the boar. It tried to take off but couldn't. Its wing was injured. It was smaller than the big vultures, but even if the vultures were the size of me, they couldn't have taken down an adult boar like that. Could it…? No.

But what if it was?

Impossible. I was still so upset. I was seeing things. I was going mad.

I rubbed my eyes and opened them again, but it was still there.

It might have been easier to convince me it was a ghost than what my eyes were showing me. This was a shadowfalcon.

Another boar charged after seeing his comrade collapse, and the falcon just barely made it out of the way. Why had it not paralyzed this boar too?

The boar charged again. This time the escape was even more narrow. The boar had bumped it through the air but missed goring it with its tusks.

No way I could miss this chance. Most people lived their entire lives without seeing one of them. No one had ever seen one up close. The few who had seen them were never believed, and here I was, nearly in reach of one, and about to stand there and watch it be gored to death by a boar? Not a chance.

I aimed the rifle, and just before the boar finished its third charge, I fired a shot that made it slide to a stop, making one attempt to return to its feet before falling again and going still.

The shot had spooked every animal around, sending a flurry of feathers into the air and boars charging in all different directions, though they didn't go far before slowly circling back. I approached the falcon, and he collapsed to the ground. He'd used their defense I'd heard about, which I had hoped wasn't true. It was said that a shadowfalcon would turn his paralysis weapon on himself and stop his own heart if he found himself cornered and unable to fight.

I walked over and picked up his body, my heart suddenly heavy again. I shouldn't have approached him like that. Then again, he'd have died anyway with his injury.

He was pitch black, and the glistening of his feathers wasn't too much unlike the starlight in the sky. His plumicorns were the only feathers on his body that weren't completely black, instead carrying a red tint. His eyes were a deep, solid green, and glowed eerily in the moonlight. Other animals with low light vision had similar eyes. His must be able to see through almost no light at all.

I sat him back on the ground and, with a heavy sigh, took a couple of steps back before something tugged at my gut. My instincts told me to look again. To look closer.

I picked him up again and realized that he was still alive, just barely. He must have used too much of his paralysis toxin against the fox and boar. Perhaps the fox's bite had startled him into using more than he realized. He had paralyzed himself completely, but his heart was still beating. If I brought him back home, I could treat his injury and heal his wing. I could come out one night and release him once he'd recovered. I needed this. I needed someone or something to need me the way this falcon needed me now.

I was going to save him.

"I'll call you…Ghost."

CHAPTER 18

I wrapped Ghost tightly in my scarf, leaving only enough room for him to breathe, and wrapped a single wrap over his eyes so he wouldn't panic as much. I had planned to hunker down and ride out the night once I'd decided I even wanted to return at all, but by then, this animal would be in a full panic and would likely end itself once it built up enough toxin again. If he was to have any chance, I needed to return home immediately, and I needed the help of my only friend—a friend who I just screamed that I would never forgive and punched in the face several times.

This was a purpose I needed, and I needed to put it above everything else—even my own safety. If I couldn't give this shadowfalcon, what I once believed was a mythological creature, a chance, then I didn't want to go on living. I had to try at least to know I'd tried. To know I didn't let my lack of nerve and courage and weak guts stop me from doing the right thing.

Linus. Linus didn't let anyone or anything stop him from doing what he thought was right. He acted selflessly, even though he claimed otherwise, and spat in the face of death itself. There were surely so few men so heroic who ever lived before or would ever live after. I didn't care what beasts, hungry for fresh meat stalked me in the night. I would give them something, but it wouldn't be meat. It would be the fury I'd held inside me. That, I would give them, and they could choke on it.

I stood to my feet, cradling Ghost under one arm, my rifle under the other, and backing away from the approaching boars. One charged, and I quickly sat Ghost onto the ground next to me, aimed, and fired. It had to be the most stubborn and aggressive animal in the whole desert. Anything else would have been long gone by now. Another charged, and I had to shoot him three times. That's…two shots left. I think. What if Linus didn't get the chance to fully load it. I had no extra rounds on me. I could come back tomorrow with some men from the village, and we'd drag all of the boar back for slaughter, if there was anything left of them, but then they'd see the snake and panic. It would be best to let the desert take them. Plenty of hungry things out there would.

I picked up Ghost again and ran. The fox still wasn't stirring, nor was the boar he'd paralyzed, so he would probably be like this for a while. I had no way of knowing for how long. The fox was a beautiful creature in its own right, and I felt a pang of guilt for not being able to take her too. I would return if I could, even though it would almost certainly be too late for her. She was probably already dead.

Cloud cover came again, and I could no longer see where I was going. Before it became completely dark, I crouched down next to a large rock and tried to focus on what I could hear. A lot of good it would probably do me, but it was all I could do. The desert was full of silent killers. Half of the things in the desert could kill you without making a sound. Some, like Ghost, could kill you without *you* even making a sound.

There was nothing but silence, occasionally interrupted by a gentle breeze. A normally gentle breeze, at night, in the desert, was anything but gentle. With everything that had happened, I didn't even have time to stop and realize how cold I was even though I was freezing. It wasn't dangerous, but it was extremely uncomfortable. Yet another reason few people ventured out at night, and no one went into the open desert like this. Was my family worried for me? Did they assume I might be already dead? Would Cara care, after what I did to her?

Oh no, what if my father and brother went out looking for me. Normally in that situation, they would request to use the village's rifle. But I had it now. No, not now. I couldn't get caught up in all of this now. I'd start thinking about Linus again, and….

I felt something shift my clothing and crawl over my leg. A snake, or maybe a lizard, or scorpion? I stood completely still, only shifting my eyes so that I could see the light returning as the clouds slowly blew past. The light came agonizingly slow as I felt whatever it was crawl even further up my leg.

When the light finally came, I found myself wishing it was any of those three things I'd considered. Even all of them. It was a terror ant. I couldn't see the nest, but I wasn't covered, so this one must've been the scout, trying to figure out what to make of me. I resisted the urge to leap to my feet and flee. I had to be patient. It would eventually crawl away from me, but the moment it did, I would have to leave. If it suspected I was edible, it would send a scent back to the nest, and I'd be swarmed.

Just as it crawled off of me, darkness came again with more clouds, but I couldn't risk staying. I would rather die by the teeth, claws, tusks, or stingers of almost anything else in the desert than to be eaten alive by terror ants. So, I ran, in total darkness, in the direction of the village. I still wasn't close. I was miles away. The snake had been near the boundary, and I was less than halfway back.

Two bullets left, with one chambered and ready to fire. I still had my knife, too. Running in the darkness was basically begging to be killed, and any number of creatures might give chase and kill something strange that obviously couldn't see where it was going as well as they could.

Ghost still hadn't stirred, so I at least had that going for me. My legs burned, and my lungs ached. I was still battered from the fight with the snake and fighting to get out of that cage. My body had all but given out on me as a reward. I couldn't allow it to. I pushed hard and found myself agonizing over the thought that the empty canteen bouncing around on my belt would offer me no relief. The cold air that filled my lungs, which was so much different from the comforting warmth I was used to, did no favors for me either.

The light was just up ahead, moving slowly to meet me across the sand, the friend I needed right now, offering me the only chance I had of making it back home alive. Once I made it a few steps in, I continued running but strained my neck to look over my shoulder, ready for anything.

Nothing was there, and it seemed that, at least for this brief moment, I had a little luck left in me after all. I slowed my pace to allow my legs a chance to make a slight recovery.

I was able to walk like this for a while. It was quiet. Too quiet. I could see Linus's face again and hear his last words. He told me I made him happy. It felt strange because I also wondered if I would ever be happy again. We'd only known each other for a few days, but I'd never felt that way about anyone before. My mood swung wildly from sadness back to anger again when I thought of the life we might've had together. The children we might have had. Grandchildren. I *hated* PanTech for taking him away from me. They *would* pay for this.

A movement far away caught my attention. It was a panther. They were strictly nocturnal and normally shied away from humans, but that was during the day. At night, I must have looked just as delicious as any other animal caught out alone, away from the rest of its herd. It walked with legs sharply bent, taking long and careful strides. I continued with my pace more or less the same. I didn't want to run, or I knew it would immediately give chase.

I'd hoped that our uneasy truce would hold, at least long enough for me to get close to the lights of the village. It would run away then, surely. But, those lights weren't in sight, and I was about to lose what little light I did have, as another inopportune cloud approached. I had seconds, and I couldn't take the chance.

I stopped, sat Ghost on the ground, and fired a shot at the panther. It jumped just as I'd raised the rifle, causing me to miss. Of all the times to miss....

It ran toward me, full power and speed, and I aimed as carefully as possible. One shot left. Just one shot. I drew in a deep breath and held it, steadying myself as much as I could, but it wasn't enough. There's just something about a black panther charging at you against a fading light, with your last shot that does something to the nerves. I fired again and missed. This was it.

No! I still had my knife, and I drew it. I still had my fingers. I'd stab it until the blade broke and gouge its eyes if I had to. I still had life in me, and as long as I had the life to breathe, I had the life to fight. I threw my rifle at it as it was about to pounce and screamed, hoping against hope that it would be startled at an unusual sound from its prey it didn't normally hunt. It wasn't. I was knocked to the ground hard, and I felt claws dig deep into my shoulders. Before it could sink its teeth into my neck, I was able to plant my knife all the way up to the hilt somewhere into its body. I'd hoped the neck. The other paw slammed into my other shoulder, not digging in as deeply, but enough that I lost grip on my knife. I slapped and clawed at the beast's face as it tried to maneuver to deliver the killing blow.

Light was coming from somewhere now, but I couldn't look away from the panther, or I was dead. After a short moment, the light was bright enough to make out the features of its face. The beast cried out and jumped backward. As it did, I saw a spear sticking out of its side, which the wielder quickly pulled back. I couldn't make out the figure. The lantern was placed on the ground, at their back, and they were only a shadow. Female, I thought, but I couldn't say for sure.

Had Cara come to rescue me?

The figure held the spear in a warrior's stance as the panther charged again. She thrust it into the beast's leg, took two steps forward with incredible finesse, and threw two more thrusts into the panther's chest before it could jump back.

Was that…?

"Mother!" I shouted.

"Run, Taylor. I'll stop it from following," she said, with surprising calmness.

"Not until I find Ghost! He's here. I just put him on the ground."

She brought the spear in closer and held it above her head, leaning forward—some kind of exotic stance I'd never seen before. The panther ran but soon turned back around. They fought this way. If they were wounded, they'd run a few steps away and turn to use their charge, and did this repeatedly. Their endurance was greater than anything else in the desert—even the boar's. "Take your time. This will be over soon, and I'll help you look."

Still calm, with a voice as even as stone. First, she knew about the PanTech armor, and now she fights with more skill than almost any man I'd seen. I had so many questions, but between what had happened with Linus and now finding and rescuing Ghost, there just wasn't room in my mind.

Just as I found him and the rifle, the panther charged Mother and pounced through the air. She stood straight, then stepped to her left, as though it were part of a dance she'd performed thousands of times, spinning the spear in an arc and slicing it across the side of the panther's neck. It must have realized the fight was not in its favor anymore because it turned immediately and ran away, off into the direction it had originally come from.

I took a step forward but fell to my knee. My body had reached its limits.

Mother ran over and caught me before I fell. "Mother, listen…this…shadowfalcon. Find Cara. Tell her to bring the small animal cage. Don't unwrap it."

I spilled all of this onto her because I thought I would pass out, but somehow I didn't.

Mother slipped my arm over her shoulder and helped me walk. We walked, and walked, and walked, but neither of us could find words for the other. At times, I would catch her looking down at me, with the saddest expression on her face. All of my mental power was invested into screaming at my legs to keep walking. One more step, then one more, until finally we'd reached the village.

Every inch of my body protested and seemed to threaten me if I chose anything other than immediate medical attention and sleep, but that's not the choice I had to make.

I glanced down at Ghost. Still calm, for now. I had to go to Cara and say whatever was needed to make her forgive me. We had a mythical beast to save.

CHAPTER 19

As we entered the village, I could feel my strength returning. At least, the illusion of strength. I had not slept, and it was nearly morning. It would be early morning for Cara when I woke her. She was nearly my age but lived alone. Her mother had died when she was very young, and her father died just a couple of years ago. She'd be more than capable of taking care of herself, but I worried for her, and I imagined she must feel very lonely.

Especially with a friend who punches her in the face....

"It's alright, Mother," I said, weakly. "I can make it to Cara's from here."

I held the rifle up toward her, but she shook her head.

"I know you. You'll bleed out trying to save that bird or wait too long to clean your wound. I'm better at cleaning and sewing wounds than you might think."

Normally, I would've been skeptical of her statement, given how pretty and delicate Mother went out of her way to be, but now…now, I wasn't sure. There was more to Mother than I realized, and for some reason, she'd kept it from me. Soon, I'd push for an explanation, even if she didn't want to give one to me. But soon felt like it was so far away. For now, I trusted her.

"I believe you," I said. "But…you don't have to. I'm sure Cara can check my wounds while I get started on Ghost."

"Ghost…I can't believe you've actually captured a shadowfalcon, Taylor. I've never seen one. Your father swore he'd seen one, as a boy, but I'd always wondered if he was mistaken."

"Mother?" I asked, after a moment of silence.

"Yes?"

"What did they do with Linus?"

She took a deep breath and let it out slowly. "Your father and your brother insisted on burying him in the village graveyard. I tried, but I couldn't talk them out of it. I spoke to the other two PanTech employees that came by later to retrieve them and told them we were planning to bury the other two next so it wouldn't look suspicious that we'd only buried Linus. They accepted my explanation, but still took the other two back with them. And shortly after," she sighed, "they returned to take Linus's body as well. I'm so sorry, Taylor."

I slowly shook my head. "No…he's gone. It doesn't matter if his meat and bones are here, or there, or wherever. They took him away from me either way…."

Mother leaned her head down and touched it to mine. We stayed that way for a moment. It caused my tears to flow again, but I sealed them off no sooner than they'd started.

"Come on," I said. "We need to move quickly."

A moment later, we were knocking on Cara's door. She opened it up almost immediately. So quickly that it startled me. When she saw it was me, she took a step back and hung her head.

"Taylor…I'm—"

"No. *I'm* sorry, Cara. Sorry for everything. I'm sorry for the things I said to you earlier. I'm sorry for hitting you. I'm sorry too for strolling into your house in the dark hours of the morning, bleeding on your floor, and with an injured animal that needs saving. Will you please help me?" I asked, tearing up yet again.

Pull it together, Taylor. You don't have time for this.

"You didn't need to ask," she said. "Tell me what you need and…wait. Is that…?"

"A shadowfalcon? Yes."

Cara put her hand over her heart, taking a step forward to get a closer look. "This is a sign from the gods, Taylor. It must be. I don't know what it means, but it means something."

"Maybe, but the gods aren't here to patch him up. Mother's going to tend to my wounds while you assist me, so I won't be moving. I need you to take me to a clean table and fetch my bag from the clinic. Bring a sheet of leather, about half an arm's length, and one of our smaller cages. I have some thick long leather gloves there as well. You know the ones. I'd been working on them to use for handling terror ant hives. I'll need them to handle him once his paralysis wears off."

She nodded with each thing I mentioned. "Got it. Anything else?"

I knew there'd be a lot of things I'd forget. Poor Cara would have to do a lot of running.

"Some water for her, please," Mother added.

Cara nodded, then motioned for us to follow her. She led us into a room with a large workbench and items made of leather hanging all around: belts, gloves, aprons, and more.

"I didn't know you did leather-working," I said.

"I do. I'd love to talk about it now, but I know there isn't time. If there's nothing else, I'm off."

I nodded. "Thank you."

I turned and leaned the rifle against the wall before laying Ghost across the clean workbench. I unwrapped my scarf from his body but leaving it over his eyes and began looking him over. Now, under the light of a brighter lantern, he looked even more amazing. But better than that, he looked alive. Completely immobilized by his own toxin, but still breathing shallow breaths. I gently extended one wing, the wing I already suspected of being healthy and studied it as a reference. I expected his other wing to be broken when I slowly, *very* slowly, extended it but was relieved to see that it wasn't.

At the same time, my mother had pulled back my shirt to check my wound. Her sigh gave away that it was a little more serious than she was hoping, but not life-threatening—just a lot of work.

I was somewhat embarrassed, but I knew I would have to take my shirt off so my mother could treat the wounds. That's just the way it would have to be. I attempted to raise my arms above my head but found that I couldn't.

"It's alright. I'll cut them off. They're destroyed anyway," Mother said, sensing my frustration at the thought of having my arms forced above my head, then potentially having to do delicate work on a shadowfalcon.

I nodded.

"Alright. Do it."

She picked up a pair of shears from one of the shelves and began cutting. I shut it out of my mind. I wouldn't let it distract me from the task at hand.

"I'm sure Cara has extra clothes for you after we finish and you're all bandaged up."

"As long as you can do it while I'm working, do whatever you need to do."

"You're going to work at the same time?" she asked.

"I don't know if it can wait that long. Just be as gentle as possible, but do what you have to do. I can take it, I promise."

I only hoped that I wasn't lying, but I needed her to believe that I knew it for a fact.

She pulled out her first aid pouch, and I recognized it as the one from earlier that she was going to use on Linus. Conscious thoughts of him started creeping back into my mind. His hand squeezing mine. His last words. The way PanTech had killed him on the street like he wasn't the great man he was. I'm glad he killed them both. I wish I could have killed them myself.

"Taylor? Are you alright?" Mother asked, noticing that I had drifted off into my own thoughts.

"No, Mother. I—"

Cara interrupted me as she burst back into the room. She immediately turned her back after seeing me. "Oh, sorry! Should I…?"

"No, Cara. Just be thankful we're not outside at the clinic or even in the tent. Put my tools on the end of the table, and fetch me some cactus wine. Mother will need it, and so will I."

Cara said nothing, just followed my instructions, placed my tools next to me, and ran out of the room. She returned quickly with the wine. Mother poured it carefully over my wounds before handing it to me. I attempted to turn it up, as I desperately wanted a drink, and thought it might help me with my nerves and a bit of the pain.

Mother put her hand under it and helped me bring it to my lips. I drank several big gulps and sat it on the table before nodding to Mother.

"I'm ready when you are," I said.

She positioned herself to my right, and Cara stood to my left. I examined his right wing carefully and found several feathers had been crushed. Unfortunately, he was bleeding from all three of them. A bird didn't have much blood to lose.

"No break—" I winced as the needle entered my shoulder. I clenched my teeth and did my best to speak through the pain. "No breaks on the…ah…wing bones, but three feathers are…ow…broken, and they are blo—" I drew in a sharp breath. Thankfully, Mother was ignoring my obvious distress, just as I'd asked her to. "They're blood feathers. I need pliers, and starch, quickly."

Cara ran out of the room, quickly returned with the starch in a small bowl, and grabbed a pair of pliers from a drawer. She grabbed the bottle of wine from the table and poured some onto the pliers, wiping them down with a clean cloth, then handing them to me. I plucked the three feathers rapidly, then reached for the wine from Cara. I nearly dropped it when Mother pulled the stitching tight and cut it.

"See, I'm even faster than you," she teased.

"Probably because I'm not as rough," I said, almost allowing myself to smile. I poured wine onto the wounds, then picked up some of the starch and stuffed it onto them. "With those feathers out, the bleeding can stop. He was—" I winced as Mother poured wine over the smaller wound on my other shoulder. "He was lucky," I finished.

"So were you by the look of it. What happened, Taylor?"

Mother had begun expertly wrapping my bandages as we spoke.

"The long story will have to wait. The short story is that the desert is a hard place to survive at night," I replied. A thought struck me. "Oh, the fox! There was a fox that was still there too. Got hit with Ghost's paralysis toxin. We need to go…in…the morning."

At first, I thought the floor in the room was rising but realized that when Mother grabbed one arm, and Cara the other, it was the other way around.

"I'll take Cara. If it's still there and alive, we can handle it. You need to rest," Mother insisted.

I sighed. "No, I…," I didn't even bother finishing that sentence. I wasn't kidding anyone. There's no way I'd be able to go out at first light, which was probably coming very soon, to check on the fox. It would be selfish of me to insist that I be the one who goes. Cara *could* handle it, and if Mother could handle herself that well at night, alone in the desert, she could certainly handle the mostly gentle creatures that roamed the desert by day. "Okay," I conceded. "You win."

"Good, so I'll cage Ghost and make sure the bandage around his eyes is tied well, and you won't need anything else."

"Hey Cara," I said.

"No, Taylor. I'm not hearing anything else from you. You're going to lie down and rest."

"That's fine but…could you at least get me a shirt?"

"Oh!" she said, wincing. "Sorry. Of course."

"And…thank you," I added. "Thank you both."

CHAPTER 20

My dream was familiar. I was lying on my back in the sand, and my skin felt comforted by its soft bed of warmth. The sun kissed my face like a loving parent and made me feel safe. A gentle breeze passed over me, giving me goosebumps and making my skin tingle in the most wonderful way. A figure approached in the distance. I could hear it screaming, but I couldn't make out what it was saying or who it was. It bent down over me and continued whatever it was doing, but I was undisturbed. A small herd of deer walked past, and I tilted my head ever so slightly to watch them attentively. They weren't scrawny like the ones I'd seen reluctantly chewing on the remains of the snake. Their coats were beautiful, and their eyes were sharp. One stopped to look back at me, chewing a mouthful of grass, as calm and at peace as I was. If I weren't so comfortable, I'd have gone out to see it. I wasn't sure how, but I knew it wouldn't flee from me; we were too content to leave what we were doing.

The figure over me was still yelling, and I could start to hear it now, almost like a whisper. "Move your hand," it seemed to say. That's what it was, a little louder this time. "Move your hand," she shouted. It was a woman, but who? She kept repeating the same thing. "Move your hand. Move your hand. Move your hand!"

My hand. My hand? I looked down, and I was holding both hands over my side. I was wearing armor, like what PanTech soldiers wear. When I saw my hands, my feeling started to change from serene comfort to agony, unlike anything I'd felt before.

"Move your hand!" she shouted again.

Finally, I listened and moved my hands. The wound was grotesque. Was I dying? Of course, I was dying. Nothing would survive a wound like this.

The girl grabbed my hand and held it tightly, her body shaking with sobs. I could almost make her out, but not quite. Her voice was certainly familiar. Very familiar. Was that…?

I could feel my body going cold, slipping into that eternal sleep we all eventually fall into. I could feel my grip loosening on her hand, but she only gripped tighter. At least I could make out all of the features of her face as the last of my strength slipped away. It was…me.

I sat up abruptly as my sleep broke, and as bad as the physical pain in my body was from having moved that quickly with my shoulders freshly wounded, the agony of sadness I felt was so much worse. At that moment, the desire to die again filled my mind and my heart. I wanted it more than anything. To die and be free of the pain. If the gods were real, and I saw Linus again, all the better.

"Glad to see you're awake, but would you mind moving a little slower. It always hurts worse the next day, so you better preserve the stitches that are in there now," Mother said.

I tried to laugh, but even though I could normally fake a laugh in any situation, all of my will couldn't summon one now. Instead, I started crying again.

"Oh, Taylor…," she said, leaning toward me. "You dreamed about Linus, didn't you? I'm sorry…."

In an instant, the switch flipped on my emotions, as they often did, and I growled with the surge of anger. "Don't be," I said, slowly lowering myself back onto the bed. I noticed something odd out of the corner of my eye. Was that…?

"Is that the fox sitting on your lap?" I asked, craning my neck to see better.

She continued stroking the fox's fur and smiled. "It is. Isn't she beautiful?"

I nodded. "She is but…is she still paralyzed?"

Mother sighed. "Completely. I've been watching both her and Ghost. Not so much as a twitch yet."

"If they don't come around soon, I'll have to force water into her. Ghost is too small for that, and he'll need to start eating soon so he can heal properly. I should have asked you to—"

"Get some of the boar meat? Oh, we did. I've saved some to feed Ghost and the fox, but we're going to have some fine meals at home too."

"Mother…?"

"Yes?" she asked, tilting her head.

"How do you know how to dress a boar, track a person through the desert night, and fight a panther off with a spear? And, how did you know about Linus's armor? The way it was supposed to come apart."

She grinned. "That's a lot of questions all at once."

"You don't have to answer them in any particular order, but could you answer them?"

She looked away, stopped stroking the fox for a moment, and seemed to contemplate on the request. "I don't like talking about it, but…you deserve an answer."

I said nothing, suddenly filling with the anxiety of thinking I knew at least some of the answers already.

"I was born in a different adversity zone. There, it was much larger than our village. It was a kingdom, and the ruler of that kingdom was called Emperor."

I held up my hand. "I'm sorry. Just…give me a moment to process that. You weren't born here? You must be the only one here who wasn't. How is that even possible?"

She smiled, but it was a pained smile. "I'll get to that part. It'll be easier if I just explain as I go."

I nodded.

"When I was a small girl, things weren't so bad for the people of the kingdom. However, when I was fifteen, the old emperor passed away, leaving his young son to rule the kingdom. Most things stayed the same at first, but it wasn't long before the differences started to reveal themselves.

"The new emperor was obsessed with surrounding himself with young, beautiful women. They worked in his palace, dressed him, prepared his meals, and even served as his private bodyguards. One day, I was out in the fields with my father, tending to our farm, when the emperor walked by with his new bodyguards. I marveled at them at first. They were so beautiful but fierce at the same time. I caught his eye, and he called for us to speak with him.

"I never saw my family again after that day, and I still don't know what happened to them. It wasn't until after I was forced to join the emperor's service that I recognized the sadness in most of those girls' eyes and came to know it well."

She sighed, dabbing her eyes with her sleeve.

"You don't have to keep going if you don't want," I offered, suddenly feeling remorse for how harshly I'd judged my Mother throughout my life. It seemed I knew very little about her.

"No. It's alright. It's been a while since I spoke about this, is all," she collected herself and continued. "At first, I was a dancer. Being so young, I wasn't much good for anything else. I quickly realized that the girls who didn't put much effort into capturing the emperor's attention were placed in the most difficult roles. I was moved to the position of assisting one of the palace's doctors after failing to capture the emperor's eyes anymore as one of his dancers.

"But, after noticing the emperor rubbed his shoulder often, I borrowed a recipe from one of the doctor's books for a salve to soothe muscle pain. I convinced the emperor to allow me to apply it and give him a massage, and before long, I tended to him daily. On my nineteenth birthday, I was moved to his personal guard and trained with the spear."

"Wait," I interrupted. "Did you decline to join PanTech after taking the exam?"

She shook her head. "The emperor had much power, but he thought he had more than he did. Every year when it was time for testing, he would hide away all the young women and forbade them from revealing themselves or taking the exam. It wasn't until I was twenty-three that PanTech soldiers marched into the palace. The emperor ordered his bodyguards to protect him, but none dared. He was dragged away screaming, and I don't know what they did with him after that.

"PanTech installed a poor young woman as the new empress, but I'm not sure what came of that. A large exam was held to accommodate all the women who had been denied in the years previous. I passed, was more than happy to leave, and was assigned to the role of soldier. As a soldier, you can leave that service young. It's actually one of the most sought-after positions in PanTech, and anyone given the role must be both exceptionally bright and physically able. I completed many years of service and met your father shortly before my time was up. Since he'd declined his invitation to join PanTech, despite his exceptional score, I made up my mind to stay here with him."

"I didn't know soldiers could do that. That means Linus really could have stayed here. I could have declined my invitation if I passed the exam. And…," I trailed off, choking back the urge to cry again.

"I'm sorry, Taylor. I wish I could've done something to stop it."

"Why did you keep this from me for all of these years? Even Father didn't tell us, and Ferris doesn't seem to know either."

"He doesn't."

"But, why?" I asked, pressing.

"I was asked not to," she said.

"Just like that?"

"Just like that. I know you don't like PanTech, but my experience with them was different than yours. They were my savior from a far worse situation. If you must be a slave, better to serve the more righteous master than the cruel one."

"Yeah, I'm not so sure I buy into that, Mother. Sorry."

"I understand. I don't expect you to. You're your own woman."

"Do you? Do you really understand? Because it sounds like you don't. I'm sorry your life was awful, but when you and Father fell in love, you were able to be together. Linus is *dead*. We can never be together now. He died because he helped me and because he saved our village from that giant snake you saw. You did see it, right?"

She sat quietly for a moment, considering everything I'd said with far more calmness than I'd expected. "So that's why they went after him. But…that shouldn't be worthy of execution, and how did they know so quickly?"

"They heard me shooting, I'm sure."

"Yes, but not him. All we heard in the village was your rifle firing, not his."

"I don't know, and I don't really feel like going to ask them at the moment. It was probably a newer tracking technology on their armor or their blasters."

"I don't think—"

As she began to speak, the fox raised her head, and we both froze to watch. No sooner than she had done so, she lowered her head again.

"The paralysis must be wearing off. That means Ghost will be moving soon if he isn't already."

"It's alright. Cara is in there with him. She came home just before you woke up. She wanted you to come and see her when you came to. She has something to show you."

CHAPTER 21

I walked into Cara's shop, closing the door behind me, and found her working on something at the table. Ghost stood up in his cage, eyeing everything with caution and curiosity but a distinct lack of fear.

"What have you tied around his legs?" I asked.

She brightened up. "So glad you asked. This should help you control him a bit on your glove. Your glove, I reinforced with two additional layers of leather, by the way."

I scrunched my chin and nodded repeatedly. "I'm…really impressed, actually. I had no idea you could do all this. What's that you're working on now?" I pointed to the leather piece she'd stretched over a wooden ball in front of her.

"Oh, this?" She held it up and spun it in her hand. "You know how birds don't really pay attention to things they can't see? I thought this would help you train him if you had him around other people."

I held up my hands. "Oh no. Absolutely not. I am *not* taking him out around other people. The hood is a good idea, but he's staying a secret for as long as I can keep it."

Cara frowned. "Why not? Ghost will give everyone hope. It's a good omen, Taylor."

"Let's say that's true. All the more reason to keep him a secret. If PanTech finds out that everyone thinks he's some kind of good omen, a sign of prosperity to come, they'll pluck him right in front of everyone. We have to maintain an optimal level of adversity, remember?"

"Okay, if you say so. You're probably right anyway." She frowned, and her shoulders sagged, but she continued stitching.

"Sorry to be so depressing, Cara. And…sorry for what I did to you. You didn't deserve—"

Cara shook her head. "No. You don't need to apologize. I'm sorry for what you went through. I can't even imagine what you must've felt, so please don't apologize to me."

I smiled and wrapped my arms around her shoulders. "Thank you, Cara. I was worried you might not forgive me."

"Oh, please," she said, playfully, returning to her stitching. She looked from the hood to Ghost, then to the hood again. "You know, maybe let's let him get more used to us before we try to put this on."

"That would probably be a good idea," I said. "Say…I wonder why the toxin doesn't immediately kill what it comes into contact with. It seems to be potent. From what I could tell, it runs from some kind of glands above his beak, onto his beak, and enters the bloodstream when he slices something with it."

She shrugged. "Maybe he measures the dosage somehow?"

"Sure, but he doesn't inject it directly, like a snake. He basically drips it onto the open wound. Then there's the rumor that they're able to turn the venom on themselves to kill themselves if they have no way to escape imminent death. Obviously, swallowing it doesn't have the same effect, or they'd accidentally contaminate themselves with it all the time. It must be some kind of backward path into their own bloodstream."

Cara sat the hood down, scratching her chin and leaning back into her chair, staring at Ghost intently. "Too bad we can't just ask him," she said.

"Hey, Ghost. We're really curious. Would you mind explaining your toxin to us?" I asked.

Ghost looked between the two of us as though he were genuinely trying to understand the sounds we were making. Maybe he was.

She sighed but smiled. "Okay, obviously we *can* ask him. Thanks for that."

"You're welcome," I retorted, my tone much brighter than it had been. I really was thankful for Cara. We were never competitive the way many girls were, despite our closeness in age and our working together. Cara always put her relationships above any kind of recognition. She preferred to live quietly and stay out of the way, attracting as little attention to herself as possible.

It's what I wanted, too, or so I thought. Either I was lying to myself, or I was just really bad at it.

A knock came at Cara's door, and a muffled voice carried over the other side. "Your brother and Father are here, Taylor, and I could also use some advice on what to do with this fox. It's alert and looking around."

Cara and I nodded at one another, and she put a small sheet over Ghost's cage before we exited the room.

Father and Ferris were both gawking at the fox when we entered the common room as Mother continued holding her. Ferris started to reach out and touch it but stopped when he noticed that Cara and I walk into the room.

"Taylor!" Ferris yelled, making the fox recoil. "You're awake."

I held my finger over my lips and pointed to the fox with my other hand. "It's a wild animal, Ferris. Please don't scare it. And, yes, I'm awake."

He and Father stepped over to me and wrapped their arms around me tightly. Too tightly, and I winced. "Do you mind?"

"Yes, do you mind?" Mother echoed. "I've already scolded her about minding her stitches, and I told the two of you only a few minutes ago."

The two of them abruptly released their hug at Mother's scolding, and Father laid his hand lightly on my shoulder. "I'm sorry, Tay. I'm sorry I wasn't there. I would've tried to help."

"Then I'm glad you weren't, and I'm sure Linus would've felt the same way. He stopped me from helping him, and he'd have found a way to stop you too. Only PanTech is to blame for this, and no one else."

The silence in the room, which extended far longer than it should've, gave away the agreement. Even Mother didn't argue with me this time, although I was sure she didn't quite feel the same way. She was a retired PanTech soldier, after all.

"Anyway…," I continued. "I have something to show you, assuming Mother hasn't ruined the surprise."

Mother beamed. "Oh no, I wouldn't dare," she said, handing the fox over to Cara, who had been standing there with her arms open, hinting that she'd like to put it away. "Just remember," she said, looking between Ferris and Father. "I was the first person who got to see it after Taylor."

"Everyone, follow me," I said, making my way back into Cara's room, leaving the door swung open behind me, allowing everyone to funnel in. "Stay at that end of the room, please," I added, looking over my shoulder as I approached the cage.

I slowly pulled the sheet from the cage, revealing a suddenly alert but seemingly fearless Ghost.

Father and Ferris stood there for a moment, frozen, and silent. Ferris leaned forward as though he was trying to stretch just a little closer to make sense of what he clearly didn't believe he was seeing.

Father dropped to his knees. "Oh, gods. I can't believe it. I always knew they were real. I saw one when I was a boy, but no one believed me. No one has ever captured one. Not as long as this village has stood. Not even PanTech has managed it. Taylor, you are…," he hesitated. "I'm sorry to say this, considering the timing, and circumstances, but you are blessed by the gods to have performed such a feat. This must be an omen, but I don't know what kind."

I'd never heard Father mention the gods so directly before. It was highly frowned upon to discuss them anymore, and Mother and Father never did all that often, even behind closed doors. Her, I could understand. They weren't her gods, after all, but I was fairly certain Father didn't even believe in them. I was even more certain that I didn't. If they existed, they clearly had less power than PanTech. "PanTech doesn't care about the gods, Father, and the gods don't care about PanTech. He will be kept a secret so he doesn't end up plucked and cooked in the town square. If I hear one more thing about how he's an omen, I'm going to lose my mind. He's a bird, albeit a rare one, but *just* a bird. Maybe I should have named him Omen instead of Ghost."

Cara shrugged and smiled.

Father rose to his feet. "Sorry. I was just a little overwhelmed. When I was a boy, many more people talked about the shadowfalcon than they do now. Some even said that the one who could tame the bird would be the chosen of the gods. I had even heard that the gods would grant them immortality."

I shuddered. "Sounds like a curse to me."

"Then you should probably stop behaving as though you're immortal, then," he said, shaking his head. "I just still can't believe it. A real shadowfalcon…, have you noticed how closely he pays attention to us? He looks between us as we're speaking. Did you notice that? Do you…?" he hesitated for a moment but continued. "Do you think he understands us?"

Despite the urge to dismiss it, I had to consider this seriously. "I have noticed, but I'm not sure. I don't think he understands us now. How could he? But maybe he is actually trying to. It's possible that he's studying our tone and our actions when we say certain words, like a small child learning their parents' language.

Or, maybe he's just curious, as most birds are, and we fascinate him. He's probably seen just as few humans as we've seen of his kind. I just expected him to be more…more—"

"Afraid?" Cara interrupted. "I expected him to be terrified. That's why I rushed to make him the hood, but now I'm not sure he'll even need it. Do you think there's something wrong with him?"

I shook my head. "No. I think bravery and stupidity may just be his blessing and curse. He reminds me of…well…Linus." I paused for a moment, not daring to continue speaking, feeling the tears welling up in my eyes and my voice choking. I closed my eyes and looked down for a long moment. "I'm going to take good care of him."

"*We're* going to take good care of him. I'll be with you every step of the way. Whenever you need help treating him, or if you need your glove repaired or new accessories for his training, just come to me, and I'll help you," Cara said, smiling.

I took a step toward Cara, my arms extended out, and embraced her in the tightest hug I could muster. It hurt *so* much, but I didn't care. I didn't deserve a friend like Cara. I'm not sure anyone did.

Mother stepped up beside us and put her arms around us both. "We're all here for you, Taylor. I don't care what PanTech says. You've had enough adversity for a lifetime."

I lost my battle with the tears, and they flowed freely from my eyes. I tried to answer but couldn't even choke out anything resembling words. I released Cara and hugged Mother just as tightly. She stroked my hair as she held me gently in her arms. I never knew for certain if she loved me, and I always doubted that she did, but between the previous night when she saved me in the desert and the way she held me at this moment, I knew for certain that she loved me so much. Everything she'd ever said or done was to help me because she knew that beauty, charm, and manipulation were weapons, just like the spear or sword. She wanted me to be able to use them effectively. I should have listened to her.

Finally, I was able to slow the tears enough to compose myself. "I love you, Mother."

Father and Ferris stepped over and joined in our growing group hug, and I couldn't help but notice the oddly curious expression in the falcon's vibrant green eyes.

CHAPTER 22

Unfortunately, I had no idea what I was doing when it came to training a falcon. Luckily, I had foundational knowledge that gave me a great place to start. I understood birds, but Ghost was no mere bird. In days, he was able to follow verbal commands. Days. Not weeks. Cara has been there with me for the first couple of nights, far out into the desert. She had to fetch leather to strengthen the glove on that first night after Ghost's talons went right through it. The end result ended up being three times as thick as before and a stiffer leather. Ghost didn't seem to mind. Then again, he didn't seem to mind anything.

Unless Ghost was just an oddity, even amongst other shadowfalcons, I found it difficult to believe that there were many of these creatures out there actively avoiding humans. Ghost had several chances to leave. On the third night, I cut the leather strap bindings from his legs, half expecting him to flee. It would have been alright with me if he had. I never liked the idea of *owning* an animal like this and keeping them against their will with no chance of escape. Yet, when I cut the bindings, he appeared completely uninterested. Did he lack the intelligence to realize that they were gone, or was he actually choosing to stay? It was surely the latter, but…why?

It went on like this for several more days. On the sixth day, I killed a rabbit, showed it to Ghost, and in hours he'd gone out and retrieved another rabbit. Dead, like the one I'd shown him.

"How do I tell you to bring it back paralyzed and not dead?" I asked.

Ghost tilted his head, first to one side, then to the other.

"Can you understand me? Are you…trying to learn to understand my language?"

A restrained chuckle came from behind me.

"What are the two of you talking about over here?" Mother asked, petting the fox she was holding in her arms.

Now that Cara had finished modifying the glove, she didn't need to come along with me every night. Mother volunteered to come instead and insisted on bringing that iron fox with her. I was sure they'd end up killing one another, but they didn't. Somehow.

"Ghost is trying to tell me something. Or, nothing. I can't figure him out. When I speak to him directly, he tilts his head. Have you noticed that?"

"Omen does that too, you know. Maybe they're just curious," she said, shrugging.

"Omen? You named her Omen? Seriously? I know you've taken to her, but I really wish you'd left her home."

"Hold on. One criticism at a time, please. Omen and I were just out taking a walk. Do you own the desert now?" she turned her head away from me in mock frustration, punctuated with an exaggerated *hmph*.

"No. Do you?" I asked.

"Not everything holds a grudge like you, Taylor. Ghost barely even notices her."

"And what about Omen?" I snapped. "She's nervous. Look at her ears pulled back and her tail tucked."

"And why do you think I brought her? Like all of us, she will need to face her fears quickly. Otherwise, she will lack confidence and be vulnerable forever. In this, we and animals are alike," she said.

"That's because we *are* animals, Mother. Also, how did she become friendly with you so quickly? You've handled foxes before, where you're from, am I right?"

Mother smiled and nodded, scratching Omen's neck before putting her down and watching her run off into the vastness of the desert. She smiled again, pulling two wooden swords from her belt.

"Why don't you send Ghost to fetch a rabbit? Since I can't reason with you to stay out of trouble, I should teach you to be better prepared for it."

I hummed a deep tone, and Ghost flew off.

"Nonverbal commands. Clever," Mother said, tapping her chin and smiling, tossing me a wooden sword with her other hand.

I let it fly past me and land on the ground. "You're letting her go?"

"She deserves to be free. She isn't like Ghost, Taylor. She's more like you. She'll never listen to anyone. She'll only be happy going her own way."

"But…she seemed to really like you," I said.

She laughed and sat down on the sand, patting the spot beside her.

I sat down next to her and rested my head on her shoulder.

"Taylor. If it's alright with you, could you tell me about Linus?"

I looked up at her, surprised. I wanted to be upset, but I couldn't find the emotion.

She seemed to notice my expression.

"You don't have to. It's just that you were never really interested in boys these past few years. Your father and I wondered if you would ever be. Your brother talks about a different girl every day, it seems. You always seemed to hate PanTech so much, and he was a soldier. I know there must be more to him than I realized. We could see how you'd fallen for him. I just want to know more about him."

I stared down at the sand for a long time, hugging my knees to my chest. Mother deserved to know more about him.

"Linus was…," I began, but my voice caught, and I found myself unable to fight back the tears.

Mother wrapped her arm around me and hugged me tightly. "It's alright. You can tell me when you're ready."

"I'm…," I sniffed and took several deep breaths. "No, I'm alright. I just need a minute."

She nodded and kept her arm around me tightly while I considered how to put it into words. Did I even know what made Linus so wonderful? I hadn't thought about it in terms that could be explained. I just…felt it.

"Linus was brave. He was bold, and somehow he put everyone else before himself and also followed his own path. No matter what the consequences were, he did what he thought was right. He went against his fellow soldiers, his commander, and even PanTech itself, and it didn't even matter to him if he won. All that mattered to him is that it was what he wanted to do, and he thought it was the right thing to do. I've never met a man like that before. It only took a few short days before I really knew him. The way he stood up to the chieftain for that girl he didn't even know, and for me. The way he went with me to fight the snake…it was my responsibility, not his. This was my village, not his. These are my friends, my family, and neighbors, not his. He did it for no other reason than because it was the right thing to do. I knew when we'd killed the snake, and he protected me from the explosion, that I loved him with all my heart. Maybe he didn't feel that way about me, not yet, but I…just knew. If we only had time…."

I lost my composure and the battle with my tears. Mother hugged me tightly.

"I knew the same with your father, Taylor. The day I met him, I asked him to show me his inventions, days before PanTech decided to destroy them. He hated me at first. He was convinced that I'd asked about his inventions as a spy and reported him. It was weeks before he would speak to me again. In the end, he found that he loved me more than he hated PanTech, and I loved him more than I loved PanTech. I'm so sorry, Taylor. I wish you could have had the same chance. It's unfair that was robbed from you. I know it doesn't seem like it now, but eventually, you will heal, and maybe you'll find another, worthy of your love."

"I know what you're saying is true, Mother, but right now it—"

I was interrupted by something suddenly appearing in front of us, slamming onto the ground. I squeaked and fell backward, and even Mother jumped a bit.

In the dim lantern light, I could see that it was a rabbit, but I was also pretty certain of the fact that they don't just fall from the sky.

"Ghost, was that you? Ghost, get down here! Bad Ghost!"

Mother held her hand over her mouth in a failed attempt to hide the growing snicker.

I put my hand on my chest and took a deep breath, then let it out. "He nearly frightened me to death. I didn't teach him to do that."

"Maybe you were right," she said once she finally managed to stop laughing.

I shook my fist at Ghost…wherever he was. "About what?" I asked.

"About him being clever. I believe he was playing with you, startling you for a bit of fun."

No way. Could he…? No. "He probably just dropped it by mistake."

Ghost suddenly appeared in front of us, landing on the ground near the rabbit, and looked up at me. He nodded toward the rabbit.

"You…want to eat it?" I asked.

He nodded toward it again several times.

"Okay. Eat it."

He walked over to the rabbit and began eating it, more slowly than I expected.

"Did you see that, Mother?"

"Do you still think he's just a mere bird?" she asked.

"I don't know what to think. What about you?"

She shrugged. "You're the expert, Taylor. Your father believes he's nearly divine, perhaps more than nearly. Cara seems to believe the same. You are in a better position than anyone else to learn the truth."

"The truth scares me sometimes," I said.

That might be the truest thing I'd ever said to Mother, except it was more than just the truth that scared me. Maybe that's why I tried so hard to appear like I was scared of absolutely nothing. Maybe I'd convinced everyone of that. Now I just needed to convince myself.

"Me too, Taylor. I think the same is true for everyone, except for maybe your father. But, enough of that. Since Ghost will be busy for a bit longer, I'll train you with the sword tonight. On one condition."

I raised my brow. "Oh? And what might that be?"

She grinned. "You have to let me teach you how to apply eye makeup."

I rolled my eyes. "Fine. Deal."

She smiled, and I felt a warmth come over me, like walking up to a fire on a cold night. This feeling was followed quickly by a sting of guilt, remembering all the times I'd disrespected Mother, and assumed she had the worst of motives that she didn't love me. That she only cared about herself and being pretty. Or that she might faint at the sight of dirt on her clothing. Although I wouldn't dare allow her to know it, I now very much looked forward to putting on makeup together.

"Wise choice," she said. "Today, it will be the sword, and tomorrow we will go over a few hand-to-hand techniques. Go ahead. Pick it up."

I leaned down and picked up the wooden sword, doing my best to copy her stance.

"Ready?" she asked.

"Ready."

CHAPTER 23

The next month went by like a blur. I continued taking Ghost out at night for training and sleeping in a couple of extra hours in the morning. I'd moved him into my room, and he'd healed up nicely. It was still much safer to have another person with me, just in case I was accidentally hit with his paralysis toxin. Not to mention his talons were sharper than any knife or spear I'd ever seen. Even though he'd never tried to hurt me on purpose, I still had to be extremely careful.

Ghost's rate of learning was nothing short of incredible. In only a few weeks, he'd gone from staying on my arm without being held, to flying back, to chasing a lure we'd made from rabbit fur, to going out and retrieving rabbits of his own and bringing them back. Now, he'd mastered attack commands and differentiated between commands to use his toxin, or not use it, and whether or not to kill. Sometimes, when I'd let Ghost hunt for a while, Mother would continue teaching me sword technique and hand-to-hand combat.

Still, she preferred to instruct me as she always had, in the arts of charm, persuasion, and beauty. Only now, I wasn't so dismissive and rebellious. Although I didn't choose to exercise these skills…well…*ever* really, I still committed them to memory, for a time when they might be practical and useful. I'd taken to wearing my hair in dreadlocks, the way Father had when I was younger. Mother helped since my hair was much different from his. To my great surprise, she approved of this new look. She said it added a layer to my unusual beauty. In reality, I valued the extra few minutes of sleep it bought me, and although I did enjoy the look, it really was more about saving time. Sacrificing beauty for a few minutes of rest, now *that* Mother probably wouldn't approve of. Then again, she did scold me for not getting enough sleep because she claimed it would cause me to get bags under my eyes. There were only so many things I could juggle at once.

My eighteenth birthday came, and Father gifted me one of his smoking pipes. The one Linus smoked the day before he…was murdered by PanTech. Despite Father's encouragement, I wasn't ready to smoke it, even though I valued it greatly. Cara had given me a pair of leather boots she'd made with the help of the village's cobbler. Mother had given me a strange black dress. She said it was one of her most prized possessions and that it was her only thing left from her home. She'd worn it when she left to join PanTech. It had ridiculously baggy sleeves and an equally ridiculously wide belt that wrapped around the waist. I thought it looked embarrassingly silly, but I didn't dare say such a thing to Mother. I accepted it with great appreciation. If nothing else, because of how much it meant to Mother. That alone made it mean something to me.

It was now only a matter of weeks until the exams started, and I would have to decide if I passed, whether or not to join PanTech and leave the village. I was leaning very strongly toward staying and continuing to run the clinic. Mother and Ferris felt very strongly that I could make a bigger difference if I joined. Maybe I could work my way up in the hierarchy after a while and change how things were run. I think I'd always believed shadowfalcons were more likely to be real than the possibility PanTech could be changed from the inside. Then again, shadowfalcons *did* turn out to be real, so I couldn't exactly dismiss that based solely on the odds of it happening. I just didn't know if I wanted to be the one to waste my life on a long shot like that. I'd be just as happy, probably happier, running the clinic for the rest of my life and personally passing it on to someone else. Or was I just lying to myself?

One week after my birthday, Cara invited me to her home. She said there was someone I should meet but left out any other details. When I arrived, a young woman was sitting at the table with Cara. She looked older than us, probably in her late twenties, and wore a warm smile that didn't seem to weaken upon my arrival.

"You must be Taylor," she said, her smile still unwavering.

I returned her smile, cautiously. "I don't know who you must be," I admitted.

"Taylor, this is Lucille," Cara offered. "She's a friend of mine, and I thought you might like to meet her. She's someone who hates PanTech just as much as you do."

I nodded but immediately felt nervous. I had a feeling I knew where this was going, but I was put in the awkward position of neither being able to say so aloud nor knowing what I'd say even when I could. "Nice to meet you, Lucille."

"Taylor, I promise I'll get to the point quickly, and I won't waste your time. I know you're a busy woman, and you were probably preparing for your exams coming up since you just turned eighteen."

I shook my head. "Not exactly. I'm thinking I'm going to refuse admission if I pass."

"Is that because you like it here or because you hate PanTech?" she asked, leaning forward, resting her elbows on the table. She was still smiling, but with a small adjustment, it took on a more mischievous feel.

"Both. After all, my father stayed, but PanTech stopped him from pursuing his work because it would reduce the adversity of children in the village. Thankfully, they don't care so much about animals. As long as the animals aren't benefitting us, I'm free to help as many as I want. My teacher actually failed the exam but was a pretty decent veterinarian anyway."

Still smiling, she shook her head. "You forgot the part about PanTech."

"I'm sorry, but I don't really want to talk about PanTech. I despise them. They took someone important away from me, and I'll never forgive them for it. Don't bring them up again, or I'm leaving." My breathing hastened, and my blood started to boil. It was an all too familiar feeling over the past month, as I struggled to keep my already bad temper, now much worse, under enough control to function from day to day.

She held up her hands in defeat, finally letting her smile fade from her face. "Not even if I offer you a chance to harm them, right here in your very own village?"

My skin tingled, and my anger gave way to knots in my stomach. "You're a rebel. One of those that PanTech is staying outside the village to collect information on."

"And yet, we're still here. Not one of us has been caught, and we've stayed one step ahead of them at every turn. We know we can't take them in a fire fight. Our sticks, and rocks, and spears are no match for their rifles and blasters. We don't have special suits to make us stronger, faster, and stabilize our wounds. We don't have vehicles to cover distant land in minutes or limitless wealth from PanTech to replenish anything lost or damaged. What we do have, is the human mind. In this, we are the same. No different at all. What we can do, Taylor, is outsmart them and outmaneuver them."

I stared at her for a moment, locking eyes, and after that moment, I was sure she'd look away. She didn't. Her smile didn't return, and she remained stoic and confident. This wasn't a pitch. This was the truth. At least, the truth as she understood it, which is all the truth is to any of us. I broke the connection first.

"Cara, why did you invite me here to meet Lucille? Are you…?" I started but thought better of finishing the question.

"No. I'm far too scared to be a rebel, Taylor. You know that. But you…you're brave. You're so smart and so brave, and most importantly, you have—"

I shook my head subtly, and fortunately, Lucille wasn't looking in my direction when I did. Don't you *dare* mention Ghost. Cara took the hint.

She continued, without doing anything to acknowledge my gesture or missing a step. "—such a kind heart."

"I'm sorry, but I'm not sure kind hearts is what a rebellion needs. I better—"

"It's not the kind heart I'm questioning, Taylor," Lucille interrupted. "It's the 'brave' part."

She eyed me up and down. I wasn't about to take the bait. "If you say so. I think I'd better go."

Lucille continued on as though I'd said nothing. "Between your pretty mother and the renowned genius of your father, I don't think you've had a truly hard day in your life."

"Uh-huh," I said, standing up. "Good evening."

"The only PanTech soldier you'll ever hurt is the blonde one you got killed."

I had only begun to turn to leave but whirled back around, took a step toward the table, and jumped into the air, stretching out my body in a drop-kicking motion aimed for Lucille's face. She slid her head to the side and wrapped her arm around my legs, pivoting and throwing me off into the floor.

I jumped to my feet as she reached for my shirt, grabbing her wrists and twisting them as best I could to throw her off balance, using her forward momentum against her, just the way Mother had shown me. It worked, sending her tripping to the floor, scraping her chin, and bloodying her nose as she landed face first while I held her wrists to prevent her from breaking her own fall. I twisted her arm behind her back, and without even realizing what I was doing, I put her in a position to dislocate her shoulder.

Before I could pull back to finish the motion, Cara grabbed me and began pulling me away.

"Taylor, stop! Please. She's just testing you," Cara said, as though that would make a difference.

"I know she's testing me, but…," I turned my attention to Lucille. "If you *ever* speak of Linus again, if you so much as whisper his name, I will *kill* you!" I shouted.

Cara put her fingers to her lips, desperate for me to lower my voice. "Shh…someone might hear."

Lucille rolled onto her back, finally finished with her moaning from what must have been an extremely painful impact to the nose. "Hah! I wasn't expecting that at all. I think I learned my lesson today. Maybe it's time to retire that tactic since I can't back it up anymore. She's right that I was testing you, and you passed."

I pulled against Cara, growling as I dragged her with me toward Lucille, ready to finish what I started.

Lucille threw up her hands, surrendering. "Wait! Before you jump on top of me and start bashing my face in, ask yourself which you hate worse: The lie I told to make you angry, that you were the one who got him killed or the people who *actually* killed him."

I stopped, feeling the motivation to fight fading from my muscles. That question was easy to answer, and it was easier to answer than I realized. If the rebels had a way to hurt PanTech, I wanted a piece of that. Maybe for every bit of pain I gave them, it would heal a part of the pain they gave me. Not that we could ever be even. It would never be enough. Even I knew that, as consumed by it as I was. But that didn't stop me from making the decision.

I didn't answer the question, only offering a question of my own. "I'd like to meet the rest of you. How soon can you introduce me?"

CHAPTER 24

It turned out there was going to be a meeting tonight, and Lucille invited me along. I was blindfolded and led through the village. I couldn't tell which house we entered, but I knew we were still in the village and that we'd entered a house. After walking through the house, a door opened, and I stepped down into a passageway where we continued walking straight for some time. Was this a tunnel? It must've been, and building a tunnel beneath the sand is no easy task. No wonder PanTech hadn't been able to find them yet. A hiding place this elaborate wasn't something they were likely to expect.

Eventually, we opened another door, and I heard several people stop talking as we entered the room. Lucille removed my blindfold, and four other people were in the room with us. Lighting was dim, and everyone sat close around a small table, with only a small candle in the middle.

"I guess it went better than you thought, huh?" a small woman said, looking to Lucille.

Lucille shrugged off the comment. "Everyone, I'd like you to meet Taylor. Taylor, meet Heather, Ludo, Lapis, and Cairn. Ludo is our leader. He and his father discovered this natural cave and turned it into what it is today."

I'm not sure what I was expecting. An army? Uniforms? PanTech soldiers held prisoner in dungeons? We were a small village. A large group would've been discovered already. I should've realized this earlier. Only a small group like this could possibly operate underneath PanTech without being discovered by now. It was stupid of me to think any different.

Ludo was a large man who must've been in his late twenties. He was easily among the biggest men I'd seen and, unlike the others, wasn't someone you'd forget if you'd seen him before. I had, of course, seen him many times. He was the cobbler Cara worked with to create the boots I was currently wearing. As though reading my mind, he spoke up in his deep voice.

"How are those boots working for you?" he asked.

"They're exceptional. I didn't think of you as a rebel type," I said, not keen on allowing the change of subject to go any further.

Lapis, a brown-haired, round-cheeked older woman, laughed. "So much for the small talk."

Ludo grinned. "What is a rebel type, Taylor?"

My mind immediately went to Linus. He was not so much a rebel but a hero; in a world where the bad guys are the ones with the power, the hero has no choice but to rebel. Someone who always has a problem following orders or believing what they're told. Someone who didn't have a problem being mean to people who were mean, and hurting people who hurt people. That's what I imagined when I thought of a rebel, but now that image only brought me pain. I wanted to say all those things aloud. Instead, I said nothing.

"Taylor?" He leaned forward, trying to get a closer look at me under the dim light that made it difficult to make out anything but the most basic of features.

I shook my head. "There's no such thing, I guess. I don't seem like a rebel type either, I bet. But, here we are because someone has to be."

Cairn, the oldest one there, spoke up. His long, graying hair was the most visible of anyone's, reflecting the candle's tiny dancing flame. "I couldn't have said it better myself."

Lucille's smile was back in full force. "Are you kidding? You say that yourself all the time."

That got at least a chuckle out of everyone—everyone except myself and Ludo.

Ludo motioned toward a chair for me to sit in, which I did. "It's probably about time we got down to business. Don't worry about something as trivial as joining a group, Taylor. If you want to help, we'll be happy to have your help. And if that help is hurting PanTech, then we're on the same team."

Everyone nodded solemnly at that.

He continued. "PanTech brings in supplies to trade with the village at least once a month. This time they brought extra, probably because of the extended stay that was planned, thanks to our little club here. Looks to be about three times as much, which does a couple of things. One, it gives us an idea of how long they plan to stay before resupplying. Two, it makes things a lot more difficult for them to keep up with, given they have the same number of soldiers as always. With three of them down, now there are only four left. It's hard to even have a rotating sleep schedule with that many soldiers. It's even harder to waste time guarding medicine, and food, and wine. We're going to sneak in, and with a simple distraction, we'll walk out with a fortune. That is, as long as the distraction can keep going for more than a few minutes."

I spoke up. "What's the distraction?"

He stared at me for a moment before answering. "Well, you just had to ask the one thing I hadn't thought out yet."

I looked down, considering whether or not I should offer up my own idea on the matter.

"You have an idea, don't you?" he asked, reading my mind yet again.

"I'll go into the camp and ask to speak to the commander. I have a lot to say to her, and it'll be interesting to the other soldiers there. I was with the three soldiers who died, and I can give her a recounting of the events that took place that no one else can. She'll listen to me, and I'm sure she'll have plenty to say. While she's speaking to me, the rest of you can sneak in to carry out as many supplies as you can before she and I finish speaking."

Ludo shook his head. "You do know she'll kill you if she realizes we're taking the supplies? That woman is as sharp as a tack, and she has an enhancement. That means she can break your neck before you realize she has her hands on it. No, we should come up with something—"

"Come up with something different if you want," I interrupted. "It's something I'm going to do anyway, so you may as well take advantage of the opportunity. Or, don't. It's up to you."

Ludo smiled. "Well, what can I say to that? I guess that plugs the hole we had, then."

Lapis shook her head. "Maybe, but is this really the kind of mission we should be bringing...well...is it really a good *first* mission?"

Cairn laughed. "*First* mission? This is the first *real* mission for any of us. PanTech doesn't exactly leave a lot of openings. We've been waiting years for a chance. She's just as ready as any of us are."

Ludo nodded several times, clearly wanting to move the conversation along. "You're both right, and she's just as capable as anyone here, from what I understand. Lucille wouldn't have brought her here otherwise, and I trust Lucille's judgment.

"Now, onto the plan of action. We are going to take a wide trip around, and the same wide trip back. We'll leave several minutes earlier than Taylor, both to avoid suspicion and also to make sure we get there just a little after she does. Cairn and I will take a look at the map tonight.

"We'll have to be quiet, which means no carts near the camp. We'll bring them with us, but they'll have to be left a good distance away to make sure they're neither heard nor spotted."

"So, how are we supposed to get anything of value if we have to make big, long trips to our carts?" Heather asked.

Ludo shrugged. "That's a limitation we have to live with, Heather. We can move quickly, but we just have to move quietly."

"Sure," she argued, "but wouldn't we be better off not bringing carts at all since they'd just slow us down, and we're probably only going to get one trip in without putting Taylor at risk anyway?"

Ludo opened his mouth to speak but stopped, and everyone sat quietly for a moment.

"She has a point," Cairn said. "Carts are going to slow us down a lot on the return trip too. If anything at all happens, we'll have to abandon them."

Ludo nodded. "Yes, probably for the best that we just go with packs and just fill up on whatever we can carry. Focus on the smaller, more valuable items. Less likely they're going to notice anything missing that way too. I doubt they pay much attention to inventory if they even keep inventory at all since nothing is ever missing."

Lucille slapped the table. "Here's a crazy idea. You ready?"

Everyone looked at her, but judging by the tired expressions on their faces, they already knew and didn't like where this was going.

She continued. "There's only four of them. We can bring our weapons, ambush them, and steal their armor and blasters. We'd have plenty of time to take the supplies, and if the suits let us leave the boundary, we can go and look for other zones to join us using their vehicle to cover a lot of distance we normally couldn't. When the next group comes in to relieve them or see what's wrong, we ambush them with our new weapons and armor, and repeat the process, maybe even with help from other zones. We could be the first step in a long march that leads all the way to headquarters."

Everyone looked back and forth between one another as a cloud of dread seemed to descend on the room. I liked the plan, personally. There are only a few problems.

"I like it, but it won't work," I said.

Lucille shot me a glare, and for a moment, I thought she might take a swing at me. "Because of the commander's enhancement? If we get the jump on her, it won't come into play. Once she's out of the way, the other three will hardly be a threat at all if we're careful."

I tapped my finger on the table, shaking my head. "That's not the problem…or at least, *maybe* that's not the problem. I don't know much about the commander, other than the fact they all see her as unbeatable. Maybe she isn't. The problem is with just about everything else. The suits can't just be taken off and put on anyone. They have to install them into the person at headquarters, and they wear them all the time. They're attached to the soldier's body. They're filled with fluid that has to be changed. They're really complicated. We'd need to study them for a long time, and even then, we wouldn't have the technology to fit them onto someone else or replace the fluid.

"Then there's the blasters. I've never seen any soldier fire another soldier's weapon. What if they're somehow unique to them too, and only that soldier can use them? Then, there's the boundary. We have no idea what allows them to go through it. It might have nothing to do with the armor. Maybe they have some kind of key put into their bodies that allows them to walk through no matter what. That's something else we'd have to study, and even if we did find some kind of key embedded into their body, there's no guarantee we'll be able to use it.

"If even one of these things goes wrong, which is almost a guarantee, the plan is going to end with all of us getting killed. Possibly the moment we attack the commander."

Lucille sighed and slammed her fist onto the table. She didn't try to argue or ask any questions. She just leaned back in her chair, seething.

"One step at a time," Ludo said. "Let's keep an eye out while we're there and see if we can learn anything new. It seems like our biggest disadvantages are always the things we don't know. Get a good night's rest. Tomorrow, for once, PanTech will get as good as they give. Let them experience some adversity for once."

CHAPTER 25

The next day, we employed our plan. I took the straight path to the PanTech camp, and the others took a wide, semicircle approach. They might've thought it bold or clever for me to come up with this distraction so quickly, but the truth was much less complex than that. I wanted to meet the commander. I wanted to see if she was open to clearing Linus's name or telling me more about him. I wanted to know if she was as terrible and scary as everyone made her out to be. Even though the truth was less complex, it was probably just as stupid. It took being curious about terror ants and digging them up to see if everything you heard about them was true.

Still, something about the commander just seemed…off. She didn't behave like a professional soldier. She was more like Linus than the others, but none of that made sense. Is that why she gave him so many chances, or did they not get along, and that's why she wanted him dead? Was he competition? Probably not, since Linus hated being a soldier. He'd never try to make commander rank. But then again, did PanTech really care what anyone wanted for themselves? When it came down to it, I just didn't expect the commander to kill me. Maybe she'd threaten me or punish me in some way, but she didn't seem to care enough.

As I approached the gate, I noticed there weren't any soldiers standing out front this time. Not wanting to startle anyone, I whistled loudly. For a few minutes, no one came. Was the camp abandoned? Did they assume that if they left it unattended, that no one would be stupid enough to walk in and take the risk? Normally, that might be a fair assumption, but they knew about the rebels. It's why they were here. Was this a trap? Did they know about this plan somehow?

I whistled again, louder this time, and shouted "hello" as loudly as I could. Again, I waited, and no one came. I fought the temptation to just walk in…for now, at least. I had to be patient. Ludo and the others may have arrived ahead of me and gotten caught. No, that shouldn't happen. We went over the pacing thoroughly. They should still be several minutes away. So, what was taking so long? I whistled a third time, and this time two soldiers came to the gate.

"State your business!" the first shouted.

Before I could answer, the second soldier spoke up. "Wait, isn't that the girl from before? The one who came to see Linus?"

"It's me," I shouted back. "Can I come closer, so we don't have to yell?"

They looked between each other for a moment before the first soldier waved me over.

I approached slowly and stopped a respectable distance away. From where I stood, I could tell that the second soldier was a woman, due to the feminine shape of her armor, which was in stark contrast with her deep voice.

"Would it be possible for me to meet with your commander?" I asked, with all the faux confidence I could muster.

"Absolutely not," the female soldier snapped. "No one can just walk in here and meet with the commander, or any of us really. The only reason you were able to meet Linus is because he wanted to meet with you. We have rules to follow and protocols to observe."

"That's right," the male soldier agreed. "Besides, we don't have time to babysit you, considering we aren't even getting breaks now, thanks to that free-for-all."

The female soldier jabbed him with her elbow. I guess this wasn't something they were supposed to admit so freely.

"Irrelevant," the female soldier said. "You should be on your way before—"

A figure stepped out of the tent behind them, revealing the beautiful, fire-haired commander.

"Oh, what's this all about?" she said, her voice overflowing with amusement.

"Ma'am!" Both soldiers shouted, spun around, and saluted in perfect unison.

"This girl—" the female soldier started.

"I wasn't asking you," she said. "I'm asking her." She pointed at me.

"I…uh, wanted to meet with you," I stammered, caught off guard by her sudden appearance and forwardness, though I shouldn't have been.

"I don't know. I like visitors as much as anyone, but that didn't work out so well for Linus, now did it?"

My cheeks flared with heat at the sudden wave of embarrassment. They really were somewhat alike, but she didn't stumble over her words the way Linus did with that kind of remark. She was quick and knew precisely what to say to throw everyone off their thoughts. She would not be easy to speak to. This was a mistake, but one too late to take back.

"I…no. I just wanted to speak with you about Linus. Would that be alright?"

She sighed and held open the tent door behind her, waving me in.

I stepped inside and tried to absorb as much of my surroundings as possible.

Tables lined the outer edges of the tent, each dedicated to a different task. Suit parts lay strewn across the longest of them, to my right. I recognized them. They belonged to Linus, Oscar, and Peter. Several pieces were damaged beyond repair, but what would I know? I'm sure PanTech has the knowledge and means to repair things I couldn't even comprehend, or reduce the pieces down to their base materials to build new armor, the way a blacksmith would melt iron and forge a new tool. Too many questions flooded my mind, but I wouldn't waste time on trivial things. I had little enough of it that it was precious, and I had to choose every question carefully.

A large tank sat in the corner with hoses attached. Was this the machine that cycled the fluid in their armor, or was it used for something else? Since it sat near the pieces of armor, I suspected it was the former. Blasters and rifles rested on the table that ran along the back of the tent. There's not much mystery there beyond the obvious ones. Along the left side table, there appeared to be several small sealed containers in boxes. Food and drinks? It couldn't be ammunition. Their guns didn't use it. Medicine?

She pointed to a chair in front of the table in the center, and I took a seat. A fourth soldier stepped into the tent, walking to the corner, only stopping for a moment to regard me. All wore their helmets except the commander, so I couldn't determine anything about their appearance beyond the bulky, dull, gray armor they wore. The soldier, who I assumed to be male based on their armor's appearance, nodded to the commander and walked into the corner, attaching one of the hoses to his armor. It seemed I'd guessed correctly. This was the machine that recycled the fluid used in their armor. It took every ounce of my willpower not to ask about it.

Four of them were in this tent. The commander was now sitting in front of me, two behind me guarding the tent's exit, and now the fourth doing maintenance on his armor. This was a good fortune I didn't expect to have, and I wasn't about to squander it. Play it smart. Play it carefully. *This is your moment, Taylor.*

"So, you aren't here to make friends, which is a shame. Just business, then?"

"What? No…I mean, yes. I wanted to talk to you about Linus."

"Right, Linus," she said, frowning. "What about him?"

"Why did you order Oscar and Peter to kill him?" I accused flatly, doing everything I could to mask the rising anger and prevent it from spilling into my voice even as I asked the question.

"That's a lie. Who told you that?" Her playful expression faded immediately, and she looked every bit as angry as I felt. Except, she made no effort to hide hers.

"Oscar and Peter said it. I heard them myself."

"I told them they were authorized to use force *only* if Linus attacked them first."

"Sounds like an obvious loophole. They tricked him into shooting first, so they could kill him. I'm *glad* they died in the process. Human garbage," I said, gripping my hands together tightly in my lap. So much for containing my temper.

She narrowed her eyes at me. "Are you calling me an idiot, girl?"

I stood up from my chair, sending it toppling over behind me. I heard both guards behind me unholster and charge their blasters, but I didn't look back at them. "I do! What kind of fool gives an order like that, knowing they already hated each other?"

She stood up and flipped the table to the side, leaving nothing but open space between us. It was done with so little effort, so little movement, that it might have been a sheet of paper or a blade of grass, yet it must've weighed hundreds of pounds.

I stood my ground, my fists clenched, not unaware of the surge of fear that left me mostly paralyzed. I could feel tears building up around my eyes, but I wasn't about to stand down.

She stomped more than stepped and stopped directly in front of me. She brought her hand down toward my face but stopped abruptly, running her fingers through my hair instead with a mischievous grin. For a moment, I couldn't believe what was happening. I couldn't move. I held my breath and thought I might faint. When at last I finally regained control of my body, I pushed myself away from her. I drew back my hand and tried to slap her with all the force I could muster, but in a blur that was impossible for my eyes to follow, she caught my hand. I stared at her grip in disbelief, but when I looked at her face, she was still smiling.

"I love it when someone has the guts to talk to me that way. So exciting. It's what I liked about Linus, too. It can be so boring around here, you know." As she let go of my hand, she pushed me back, sending me falling to the ground. "You got what you came for. Linus was wrongfully murdered by his fellow soldiers. I'll amend the report and clear his name."

"T-thank you," I stammered. "May I go now?"

She laughed and shook her head. "It's my turn. I have some questions of my own, so listen closely."

I nodded, trying not to show my fear, but by now, I'm sure it was written all over my body.

She continued. "Your village has a bit of a rebel problem, as you know. Do you know them?"

I shook my head.

She laughed again, louder this time. "You're lying. I can tell. Doesn't matter, though. I want you to be my informant. My pretty little bird that flies in and listens to the important details then flaps her way back to me to sing the whole song. They'll talk to one of their own. Will you do it?"

"N-no!" I said, probably more surprised at my own words than she was.

"Fair enough. How rude of me. Let me make you an offer. I'm one of the few in PanTech who can order a physical enhancer, like the one I'm fitted with, when I deem it necessary. How would you like to have one? Don't answer. Let me sweeten the deal even more. You're a veterinarian, so assuming you pass your exam, I'll let you bring a species of your choice back to study. Surely that appeals to your scientific mind. This is an opportunity rarer than you realize, but you see, I'm fairly lazy as an adversity zone manager, and I prefer to just let things run themselves. You could save me a lot of work. You scratch my back, and I'll scratch yours. What do you say?

I opened my mouth, but my throat caught. Ghost. I could bring Ghost with me, but what was I thinking? I wanted to destroy PanTech, regardless of whether she was telling the truth about Linus or not.

"You still hesitate? Fine, think about it. The offer stands until you refuse it, so I'll advise you not to rush. Go on; you're free to go." She nodded to the soldiers standing behind me, who I'd forgotten about. "Escort this pretty little firebrand out of my camp."

The soldier who had been standing in the corner the entire time remained stoic. I could only imagine the expression they must be wearing on their faces. Oh, how I hated those helmets.

I gritted my teeth as both soldiers came up behind me and grabbed an arm each. I didn't dare fight them. I'd already gotten far too lucky. She was every bit as dangerous and unpredictable as I thought she'd be, but not quite as cruel, somehow.

I walked quietly with the two soldiers to the exit of the camp, where I was assisted with a generous shove that sent me toppling to my knees. That had taken a while, for sure, but I was playing with fire. More than I could likely handle, but that wasn't what mattered at the moment.

They had plenty of time to grab all the supplies they could carry.

My work here was done, and then some.

CHAPTER 26

It turned out Ludo and the others were able to get their hands on a lot of supplies and were probably gone long before the commander and I finished our conversation. Food, medicine, clean water, cloth, leather, iron, and more. Ludo promised they'd begin distributing the supplies to the people of the village in need of them as soon as possible, and I felt good that I was finally a part of something that dealt even the smallest blow to PanTech, while helping the people of the village. However, the excitement was short-lived because the very next day, Ferris and I heard the news that the testing personnel had arrived and began mandatory registrations for the upcoming exams, and that meant us.

Arriving at the registration tent just outside the village, we found ourselves waiting in a short but very slow moving line. Everyone that had turned eighteen years old since the last time they came was here, and thanks to sleepyhead Ferris, we caught the tail end of it. Some of those standing in line looked overwhelmed with excitement and wonder. They couldn't wait to take the exam, and a part of me understood what they were thinking. If they'd never had personal dealings with PanTech, and didn't ask many questions, PanTech probably seemed like some kind of abstract, harmless manifestation of benevolent gods.

In reality, if it was a manifestation of anything, it was cruel and tyrannical gods who were only kind to those who obeyed and worshipped them absolutely. They hurt you for your own good; they'd say, to the twisted gratitude of their subjects. And, they weren't likely to be going anywhere anytime soon. I considered Lucille's plan. Even though there were problems, I was excited to think about how easy it might be under the correct circumstances. If she had been right in her assumptions about the commander, their armor, weapons, and the boundary, her plan might have actually worked. Or was I just dreaming too?

"I need more testing kits," the balding, bespectacled man in a white lab coat said to the soldier standing beside him.

"This is the last box," the soldier replied quietly.

"Last box?" he shouted. "I had twice this much ordered. What do you mean this is the last box?"

The soldier wasn't about to be intimidated by the man's shouting. "I mean this is the last box."

"Well, what happened to them? This is ridiculous. If I don't perform blood tests on these applicants, their transfer to PanTech could be delayed by as much as a week. This is an embarrassment."

A quiet sigh escaped the soldier's helmet. "They were stolen from our camp. Make do with what you have."

The man turned back around to the girl standing in front of him. "Alright, be sure to hold still. If we fail this test, I'm not sure I'll have enough to test everyone else here."

The soldier sighed again, but I'm fairly certain the overly stressed man in the lab coat didn't even notice.

I looked up to realize Ferris was staring at me with his brow furrowed.

"Taylor…," he started but thought better of continuing his sentence. Ferris was a lot of things but, stupidity is not one of them. Something on my face must have given me away—that, or the fact that I'd gone out at night without taking Ghost with me.

"State your desired post. Your exam will be tailored to your area of interest."

The woman stared down at her feet, hesitating.

"Go on. Don't be shy."

More silence.

"I know it's stupid, but can someone be a dancer? I told you it was stupid…."

"Dancer. Alright, testing for dancer. Don't be silly, girl. There are many dancers."

Wow. Dancers? Really? I had seen some cultural dancing in our village before, but not often. It was considered to be mostly a waste of time unless there was a specific celebration. Celebrations had gotten fewer and further between. I remembered that Mother's adversity zone had professional dancers. It made sense because the emperor was so pampered and surrounded by beautiful women whose sole purpose was to entertain him. What if this girl's request landed her into the servitude of the same sort of horrible human being? Then again, what was I thinking? It's PanTech. Of course, they're awful human beings.

He shooed the girl away and waved up the next person, a young man.

"Hold out your finger. You'll feel a small prick."

The young man complied, but it didn't seem to hurt him much. "Soldier," he said.

"Well, I hadn't asked you that yet, but alright, soldier. I'm obligated to tell you that being a soldier is one of the more difficult positions to achieve. You must pass based on both intellectual and physical markers. Despite what you may think, the role of a soldier is one of the most revered positions in all of PanTech."

A loud cough came from the soldier behind him.

"Oh, would you shut up," the man in the coat said, turning to scold the soldier.

The soldier did not indicate how he received the man's remarks, hidden beneath his expressionless helmet.

"I'm sure. Soldier," the boy said, ignoring the apparent spat.

"Soldier, then. Next."

This continued with several others, until finally it was my turn.

"Sorry, I don't have any more tests for the two of you. I'm afraid you should've shown up earlier instead of dragging your feet," he said, adjusting his glasses. "All the same, choose your desired occupation."

"Test registration taker," I said.

He narrowed his eyes and leaned in. "Excuse me?"

"I'll get to sit at a table and be grumpy all day, right?"

The man started to open his mouth, but the soldier behind him interrupted whatever he'd planned to say with a loud and very unprofessional chuckle. Just one chuckle, but his helmet wasn't hiding this for him.

"Alright, if you want the most stressful and thankless job in all of PanTech—"

Ferris kicked me so hard in the back of the foot that I thought my feet were going to be swept out from under me.

"Alright," I said, bracing myself on the table to keep from stumbling forward. "Animal studies. I'm the veterinarian here. I want to continue researching animal medicine."

A lie, of course. I hadn't discussed my decision not to join PanTech with anyone and didn't plan to. I didn't want to have another argument with my mother or disappoint her. Ferris, too. I'd have to keep up appearances.

"Animal research. I've heard a rumor that the scientists there are about to begin some very exciting research. It is a rarely requested position, but perhaps it's the most ideal time to pursue it. Let's hope your brain is as smart as your mouth. If so, you should be fine. Next."

I stood aside and let Ferris step up. We really were the last ones to register. About time, too. I couldn't wait to get out of here.

"Desired occupation?"

"Soldier," Ferris said.

"What?" I breathed, so surprised that it's a wonder I was able to say anything at all. "Soldier?"

"Soldier," he repeated.

"But, Mother thought you'd want to pursue mathematics."

"I know. I'm good at it, too. Inherited the knack for it from Father, I suppose. Still, Soldier."

"Soldier," the man in the coat said, confirming. "I'm obligated to tell you that—"

"I overheard the warning earlier."

"I am obligated," the man continued, his eye twitching, "to tell you that the testing for the role of a soldier requires both intellectual and physical markers to be met. It is a prestigious position in the organization and is not easy to get. You may be given a choice to transfer into a different position if you fail only the physical marker. No one is transferred into the position of a soldier unless they apply for it."

"That's a lie," I said.

The man's face turned as red as the commander's hair. "Girl, I'm about to have you removed from the testing. How dare you call me a liar?"

"Are you saying it's never happened? I know of a soldier who transferred to the position after his exam."

"For a soldier to transfer into the position after the exam, it must be because he excelled to such a degree that PanTech felt it would be such a monumental waste of opportunity not to place them in the position. Such individuals typically, receive high ranks and renown."

My heart sank, knowing that Linus resisted the system he was placed into. He renounced a road to power and fame.

"I'm sorry…I…just catch up to me, Ferris. I want to be alone for a few minutes."

I turned and walked quickly away, stopping between the tent and the village to wait for Ferris, wiping my eyes in hopes they'd be dry by the time Ferris came back.

A few minutes later, they still weren't.

Ferris caught up to me and hugged me tightly. "I understand why he didn't want that life."

"Do you?" I shouted. "It seems that you don't, since you chose it as your profession. Do you want to go around making things hard for children of other zones, taking away their food if they have too much, introducing predators if they're too safe? *Do* you understand, Ferris?"

He looked to the side, taking a deep breath before meeting my gaze again. "I do. I want to make sure there are as many sympathetic soldiers as possible. I want to be like Linus. Think about what would've happened if that giant snake had been set loose upon us, and there was no Linus to stand up to them and help you deal with it."

"Linus *died* doing that!" I was nearly screaming now, grabbing onto his shirt, before lowering my voice, remembering that we were out of hearing distance of everyone at the moment, but maybe not shouting distance. "I don't want you to die."

"I can do small things, Taylor. I don't have to be the big hero Linus was, but little things make a difference too. I'll be careful. I won't get myself killed or get into too much trouble, but I'll make a difference. The night he stayed with us, Linus told me many stories about things he'd done and gotten away with. There's a line, and you can stay just behind it."

Remembering what the commander said to me, I think I understood the real reason Linus got away with so much. The commander liked having him around. She didn't find him boring, and she found that…attractive…I suppose. I shuddered at the thought.

"You're a man, Ferris. You can decide. I'm sorry for judging you."

"It's alright," he said, "because I have something to say to you too. Consider us even after I do. I think you were involved in stealing the supplies. Taylor, *please*, if you're involved with the rebels, stop before it's too late. It won't end well. I could tell by how you were so relaxed and gave that sarcastic answer that you don't really plan on joining. But, please, just think about it. We can make a difference, Taylor. You heard what he said. There's something major coming to animal research. What if you can influence that research to make a difference? So much of a difference that even PanTech can't stop it from helping everyone. Even Father would approve of that. Please, you don't have to say anything, but think about it. It's all I'm asking."

I didn't say anything. I'd already made up my mind. Even if I found a way to cure every disease and sickness known, make everyone immortal, and make rainbows show up in the sky every day, PanTech would still find some way to use it to harm everyone. They'd cure only those in their service, make their leaders immortal, and I'm not sure what they'd do with rainbows, but they'd find something. No, if I learned one thing from Linus, it was that no good could come from the inside. They needed to be destroyed from the outside. It was time to go speak to Ludo and the others and tell them I'd made my decision.

CHAPTER 27

I didn't wait until nightfall. Instead, I walked directly into Ludo's shop, where he also lived, midday. I could estimate with confidence that's where the secret cave was located, so the blindfolding was more or less pointless. Then again, it might have actually mattered if Lucille hadn't revealed who furnished the cave, and who their leader was the moment my blindfold was removed. Lucille didn't seem to be the careful type, but bold and definitely smarter than she let on.

Ludo was occupied by whatever was on his workbench when I entered, and the bell on the door rang, resonating throughout the small room. "Welcome," he said, still not looking up. "I've got some new boots in the corner over there, to your right, if you'd like to give them a look-over. Sized for men and women, and if I don't have your size, I'll make it in your size."

I humored him for a moment, walking to the corner without a word, glancing at the boots. Impeccable quality. Despite the fact Ludo was basically the only serious cobbler in the village, he didn't let that affect his sense of pride in his work. Even if there'd been a dozen others, odds were good he'd still be the best, and probably by no small margin. Hopefully, the same was true for me. I'd like to think so. "You know, they're great, but I think I like the pair I'm wearing better. They fit like they were made just for my feet and legs."

He looked up and grinned, trying to hide his surprise that I'd just dropped in unannounced like this. "That's because they *were* made to fit your feet and legs. Cara's estimations were spot on. I believe I told you that you won't find a better pair for as long as you live, especially if you keep living here."

"It's funny you say that. Would you mind closing up your shop for a few minutes and heading into the back with me?"

He hesitated for a moment but obliged. "Sure, I'll flip the sign, and we'll head into the back. If anyone asks, I was showing you some of my new materials."

After flipping the sign and locking the door, Ludo led me through a door in the back and then through a hidden door in the floor under a table and rug. It was clever. The handle on the door was recessed in the door itself, so you couldn't see any suspicious shapes poking out from under the rug. The tunnel leading down was rough and unfinished, stone probably almost as old as the sand itself made one path forward, eventually leading into a larger stone space that opened up several times larger than the tunnel itself. The ceiling was taller than I could reach, but Ludo could reach up and touch it easily. I looked around and saw supplies lining the walls the whole way around.

I didn't understand, but I wanted to assume the best. "Why are the supplies still here?" I asked.

"We're keeping them," he said flatly and offered no hint of a further explanation.

"Wait…why? I thought the entire plan was to distribute these supplies to villagers in need. There's medicine here, and food and water. You could sneak these into homes where PanTech has taken food away from children. The food's eaten. It's not like they can trace that back to us."

"Us? So, you've decided to join us then?"

I shouldn't have given him the opening to change the subject the way I had. That was stupid of me. Still, I'd be diplomatic and circle back to it.

"Yes, I've decided that I'm going to stay here in the village, regardless of my test results, and continue running the clinic and helping with our cause. Speaking of our cause, when exactly do you intend to distribute these supplies to villagers?"

"We're keeping them," he repeated. "What helped you to make your decision? Was the commander that rough on you?"

Another deflection, but memories of my interaction with the commander made me feel immediately uncomfortable.

"She wasn't so bad," I lied. "She agreed to amend her report about Linus. Not that it really matters. Probably just a trivial gesture to make me go away and give up my vengeful thoughts."

"And have you given them up?" he asked.

"No," I snapped. "I have not. Now, please stop dodging the question. Why aren't you giving these supplies to the villagers like you said you were going to?"

"Maybe I will, eventually. For now, they'd just go to waste. Think about it, Taylor. For the most part, they're just a bunch of PanTech worshipers. Doesn't that make them just as bad as PanTech, in just about every way that counts?"

"What? No…they're just afraid."

"Oh? How many of them stepped in to help your Linus when he needed them? You and he had just saved the village. He was their savior, and yet, all they could manage was to gather around and gawk as he lay dying on the ground. In fact, it wasn't until your Father learned about what happened that he came and took care of his body. Of course, PanTech dug him up anyway."

"They were afraid to help. PanTech soldiers would have stepped in and blown them to pieces."

He shook his head. "Then why should we give them what they were too afraid to take for themselves? Why shouldn't we benefit from the supplies? Swell our numbers? Expand our operations? Be better prepared to strike PanTech when the opportunity arises? Why risk being reported to help trembling idiots who are too afraid to even help themselves, and *still* find it in their hearts to thank PanTech for all the misery they inflict on their children?"

What was there to argue about? He was right, in a way, but although he was right, that didn't make what he was doing right. I couldn't come up with a rebuttal. I just stood there, thinking over everything in silence.

"Am I wrong? Not everyone is like you and me, Taylor. We don't need the weak around us clinging to us with their open hands outstretched, weighing us down, when our goal is to battle with the strong."

"You're not wrong," I said, finally. "I'm going to go. I have a lot to do today. I just wanted to stop by and check on the supplies."

Ludo looked at me, and something in his eyes felt untrusting. "Alright. Come by again soon. We should begin discussing our next move. We don't want to miss any opportunities."

I just nodded and left, making my way home. All I wanted to do now was check on Ghost and sit alone in my room for as long as possible.

It seemed I wouldn't be able to be the hero I wanted to be no matter what path I chose, and all those I thought might be heroes were never heroes at all, except for the only one I ever knew, who was now dead. My heart ached, thinking of him again. I wondered if I'd ever stop feeling his hand in mine and if his smile would ever fade. It seemed to only get clearer as time passed, but only anger could be found where fondness should be. As much as I loved him, I hated those who took him away from me more than that.

When I stepped through the door into my home, Mother was sitting at the table. She'd been waiting for me.

"Welcome home," she said, smiling.

"Thank you. I'm going to be in my room for a bit if you need me."

She patted the seat next to her. I knew what was coming, or at least I thought I did, and I wasn't really in the mood for it, but I obeyed and sat. I hoped I'd be able to brush her off quickly, though I immediately disliked myself for thinking that.

She reached out and grabbed my hand, squeezing it tightly. I jerked away quickly, my mind going back to the exact moment where the commander grabbed my hand as I was about to slap her. I gathered myself, took a deep breath, and placed my hand back on the table next to hers. "Taylor? Are you alright?"

I shook my head. "I'm alright, Mother. Sorry. What did you want to talk about?"

She frowned. Clearly, she did not believe I was alright but didn't want to argue with me.

She was right, though. I wasn't alright. I was far from it and I wondered if I'd ever be alright again for as long as I lived.

"I spoke to Ferris when he returned. He wanted me to talk to you. *I* wanted to talk to you, and your father agreed to let me do it with just the two of us so you wouldn't feel ganged up on. I sent them out for a while to run some errands." She reached out and moved a strand of hair out of my eyes, and I again felt uncomfortable remembering my meeting with the commander. "We're really worried about you, Taylor."

It was always Mother's way to scold and demand, rarely to ask and be kind. She must have truly been afraid for me, for her to speak this way.

"I'm alright, Mother. Just…the exams coming up, and everything that happened with Linus, and having to lose sleep to go out and train Ghost…I'm just under a lot of stress, you know?" I lied.

"If you were in trouble, you would come to us for help, right? I always wanted you to see PanTech the way they ask us to see them, the way I saw them when they saved me from the awful life I was living because I knew that would make your life easier and make you less conflicted about your path forward in life. Now that I see that you're determined to think differently, I want you to know that I support you anyway, that your father and I love you, and that Ferris loves you too."

My fingers began to tremble without realizing it, and my vision became blurry with the tears that had started to flow. I flung my arms around her and released my pent-up emotions on her like a sandstorm.

"Oh, Mother. I don't know what to do anymore. I don't know what's right and what's wrong. I don't know who's good and who's evil. I can't tell the right path from the wrong one, and I hate…everything! I hate so much. I'm so angry. I want them to pay for what they did to Linus, but I still want to help people. I still see his face every day. Every time I close my eyes, I see his death, and I feel his kiss on my lips, and that wound, I see him dying, and it makes me so…angry, but so sad too. I…I don't know who I am anymore."

She wrapped her arms around me and stroked my hair. "Shh. It's alright. When you can't make sense of the world around you, always remember to trust yourself most of all. Don't believe what you see, or what you hear, if your gut tells you that it's wrong."

I nodded. My gut wasn't telling me much. All it wanted to do was tie itself into knots and make me feel sick. It didn't even want food anymore like a normal gut should. How was I supposed to trust that?

"Thank you. I think I'm going to go rest in my room for a while."

She nodded, moving her hand to my shoulder before letting me go completely. "That's good. If you haven't heard, testing is tomorrow. You should get some rest. Ferris said you declared animal medicine. I'm sure you'll make everyone proud, but make yourself proud first. Don't worry about what everyone else wants until you get what you want."

"Tomorrow?" I asked, surprised. I hadn't realized it would be so soon. Would Mother really not be disappointed when she found out that, even if I passed, I was rejecting the invitation and staying in the village? I was too tired to think about it anymore.

I went to my room, and in the privacy behind my closed door, told Ghost everything about what happened. It was somehow therapeutic to give the full, unabridged truth to someone who couldn't repeat it.

Exhausted, I quickly drifted off into sleep.

CHAPTER 28

At last, the day had arrived. The day we were all told to look forward to, but filled nearly all of us with endless dread. The exam was extremely difficult to pass, and only a few passed each year. Sometimes, none at all. You only had one shot, and if you failed, you failed forever. There were no retakes. No do-overs. No second chances. Some were insane enough to revoke their admission into PanTech. The only person I'd ever heard of to do this was my father. A brilliant inventor who was dedicated to improving the lives of everyone in the village soon after barred from building anything that would reduce the adversity score of our village's children. If he didn't? Soldiers would have to create more adversity themselves to fill the gap. Confiscating food, sabotaging our drinking systems, or worse. Who wouldn't want to leave such a place to join a different world? A world of infinite technological advancement. A world without adversity scores, where it was decided that you'd already paid your dues and you could now live in comfort and luxury; scientific discovery and power, unlike anything any of us could even conceive of…and I'd decided to forsake it all.

Despite that, I still needed to do my best on the exam. Otherwise, what meaning would the gesture have? If I failed the exam and decided to stay, it would mean nothing. Leaving wouldn't be offered. No. I had to pass and throw the best score I could manage into their faces.

Ferris was up before me, as unpredictable as ever, and had made all of us breakfast, including Father, who was his usual quiet self this morning. He puffed on his pipe but wasn't reading or writing this time. Simply absorbed in an apparent daydream, which he was unable to escape from, save for the absolutely minimal effort required to lift his pipe to his lips and pull a few puffs from it.

"Father, are you alright?" I asked.

At first, he didn't answer, still trapped in whatever waking dream held him.

"Father?" I spoke again, louder this time, as I sat down at the table.

He heard me that time, smiling and nodding, before going quiet again.

"You seem troubled. Are you worried for Ferris and I?"

He sighed and sat down his pipe on the small leather stand in front of him. "Not worried. Just sad, I suppose, in a way. There's a chance that both of my children will be leaving forever, and I'll never see them again."

"Will you be upset if we join PanTech?" I asked, genuinely curious. It was a question I'd been wondering the answer to, but given everything that had happened recently, I hadn't had the chance to ask.

"Your mother and I discussed it. We've agreed that our personal feelings about this decision should be secondary to your own. We will support you, pass or fail, go or stay."

Mother walked over behind him and placed both hands on his shoulders. He brought his hand up and squeezed hers.

I'd prepared myself for uncomfortable questions from everyone this morning but hoped they wouldn't come. As we all sat around the table, eating our breakfast, tension filled my stomach, both with the anticipation of the upcoming event and knowing that these questions from my family could still come at any time. But, after we'd finished our breakfast and Ferris and I prepared our packs for whatever was to come, the questions never came. In fact, nothing ever came. Beyond my brief exchange with Father at the table when I first arrived, not another word was uttered.

Ferris and I continued to walk in silence slowly out the village and toward the tent set up for testing. There were two tents now, instead of just the one, and we soon found out why. Testing was divided among those seeking to become soldiers and everyone else. Soldier candidates would also be supervised by the commander and submitted to an intense physical trial. Ferris was lighthearted, but as all the young women in the village liked to remind me of frequently, he was also a physical specimen. He hadn't chosen a profession in the village, but he found enjoyment in hard labor. If something broke, he was first in line to help fix it. If heavy things needed to be moved from one place to another, he was happy to help. And, unfortunately, if someone were to call out for a young man to remove his shirt and be gawked at by all the pretty young women in the village…he'd probably be at the front of that line too.

As for me, I was happy that I wouldn't have to see the commander today. Though, I'd prefer it if it were never again.

We sat at desks, and a stack of paper was thrown down in front of us.

The same older man in the white coat and glasses from yesterday paced in front of us, his hands clasped behind his back. "This is going to take all day, perhaps into the night, so I'd advise you to get comfortable and begin thinking of how you'll resist complaint. This will either be the proudest or, for many of you, the most disappointing day in your life. The majority of you will likely fail this exam. There is no shame in that. I wish only to instill in you a comprehension of the seriousness of each and every question. Each test has been tailored specifically to each of you, based on your declared focus of study. If you find that any questions are unfair, you are mistaken. If you find them to be too difficult, you are right. If you have any questions, that is too bad. I will not be answering them. Once you complete your exam, you will wait until everyone else has as well. Results are produced instantly. Curious how that is possible? If you pass, you will learn that and more, and if you fail, you will never know, nor will you ever need to know. Begin."

I opened the paper packet and held the first sheet up to the light, which drew an instant and intense glare from the man. Hoping to avoid any confrontations with him today, I gave up on that little experiment pretty quickly. Though I could've sworn I saw something woven inside the paper. This was no doubt some sort of PanTech advanced technology and had something to do with how the results were determined instantly. After I sat the paper back down in front of me, I could've sworn I saw the man grinning at his desk, still looking at me.

Two soldiers were in the tent with us, no doubt to protect those administering the tests from a potential rebel attack. Including the commander and assuming there was another soldier in that tent, meant that all available soldiers were preoccupied with testing. It's a shame Ludo and the others didn't know that. What a golden opportunity. One that would, no doubt, go to waste.

As I moved through each sheet answering questions, I couldn't help but be distracted by the thoughts of Ludo and what he'd done, or more specifically, not done with the supplies, and what he'd said about the other villagers. He'd lied to me. He didn't want to help the villagers. He only wanted to help himself. Helping them was just an unintended consequence if he ever helped them at all. Was this really any different from the hubris of PanTech? Then again, Ludo wasn't my enemy. PanTech was. So, it didn't matter.

I remained focused throughout the remainder of my exam, sure to give everything I had to each and every question, reading and rereading each one. I was prepared to take all night if I had to and make everyone wait for me to finish, but it did not come to that. To my surprise, I was the first to finish. I handed the man my stack of papers, and he only pointed to my seat in return.

For hours I sat, letting my mind wander to all the places it had taken refuge over the past weeks. Thoughts of Linus, mostly, filled my mind. I saw him everywhere, and everything seemed to remind me of him. I wondered if I would ever be able to go a day without mourning him, but I knew that such a day would eventually come, even if I didn't feel like it would right now. Time heals wounds, but not always. Sometimes time spreads them wide and allows things to enter and fester, only deepening the wound and making them worse. Even time couldn't be counted on.

At last, in the late hours of the evening, the final villager handed in their exam. Everyone had begun chattering amongst themselves, including the soldiers who stood behind the man overseeing the exams.

At first, I thought hearing Linus's name was just my thoughts echoing from inside my mind. I nearly dismissed it outright, but listening closely, even from the back of the line, I heard it again.

"Linus was supposed to be overseeing this. I had the night scheduled off," a male soldier remarked.

"Found a way to be a pain in the backside even in death. I'm impressed," replied the female soldier's voice.

"Yeah…truth be told, I miss him. Can't say the same for Peter. It's a shame that cobbler reported Linus. Otherwise, the commander would've never sent Peter and Oscar to collect him. He'd still be here, and I'd be back at camp enjoying some drinks."

My blood ran cold, and I froze in place. Every cell of my blood seemed to catch fire all at once, and I thought my skin might melt off my body or burst into flames too. The room began to sway, and

I fought the feeling that I might faint. My mind collapsed in on itself, and the room went deathly quiet. I couldn't hear the soldiers, nor the villagers, nor the man give the results to each eager person standing in line. I didn't notice the excitement or the disappointment. I didn't feel the hurt in their voices or the life-changing happiness. I only felt rage, and it threatened to burn me to ashes.

I turned and started to walk from the tent.

"Where are you going?" the man shouted behind me. "You're not allowed to leave until everyone receives their results. Get back in line."

I ignored him completely, running from the tent toward home. I didn't slow down until I got to the door, where I took a deep breath and fought for the last shreds of composure I could muster so as not to alarm Mother and Father. I stepped inside.

"Welcome home, Taylor. How did it go?" Mother asked.

"Oh, I'll be getting my results soon. I was worried I forgot to lock Ghost's cage properly in the excitement of the morning, and the man overseeing the tests was nice enough to let me run home. I'm afraid I can't stay long, though. Sorry."

I didn't wait for an answer. I ran into my room and collected two of my knives. One I hid in my pack, and the other I stuffed into my boot. I looked at Ghost, who was noticeably distressed and spoke to him in a quiet voice.

"It's okay, my friend. It's likely I won't be back, but this is good news for you." I reached out and opened the door of his cage, and he tilted his head in response. I then raised the small window on the wall near my ceiling, just large enough for him to fit through. "I'm setting you free. Thank you for everything. Thank you for the purpose you've given me. For all that you've given me, and…and, I'm sorry. I love you, Ghost. May your hunts always succeed, and may your kills always be swift. But…maybe avoid foxes from now on."

I reached gently into the cage, hesitating at first, knowing one tiny drop of his toxin would paralyze me for a full day at best, but he didn't appear alarmed. I stroked his back, then turned, and left the room, my rage finally tempered by the sorrow that I'd never see my friend again.

CHAPTER 29

Many were still outside their homes, waiting to comfort or potentially congratulate their children, their child's friend, or neighbor. It was impossible to be subtle right now, but right now was the time I had, and nothing was going to stop me from doing what I needed to do. But…what did I need to do? What did I want to do? I could sneak up behind him and bury my knife into his back, but more than anything else, I wanted to know why. Why, if he knew what Linus was doing, would he report him and set the events in motion that would kill him? He was helping me. He was helping the village. He saved so many and was willing to risk his life to do it. He had to pay. There was no forgiving this. There was no letting it go.

I stood in front of his door. I checked the handle. Locked, and the sign said closed. I hammered the wooden door with my fist. "Ludo! Get out here!" I shouted.

"We're closed; come back tomorrow!" he shouted in return.

I hammered on the door again. "It's Taylor. Get out here, now!" I heard him unlocking the door and stepped back several steps to give myself distance. Ludo was almost triple my size, and there'd be no escape if he grabbed me.

He stepped outside, looking around at all the onlookers who had started watching us now. "Can't this wait until tomorrow?" he asked nervously.

"No. It can't wait another second. Why did you report Linus? If you'd been watching us, you knew what he was doing. Why did you do it?"

He laughed, watching the faces of everyone around him. "I don't know what you're talking about. Go home, Taylor."

He turned to walk back into his house, and I threw my knife into his door. He turned around slowly, clenching his teeth.

"Because he was PanTech scum, Taylor. What more reason do I need?"

"Scum? He saved everyone from the giant snake PanTech brought. If you knew enough to report him, I know you knew about it! He was on our side. He risked his life for us. For you!"

"For me? When my father was dying and needed medicine, where was Linus when the soldiers refused to trade for it? Where was Linus when PanTech decided I'd had things too easy? Maybe seeing my father die an agonizing death would toughen me up. Well, it did toughen me up, Taylor. So long as he wore that armor, he was my enemy. We got three of them with one trick by pitting them against each other. That's a good start, but now you've gone and ruined all of that. All of our plans, all of our progress, all because you wanted to make a spectacle of everything. So, you've come here to kill me, have you? Here I am!"

He reached onto his belt and pulled out his knife as I pulled mine from my boot. He took several steps toward me, but I held my ground, ready for any opening I could find. He broke out into a run, holding his knife above his head. I held mine in front of me and braced the hilt with my other hand. If I landed the hit, it needed to go deep. I lunged forward and extended my arms, hoping my speed advantage would end the fight quickly.

But, the speed advantage I thought I had turned out to be wishful thinking. He blocked the thrust with his left hand, taking the knife blade into his palm, all the way to the hilt. Blood dripped from his hand onto the knife and my hands. He brought his knife down above me. I raised my leg and slammed my foot into the side of his knee, causing him to miss my neck, but the knife slashed deep across the back of my shoulder.

I bit into his right arm and held tight. I thought my teeth would come out as he tried to pull away. Out of the corner of my eye, I saw his headbutt coming, but there was nothing I could do. It was better than getting stabbed by the knife. The first hit gave me a false sense of confidence that I could take it, but the second one sent me to my knees, and I lost my grip on both his arm and my knife.

"Someone help her!" I thought I heard someone shout.

"But she attacked him first," shouted another.

"Hurry, get the soldiers!" another voice boomed.

He brought his knife down again, and I shot my palm up into his nose, sending him stumbling back a couple of steps, but he countered quickly with a punch to my jaw, and I thought again that I'd lose consciousness. Somehow I didn't, but it didn't matter. I felt dead on my feet. My arms were numb, and I couldn't lift them. My vision was blurry, and I swayed on my feet. Another punch hit me in the face, and blood poured out of my nose onto the ground in front of me, sending me stumbling backward. Only Ludo caught me before I could fall to the ground, holding both hands tightly around my neck, squeezing.

The shouting of the people around us intensified as the crowd grew. Several people tried to step in and stop him, but they weren't able to pull his hands free. Before enough of them could grab him, I saw the other rebels run out of the door and begin fighting them off. Even without knowing what was going on, they ran to their leader's aid. But, who was I kidding? They knew exactly what was going on. This seemed like a plan Lucille would come up with. This one didn't have any fatal flaws, it had worked. But that couldn't be right. Most likely, she would have never risked recruiting me, which could only mean one thing: She was unaware. This was all Ludo's doing, and he assumed I would never find out. I almost didn't.

All at once, his grip loosened. I choked and coughed as I was able to breathe again, all of my blood flowing into my head again. My eyes began to clear, and I could see what happened but couldn't make sense of it. Ludo's neck had a horrible wound, and blood ran down onto his shoulder. He was frozen in place. He faced straight ahead, his arms falling loose to his side. His eyes were full of fear as he looked around in horror, unable to process what had happened to him.

Wing beats boomed as the falcon slowed on his next circle around, and he landed down onto my arm, sinking his claws in deep. The blood from Ludo's neck slowed as he collapsed onto the ground. Lucille screamed and raised her knife, starting to rush toward me. Ghost beat his wings at her approach, and upon seeing him clearly, she immediately dropped her knife and fell backward. Cairn, who had been next to her, did the same.

"That's…," he started to speak but stopped and scrambled to his knees. "Oh, gods…," he said, clasping his hands together.

Lucille gathered herself and reached for her knife, but Cairn grabbed her arm.

"No. Don't you see what that is? This is an omen. The gods have spoken. Don't provoke their wrath, please," he begged.

I looked behind me, saw Heather and Lapis being held on the ground, and realized it was Mother who was holding them there. I hadn't even noticed she'd arrived. Father was standing behind her but was breathing hard enough that I could tell he'd only just caught up. Did Mother really disable both of them that quickly?

Before I could speak, the loud stomping of armored feet filled the momentarily quiet air with the sound of a new threat.

The commander arrived with two soldiers, as well as Ferris. "Hah!" the commander bellowed. "You did it. You had me fooled. I never thought— What's that?" she asked, nodding to Ghost. "A new species for me to send to the university."

"No!" I shouted. "He's mine. He's staying with me. You said I could bring a native animal with me to study. This is it. I choose the shadowfalcon."

"First of all, girl, those aren't real...," she said, almost reflexively. "We've looked for them. What's this, some kind of cleverly disguised vulture? Second of all, how do you know you even passed your exam?"

I didn't answer, the blood from my arm stained the sand below me where Ghost's talons sank in.

"Alright, well...regardless, I keep my promises." She looked to the soldiers beside her. "Arrest these rebels, and the chieftain, for his incompetence. We'll find someone better to do the job this time. And this village used to be so well-behaved...." As she was walking away, she looked back over her shoulder. "Of course you passed, by the way. You'll be going to the university. You can take that...whatever it is, with you."

One of the soldiers flung Ludo over his shoulder and held the other rebels at gunpoint, ordering them to walk in front of him.

Once they were gone, everyone continued to stand around me. At first, I was oblivious, but after a few minutes, I realized everyone was waiting for me to say something. Several people had already gotten onto their knees and clasped their hands together, especially the older villagers, in reverence to Ghost. Do I speak honestly to them? Do I tell them he's just a bird and, even when I set him free, he simply reverted to his training? Only...I'd given him no command. Did I really believe what I'd been saying anymore? There was definitely more to Ghost than I'd originally thought. How much more, and what, I didn't know.

No, sometimes hope in a lie was better than no hope at all.

"Everyone...what you see before you is real. An omen of hope in a bright future to come. A shadowfalcon. He has chosen me to bring about this new future, and he will accompany me along the way. Better days are ahead, not just for the village but for the entire world. I'll be leaving soon, but I will never forget all of you. Please, be good to each other."

Once home, Mother tended to my wounds again. Ferris and I said our goodbyes to everyone. Cara apologized to me endlessly again for what Ludo had done. She hadn't known about any of it.

Five of us had passed the exam this year, including Ferris and the other soldier, but it was unlikely any of us would ever see each other again.

I was both excited to take part in this groundbreaking animal research and terrified at the same time of what it might mean. The events of the recent days made me feel as though the decision had been made for me by some…higher power, chance, the universe, whatever you'd want to call it. But I was going to make the most of it. Other heroes had made a difference in my life, and I would never forget them. It was time for me to become the hero of my own story.

PanTech, you'd better get ready, because I'm coming for you.

EPILOGUE

"Come on, it's not like you don't know how pointless this is to have as a vanity project. Put your own ambitions aside, and let the military take charge." The giant man ran his hand over his long, black beard, patiently waiting to see if his adversary would take the bait.

"Hah," the thin, bespectacled man chuckled. "Vanity project, you say? Ambition, you say? You are one to talk, General. Your post is as useless as you are, and your words are as hollow as the paper enemies you imagine. Why the president keeps you around is beyond my ability to comprehend. The project will remain with me, and if you speak to me with due respect, you will perhaps benefit from my research."

Struggling at his own game, the General clenched his teeth, fighting to maintain his composure. "The president keeps me around, Lab Coat, because I keep him around. I monitor every uprising attempt reported by every commander in my service, from the small but disciplined armies to the back alley riffraff. I know about it all, and I make sure it is dealt with swiftly and productively. And, don't forget, I make sure we stay prepared for another incident like we had a hundred years ago."

"Lab Coat? My, you are so, so very clever, General. You mean the eastern invasion? Be careful; you'll sprain your shoulder trying so hard to pat your own back. Not only was that before our time, but it was also an incident hardly worthy of note. By the way, 'Professor' would be far more dignified on your part, would it not? You wouldn't want your soldiers to hear you be so disrespectful to a man of high station, such as myself, would you? Imagine the scandal."

The General sighed. "I'll speak to the president...Professor. We'll see what he has to say about all of this. If the eastern invasion were such a trivial matter, then why are we still talking about it a hundred years later?"

"General, you are trying my patience, as I'm sure is your intent. At least you will find my agreement that you are indeed good at something. PanTech controls all territories on the planet now. There are no longer any independent, foreign territories. Who do you suppose will threaten us, some remote, indigenous tribe somewhere that we've somehow not accounted for? Really, you should be in charge of the College of Theater, not Adversity Management. Your flair for the dramatic is truly a spectacle worthy of marvel." The thin man flipped his blonde ponytail from his shoulder to his back, and despite his thinner frame, seemed to be enjoying his nearly full head of height advantage over the general a bit too much.

"Fine. Clearly, you have a lot invested in this project. After all, it is the single greatest possible advancement to the College of Animal Studies. I'd imagine it is frustrating for you, being a man of genius and so poorly regarded by our president, that you are relegated to animals, leaving the human studies to more capable men and women. And the purpose of the project? What a joke. How could you possibly take pride in creating designer pets? A man of your genius, cleaning out litter boxes and dog kennels all day?"

The blonde man sighed and pushed up his glasses. "General…while it may be true that you are the preferred lapdog of the president, you have whispered paranoia into his ear for so many years. But I'll have you know that because of my research, PanTech will mark one of its greatest scientific breakthroughs in the past fifty years. This will have an impact far beyond my dying day, which I'm sure you hope will be soon, and my name will be written in our history books and taught in our classrooms, while yours…well, for what purpose would yours be included? Wasting our resources on over-preparation for another invasion that will never come is hardly, *hardly* noteworthy, wouldn't you agree?"

"Without me, are you certain your name will be worth writing either? A designer cat, capable of saying 'hello' to his lazy, over-indulged owner, while impressive from a scientific standpoint, is not the sort of thing you remember who was responsible for. Now, take, for instance, war dogs that are capable of following and understanding commands. And—"

"Talking war dogs? Really, General? I thought you had no interest in talking to animals."

"You didn't let me finish, Professor. You want me to stop being so paranoid? Imagine the potential to monitor adversity zones if we were able to send in, say…a bird who could listen to conversations and report back her findings. A mouse, crawling beneath the boards of a home, who hears the very moment a man speaks to his family about creating any sort of uprising. You want me to be less paranoid? What better way than this? I'd no longer have to worry, knowing that everything was being effectively monitored and well in hand. No more surprises, like we keep running into. They aren't threatening now, but if you let any problem go long enough ignored, it will fester. Sooner or later, they will become emboldened and find a way to operate outside of our knowledge, *just* as they did a hundred years ago. However, this time, we'd know about it long before it mattered. We could all relax, but most of all, the president could relax. Don't you want him to focus more of his attention on scientific endeavors again rather than my military projects? This could be your way to earn his favor and set yourself up for approval of your future project proposals. How many of them have been turned down in the past decade alone, Professor?"

The professor sat quietly for a long time and began to gently tap on the wooden desk in front of him, his eyes locked with the general's. "I'm not an unreasonable man, General. If you speak reason to me, I am certainly open to changing my mind. Let's say I accept your logic in this particular circumstance. What do you propose?"

The general removed his hat and rubbed his hand along his slicked-back hair, fixing the few strays that had begun to jut out.

"I'm so glad you asked, Professor. I saw the sparkle in your eye when I mentioned the animal spying idea. What if we repurpose your Animal Intelligence Evolution Project to this goal, ensuring PanTech is safe for many years to come?"

The professor shook his head. "No, I'm afraid I need to remain true to the original stated goal, which is to produce intelligent pets who provide a more complete companionship for their caretakers. If I change the scope of the project, I will have to apply again. If I do that, I risk being denied yet again, and even with your support, I simply cannot risk it."

The general sighed, tapping his finger on his chin. "I see...."

"However," the professor said, holding up his finger with a grin. "If we consider this project to have the true purpose of placing these intelligent pets in homes across PanTech, and, out of our shared interest in maintaining PanTech's goal of controlled adversity, we extend these pets to many homes within the adversity zones as well...."

The general grinned. "Thereby remaining true to the original stated goal of the project. I see. Professor, you are indeed as clever and capable as everyone says you are. I apologize for my earlier disrespect. Clearly, I have not spent enough time around you in person, and in error, I seem to have misjudged you."

"Likewise, General. I will offer you the same apology. Together, let us solidify the happiness of all PanTech employees."

"And the efficient control of all its citizens, guaranteeing we continue to become stronger through adversity," the general added.

The professor smiled and reached into his desk, pulling out a bottle and two glasses. "A toast?"

The general smiled to his new friend. "Of course."

After pouring the two glasses nearly full, the professor slid one toward the uniformed man who sat across from him, a symbol of his new respect.

"To friends?" the professor tilted his head slightly, his glass outstretched.

"To friends. To partners. To strength through adversity."

"Strength through adversity!" the two men shouted in nearly one voice, bringing the glasses to their lips and drinking the contents dry.

PANTECH CHRONICLES

INSURRECTION

BOOK 2

CHAPTER 1

"Would any of you like to share a way adversity has affected your life for the better?"

The bespectacled professor standing in the front of the group had a disturbingly chipper tone. Disturbing in its consistency, at least. Her smile was always bright, and her springy, short, brown hair seemed to bounce as she nodded along with every answer.

I hated this part the most. It had only been a few months since I left my parents behind to join PanTech's animal research division, and I've spent most of the time studying independently. They'd given us a tailored curriculum based on our individual abilities, designed to catch us up quickly to everyone else.

It was those times, sitting quietly at my desk in my room, talking to Ghost and thinking about Mother and Father, that I found something resembling comfort. I'd learned a great deal about the world's history, PanTech's rise to power, and their wonderful idea of cramming people into historically themed habitats and making their lives miserable like psychopathic pet owners. I could see that it wasn't always smooth sailing. Though history is, of course, written by the victor. PanTech had won it all.

"Taylor? Would you like to share?"

My mind snapped back to reality.

I fumbled, looking nervously at those around me, hoping to discern some hint from their expression. No such luck.

"Sorry. What was the question?" I asked, bracing myself for her response.

There was something so apathetic, bitter, and worn in that woman's voice and jovial expression that I think I'd have preferred it if she'd screamed at me or thrown something. Instead, her reactions were so unfitting and predictable that I sometimes questioned if she was a real person. Or if any of this was real. PanTech was nothing like the village I'd come from, with tiny homes in the desert, blades as the most advanced weapon, sicknesses and disease so common. PanTech was a bright, inspiring utopia… or at least that's how they sold it to us.

"Oh, it's alright. Don't be embarrassed. I just asked if you could share a way adversity has affected your life for the better."

Should've guessed that's what she'd asked. I had a feeling.

The one and only group class that meets once a week, and I get called on every time… and always with questions that made me want to march up to her and sock her in the jaw. At least this would be the last one. Thank goodness.

"I'd rather not share if that's alright."

"You can't think of a single time adversity has affected your life for the better?"

That's not what I said, and she knew it. She was testing me. Getting under my skin. Maybe that was it. Her one sick pleasure she had to look forward to every day… making people squirm.

"One time I bumped my elbow walking through a door. The next time I walked through a door I was more careful."

She stared at me. Her smile was unchanging except for a tiny, teensy bit, just around the eyes.

As she opened her mouth to speak, a laugh echoed throughout the room, and quickly silenced itself.

Her eyes darted around the room, seizing upon the culprit.

"Linda, it seems you'd like our attention. Has Taylor's answer reminded you of a story of your own?"

Linda stood up, clearing her throat.

"No. Sorry. Involuntary reaction."

"It seems you haven't experienced the level of adversity some others here have, seeing as you are quick to laugh at the misfortune and challenges of others. I suggest you reflect on where your character is lacking and consider how it might be improved."

This time, it was me fighting back a laugh. Though, unlike Linda, I'd held it in.

Linda went rigid, terrified, sending a glance my way that seemed to beg for help. Linda was taller than most men, with platinum blonde hair, sky-blue eyes, and a slight but chiseled frame. Yet, from the way she acted, you'd think she was the tiniest person in the world. She was extremely timid. Still, she'd become one of my only friends here, and had been kind to me since the moment we first met.

"It sounds like that's what you're doing, professor. Linda just has a hard time controlling her reactions to things. How about some sympathy?" I asked, tilting my head.

I heard a squeak and turned my head around to see Linda shriveling into herself, looking as though she'd seen a ghost. This was *not* the help she was hoping for.

"Oh, thank you so much, Taylor. It's wonderful when new employees are so helpful, sharing their fresh perspectives with everyone. Therefore, we meet in a group for this class on PanTech values and philosophy. I learn so much every day from all of you. I apologize to you, Linda, if my criticism sounded judgmental."

I seethed. Was she serious? PanTech certainly picked the right woman for the job.

"It's alright. No harm done," Linda said meekly, looking down at her feet.

I sighed. There's just no helping some people. I certainly wasn't the first one to try.

Just as the thought of this other person popped into my mind, their voice emerged, as if on cue. This time, my friend Joyce spoke up, clearing her throat and standing.

"I would like to share if you don't have an objection."

The professor nodded, still smiling.

Joyce's skin was several shades darker than mine, and she had bouncy black curls almost exactly like the professor's. However, those were the things you noticed about Joyce before she spoke. After she spoke....

"Even the tense moments we have in these meetings are a sign of 'Strength Through Adversity' at work. Our differences bring us closer together, and our different ways of speaking will be internalized by one another and adopted as our own over time, without us even realizing it. Bit by bit, the pieces make the whole. Even this meeting is designed by PanTech to challenge our tolerance of one another's differences, and we will admire traits we once thought we hated. I just wanted to say that, despite the difficulty we all have with sitting through these meetings, it is easy for me to see how it is improving us as employees of PanTech. Soon—"

A buzzer interrupted her as she had likely planned, sparing Linda and me further negative attention from the professor. Everyone both admired Joyce and suspected her in equal parts. As they liked to say in my village, she had a tongue of solid silver. She could sell adversity to PanTech. More difficult than that, she'd made friends with me.

As we all poured into the hallway outside the room, Linda put one arm over Joyce's shoulder, and the other arm over mine.

"I owe you one, Taylor," she said, returning to her usual

energetic self.

"I'm not the one you should thank," I said.

"Why do you think Pinta has it out for me, anyway?" she asked, looping her finger around and sticking it into my nose, prompting me to swat her hand away.

"Swing and a miss!" Joyce said, smiling. "It's not you she has it out for, goof."

"I'm not sure I follow," Linda admitted.

"Come on, girls. Shouldn't we grab lunch before we head back to the lab?" Joyce whined, ignoring Linda's statement completely.

"I'd rather not. I've already left Ghost alone for a while to go to this stupid meeting. He hates being cooped up in that room all day," I said.

"Then how about we *all* go check on your bird, *then* we can go to lunch," Linda offered excitedly, craning her head down to smile at me.

"And how do I know you won't try to make him your lunch, Linda, like you did the first time we met?" I asked, teasing her. Though, I had to admit, I was still a little sore about the whole thing.

"Hey! I didn't know he was your pet. It's not like newcomers are running around with pets straight off the transport, you know. I thought he'd flown in. Birds like that are a delicacy in my zone."

"Oh, she's just yankin' your chain, Ice Princess. Don't get all bent out of shape," Joyce said, holding back a laugh.

"Yanking my what? If you keep purposely using phrases I'm not familiar with, maybe I'll bend *you* out of shape."

"Oh my, our Ice Princess is discovering humor, and she's quite good at it for a beginner!" Joyce said, reaching up awkwardly high to pat Linda on the head.

I continued to guide them, probably without them even realizing it, toward my living quarters. The one thing they had in common was how easily they got absorbed into conversations. Especially when it involved delivering jabs to one another.

"You know, if we keep irritating Professor Pinta like that, they're going to end up sending us over to Adversity Management. Maybe not Joyce, though. Look at these soft muscles," Linda said, poking into Joyce's bicep.

"Well, we didn't exactly go around fighting everyone in my zone. I was a lawyer, you know. We helped resolve problems in the courts, through speaking, not by literally bending our enemies out of shape."

"How did you handle enemies in your zone, Taylor?" Linda asked, turning her attention to me, ignoring Joyce.

"Um, we didn't really have any. Remember how I told you we were just a small village?"

Linda frowned. "So, I guess you've never killed anyone before, then? Only seven for me, truth be told."

My memories came flooding back to me. The night of the exams, when I confronted the leader of our village's rebel group, Ludo, about dooming Linus to death. Whether Ghost landed the killing blow doesn't even matter. I was responsible for it. Yet, his death had bothered me far less than Linus's. Then again, it was Linus I was in love with, not Ludo. Thankfully, I'd thought about all of it less and less now that I had complicated work to keep me busy. Until someone said something to bring it all back to me, that is. Not that I'd ever truly forget. I hadn't bothered telling anyone else about it. On the surface, a girl getting revenge on a rebel for harming a PanTech soldier makes me look like the perfect little loyal PanTech employee. Never mind the fact that the reality was the opposite. I didn't have the energy to explain.

I zoned out and walked past my door without even realizing it.

"Taylor…," Joyce said, leaning around Linda.

"Huh?" I replied, snapping back to the present.

"Are you alright?"

She was frowning now. The question was obviously rhetorical.

"Yeah. Why?" I attempted to lie, anyway.

Joyce pointed back behind us. "Don't you live back there?"

"Oh…," I hung my head, accepting my defeat. "Yeah, I do."

"Way to go, Ice Princess," Joyce scolded, flinging Linda's arm off her shoulder.

Linda released me with her other arm, placing both hands on her hips, squaring up with Joyce. "Oh, you want to make a go of it, do you? Come on. You and me, right here. Loser buys everyone lunch."

"We don't even buy lunch here, Frost Giantess! There's no currency. I swear, it's like you just got here today. But let an authority figure show up, and you turn into a wet noodle."

"Alright, that does it!" Linda shouted, taking a step toward Joyce.

Before she could take another step, the entire corridor filled with laughter. I recognized the source right away.

"Well, if it isn't my three prodigies. So glad I ran into you here," the man said, turning the corner.

He'd probably been listening the whole time.

Great….

CHAPTER 2

"Pro-pr-prof…" Linda stammered, taking a step back.

Professor Barth looked as though he could be Linda's father. A tall, slender man, with blonde hair he kept in a tight ponytail, and ice-blue eyes. His demeanor was even like hers when no authority figures were around. That, and unlike Linda's playful boasting, Barth was genuinely arrogant. It would annoy me had I not gotten to know the man so well over the past couple of months. His arrogance was well-earned.

"Just the three unwilling participants I was looking for. I'm flirting with a breakthrough and need some outside hours assistance in the lab if anyone would like to volunteer. Of course, I'm forbidden from forcing you."

"Good, because we were just about to go to lunch. I'm sure it can wait," Joyce said, giving the proposition no thought.

"You're such a spoilsport, Joyce. Linda, what about you?"

"Uh… I'm…"

"Ah, I'm sorry. I think you're still a bit too nervous to come by yourself. Give it some time. You'll adjust before long. Taylor?"

I took in a deep breath. Of course, the last person to offer an excuse sounds the worst. I shook my head. "I don't mind skipping lunch, but I need to check up on Ghost. Maybe in a couple of hours?"

He clutched his chin and jaw with his entire hand, looking the three of us up and down. No doubt he was grappling with his disappointment. Many of the newcomers speculated he was so thin because he rarely sat down for a proper meal. He relied almost entirely on nutrition packs while he was working. These little packs had everything a human needed to be fit and healthy and provided enough energy that sleep was almost unnecessary. They had all these magical qualities, except for an important one. Regardless of flavoring, they just weren't as appetizing as actual food. We were told we'd get used to the synthetic stuff, and it seemed most did. We newcomers struggled the most.

"Right. I know it's difficult for new employees to juggle all their responsibilities. Tomorrow, perhaps?"

I nodded. "Or later if I get the time."

"Well, you know where to find me."

"Right," I said.

I definitely knew. This was the first time I'd seen him outside the lab or his office.

He waved at us and continued to walk by, disappearing around the other end of the corridor.

"Okay, did anyone else find that strange?" Linda quickly returned to her normal self.

"That your nickname has two meanings? That you're the princess of an icy land, and you freeze like a block of ice as soon as someone who outranks you appears?" Joyce teased. This time, Linda didn't take the bait.

"I'm serious," she pressed.

"Well, I agree with her," I said. "I don't think it was a casual request. I think if he was out here looking for assistants, he really must be on the edge of a breakthrough. The project is already ambitious."

Joyce wrinkled her nose. "I'm not sure I'd call designer pets ambitious, Taylor. In fact, I think having an animal walking around with me that's almost as intelligent as a human is downright creepy. Can you imagine? 'Good morning, Master. I brought you this dead bird. Hope you like it.' Just think about it."

"I think it's us putting ourselves as gods. Science should enhance nature, not rewrite it in our own image. That's the folly of gods," Linda said, punctuating the statement with a shiver.

"Ooh, look at you. Very profound," Joyce grinned. I wasn't sure if it was teasing or genuine praise.

"Look around you. Do you see any gods here?" I asked, raising my voice. "What do you suggest we study instead? A cure for diseases? PanTech has already cured them all. Genetic defects? PanTech has already corrected them. Cancer? Eliminated for hundreds of years. A better treatment for injuries? Short of making someone invincible, PanTech can stabilize and treat almost any injury you can imagine if the right kit is available, and a medic can administer it. PanTech can even regrow new organs if one is damaged. This isn't an adversity zone."

Linda frowned, likely missing home. She needed the reality check. They both did. The feeling, though, I knew well.

Upon arriving here, they brought us up to speed on so many important things, and there was still so much left to learn. The very things that plagued us in our adversity zones did not exist here.

They solved most problems a long time ago. This included all supplies and materials.

Every type of resource is mined and processed with very little human involvement, and the same process replenishes them. Nearly all done by machines. Manufacturing was completely automated, and they could adjust it to meet any demand at the slightest whim. Algorithms could solve deep mathematical questions in machines with programs called real-time adaptive integrated learners, or RAIL. Creativity and imagination were all that remained.

Ironic… so ironic, that the organization with the slogan "Strength Through Adversity" had now eliminated nearly all adversity from the human experience. To the point they needed to manufacture it in order to give human beings any sense of purpose at all.

"Rights and ethics are an ever-evolving problem, Taylor. Take it from me. I was an animal rights lawyer, remember? That is a problem that will never be solved, so long as we and animals exist in the world," Joyce said. Seemed she'd taken my outburst a bit personally. I shouldn't have said it that way….

"You're right, but that's not what I meant," I said, taking a deep breath and lowering my voice. "I just mean that in the context of where we are, it matters. It's important. Also, I don't find it creepy or problematic at all."

"I was a handler in my zone," Linda chimed in, smiling at the opportunity to mention it again. "I tamed a thunder bear. Sixteen feet tall, they are. I first think to myself that there'd be no need for a trainer if animals are as smart as humans. But then I ask myself the more important question. The one I should've asked from the start. What would the world look like if thunder bears were as intelligent as us?"

I sighed. Everyone struggled to adapt. To recognize that their past lives no longer reflected the reality of the world.

Linda lowered her head and clutched her left elbow with her right hand. *Gah! Stupid, stupid Taylor! One of my only friends, and I was making her feel terrible.*

"Sorry. It's a good question. It's just that you have to remember the weapons and military capabilities PanTech has. There are labs here that can code viruses to wipe out their entire species, so contagious and with such a high kill rate that they'll cease to exist within a year. Maybe five if they're spread out enough. There are weapons and armor… well, you've probably seen them. And advancements in those currently being developed. That's not even to mention—"

"That's enough, Taylor. Sheesh. You're making me want to go jump out of a window," Joyce snapped.

"But she's right, you know. We need to study the real world more and accept that things aren't like they were back home. We have to adapt, or we'll just end up fish out of water here," Linda said, offering me a half-smile.

"You too? Well, they haven't figured out a way to make me not hungry yet. That's a problem with an obvious solution that can be dealt with right now. Now, are you big-brained ladies with me, or against me?"

"With you! For once," Linda cheered.

"For once? What's that supposed to mean? I'm not sure why I love the two of you so much. You don't make it easy," Joyce said, jabbing her elbow into Linda's arm.

"Sorry, girls. I really need to check on Ghost. He's going to be upset with me as it is. How about you go ahead without me today?"

Linda narrowed her eyes at me. "Are you sure? We went this way in the first place because we said we'd go check on him with you, *then* go to lunch together."

"Yes, I'm sure. I think I'm going to do some extra studying, then go see what Barth was so excited about. I promise we'll go tomorrow."

Joyce threw her head back and sighed loudly. "Borrring. Come on, Taylor. You can study any time. Let's check on Ghost, then eat. You're going to turn seventy by the time you're twenty at this rate."

"Um…" Linda started.

"Tomorrow," I repeated.

"That's our Taylor. Completely immune to peer pressure. And fun," Joyce teased. "But okay, we'll think of you while we're enjoying actual food."

"Bye Taylor," Linda said, smiling and waving.

I turned and walked the short distance back to my living quarters, holding my hand up to the door and watching it open in front of me. Using only the blood sample they'd taken on testing day back at the village, now everything that was assigned to me could be opened with only a wave of my hand if it was locked. I shuddered to think of what else they might've used the blood sample for.

Stepping inside, I dropped my shoulder bag onto the closest table, unbuttoning the top two buttons of my shirt and stretching my arms out, enjoying the moment of freedom as much as I could.

"Sorry for running out on you, Ghost. Stupid meeting again," I said, pushing open the door into my bedroom.

Ghost seemed on-edge, which shouldn't really be that surprising, I suppose. Between the meeting and the spectacle in the hallway, this was the longest I'd left him alone since arriving.

He eyed me, then glanced behind me.

"No, I will not go out again tonight. Going to eat one of these gross nutrition packs and catch up on some reading. That alright with you?" I picked up the canister off my nightstand, holding it up in front of him. "See? Apple flavor. I don't know about you, Ghost, but I think I'd rather just eat apples and suffer malnutrition."

He looked at me, then behind me again, this time more frantically.

I sighed. "Seriously. I'm sorry. Starting next month, we may be able to travel outside, and I'm going to see about tagging along with the soldiers to different zones. I make it seem like I'm adjusting well, but all I ever think about is getting out of this stuffy place. Oh, and no more of this company culture meeting garbage. It's not that I dislike the research. I just don't think I can lock myself up in a lab all day, every day, like Barth does. I need to get out in the field sometimes, too. What do you think, Ghost?"

He flared out his wings, looking behind me. It didn't seem like I'd upset him. He was trying to tell me something.

I spun around, instinctively flowing into the fighting stance Mother had shown me. As quick as I turned, I felt a firm grip on both of my wrists before I could even focus on the face, sending me falling back onto the bed. It was a woman, with bright red hair and green eyes, her face covered in freckles. A face I was very familiar with. I almost didn't recognize her outside the armor.

She pinned my arms above me and smiled. Fighting back was impossible against this woman, with the strength of the enhancer in her body. I shouldn't be afraid of her anymore. I knew the rules forbade her from hurting me now, but too many memories lingered of our previous encounters.

"I don't enjoy being ignored, Taylor. How are you going to make it up to me? Hmm?"

"You're hurting me…," I said, intending the words to be a roar. Instead, they were barely a whisper.

"Oh, I can hurt you a lot more than this," she growled, nearly touching her nose to mine, her hair falling around my face. "This is nothing."

I sucked in a deep breath. *You don't need to be afraid of this psychopath anymore, Taylor. Show her you won't be pushed around. Linus wouldn't have let her treat him this way.*

"Let go of me. Now!" I shouted.

Her smile faded, her eyes widened, and she loosened her grip on my wrists.

I pulled my hands free and shove her back, sending her off me far enough to allow me to sit up.

"I—" she nearly spoke, but I interrupted.

"Why are you here?" I growled.

"To keep my promise," she said.

CHAPTER 3

"Your promise, huh? I'm listening," I said, crossing my arms. She needed to see me keeping a level head. Not being afraid. Not getting angry. It was all a farce, of course. All I wanted to do was cry. This woman was explosive and unpredictable and could easily rip me in half with her bare hands. She didn't seem like an evil person, but evil people aren't the most frightening. It's unpredictable people, by a landslide.

"Well, your bird is here. Had me fooled on that one. Thought it was a cleverly disguised vulture, but here he is… a real, genuine shadowfalcon. I thought it was just something you backward desert people made up for your tall tales."

"Should I release him from his cage and give you a closer look?" I said, in the most threatening tone I could fabricate.

She laughed. "You think I couldn't swat him from the air like an annoying fly before he performs his little trick?"

"I don't know that for sure, no. Remember the state you found the man I killed? Paralyzed and bled to death in seconds. Never saw it coming."

She walked toward me, slowly. I took a step back before steeling myself. She circled behind me, leaning in close, whispering. "Your heart is racing. I can hear it. Your slow breathing is forced, and I can see the sweat forming on your skin. My physical strength isn't all that's heightened by my implant. My senses can be tuned as well. It can be a little overwhelming at first, but in time you'll get used to it."

I turned around to face her again. It seemed she wasn't here to hurt me after all. Considering how calm Ghost had been through this conversation, he must've come to the same conclusion. "How did you convince the higher ups to allow something like that?"

She laughed again, but even harder this time. "Convince the higher ups? Are you daft? I didn't walk into the president's office or submit a formal request form, if that's what you're wondering. It was more that I called in a favor with the military science division. I was their little test subject for this device, after all. And, I suppose you wouldn't know since you're in Animal Research, but I was the first."

"The first? You mean——"

"Yes, I mean I was the first to be outfitted with one of these little monstrosities, which means long-term side-effects are unknown. Excited yet?"

I took a deep breath. This changed nothing. "I still want one."

She grinned, opening the door to my room and waving me out. "Brave, bold little Taylor. You're a wild one, aren't you? All your friends think you're like them, but you're not. I know you better than anyone. Better than yourself. There's no chain strong enough to bind you. That's something you and I have in common."

"You and I are nothing alike," I snapped, correcting her. "This is only the third time we've ever talked. The first time we've talked privately. You don't know me at all."

She shrugged, still grinning. "If you say so, Taylor. If you say so."

We left my living quarters and made our way to the opposite end of the building, where I hadn't been before. When she said the military science division, I assumed it would be in the same massive structure as all the other science divisions. That wasn't the case. We had to board a transport pod that shot us through a series of tunnels, landing us several miles away. I couldn't say how many. The distance traveled in mere moments, and it was impossible to make out anything aside from colored blurs through the clear windows. The travel pods were designed to eliminate the effects of fast travel on the body, but they still made me feel dizzy when I stepped off them. I'd only traveled in one once, and that was when we first arrived.

I had mixed feelings about whether I wanted to run into my brother Ferris here. It was too short notice to warn him I was coming, and he probably wouldn't support me getting this implant. The commander would probably run her big mouth and then he'd try to stop me. He always was protective, but I didn't need protecting and neither did he. He was my older brother by a little more than a year, but he took the role of big brother seriously... even though it was me bailing him out of trouble more often than the other way around.

"First time here?" she asked, grabbing me by the arm and

leading me out of the pod as I struggled to stand stable. I thought at first she was going to throw me out, but she was surprisingly gentle.

"You know… I've never asked your name," I said.

"Oh, you care about me enough now to want to know my name? What an exciting development. I'm not growing on you, am I?" She smiled when she asked, a little too widely. She was the last friend I probably needed here if I planned to stay out of trouble. For once. In fact, thankful as I was for her help, I really hoped this would be the last time I ever saw her.

"No, it just seems strange that I never heard it and never asked. I only know you as *commander*. I know that's not your name."

"Frelya, and that's alright. Very few people know my name. I don't give it to just anyone, you know. You're special, Taylor. *Very* special."

"Um… thanks. Mind letting go of my arm now?" I asked, noticing she hadn't released it, even after we'd stepped out of the pod.

"What? Oh, right." She quickly dropped her hand, walking toward the enormous building in front of us.

Familiar architecture. The building stood with enormous stone pillars in the front, supporting a covered, common area filled with uniform tables. Empty, of course. We had the same thing on my campus, also empty. Everyone preferred the simulated reality rooms to the real outdoors. I was told you could sit in any environment. Just sit in the chair and put on a lightweight headband, and suddenly you were transported to anywhere you wanted to be. It was almost as real as… reality itself. I tried it once, but the feeling I got from it wasn't the feeling of amazement it promised me. I felt disconnected. It made me question reality itself. It was so close to real that it was nearly impossible to tell the difference. You could even sync with other users and they could accompany you. No, my feeling was a disjointed horror that made me feel less human. I never used it again.

"Do you ever sit outside, Frelya?" I asked, prompting her to stop her hurried steps.

"You mean out here, at these tables?" She twisted around, tilting her head. Yeah, it was probably a dumb question.

"Or do you use the simulation room to relax?"

"The simulation room is stupid. Besides, I've kept a very close eye on you since you've arrived. What would you know about relaxing? I've looked through your access logs too. Seems you use all your time to study. You're like that beanpole professor you study under."

She turned around and continued into the building, not waiting for me to add anything, but I did anyway. I caught up to her and walked by her side. There was no reason to lead me around anymore. I wasn't a villager in one of her adversity zones anymore.

"What's the matter? You seem to love getting into my business and learning about me. Don't like it when I ask personal questions?"

"That's right. I want to know everything there is to know about you, but I'm not interested in answering your questions. So what?"

Why did I even want to know, anyway? It was silly to have even asked.

"Good afternoon, Frelya," an older man in a lab coat said as he walked by us.

"Where do you think you're going, Jer?" she asked, grabbing his arm just before he could make it out of reach.

"Uh… home?"

"Uh… no," she said. "Remember the little favor I asked you for?"

He yanked his arm away and walked back around to face us. He eyed me up and down before grinning at Frelya, then laughed.

"You must be kidding. This… animal division student?"

"Do you want me to knock that smile off your lips along with the head it's attached to, or will you show me the proper respect?"

He stood rigid. "Sorry, Commander Frelya. Forgive me for second-guessing you."

"I will, but only because you're useful. You are… useful, aren't you?"

"Please… when have I ever let you down?" he asked, adjusting his thick-framed glasses. Vision was easily corrected here by a simple two-minute procedure, so glasses were more often used as a visual tool for referencing data. Or a fashion choice.

If I were back home in my village, I'd have said the man was in his sixties. Here, it was impossible to tell. Occasionally, someone in our village would live to see a hundred. Very occasionally. They looked it, though. Here, I'd met several people nearing two hundred, and they didn't look a day over eighty. Still walking around. Still communicating clearly. All their hair. No cognitive deterioration. Everything here was indistinguishable from magic. Yet, there was no magic to be found.

"See that it stays that way, Jer. Follow us. I need you to install the implant."

He looked at me, then back at her. His face went pale. "I don't mean to second-guess you after I just said I wouldn't, but… no acclimation period? No staging? It will be… uncomfortable or worse."

She put a hand on my shoulder. "Do you think I need you telling me that? Nowadays, any weakling can withstand the process. You don't need to be a true warrior anymore. What the general and I went through… now that took guts."

"With all due respect—"

"With all due nothing. Taylor will either be truly worthy of it, or she'll die during the adjustment. Or I suppose she could change her mind." She turned her attention to me, smiling. "Well, Taylor? Not afraid of a little agonizing pain, are you?"

"It's not the stress on the psyche that's more problematic. You are… unique. This girl, I fear—" Jer protested.

"Fear is something you're going to become very familiar with if you continue to argue with me, Jer."

"I'll do it," I said, interrupting them. "If Frelya can handle it, so can I. I'm not afraid."

Frelya squeezed my shoulder and smiled. "Everyone here has forgotten what 'strength through adversity' really means. They've gotten soft and they turn away from pain like cowards, fearing what's just beyond it. They get here and stop pushing their limits."

She reached out and grabbed Jer by the collar of his coat, yanking him forward, leading me gently by the shoulder with her other hand.

We passed several other employees as we walked, but they treated this as a common sight. Perhaps it was, if Frelya was here often enough. Finally, we came upon a room with several chairs lined up side by side, those simulation headbands dangling from the ceiling.

"Strap her into the center chair."

I swallowed hard. Strapped in? No, I wouldn't back out, no matter what. I needed to remind myself why I was doing this. This was to give me any edge I could get against PanTech. They saw me as the girl who squashed a rebellion in her village, so they trusted me. But I'd never forgive them for what they did to Linus. Never.

I sat down and waited for the multiple straps to be secured around all my limbs.

"I will now insert the device into your brain, but don't worry. That's not the uncomfortable part," Jer assured me. Or at least he meant to assure me. It had the opposite effect.

"Stop dillydallying, Jer. We don't have all day!" Frelya scolded.

"Are you ready, Taylor? Beyond this point, there's no turning back," he asked, almost pleading.

"I'm ready. Please proceed," I said.

I took a deep breath, then another, and another.

You can do this, Taylor.

CHAPTER 4

Without warning, he slipped the headband over my head, and I found myself sitting in darkness.

No, not even darkness. Nothingness. I remembered why I hated these things so much, and it took this moment to illuminate it. Even with a world generated all around me, something inside my mind always felt unsettled. In an instant, a lush green forest appeared around me, and I was sitting in a clearing. I'd never seen such a place before.

"Do you like it?" Frelya's voice asked, just before she appeared in front of me.

"Where is this? I don't recognize it from the company catalog," I said, noticing how realistic the environment appeared. Not lifelike, but more convincing.

"Extracted from my memories. Well, my nightmares, to be more specific. I like to relive them, to remind myself where my strength came from, so I don't become soft like the others."

"Why would you…" I stopped speaking, noticing a burning sensation washing over me. Comforting, in a way. It was warm, like lying in the mid-day sun. "Why am I feeling things in here?"

She grinned. "You are and you aren't. That sensation you're feeling of your body heating, it's going to get worse. Much worse. You're going to feel like your skin is literally on fire. Your brain will feel like it's being boiled inside of your skull. You'll want to tear off your own flesh just to escape it. There are only two ways to escape it. The way I did it, and the way the three who came after me did it."

I could feel the heat intensifying and tried to brace myself. It only took a few seconds to realize that bracing myself would be useless.

"Just tell me!" I shouted.

"Overcome it or die."

"What?" I clutched my sides, finding it hard to even arrange my thoughts, much less speak them into words. "You never said—"

"My memories will help you focus on that fire burning in you now. It will become your killer, or your weapon. It should only belong to the worthy. The power is wasted on the weak!"

I opened my mouth to argue with her, but another voice interrupted me.

"So, this is where you were hiding, eh Frelya?"

Two men entered the clearing, wearing only furs to cover them below the waist. They were some of the largest men I'd ever seen and muscled as though they'd been given stimulants. Both their bodies were covered in terrible wounds, but they seemed completely unaffected. They spoke to Frelya but looked at me. That's right… this was her memory!

"We're the only two left, but they said there was a third. We knew no true warrior would hide, so we came to deal with the coward. Having someone ambush the victor would be an embarrassment for our people."

Frelya mouthed the words that came next, her face expressionless. The voice sounded like it was coming from me.

"I'm sorry. Someone shoved me in at the last second. I don't want to fight. Please!"

One man approached me and clutched my throat. He lifted me into the air as if I were a cloud. The pain shot through my body now, nearly unbearable.

"You'll feel pain here too, you know. I designed it that way," Frelya warned, a bit too late.

I clutched the man's hand as I struggled to breathe, but he ignored me like an insect biting him. He drew back his fist and slammed it into my face. My vision blurred. I could feel every bone in my face shatter in real time. He dropped me to the ground, and before I could fall, kicked me into a tree that was behind me.

"So small and frail. If only you had more strength. More power. If only you could take that rage inside you and synchronize it with your muscles."

My vision went completely dark for a moment, before I found myself jolted into the same position I started in, kneeling in the clearing.

Before I considered what was happening, the pain intensified again.

"So, this is where you were hiding, eh Frelya?"

This time I jump to my feet, picking up a stick from the forest floor.

"That's right. Your imagination can alter this reality within the realm of possibility. But your half-hearted gesture will yield pathetic results."

Frelya's commentary didn't exactly help. It felt more like she was antagonizing me than supporting me.

I swung the stick at the man who punched me last time, but the other grabbed it from my hand like I was a child, driving his own fist into my face. Blackness, again.

This time, I grabbed a handful of dirt, waiting for them to appear. Before they could acknowledge me, I threw it in their faces and went for the knife on one man's belt. He caught my hand and snapped my wrist. The pain felt real but paled compared to the rising heat in my body.

Blackness.

"Not every fight can be won by outsmarting your opponent. Intelligence can help you avoid a fight, but when fights are unavoidable, it's strength that allows you to win them."

Another lecture from Frelya.

She was really… making me angry. The burning sensation was familiar. Not the same, but like burning rage—if it was allowed to leave the mind and take a physical form in my muscles.

The men appeared in front of me, and I allowed myself to feel all the suppressed anger I'd been bottling up. I'd always seen it as my problem. For once, it might be my solution.

I ran toward them, screaming at the top of my lungs. With all my might, I swung at one man's stomach. It landed without effect, and with one swift kick, I was sent against the tree again.

"It's not enough to be angry, Taylor! Anger from the weak is like a puff of smoke in a tornado. It means nothing!"

Blackness again but I immediately ran upon the world resetting. I cried out, charging from the clearing and in the direction I knew the men would come. They were facing one another, speaking, and it alarmed them to hear my voice. I picked up a rock, then jumped on one man's shoulders, slamming the rock into his head. He collapsed to one knee, but the other man quickly tore me away from him and slammed me into the ground, beating me unconscious.

"Control your breathing. Let your rage fill your body. They're bigger, but only appear stronger. That's the real illusion. Understand that you are a goddess before mortals. Your mind only has to accept it for it to be true."

I ran forward again, but this time I imagined myself faster, like the panther from my homeland that nearly killed me. It could leap through the air, the height of three men, but now I could too. I jumped up into the trees and kept quiet. Dropping down, I choked the man, nearly crushing his neck, every bit as strong as they were. There was a struggle that went on for a while before both men took me to the ground.

Blackness, again. It wasn't enough. I needed more.

"Is that all the ambition you have? You can push your body beyond limits you could only dream of, and you choose to be the equal of what men have been capable of for thousands of years. At this rate, you'll—"

I ran off before she could finish. I couldn't focus on a single word she said anymore. Never had I felt so much pain in my life. It made terror ants seem like nothing.

I ran into the men and punched with both my fists at once, sending them onto their backs and incapacitated.

Blackness, but why? I'd beaten them this time.

"Frelya? Can you hear me?"

"The scenario is resetting. I'm not sure why. Focus on your breathing," she replied.

A scene materialized in front of us, and I nearly fainted at the sight.

Before us was the giant snake Linus and I fought on the outskirts of my village. Though we'd killed it, it lived on in my nightmares, second only to one far worse.

"Taylor! You're willing this memory into the system. That's unexpected, but good. You can win this fight now, too. Alone."

The snake's eyes peered right through me as it flicked out its tongue. It coiled, and I knew all too well the signs before the strike.

It struck at me with incredible speed and power, but I was ready. Planting my feet firmly into the sand, I grabbed both fangs when it was upon me. They were hard as stone and allowed me to stop the beast in its tracks. I held even with it at first before twisting it with all my might. Despite my new strength, this behemoth proved too much to overpower. Still holding onto the fangs, I ripped them from its mouth, sending it flailing onto the ground. I landed hard on the sand, but quickly rolled back onto my feet, leaping through the air and slamming both fangs into its skull, deep enough to enter its brain. It raised its head high into the air before collapsing, dead. I landed on my feet.

Blackness. Would this ever end? I hated PanTech, and it seemed I'd forgotten just how much. I'd pushed the memories deep down and told myself I shouldn't feel them anymore. Had this only made it worse?

The scene manifested again. It was the worst nightmare of all, and I wasn't ready to see it.

"Turn it off!" I screamed. "Frelya, I don't want to see this."

Frelya seemed just as shocked as I was and offered no answer. She looked on with clenched fists.

"So, this is what it looked like, huh? If you were strong enough—"

"No!" I screamed, putting my hands over my ears. "Turn it off!"

She ran over to me, yanking my hands away.

"If you were strong enough, you could have fought at his side. You could have saved him. These events aren't once in a lifetime, Taylor. Trust me. Do you want to watch something like this happen again? Be strong. Choose strength!"

"But these are PanTech soldiers in power armor. They're too strong."

"Accept your gift. Those who were strong before have now become weak."

As the scene played out, I found myself locked in the large animal cage, just as I was before.

"If you let her out, I'll kill you," Linus said to no one. Cara wasn't here. Only Frelya and I.

Would I really have to watch this again? I couldn't.

I wouldn't....

Peter raised his gun to shoot Linus, but just as before, Linus was too quick. He shot him. Peter's blaster fired prematurely into the desert sand below, sending up a cloud.

I kicked the heavy door off the cage and ran toward them.

Oscar activated his blaster, and I could hear the low hum as though I had enhanced my hearing a hundred times. But the distance was so much to cover, and this would all play out so quickly. I ran faster. It felt as though I was manipulating time, slowing the surrounding events, rather than speeding myself up.

He raised the blaster, but before he could level it, I grabbed his hand.

"You!" he shouted, grabbing my wrist with his left hand,

trying to free himself. Even with the strength of the armor, he couldn't budge me at all. "But how…."

I tightened my grip on his hand, causing the armor to split, then break, crushing his hand along with it. He shrieked in pain, letting go of my wrist and throwing a punch at me. I dodged it easily, moving around to his side, wrapping my arm around his neck and squeezing it. With almost no effort, I heard a loud snap, and he fell to the ground.

I looked up, desperately trying to see through the cloud. Was Linus still there? Was he alive?

When my heart had slowed and my eyes focused, I saw him standing there, balancing the rifle on his shoulder. He tipped his hat forward with the other hand and smiled.

"We did it…," he said.

"We—" I tried to repeat the same thing but choked on the words. Tears poured from my eyes. I ran toward him.

But no matter how fast I ran, he got no closer. He was frozen there, smiling, tipping his hat to me.

Blackness.

I didn't care anymore.

My anger no longer burned, extinguished by the tears.

All I could do was cry.

CHAPTER 5

A painful grip on both my shoulders pulled me back into reality. "For what it's worth, I'm sorry," Frelya said.

My eyes slowly adjusted. I felt terrible. Like I'd fallen out of a tall building and was being kept alive with technology, though I should've been dead.

"Wh—what?"

"For what happened to Linus. This is the last time I'll say it. I'm sorry."

"I don't need your apology, but… thanks anyway," I said.

I wanted to say a lot more than that but thought better of it. I couldn't exactly tell her, a PanTech commander, how much I hated PanTech. It was their fault. *All* of this was their fault.

"Strength through adversity. We say it, but few of us understand it, and most of those who know forget quickly when dropped into comfort and luxury beyond anything imagined in their homelands."

"How do you feel?" Jer interjected. Thank goodness.

"Awful," I replied. Understatement.

"You should recover quickly. I've already administered a restoration cocktail to heal the damage you caused your muscles during the synchronization. The small amount of damage caused during the implantation process is already healed."

I looked at Frelya. "Will I really be able to do all of those things I did in the simulation?"

She grinned. "Not unless you wanted to get all your organics replaced with synthetics. Short of that… hardly. Considering the stress it places on your body, you really must pick carefully when to activate it. Synchronization joins its function with your thoughts for simple activation. If you don't specifically call upon it to increase a function of your body or mind, it is always dormant. Small increases in your strength can be used regularly. Big ones, well… say hello to torn ligaments, pulled muscles, and broken bones. The enhancer can help you heal those much more quickly than the average person, but nothing close to instantly. Sorry, Taylor. You're not a superhero."

"So… what? Are you bluffing all the time?" I asked. Seemed the best way to get answers out of Frelya was by antagonizing her, as dangerous as that was.

"Oh, dear Taylor, I'm never bluffing. I know exactly what the device is capable of. Don't forget, I've had it longer than anyone. Besides, I'm the one who invented it."

I was stunned. This brutish woman? Even if you'd given me a hundred guesses, I would've never picked her as the inventor of such a complex and powerful device.

"You… invented it?" I asked, my voice nearly a whisper, as though it were a secret.

She huffed, narrowing her eyes at me. "Did you forget anyone accepted into PanTech must also possess high intelligence? Did you think I was the only idiot at headquarters? Honestly, Taylor, I thought you and I understood one another better than this. Besides, I only made this because they denied all my other proposals. PanTech's higher ups really, really hate mixing human and machine. A long time ago everyone was doing it, and the consequences were catastrophic… or so we're told. You know how tight-lipped they are about embarrassing history. I've seen your search activity, remember?"

I'd forgotten about that. Does this mean Frelya had gone down the rabbit hole too, searching for PanTech's weaknesses? *No, assume nothing. She may have been searching for the weaknesses so she could improve them. She seems loyal to PanTech. Don't trust her. She did you a favor for a favor. That doesn't make you friends. Keep a level head, Taylor.*

"Why was this allowed if cybernetics weren't?"

"It pushes the limits of what our bodies are capable of but doesn't go beyond. General Markus also helped convince the president we needed it to give the military an edge over any potential insurrection. You know the other part of PanTech's history that's clouded? Seems the adversity zones mounted a pretty good one a little over a hundred years ago with the help of the last remaining country not under PanTech's control to the east."

"Doesn't matter what the details are. We know the ones that matter. They tried it, and they lost," I said, trying to mask my irritation.

I'd done everything I could to find out what happened back then. The offensive lasted almost a month. They dealt heavy damage to PanTech during the first week, and it seemed they might have a chance. A week was all it took to mobilize PanTech's weapons, and all opposition was obliterated. Outnumbered thousands to one, PanTech ripped them apart in weeks. Days, really. It just took weeks to hunt down those who attempted to go into hiding. But what was the technology? How was it deployed? What reasons did the enemy state for the invasion? How did they track down those who tried to hide? All a giant blank space in the archive, which only meant the truth was inconvenient. It just meant that Frelya was right about one thing she'd said. No one wants to rock the boat. They have it too good here. Every luxury and comfort you could ever imagine. Completely free to pursue your desires, whatever they are, as long as they don't endanger PanTech.

I'd hoped to get Frelya talking about those secrets sometime. I'd hoped that as a commander, she'd know all the details. Seems I was wrong. She knew no more than I did. There were PanTech employees old enough to remember the battle, but I had a feeling they wouldn't be of much help either. I'd been told that most of them stayed in their quarters most of the time, hooked up to simulations, reliving old memories, no longer interested in creating new ones.

"Nonsense!" Frelya shouted. "How are you supposed to avoid a repeat of history, or worse, if you don't know what went wrong in the first place?"

I sat forward in my seat, hopping off the edge and landing on my feet. "What? You mean like killing probably everyone involved and locking down the adversity zones so tightly they couldn't sneeze without the adversity management people knowing about it? I'd say they tied up their loose ends pretty well."

She took a step toward me, putting her hand on my cheek. "You're adorable when you think you have everything figured out, Taylor. That's what makes humans human, after all. When we're up against something impossible, it only makes us want to do it more. I've watched your little village, Taylor, and I've seen others. They're practically salivating for a chance to march in here and skin us alive. Oh, and you'd better get used to the idea that you're not one of them anymore, Taylor. You're one of us now."

I grabbed her wrist, feeling right now was as good a time to test the implant as any. *A little more strength. Just a bit. Just enough to remind her,* I thought to myself. I yanked her arm away from my face, and she clenched her teeth, taking a step to the side to gain her balance.

"Good. You're a quick learner," she said with a smirk.

"I had an excellent teacher."

"Things have been quiet in your zone, so I have time on my hands here. Thanks to you. How about we meet here and do more training tomorrow?" she asked. Though, her tone was a bit more gentle than usual.

Was she lonely and just wanted someone she saw as being like herself to spend time with? It's not like she'd give me a straight answer if I asked. I still hadn't decided if I should stay as far away from her as possible now that I had what I wanted. Staying close to her would have its benefits, but would it be worth the danger?

"No, I want to stop by Professor Barth's office and help him with the big project at Animal Research. I promised him I would come by later if I had time. I'm not sure how long we'll be working on it. Could be days, or months. If I have extra time, I'll stop by."

"I've added travel clearance for you to come here. This implant can also help you with thinking more deeply, quickly, and about multiple variables at once. It's one of the bigger benefits because it's hidden. Use it conservatively. It can cause some pretty serious headaches and cause you to become unstable if you use it with too much power or for too long. Experiment. I've found that I can lose a bit more sleep when needed. It's like a super capacitor embedded in your brain. It saps a small amount of energy from you passively and stores it. That's another reason time has to pass between major uses. Don't get carried away is what I'm saying."

Before I could answer, Jer interjected. "We'll be collecting data like we do from all of them, so we can learn more about what they're capable of. Your vitals and location data are part of that."

"I didn't give you permission to do that!" I growled, putting my finger in his face, backing him against the console beside the chair.

"It's standard. Th-they all have it!" he said, raising his hands in the air.

"Even mine," Frelya said, probably trying to reassure me. It wasn't working, but what could I do about it now? In fact, my little outburst probably only made it look like I had something to hide. I was being tracked all over this campus and headquarters anyway. I already knew that. Of course, they'd track these devices in case they'd need to recover them in the field. *Deep breaths, Taylor.*

"It's understandable. I just don't like surprises. That's all."

"You're the one who agreed to have experimental technology implanted in your body. No one forced you. Remember that," Frelya said, resting her hands on her hips.

"You're right. I'll remember…. If that's all, I'll be going now."

"Have fun with your new toy," Frelya said.

Jer raised his hand. "Come back here if you experience side effects. Especially a rise in body temperature, loss of feeling in your extremities, seizures, and that sort of thing. It will trigger an automatic alarm here, but it will still be quicker if you come to us. Most of the scientists here can check—"

Frelya interrupted. "I'd prefer if only Jer and I knew about this for now. Not that I care what the others think. I just don't have the patience to answer the long list of idiotic questions I'll no doubt be buried in. Jer's were already bad enough."

I considered protesting, saying something about how they should've maybe told me about the potential for these side effects before sticking the thing in my brain. Once again, I had to accept the responsibility for everything that might come along with it. It was easy to get angry with Frelya, but I didn't exactly ask her questions. Whether she'd have answered them would be a different story, but I should've asked.

It wouldn't have made any difference. I now had an advantage over everyone short of Adversity Management commanders. Frelya was keeping it a secret from everyone who didn't need to know for convenience, and I could definitely use that. If I could keep this to myself, the advantage is that much greater.

"No problem. I'd prefer to keep it quiet too, for the same reasons. My friends would ask way too many questions. If I feel anything going wrong, I'll come right away."

"Good. Get back to work, Jer. I have other things to do too. Good luck with your… animal experiments, Taylor."

Her tone was pure disgust. I'm sure in her mind she couldn't possibly understand why I'd choose the animal experiments over sharpening what's just short of a superpower. The reason was simple. Even though I hated PanTech, I joined the College of Animal Research for a reason. I wanted to be a part of the groundbreaking research currently underway, genuinely, and I was going to do everything I could to keep PanTech from perverting it into something used to make everyone's lives more difficult. This was how I'd make a difference. Now, with this implant, I could even more easily impress Professor Barth with my mind and gain his trust.

Things were finally going my way. Though, I couldn't help but ask myself one important question:

How long would it last?

CHAPTER 6

By the time I made it back to my living quarters, it was late. Most employees would be snoring right about now. I really, really felt like doing the same. Every muscle in my body ached, like everyone in PanTech took turns hitting me like a piñata.

I stood in front of the door, thinking the whole situation over. I could head to bed now. Get an early start. Get the much-needed rest. That would be the wise, responsible, and reasonable thing to do. But since when have I ever considered all of that when deciding something? No point starting now.

Professor Barth had said earlier he was on the verge of a breakthrough. That meant one thing was almost certain. He was not in bed, and probably hadn't seen a bed in days. He'd probably choked down synthetic nutrition paste and was slumped over his notes, trying not to fall asleep.

Or maybe none of that was true, but showing up this late might be a move that impresses him. Taking a step back, I headed down the other end of the corridor and wound my way through the tight hallways that wormed their way through this enormous campus. It was so easy to get lost in here, and new recruits were doing it all the time. Spending so much time in the desert, my sense of direction was pretty sharp. Some were much sharper than mine. I'd already noticed an obvious pattern that gave it away. The higher level of technology available in their adversity zone, the less able they were to function independently of it. Things like remembering directions or performing complex calculations in your head became extremely difficult.

Every day, I'd feel myself slipping, just like Frelya warned, thinking thoughts like these. For a moment, I was thankful that I'd grown up spending so much time outdoors and had only primitive tools. I was thankful, yes, but it shouldn't have been forced on me. Judging by that simulation she manifested, Frelya's adversity zone must've been some kind of kill or be killed nightmare. It had turned her into a model PanTech citizen, praising the strength she'd gained through surviving those nightmares, and valuing suffering and the strength gained from it above all else. She didn't seem to like anyone aside from me and supposedly Linus. At any moment, she could snap over the smallest thing. Seemingly nothing. Was this what PanTech wanted? She could've been a normal girl. That's probably all she wanted when she was a child. So could I. PanTech takes from you with one breath, then asks you to thank them for it in the next.

I stopped short of walking straight into the wall, lost in my thoughts.

"Animal Studies Lab 3" was etched into the metal plate on the door. The room was dimly lit. Almost dark. I nearly walked away before I glimpsed Professor Barth's head rising above the high-backed chairs lining the opposite wall. I considered knocking, but I could tell he was in deep concentration. There was no evidence of it I could see, but I guessed by the way he was leaning back in his chair and gesturing to no one at all that he was deep in some sort of calculation or organizing information, running probability tests, or something like that. The only odd thing about it was the fact that gesturing was completely unnecessary. According to him, the version he was used to required it, and he didn't want to change to only using his eyes. I guess even PanTech employees can get set in their ways and resist new tech. Ironic, in a way. Downright blasphemous in another.

I opened the door as quietly as I could and let myself inside, looking around for anyone else that might be there too. The room was empty, save for a row of animals in spacious cages, already deep in some kind of soothing simulation of their own. I'd been quiet enough not to alert any of them at least. Including Professor Barth.

"Ahem." I cleared my throat, in as low a volume as I could manage. Nothing. He continued throwing his hands about rapidly and mumbling. "Professor Barth," I said, a little louder this time.

Without removing his magic glasses, he finally acknowledged me.

"Taylor! Well, well… it took you long enough. Better late than never, I say. Well, don't just stand there like you're one of those empty chairs. Grab an optic aid and we'll sync up. You need to see this!"

Following his instructions, I picked one up off the table and placed it on my face. I was clumsy with these. It was one thing that really freaked me out when I first got here, but I was really getting the hang of them now. The implant would definitely help with the rapid eye movements. Just hopefully not too much. I booted up and gave a verbal command to sync to the nearest device, which happened instantly. Immediately, it flooded me with information. Piles of it. In every corner of my vision and beyond. By simply thinking it, I could move the space around in my vision, and my eye focus triggered a clearer look at each bit of information. Not that it helped. Though, this wasn't far off from what I expected the cluttered mind of a genius to look like.

"Um… what am I looking at, Professor?"

"Cell thirteen. Look at the results of the simulation I ran on the compression of usable brain tissue and related energy targets."

I squinted, looking at it carefully. Aside from the one he mentioned, I saw thousands of previous attempts with different variables. This one was unique. Also a failure, but…

"This dog's brain, using these calculations and procedures, becomes virtually identical in function and capacity to a human brain. Does this mean that—"

"No! Look at the results. Failure at the moment after success is still failure. It will complete, but the subject won't survive long enough to make even the slightest use of his or her capability. It is born and dies, no more advanced than an infant, and developmentally almost identical. Do you see my problem? In particular, do you see *the* problem?"

"Natural reproduction is impossible," I pointed out.

"No. No. You're thinking small, Taylor. *Why* is that the case?"

I studied it carefully. I knew the question was intentionally near impossible to answer. He was testing me. He expected me to ask him what the problem was after failing to find it. I needed to use the implant to do it a little faster than he expects. Only a little. Dig deep down into the data to find the issue.

I scanned the information rapidly. It was like speed reading, but many times faster, and with no change in how much information I could absorb.

"There's a sub-helix incompatibility on the omega strand. It doesn't respond to the procedure, creating a weak link that—"

Barth excitedly rose to his feet, finishing the statement. "It creates an energy imbalance because it cannot adapt to the new energy expenditure. Though it takes the same amount of space, the evolved brain's density means it requires a higher intake of energy. It throws off the entire metabolism which, if off even a slight amount, causes the body to fail quickly. Especially with the improper allocation of the body's resources. Well done, Taylor. However…"

My whole body tensed. Had I slipped up already?

"I know you've worked hard, but you have to take your time and be more thorough in your analysis. Don't think I didn't notice how quickly you went through the data, only to stumble upon the correct conclusion by chance. You must resist the temptation to seek the quick answer, and always choose to be thorough."

I'd guessed wrong. He was actually wanting me to slow down and focus under pressure, and I'd misread him.

"Sorry. You're right, of course. I'll do better from now on."

He laughed and removed the device from his head, tossing it on the desk in front of him. "Nonsense. Considering the technology rating of your adversity zone, and the short time you've been here, your adaptation to modern science and practices has been nothing short of astounding. These days, there are very few dedicated to animal research with the passion you and I have. It receives the least amount of praise from the higher ups, and even on the cusp of such an amazing advancement, they still consider us the least important division. In fact…"

He stood, motioning for me to follow him. I removed the glasses and scrambled to keep up since he was already halfway across the room. We walked a short distance to his office, where he motioned for me to sit down. He snapped his finger, and a light background music played. Nothing I recognized. It seemed Barth was probably more sentimental than I'd realized. I should attempt to learn about the adversity zone he came from.

He walked over to a cabinet in the room's corner, opening the door and pulling out a bottle and a glass.

"Drink?" he asked, waving the glass.

Just as I opened my mouth to refuse, I reconsidered. The cabinet was ornate, and obviously carved from a high-quality wood. It took a moment for me to realize what that meant here. I had scarcely seen anything made of wood since I got here. Everything was custom-fabricated by large machines to exact specifications, made of synthetic look-alike materials. Focusing on the grain of the wood, this was genuine. If my theory was correct…

"That cabinet. It's beautiful. Is this the belonging you took with you when you left your adversity zone and came here."

He froze in place, and for a moment, his smile faded. Only for a moment, though, before returning at double the intensity.

"In all the years I've been here, you are one of only a handful to notice and comment on it. That attention to detail will serve you well."

"You give me too much praise. And sure, I'll have a drink too."

His smile warmed even more as he poured us both a drink before returning the bottle to the cabinet and sitting. He took a sip, and I could sense the beginnings of a speech boiling just behind his lips.

"I won't mislead you, Taylor. You should know I am a glory chaser. I'd like to sit here in front of you and boldly proclaim that I care only for the science, and I enjoy the lack of oversight that comes with not being the center of attention. With your perception, you'd see right through such an obvious lie. I know myself very well. In the beginning, I believed that was true. I was already a scientist before coming here. One of the youngest ever in my zone. They heaped praise upon me left and right. Every night, I had dinner with a different politician or celebrity. It seemed like every month I was accepting a new award.

"I told myself it was all tiring and excessive. That it was impeding my research. Then, the testing came, and shortly after, the world around me completely changed. I was no longer the biggest fish in a tiny pond. I was… average. No more awards. No special treatment. Did you know that I've never met with the president of PanTech, even once? It's true. All he cares about anymore is the military now that the 'general' is in his ear every day, feeding his paranoia of another uprising."

He made air quotes with his fingers when he said "general." Clearly, he disliked this man. Frelya didn't really talk about him much, beyond her admiration of his strength. Maybe he deserved the praise, and Barth was only bitter. Still, I needed to be very careful. Clearly, the professor had an ego. Unlike most, he wasn't even hesitant to admit it. This was another test.

Think carefully before you speak.

"That's short-sighted," I said, taking a sip of my drink. "You're the head of your own research division. You work harder than anyone I've met here."

This was true, even if I mistook his motivations. In the end, it probably didn't matter. PanTech would use whatever breakthroughs made to either enrich the lives of those here or hurt those in the adversity zones. It's not like that would ever change.

No… I needed to stop thinking that way. Or else why did I even come here? Frelya had taken a liking to me. She's a commander and a military scientist. Commanders work directly beneath the general. Barth was the head of Animal Research. What if I could take his place someday? I could sabotage harmful research or discourage the military from using it. Maybe Frelya could have her part to play in that.

I remembered the teachings of my mother. Stop being so stubborn and callous. Use charm. Manipulate your enemies into defeating themselves.

"Yes, well, at least someone around here noticed. And you've been here, what… a mere handful of months? We've placed human and military research on such a pedestal that we've forgotten that we make up only a fraction of living things on this planet. With human population absent in so many large parts of the world now, new species of plants and animals are emerging at an alarming rate. What could we learn by studying them? It was *my* research, using the same process antlered mammals use to regrow their horns quickly, that we have to thank for broken bones being mended in *days*! What a historic accomplishment this was. To have one injection heal a broken bone. But do you think I got a visit from the president? An award? A medal? A structure renamed in my honor? Hah! If you guessed 'nothing,' you'd be correct."

This strategy was the correct one. Give a big-talking ego like Barth the tiniest prompt, and he could talk about himself for days.

I set my glass down on the desk, hard, raising an eyebrow. "That's amazing. If something like *that* wasn't enough to get the president's attention, what were the other divisions creating?"

He shook his head, standing and facing toward the wall behind him.

"That's the most insulting part of that entire event. That same week, General Markus, along with other top scientists in the military division, unveiled the newly designed power suits. Unlike the previous version, the new one was… well, I'm sure you've seen them. The fluid inside would enable the soldiers to be comfortable in any environment, and it contained available treatments for wounds and ailments of all sorts. They were also more powerful. Not that it was necessary considering half of the apes in these adversity zones have barely advanced beyond hurling stones or firing arrows from longbows. Perhaps you can guess what happened next."

Apes, huh? Barth really wears his heart on his sleeve. He doesn't even see most of the population as human. They're lesser creatures to him. Apes. Disposable. My blood boiled, and I struggled to keep my cool. Yet, that's what I had to do. I knew this meeting was a rare opportunity, and I had to seize it. I had to do everything right. No mistakes.

I shook my head, taking another sip of my drink. "I suppose everyone was so enamored by the military advancements that they didn't even notice something as groundbreaking as your invention."

Barth laughed, placing his hand on his forehead before turning back around to face me, smiling widely.

"Oh, if only that were the case, Taylor. Far worse than that. They considered my research the ideal supplement, accessory even, to the military's new technology. After all, it was so easy to add my technology to the fluid of the suits. Now soldiers, in the mostly imaginary scenarios where they might have their bones broken, would receive immediate treatment that would have them back in the fight in no time. You could ask yourself what fight that may be. Well, that would be a fair question. The truth of the matter is, as you could likely guess, that there is no war and hasn't been a war in ages. The last rebellion was squashed so decisively that another one is all but impossible."

"Yet the president fears it anyway and gives all his personal attention to the military's waste of resources and personnel," I said, punctuating the statement with a deep sigh.

He sat back down in his chair, downing the rest of his drink in one swift movement. His skin was flushed from his tirade, but he seemed to be calming down.

"It feels good to sit down and talk to someone who sees things for what they are. It's a rare event indeed. I hope you don't give in to laziness, just as most others do when they transfer to PanTech."

This was it. This was the opening I'd been waiting for.

"Actually, I'd like to be more involved. Since you were so honest with me, I'll be just as honest with you. I was a veterinarian in my adversity zone. It was a thankless job, but it was something I really cared about. There were a lot of distractions in my zone leading up to my testing, and… I hope you won't be upset by my saying this, but I was hoping to become more involved in this important breakthrough research I heard so much about. I've done so much studying since I've arrived. You can see how much I've learned in just a few months. I've met people who have been here for years that are behind me already.

"You and I are different, but in a way, I think will complement each other well. I hate the attention that comes with major discoveries, and I only care about the work itself. I would be more than happy to give you the credit for anything I find or help with. All of it. One commander has taken a liking to me, and I can go on expeditions with her to bring back samples from any species you think we should study."

He nodded slowly, looking down at his desk. None of this had really been a lie, after all. Only our end goals were different. He wanted to be a shining example of PanTech, with a statue of himself erected in the president's office. Me? I wanted to see the whole thing collapsed in on itself. PanTech could become its own adversity zone, no longer above the many they looked down upon. They could taste the adversity they'd so long forgotten and see if it still seemed worth it to them.

"Yes, I think I'm inclined to agree with you. That arrangement would be suitable. So much work needs to be done in the field, perhaps even in cooperation with other divisions. I prefer the deeper scientific work done in the lab, but if you were serious about the rest…"

I nodded. "More field work and working with other divisions sounds like it would be great for the reputation of the College of Animal Studies. It would give me a chance to get away from this stuffy campus from time to time and talk you and our division up to the others."

He tapped his finger on his desk, followed by more nodding.

"Yes. Yes, I think this will work out well for me… and you, of course."

I finished my drink with a quick gulp, hoping to wrap up this meeting soon. I was exhausted and still felt as though I'd fallen off a cliff and landed in a nice pile of rocks below. The discomfort was reaching a point where it was difficult to mask.

"Then I'll leave you to the planning. If you could make me a list of animals and the zones they live in, and the divisions and contacts you'd like me to speak to, I can get started as soon as you'd like me to."

I stood and turned toward the door.

"Wait. Please, sit for a moment longer, if you have the time."

I nodded, complying with his request. Had I given something away? No… come to think of it, this was way too easy from the start. Now would come the punchline.

"You are probably wondering why it was so easy for a new arrival like yourself to walk right in here and secure such a vital role in my division, after only one, albeit productive, one-on-one meeting. Would you care to guess the reason?"

Oh, no… I should've guessed the reason already.

Play dumb. Cross your fingers and hope you're wrong. I'm such an idiot for not considering this from the start. I should've waited. Found a better opening. Taylor, you should've never underestimated this guy. You've walked right into his trap, and all the while, he let you think you were setting one for him.

"Because I actually care about animal research, and most of the people who come in here just want the same thing you do. They're competition," I said with noticeable strain, the lie clear as day as it left my lips.

He grinned and let the hint of a laugh slip.

"Not untrue. Certainly, that is a consideration. However, there is one species I've been dying to study for quite some time. Since I first arrived, the mystique behind it intrigued me. Reliable sightings had been documented, but those records were nearly a thousand years old. No hard evidence existed. The scientists who described their sightings predated PanTech itself, and their peers laughed them out of the room when they presented it. Anything in the last five hundred years was only anecdotal and only spread through word of mouth by your primitive sand people. No offense to the present company, of course."

My jaw clenched, but I could feel his eyes focusing on my face, looking for any sign of irritation. I was clearly on the defensive now. I had been from the start. With great difficulty, I relaxed. On the outside, at least.

"None taken. I have to accept that they aren't my people anymore, just like you don't belong to yours anymore."

"Very true. But back to the far more important matter at hand. I believe there's no need to make myself clearer unless you intend to continue playing coy. I could spell it out for you, but what's the point?"

Of course. How could I have walked into this room and not seen this outcome from the very start? I'm such a fool. I should be ashamed by how overconfident I allowed myself to become. Even with this enhancement, Professor Barth was much older, far more experienced, and a genius. I was new to this way of thinking. Using others as pawns for your own goals. Barth had likely perfected it.

"No, I'll not pretend any longer. You're talking about the shadowfalcon. But, even more important than that, you're talking about Ghost."

He narrowed his eyes. "Ghost? You named the creature? Is it your pet?"

"Companion," I corrected. "Please take that into consideration when you make your request. I'm under no obligation to give him to you. No more than I would be to take your cabinet over there. I'm familiar with the rules."

"I'd expect no less from you. Of course, if I had the means, I would already have seized the shadowfalcon at the moment of your arrival. I need your permission to study it."

"*Him*, and the answer is no."

He leaned back in his chair, his face growing flush despite his effort to conceal his irritation, taken aback by my refusal.

"No?"

"That's right," I confirmed. "No."

He scratched his chin and sat quietly for a moment, before the confident smile returned to his lips.

"Allow me to make a point, and then to offer a concession. The military, as you know, may seize anything for its use. I don't need to tell you what the creature… I mean, Ghost's neurotoxin would mean to the military should they discover its existence. Under my care, I could protect him. *We* could protect him. I have no interest in his toxin at the moment. I'm more interested in the bird's rumored intelligence. It's more relevant to our current project. Or should I say... *your* project? I would ask only to influence *your* study of Ghost, merely to make suggestions based on my knowledge. What would you say to that? You could call it my last offer."

I could call it that, and should, because that's what it was. Even though it wasn't direct, his comment about the military was clearly a threat. I'd messed up. Badly. I felt like such an idiot. I walked right into it. But if the neurotoxin would be such a prize to the military, then why hadn't they seized him already? Frelya knew about it. That could only mean she hadn't told them. But why?

One question at a time...

"Professor... we have a deal."

At least it was over, for now, and I could finally get some sleep.

CHAPTER 8

The warm sun beamed down, directly into my senses, like the kind words of a friend. It made me feel energetic yet too lazy to move. Lying in the scorching sands of my homeland, I felt truly at ease.

"Taylor," a gentle voice called out to me. One I recognized.

I couldn't answer. Didn't want to. For once, I knew I was in a dream and had no desire to rush it along.

"Taylor," she called again.

Mother. A woman I'd spent my entire life despising, often hating, with a fiery passion. Now, several months away from home, I wanted to see her more than anyone.

I tightened my eyelids shut, fearing what I might see.

"It's alright. Open your eyes. Don't you smell it?"

She spoke again, unrelenting. I focused on my sense of smell. I smelled it now. What was it? That's right… freshly baked bread, a stew my father loved, and cactus wine. A smell that once made my stomach feel uneasy now filled me with a joy I could barely withstand.

Finally, I opened my eyes and looked up at her. She was even more beautiful than I remembered. Her long, raven hair blew loosely in the desert wind. Her narrow, dark eyes glistened in the desert sun as she looked down at me. A pale hand extended, calloused from training yet somehow delicate in appearance. I took it.

"Good. I'm glad you finally stopped lounging around all day. I know your work is done, but we still have the victory celebration to go to. We're already late."

"Victory celebration?" I asked as I dusted the sand from my plain clothes.

"Yes. Finally. You played such an important role in the rebellion. It would be an insult to everyone if you were to miss it. Let me brush your hair, at least."

"Mother…" I looked at the empty village around me. "Where is everyone?"

She pulled me toward her by the arm, spinning me around, and hurriedly pulling a comb through my hair.

"At the celebration! I did mention we were late. Now, hurry.

We're going straight there."

She put the comb away and clutched my hand, pulling me along behind her.

"It's out in the desert? Why not in the village?" I asked.

She didn't answer. She only kept pulling me along. Further and further into the desert. With every step, the sky seemed to fill with more clouds, as though a great storm were approaching.

"It's just up ahead," she said. "Just around those rocks."

As we rounded the turn and up a small hill, the full sight entered my vision all at once. In that moment, it gripped me with a horror that felt so real.

A crack of thunder startled me as the sky darkened once again. The air, only moments ago feeling so warm and comforting, took on a cold, damp oppressiveness. My breath caught in my chest, and my lungs halted their duty.

The ground was soaked in blood and covered in the bodies of so many villagers. Nearly all were dead. A few were alive, shackled in so many chains they could barely stay upright on their knees, too weighed down to stand. PanTech soldiers, their armor speckled red, stood above them with their helmets obscuring their faces. Their rifles were drawn, ready to be fired at a moment's notice. At the slightest whim.

"Do you see, Taylor? PanTech's glorious victory against the last rebellion. It's all thanks to you. You did this!"

"No!" I screamed, falling to my knees. "I didn't! I didn't…"

Mother grabbed me by the chin, forcing me to look up at her.

"Don't be so modest. Wasn't it you who fell in love with a PanTech soldier and stopped the rebels in our village? Wasn't it you who brought the shadowfalcon to PanTech and turned a symbol of these people's freedom into a weapon of war to be used against them? None of this would have been possible if it weren't for you. Don't just look at the ground. Look above you. Ghost's final proclamation!"

She pointed to a pillar not far ahead. My eyes slowly rose to the top. I became sick, and I looked away. Mother grabbed my head and forced it back toward the top of the pillar. There was Ghost, dead, pinned like a butterfly in someone's collection. I screamed, rising to my feet, and running toward the pillar.

Mother grabbed me. "Taylor, it's alright! It's just me. Pull yourself together."

I fought against her. I'd tear this pillar from the ground. Then I'd take one of their weapons. Somehow, I was going to kill every PanTech soldier here.

But Mother's grip was so strong, and her voice felt different. I could feel myself being pulled away, but I kept fighting.

"I'll make them pay for this!" I shouted, gripping my hands on her shoulder, pushing her away. She moved only a little before overpowering me again. "Let me go!"

"Taylor! Snap out of it. I've got you. I'm here!"

The hands gripped me tightly again, shaking me. The clouds above me disappeared, and my senses slowly returned. I knew it was a dream. I knew, but I couldn't stop it. Couldn't escape it. I looked up, finding Frelya gripping my arms.

"Taylor! Are you back yet? Your vitals were off the charts. I thought you were in an actual fight. If one of your friends found you like this, you might've accidentally killed them."

I grabbed her by the shirt and pulled her close to me. For a moment, I thought I might punch her with all my strength, but in that same moment the weight of everything finally collapsed onto my shoulders. I pulled her close, buried my face into her shoulder, and sobbed loudly.

I waited for her to shove me away, or hit me, or berate me. Instead, I felt her arms wrap around me and pull me closer.

"I'm sorry," was all I could squeak out between deep breaths. She sighed.

"I used to have them too, you know. The nightmares. Like you, I would wake up and cry in my room. You're the only person I've ever told. It gets better. One day, I stopped crying."

"How?" I asked, after sniffing so hard it hurt my head.

"One day, I think I just ran out of tears."

I smiled, then a chuckle slipped out, surprising me as much as it did her. Within seconds, it had devolved into full-blown laughter. Frelya joined me, and the two of us laughed until our sides hurt, and we had no choice but to stop so we could breathe again.

She picked her hands up off my shoulders and slammed them back down again, squeezing tightly. "I was never here, and never let me hear you apologize again."

I nodded and felt awkwardly stuck on what I should say in reply. Before I could come up with anything, she was gone, and I fell back into my pillow. It took only a few minutes for me to fall back asleep. By the time I woke up, I questioned whether any of it really had happened after all, or if it was just part of the dream.

I awoke the next morning, not feeling refreshed. Better physically, at least. After grabbing a quick shower, I ran out the door, hoping to get to the lab ahead of most of the other students. I bolted out of my door the moment it opened, nearly flying straight into Linda and Joyce.

"Wow, Taylor. Is your room on fire or something?" Joyce teased, taking a step back to avoid a collision.

"Maybe she heard us coming and was trying to avoid us... again," Linda said. An obvious jab about yesterday's lunch.

Wow, was that really yesterday? So much happened in a single day. It felt more like weeks.

"I'll tell you what... if you girls agree to help me out with something long-term, lunch is on me today. And I'll actually show up."

Joyce tapped her cheek with her index finger. "Ignoring the fact that everything is free here, what kind of absolutely insane mess have you gotten yourself into?"

"Yeah, and it's so bad that you're asking *us* to help you out of it. About once or twice a week, I agree with Joyce, and I think this is one of those times. Spill it!" Linda said, poking my shoulder with a big grin on her face.

"I... kind of volunteered myself to play a lead role in this animal intelligence research breakthrough we're all working on. You remember how Professor Barth was looking for someone to help him with something? Well, I went to the lab late yesterday, and we made some interesting discoveries. He wants me to handle cooperation with other divisions, and field work."

"Ooh, how interesting? Did it involve a kiss?" Joyce said, puckering her lips.

"Joyce..." I said, crossing my arms.

"Oh... that's right. Sorry, Taylor. I said that even though you told us what happened in your zone. I just let that slip without thinking." She reached out and touched my forearm, and I instinctively recoiled.

"No, it's alright. I'm okay now. Just still hurts a lot sometimes, you know?"

Linda frowned but said nothing.

"Wait, does this mean Linda's going to be walking around being afraid of you since you're technically playing a senior role in the project now?" Joyce asked, eager to change the subject.

"Hey, that's not nice either, Joyce. Besides, Taylor is different," Linda said, pounding her fist into her palm.

"Hear that, Taylor? You're not scary at all," Joyce said.

"I guess… that's a good thing? So, does that mean both of you will help me? I need people I can trust, and you two are the only friends I have in Animal Research."

"Hear that, Linda? In Animal Research. That means she's going off and making friends without us in other divisions. Our Taylor is really growing up fast."

Linda nodded. "I'm not the most skilled analyst in the program. Joyce I can understand, but are you sure you wouldn't rather pick someone else besides me?"

I shook my head. "You have great instincts. You know the stuff better than most of us, and don't even know you know it. Know what I mean?"

"Uh… I guess so. I knew enough to get me here, I suppose."

Joyce laughed. "I think she's just faking the muscle head thing and she's probably the biggest genius here. Just lying low and not attracting too much attention. Avoiding those higher-ups, she's so afraid of."

"Are you teasing me again?" Linda asked, lowering her head and biting at her cheek.

"Only a little. If you're here, it's not by accident. Besides, you know I only tease you because I like you so much. C'mere!" Joyce took a few steps to the side and jumped on Linda's back, nearly toppling both of them over, hugging her tightly from behind. Or maybe it was a choke hold. It was hard to tell the difference.

"Joyce! Who's the muscle head now? Besides, shouldn't you answer Taylor's question? We showed up here early to make Taylor eat breakfast, remember? We were going to gang up on her, not me."

Joyce released her and landed gracefully back on her feet. "Oh, that's right! And of course, Taylor. I was getting really bored here. Building relationships with other divisions sounds like my cup of tea."

"And I can't wait for the field work!" Linda added with even greater enthusiasm.

"Then I guess I can't skip breakfast like I'd planned then, huh?" I asked. A rhetorical question.

"No!" they both shouted at once.

CHAPTER 9

Two Weeks Later

"Look, I think it's working!" Joyce said, her voice shaking from the excitement.

It was rare to see her this excited about anything, but this research had ignited a spark within her again.

"The data simulations show it should reach peak adjustment today. This very hour, to be exact. One week since we started the process on this little rat, and she's done so well," I agreed. I was repeating the plan more for myself than anyone else. This was the first proper test of the cleaned-up process. Barth had put in countless hours, as had the rest of us. Simulations produced excellent results, but simulations can't consider all factors.

"I… something doesn't feel right," Linda said, tilting her head at the rat in the cage.

"What do you mean?" Joyce scolded. "Don't be so negative without good reason. If there's a problem, at least articulate it."

"No. If she has a feeling, there's a problem. We should play it safe," I said. "Let's run a few more physical tests before we start the rapid learning protocol."

"Are you sure this is a good idea while Professor Barth isn't here?" Linda asked, leaning in closer to examine the rat.

I nodded. "I'm positive. Also, I'd prefer not to take any chances on a first impression."

"So, you have your doubts too, huh? You two are such cynics." Joyce said, shaking her head.

She was teasing us, but part of her meant it. I wanted to be optimistic about everything too, but with Ghost next in line for this procedure… I just didn't want to take any chances at all. I wanted to be completely sure, with no doubts. At all. In just a few days, we'd be scanning him. Barth would pressure me to produce results quickly. I needed to prepare as much as possible ahead of that.

"Safety takes priority. You know that," I said.

"Right. As you say, Assistant Professor," Joyce said, grinning.

"Ugh, could you please stop calling me that?"

"But you like it so much!" she said, reaching over and grabbing a handful of my cheek, giving it a gentle pull.

I swatted her hand away, but I couldn't help laughing a little.

"It's better than Ice Princess," Linda said.

"Oh, don't be jealous, little Ice Princess. You're very cute too. Come here. Give me those cheeks!"

Joyce lunged at Linda, reaching up and grabbing both her cheeks, pulling them roughly in all different directions.

Linda grabbed her wrists and pulled her hands away.

"Hey! You weren't nearly that rough on Taylor. You're going to make my cheeks red for hours."

"That's because she's not a big, tough Ice Princess like you. I'm surprised you even felt that."

I sighed, waving both of my hands high in the air. "Hello? Could you two knock it off? We need to—"

Before I could finish the sentence, a loud slam startled me.

The three of us froze, trying to make sense of what we were seeing. The rat had run into the cage so hard it was bleeding. It backed up quickly and charged again.

"Hurry, stun it before it hurts itself!" I shouted at Linda, who was standing next to the small cylinder.

Without hesitation, she grabbed it and held it up toward the cage. It emitted a barely audible sound and froze the rat in place. I ran to the cabinet, digging through vials until I found the one I was looking for. She just needed to be sedated for a while until we could figure everything out. I filled the small needle, opened the cage, and injected the rat. It slumped to the floor and was still.

"You can stop now," I said, nodding to the immobilizer in Linda's hand. "I wish we had that thing in my zone."

"No kidding. There were many people I would've liked to use something like that on," Joyce said.

"What do you think happened, Taylor?" Linda asked, ignoring her comment.

"I… don't know. Everything was looking perfect until just now. We need to wrap it so it can't hurt itself and run some tests. Joyce, do that while I calibrate the scanner."

I picked up another cylinder, no bigger than the immobilizer sound device, and linked up to adjust the settings. I wouldn't trust the automatic detection feature this time. No room for error.

Once she finished wrapping her, I held the scanner above and pressed the button on top, producing an audible click. I changed the angle and did it again. Then one more time.

"Do you think we're dealing with brain tumors?" Joyce asked.

"Let's just look at the scan," I said, dropping the cylinder into a slot near the wall. A lifelike hologram popped up from the table. I moved my hand to the side, spinning it. Holding both of my hands up and moving them further apart expanded the image. Pinching my index fingers and thumbs together moved a layer deeper.

We went slowly, layer by layer, looking for anything. When we finally reached the brain, we zoomed in completely, until the image was twice the size of our own heads. Thin layer by thin layer, we slowly flipped through until we reached the very center. Nearly an hour.

"Do you think we missed something?" Linda asked, wringing her hands.

"I don't get it. We couldn't have," Joyce added. "We went frame by frame, meticulously. All three of us were looking from different angles."

I sighed, leaning back against a table behind me. What if this had been Ghost? Would he have gone crazy too? I didn't know what to say.

"Get a blood sample," Linda said.

"I mean… sure, but why?" Joyce asked as she picked up a smaller cylinder with a clear window on the side and held it against the rat. A small click, and it filled with a tiny amount of blood. Barely a drop. With this technology, it was more than enough.

"We should check stress levels, hormones, and things like that. I'm not convinced it went crazy. Maybe it was scared, or maybe it didn't want to be in a cage anymore. Maybe it thought we were fighting and wanted to fight too. You were a veterinarian, Taylor. You know. Animals have a lot of complex thoughts already. This rat should've had the intelligence of a human child at this point in the procedure. We don't know what she was thinking. She wasn't a normal rat anymore."

I slapped both hands on my face and dragged them down. "Now I'm really glad Professor Barth wasn't here."

"Hey, so you're supposed to handle cooperation with other divisions now, right? Why not take this over to the people in Neuroscience? They're much better equipped to diagnose this than we are. Even though it's an animal, we're dealing with a more human-like brain now. It's something completely new. They'll eat it up!" Joyce said.

"You're not wrong, but Professor Barth said involving the

human medical divisions would be a bad idea."

"But he didn't say you *couldn't* involve them, right?" Joyce said, leaning down and grabbing my shoulders, forcing me to look up and see the big grin on her face.

"No, he didn't. That's true." I conceded.

"And!" Joyce stood up straight and paced slowly. A habit she'd still not given up from her time as an attorney. "This is the perfect olive branch to offer those snobs. Humans have barely changed over thousands of years. So what if they like to look down on us? It must be a bore studying one species all the time that barely changes. We're giving them the excuse to do something fun for once, and with the promise of there being even more where this came from."

"She has a point," Linda said. "As much as I really, *really* don't want to go over there."

"Fine. I hope we don't regret this. Get the rat in a portable unit. She shouldn't wake up for several hours with the dosage I gave her. That will give them plenty of time to run their own tests if we forgot something."

Linda nodded, and began rummaging through a nearby cabinet, pulling out a smaller box with clear windows on each side.

"One without windows, please. I'd rather not attract unwanted attention."

"Right," she said, swapping it out for another before gently placing the rat inside and locking the top.

I took several deep breaths, trying to shake the flood of stress that was filling my body. Barth had said the military division was on top because they were the president's personal favorites. They could look down on everyone.

The robotics scientists and engineers over in resource gathering and processing facilities were basically recluses. I'd never even met one of them. I was told it was almost all automated now, anyway. Resources were harvested, processed, then renewed through a completely automatic process using machines and facilities that required almost no oversight. Only the allocation was handled by humans now, and the occasional change based on our needs. Thanks to them, there was no more supply and demand. We should consider them the actual heroes of PanTech. Yet, somehow, the military was even more favored.

And knowing that, Frelya still treated me the way she did?

What was her angle, anyway?

"Taylor?" Linda asked, tilting her head. "Are you okay?"

"Yes… No… I don't know. Let's just get this over with. My pass should allow us to go almost anywhere now. We don't need anyone to escort us over."

"Come on. Cheer up. We'll have this wrapped up by lunchtime. I bet these neuroscience people will invite us to eat with them because we're so fascinating and do such interesting work."

"All you ever think about is eating," I said, smiling.

"Well, of course. Do you think these curves are going to just maintain themselves?"

There was probably some truth to that. Despite her constant teasing of Linda, the two both exercised together almost religiously. Linda was obsessed with maintaining her strength as a warrior, while Joyce was more concerned with appearance. I never seemed to find the time despite them regularly inviting me. Or *make* the time, as they often liked to correct. My constant activity kept me in decent enough condition, I suppose.

Frelya's voice seemed to appear in my mind. Training. Right. Now there was someone else pushing me to regain my athleticism. It was even more important now with the implant. My muscles needed to handle additional load at a moment's notice without exploding. Frelya's muscles were… really something, come to think of it.

"Right. Sure, those curves are important…" I mumbled.

Joyce sighed, leaning on the table next to me.

"Are you sure you're going to be okay? I'm worried about you. These kinds of setbacks are normal, but it feels like you're taking this one personally."

"I'm under a lot of pressure to run this procedure with Ghost. Outcomes like this out of the blue… well, they're just really scary. Ghost is more than just a rare species to me. He's like family. I just don't want to think about what might've happened if this had been him instead."

Joyce wrapped her arms around me, hugging me tightly.

"Oh, honey, why didn't you tell us that? Look at it another way. It *didn't* happen to Ghost, right? And we're going to figure out what happened, so it doesn't happen to any other participants either."

Linda put her arms around both of us. "Group hug!"

"Okay. I get it. See? Look, I'm smiling," I said, forcing the biggest fake smile I could manage.

"Wow... don't hurt yourself," Joyce said.

"Let's get going. We're aiming to get this done before lunch after all, right?" I said, standing upright.

"Let's go make some new friends," Joyce said, pumping her fist into the air.

New friends...

I had my doubts.

CHAPTER 10

The College of Neuroscience was only seconds away on the faculty rapid transit pod, but it may as well have been on the moon. After stepping off, once I took a moment to reorient myself, the differences were apparent. The three of us stood speechless. It was as though we'd been living in a scaled-down version of the real thing. Everything was just… bigger. In every sense of the word.

They still made the walls and floors of the same glossy white synthetic material that could be found all over PanTech, but all areas of the surface, from the floor to the ceiling, were polished regularly. That theory was confirmed when a small machine stopped in front of us. It was just a few feet tall and shaped like a puck. A small compartment opened and extended toward me.

"Welcome. I will clean your shoes. Please respect all guidelines while visiting the College of Neuroscience. Please wait for a visitation supervisor before continuing. One will be alerted, assigned, and shall arrive shortly. Enjoy your visit to the prestigious College of Neuroscience."

"Hey… why don't we get a robot greeter?" Joyce said, far too loudly, while bending over and examining the machine.

I simply shrugged. I was glad. These things really creeped me out. In fact, I was only surprised to see it here because I'd heard the president really didn't like having them on campus due to, unsurprisingly, mysterious past events. Probably linked to the rebellion. The people in Neuroscience must really be able to pull some strings to have this much mechanical assistance.

"What's even worse is we barely have any animals over in Animal Research," Linda said.

Good point. I had given little thought, but most of us were animal lovers, and pets were rare. Aside from me, I wasn't aware of anyone else having an animal with them. Briefly, I had an idea about purposing our current research to allow Animal Research employees to have an intelligent animal companion. Maybe that would keep it out of the military's hands. Then again, the obvious hurdle would be the distinct lack of glory and recognition. Unless the president himself wanted one, he'd likely have no interest what-so-ever.

"Guess I never thought of that," I conceded. "I have Ghost."

"Ghost is so cool, too," Joyce said. "I should go to your zone when we start field research and get one for myself. How long do you think it would take me to capture one?"

I considered the question honestly, crossing my arms and tapping my elbow. That would be quite the task, but surely there were more somewhere. Ghost didn't just spontaneously pop into existence. "I don't know… using all of our current technology… a hundred years, maybe? You know I named him 'Ghost' for a reason, right? They don't exist."

Linda shook her head and raised her hand in protest.

"Oh, I beg to differ."

Joyce narrowed her eyes. "Seriously?"

"Seriously," Linda said, her expression still stoic. "One time, I—"

"'Seriously' is right. The notification said you three are from Animal Research. Are you lost?"

A tall, blonde woman only a few years older than us approached, stomping her heels loudly. Who even wore heels anymore? I'd heard they were an odd fashion choice abandoned centuries ago. Highly impractical, I might add. How did anyone get anything done in those? Her shirt was at least one size too small, and her skirt was… uncomfortably short. Not uncomfortable for her, probably, but definitely for me. How could she even sit wearing that?

"We're, uh…" What was the best way to phrase this without sounding stupid? Guess I should've thought about that on the ride over… all three seconds of it.

"Uh… uh…" she said, mimicking my voice. "Are you three of the animals, perhaps, disguised as humans? Why are you staring at me like that? If you want to study me that badly you should check in with the anatomy people. We deal with brains over here, and it appears yours aren't in good working order."

Oh, now I was definitely interested in her anatomy. I wanted to rearrange her face with my fists. "Listen—" My boiling blood sent my mouth wide open, ready to have it out right here, just a few steps out of the transportation pod. Joyce, thankfully, was quick to step in front of me and interrupt.

"My apologies. We were just taking in the sights here, and it's disorienting for us. I'm not sure if you've visited Animal Research, but our facilities are more different from what you might think. We actually have an interesting challenge we thought our counterparts at Neuroscience would be much better trained and equipped to analyze and explain. Thank you for taking the time to meet with us."

The woman pulled down her thick-framed glasses, eying Joyce with a grin. "Oh, so one of you possesses something resembling what could be called manners. More clumsy flattery, perhaps. But better than staring at me and saying nothing. I can give you fifteen minutes with one of the assistant professors to make your case. I do like flattery, after all."

"You don't say…" Linda mumbled.

I elbowed her before taking a step forward to be alongside Joyce. "Thank you. We understand how important the work is here, so fifteen minutes is more than generous. Do we need to schedule an appointment?" I tried to cool my temper. This woman had spent at least a few years working in neuroscience. It was just as likely she was having fun with us, trying to goad a reaction to test our professionalism. Giving her one would have been a poor choice. Thank goodness for Joyce. That rhetoric skill set came in handy after all, and this probably won't be the last time it does.

"I thought you said this was important and interesting? Of course, you don't need to make an appointment. I just hope you don't mind waiting."

She spun on her heels and stepped with an exaggerated bounce in the opposite direction. We followed closely, trying to ignore the stares from everyone we passed going through the multiple corridors, twists, and turns. We'd need a map to navigate this place. There's no way we could find our way back out of here again without one. Nothing like the military facilities that I barely saw even a glimpse of, but much bigger than Animal Research.

Eventually, we arrived at a small room with bench-style seats lining the walls. She pointed inside.

"Have a seat in there. An assistant professor will be here to see you once they have time to spare. Minutes, hours, days, I don't know. Whenever one of them has nothing better to do."

"It's nice to see the manners go both ways. Are those glasses even real?" Linda blurted.

The woman pulled those glasses down her nose again, raising an eyebrow at the comment. "Except for you. You're coming with me. You can catch up to your friends later."

Stunned, Linda looked at me. Her eyes pleaded for help. It was almost as obvious as the horrible grin spreading across Joyce's face, taking an almost frightening amount of humor from the turn of events. If I didn't know these two as well as I did, I'd think they were bitter rivals, not great, close friends.

Arguing with her at this point would be a bad idea. It's not like she was going to hurt Linda as any forms of clear bullying weren't allowed. She was probably going to be embarrassed a little, then meet back with us later. If she could tolerate Joyce's relentless teasing, surely this woman would be nothing. Maybe they'd become friends.

"It's alright. The two of us are familiar enough with the issue we're facing. You can borrow Linda for a bit."

"Delightful!" the woman exclaimed. "I wasn't asking permission, of course. Good luck to the two of you."

She stepped alongside Linda and motioned for her to follow. With the two of them so close together, our eccentric tour guide stood several inches taller than Linda. That was impressive, even with heels. Linda was nearly six feet tall.

Joyce and I stepped into the room and waited. Then waited more. And more.

Before we knew it, two hours had passed. There weren't even any other people in the room with us. Just a big, blank space that seemed to get smaller as the time went on. No music. No snacks. Just a small information unit that contained those foretold guidelines the robot warned us about, sitting on a small table in the center of the room. I read them... six times. Super obvious. Extremely boring.

Joyce had the right idea, and had been napping for at least the last half-hour. I didn't want to risk someone walking in to see us, finding us asleep, then just walking out.

About ten more minutes passed before a bearded man abruptly opened the door, causing us both to jump in our seats.

"I'm supposed to see two from Animal Studies. I assume that's you two?"

"Yes, that's us." I said, giving Joyce the chance to rub her eyes and adjust back to the waking world.

He walked over to the table and held his hand on top of the information unit. "Let's see what you have. You can explain as you show it to me. I'm very busy, as I assume is the case for you, so let's be efficient with our time please."

Right to the point. Still rude, but I could work with this.

Joyce and I took turns explaining the situation, our research, and the roadblock we were facing. We tried to stick to facts only. Several times Joyce tried to elaborate further, and both times he waved his hand and dismissed her with a huff, reminding us to stick to what was relevant. A real charming man, this one. Still liked him better than the woman.

"Unexpected," he said, with no hint of the meaning in his voice.

"How so?" I asked.

He eyed the small box we were carrying for a moment. "Is it in there?"

"It is," I said, still trying to read him, with no success.

"Unexpected. It was supposed to be important and interesting, and to my surprise, it was perhaps both things. Amazing, coming from a waste of space like Animal Research."

My mouth was quick to fly open, instinctively, but Joyce was a step ahead of me, shaking her head with a silent warning to hold back again.

"We appreciate the compliment, Assistant Professor," I said, in a likely very unconvincing cheerful voice.

He tapped something on his wrist. "Down the hall, to the room at the very end, straight ahead. Take a right when you exit the room. Please be respectful of Professor Elise's time. Despite how she behaves, her time is precious. She's been alerted, so just walk right in. Good day."

Without waiting for our reply, he rushed out the door. Joyce shrugged, and we followed his directions down the hallway.

When we arrived, I took several deep breaths in front of the door.

"It'll be alright," Joyce said, putting a hand on my shoulder. "You're doing fine. Just keep that temper in check. Everyone around here seems to enjoy testing you, so you should expect it."

"Thanks, Joyce. Here goes," I said, giving the door a push.

Was this the wrong place?

Two familiar faces sat across a table, teacups in their hands, both laughing as we opened the door.

"L-Linda?" I asked as my jaw dropped, nearly choking on the name.

CHAPTER 11

"Oh, hey Taylor. Hey Joyce," Linda said, no hint of surprise in her voice.

"So, they sent you to me after all? That's surprising. Not a lot gets through these days," said our tall blonde tour guide, sitting in the chair across from Linda.

"So, you… that means… but wait a minute," I said, looking at Joyce, who only shrugged.

"I'll help you with your stumbling thought process, since we don't have all day. Yes, I'm Professor Elise. Yes, it turns out that the way a person looks and dresses has no bearing on their intellect. Unless you want to avoid being a distraction. I don't. I only care about what I want," Elise said, rattling the words off as though she were speed-reading it off a script. She'd probably repeated it pretty often to new arrivals. I was seeing the purpose of the group meetings to assimilate us into PanTech culture.

"But you're so young!" Joyce blurted.

"I'm forty-seven. In one month, I'll have been the head of Neuroscience for twenty years."

"You're… *what*?" Joyce's jaw dropped again, wide-eyed as she approached the professor, examining her like a statue. "How is this possible?"

Age was impossible to gauge here. I knew it was a possibility the moment I saw her, but that was true for everyone we met here. Someone who looked sixty might be well over a hundred.

"I invest heavily in my appearance. Other divisions always need my help, and I get to partake in innovative research. Most of how we perceive age depends on the appearance of our skin. Professor Dari over in Biology is studying a procedure that recalibrates the regeneration rate to compensate for aging. Oh, and my hair. I assume most of your adversity zones would require dye to change the color of your hair. Mine grows this shade of blonde. I invited your friend here to take a sample of her hair because I adore her shade. I may change to that next time. A slight alteration to that genetic attribute, and your hair can grow a different color."

Wow. For someone so busy and short on time, she sure loves talking about herself. It was like talking to the female version of Barth in a way. Come to think of it, I bet they're all like that. Self-absorbed, apathetic, and vain. You'd have to be, knowing what the rest of humanity is going through at the hands of your organization. Even when *you* went through it yourself. How does everyone forget so easily?

"So, what made you study neuroscience instead of biology?" I asked.

"Isn't that obvious? Understanding the mind is above all other knowledge. Changing something about your appearance would be completely random if you didn't understand how it would be perceived by others. Far deeper, how that perception is influenced by the mechanics and composition of our brain itself. What might be a lucky guess for someone like the three of you is a calculated prediction for me. Especially if I've seen a scan of your brain, which I could easily look up. You caught me a bit by surprise today, so this is fun. I can't predict your thoughts and reactions the way I might normally."

"How… comforting," I said, trying not to let the chill that went down my spine take physical form.

"Why is that comforting? Something you wouldn't want me seeing?" she asked, motioning to one of two empty teacups next to the pot on the table. "Tea?"

No. She was worse than Barth. Didn't expect us? Then why were two empty teacups already sitting on the table. The table had four chairs. Not only had she expected we'd end up here and had time to prepare, but she made the most subtle of gestures at just the right moment to make me realize it. And… the smile forming on her lips just proves it.

"Yes, please," I said, pulling out a chair, prompting Joyce to do the same.

If she was going to be this perceptive, then maybe I should try behaving differently. Unpredictably.

"She's reading me so well. I should do unexpected things to throw her off. Would that work?" She smiled again, but it wasn't a devious smile. I wasn't sure what it was. "Does that sum it up pretty well, Taylor?"

There was no point in lying.

"Yes, actually. But why make that point?"

Linda and Joyce looked completely lost on what was happening.

"Because that's not the question you should ask yourself. The question you should ask yourself is: Why am I thinking that way? You're a competitive one, Taylor. You don't like to lose at anything. But you should remember that everyone was a big fish in a small pond before coming to PanTech. Here, you're in the ocean. All the small fish are gone. The biggest adjustment is realizing you're now the small fish."

"Sharks," I said.

I shouldn't have said that.

That was such a stupid thing to say.

Way to go, Taylor. Tell this perceptive woman exactly the way you see PanTech.

"Interesting," she said, taking a sip of her tea.

"Speaking of interesting!" Joyce blurted. *Thank you, Joyce.* "Would you like to see our little research project?"

Elise winked at me, then turned to Joyce. "That's why you're here, after all."

She grabbed a small device off her desk, within arm's reach, and placed it at the center of the table after sliding the teapot out of the way. "Let's see it."

We spent the next several minutes explaining the research to her, and the issue we'd run into. About how the rat went crazy and started slamming itself into the cage. We showed her all the scans, data from the blood samples. She even examined the rat, still sedated, taking a brain scan of her own from a tiny device she had in her shirt pocket, taking another blood sample as well.

"Silly girls. Your experiment didn't fail at all. This is amazing, truly. A remarkable new way of applying the field of neuroscience outside the human species. Look, see how these markers are elevated in the blood and brain scan you took, but are different on the fresh scan and sample I just took?"

I scratched my head, trying to follow. "So, you're telling us she didn't suddenly go crazy and start bashing herself against the cage as a side-effect of the procedure she'd undergone?"

Professor Elise sighed. "Please pay attention. That's not what I said. All I said was that the experiment was a success. You could call this a side-effect. Just not what you're thinking. The rat didn't suddenly go berserk out of nowhere. Based on your sample, I can see the markers surged. Based on the timeline you gave me, these stress levels didn't rise until *after* it had slammed itself against the cage. About the time you used the equipment in your lab to immobilize, then sedate it."

Linda slammed both hands down on the table, smiling. "It was trying to trick us into opening the cage, so it could escape!"

Elise pointed to Linda with a big grin of her own, leaning back in her chair. "Someone is paying attention. That's exactly what I'm saying. You're the animal experts. I'm sure you can come up with a reason a rat was not the best of choices for this experimental procedure. Or do I need to explain that to you as well?"

I sighed, rubbing my face with my hands. It should have been obvious.

"Rats are already crafty tricksters, and natural problem solvers. This one wasn't domesticated as a pet. It didn't trust us. It saw us as giants imprisoning it. They don't like being stuck out in the open, either. Wow."

"We should use a dog," Joyce said.

Elise nodded in agreement.

"You haven't seen a dog in person yet, have you Taylor? You said they weren't in your zone," Linda said.

"I actually expected to see lots of new animals when I arrived at Animal Research."

Elise nodded. No doubt another thing she's had to explain many times.

"PanTech's use of simulations virtually eliminates the need for actual subjects until the final stage of the experiment, if then. Most of the time, they're never needed at all. There are plenty of volunteers in all the divisions for human research because of the level of safety, but your division is a special case. However, I would suggest it's necessary. As for why pets aren't more common, that should be obvious to you."

"Why would that be obvious?" I asked. It certainly wasn't obvious to me.

"When you arrived here, didn't you see all the cleaning and maintenance machines rolling around? If you were considered a higher-level division, you'd have them. Being a lower-level division, you're expected to operate in minimal space and with minimal resources. Our living quarters here are much larger than yours as well."

"Wonderful," Linda said, sipping her tea.

"Is Animal Research really considered a lower-level division? I didn't know that," I said, confused why I didn't know already.

I'd been here for months. Shouldn't it have come up at some point?

"Are you kidding? Barth? Admit to being the head of a lower-level division. Hah! That'll be the day." Elise giggled almost as much as she spoke. I guessed she and Barth had a history somehow, but the last thing I wanted to do was get into that.

"I take it you'd like to be involved," I said, hoping to steer the conversation back to the topic at hand. I could feel another monologue coming. If she thought she was very much different from Barth, she was kidding herself.

"Oh yes. I'd like to observe this experiment for my own purposes. Someone should socialize this dog with humans both before and throughout the procedure. You should show them educational imagery as the process takes place. No surprises. No cages. One of you can care for it and watch it around the clock. Beagles were often used a long time ago for experiments because of their calm, trusting natures. One of them would probably be a good choice."

Linda raised her hand, looking at me with her eyes practically sparkling. "I'll do it. I cared for my clan's animals in my zone and trained them. That included dogs."

"If it's a beagle, his name's going to be Henry," Joyce blurted, drawing everyone's attention.

"Henry?" I asked. "What if the one we get is a female?"

"Henrietta, then."

"You'll need to petition the Adversity Management to bring one back for you," Elise said. I forgot about the fact they only used military jargon within the division. Others referred to them as Adversity Management, unless they didn't like them, like Barth. Commanders were Adversity Managers, Adversity Management Specialists… something like that. I hated the corporate lingo that was used here.

"I know a couple of people there, so it shouldn't be a problem," I said. That was close. I nearly said I had a friend there but caught myself. I hadn't yet decided if Frelya was a friend and didn't want to get caught calling her one. "But Barth *really* won't enjoy asking the militar—I mean, Adversity Management for something like this."

"Oh, he will when he finds out the president and other professors will be there for the unveiling of your first successful subject to be shown to other divisions. Barth *loves* that kind of thing. He's been wanting to meet the president since he became a professor. Poor guy. We'll make his dream come true, and he'll do whatever you ask. Trust me. Once you've secured your subject, plan for one month of preparation. If we can achieve a small amount of speech, it will really wow the crowd."

"Do you really think speech is possible?" Joyce asked, looking concerned. "I mean… that's a little creepy. Talking animals?"

"Don't get cold feet now, Joyce," I said, refilling everyone's teacup. "Professor Elise, thank you for your help. I hope this is the beginning of a long, and prosperous partnership."

She smiled, holding out her teacup for everyone else to touch with theirs.

And with that, we'd sealed the deal with Neuroscience.

I just hoped it wasn't a huge mistake that would come back to haunt me.

CHAPTER 12

The next month went by like a blur. I went to see Frelya, who sent out the request to another commander to bring back a beagle when they returned to headquarters. Just a couple of days later, the creature arrived. It wasn't long before I realized why so many of the others talked about dogs so much. He was adorable! We took him out to play during the day, and Linda kept him during the nights. Professor Barth and I formulated the injection he received with some input from Professor Elise, who was now a frequent visitor. Much to Barth's irritation.

Part of me thought, with a woman as alluring as Elise coming to see him, he might welcome her presence with enthusiasm. Not at all the case. Privately, he voiced his concern that she would likely try to steal some of the credit for the research. The brain density concept was something Elise had come up with herself many years before for use on human subjects, but the president denied the proposal. Knowing that, didn't she deserve part of the credit? That's not the way Barth saw things. In his mind, his position was already prestigious enough. He wanted all the credit. However, like Elise had predicted, the party she planned to throw him was enough to convince him to tolerate her presence. Especially when she mentioned it would include the attendance of other professors and the president himself.

When I had time, I went to train with Frelya at Adversity Management. It turned out to be more structured and focused than I expected from her. Then again, I was long overdue to change many of the impressions I had of the woman. She wasn't rash or foolish. At least, not to the degree she pretended to be. It was a persona she'd created. An appearance for others. Partly, anyway. If the simulation I'd seen giving me a glimpse of her past was any sign, she'd had a very traumatic history. Still, sometimes I'd catch her smiling or laughing when she thought I wasn't looking. When I couldn't quite pick up the object I was trying to lift, or make the jump I was trying to make, and I would get frustrated. Little by little, thanks to her, I was becoming familiar with the real-world applications of this implant.

Henry, the beagle, evolved quickly. His understanding of words and gestures was easily on the level of a human child within the first couple of weeks. He knew all our names, the names of his toys. By the third week, things got a little stranger. He started practicing walking upright for longer and longer distances. A few days after that, he began pawing at Linda's clean uniforms and whining. When we had a few sized for him, he was thrilled, and struggled to get them on himself. Just before they'd arrived, he learned to use the human toilet. Linda was clearly the right person for this job. It even impressed Elise, who urged us to be accepting of Henry's explorations, like the one with human clothes. She urged us to see him as he sees himself, which was transforming.

Barth was, of course, overjoyed about the clothing and upright walking. He took Henry himself to be fit with for a fancy suit to wear at the party. He liked the optics. Many times he reminded Henry that the party was in his honor, and everyone couldn't wait to see him.

By the third week, speech experts were spending several hours a day with Henry and Linda, helping him create sounds that are more difficult for a dog to make. Progress came quickly, but he sounded hilarious when he spoke. His tone could barely change, because of his limited anatomy for speech. Barth and I made notes on the changes we'd have to make for the next subjects. More human-like anatomy for speech, and slight altering of the paws to make it easier to grasp objects or use tools. These changes would be easier in earlier development. Preferably while still in the womb.

Nearing the end of the third week, Henry's speech, comical as it was, was more or less understandable. It needed continued work over the coming months, but he was ready for his big debut.

Barth was especially polite to Elise in the final days, asking her to help upgrade their venue to accommodate employees as well. He was pleased with the results. So happy he was beside himself. Our party and reveal would take place in a giant concert hall. Almost as big as Barth's ego, but not quite.

I sent Joyce to oversee decorations, which I was told she was quite good at. Told by her. Many times.

Linda had gone from rowdy warrior woman to concerned parent in a matter of weeks. Despite the rest of us reassuring her, she worried we were pushing him too hard, and that he might be feeling too much pressure.

Henry was almost as excited as Barth about the party. He

strutted down the halls like he was a professor and was treated like one. Everyone stopped to say hello when they passed him. Everyone on their way to lunch invited him along, which he almost always happily accepted. In fact, he'd accepted those invitations so often that his suit had to be resized at the last minute to accommodate his growing waistline. Beagles have an insatiable appetite. Something we'd failed to plan for. Though there'd be plenty of time to teach him about diet and exercise later.

Barth called us all of Animal Research together on the night before, giving everyone instructions on when to cheer, when to gasp, when to say "aww," and more based on his subtle hand signals. After that, we were all dismissed for one final good night of sleep before the big event. The day had finally arrived.

Professor Barth ushered all the guests in, one after another, as they showed up at the door. Some even had dates. It would've made sense for me to stay up front with him to meet everyone coming in, since that was part of my role now, but being backstage with Henry was a higher priority. To me, at least. Not for Barth.

"Do you think everyone will like me?" Henry asked, pawing at Linda.

"Well, you *are* the whole reason for this party," she said, patting him on the head.

"I think everyone will like me," he said, practicing his best smile, tongue hanging out. After a quiet moment, he asked another question. "What will happen to me after this?"

"Well, everyone might not be as excited as they are right now," I said, trying to handle the question delicately. "But you're a part of Animal Research now. You'll continue to receive your lessons. I'll keep visiting you. Maybe you can have a place to stay on your own. Would you like that?"

"I want to stay with Linda. I love Linda. She's nice. She is my friend."

Linda snatched him up, giving him a big hug. "Of course you can stay with me! You can be my personal assistant. How about that?"

"I will help!" Henry said, bobbing his head up and down,

causing his ears to flop.

"You're a good boy, Henry," I said, patting him on the head.

"I'm a good boy," he repeated.

Despite the difference in intelligence, so much of his inherent behaviors as a dog remained. Elise had asked to keep the rat for observation, and we'd agreed, but she hadn't spoken about her much since. Only to say she was doing fine, and we shouldn't worry.

"I think we should go over some nutrition basics with you, Henry, and maybe take you with us for some exercise," Joyce said, poking him in the gut.

Henry wagged his tail. "The food is too good. That is the problem. Too good and too many kinds. I want them all."

We all laughed. I'd never heard anyone refer to the food here as "good" before, but Henry certainly meant it.

One of our coworkers stepped behind the curtain.

"Taylor, you're next. Then Linda and Joyce will bring Henry out after a brief announcement."

I nodded, then looked back at Henry.

"Good luck, Henry. I know you'll do great in your interview."

"You will do great too, Taylor. You're a good girl!"

I put my hand over my mouth, fighting back a giggle. I didn't think anyone called me a good girl since my father, when I was little. The thought made me miss him terribly. We'd always been so close, and I knew how much he hated PanTech. He was one of the few who seemed to hate them more than me. With Ferris and I both gone now, was Father lonely? No, he probably sat outside and smoked his pipe for hours now, reading his favorite books. Maybe he'd even started writing one by now. And he still had Mother.

I had to admit to myself, with Frelya as their zone manager, I worried less than I would have otherwise. The giant snake was a decision the general himself had made. One she'd opposed. She'd warned me about the general, while she seemed to speak highly of him in some regards. She said he was one of the last true warriors. He'd accepted the implant as Frelya had. No simulation or process in place to aid it and survived. I didn't have the full process, but I had Frelya's guidance and the simulation. Frelya said it was close enough, but was it? Why had she warned me to avoid the general if he was such a great man?

"Taylor? You look sad. You don't want to be a good girl?"

Henry asked, tilting his head.

"Sorry, Henry. I'm just a little overwhelmed by my turn coming up, and I have a lot on my mind. I'm okay with being a good girl… sometimes," I said, smiling at him.

"You're always a good girl, Taylor. You will do great."

"Aww, Taylor, you are such a good girl. I love you so much," Joyce said, bouncing up behind me and hugging me.

"Kisses, kisses, kisses," Linda said, taking advantage of Joyce holding me still and kissing me several times on the top of my head.

"Yay! I will hug Taylor too!" Henry said, hugging my leg.

I felt my cheeks get hot from the embarrassment, and they were going to call me out at any moment. I fought the urge to use the implant's help to break free.

"And now I'd like to call out one more individual before the main event, if you'd all be so patient. Taylor, please come on out!" Barth shouted in his best announcer voice.

I stepped out from behind the curtain, and the lights nearly blinded me. It was my first time being on stage. I'd gotten used to them during our rehearsal but walking into them suddenly made me freeze for a moment to give myself time to adjust.

"Oh, don't be shy, come on out!" Barth said, grabbing my arm and pulling me along. I could make out some faces in the front, but not where the higher-ups were sitting, on an upper balcony in the center.

"Thank you for the warm welcome, Professor," I said, putting on my fake smile.

"Sorry to pull you away from your work. I know you were getting Henry ready, but I wanted to announce that I've made your position official and expect you to continue representing Animal Research regarding the other divisions. Doing this on stage lets everyone see your face and recognize you when you visit the places you haven't been to yet. What do you say, Assistant Professor Taylor?" he asked, putting his arm around my shoulder.

What could I say? It was a rhetorical question, but I would've accepted even if it wasn't. Freedom of movement was exactly the thing I needed.

"Thank you so much, Professor. I'm honored. I've learned so much from you, and your amazing ideas have inspired me. Obviously I'm so excited, and I can't wait!"

Even as I spoke the words, I felt like another person. Thankfully, I'd listened to Mother when she instructed me. I knew how to look pretty, to flatter, and how to sound gracious when I needed to. When it would get me what I wanted.

I could see a man standing in the very center, at the top. As my eyes finally adjusted, I could see him clearly. His blue eyes were visible, even at this distance, and his jet-black hair was slicked back neatly. His beard was thick, but meticulously combed and trimmed. The man himself was a giant. Despite being a little shorter than Barth, he was incredibly muscled. It would take two Barths standing side by side to match his width. One of his biceps was the size of my head.

Slowly, he clapped, his eyes locked with mine. His expression never brightened. I could feel an intense fear bubbling up within me, and I didn't understand why. My legs felt weak, and I worried they might tremble. Was it his size? No, not that. He wasn't even in a power suit after all, and I'd been face to face with aggressive soldiers wearing them, with guns. Ludo, the rebel leader I'd fought in hand-to-hand combat, despite being much stronger than me, didn't make me feel this way.

Everyone in the area below turned to look at him instead of me. Immediately, they all stood with him, clapping wildly. It was only a small thing, but I took notice of it. Everyone respected this man. I'd been so focused on him I hadn't noticed the ancient man standing beside him, resting both hands on his cane. That must've been the president. But no, I still couldn't look away. If this man was standing next to the president, I knew who he was.

"Thank you, Taylor," Barth said. "You can go back and help Henry prepare to come out in just a moment." He said it without the amplification, still plenty loud enough for me to hear, but my eyes remained locked with the man on the balcony. I was determined to hold eye contact. He wouldn't intimidate me. I wouldn't look away.

"Taylor. Didn't you hear me? Get off the stage," Barth said, pulling me by the arm.

The man with the black beard stopped clapping, and as he sat, I saw the hint of a smile.

I smiled back.

So, this was the great General Markus…

CHAPTER 13

Henry's interview mostly created laughs, and the occasional gasp from the crowd. His speech made everyone smile at first, but the impressiveness of a talking dog, walking upright, in a suit, eventually sank in. Barth got his fifteen minutes of fame he's been searching for since he arrived at PanTech, and there was no doubt he'd be grateful for it.

Now that Barth had appointed me his only assistant professor, I wanted to believe that this was a time for me to take a step back and breathe. Only, I felt nothing but unease. Was it because I'd met General Markus? No, I hadn't even *met* the man. Only made eye contact with him from across the enormous space of the room. And yet, my entire body felt icy. Had he learned to use his implant to create this kind of effect on the people he looked at? No, that wouldn't be possible. It only affects our own bodies. Why was I even thinking about this now? I needed to take a deep breath and enjoy the rest of the night with my friends and go over my ideas with Barth tomorrow.

If I could just keep him focused on his own ego and fame, I could keep these experiments from being used to harm innocent citizens. No one else like Linus would have to die either, trying to set things right. Though, part of me would never rest until this general got what was coming to him. He was indirectly responsible for Linus's death, and who knows how many others. Given the chance, I'd make him pay for it. Someday.

Stop thinking about it, Taylor. Why can't you stop thinking about it? You've won this battle. Worry about the war tomorrow.

Except I couldn't.

By the time I'd helped take care of everything behind the scenes, most of the attendees had left. Those who remained, I'd already met. With the larger venue, many of the commanders were in attendance as well, but I didn't remember seeing Frelya. Why didn't she come? I felt the slightest tinge of pain from that thought, but quickly shook it off. She'd not proven herself a friend beyond any doubt. Not yet. I couldn't allow myself to think of her as one, or it would leave me vulnerable. She was still loyal to PanTech, and her general, who she seemed to admire.

I couldn't focus and turned in early. Everyone who tried to

speak to me went in one ear and out the other. I needed to get some sleep and hope to put my finger on what was bothering me in the morning.

As I reached my door, I stood in front of it for several minutes. I should see Barth before turning in. He'd probably appreciate if I showed up at his office to congratulate him. No doubt he'll want to tell me all about meeting the president, and rant more about how much he hates the general. In fact, this would be a golden opportunity to let him talk on just that subject with the experience fresh in his mind.

I turned and hurried back toward his office. I should've just gone there first. Why was I being so scatterbrained? Was it the excitement of the evening? Was this a side-effect of the implant, maybe?

Stop thinking about it.

I finally made it to his office door and reached for the handle. Before I could grasp it, the door opened in front of me, causing me to nearly fall inside. I stumbled forward and hit against a man's chest. I looked up and felt my stomach twist into knots. It was General Markus, and I'd just walked right into him.

"Taylor, was it? You should watch where you're going. For your own safety."

I could say the same to you, General.

That's what I'd wanted to say. My throat felt constricted, like I was dehydrated, and I could barely force out words.

"Excuse me," was what I actually said.

His black uniform was adorned with many medals, but that made little sense. The rebellion was supposed to have taken place over a hundred years ago. What could he have received them for? So little has been talked about regarding the military and their exploits. Everything was mysterious. Hidden.

He adjusted his hat and grunted.

"You and I will see a lot more of one another. I look forward to working with you," he said as he walked out, shutting the door behind him.

What did he mean by that? I wanted to chase after him and ask him what he'd meant, but I was far more likely to get answers from Barth.

"Professor, what was he talking about? Is he having me transferred out of Animal Research and into Adversity

Management to spite you?"

Barth laughed and waved me over to his desk.

"Come now. That's no way to speak about a good friend of mine, is it?"

"Good… friend? But you…"

"Hated him before? Yes, I did. Very much. That was before he made such a generous offer to bring my research to the forefront of all PanTech's current scientific research. Just think of it, Taylor. Use your imagination. Intelligent spies, blending into homes across every adversity zone, reporting in regularly. How many rebellions could be stopped before they started? How many traitors could be ousted before they even claimed a single victim, roused a single crowd, or even carried the idea away from their dinner table? You stopped quite the nasty one, from what I hear, though only barely developed. If, at the very first meeting, one of our little birds could be perched on a window, what might've happened then? A nearby cat drinking from a bowl. A dog playing with a toy. A mouse scurrying through a cabinet beneath a sink."

I struggled to control my emotions. It was taking every ounce of control I could muster. I wanted to crush this man's throat in my hands, and resisting that urge was even more difficult knowing I easily could.

"Professor… why? The military is going to steal all the credit. It'll be the general's project now, not yours. They will steal your research from you, and you'll get nothing more than a pat on the back, while the general rises higher and higher."

Barth opened the bottle sitting on his desk, refilling the glass in front of him.

"Oh, Taylor, you're such a cynic. One with a mind for science must change their mind in the face of recent evidence. He would do exactly what you say, if he could. Of this, I know. Consider the evidence. Now, everyone has seen our unveiling of this experiment. We've showed it to all of PanTech. The president himself was in attendance. It's no longer possible for our role to be swept under the rug and ignored. If our research is used, all will know its origin."

"Was that the mistake Professor Elise made with her brain density research?" I asked.

He stared at me blankly for an uncomfortably long moment, tightening his grip on the glass.

"I see. So, you've heard about that, have you? You realize there's no way for her to use the research. They declined her proposal. As most of mine have been. You could call it 'inspiration,' if you prefer. A much more appropriate use of the procedure, I'm sure everyone will agree. After all, she helped us. Clearly, she harbors no ill will."

I nodded. I was asking the wrong questions. Again.

"Sorry if I sounded accusatory, Professor. I only meant to illustrate the fact that others were aware of her research, but another division could use a similar process and receive full credit despite that. No one objected tonight or demanded Professor Elise receive proper credit for the role her own research played. How can you be sure the general isn't planning to do the same thing with us if we allow his foot in the door?"

Barth sighed, taking a sip of his drink.

"Assistant Professor, please consider that I have been playing this game far longer than you have. There's still a lot you can learn from me. While it's true that many pieces played their role in today's game victory, it was I who moved those pieces into their proper place. I couldn't have predicted the future. I certainly didn't expect the general to be cooperative rather than adversarial, but when the board changes, you must be ready, in an instant, to play a brand-new game with brand new rules. If you object or try to revert the game to its original form, you lose the first move to your opponent. I would suggest you prepare yourself for the new game."

No, I'm still asking the wrong questions!

"Professor, what did he mean by what he said to me?"

"If you think I'm simply betraying you for my gain, I can't stop you from concluding that. Really, I couldn't even blame you for it. However, as my representative in this joint project, I am still placing a large role in your hands. A role where you can still influence the outcome. Assistant Professor, I cannot possibly be clearer about this. General Markus can do whatever he wants whenever he wants. I have told you this before. If he wanted, he could simply snatch up Ghost and seize control of this project for the military. You could never see him again. With too much resistance, he would do just that. It would be such a disappointment if you turned out to be so obtuse. Consider yourself fortunate that your presence and involvement was requested."

I shot to my feet.

"Wait! He has Ghost?" I shouted, nearly knocking the general's empty glass onto the floor.

"The president is upgrading us to a higher-level division, Taylor. Do you expect me to choose you and your pet over my career? Do you think I could stop them even if I wanted to? Even if I tried? Really, get your emotions in check, Taylor. If you don't, you're bound to act rashly and make things much more difficult for yourself. And Ghost too. He still has you, at least, so long as you don't overstep."

I shook my head, trying to hold in the tears I could feel rising to the surface. No. No, no, no. Why did I think I could just outsmart these people so easily? Why did I let myself believe I'd "won" anything? I was so angry with Barth at this moment, but his way of thinking came from many years of sitting in that chair and playing every opportunity that presented itself to him. Myself included. If I were to have any chance, I had to adapt even more. I had to let go of even more.

But *not* Ghost.

"I'm sorry, Professor. I..."

What was I going to do? What could I do?

"Take a deep breath. Do you really think the general will harm such a valuable specimen? One he can't possibly analyze or understand without our help? He is safe."

I wasn't sure I agreed with that. After seeing what happened to that snake, and now with his new plan to use intelligent animals as spies, it seemed no one would be safe anymore or ever again. Least of all the animals.

I still had time. I couldn't explode and kick in the door, demanding Ghost be returned, only to be rushed by dozens of suited soldiers, stripped of my new position, and sent for re-education. Even if that's exactly what I really, *really* wanted to do.

I walked out of the office and made the lonely walk back to my quarters. Nothing appeared to be touched, but Ghost was missing.

I buried my face in my pillow and cried.

CHAPTER 14

The next morning, I awoke to my door opening and several uniformed members of Adversity Management waltzing in like it was their quarters. At first, I thought they were coming to collect me, but then I saw the covered cart they were rolling in behind them. Without a word, they left as quickly as they came. Not even a hello or good morning.

Removing the cover, Ghost was calm. All things considered, I wished I'd never brought him. He would've been safer back at the village, with Mother and Father. They could've taken care of him, and PanTech would've overlooked him. Especially with Frelya being the zone commander. She never thought they were real in the first place and didn't even believe me when I told her.

I looked him over and didn't find any kind of wound or marking to give me a sign of what they'd done. If they'd extracted his toxin, I could tell. It would've needed to be done by force. My guess was they'd scanned him, taken blood, and done a visual inspection. They're lucky he'd become so calm around people.

I knew better than to feel any kind of relief, other than the most temporary kind. It would buy me some time to react. After checking Ghost over, the first place I went to was Professor Barth's office. He was busy entertaining visitors, which would likely be a new trend going forward.

I barged right in. "Excuse us for a moment," I said to the man and woman sitting in front of him. "This won't take long, so you can just wait outside."

They nodded, appearing more surprised than annoyed, and stepped outside the door, which I closed behind them.

"Is this how you show your gratitude? By interrupting my plans for the upgrading of our division?" he asked, crossing his arms.

"It'll only take a minute and—" I paused for a moment, considering his choice of words. "So, you had Ghost brought back?"

"I'd originally tried to prevent them from taking him at all, for the time being, but they insisted on tests, scans, and a physical examination. He'll be transferred permanently in two weeks for longer-term study. I attempted to explain everything to you yesterday, but as you were in such a frantic state, I thought it best to leave out any unknowns. I didn't get word back from the general until this morning that he'd approved my request. You've slept in late, or have you even realized that yet?"

I hadn't. I needed to keep my head straight. Losing track of details like this would not do me any favors.

"I get your point, and thank you. One more thing."

"It's not like I'm busy, right? Go ahead."

I held up my hands, trying to use more relaxed body language. Whether it was working was a different story. "Sorry. Sorry. I'll be brief. We discussed expeditions to get samples. Since I only have a couple of weeks, I know I won't be able to go to any of the zones. But what if I went to the surrounding area, outside headquarters? No one's been there in a while, right? It would give Ghost a chance to get out and actually hunt, rather than just be fed. Being cooped up so much isn't good for him, and I can't know for sure the Adversity Management scientists will be as reasonable as you about an animal's needs."

He looked at me for a moment, quietly, most likely trying to decipher my intentions. "You're not planning on making a run for it, are you? PanTech is very good at finding people, and you wouldn't be the first to attempt it."

I hadn't considered that. As tempting as it was, I'd already assumed something like that would be beyond impossible.

I laughed, shaking my head. "No… of course, I won't make a run for it to live my life alone in the vast wilderness. It's an interesting thought. I just wanted to document the wildlife and changes to the ecosystem because of the area being abandoned for so long. I can bring a tranquilizer set and collect blood samples too and collect scans."

He nodded. "Well, it's not as though it's a bad idea. It's long overdue, after all. Everyone just keeps getting distracted, and no one wants to do dangerous expeditions anymore. As long as you can promise to have Ghost back before the scheduled transfer, I suppose it wouldn't hurt anything. I won't have you all to myself again until after the current joint project completes and that could be quite some time. I'll inform the security personnel stationed at the gate to expect you tomorrow, and possibly a companion. Yes, I'd strongly suggest taking someone, regardless of how capable you are. There's a remote possibility you'll encounter something dangerous, given… events that have taken place in that area."

"Thank you, Professor. I'll consider companions for the expeditions, and plan for the supplies I'll need. Sorry again for interrupting your meeting."

"Yes, well, tell them they can come back in and apologize while you're at it. This place will look different when you get back, thanks to them."

"I will!"

I stepped out and quickly bowed to the man and woman waiting outside, who laughed and bowed back before heading back in. Thankfully, they weren't as snobby as the people I'd met from Neuroscience, or as uppity as the people from Adversity Management.

I ran through the corridors, hoping I'd be lucky enough to catch Linda and Joyce waiting at my door. Thankfully, that's exactly where they were.

"Both of you, come inside for a moment," I said, waving them in quickly behind me.

"Uh, breakfast?" Joyce said.

"Just for a minute," I said, pleading with them to hurry.

Not wanting to look suspicious, I was as brief and straight-to-the-point as possible.

"I need you two to help formulate the procedure for Ghost. I want to get a head start on it before the project transfers to Adversity Management."

Joyce shifted uncomfortably. "I heard about that, but Taylor… if Adversity Management took over the project, the decision making is going to be up to Professor Barth and General Markus. Are you sure you should do this on your own? *And*… it sounds to me like you're keeping this under wraps. Why are you *really* doing this?"

I hated lying to my friends, and yet I always did. Was I ever honest with anyone?

"I don't have time to go through all the back-and-forth with everyone, Joyce. I'm leaving tomorrow for an expedition outside the wall and—"

"Wait, you're what?" Linda interrupted. "Since when?"

"Since five minutes ago. Barth already cleared it. Understand now?"

Linda was still trying to absorb the situation. Joyce was still skeptical.

"Why didn't you bring up the procedure with Barth while you were talking to him. You know… all of five minutes ago?"

"Because it's something I came up with on my way here, and for the reasons I already mentioned. Look, you don't have to help if you don't want to Joyce. It's harmless, but I *am* kind of overstepping my authority a bit here."

"I don't see how," Linda said. "Aren't you the assistant professor for Animal Research now? You're basically assigned to overseeing this project. So what if they don't like that you decided without their input? Isn't it something they have planned to do soon, anyway? Starting the process early will just save them time, and it'll be easier to adjust him to the changes while in the field. I don't think they'll be *that* upset about it. I'm in."

"We'd know exactly how upset they'd be about it if we asked beforehand. Obviously, Taylor's afraid they'll refuse. She's keeping things from us, Linda. It's obvious," Joyce said.

"I'm sure she has her reasons, and she'll tell us when she's comfortable. We're all friends, so why not trust her?"

Joyce inhaled sharply through clenched teeth. "I trust her. It's just… Taylor, I just wish you'd have told us to do it rather than frame the conversation this way. Then I could just say I was following my Assistant Professor's instructions. Now, I get the uneasy feeling I'm doing something I'm not supposed to be doing, and it's going to come back to bite me later. I'll help you with this, but I'm not sure I will next time. Got me?"

I nodded. "Sorry. You're right. Guess I made it awkward. You guys are my friends is all. I don't like just telling you to do things. I want to ask, and I want to hear your thoughts, just like now. Sorry, I just don't feel comfortable ordering you around."

"Forget it," Joyce said, rubbing the back of her neck. "I'm sorry too. I just don't want to get in trouble. As much as I tease the two of you, I'm the most afraid of authority out of the three of us. I like to keep my nose clean. I don't like to take risks. In my zone, things like this often ended up with people dead."

"We know you just tease us because you love us," Linda said, elbowing Joyce. "You're overthinking this. Adversity Management didn't give us permission to change the rat, or Henry either. Even Barth didn't. Ghost is Taylor's companion. If she's comfortable doing it, then I am too."

Joyce only nodded. I should've remembered she was from a high-crime zone, and something like this would concern her. Now, I regretted asking her at all. Now that I already had, I had to follow through. There wasn't enough time.

"We'll scan Ghost here and get his samples. We've already moved him around enough as it is. He needs to settle down before we depart tomorrow. We'll prepare the injection at the lab, and I'll give it to him tonight."

"I'm not really the outdoorsy type, so I'll just be dead weight. I can always babysit Henry for Linda if she wants to go," Joyce said, trying to sound more like her usual self, and failing.

"Oh, there's no question. If you'll have me along, I'd love to come. I've been getting sick with wanderlust since we got here, probably more than you, Taylor. I'm coming whether you want me to or not. We can arm-wrestle for it!"

Probably not a great proposition for me when we first arrived. Little did she know that was a challenge I could easily win now.

"No, I was going to ask both of you, and go by myself if I had to. Professor Barth suggested I bring someone with me because no one's been out there in a while."

"Oh, no one's been there in a while? That's going to be fun. I'll bring my sword!"

"Your… sword?" Joyce asked. "That was your item you brought with you?"

"You bet it was, and she's a fine blade, too. I call her Twisted Key."

"*Her* and *Twisted Key*? Why? No, I'm afraid to ask. No, never mind. I'm too curious now. Tell me. I'm going to regret asking you. I just know it," Joyce said.

"We believe that the one who gifts us our weapons, or the one who forges it, gives part of their soul in every blade. Our own soul becomes infused with it, too. Along with those we kill. They become closer and closer to a living thing every time they're used. As for Twisted Key, well… she's so sharp that all you have to do is stick her in and she'll open up just about anything."

I raised my eyebrows, not sure what to say.

"That's… some very dark humor, Linda. I worry about you sometimes," Joyce said, gently patting her on the shoulder.

"Oh, I know you do!" Linda said, suddenly grabbing both of us in headlocks and rubbing her knuckles against our heads.

CHAPTER 15

The thing is, we didn't really know exactly how to prepare for this little vacation. Very little information existed about the outer wall, and from everything we knew, no one had been there in quite a while. That could only mean one thing: Whatever was out there was inconvenient to PanTech's story of a perfect utopia.

Henry had insisted on coming along despite Linda's best efforts to convince him otherwise. He argued that dogs always went along on these expeditions. He'd read up on it! Although his intelligence had peaked a couple of weeks into the process, he had so much learning to catch up on, and his personality rapidly changed. He matured. For him, this was something important too, and he wanted to keep Linda safe. Reluctantly, I agreed. I was bringing Ghost along, after all.

Ghost's demeanor changed just as quickly as the scenery. As I suspected, keeping a bird like him locked up in a room for months had not been good for him. Thankfully, he never seemed to hold it against me. He perched on my shoulder, just as we had done back at the village. I wore my old leather handling gear, passing up the chance for new equipment. At least for now.

As we neared the gate at the edge of the boundary, two guards approached us.

"It's not every day we see someone out here. Pretty boring, actually. The two of you come to look at the wall? I'd keep a safe distance if I were you. No one's been past there in a while," the first guard said. A young man… or at least he appeared to be a young man.

I had long stopped assuming. What was strange to me was his casual approach. No demand for us to state our business. No ordering us to prove authorization to be here. Nothing. The other guard, a similarly young-looking woman, seemed even less interested than he did, only offering us a smile and a nod, letting her partner handle the rest.

That could only mean that not only had no one been out this far in a while, but also that no one had even tried. Then again, why would they? Endless comforts, indulgences, resources, food. Anything. Why would someone want to leave that to go explore some decrepit ruins of a time long before them? For all the adversity experienced by everyone before coming here, it didn't seem to take long for their hardships to be forgotten. They'd get lazy within years, or sometimes months. Was it even worse before the adversity zones? Was it happening to me, too?

"We're here because we're departing on an expedition beyond the wall," I said. Linda nodded in confirmation.

"I am going too!" Henry exclaimed, prompting the stunned guard to smile.

"Hey, you're Henry! My friend told me about you. I couldn't leave my post to come see the big reveal, but they're talking about you all over PanTech. It's great to meet you," the man said, kneeling down to Henry's height.

Henry snatched up the man's hand in his paw, making a shaking motion.

"I am glad too! I'm sorry you could not make it to the party. It was fun," Henry said, in his adorable, even tone.

The other guard came over. Seemed Henry was enough to get her attention. Now that she was close, I could see that the two were twins. How fortunate that they could remain together like this. Ferris and I were lucky enough to arrive together too, but I hadn't seen him in months. Now that I was overseeing the cooperative project with Adversity Management, maybe I could bring him in too.

"What is that bird you have?" she asked, shaking me from the thought.

Ghost was so quiet, I'd nearly forgotten about him.

"He's a falcon. His name is Ghost," I said, hoping she'd let the topic go. Henry, the very nice dog, was standing right here. Was it too much to ask, hoping they'd ignore Ghost?

She eyed him with a keen stare. "I've seen many falcons in my zone. I hunted small game with one for years. This one is unlike any other I've ever seen. His black feathers glisten in the light, and his emerald eyes seem to glow. He has plumicorns, not unlike an owl's, but smaller, and they're the color of crimson blood. He's much larger than the ones I've seen too."

She'd gone from complete disinterest to so much enthusiasm. As much of a hurry as I was in, she was one of the only falconers I'd ever met. It took a great deal of willpower to pry myself away. There were questions I wanted to ask her. Maybe I'd have to come back here and visit with her sometime.

"I'm Taylor, and this is Linda. Henry here is a beagle dog, and Ghost is a shadowfalcon."

"I'm Glimmer, and this is Farle. It's obvious, but we're twins. Normally he's the talker and I'm the listener, but your falcon drew me over."

"Nice to meet you," Linda said with a smile and wave.

"Your names are beautiful," I said, causing the brother to turn his head away, rubbing the back of his neck. Blushing? Good grief. Had no one ever paid the man a compliment before? I reflected on that thought for a moment. Possibly not. These two seemed to be all business and no play. Especially the sister.

"We were expecting the two of you," he finally said. "You can proceed as soon as you're ready, but be careful. I see you have a blaster, and your friend carries a sword. You likely won't need them but keep them ready. We sometimes hear a roar on the other side. A cat, or perhaps a bear."

"Oh, looks like he's already under your spell, Taylor. He's awfully concerned about you suddenly," Linda teased.

"Linda!" I shouted, genuinely irritated.

Glimmer laughed, patting him on the back. "Oh, don't worry about my brother. He's still heartbroken over leaving his three promised wives behind to come here."

His expression hardened. "'Heartbroken' isn't the word I'd use," he said grimly. "'Relief' would be a much better one."

"Linda here likes to tease everyone. Please ignore her," I said, waving my hands, doing my best not to get flustered at the rapidly devolving situation.

"He's a bit short, but otherwise he's a catch. You sure you're not interested, Taylor?"

"Linda, I am going to sock you in the mouth if you don't shut it. We just met these people. You don't have any shame. Also, everyone's short compared to you."

She was right, though, at least partly. His skin was a bit darker than Mother's, but he had the same narrow, dark eyes and long, black hair. Every time I thought about someone in that way, the pain would just resurface. It was an open wound that refused to heal. Destroying PanTech, maybe starting with General Markus, would probably go a long way.

"Okay, sorry. We're going to be spending a lot of time together over the next couple of weeks. I'd rather you not start hitting me before we even officially start," Linda said, clasping her hands together and bowing.

Realizing how far away from Ghost the current topic was, I felt a lot less angry. Had she done that on purpose? Knowing Linda, probably not.

"Fine, but we'd better get moving. Daylight's burning, right?" I said, taking a few steps and waving her to do the same.

"The two of you seem light on provisions. Are you sure you don't want to stock up a bit more?" Glimmer asked loudly, as we almost made it out of earshot.

"It'll be fine. We carried light rather than comfortable. We have concentrated nutrition pods to spare, and everything else we'll need," I shouted back.

I hoped that was true. The thing is, I hadn't been out on my own like this in a while, and my trips out never lasted this long. I was also familiar with my homeland and knew what to avoid and what was helpful. Linda boasted the same, but neither of us knew what this environment was like, and it was impossible to study. A long time ago, it was dense forest, and steep mountains, but terraforming is a simple process with PanTech's technology. Without an updated log, there was no telling what the environment was anymore. With new environments come new plants and animals. Weather, even. All controlled to perfection without PanTech's headquarters boundary.

We reached the gate, and it opened as we approached. Activated remotely.

I turned back to see the twins waving at us.

"I am scared, but also very excited!" Henry said bluntly, as he said everything.

"Not too late to turn back now," Linda said, patting him on the head.

"I am a good boy. I will be very brave."

"You're definitely a good boy, and by the time this is over, you'll have experience and won't have to be as afraid the next time," I said. "Same for you, Ghost, if you can understand me yet."

Ghost snapped his gaze to me, like he always did, paying careful attention to every word I said. He always seemed to understand me, even from the very beginning. Verbal commands took him no time at all. Yet, it had been a full day since I gave him the injection to start the process, and he didn't seem any different at all. Henry showed changes in his awareness and responses. Ghost is… Ghost. Had we miscalculated?

"You are right, Taylor! I will be even more brave next time!" Henry said, raising his paw into the air.

"Is everyone ready?" I asked.

Ghost stared at me with the usual intensity. Henry and Linda nodded.

"Let the expedition begin," I said.

I adjusted the straps on my backpack and took the first step into the unknown.

CHAPTER 16

The world between these two walls was unlike anything else we'd seen while at PanTech… and I got the distinct feeling it was something we shouldn't have been seeing at all. Likely, Barth knew little more about it than we did, being a professor of a lower-level division and younger… relative to some of the other occupants that may well remember what happened to this place. And, for some reason, encouraged not to speak of it to anyone else.

Vines had grown over the outer walls, and many parts of the ceiling had collapsed, with pieces of it lying on the floor. It was almost an open-air funnel that looped around possibly the entirety of headquarters. We were immediately hit with a burst of heat, now beyond the climate control present inside the wall. Instead of being uncomfortable, I found it almost refreshing. I'd adjusted to being away from the desert heat for all this time, but the nostalgia was still something that took hold of me. I never thought I'd miss that place so much, but now… Looking up at the sun. Feeling its intense warmth. The hint of an authentic breeze hitting my skin. I'd almost forgotten the way it felt. It was the sensation of freedom. Of living.

The suffering PanTech held in such high regard, holding it up as the origin of all virtue, was ironically absent within its walls. One didn't even have to fear the danger of a sunburn, or the discomfort of a cool night. There was never any rain, or storms, snow, or total darkness. Only comfort, luxury, and limitless resources. All while systematically oppressing most of the population in cages they called Adversity Zones. Any comforts were meticulously controlled and rationed. If life became too easy, they made it harder. If anyone tried to live truly free, they could no longer live at all.

"It's as hot as a forge out here. Gods in the mountains, and I thought it was hot inside!" Linda exclaimed.

"Gods in the mountains? I've never heard you use that expression before. Did your people believe in gods?" I asked, surprised.

"You think we believe things like spirits living in swords, but not gods? No, we… well, they believed in all kinds of gods. I stopped believing myself when PanTech had either defeated them, or our gods were too afraid to fight. Either way, they aren't much of gods then, are they?"

I nodded, remembering my own thoughts about my people's gods. Especially when they tried to link Ghost to some kind of prophetic notion that he was a symbol of freedom. Absurd. Freedom, huh? As if such a thing could be allowed to exist in this world anymore. Golden shackles were the closest it came.

"I had the same thoughts, actually. Since you're only saying it out here, I guess your people also kept their ideas about the gods private. Ironic, that it was probably PanTech that placed those ideas within the culture in the first place before later changing their minds and wanting it gone."

"Woah," Linda said, snapping her fingers loudly. "You know, I'd never thought about that, but I'll bet you're right. I wonder how high up the food chain you have to go to get access to information on specific zones. I'm guessing adversity managers have that kind of reach, and of course the general… and the president. Probably not any of the other professors unless it's about their own zone. Maybe we should interview other new arrivals and find out about their homes."

"I'll bet most of them are so happy to get away from the pain of their previous lives that they won't even want to talk about it. Besides, the information we're talking about is accumulated over long periods of time from multiple sources. We could probably find out which zones could take part in the mysterious rebellion. I'd give anything to find just a sliver of information about it," I said, sighing. Fat chance.

Linda grinned. "What would you give, exactly? I'm curious."

"Now that you're grinning like that, I'm going to say 'nothing' is probably the correct answer."

"You know what PanTech's structures are made of. Look around you. Do you think something natural caused this damage?" she asked, pointing to the outer-most wall.

I could see that the damaged worsened much further ahead, but there was enough evidence right where we were standing. Holes in the wall. Pieces that didn't belong in the places they were lying, and too heavy to have bounced there. Linda had great intuition, and she was definitely onto something here.

"I do not like this. This place feels very scary. It does not smell right," Henry said, fidgeting with his paws.

"Oh, don't worry, Henry. This is your first time out of PanTech since you had your procedure. I'm sure everything feels scary."

Henry shook his head from side to side, his ears flapping as he did.

"No. I can tell. There are weird smells up ahead."

Linda and I looked at one another, understanding, but not saying anything aloud. Henry was nervous, and I was thinking I'd made a mistake bringing him along.

"I'm sure we could get the guards to escort you back, Henry. I know we said it wasn't too late at the gate, but it's not too late now either. If you think you're not ready for an expedition, maybe you can come along with us on the next one," Linda said, reaching down and patting him on the head.

"I will stay even though I am scared. I will help. I can smell things up ahead. You can't," Henry said, nodding as he did, causing his ears to flop more.

"Don't you think we're getting excited a little early, Linda? We're going to be out here for two weeks, and hopefully we'll move past this spot by the time it's over," I said.

"Oh, have a bit of compassion, Taylor. Not everyone's had blood that flows of molten steel like you and Ghost."

Ghost tilted his head, probably because of the mention of his name.

"Better be careful. Ghost has even less patience than I do."

"You heard me, birdie," Linda said, sticking her tongue out at him. "You're not scared at all, are you?"

Ghost only continued to stare at her, his eyes locked with her as his head remained cocked to the side.

"Please don't rub off on him while we're out here, Linda," I said, smiling and shaking my head.

"Hey!" she said, placing her hands on her hips. "I'm not so bad."

"Linda is great. She is a good mentor."

"Okay. Fine. Let's get moving before her head swells up too much to fit between the walls," I said, taking a few steps forward. They could stay here and chat if they wanted, but I wanted to create distance between myself and that door. The last thing I wanted was for the thing to come flying open with a panicked Barth running through, telling us he'd made a terrible mistake and we needed to come back.

"Oh no! Does that happen to humans if they get too many compliments? Their head gets really big?" Henry asked, putting his paws over his mouth.

"It's a metaphor," I said. "I mean her ego, not her actual head. Now please come on, you two. I'm really curious about those ominous smells up ahead Henry warned us about."

"Ohhh…" Henry moaned, jogging a few steps to catch up. "Now I wish I did not say that."

~~o~o~o~~

We continued walking for a while, with not much change. Suddenly, Henry stopped in his tracks and trembled.

"The smells that are not right are just ahead," he said.

"Can you tell what it is?" I asked. "Something dangerous?"

"It is not alive. It is d-d-dead," he finally said, his teeth shattering for dramatic effect. Whether it was involuntary or if he was just playing it up, I couldn't say, with Linda being his *mentor* and all.

"Dead? That's good. Better to come across something scary dead than alive, right?" Linda said, patting him on the back.

"I do not know if I agree," he said.

"Well, I know *I* don't agree. We're here to study living things if possible. Something dead being the first thing we come across isn't the best sign."

Linda nodded. "Good point. Let's find out what it is."

Only a few more steps ahead, and the scenery took a sharp contrast. There was a large hole in the wall, big enough for us to walk through, and… were those what I thought they were?

"Bodies?" Linda said. Though it was more of a statement than a question. "Lots of them. At least a dozen. They're all holding guns, but they don't look like PanTech's. What uniforms are these? They've been dead for a long time. I'd say—"

"A little over a hundred years…" I said, finishing her sentence.

I wasn't sure before, but now I knew we weren't supposed to be here. Had Barth expected us to just scale the wall as soon as we exited the main gate? Did he even know about this?

"This was a fight that happened during the rebellion. These bodies… they're scattered everywhere," Linda said, walking through them, unfazed.

I bent down and took a closer look. The damage was unreal. Some of these bodies were cut in half. Some even more sections. No signs of animals bothering with them. In fact, I hadn't seen so much as a mouse or rat since we'd been out here. Had PanTech's rifles blown them apart?

No… there aren't any burn marks on their clothes or bones. They were literally ripped to shreds. Did PanTech kill them so brutally just to make an example? To terrorize them? To show how cruel they could really be?

Oh, I knew they could be cruel, but—

"Look, this one's arm is a machine arm," Linda said, holding it out in front of her.

"Linda… we can't mention this when we get back. Not to anyone, understand? That goes for you too, Henry. I know you're a sweet dog who doesn't like to lie, but we could find ourselves with a lot more problems because of this."

"I will not tell anyone. I will not mention it if it will cause Linda problems," Henry said, revealing his eyes that his paws had covered. What a scaredy dog…

"Henry, can you smell any more of these here? Maybe that smell different, like familiar smells inside, or just different?"

"No other smells. It is safe," he said, trying to reassure us.

Though, I wasn't sure if the lack of other smells made me feel any safer. Had they not claimed a single PanTech soldier in this skirmish?

I walked through the large hole in the wall, welcoming the sight.

The dense forest that was rumored to be here had remained, and I could already see signs of life. Several birds flew from one tree to another, and a squirrel climbed up one of them. When I closed my eyes and concentrated, I could hear the faint sound of a water source nearby.

"The animals won't come in here. Without knowing why, I think we should camp just outside this big opening tonight. Tomorrow, we'll start dividing our time between the massive corridors looping around headquarters between these walls and the wilderness outside. We'll keep what we find within this section between the inner and outer wall to ourselves," I said. Hearing myself, it sounded more like orders. Linda must've felt the same.

"Yes, ma'am. I'll clear out a spot for us to get some rest. This is probably enough excitement for the first day. We should start teaching Ghost some things too. Don't forget to divide some time for that."

I nodded in agreement. For a moment, I'd almost forgotten about the procedure.

Soon, things would change for Ghost.

Maybe for all of us.

CHAPTER 17

One Week Later

"Do I really need to continue cataloguing the squirrels, Taylor? There are seven different variations so far. How about we just write 'multiple species of squirrel' and be done with it?" Linda asked, going over the data from the previous day's samples.

"Because then we sound like tourists, Linda. We're supposed to be scientists, remember? Thorough," I said, doing my best to sound like I was scolding. Failing miserably.

"Aye, Assistant Professor!" Linda said, flicking through the samples on her recorder, associating them with the images and temporary names we'd given them.

"How many of them do you think are new? Either completely new or new to this area?" I asked.

"Hard to say. I'm going to say none, given how untouched this place seems to be. It's amazing how much the planet can heal itself in such a short amount of time."

"I believe Ghost has eaten one of every squirrel! He will not eat the food you brought him at all!" Henry said, throwing up his paws in exasperation. He'd gotten increasingly frustrated with Ghost's free spirit.

"Speaking of Ghost… Taylor, I think we may have messed up the formula. He's…" Linda trailed off.

"Acting like he always does, right? He's listening to everything we teach him throughout the day, and he watches us when we show him things. He gives us his undivided attention when we play the rapid education material for him. In fact, he hardly blinks."

"Exactly! We've been out here for a week, and I haven't seen any changes. It's time to accept that we screwed up. I don't know how. Before, I was just as confident as you we'd measured everything flawlessly. I don't see how we could have possibly miscalculated, but maybe his toxin negates it somehow, or there's some element of his genetics we hadn't uncovered that makes him resistant. Regardless…"

"Well, it's done. I don't know what you want me to say, or why you keep bringing it up like beating it into my brain is going to change the results. I can see the way he acts just the same as you, except I know him a lot better than you. So, how about you keep the pessimism to yourself?"

"How about you make me, *Assistant Professor*?" Linda said, standing up and punching her palm.

"Grrr! I may not be a warrior like you, but that won't stop me from taking you up on that offer," I said, bolting to my feet. I was sure she was mostly teasing me, but I wasn't in the mood for it anyway.

"No, no! We are friends. Do not fight," Henry said, running between us waving his arms around. He tripped on a rock and landed on his face. Immediately, he stood on all fours and let out a long, continuous bark, catching both of us by surprise. So, when he gets riled up enough, he still follows his instincts.

The sight was enough to make Linda and I forget all about our meaningless argument, and we laughed so hard we nearly fell over. Henry stood up and joined in the laughing... as best he could, anyway.

Ghost only stared ahead, eyes darting between each of us, as though we'd gone mad, and he was the only sane one remaining.

"Sorry, Linda. You were just teasing, and I got carried away," I said. "My temper has always gotten the better of me."

"I wasn't teasing you. A good fight can often bring friends even closer together where I'm from. Friends fight all the time! But yeah... I'm sorry too. You're under a lot of stress."

She might not have been bluffing, but I sure was. The last thing I wanted to do was fail to control this implant properly and accidentally kill one of my only friends.

Ghost took off again without warning. A *word* of warning would have been nice, too.

Oh, Ghost... I'm sorry I failed you.

"Say... haven't you noticed something strange about the animals?" Linda asked, her tone becoming more even.

"A few things, but it might save us time if you actually cut to the chase."

"Have we encountered a single ground mammal, or a single ground animal at all besides insects or the occasional tree-dweller making a quick trip to the ground before climbing back up?"

I sat quietly, contemplating. We'd documented hundreds of species. Many birds, squirrels, some reptiles that lived in the trees, a small bear that... lived in the trees.

Ghost shrieked, making me jump so hard I nearly fell over. He was so high in the sky that I had to stare for a moment to be sure it was even him. I shielded my eyes, squinting. It had to be him.

"Was that Ghost?" Linda asked, her voice trembling from the sudden shock.

"I've never heard him make a sound like that before. Get everything dismantled. We're getting out of here," I whispered. "And do it quietly."

Linda rushed to collapse our tent, which could thankfully be done as easily as a button press. She'd stuffed the data logger she'd been using in her pocket.

"Henry, do you smell anything?" she asked.

Unfortunately, Henry was bad at whispering, despite trying.

"I smell something weird. It's what I smelled when we found the bodies, but closer now."

"You mean the bodies weren't what you were smelling?" I asked.

"No. I thought so, but this is the smell. It's stronger now. I'm scared," he said, lying down and curling into a ball.

Ghost swooped through, knocking the tent out of Linda's hand, nearly knocking her onto the ground with it.

"Hey, you featherbrain! What's that for?" she asked, scrambling to pick it up.

He circled back around, knocking it from her hand again just as she'd retrieved it.

"Ghost!" I shouted. "What's wrong?"

He landed at high speed, taking several steps to slow himself once on the ground.

"It's too fast to run from. Drop everything. You have to fight. I flew as fast as I could, but it is coming," he said.

I froze in place. His voice was clear. Distinct. He spoke the words nearly as well as a person could. Not at all like Henry.

"It smells strong now. It's close! That's… not an animal, or person, or—"

Henry hadn't finished the sentence when we heard it. A rumbling of the ground. We looked in the direction it came from and saw small trees toppling as though they were dominos. Whatever this was, it frightened Ghost.

Nothing had ever frightened Ghost.

I sucked in air through my nose, and breathed out quickly,

repeating it several more times before my hand was steady enough to grip the blaster on my hip. I toggled the charge, only slightly reassured by the audible hum.

"Oh, gods in the mountains… stay behind me, Henry," Linda said, drawing her sword.

I should've made her bring a better weapon.

I should've been a better leader and prepared for something like this.

I was going to get us killed. It was going to be my fault.

I shook my head furiously as the rumble neared. The rumble wasn't coming from the ground. It wasn't coming from the trees falling because they'd ceased to fall. It was coming from the monster approaching us.

It was like the snake all over again.

Pull it together, Taylor. You won that fight. Remember the physical enhancer. Remember that you've been through this before. Whatever it is, you can beat it. And no matter what… No matter what it takes… Do not let another person die trying to save you!

The beast erupted from the forest, no less than ten feet tall. A spider? No way…

A red light erupted from its head, pointing straight into the air before spreading out into a dome that slowly fell around it, enveloping us with its sinister light. The hum never stopped. My lungs ached from the resonance. The deep tones were below what I could hear, but also deafening. My bones felt as though they'd rattle into pieces. My vision blurred.

Ghost shot into the air and rose quickly. I couldn't follow him with my vision. It was unbelievable he could still fly through the sound. If he'd fled, I couldn't blame him. Ghost wouldn't be of any help in this fight. As the creature came closer, I could see clearly what it was we were facing.

One of the fabled machines. PanTech's hypocrisy in physical form. A machine made for nothing but killing, heavy with rust. This was what slaughtered those men and women. This was why there wasn't a single PanTech casualty on these grounds. Heavy guns pointed in all directions, long empty of ammunition. Long tubes protruded from its body above them. Rockets once fired from these, or perhaps grenades. The specifics didn't matter.

"What's the plan?" a distant voice said. I couldn't register it.

It may as well have been a thousand miles away.

It really resembled a spider. Eight legs, each section the length of my body, held the body into the air.

"Taylor!" it screamed. The voice again. "Taylor, we have to fight!"

It had stopped, but why? Now was the time to act.

"Don't move!" I screamed. "Ghost said we couldn't outrun it. Maybe once it sees we're with PanTech, it will stand down. We don't want to fight that thing if we don't have to. It's the reason there aren't any ground animals."

"But just in case it doesn't, what's the plan?"

"You'll have to scale it somehow. Cut anything that looks like a wire, cable, hose, tube, whatever. I'll aim for anything that looks like a sensor or motor. Henry, run away."

"I will fight!" barked Henry. I didn't argue with him.

"And if that fails… it was an honor, Taylor. I'll have no regrets about dying to such a worthy foe," Linda said.

Images of Linus lying on the ground with blood pouring from his wound flooded my mind.

I would rather die myself than to go through that ever again. I'll push this implant to the bitter limit, even if it kills me.

"Do you know how these blasters work?" I asked her, as the rumbling sound slowly subsided.

"Well… yes, but—"

"I'm throwing you my blaster. Give me your sword."

"But it's my—"

"Give me your sword!" I shouted. I'd let tears slip from my eyes. Now, at the most useless of time for tears.

She hesitated for a moment, opening her mouth to argue, but finding no words. She undid her belt and threw the whole thing at me. I did the same with the blaster, throwing it to her and putting the sword on my waist. It barely fit.

Why was it still standing there? Why hadn't it advanced since it scanned us? Did it recognize us as an ally? If it was there to kill the invaders, it should have done just that.

A rattling of the large metal open tubes made me brace myself. No projectiles. The guns pointed to Linda and me and spun with a furious whistle. Nothing came out.

It crouched, leaned back, and paused.

"It's going to leap!" I said, drawing the sword.

Linda pulled the blaster from the belt, not bothering to put it on. "Ready!"

It had been so far from us, but it catapulted forward, closing the distance as though it was never there, and at horrifying speed.

This was it.

No one was going to die for me.

CHAPTER 18

Time seemed to slow as the machine flew through the air, landing hard enough to knock me off my feet. The low-frequency hum that had been driving me crazy suddenly stopped, replaced by an absolute silence. Had it destroyed our hearing? I felt no pain. I wasn't bleeding from my ears. What could be happening?

I looked over to see Linda shouting at me as she steadied herself again. That only confirmed it. I saw her mouth move but heard nothing. Henry was on all fours, snarling. I couldn't hear it.

A blur passed through my vision. I couldn't make out what it was. The speed was beyond anything my eyes could track, enhanced or not. I knew it was Ghost. His toxin wouldn't be effective against this enemy. Made of steel, and rubber, and rusted by the many years it had been out here… and no doubt the human blood that had once covered it.

It stomped toward me so quickly I barely dodged it, even with the enhancement. Linda wouldn't be able to do it.

"Run!" I shouted, knowing she wouldn't be able to hear me. It was more instinctive than anything. I was thinking out loud. Nothing would make me happier than for her to abandon me right now, grab Henry and make a run for it. But that wasn't Linda. She wouldn't run if there were a thousand of these things. She'd stare them down without fear. I nearly lost my composure, but she didn't flinch.

I saw a blast hit it directly in one of the large lenses protruding from its side. Great shot! It shifted slightly from the blast, taking a step to balance itself. The lens was cracked now. I could see it.

Its torso rotated in place, and it stepped toward her. I couldn't let it stomp her. She wouldn't be able to dodge. It lifted a leg. Time to act.

I sent power into my legs. A lot of it. I jumped so quickly that my legs instantly felt as though I had yanked them from my body, and I nearly overshot the creature. Luckily, it had moved since I launched, closer to Linda. I drew the sword and diverted the strength into my arms. Less this time. I slammed the blade into the crack of the lens, and it shattered. Wrapping my arms around one of the large hoses near where I landed, I pulled back with the blade, making sawing motions as I did.

It rotated quickly and would've thrown me off if I hadn't been holding tighter than any human could. My fingers on the hand I was gripping the blade with were cut deeply. To the bone.

Another shot hit the opening where the lens had been. Linda was an ace shot with that thing. Even I couldn't have made a shot like that twice in a row. If it was just luck, I'd take it.

Fire erupted from it, and a high-pitched whine entered my ears. The first sound I'd heard since the world went silent. I let go of the hose and slammed Twisted Key into the opening where Linda had just shot, removing and slamming it in again and again, like I was opening up a rock with a mining pick.

It leaped into the air and rotated so that its legs were facing the sky. It meant to smash me!

I tried once to remove the sword, but it was stuck. How had this thing even stayed in one piece? Any sword I'd ever seen would've broken by now. I was forced to abandon it and put the power back into my legs again to repel myself away from it. My muscles cried out in protest. The damage from earlier had been done, and it was now compounded with every movement I made. I could deal with the pain later if I survived. The medical supplies we had with us could heal any wound that wasn't lethal, given a bit of time. Time we didn't have at the moment. At least my bones were still intact. For now.

I'd made it far enough away to avoid the body crushing me but was pinned beneath a leg instead. I pushed against it with everything I had but couldn't get away. Had I exhausted the limits of the enhancer already?

I felt a tug on my shoulder and looked up to see Henry had grabbed my shirt and was trying to pull me free. Linda came over and grabbed the other arm. I screamed. My ribs were badly broken. The leg moved. Only a little, but it was enough to allow them to pull me free.

With a rapid spin of its body, it burrowed itself several feet into the ground. I could hear again.

"It's canceling out all sound!" Linda said. "We need to run. Can you move?"

I tried to stand but collapsed the moment I did. "Just leave me. Go!" I screamed. I couldn't use the enhancer anymore. I abused it at the start of the fight, and now I'd missed my chanced to win with it.

"I'm going to carry you. I won't—"

As she bent down, the legs began to spin rapidly. One leg hit Linda, and she was stuck on it momentarily before slipping off and flying, landing on the ground several yards away. Her arm was broken, but she was conscious. I could see her struggling to get back to her feet.

Henry grabbed me again, dragging me on the ground, but he couldn't move quickly.

I forced one more surge of strength into my arm. One arm was all I could manage. I grabbed Henry by the scruff of the neck and threw him out of range of the legs.

"Run! Now!" I screamed with everything I had, my voice fading as I lost blood.

"We won't leave—" Linda said, rising to her feet, covered in scrapes, blood dripping from her shattered arm.

"Please!" I said. The tears came back again. It would flip over soon, and I'd have to watch it kill them both if it didn't kill me first.

It was happening again. Even with all the time that had passed. Even with the enhancer implant and training. Even with the promise to myself that I would never let it happen again, it was happening again anyway.

"If you have the strength to cry, you have the strength to crawl," Ghost said, landing on its underbelly and grabbing a talon full of wires. The hose I'd been cutting earlier had been cut after all, and it was protecting them. Ghost had been hovering above, watching for an opportunity, and dove in when he spotted it.

It took several yanks, but he ripped several of them apart. The legs stopped spinning and began flopping around wildly. I turned onto my stomach and clawed my fingers into the dirt, pulling myself just inches at a time. Ghost was right. If I could cry, I could crawl. My head felt hot. I was getting dangerously close to overloading the implant, but if I didn't make it away, it wouldn't matter anyway. Better to take my chances with the less certain death. I concentrated and focused on one arm again, pulling myself away. It was still slow. A leg came down and crushed my foot, causing me to scream out in pain. I wouldn't make it.

Henry rushed in through the deathtrap of hulking metal legs flailing. Any of them could crush him to death instantly, but there he was. He grabbed onto my other hand, sinking his teeth in, and pulled along with me. A few terrifying seconds and one miracle later, we'd escaped the range of the legs.

"There's a square seam just left of where the cables connect to the body. Shoot it Linda," Ghost said, flying straight into the air to get clear.

Linda raised the gun with her only good hand and fired once. She missed. She charged and fired again, hitting just along the edge of the seam.

The machine reacted by flipping its legs around, so that what was the top before was now the bottom, and stomped down with every limb, freeing its body from the ground. Twisted Key fell to the ground, jarred loose by the sudden motion.

Rather than attack, it fled as quickly as it had arrived.

Henry let go of my hand and ran to grab our supplies. Thankfully, they hadn't been destroyed in the fight.

"Hey… if you're going to borrow my sword, the least you could do is not drop it," she said, pointing to the glimmering blade lying on the ground near where I'd fallen.

Even though it hurt every single fiber of my body, I couldn't help but laugh.

"I probably got fingerprints on it, too. I'm really sorry," I said, forcing a smile. My voice was hoarse, and even speaking normal volume felt like shouting.

No tears from Linda. Cracking jokes in the face of death. Part of me wished I could be like that someday, but the other part of me hoped it would never come to that. This encounter was enough to last me for a while. A lifetime, maybe.

Henry came running back, just as Ghost landed beside me.

"I don't know how to use these. They are complicated. I will learn first aid soon. Oh no…" Henry said, rummaging through the pack.

"I'm okay to do it, Henry. Thank you. You did enough. You're such a brave, good boy."

"I was brave because you were brave, Linda and Taylor. You too, Ghost. You were brave too. You are a good boy too."

Ghost just stared at him with no sign of emotion.

"I will have to sedate Taylor, and we can't move her for the next couple of hours while her bones regenerate. After that, we're getting out of here," Linda said, grabbing a vial from the pack and tearing off the seal with her teeth.

"It won't be back. Not after that. It's going to repair itself and that will take time. I'm sure it works the same way as the resource gathering machines do. They maintain themselves and swap out with another. Ghost, are there any other machines here?"

"No. Linda, before you sedate Taylor, there is something I need to say to her. They implanted me with a monitoring device, but I could feel it shutting down when the machine appeared. Before it returns, I have to tell you something I overheard General Markus saying to others."

It was strange to hear Ghost speak like this. He'd been my companion for so long. I was tempted to explain it away as a concussion.

"I can only imagine what he said."

"No, you can't. He is planning to seize PanTech by force. This will be my last opportunity to tell you this. Once this implant comes back online, he will listen again. He and several commanders are going to use these devices against the other divisions, and once they're planted, they plan to seize control so quickly that no one has time to react. If they react, the general will know and respond so quickly that it won't matter. He plans to send away all PanTech's most loyal commanders just before he does, so they won't be at headquarters. Only the commanders supporting his plan will remain."

The four of us didn't move or respond. There was nothing but stunned silence. I knew that General Markus was bad news, but an insurrection? The president thought so highly of him. He'll never expect his most loyal employee would do something like this. His reputation is that he's fiercely loyal to the president and PanTech. I thought he'd be its most steadfast protector. If there was one way to make PanTech even worse than it already was, it was by turning it into a military dictatorship with Markus at the helm. Now that the four of us knew, we had no choice but to stop it. If I told anyone, they'd just assume I was lying to make the general look bad. The president would believe no one without proof.

I took in a deep, painful breath and sighed.

"Alright. We won't mention this again in your presence. We'll carry on like none of us knows. Thank you, Ghost."

Linda and Henry just nodded in agreement, probably still in disbelief.

Every step forward came with twenty steps back…

CHAPTER 19

Six Days Later

PanTech's technology was beyond what anyone could have imagined from my village. What would Father say if he knew there was a simple injection that could start a rapid regrowth of damaged bone and tissue?

I knew what he'd say. I'm confident he'd curse PanTech for keeping it to themselves, while others died of injuries or suffered months of grueling recovery in bed, wearing casts, and physical therapy. He'd remember the times PanTech halted his own research and inventions, all of which paled compared to what was available to them. He'd be right. And yet, here I was…

These injuries would have been life threatening if I'd sustained them in my village. One week later, only an enormous appetite and a bit of soreness remained. While the treatment was working its magic, it needed constant energy to fuel it. We'd packed so many nutrition packs just in case, and we'd nearly emptied them all, plus Ghost's constant hunting for us and Henry's cooking and feeding us.

Most of us have met people in our lives that make you wonder how they ever became friends. Two individuals so different in every way that it would seem impossible. Many times, events like this were the reason. Henry and Ghost fit that description. Henry felt uneasy around Ghost from the very start, and Ghost found Henry's cheerful optimism annoying. Before this expedition ended, they were coordinating like old friends. Exchanging instructions and taking care of Linda and me as well as anyone could've. Being unsure of whether bringing Henry along was the right thing to do, all doubt had left me now. I might've been dead if it wasn't for him dragging me out of harm's way.

Ghost had warned us of danger and gave us time to put up our guard. He helped in the fight. He hunted the food for Henry to keep us fed so our bodies could heal. This was the true vision of what these animal companions could mean for their human counterparts. No matter what happened, I couldn't let General Markus pervert it into just another military weapon project. More than anything, I couldn't let a man like that seize control of PanTech. As corrupt as the entire organization was, there were still parts of it that were mostly harmless, or even helpful. General Markus would turn something mostly bad into something completely bad. Everything would be converted into a weapon idea. He was paranoid about the Adversity Zones, and he'd probably tighten restrictions and lock them under complete, violent control. The image of armed troops marching through my village, ordering everyone around at gunpoint sent a chill down my spine. It couldn't happen. It just couldn't.

"Fried squirrel with squirrel gravy, topped with nutrition supplement crumbs. Wow, what a great breakfast!" Henry cheered.

From anyone else, I'd have assumed it was sarcasm. From Henry? Sarcasm just didn't come naturally. Or at all.

"Wow… yeah. I really loved it yesterday too, and the day before that, and the day before that," Linda said, demonstrating sarcasm perfectly.

"What about you, Ghost?" Henry asked, holding up a bowl.

"I don't need to eat like a human," Ghost said coldly, pulling apart a squirrel he'd just caught.

"Okay. It is your choice. There will be enough for Linda and Taylor to have seconds!"

It felt so awkward not to discuss anything Ghost had told us. We couldn't. Not as long as he was present, and the spying devices they equipped him with were likely back online. There were so many things I wish I could've stayed conscious long enough to ask him. For example… what did the other insurrectionists look like? Was Frelya among them? I could've asked for more details on their plans, or where they meet.

Could've. Would've. Should've. No point in worrying about that now. Ghost told us the most important things he could in the short time he had to do it. I'd have to work with it, and quickly. As long as I exposed him before the animal research concludes and innocent animals are deployed into the field, that's all that matters.

"I'm going to join you with the joint project, Taylor," Linda said, as though reading my mind. "I'm sure you already guessed that I would."

"I wasn't sure, and I wouldn't ask. It's outside of what we were originally planning, so…"

I trailed off, careful not to say too much.

"I also have something to give you," she said, reaching behind her and producing her sword. "Twisted Key is yours now. I want you to have it, but on one condition—"

"Thanks!" I said, before turning to Ghost. "Speaking of gifts, I think I'd like to bring some of that squirrel back with us and have the kitchen do something proper with it. Do you think you could capture about ten more for us, Ghost, and leave them by the wall so we can bring them in later?"

Ghost nodded, finishing his bite and flying away.

I watched for a moment, making sure he was long gone before speaking.

"Okay, why are you giving me your sword? This is important to you. *Really* important, considering that explanation you gave me about the souls being in it."

Linda sighed, partially drawing the blade to inspect it, then sheathing it again.

"I can tell that it's going to be far more at home with you than with me and my new life here. You could say the sword is asking me to give it to you… in a way. I just want you to be honest with me, for once. Can you do that?"

Henry attempted a throat clearing sound, which ended up sounding more like a burp.

"Oh look, there is a better spot for me to wash these squirrels over there. I will go there and come back soon," he said.

Linda and I laughed, but it really was thoughtful of him. Something else he was learning.

"I'm sorry, Linda… it's not that I didn't want to tell you. I just didn't want to involve anyone else in my personal problems. It's all really complicated, too. PanTech…" I swallowed hard. The tears were already threatening to emerge. When did I become such a crybaby? "PanTech soldiers killed the man I loved… but he was also a PanTech soldier. I hated his commander for failing to do more, and now she's become my friend… I think. When I was still in my village, there were rebels there. She offered me the chance to bring Ghost with me, and also to be given a physical enhancement implant, like the commanders get. I found out the rebels sold out Linus and they were the reason he died, and I snapped. I confronted them out in the open. Ghost and I killed the leader, and PanTech arrested the others. And here I am… and now there's a military coup brewing that only I know about, and—"

"*We* know, Taylor. *We* know about it. Besides, I don't know why you're so worried about being out in the open about the other things. You sound like a model PanTech citizen, protecting their interests."

"I don't want to be a model PanTech citizen, Linda. You want me to be honest with you? I want to see them destroyed. I hate PanTech. I hate what they do to people, forcing them through pain and suffering, while they… Look at the medicine we just used. How many have you seen die in your own zone who could've been saved by something like this? I had life-threatening, life-altering injuries a *week* ago, and I'm completely healed. Limitless resources. Never-ending food we don't even need… while others starve according to plan."

"Stop…" Linda said, pushing the sword into my chest. "I've heard enough."

I grabbed her arm as she took a step back. "Are you sure? I think about this all the time. I could keep going."

"That's enough!" she said, jerking her arm away. "I need… Sorry, I just need time to think about all this. It's just… do you hear yourself, Taylor? Are you insane? PanTech isn't just a ragtag group of rebels you can outsmart. They have things like, you know… medicine that can heal life-threatening injuries in days, limitless resources, never-ending food and never-ending *guns*! Didn't you see all those bodies in the wall? The machine probably did that. We almost died, and we didn't even disable it. One machine. They probably have hundreds, maybe thousands of them in the uninhabited wilderness that stretches beyond here. What you want to do, you *cannot* do!"

"Don't tell me what I can't do! You may be too much of a coward to even try, but I won't rest until things change."

Immediately, I felt the stab of regret, but I was too angry to take it back.

Linda's eyes watered, and she rubbed one of them before forcing a laugh.

"Me? A coward? I was ready to fight alongside you to the death. And you call me a coward? There is no greater insult to my people, and yet you call me, your *friend*, that so easily. Do you hear anything you say? If I'm a coward, then you're a fool. If courage was enough to accomplish the impossible, Linus would still be alive!"

I drew back the sword and threw it on the ground at her feet.

My skin felt as though it was about to boil right off my bones. Though the rage didn't stop the tears from flowing. It only made them feel hot against my cheeks. With one punch, I could hit her so hard in the face it would break her neck. Only I knew she was right. It changed nothing, but she was right. Linus was a master with the gun, but died because he was injured, had two opponents, and an inferior weapon. At least... that's what I told myself. Maybe it was because the person with him was too weak to be of any help. As I am now, I could've helped him. I could've killed them both, and he wouldn't have even needed to lift a finger.

Maybe he was a fool too, trying to do the impossible. If that's what it means to be a fool, then a fool was what I wanted to be. I'd accept that label proudly. Even if I had to continue on that path alone.

I turned and was about to stomp off when I felt a hand grip my wrist.

"I'm sorry..." Linda said, shoving the sword into my hand.

When I turned, she wouldn't meet my gaze. Instead, she looked down at her feet.

"I'm sorry," I said. "You're not a coward. I was wrong to call you one."

"I'm only sorry about what I said about Linus. You are *definitely* a fool... but you're my friend, and foolishness and bravery are the same thing, just a little different flavor. What you said just caught me off guard is all. I'm with you. If you need my help, you only need to ask. You don't have to keep doing everything alone and hiding things."

I turned and wrapped my arms around her and probably looked like a child hugging her mother, considering our height difference.

"Oh, this is good. I'm glad you two aren't angry now. I will join the hug too!" Henry said, running toward us with his arms wide.

The seriousness of the moment couldn't survive Henry. We were both laughing before we knew it.

CHAPTER 20

Having had just about enough of our so-called vacation, we made our way back to the inner wall a day earlier than planned. We'd collected more than enough data to keep Barth entertained for a while, and we were depleted of our first aid supplies. Unlikely as it was for that machine to come back for us again, it wasn't a chance we would take now that we'd fully recovered.

I'd kept Ghost away from the general and his goons long enough for the procedure to take effect. He'd progressed far faster than Henry had, and seemed to exceed human intelligence in certain ways, though he lacked the communication of emotion Henry had developed. Like some humans, I just saw this as part of his personality. I liked the stoic, cool-headed Ghost. I knew him far better than anyone else, and this was always his personality. He'd been observing and studying, even though he couldn't completely understand. He'd committed words and phrases to memory even without grasping their whole meaning. It seemed he truly was special.

Nearing the gate, he perched on my shoulder. Henry seemed agitated.

"I smell Joyce. She is nervous. Something is wrong."

I shot him a glance, more out of surprise than skepticism. He was getting much better at articulating his instincts.

"Are you sure?" I asked. "You can tell she's nervous?"

"I can. It's hard to explain. I just know."

"Maybe she's just worried about us. I mean, it *has* been almost two weeks after all. You'd worry about me if I was gone for a while too, right?"

"I was worried just thinking about you being gone!" Henry agreed, nodding vigorously, causing his ears to flop around.

I smiled, pressing a button on the gate to alert the guards nearby. My finger had only barely touched it when it flung open, surprising all of us into taking a step back. Joyce was standing there alone, her eyes wide.

"Taylor! This is bad. I'm glad I got to you before they did," she said, running forward and grabbing my shoulders. "This is terrible. I don't know what to do. Barth said there's nothing we *can* do."

"Joyce. Breathe. Slow down. What's bad? Who wants to get to us?"

"Not us, Taylor. You. General Markus is stomping around Animal Research like it's his division, impeding the upgrade process, and irritating Barth to no end. He was livid that you went on that expedition without his permission."

I shrugged. "Well, I can't say I didn't expect this might happen. I suppose he has the right to come after me if he thinks I broke the rules."

I took a step forward, and Joyce pushed me back again. "No, Taylor, he doesn't. I haven't mentioned this, but my father is an investigator, detective, whatever you want to call it at the Division of Investigation. They look into rule-breakers, stolen items, and things like that. That's their jurisdiction. The general is head of Adversity Management. He only has that kind of authority over those in his own division, or the zones. He's acting completely outside his authority!"

"Not that it matters when he's all buddy-buddy with the president," Linda said.

"Exactly. No one can hide here, and it'll just make things worse if I avoid him. I'll go straight to him and just see what he wants. There's no use in us getting bent out of shape until we find out what's got *him* bent out of shape," I said, surprised at my calm demeanor. That's what happens after a brush with death. Kind of makes everything else feel trivial.

"I'll go with you," Linda said, putting a hand on my shoulder.

I shook my head. "No. I can handle him on my own. There's only so much he can do to me right here in headquarters."

"I wonder…" Joyce said, nervously tapping her foot.

"Ghost, go with Linda. I'll catch up with all of you later. Maybe we can get some dinner for once."

"I like dinner," Henry said, licking his lips.

"We know you do, Henry," Linda said, patting him on the head. "And sure, I'll take Ghost with me. Please don't eat me, Ghost."

Ghost said nothing. Not even a nod. Linda shuddered.

I gave Joyce a pat on the shoulder and continued walking past her, and past the guards who had spoken to us almost two weeks prior. They both offered a smile and a nod, but seeing that I was walking with purpose, didn't speak to me or otherwise hold me up.

I continued walking like this all the way to the transport, boarding it for Animal Research. As soon as I stepped off, Barth spotted me and almost sprinted in my direction. It was almost funny, given I'd never seen the man go any faster than his usual confident stride. This looked anything but confident.

"Taylor! Thank goodness you're in one piece. I made a huge mistake allowing your expedition. The general gave me an earful. I tried to make it look like I was certain you'd return, but I was anything but certain once he told me what existed beyond the wall. You need to go see him right now, down in Adversity Management."

I held up my hand. "Take it easy, Professor. As you can see, I made it back just fine, and so did Linda, Henry, and Ghost. Linda will be here soon with our data we collected. You're going to love it. The machine that was out there has had a tremendous influence on the ecosystem. For example, there are no animals who live primarily on the ground."

He tilted his head. I had his attention now and distracted him from his panic.

"Truly? That's remarkable. Did you happen to… No. You need to go see the general. Once you're done, resume your work on the joint project."

He waved both hands, shooing me back into the transport.

I hadn't recovered from the first trip. I really should've taken a few minutes break, but I didn't. Of course, I paid for it when I arrived at Adversity Management. Immediately after stepping out of the pod, I ran to the nearest waste canister to hurl. I *hated* these things… I wondered if there was a long way I could take next time.

With that bit of business out of the way, I continued my walk toward the main building. I'd been inside the science building already, but never this one. It dwarfed every other division I knew of. I was understanding why it was on the ground, too. At least, I had a theory. If there's a fight, it's best for the people with all the armor and guns to get there first.

"Stop right there." A voice called out from my right. He stepped quickly toward me. "State your business or—" He stopped in his tracks once he was close enough to get a good look at me. "Wait, Taylor?"

"Ferris?" I said, trying to conceal my excitement. It sounded like him, but it was hard to tell through the helmet's speaker, and everyone looked like a robot with those helmets on.

He pulled off his helmet, and sure enough, it was him! I almost wasn't sure, even after seeing his face. He'd matured so much in these past months, already growing a beard. He looked so much like Father, and it made my heart swell.

I ran toward him, jumping the extra height his suit gave and hanging off his neck while hugging him tightly. "Ferris! It's really you!"

I could barely contain my excitement. I hadn't spoken to my brother since we arrived. Lately, I wasn't sure when I'd ever get to see him again.

"Well, well, well… if it isn't the big shot herself. I swear, I go to an entirely different division to get away from you, but I end up hearing your name all the time anyway. The last couple of weeks, at least."

I let go of his neck, dropping back to my feet, giving him a shove that hit harder than I intended. "Oh, I'm sorry, does your ego hurt? And speaking of apologies, where's mine? Why haven't I heard from you? There's instant communication technology here, you know. Have you heard of it? And those awful transports."

"Ah, now that's the sister I remember. Well, first of all, not everyone's as special as you and gets to go on those things freely. Second, the general doesn't like us being distracted when we first arrive until after we finish our basic training. After that, we immediately get shipped out on our first mission. I haven't been out long. The day after you did whatever you did to ruffle General Markus's feathers, apparently. I wish I could've gone with you. They made it sound like it was dangerous. Were they mistaken?"

I shook my head. "No, they weren't mistaken. We almost died. Probably would've if I had to carry dead weight like you around, so I'm glad things worked out the way they did."

"Oh. Ha ha ha. You're so funny, Taylor. By the way, how do you like my whiskers? Came in pretty well, huh? I think I look like Father now."

"Do you think Mother and Father are doing okay?" I said, my voice low.

"It's Mother and Father. Of course they're doing okay. And all jokes aside, I'm really happy to see you again."

"Me too, Ferris. So much has happened. I wish I could tell you everything, but it would take more time than I have now. Speaking of which, I'd much prefer to find the general before he finds me. I get the feeling things are a lot more likely to go better for me if I do. Offer your sister an escort?"

He smiled, fitting his helmet back on. "It would be my pleasure, Assistant Professor. Right this way."

He stepped toward the massive building, and I followed. I quickly realized I would've gotten lost without him, as it took us a full twenty-minute walk to reach the other side. Much of the building comprised different training areas. Some were simulated to look like the outdoors. Other areas we passed were clearly stocked with equipment and even vehicles. Most of which I'd never seen before and couldn't even guess the capabilities. I was sure that somewhere around here there were more of those horrible machines, but likely somewhere my brother wouldn't be allowed to go.

Finally, we reached a large room that looked like something out of a fantasy tale, with maps adorning the walls and shelves filled with real paper books. A massive table sat at the center, with a model of the entire PanTech headquarters and the land beyond. Sitting at a large wooden desk on the other side was General Markus, arms crossed with a smile on his lips. He nodded impatiently at Ferris, who quickly remembered protocol, snapping to salute, his left fist resting on his lower back and his right fist on his chest.

"Sir! Assistant Professor Taylor from Animal Research is here to see you!"

"Thank you for escorting her here, recruit. Dismissed."

Ferris gave me a subtle nod before quickly leaving the room.

"How thoughtful of you to come straight here to see me, Assistant Professor. Please, join me at the table," he said, standing and walking to its edge.

Suddenly, that uneasy feeling returned. Even my brush with death wasn't enough to bring me to take this man lightly. I had to choose my words carefully, or I'd give away the fact that I knew more than I should.

I walked around the table and stood at his side, following his eyes to the familiar battered section of the outer wall. He's waiting for me to speak first.

Here goes nothing…

CHAPTER 21

He'll expect me to try being diplomatic and weasel my way out. I'll surprise him by hitting the touchiest subject first, and direct.

"You'll be pleased to know I already started the intelligence procedure on Ghost, and he already has a surprisingly good grasp of language."

He nodded, still looking down at the model.

"I appreciate someone who can think on their feet and doesn't fear reprimand. Even with the stir I've been causing in your division, you still came straight here to meet me. Bold, and a touch of recklessness. I see Frelya is still a fine judge of character."

Does he really mean what he's saying? Is he actually happy I started the procedure without his order? No. He's the one being diplomatic, trying to throw me off… and he's good. He has the best poker face I've ever seen. No matter how closely I observe him, I can't detect even a hint of deception.

"Thank you… I wish I could say the same for myself. Every time I think I have someone figured out, they surprise me."

He laughed, leaning forward and gripping the edge of the table.

"I assume you mean me? I'm the head of Adversity Management. No different from Professor Barth to Animal Research. To call me 'general' is an outdated formality. You may call me Professor Markus if it put you more at ease. My priority is philosophy and the human spirit, and how to make it thrive. We are nurturers of what makes human beings the best they can be, and only when necessary do we fight."

"An awful lot of armor and guns for philosophers," I said, a little more quickly and sharply than I meant. He was provoking me, and I realized it only a little too late.

"It would surprise you how seldom force has to be used when the power you wield is overwhelming. Strength is the shortest path to peace, otherwise you're always being tested. Challenged. I can hear it in your voice that you don't yet believe me, but in time you'll learn."

It's not that I can't detect the deception. There just isn't any. This is a man who believes his own self-important words.

"I see your model has the hole in the outer wall we encountered. Interesting," I said. This time, I'd leave the opening for him to speak first.

"Judging by the fact you're here speaking to me, I suppose you didn't encounter one of the old defensive units. Unless… you did and somehow survived?"

He looked up at me, faster than I'd expected, and locked eyes with me. My first instinct was to look away, but I resisted. Surely, he was aware of the encounter.

"We encountered it but escaped. Why is that thing there, and why did it attack us?" I asked, finding my nerve again.

He sighed, opening a small box sitting on the edge of the table and pulling out a figure that looked identical to the machine we encountered, putting it down in the wilderness area outside the wall.

"This machine is a prototype. Originally, they were programmed not to attack those who carried the friendly tag given to all PanTech defenders. However, everything happened in a hurry, as you could imagine. There was no time to test things thoroughly, implement changes, and update these machines. Their primary purpose was to prevent loss of life, and that meant keeping them in the field. Many deserters showed themselves within our ranks, and the tags became useless. Traitors could simply walk up to the machines and casually disable them. So, the ability to differentiate friend from foe was removed, and all defenders were withdrawn. The machines proved to be more than sufficient to stop their advance."

Despite being tempted to point out the obvious contradiction in the purpose of these machines being to prevent loss of life, I bit my tongue.

"Then why are they still active? This conflict took place a hundred years ago."

"They sent a deactivation signal out to all the units. However, some were damaged in the conflict and could no longer send or receive a signal. These units continued to patrol."

"And kill or drive out every living thing on the ground. Did you know that?" I asked, having trouble hiding my irritation again. "There are no more ground animals there. It's altered the entire ecosystem."

"An unforeseen consequence, but an acceptable loss. You

may disagree, but human life comes first here. I'm not angry with you. I understand that you've only experienced one side of what Adversity Management does. You should see it from the other."

"I'm not interested in transferring to Adversity Management if that's what you're suggesting. I'm perfectly happy in Animal Research, though I appreciate the offer."

He smiled, gesturing to the areas beyond the model.

"Though you'd be welcome to transfer, that's not what I meant. There's someone I'd like you to meet."

He tapped a button on his jacket. "Manager Pauline, please report in-person to be briefed on your next assignment."

I stared at the button, waiting for sound to come out, but it didn't. He noticed my expression and grinned.

"Oh. There's a small device in my ear. She confirmed and will be here shortly. You'll like Pauline. She has spirit, like you, but she's old enough to be your great grandmother. A lot of wisdom comes with that kind of experience."

Where was he going with all of this, and why was he being so casual and friendly? It wasn't just unusual considering his reputation and rank, but also my reason for coming here. I expected I'd at least get a lecture, or a cold reprimand. He was treating me like an old friend, or a young trainee he was taking under his wing. He didn't seem angry with me at all.

A fully suited soldier entered the room and saluted. "Reporting, General," a female voice said.

"You can remove your helmet. There's someone I'd like you to meet," he said, nodding toward me.

She looked between us several times before reluctantly removing her helmet.

At first, I thought she was furious, but I quickly realized she wouldn't wear such an expression in the presence of the general, given her etiquette. This was just her face. All the time.

"Well, go on, girl. Introduce yourself to me, or do you think that scientist's jacket means you don't have to observe manners?"

I quickly saluted. I'd assumed someone else was just posturing or trying to play games with me. This woman didn't seem the type. Clearly, she was a stickler for protocol.

"I'm Assistant Professor Taylor, from Animal Research. It's a pleasure to meet you," I said.

"Save your flattery, girl. A simple introduction would suffice.

I don't need to know what does or doesn't give you pleasure. We aren't that close."

My jaw nearly dropped. So much for impeccable manners.

Markus burst into laughter, giving me a pat on the back.

"See what I mean? You two are going to get along great."

Before I could ask what he meant, she spoke again.

"I am Commander Pauline, and meeting you is not a pleasure, but an inconvenience I will bear because General Markus has asked it of me, and because I trust his judgment."

Could this woman be part of his inner circle, and the plot to take over PanTech with military rule? It was hard to venture a guess. On one hand, she would clearly follow all orders without hesitation. On the other hand, that probably meant she was loyal first to the organization, with everything else coming second. She respected protocol and the structure of command. She'd obey the president over the general in an instant. Doubtful someone like this was in on it.

"I always appreciate your candor, Pauline. You and this girl have that in common. A rare trait these days, especially among newcomers. It's why I chose you to take her along on your next deployment, seeing as it's happening soon and will be short. It will do Taylor some good to experience the perspective of an adversity manager firsthand. She's also cooperating with our division to create assets that will ultimately make us more effective in the field. Shadowing you will give her a better understanding of how best to guide this research and implement it."

Not only is he not trying to keep me close to him, but he's sending me away again so soon?

"I've sent Ghost with Linda, and she should stay with him for monitoring. He behaved strangely after the encounter with the machine. Until we can rule out any behavioral complications, he should stay out of the field."

Markus nodded along, as though he didn't understand why I'd even brought it up. This man was making me doubt things I knew to be true.

"He's your companion. Of course, I will trust your judgment. Let me know when you're comfortable and we'll transfer him to our facilities for monitoring. It can certainly wait until you return."

"Ghost? Companion?" Pauline asked, looking at me, then to the general.

"Ghost is her falcon, and one of the first test subjects for our joint project with Animal Research."

Pauline's eyes were glazing over with each word. Clearly, she had no interest in discussing science.

"Understood. I suggest you stick close when we arrive. These primitives can be rowdy when we show up. These days we roll in with guns hot and don't get a lot of arrows shot our way anymore. They're smart enough to figure out that guns beat bows, I guess."

I could feel my body's urge to tense and resisted. This woman may have some of the wisdom that comes with age, but her narrow-mindedness and sense of superiority overshadowed it.

"Now, Pauline, you understand even your zone is cultivating PanTech's future youth," General Markus said, with a hint of reprimand in his tone. It was a statement, rather than a question.

"Oh, I understand that very well, General. Those that come out of that place are truly worthy of being called diamonds in the rough. The poor souls. At any rate, with your permission, I'll return to my preparations."

General Markus nodded, resting his hands behind his back. "Dismissed."

Without a word, Pauline turned to leave but only made it as far as the door before stopping and turning to look at me.

"Do you think we're racing, and you're giving me a head start? Why are you just standing there?"

General Markus nodded. "Good luck on the mission, both of you. Assistant Professor, please come see me immediately upon your return."

I turned and saluted him. The involuntary nature of the movement startled me. In only this brief conversation, it seemed his charisma had already infected me. I'd have to be truly careful from now on. Exposing this man would be nearly impossible. Without irrefutable proof, no one in this world would believe me. After all, I'd nearly doubted it myself.

CHAPTER 22

Unfortunately, I didn't have time to warn Linda and Joyce before I joined Commander Pauline's team, but Ferris promised to get the message to them somehow. I wondered when his next deployment was, and how long he'd be gone. I'd hoped we'd be able to see each other more than we had. Despite PanTech being larger than I envisioned, he was only a few seconds' ride away on the transport. In that way, PanTech felt smaller than it was.

I wondered, too, what Markus's true purpose was for sending me on this mission. Was there a different reason than the one he stated? With him, it would be impossible to tell. Where most give hints to their true meaning through body language or tone of voice, General Markus showed none of these weaknesses. Many times already I'd doubted what Ghost had told me. I couldn't imagine this man, upright and loyal friend of the president, as the leader of a military coup. It felt like trying to imagine the sun as actually being the moon if someone you really trusted told you so.

"Rise and shine lab coat," a male soldier said, nudging me with his leg.

I sat up in my cot. Despite falling asleep in a rapidly moving vehicle, I slept soundly. From the inside, it was difficult to tell the thing was moving at all. From the outside, you could see it coming from miles away. It reminded me of something that belonged on the water more than on land, and I was told it could manage both. Air capabilities were there too if the need arose. Not sure what that would mean, exactly. I assumed that meant more for broken roads and bridges, rather than retreating. Soldiers referring to it lovingly as the "RB", short for rolling barracks. It lived up to its name.

"It's Taylor, armor face," I said, sitting up and stretching my arms.

"Armor face? I love it, considering I don't even have my helmet on right now. I'm Zel, by the way. Sniper and man of very few words, as you can tell," he winked, brushing the long, dark hair out of his blue eyes.

"Clearly, you're the best choice for a sniper. I couldn't even tell you were here until just now. I didn't hear you bragging about your rifle upgrades last night for close to an hour, or trying to convince your female teammate that you were the best kisser ever and you'd wager your rifle in a bet to prove it. Also, I didn't hear you chatting with the chef all morning about how his breakfast reminded you of your mother's cooking. I didn't hear you tell your friend sitting across the room there... what was it now? Something about me being a cute one and how you're going to come over here and try the old insult and compliment trick, and how it works every time. You're basically invisible."

He took a step back and looked around to see who'd heard, and his face turned red.

His friend across the room clapped his hands together and started laughing so hard he fell backward into his cot.

"Smooth as spider silk, my brother! She's practically already your wife!"

"Shut it, Zeek!" Zel shouted, before clearing his throat and turning back to me.

Twins, though they didn't seem that much alike.

"Where's my ring?" I asked. "It's a custom in my zone. You're supposed to offer a ring to the one you intend to marry."

Zel crossed his arms, his face slowly returning to normal color. "Oh, you're just as bad as my brother. Can't tell a joke around here without getting interrogated by the anti-fun division. Forget it. I bet you're more into the science types anyway," he said, punctuating it with a humph sound and turning his head away.

It was so unexpected, I let out a small giggle. I was understanding his humor a bit... sort of. "I'm not sure why everyone does that. Everyone here passed their entrance exams. You're a 'science type' too, actually."

"Does that mean you're into me after all?" he said, waggling his eyebrows.

"Quit while you're ahead, Brother. You made her laugh. Don't make her vomit right after."

"Fine. Breakfast is served, lab coat. The others said I shouldn't get too attached to you, since lab coats have died on these missions from time to time. I didn't think that was fair, so here I am. Stick by me and I'll keep you breathing."

He extended his hand, holding a small bowl covered with a lid. Removing the lid, the smell was almost overwhelming. I expected worse, but this food was certainly better than the synthetic stuff we ate at Animal Research.

I narrowed my eyes, not sure whether to feel anger or

appreciation. Was this the true reason he asked me to tag along? Because lab coats die on these missions sometimes?

"If you're wondering why this food looks so good, it's because we trade with the citizens of the zone. I'm sure you remember, as most low-tech zones have the custom, and most zones are very low tech."

"Eggs and bacon? Real eggs and bacon?" I asked, still in disbelief.

"Yep," he said, smiling from ear to ear.

"Five minutes until landing!" a voice echoed over the auditory system.

"Better make quick work of that," he said, placing the bowl in my hand and sitting down across from me.

"Thanks," I said, resisting the urge to ask more questions in favor of getting my food down. Linda and Joyce, the culinary enthusiasts they are, would be so envious right now. It's a shame I had to eat such good food so quickly.

"I meant it," Zel said. "I was with one of those lab coats who died. We won't let it happen to you. Forget all that other stuff I said. Was just trying to make conversation and I'm not very good at it."

"Thank you, Zel, but I have a feeling I'll be okay," I said between bites, not elaborating further.

"Aren't you curious why you weren't assigned a power suit?" Zeek asked, his voice even and low.

I finished my bowl and handed it back to Zel, considering Zeek's words. Of course. Why not send me on another expedition that wasn't leaving so quickly, to give me time to be fitted for a suit? Answers always come with questions. Am I being sent here to be disposed of or to be tested? I knew that even if I survived, I could never read the answer on his face. That left only one goal in front of me: Survive. Return. Expose him… somehow. That part wouldn't be easy. Assuming it was even possible.

"Arrival!" the disembodied voice called again.

The three of us moved up several rooms until finally we arrived in the main area with about twenty other soldiers. Pauline stood in the front.

"It's been one month since our last visit. Civil unrest has been reported, and another attempt has been made on the life of the appointed king. This time, successfully. The people have installed their own king. We are here to evaluate whether that king is suitable. If he isn't, we will remove him and install a more appropriate one. But you should be prepared for bloodshed. We will not tolerate resistance. Questions?"

I raised my hand.

"Taylor," she said, waving her hand toward me.

"Why not just let them keep the king they've chosen and avoid the bloodshed?" I asked.

"Ah! A perfectly reasonable question. Who doesn't want to avoid bloodshed, after all?" she asked, clearly mocking me. "Well, I'll tell you. The new king is likely to be hostile to PanTech's presence. If he is, he'll use his new power to form a resistance effort and attack us on our next deployment. That's assuming an attack isn't already lying in wait. This little 'war' of theirs will cause many of their own deaths. Or, even worse, one of our own could get hurt. The cattle don't get to make the rules for the farm, to use an animal metaphor. That should help you understand, since you're from Animal Research."

I wanted to argue, but I could feel how pointless that would be. Instead, I clenched my fists and did everything I could to look satisfied with her answer. No other answer would have been any better.

"What was the point in bringing along another lab coat?" a woman near the front asked. "Didn't the last one take an arrow to the eye?"

Pauline sighed. "Fair warning, this is the last stupid question I answer. The general has faith in Taylor's ability to keep herself alive and recommended her for this mission personally. Let me say that again… He nominated her for this mission *personally*. Would anyone like to express further doubt in his judgment? I can always bring it to his attention when we return. I'm sure he'd love to listen to your advice on how to better lead our division."

Only silence followed. A long, awkward silence. Pauline was exactly the kind of commander I hated. It made me really appreciate Frelya even more.

"Good! Now get out. We'll be getting many visitors, so handle them as you see fit. We'll spend the morning here before going to see the new 'king' of their people."

Everyone stepped off the RB in an unorganized fashion and spilled out into the main gate of the city. I braced myself for hostility but was met with the opposite. It seems I wasn't the only one surprised, as nervous, confused glances were exchanged between the soldiers as they flung flowers at us. A large, cheering crowd had gathered, and had likely been waiting there for some time.

More surprises that should have never been surprises. Of course, the new king would recognize the biggest threat to his recently gained throne wouldn't be a competitor from within the zone, but PanTech. Smart. No doubt this crowd had formed on the king's orders.

As for their intention, that was yet to be known.

CHAPTER 23

I couldn't tell if Pauline was more disgusted or disappointed by the warm reception. Only that she didn't like it. Most of the soldiers hadn't put on their helmets, and after some hesitancy, some present had approached the soldiers individually and offered them gifts. They ranged from more flowers, to snacks, to something even more bold. Themselves.

Two young women approached Zel, and one wrapped herself around each arm, both giggling as they dragged him away down the busy street. They were beautiful. Everything about this was becoming far too obvious, as if it wasn't obvious already. Though these young men and women were trained and equipped to win any battle, they stood on an even playing field in a battle of wits. I knew firsthand what it was like to play on the heartstrings of one of these soldiers. No matter the intent, it's always our hearts that get us into the most trouble. I really hoped that Zel would be alright. Maybe I should—

"Hi!"

I looked down to see a little girl standing in front of me. Her smile felt a little more genuine than the others.

"Hello there, little one. Lots of people here today, huh?" I said, suddenly realizing how long it had been since I'd seen, let alone spoke to an actual child.

"Have you seen my cat? Her name's Milda. She's really little. Gray with lots of stripes. She always follows me to the market, but the big cart scared her. She ran away."

I looked around, but there was no sign of the cat anywhere in this area. Unless this was a trick, the little thing most likely hid itself under something close to where she was scared. I looked around again. This time not for the cat, but for Zel and Zeek. Both were long gone. So much for my heroes. Though, I was eager to explore this zone and learn more about the culture without bloodthirsty, armored soldiers standing next to me. If the others could sneak off, I'm sure I could get away with it too. If I was going to take my chances of getting dragged off by someone, better a child than some handsome stranger offering to feed me, then swindling me out of supplies or a favor after feeding me his sob story instead.

"I'll help you find your kitty," I said, reaching down and taking her hand.

She smiled brightly, and we began walking down the street.

"You're really pretty, and you don't wear the big armor, but your clothes are kind of strange. Are you with the oppress—I mean, PanTech, or are you from here?"

"Well, thank you. And don't worry about that little slip just now. Though you'd better be careful. Some others might get angry or worse."

"Sorry…" she said, tightening her grip on my hand.

I gave her a pat on the head. "Let's just focus on finding your kitty."

As if on cue, she pointed to a man and woman standing and talking in front of a building. The woman was holding and petting a kitten. Sure enough, gray with stripes.

"There she is. There's Milda!" she shouted, letting go of my hand and running toward the couple. I walked quickly behind her, looking around for potential ambushers. These all seemed like regular people. However, I knew full well that ordinary people can do extraordinary things when their backs are against the wall.

"Is this your cat? She sneaked into my shop this morning and got into my fresh meat!" the man said, shaking his fist. "I thought she belonged to this woman, but I can see now she's yours. Come inside and I will show you what your parents owe me."

Without warning, he grabbed the little girl by the arm and pulled her inside, much to the dismay of the woman holding the kitten, who seemed just as surprised as me.

I took a step inside and stopped when the door closed behind me, and I turned just in time to see a large board fall in behind it, locking it from the inside, dropped by a large man who had been waiting. I couldn't muster up enough enthusiasm to even feign surprise.

"I'm sorry! They have my mommy, and that really is my cat, Milda! He said he'd chop her up and sell her in his meat tomorrow and hurt my mommy too if I didn't help. I didn't have a choice."

I held my finger to my lips.

"Shh. It's alright. I'm not mad at you."

A third man jumped out from behind the counter. Just how many were they? Before I could react, he had a blade to my neck. I didn't resist, just observed. His hands were trembling, and tears were welling up in his eyes. "Now come along and don't make a fuss, or I'll gut ya like a fish!"

"Right…" I said, raising my hands in the air. "Just tell me where to go. Clearly, you've got something on your mind. Let's just talk."

"Go upstairs, and don't make a break for it or I'll cut you, I swear! Me and these boys are knights who served under the true king, recently murdered and replaced by your puppet!"

"Our puppet? But we didn't—"

"Shut it!" the man standing by the door said, drawing his sword. "And we know you PanTech tyrants have fancy tricks up your sleeves, so make one wrong move or reach for anything and you'll be dead before you grab whatever it is."

"Alright, I'm not reaching for anything. Look, I'm walking upstairs," I said, stepping slowly up the stairs, my hands still above my head. Should I use my implant and pummel these guys, then make a run for it? No, not yet. I had a morbid curiosity. I wanted to hear what drove these men to do something they clearly didn't want to do.

The butcher walked up the stairs last, joining the three of us in the small attic. The sun shone through, and it was a beautiful view. Any other situation, and I'd have enjoyed sitting here for a few minutes, away from all the insanity I'd entangled myself in. Instead, I was here with a knife to my throat, entangled in yet even more.

The man with the knife pointed to a chair. "There. Sit."

I stopped and turned to face him. "I'll sit, but I'm not letting you tie me up. Understand?"

We stared each other down for a moment, before the butcher spoke up.

"She's not going anywhere. I locked the hatch. The door downstairs is barred. She's just a lone woman, and no one followed her here or they'd have already busted in to save her. Just humor the girl and leave her untied."

The tears finally flowed from the man with the knife's face.

"Let's just let her go. We were knights in the king's guard. Men of honor. We shouldn't be kidnapping girls off the street."

"Shut your mouth!" the man with the sword shouted. "The rules changed when they assassinated the king. Now we do what we must, for our kingdom."

The man with the knife dropped his weapon, letting it bounce across the floor.

"I won't kill an innocent woman just to sabotage the usurper."

"Innocent?" the butcher asked with a laugh. "Innocent, you say? She is one of the oppressors who installed the traitor. How is she innocent?"

"We didn't—" I tried to speak but was interrupted again.

"So, you will deny it?" he said, taking a step toward me and crossing his arm.

"On our way here, I was told that this change in leadership was unexpected, and that we were going to meet with the new king to assess the situation. PanTech plans to remove him if he is unfriendly toward them and replace him with yet another king. Maybe I was lied to, but it didn't sound to me like this was a planned change."

The men looked at one another. I could see in their eyes that they didn't believe me.

The man with the sword took a step forward, grabbing me by the hair and pressed the tip of his blade into my chest. This man wasn't trembling. He had the will to do what he claimed he would do. Still, maybe I could find out more and talk my way out of this. Even if this man was willing to kill me, the root of it was still a misunderstanding.

A glint in my peripheral vision caught my attention. Could it be? I activated the implant, forcing my eyes to focus harder on the object in the distance. I couldn't be certain, but I had a feeling. It was Zel, and his rifle was pointed directly toward us. He kneeled and was in position to take a shot. I had to act now, or these men would be dead in the next few seconds.

All three of the men were distracted now by my focus on the window, and I took advantage of this to grab the blade of the sword, redirecting it away from me. Just a little strength. Just enough to make this simple, but not enough to seem impossible. That's all I needed. As he fell toward me, I grabbed his arm and rotated my torso, slamming him hard onto the floor. He gasped and remained conscious, but lost hold of his sword and didn't move.

The butcher lunged forward next, and I met him with a quick jab to his throat. When his arms reached involuntarily, I followed it up with a kick to his stomach. He fell hard against the wall and rolled to his side, writhing in pain on the floor.

"Get down!" I shouted at the man who had dropped his knife, standing there in shock at what had occurred. He didn't listen to my command. I lunged toward him, tackling him to the floor. In that exact moment, something blew through the glass and left a gaping hole in the wall across. It sounded like a thunderclap inside the room, and everything went silent before my ears started ringing.

"You… you saved us from someone watching the room. Someone was watching after all."

"You're fools to go up against PanTech this way!" I said, slapping him across the face as he sat up, knocking him to the floor again.

He clutched his cheek with his palm. "And yet… what can we do but fight back? You're saying our safety is more important than our freedom, but nothing is more important than freedom. Not even our lives. The old king didn't even understand that. This one is even worse. What choice do we have but to fight?"

I didn't have an answer. In fact, his words left me feeling empty. What were they supposed to do? Did I have an answer?

I didn't.

A loud bang came from below, followed a second later by a fist flying through the attic door and knocking it open.

"Oh, looks like you've got it covered. Didn't mean to step on your toes, Taylor."

It was Zeek. Zel was still watching us from a distance and was covering him.

"I thought your brother was too busy to be bothered to help," I said.

Zeek laughed. "Oh, you mean the girls? Truth is, Zel is a lot smarter than he looks. He was only gone for a couple of minutes before he came back, noticed you were gone, and tracked you here. We have your blood signature, obviously."

I'd forgotten about that. My blood signature. Of course. Someone was going to come, eventually.

"These men confessed to not working for the new king. They were trying to set him up by killing me and making it look like the new king had ordered it, giving their lives in the process and letting the secret die with them."

"Oh, well done! Zel is more of the shoot first and ask questions later type. This could have been bad if you hadn't handled things the way you did. Stand behind me, please."

I walked behind Zel, and he held up a device in front of him. When he activated it, the three men fell unconscious. Some kind of weapon I hadn't seen before.

"Don't worry," he said. "They're not dead. We'll bring them in and wake them up for questioning."

If I'd had a hidden recording device on me, like the soldiers' helmets, I could've broadcast their confessions. Then, no one would have to be convinced. Pauline still might not believe me and—

Ah, that's it…

CHAPTER 24

The mission turned out to be a short one, as expected. With the testimony of the would-be saboteurs considered, and after several meetings with the new king and his advisers, Pauline left the new ruler in place rather than destabilize the zone further with its third king in almost as many days.

Zel and Zeek were not reprimanded, as far as I knew. It was strange, considering I was likely sent there to disappear. It's possible that either Pauline didn't know about this intention, or they just didn't care about the outcome.

As promised, I went straight to see the general. I tried to remind myself that his expression would be meaningless but got caught up in it anyway. He genuinely looked so pleased that I'd returned. I'd seen that look so many times on my father's face when I'd return home. Markus's expression looked as real as his.

"Welcome back, Taylor. I'm told you ran into some trouble. Nothing you couldn't handle, I see," he said, leaning over the table and looking down at the broken wall as he'd done before. He clearly wants me to ask him about it.

"I see Pauline must've contacted you after the event. It was really no trouble at all. As you said, much needed field experience. It's easy to make assumptions being on the other end of things. I never really appreciated how difficult it is for PanTech to manage these zones."

"Go on," he said, his eyes meeting mine.

"To be frank, it seems like Adversity Management is the backbone of PanTech. The rest of the divisions are isolated and seem to be more focused on what happens here. Only Adversity Management deals with citizens across our territories."

Even as I said it, it didn't feel like the lie I'd intended it to be. Was I believing it?

He scratched his chin, as if to ponder my words. "It can seem that way, but looking deeper, that's almost like saying your skin is the only important part of your body because it's what everyone sees. We represent PanTech to those who live in the zones, and we nurture their adversity to make them the highest quality humans they can be. However, it's the president's office, and all the scientific divisions that make this a place worthy of reaching. A reward for those who have suffered and are worthy."

"But doesn't reward rob us of adversity? Injections that can heal broken bones in days. Simulated realities that feel like the real thing. Machines that can build in hours what would take men years. Free, nutritious food that can taste like anything. Limitless resources of all kinds that have made the exchange of goods, something that has existed as long as humanity itself, obsolete. Invincible protectors that guard the walls. I could go on."

"Feel free," he said, not a hint of emotion in his words.

"I'm curious what you think," I said, suddenly cautious that I'd gone too far.

"I will speak gently and assume your intentions are pure. I enjoy a discussion of philosophy as much as the next person. After all, it's at the very core of Adversity Management. Not violence. However, I'd say your words border on dangerous. They almost sound rebellious. Of course, that's not at all what you mean. I just want to caution you against… speaking so freely in the presence of others who may not understand."

And just like that, the gate slams shut. I'd hoped for an opening. Of course, it would never work. It was too early, and I simply didn't have time to go for another inside approach. By the time I gained his trust, PanTech would be a military dictatorship, and things will be much worse for everyone. Worse. Hard to imagine, and steeped in irony.

"You're right. I should have considered how it sounded before I spoke so freely. That's good advice. Thank you. By the way…" I said, looking down at the wall. It was small, but I saw it. What was that? A twitch? A tap of his finger? I barely caught it, but I suddenly couldn't help but feel this was a trap. He's baiting me into showing my true colors. He gave me the rope to hang myself, and I threaded the noose with my words about Adversity Management being the backbone of PanTech. Seems he was far better than me at this. I had to be careful. Being close to him like this was not a good idea.

"Yes? You were about to ask me something?"

I need to pivot to something believable. I was looking right at the wall.

"I was just thinking about how the members of Pauline's unit tracked me down so quickly. Of all the things I've seen since I arrived here, the technology surrounding our blood being used to open doors, identify us from a distance, or track our movements seems so far beyond even the latest science. Who invented it?"

"That would be the president, a little over 200 years ago."

I was stunned. How long ago did he say? 200 years? Impossible.

"Did you say…" I started.

"200 years? Yes. Surprised? He's much older than that."

"Are there others that old in PanTech?"

"No. He's by far the oldest. I'm 163 myself, but that's not uncommon for those with the goal of a long life. Though, even that isn't as common as you probably think. In the Age of Steel, very old ages were common. It was catastrophic for humanity, as you might imagine. You're a smart girl. I'm sure you could think of many reasons."

"Arrogance. Power. Not sure what a long life would do to make it worse," I said. Something felt out of place. His explanations feel indirect. Like he's purposely leaving them unclear, allowing me to make assumptions that are untrue?

"If you were to have the power to create the perfect world, what would that world look like, Taylor?"

"A perfect world isn't achievable. I wouldn't try. It should be up to each individual to create their own idea of a perfect world," I said, trying to choose words carefully. Philosophy again?

"And if their ideal world involves them preying on others? And if another's ideal world involved not being preyed upon? Which one deserves their ideal world more? Who decides?"

"People can look out for one another. Band together against those who want to do them harm," I said.

"Right. They band together. Agree on rules. Agree on how those rules will be enforced. Designate protectors. Enforce the rules. By enforcing the rules, they are no longer free to choose their own ideal world. Do you understand? A world where everyone chooses for themselves isn't possible."

"But in your description, isn't it the enforcers who ultimately decide? The creators of the rules only think they're deciding, but the enforcers actually create the society and maintain it. The enforcers naturally become the rulers in time, whether or not it looks that way."

He sighed, turning and strolling back to his desk. "You've missed the point, Taylor. For today, at least. Not to worry, though.

You have a long life ahead of you, but you should concern yourself with the long day ahead of you first. We have a thousand dogs and cats who began the process yesterday, and you'll need to oversee them. I assume you'll want to catch up with your friends as well. You've had a very busy couple of weeks, after all."

I see. He played my card against me to make a point. I began the process with Ghost early, without advising him. Now he's started the process on a thousand dogs and cats while I was gone. What can I say? Nothing. I did the same thing. I can't object, or even show signs of being upset. It would expose me as a hypocrite who had other motives with Ghost. It would show that I didn't trust him, and that he shouldn't trust me. This man is far more cunning and dangerous than I ever gave him credit for. I couldn't waste any more time.

"I hope we can continue our conversation again soon. I'll think about your question in the meantime."

He smiled, nodded, and turned his attention to his desk. My cue to leave.

I'd only just made it outside when Frelya approached me. She'd been waiting for me. I'd expected her to look happy, but she wasn't even making eye contact. Was she feeling well? Still, she was exactly the person I wanted to see, and she'd saved me the trouble of finding her.

"Frelya, is there somewhere private we can go? Maybe to your training grounds? There's something I want to talk to you about…"

She made eye contact with me briefly before looking away again. She seemed even more uncomfortable than before. "Oh? Sure, I suppose we can. You're behind on your training, anyway."

Frelya was the only type of person more difficult to read than the general. She was completely unpredictable, and sometimes her reactions or things she would do didn't even make sense. Her antics would make you think she hated you one minute and loved you the next. I wanted to believe that she was my friend, after everything she'd done for me. She mentioned so many times that she thought we were alike. I was about to find out just how alike we really were.

CHAPTER 25

Frelya didn't speak to me on the entire walk to the training grounds. Something about that scared me, and although I never make small talk with people, I tried with her and received nothing but yes or no answers, or the occasional grunt. Once we arrived, she set up everything as she always did, but without all the enthusiastic rants about reaching my potential or a flood of questions about what I'd learned about controlling the implant. Today, of all days, the questions would make sense. After all, I'd been in several life-threatening situations since the last time we'd met. There were many things we could go over. Though, it wasn't the implant I wanted to go over today.

After a few minutes of watching her set up jumping platforms in silence, I couldn't take it anymore.

"What's wrong?" I asked.

"Nothing…" she said, continuing to adjust the distance between platforms.

"It's not nothing. Something's bothering you. Just say what's on your mind. It's not like you to act this way."

She stopped what she was doing, walked over to me, and shoved me to the ground.

"Don't act like you care about me! If I want you to know something, I'll tell you. Got it?"

She clenched her fists and paced in front of me, growling. The question was almost a scream.

"You're right. I shouldn't have pried. Sorry," I said, standing up and dusting myself off.

With no warning, she ran up to me again. I braced myself, not sure what would be coming. Rather than an attack, she embraced me tightly.

"When I heard they deployed you with Pauline, I was afraid… I was afraid you…"

In this moment, I finally felt like I understood her better, and it made me feel so much pity for her. She would have been angry to know that's how I felt, but it's the feeling that came naturally to me. This was someone who might've been an average woman, living a normal life. Instead, her experiences warped her into a warrior, and her mind showed signs of massive strain and fractures. Something even PanTech lacked the ability to repair. You could treat the symptoms of mental damage, but you couldn't undo time. You couldn't reverse someone's experience. No one could go back and protect the young girl who was accidentally pulled into the selection process, though I felt I would if I could. I wanted to cry for her… instead, I would do what I always did. I would just use her to accomplish my own goals. Just like I did Linus. What kind of person did that make me? At this moment, someone awful…

"It's okay," I said, returning her hug. "I survived. Oh, and I missed you too. I became a lot more familiar with the implant, but if it's alright, I'd like to go over that another time. Today, I have something to ask you, and you're not going to like it. I need to ask you anyway, so here goes…"

She let go of me and took a step back, wiping her eyes. She didn't say a word. Oh, Frelya… I'm so sorry.

"Ask your question," she said.

"Is this place under surveillance? Answer truthfully."

"It's not… Taylor, why—"

"Are you part of the group planning to help General Markus with a military coup?"

I couldn't think of any way of asking that would make it any easier to ask or hear, so I said it outright, as though I were reading it out of a book.

"Why have you done this to me, Taylor? Why? I'll answer you truthfully. I am, but you're smart enough to know what happens next. You know I can't let you live now. I'll never forgive you for this. I—"

I held out my hands. "Hear me out, please! I trust you, so… I want to give you my secrets too. I want to destroy PanTech. It was my reason for joining. When I fought with the rebel leader in my village, I was originally helping them. I only attacked him because he reported Linus. When I found out, I was so angry I had to kill him, no matter what the consequences were. I blamed you too. I let you believe I helped you because, since things went the way they did, I saw no reason to not take advantage of your offer. You let me get the implant and take Ghost along. But now…"

"But now? But now? Taylor, please don't make this any harder than it already is. Don't say anything else." She reached to her side, unbuckling her blaster.

"But now I see we *are* alike, just like you said! I just need to make you see… that the answer isn't military rule. It's freedom! Zones should be free. They need to experience their own natural adversity, like every human does, not have it artificially forced on them by scientists… or generals in ivory towers."

"I hate you…" she muttered, lowering her head. She gripped the blaster but made no effort to draw it. "I hate you because your softness has made me soft. A lifetime of hardening my warrior's heart, undone by one girl. I will fix that here, and now."

She drew her blaster, quickly and cleanly, leveling it at my head in an instant. I tensed. Was this it? I'd made the wrong gamble, after all. I had to try.

Our eyes locked for a long time, and neither of us moved.

"I need your help to expose him. Frelya, I'm asking you… but I won't beg. Do what you have to do."

Her hardened expression gave way to a smile, then she erupted into full-blown laughter. She laughed so hard that she nearly couldn't catch her breath when she was done.

"Fine," she said, tossing her blaster aside. "We have the same implant. I have no other weapons on me. We will fight to the death, and the truth will side with the winner. The loser will be the one with the weakest resolve. I'm going to show you what softness brings."

As soon as she finished speaking, she gave me no chance to respond. No option to agree to the terms, or to negotiate.

Her first strike came at normal strength and speed. I'd not neglected my body, but Frelya was stronger and faster than me. I activated a minuscule amount of the implant's power, and easily dodged, countering with a kick straight to her chest. Rather than dodge, she met it with an attack of her own. A palm strike grazed my knee before my foot connected with her. She stumbled back and clutched her chest.

When I brought my leg down, the pain surged through me immediately. She'd dislocated my knee, with what felt like the lightest touch.

"We don't have to do this, Frelya. Please, stop! Listen to me."

Ignoring me, she lunged forward with another attack. Another punch, this time sped up considerably. I'd have to dodge or block it, but dodging was the only way to avoid damage. Activating a larger portion of my implant, I stepped back the same way I did before. My knee buckled under me, and I nearly went down to the ground. The pain was more agonizing than I could've expected. The weakness she'd created prevented me from putting more strain on my leg. I'd successfully dodged the punch but couldn't recover quickly enough to follow up with a counterattack!

She grabbed the collar of my shirt and pressed me down, creating even more weight on my knee. My eyes produced tears involuntarily, and I squeaked as I tried to suppress my voice. I couldn't stop. I had to ignore it. Could the implant be used to disable the sensation of pain? In theory…

I focused on just that, rising back to my feet and threading my arms between hers, launching them upward and spreading them out in a wide, outward arc. I slammed both elbows down on my sides, prying her hands away. Then I stepped forward, throwing out a punch as quickly as I could while she was off balance. It had to land, but it couldn't kill her. I could use everything I had left in the implant and knock her head off, and I'd survive with the side-effects making me unconscious for a while. But I needed her for what I had planned, and what's more than that… I wanted her to live. The thought of her dying made me feel a sensation of sadness far stronger than I'd expected.

Just enough to knock her out, or down. I could follow up quickly to immobilize her if the punch didn't do the job.

My fist connected with her jaw, and time seemed to slow. The effects of the implant operating at higher power. I understood this feeling. It was like time slowed, but it was really me who was moving faster.

With a scream, Frelya's jaw cracked beneath my knuckles. More cracking. It wasn't just her jaw. It was my fingers too, and my hand! I used too much! Yet, she still stood, her battle cry causing my ears to ring. She grabbed my wrist and twisted, flinging me over her shoulder and hard onto the ground. I felt several bones break. My wrist was broken from her grip. She placed her foot on my back and bent down, pulling my arm behind me. The implant couldn't suppress the pain anymore. I'd used up nearly all of its power. Using more from this point on would be dangerous. Life-threatening, even.

"Using the implant to override functions of the brain uses far more power than sending signals directly to the muscles. You lose, Taylor!"

The way she said the words, you'd think we were never friends at all. I was an enemy now. So much for getting through to her.

No! I couldn't lose. But the pain… I screamed out as I allowed it in. I had to release the effects of the implant to conserve the last bit of power it had available. I'd never felt this much pain in my life. My shoulder was being ripped from the socket, and I had trouble breathing through it.

No matter what it took, and no matter the cost. No matter the price that had to be paid. I couldn't let it end here. If using the implant to suppress my pain used more energy, then that meant I had more of a supply than I realized available to send to my muscles.

I screamed as I felt my shoulder tear, but I rose to one knee. With everything I could muster, I reached along my side and grabbed her by the waist of her pants. I twisted so far that my other arm was now bent at an inhuman angle. I saw her face. Her eyes were wide with surprise. This would have to work!

I yanked her to the ground and leaped on top of her. She struggled to maneuver away, but I fell against her, landing several headbutts to her face. Blood from my face dripped onto hers as I struggled to stay conscious. I'd gone up against my limit, and several steps beyond.

Frelya stared up at me, her nose broken and bloody, and I could no longer see any of the anger and hatred I'd seen before. Nor did I see a fear of death, or a fear of anything. She looked distracted, as though she was deep in thought, attempting to solve a puzzle.

I brushed her hair out of her face and smiled.

"I won, Frelya," I said.

It was the last thing I remembered doing before my eyes drifted closed and I collapsed into darkness.

CHAPTER 26

In my dream, my father stood above me, smiling. He reached out his hand when he saw my eyes open and helped me sit up.

"You're awake. Good. I worried you would sleep forever," he said, still smiling.

"This is all a dream," I said, surprised I could say such a thing. An unusual dream for me, where I normally have no control even if I'm aware I'm dreaming.

"I suppose you must be missing me, or perhaps it all means something else," he said, offering no reaction to my accusation of him being a figment of my imagination.

"Of course I miss you, Father. Only I'll never see you again. So many times I've wanted to ask for your advice. You're always so wise, and you know what needs to be done. You hate PanTech just as much as I do. Oh no… am I dead?" I asked.

He snickered, looking around him before looking back to me, as though I'd asked someone else or something around us held the answer. "Dead? How should I know? Maybe you are. Dreams are a funny thing, though. They give you wonderful answers, but never directly. If this is a dream, shouldn't you be focused on the message?"

"Wow, it's almost like Mother is standing over your shoulder, ready to scold you for revealing too much. Since she isn't here, I know it's a dream for sure now. Father would've just told me his opinion without all the smoke and mirrors."

"Smoke and mirrors are hard to fight, aren't they?" he said, running his hand through his long beard.

I looked around, finally realizing we were flying through the night sky. We passed through several clouds before the path cleared and I could see below. We were riding on a giant shadowfalcon, the desert floor a blur beneath us.

"If you're fighting the smoke and mirrors, you've already lost," I said. "It means you've taken the bait, and lost sight of the real opponent."

He nodded. "Well said. I'm proud of you, by the way."

I missed so much hearing those words that I was taken aback. I had to gather myself before answering.

"For what?" I asked.

"You finally put faith in your friends. Only a few years ago, I worried you might never find the courage to rely on others and try to go it alone your whole life. You've really changed, Taylor. You've become a stronger woman, and you've made strong, resourceful friends who support you and make you a better person. Linda is courageous and has good instincts. Joyce is charismatic and cunning. Frelya has a focused fury, and an unbending will. What made you trust her? Frelya could have killed you. As you pointed out, maybe she did."

"Frelya… is like a version of me if my life had gone just a little different. I feel such a strong pity for her, but when I acknowledge that, it's almost like I'm feeling sorry for myself. Trauma fractures her mind, but I fight against the same demons. What PanTech did to her… it's not right. It's worse than what they did to Linus. Getting to know her, despite her support for them… it's made me want to stop them more. Not less."

"Sounds like your mother, doesn't it?" he asked, raising his eyebrow.

"Yes… it does." I paused, considering my surroundings again. "Is this a vision? Are you one of the gods?"

A chuckle.

"That would be convenient, wouldn't it? Perhaps I am. Perhaps it is. Perhaps I'm not and it isn't. After all, many have suggested that the concept of a god or gods is nothing more than a manifestation of one's own internal ego, or aspects of it. There is no wrong answer to the question you've asked. There's no wrong answer to any of it. It's one precise message you need, but many interpretations of it. None of which is wrong. Do you understand?"

"I suppose. If you were a god, it's not like you would say so. Regardless, I think I understand the meaning of the dream. The face it used to give the message. My surroundings here. The things you've mentioned. It all ultimately means nothing, and yet I feel better. I believe I've done the right thing. If I've died for it, then so be it."

My father reached down and clasped my hand. "What do I mean to you, exactly, Taylor?"

"I…"

~~o~o~o~~

The room changed as I opened my eyes to reality, but the sensation of the hand remained. The one sitting with me was Frelya. It must've been her voice that asked the question. The fact she was sitting here, and I wasn't dead… she'd changed her mind. Something about the way things happened caused her to reconsider. I gripped her hand tightly in mine.

"You're the last friend I thought I'd make. I thought we'd be enemies. You thought the same, I guess. But you're sitting here… because you must have helped me."

"Your friend. Okay then. I'm happy with that. Don't laugh. No… you wouldn't laugh. I helped you because you helped me… see me for what I really was. I thought I was different. How foolish. I thought I was some kind of hardened warrior who was better than others. But lab coats like you, I didn't expect you to— I'm sorry. I'm having trouble putting it into words."

I'm worse off than I thought. My limbs are heavy. I've been treated, but still haven't recovered. I'm somewhere else, so I must've been out for at least long enough to be moved. No one else is here… this must be her quarters. No, they would be monitored. So where… No, now isn't the time. Frelya is trying to be genuine. I need to listen and not be distracted. I'm only here, wherever that is, because of her.

"It's fine. Just take your time and keep trying."

"It's not fine!" she growled, trying to yank her hand away, but I held on tight.

"It doesn't matter. Just keep talking. Say it before you lose the feeling and can't," I said.

She stopped trying to pull away and took a deep breath. "You're right. I'll keep going. It's… the general believes the same thing. What I thought I did. That we soldiers are different, and better suited to guide humanity to its roots because we hadn't lost what we'd gained from true adversity. Because we were the only ones who truly understood it. That truth made us immune to the disease that had afflicted everyone else here. The softness and self-absorbed indulgences. Dulled senses and a lack of resolve. Something a life of ease and comfort brings. But you…"

She faltered again, stopping when the tears flowed from her eyes. She hated them. I could tell. She wanted them to stop, but she knew they were necessary to stay connected to the feeling.

"I'm here. Please, go on," I said, squeezing her hand again as it trembled.

"I really meant to kill you, but seeing you fight the way you did… It was like seeing myself fighting for my life when they included me in our selection. When they came after me, I led the last two men between a mother bear and her cubs in the forest. I knew the woods better than they did. They had weapons, so they killed her, but both were so terribly mauled they were barely alive. I knew only one winner would be allowed to leave, so I came up behind the one who fared better and bashed his head in with a stone before he could react. The other was already blinded and dying from the attack, so I did the same to him as he begged me for water.

"It's not that I forgot about it, but seeing you fight that way brought the memory back so clearly. What they did to me… I'd convinced myself it made me better but seeing you in my place made me realize it was wrong. It was always wrong. I wasn't the beneficiary of some great gift. I was a victim. Taylor, it hurts to see it for what it is. I feel like everything I am is a lie."

"I know…" I said, though I'd wanted to say more. Wise words like my father would've said, or something to bring clarity, like my mother might have said. I didn't have their gift for words. "Thank you for saving me."

"What you did was foolish. I had to use battlefield trauma treatment to save your bones and tendons. What we have is stronger and works more quickly than what's available to the science divisions, and there are side-effects. You nearly drained your implant, and you're lucky it didn't cook your brain from the inside. I noticed you had other injuries that weren't completely healed yet. Science isn't magic, Taylor. If you do this too often, there'll be consequences. You could drop dead from exhaustion and not even see it coming."

As much as I tried to pay attention to what she was saying, I found her tone amusing.

"Wow, you make a convincing doctor suddenly. Okay, Doc. I'll take all your advice under consideration and try to avoid any other deadly encounters for the next couple of days."

She yanked her hand away from mine.

"Don't lie to me, Taylor. We both know you won't listen to my advice or anyone else's. It's one of those things I like so much about you," she said, finally showing her more typical toothy smile.

I tried to sit up but found I couldn't.

"Frelya… why can't I move?"

"Rapid repair is nearly as painful as rapid damage. Your muscles are selectively isolated, pain relievers applied, and a relaxing agent mixed in. You can't stress them while they're repairing. Remember how I mentioned side-effects? You can't just inject this stuff and go about your business. If it's not done perfectly, damage can be permanent. You should be able to move around in a few hours. Other side-effects will continue for several days, but you'll be able to conceal most of them with effort or blame them on something else."

I breathed a sigh of relief and allowed myself to relax. This was for the best. I was so lucky to have made such wonderful friends. Joyce, Linda, and Frelya. I could trust them with anything. I took a risk by revealing more to Frelya than I ever had anyone else, but that paid off too. None of this would be possible without her. Especially my plan for General Markus.

"You're a genius, Frelya. Speaking of which, there's something I need your help with, and I only trust you to be capable enough to do it. It's asking a lot. So, if you don't want to, I'll—"

"Spare me the lecture. You want me to sabotage the General's big plans. Now that I see things more clearly, I'll help you. Just tell me what you need."

CHAPTER 27

I expected to face skepticism over my overnight training session with Frelya, but no one seemed to find it unusual at all. They weren't even curious. I gathered it was because she'd spent the night there often, but since no one asked me questions, I didn't ask any either.

My first order of business was to inspect the five hundred cats and five hundred dogs beginning the process. It was still early, so they weren't behaving any differently than a regular dog or cat. I wasn't an expert on their behavior in the first place and was happy to let the students from Animal Research looking after them continue to do so. I checked reports, signed off on various things, and found the first half of the day had flown by despite the early start.

My muscles and joints felt miserable, and I remembered the complaints from the elderly people in my village about their various aches and pains. I was still technically a teen, and I empathized with them. I had to step away a few times to vomit, and once I became light-headed and had to sit down. When I was questioned about it by the other Animal Research students, I just said Professor Barth was rubbing off on me, and I was neglecting sleep.

Observing the students now, it was like night and day. Previously, many joined Animal Research because it had a reputation for going easy on those who, while initially joining for the right reasons, just wanted to lounge around and drift through life once they were exposed to the endless luxuries life at PanTech afforded them. Many students spent most of their days in simulations, and Barth had a strict policy that labs were for volunteers only. Now that Animal Research's status had been upgraded, many had been reminded of their passion for animals and crawled out of the woodwork to embrace their new importance. It was good to see, but disheartening that fame motivated so many.

Seeing these cats and dogs made me think of Henry, and I knew they would soon use many of these wonderful creatures as tools of espionage. I could not allow that.

As soon as I was able, I tried to slip away. I needed to find

Joyce. Fortunately for me, I ran straight into her and Linda on my way to the transport.

"Taylor!" Joyce shouted, running and jumping into my arms, hanging off my neck.

Any other time, I'd have wrestled with her and laughed, but the immediate shock of pain that went through my body was almost unbearable. My vision went blurry, and I nearly collapsed. Linda rushed forward and wrapped her arms around my waist to hold me up, prompting Joyce to let go and jump back.

"Taylor, are you alright?" Linda snapped. "What's wrong?"

I shook my head and put a finger over my lips. My first instinct was to lie and say nothing was wrong, but that wouldn't be fair to them.

"I'm pretty beat up, but it's fine now. It's a long story and I'll tell you all of it later. The short of it is I had a long training session with Frelya, and things got a little rough. I was actually on my way to see Joyce."

Linda made a fist and punched her palm. "Where is Frelya? I'm going to have a talk with that crazy woman."

I grabbed her arm, stopping her as she stomped off, causing another surge of pain to shoot through me. This was going to be a little harder to hide than I thought.

"No, you're not, and Frelya is my friend, so please don't say things like that about her. If you get to know her, you'll like her."

"But—" A sharp elbow from Joyce made her stop speaking. "Ouch, what was that—"

"Ignore Ice Princess. I think she's just jealous of how much time you've been spending with Fire Princess," Joyce said.

Why did I have a feeling Frelya would *not* appreciate Joyce's nicknames?

"You said your father worked for the Division of Investigation, right? Let's go see him today, before I get too swamped with these subjects maturing at the same time. I'd love to meet him."

Joyce eyed me with incredulity.

"Say what now? Why do you want to go there of all places?"

I thought of giving them a hint that I worried about being watched. Some kind of subtle nod or twitch. The problem was any of that could be picked up and seen by anyone with access. And one of those people was, of course, General Markus.

"I've been thinking about the whole situation between Professor Barth and Professor Elise, and something just doesn't sit right with me. If Barth stole this research from Elise, then why was she so quiet about it when he gained so much recognition because of it. What if Barth originally did the research, but was afraid to say anything because Elise was the professor of a higher-level division?"

"Um, then why not just ask him, Taylor?" Joyce asked. A frustratingly fair question.

"He won't want to rock the boat, so he'll never tell the truth about it. Things are going too well for him right now to stir up anything. Besides, Elise helped us a lot with adapting this research on animals."

"Then why rock the boat ourselves, Taylor? Even if Barth did the original research, if he's content with leaving it alone, then why wouldn't we?"

I should've known I couldn't win a debate with Joyce…

"Look, what if I told you it was all an excuse to give you a chance to go meet your father without having to go through all the red tape? I'm an assistant professor, so I can walk you straight there with no questions asked. You also made him sound like a really interesting man, and he sounds a lot like my father. I'd like to meet him. Is that a strong enough hint for you?"

Joyce rubbed her forehead. "Sometimes I just don't get you, Taylor, but you're so sweet sometimes I could just lick you. Okay, let's do it. Linda will be right at home with the rough crowd here anyway. By the time we get back, she'll be walking around in a power suit asking us to state our business."

"Or maybe they'll be so impressed with my intellect that they'll wonder why they needed you here. They may tell you to go back to Animal Research and catch a nap while the real prodigy handles things."

Joyce gave Linda a hug, surprising her.

"You be a good girl while we're gone, okay? Don't get into trouble. Look, I'm not joking. You and Taylor are losing your minds and running all over the place, when you should just be enjoying a peaceful life. When am I going to get dragged into one of these big adventures, anyway? I'm feeling kind of left out."

Oh, if only she knew…

~~o~o~o~~

The Division of Investigation was so empty, I nearly thought I was in the wrong place. It was still larger than any building I'd seen before transferring here, but even Animal Research dwarfed it by comparison. Unlike other divisions we'd visited, no one was even there to greet us when we stepped off the transport. We waited several minutes before a young man walked by with a cup of coffee in his hand, thinking of a faraway place. He walked right by us without even noticing.

"Ahem!" Joyce shouted. I wasn't sure if that was supposed to sound like clearing her throat, but it came out more like her just yelling the word.

The young man jumped, spilling a bit of coffee on his suit.

"Hey! Do you mind?" he said, frantically pulling a cloth from his jacket pocket and dabbing off the drops of coffee.

"Mind what?" Joyce asked, stomping her foot. "Are you so busy you don't even notice two beautiful young ladies standing here waiting for help?"

The man pushed his glasses up his nose and ran his fingers through his curly red hair, pushing it back into place. His demeanor changed completely. He looked both of us up and down with his cold blue eyes.

"Oh, my goodness, please forgive me. I didn't realize there were two beautiful young women here to see little me, and you look to be about my age. So, which one of you is my date… or is it both? Sounds like a lot of work, but I'm fine with that. Lot of men in this place, so the choices are slim. I'll be the talk of the entire division with a pretty girl on each arm."

"Oh, would you…" Joyce held up her finger, but for once couldn't find the words to finish her sentence.

"Oh, I see. Then how about you two beauties walk about a hundred steps forward and look at the big sign in the middle of the floor. It has every investigator's name and office number. Help yourself."

He adjusted his tie and walked away, mumbling something about his new suit.

Joyce looked at me and shook her head.

"Don't look at me. You're the one that pulled the beauty

card," I said, smiling. "I'm going to guess he had something besides girls on his mind."

"Apparently. Well, he helped us at least. My father's name is Croshaw. Let's go find his name on the board."

We found the board and found his name close to the top.

"A senior investigator, huh? Are you excited to see him?" I asked.

"Not really. No more excited than I would be to meet anyone else. He left Mom and I to join PanTech when my mom was pregnant. He didn't even know about me, and probably still doesn't. It's not like I know him. I have pictures from when he was eighteen, but he probably looks a lot different now. Mother always went on and on about what a great man he was, but… your stories about your dad sound a lot more interesting."

Uh, Taylor, you're such an idiot sometimes… Of course, if he's here, she must've grown up without him.

I was so distracted with everything going on that something this obvious slipped right past me.

"I'm sorry, Joyce… do you want to go back?" I asked.

She shook her head and punched me in the shoulder. I did my best to conceal the pain, but she immediately apologized.

"Sorry! And no, I really want to meet him. I'm sad about growing up without him but holding that against him would be unfair. My mom said she encouraged him to go, even though she failed the exam. She didn't realize she was pregnant until after he left, so how could I blame him? It's time for me to let those bitter feelings go and give him a chance, you know? It's rare for someone to have parents here, for obvious reasons. We can't have children once we join, so they had to have the kids while still in their zone."

"Okay, well, I'm here for you," I said, awkwardly maneuvering to hug her in a way that didn't make my bones feel like they were exploding. It only somewhat worked.

She smiled and nodded, and we made our way to his office.

When we arrived, we both looked at each other and I gestured to the door.

Joyce smiled and took a deep breath before knocking.

"Come in," a deep voice came from the other side.

With another deep breath and exhale, then another, Joyce opened the door.

CHAPTER 28

Without looking up, the man at the desk clicked away at a long, flat device with his fingertips. He stared intently at a screen in front of him, as though he couldn't spare even a moment of time. Not even for important visitors. His own daughter, even. His appearance was striking. He was an unusually handsome man, and I immediately saw the connection with Joyce. Despite his dark expression, he looked very young. Far too young to be the father of my friend standing next to me. Then again, he would only be in his mid-thirties.

"Investigator Croshaw?" I asked, just breaking the silence.

"Just like the sign on the door says," he replied, finally looking up. "How can I help—"

He froze as his eyes moved from me to Joyce.

Joyce opened her mouth to speak with a smile, but the smile quickly faded, and she looked away.

An uncomfortable silence filled the room, and I didn't have the courage to break it, despite the urgency of the visit. I just stood there, looking down at my feet, waiting for one of them to find the words. After a full minute, Croshaw spoke first.

"Do you hate me?" he asked, his voice soft and quiet.

"Do you feel anything for me at all? Based on your question, you knew I was here and who I was. Investigators can move freely between nearly all divisions. Why didn't you come find me?" Joyce snapped.

More uncomfortable silence.

"I didn't think you'd want to see me. Besides a blood connection, no other connection exists between us. We're no different from any other strangers meeting. You left behind a promising career as an attorney and animal rights activist, so you understand what it means to cut ties."

His tone was so cold, but it didn't match his words.

"Do you research the history of every new arrival at PanTech like that?" I asked.

More silence. This man didn't like to speak before he considered his words.

"I'm sorry. For having to grow up without a father, not my actions. Lost time can't be made up for, and it's pointless to apologize for a choice I didn't make," he said.

"I didn't come here to make you apologize or guilt trip you! I know it wasn't your fault. Don't put words in my mouth. Did I say one word about your past? I just wanted to meet my dad, because Mom made you sound like the coolest guy who ever lived," Joyce said, raising her voice to a shout. She clenched her fists tightly, so I placed my hand on her shoulder.

He was quiet again. It must make everyone uncomfortable, the way he would pause so long between responses. Maybe it's something he's developed over time.

"Your mom was the coolest person I'd ever met. Way cooler than me. I've been afraid to ask, but could you tell me if she's had a good life?"

Joyce nodded. "We struggled at first, but Mom is happiest when she makes the people around her happy. She passed her exam to practice law on her fifth attempt. I chose that path because of her. She was always so proud of you for having the courage to leave your life behind and join PanTech, and she was excited for me, too. Didn't just pretend to be. She really was. Said she hoped you moved on and found someone else, and not to mention her to you if we met."

He laughed, and the smile stuck.

"See? How in the world am I ever supposed to move on after being with a woman like that? She's ruined my expectations. No other woman I've met has compared. That'll be my one complaint to her if I ever see her again. I've married my work instead."

Joyce mirrored his smile. "No offense, but I have to agree. Mom is definitely cooler than you."

"None taken. Now, would the two of you like to have a seat?"

Joyce nodded, and the two of us sat down in the leather chairs in front of his desk.

"What's that thing you were clicking on when we came in?" I asked.

"Oh, this? It's called a keyboard. Ancient relic as far as PanTech is concerned, but it was what I got used to in my zone. I'm one of those old-fashioned men who can never adapt to certain things. Set in my ways. Fortunately, they accommodate me and adapted my system to the current interface. But I assume that's not why you're here."

"We're here because, for some strange reason, my friend here wants to investigate the origin of the foundational research we used for the animal evolution project we're currently overseeing with Adversity Management," Joyce said, tilting her head toward me.

"Oh? Well, we're not private investigators here, and I can't spare the time for unofficial work. Sorry you came all this way."

Now it was my turn to be uncomfortably silent.

"Are you okay, Taylor?" Joyce asked.

"Investigator Croshaw, is this room under surveillance? Sorry, I just don't want to implicate my division. You understand. I'm an assistant professor, after all."

He reached under his desk, and I heard a click.

"As I said, I'm old-fashioned. From now, you can speak freely. I've shut off all monitoring in this room."

I breathed a sigh of relief, reached into my pocket, and tossed a device no bigger than a coin on his desk.

"Do you know what that is?" I asked.

"You didn't come here to talk about some dispute between professors, did you?"

I shook my head, and Joyce twisted in her chair, giving me a look of pure shock.

"You mean you lied to me about all that?" Joyce asked, sounding hurt.

"I didn't have a choice. Besides, didn't you ask when I was going to involve you in one of our crazy adventures? Well, this is the craziest one yet, and you're involved. Congratulations."

Joyce stood up, ruffling her big, curly hair.

"I was being sarcastic. Oh man, this is big, isn't it? You and Linda, then Frelya, now me... what have you gotten yourself into?"

Croshaw nodded, signaling his agreement with Joyce's question. However, his expression changed again. He looked sharp. Excited, even. Not the least bit distracted anymore.

"General Markus is plotting a military coup of PanTech," I said.

Croshaw burst out laughing. "That old reliable pillar of the PanTech community? The president's dear friend and most loyal division leader? Here I thought I was boring, but compared to that guy, I'm basically a party animal. You must be pulling my leg here."

I shook my head. "Sorry. I'm not."

"Okay then. Tell me how you know," he said, leaning back in his chair and crossing his arms.

"…My falcon told me," I said, knowing full well how it would sound.

Croshaw put his hand over his mouth, then looked to Joyce.

"Where did you find this one? You have some interesting friends. You're literally saying a little birdie told you? Never heard that used other than a figure of speech, or is that how you mean it? You don't want to reveal your source, then?"

Joyce sighed. "No, Dad, she actually means an actual bird, and not just any bird. It's a shadowfalcon. Basically, a mythical creature that was a legend in her zone. He was the third animal we used in the evolution project. He can talk. In fact, he's probably more intelligent than we are."

Croshaw's smile faded, and his arms slowly relaxed to his side. Time for more uncomfortable silence.

"When is this insurrection to occur?"

"I don't know," I said. "I have someone on the inside of Adversity Management, part of his inner circle, who will use my falcon to monitor their next meeting."

"How in the world did you install such advanced surveillance technology into the nervous system of this animal without the general knowing? This is cutting edge. Even by PanTech's standards, I've seen nothing like it. Does Adversity Management really have someone like that designing their tech?"

"They have two people like that. At least," I said.

"Two?" he repeated.

"The general, I assume, designed the technology himself. He's been wanting to use it for some time to spy on residents of adversity zones. He saw our research as an opportunity to make that a reality. Intelligent animals are the perfect spies to carry this technology and spread it throughout those communities, and probably here too eventually. My falcon is the first to be outfitted with it."

Croshaw rubbed his temples. "I have so many questions, but let's go with the most important two. How did your falcon tell you if he's constantly under surveillance, and how did you get your hands on a device that can monitor it in real time?"

"Ghost is his name," I said. "Now that I've explained *what* he is, let's call him that from now on. He could tell me because we were attacked by an electromagnetic jammer outside the walls by one of the lost old machines that patrols out there. As for the device that monitors in real time—"

Croshaw held up his hands. "Slow down. Give me a moment to process all this before we move on to the next thing. I have to go through this slowly or I'll lose details. I can't take notes on this, obviously."

He sat quietly for another couple of minutes, looking down at his hands, almost meditating.

"Okay, the device," he said, waving his hand for me to continue.

"My friend inside Adversity Management put together the device. She reverse engineered the tech and created an undetectable way to monitor it in real time. Essentially, it's a way of doubling the signal, and rerouting the second signal somewhere else. I didn't want it to be stored and delivered, even though that would be safer. Too many ways to claim it's been fabricated. It needed to be seen in real time and by a particular person. That's why I'm here."

Croshaw passed a hand over his clean-shaven face, rubbing several times over his short hair. "You want *me*, a simple investigator, to somehow have this chip in the president's presence. At the time of the next meeting, and you don't know when it will happen."

"Sorry," I said. "I don't know what else to do. If anyone else relays the news to the president, he won't believe it. Markus is his friend. His only real friend, as far as I can tell. He's lived a long time, too. He will be skeptical of anything other than his own eyes and ears."

"I hate to disappoint you, but this is impossible for me," he said.

Joyce and I looked at one another, but neither of us knew what to say. All this planning, and with so much on the line, only to reach a dead end.

"I'll think of something…" I said, rising to my feet. "I have good friends like your daughter who have helped me through everything so far. Somehow… I don't know. I'll find some other way."

Croshaw grinned and pointed to the chair. "Have a seat. I only said that *I* couldn't do it, not that I couldn't see it done." He pressed a finger to his lips, and with the other hand, pressed a button on top of his desk. "Daniel, please come to my office. I've got an assignment for you."

"It's about time!" a voice broadcast through a small speaker. He really was old-fashioned. Not even a sound field in here.

Only a few seconds later, the door opened wide, revealing the red-haired man we'd met from before. Joyce immediately shielded her face with her hands, embarrassed.

"Well, if it isn't the pair of visiting beauties. How can I be of service to such esteemed guests?" he said, clearly enjoying his unexpected opportunity to rub in Joyce's comment from before.

"Careful, Daniel, the one covering her face is my daughter. I expect you to be on your best behavior," Croshaw said, pointing at Daniel, his stern voice surprising everyone.

Then he and Daniel both broke out into laughter. What was happening?

Joyce was now covering her face completely. I thought nothing in the entire world could embarrass her. Seems Croshaw instinctively knew his daughter better than I did, without even meeting her before.

"Kill me now," Daniel said. "What have I done to deserve this? But first, tell me what *this* is."

"Oh, you're going to want to be sitting down for this. Go ahead. Tell him everything you just told me," Croshaw said, as Daniel sat in a chair on the side of the room and crossed his legs.

CHAPTER 29

A few days had passed, and I was becoming anxious. It gave me opportunities to explain everything to Linda, at least, but the longer it took for the general to call together his loyalists for their next meeting, the more likely it became for him to figure out something was up. I handed Ghost over to Frelya to "complete his rehabilitation," and he seemed instinctively to understand. He never once slipped up or said anything that would even remotely raise suspicion. I underestimated his intelligence when doing the procedure on him, and I suspected we ended up with a higher than human level of intelligence. It might irritate Barth, but I was relieved to have allies who were smarter than me. I wouldn't have made it this far if that wasn't the case.

As for Daniel, it turned out he once worked in the president's building. There, he foiled a flimsy plot to poison him. After that, Daniel realized he enjoyed that kind of thing and asked to be transferred to the Department of Investigations, only to find himself disappointed by the lack of action there. Since he once worked there and the president was fond of him, it wouldn't raise suspicion for him to go there. Though, it surprised all of us when Daniel insisted he would need a partner to make sure he could pull all of this off, and then insisted that partner be Joyce. Joyce, always a clever opportunist, agreed before he had a chance to call it a joke or change his mind. They've even been producing a fake paper trail about the origins of the brain density research and prying eyes had already started spreading rumors about it. Though, like everything else, if something didn't happen soon, it would become a problem to keep it up for a long time.

Fortunately, that day never came.

In the late-night hours, a signal was sent to activate the monitoring device in my possession. I could only assume the other one I'd given to Daniel was activated as well. I had to hope that he and Joyce got it to the president or placed it somewhere it would get his attention.

I jolted to sitting in my bed and shook Linda awake beside me. She had insisted on being by my side until the time came and was afraid she'd miss out on the action. She'd left Henry alone, and despite his protest, he was doing fine. With the building anxiety, I had to admit it was a relief to have someone with me.

"What is it? Is it time?" she asked casually, rubbing her eyes.

I fumbled with the glasses beside my bed, dropping them twice on my lap while trying to sync them with the monitoring device. "Yes. Yes. I think so."

Linda placed her hand on my forearm. "Breathe, Taylor. It's going to be alright."

I took several deep breaths, trying to slow myself down. Once my glasses were activated, I grabbed the second pair and synced them for Linda.

I could see and hear what Ghost saw and heard. It was disorienting, how real it was, and difficult to focus on what was actually in front of me, although the image was transparent.

I knew PanTech could monitor the room, so I held my tongue. I was scared, but I trusted Frelya and Ghost to pull it off. So many things could go wrong.

Ghost perched on Frelya's shoulder, bouncing slightly as they walked. She didn't walk far. I recognized this place. Frelya's training ground! No wonder there wasn't any surveillance there. Several commanders were already there, sitting and talking amongst themselves. They nodded politely to Frelya and continued their chat. In the next few moments, several more arrived. There were so many. I hadn't expected he'd created such a large group of supporters for his scheme. If this many armed commanders were to attack all at once, without warning, they might succeed even if they launched the attack tonight. Many of them had physical enhancer implants. No, most likely these did.

"Look sharp, Neri. Brevin. The general will be here shortly, and the two of you look like you're having a picnic under the moonlight. You're supposed to be our lookouts. Act like it," Frelya said sharply.

"Why don't you just use the bird for that, *Your Royal Highness*?" the blonde-haired woman called Neri said. "Besides, unless some moron gets followed, no one's going to stumble upon this place. So, take your tough-girl attitude and shove it."

"What did you say to me?" Frelya snapped. "Stand up and

show me if you can back up your insults."

I appreciated Frelya's dedicated to not being suspicious, but a fight right now might seriously endanger this whole thing. What should I do?

No. Calm down, Taylor. Trust her. She knows what she's doing.

Neri snapped to her feet, with Brevin grabbing her arm.

"She's just goading you. Stop taking everything so personally. Do you really think she's going to fight you with that precious falcon on her shoulder? And what would the general say if you accidentally killed it? Just sit back down."

With a dramatic sigh, she did just that.

With the sudden rush of relief, I let out an enormous sigh of my own.

"Stop bickering. What part of 'wait quietly' do all of you not understand?"

Another commander, with about eight more Ghost hadn't spotted yet. He scanned the area, as though he were reading my mind. Ten. Thirteen. No, seventeen commanders. Another just walked in. Eighteen. Oh no…

Linda gripped my arm, and I could feel her hand trembling.

If Frelya gets caught now, she'll die for sure.

Please don't get caught. Please don't get caught. This can't happen again.

Thoughts of Linus filled my mind, as they often did, but now wasn't the time to get caught up in them. I would never let that happen again. I grabbed my blanket and threw it off, but Linda's grip tightened on my arm. Instinctively, I tried to yank it away, but she held firm.

I looked at her, but she only shook her head.

I clenched my fists, but I understood. I kept telling myself to trust Frelya. Trust my friends.

A familiar voice.

"That's alright, Olaf. It's a character trait I admire in them. They are fiery and bold. Many wars have been won on the backs of such warriors."

It was the general, and he didn't appear to be suspicious at all, but would he? Even if he knew everything, would even a muscle on his face move to give it away?

He was in his power armor, but so was everyone else, Frelya

included. It seemed they were prepared to fight if they were to be discovered. Twenty-five commanders and the general.

"It looks like everyone is here, so let's begin as we always do," he said, snapping to a sharp salute, which everyone mirrored in perfect unity. "While others may call us traitors, those of us here are the most loyal members of PanTech. We adhere to the core values of what made this organization great, and saw it rise to rule the world. Though others have lost their way, burying their nose in scientific experiments that make us stray further and further from our grit, we steel ourselves and keep the philosophy of adversity close to our hearts. We shield ourselves from excess and train our bodies and minds to remain strong. Soon, we will renew this ideal humanity across all PanTech and create an environment of true adversity for the zones we manage. They exist for no other reason than to facilitate growth of the ideal human being, and it is time we remember that."

He smiled, nodding his head. "But that's not what all of you want to hear. You already know all of this. Strategy. A date and time for true action. That's what excellent soldiers concern themselves with. I ask all of you to be a bit more patient. If we were to attack now, we would no doubt suffer casualties, and with such a small group, we cannot afford to lose even a single one of you. You are too precious. However, we are close. Twenty-five of you, there are currently. I am scouting two more commanders presently, and I'm reviewing your suggestions regularly. With five more commanders, we should be able to accomplish a perfect victory without a single human loss."

Several of the commanders looked at each other but hesitated to speak.

"General, not to contradict you, but…" Neri said, gathering her thoughts.

"Don't be afraid to speak freely, Neri. You wouldn't be here if you weren't worthy of having your thoughts heard."

"It's just that I don't understand how we'll be able to do something like that without a single casualty."

General Markus raised his finger into the air. "Ah, but you didn't listen carefully, Neri. I didn't say there wouldn't be casualties."

Neri tilted her head, trying to understand.

"You mean…"

"Yes, in one month we will have about a thousand new recruits. Within two months, they will be trained. Within three, they will be armed. The best time to act is when victory is certain."

I felt faint. I felt sick. He never intended to use them for spying. Only Ghost was outfitted that way. He always meant the rest to be highly impressionable, intelligent, and expendable soldiers to accomplish his military coup with an overwhelming victory. This was far worse than I could have ever imagined. Those poor animals, slaves to such an evil man without even knowing. He was going to sacrifice them, and then use whatever's left to do something with the zones. No, he'll make even more! Tens of thousands could be ready in less than a year. Would he use them for his sick war games he mentioned for the zones? I never imagined it could be this bad… I had to—

"Stop. Silent, everyone," he said, lowering his head. After a moment of silence, he mumbled. "But how… Everyone, leave this area immediately, but quietly and orderly."

Neri was the closest to the entrance and raised her hand to open the gate. It wouldn't budge.

"General?" she asked, looking panicked.

His attention snapped to Ghost. "Frelya, kill that bird right now!"

"Fly, Ghost. You know what to do!" Frelya shouted, shaking Ghost from her arm and sending him into the air.

In an instant, the broadcast changed from Ghost's eyes to Frelya's helmet.

The general drew his sidearm and aimed, then fired. I held my breath and clenched my teeth. I felt time stand still.

But, by some miracle, he missed. No, not a miracle.

"What's happening to our suits?" one commander shouted.

Then, the general showed emotion for the first time since I'd met him. I could hear the subtle change in his voice as he pointed to Frelya.

"Our suits have been forced into low-power mode, and we can't switch out. But don't panic! There's twenty-five of us, and only one of her. Even at full power, she can't kill more than three or four of us before we take her down. Frelya!"

"Come on, then! By the time I'm done with all of you, there won't be enough ashes to spread into the wind!" Frelya shouted.

Another shot. This one hit true, right into the face of Frelya's helmet. Everything went dark.

I flung myself from my bed, falling onto the floor before making it to my feet. I grabbed Twisted Key and rushed for the door, Linda not three steps behind me, sprinting to keep up.

I had to make it in time. I had to. Even if I could only make a slight difference, this time I wouldn't let anyone hold me back. No one else was going to die for my choices.

Just hang on, Frelya!

CHAPTER 30

Each leg of the trip took only seconds, but they passed so slowly they could've been hours. I hadn't even taken the time to change clothes, so Linda and I were rushing into battle wearing only our pajamas and bare feet. Linda never hesitated, even for one moment, to follow me. She only took a moment to pick up a blaster she'd kept from our encounter with the machine. Twenty-four commanders and the general… what were we doing? There was no way we were going to make it out of this alive.

No, it didn't matter. We had to. Somehow, we had to. We just needed to buy time. Keep them there until the president sent someone to help. Surely there was someone he could send.

For the first time since coming here, I wished the transport pod would move faster. When the doors opened, I jumped through them.

"We need to avoid being seen if we can, and don't talk to anyone," I said.

"What? Shouldn't we tell everyone?" Linda said, nearly shouting before lowering her voice.

"Think about it. None of them will know anything about the general's plan. If other commanders show up, he'll just say Frelya is a traitor, and the commanders will help him and make everything worse. We have to do this ourselves."

Linda nodded as we continued to run.

When we arrived at the door leading into the training area, Ghost swooped down in front of us.

"Enter quickly if you must, but it will shut tight behind you and you won't be able to leave," he said.

"Is Frelya still alive?" I asked.

"She is alive," he replied calmly.

"Then we're going in. Ghost, I'm going to create an opening in General Markus's armor. Do you think you can apply your toxin if I can?"

"I will read your intentions and act as I always have. Waste no more time speaking to me," he said, taking to the air again.

He was right. I never needed to have a conversation with him to discuss plans before, and I didn't need to now. There wasn't time.

We rushed through the door, and I immediately tripped over something and fell to the ground. Linda jumped over me and reached out her hand to help me to my feet. It was a body. Several. There were three by the door. Frelya must've used it as bait and killed them as they tried to open it.

General Markus immediately noticed as we entered, as he exchanged gunfire with Frelya from behind a pillar for cover. I didn't expect him to be so concerned with defense. It must be because his suit can't compete with one running at full power, despite his being unique. It was larger than the others, and deep black. Additional machinery flowed beneath the heavily armored plates. I could see several burned spots on the torso of his armor, even from the gate. Direct hits had done no damage.

I prepared myself to rush in for an attack while Frelya had him pinned down, but we immediately started taking fire from the other commanders. Linda retreated behind a pillar, and I was about to do the same.

"Taylor, clear the door!" Frelya shouted. She'd discarded her helmet, and her suit showed signs of heavy damage. She held a long rifle in each hand and was shooting in different directions. Her flame-red hair blew around with each shot. She looked... amazing. Like a fictional hero.

"Now! Use this chance to jam the door," Markus shouted.

A soldier ran toward the door as I crouched behind the bodies for cover. A shot to the head ended his charge, and he fell near the others.

"Neri, go! I'll handle Frelya!" he shouted, finally coming out from behind the cover to advance. His movements were much quicker now. Somehow, he'd brought his suit out of low-power mode. It didn't seem it had returned to full, but he was undoing it.

I couldn't tell any of them apart, but I remembered Neri as the blonde-haired woman Frelya argued with earlier. Now, she had her helmet on, though part of her face was visible through the damage.

As General Markus took shot after shot from Frelya and continued advancing toward her, she had no choice but to flee to a different spot. It was no good. My surprise attack I'd meant for the general would have to be used for her. Then I'd have to clear the door. The shots in my direction ceased as she approached, and she stood above me.

"Come to battle with that old sword in your pajamas? I'd let you go out of pity, but I'm aware of who you are, and I know you had something to do with all this or you wouldn't be here."

She raised her blaster. As she did, I focused every ounce of power the implant could provide on my left leg and right arm. I didn't care if it destroyed my limbs or killed me. I would get only one chance at this. There was no room for error.

I stepped forward, propelled by my left foot. A pain shot through my leg, and then through my entire body. It felt as though I'd kicked the world behind me. I could barely keep up with my own speed. I'd have to aim for a weak spot in the armor. The small seam in her torso, a crack from one of Frelya's shots, would serve as an almost impossibly small target. The momentum carried me into range. I couldn't afford to lose the power by manipulating my nervous system, so I'd have to withstand the pain. With my right arm, I thrust the blade forward. My wrist broke as the tip of the blade met resistance, but I commanded every muscle to continue gripping the sword tightly. In an instant, the armor gave way and the sword pierced her chest. Once it had penetrated, I turned the blade toward her heart. I found my mark and withdrew it quickly.

"How… When…" she choked out the words before collapsing to the ground, dead. My face felt as if it would melt, and my left leg collapsed. The hum of the gate's motor pressed it against the body that had fallen in the way. I had to clear it. Somehow. Instinctively, I tried to grab it with my right arm, but it didn't respond at all. I'd have to use the left. Just a little more. I only needed a little more. I gripped the soldier's leg with my left hand and sweat poured from my face. How high was my body temperature now? It didn't matter. I pulled with all my might and cleared the body from the door, punctuated by the gate's slam echoing through the area.

This was it. I tried to stand but couldn't. All I'd done was fall in between two of the bodies to save myself from the resumed firing of blaster shots. I tried to control my breathing and hoped I wouldn't go into shock. This must be what it felt like to burn alive. All I could do was watch now.

Linda would carefully fire from behind her cover occasionally to distract the other commanders, but it was still Frelya doing most of the real fighting. She must've had some suspicion things would turn out this way because she rigged the entire area with traps. From what I could tell, eight commanders were dead. Nine, counting the one I killed. Many others were badly wounded and relying on their suits to keep them alive, which weakened their function even further. They worked together brilliantly to pursue her but couldn't rush her blindly. She stayed one step ahead, firing shots only in obvious opportunities.

I was being ignored completely now that everyone realized I was no longer a threat.

In a blur, the general appeared in my peripheral vision. With a swipe of his arm, he shattered the pillar Linda was hiding behind, sending her flying back with the debris. She landed hard on her back, but held up the blaster, aiming carefully. She placed two shots at the lower front of his helmet as he stepped forward, crushing one of her legs. She screamed, but still got a third shot on his helmet.

"I've restored my suit's power, so this will only take a moment more. I suppose you're aiming for my respirator to force me to remove my helmet, but it will take a lot more than the power from that blaster to even leave a scratch. You're a true prodigy with that blaster, it seems, which makes this even more painful for me," he said, reaching down and grabbing her hand, still holding the blaster. With a squeeze, he crushed the blaster and her hand along with it. She screamed again, but all I could do was scream too.

A massive blast hit the general and knocked him to the ground. I could see Frelya standing on a pillar on the opposite end of the training grounds. She was holding an even bigger rifle. Surely that did something!

Despite a direct hit, he stood up quickly. Although smoke billowed from the surface of his armor, it was completely undamaged.

"Enough of this! Everyone, discard your blasters and attack Frelya all at once. She's the only threat. We don't have time to waste. I'll take care of the gate while the rest of you handle her. She's just one woman."

Seeing the charge of all the remaining commanders was truly frightening. There's no way she could take them all at once, even if her traps killed many of them. With another shot of the huge rifle, another commander fell where they stood, their armor obliterated. Another shot, then another dead. The general's armor must be something amazing to have taken no damage.

He kicked the bodies aside, and me with it.

"Don't worry. Once I get this door open, I'll still make time to take care of you, Taylor. Directly, as I should've done before." He slipped his fingers into the gate's seam and pried. Nothing happened at first, but then it spread apart little by little. It was no use. He was going to win. He was going to get away.

A loud slam echoed behind him. As he turned to see what it was, Frelya swung the rifle into the side of his head like a giant club, knocking him to the ground again. She fired three pointblank shots into his helmet, wounding herself in the process and filling the area with smoke and dust.

I wanted to believe that was enough to kill him, but I had a sinking feeling it wasn't.

Frelya had activated a partition in the training ground and had trapped all the other commanders on the other side of it. Now it was only us and the general.

A hand emerged and grabbed her by the neck, lifting her into the air.

"Frelya!" I shouted. I had to do something. I couldn't let this happen.

I crawled over and grabbed the leg of his armor. My vision doubled, and I vomited. All my limbs were numb, but I was still holding on to him. My sensation of touch was gone. I knew this feeling. I might die soon.

"Why, Frelya? You were the most loyal of everyone. I thought you understood. I treated you like my daughter. Your betrayal is the worst pain I could ever feel."

Frelya let go of his gauntlet and reached toward me. I couldn't make her hand out clearly, and he hadn't even noticed. Instead of answering, she spat in his face.

"I see. It turns out you were never brave. You're just wild, like a rabid animal. You lash out and fight randomly, and, worst of all, you were swayed by the lies of one girl."

Something propelled the tip of Twisted Key upward. The bulk of the general's armor had limited his ability to see her arm's movement so close. I had been holding the sword in my hand and didn't even realize it. I didn't even feel her pull it from my grasp. It stabbed against the front of his helmet but couldn't penetrate it. Even with the unusual durability of the sword, and Frelya's amazing strength behind it, it wasn't enough!

"Oh well, it was a nice effort on your part. Your plan nearly worked. This battle has helped me realize my new suit is powerful enough for me to accomplish this takeover all on my own. Goodbye, Frel—"

I couldn't see what it was. A shift in the light. A puff of smoke. Something passed between them.

General Markus made a horrible noise, like he was trying to blow his nose inside his helmet. He dropped Frelya and threw his hands up to his face. He tried to remove it, but his hands froze.

"What… was…? I can't…."

Ghost landed next to me. Had he done something?

The general turned and looked down at both of us but froze in place. He couldn't move. A liquid dripped from the respirator on his helmet. I understood! Ghost must have splashed his neurotoxin into the respirator, and he'd absorbed it into his bloodstream. No, that wasn't it… It was more than that.

Markus coughed but managed a laugh. Faint at first, then louder and louder.

"You're through," I said. "No one can move with Ghost's toxin in their bloodstream."

"Silly child. All I require is brain function to pilot this suit. This is only a mild discomfort. If I stay in my suit until it wears off, your last-ditch trick has accomplished nothing. Though I have no more time to waste on you. It looks like you have little time left yourself," he said, stepping over me, back to the door.

With a surge of power, he opened the doors wide. He took one step through them and fell forward.

He didn't move.

No one knew Ghost better than me. My people had stories about shadowfalcons, and this particular one turned out to be true. Dripped into a wound, their toxin would paralyze its victim. But whenever the shadowfalcon was about to be killed, it would swallow its own toxin, and when it did, their heart would stop soon after.

I closed my eyes as the sound of countless footsteps approached.

We'd done it.

We'd won.

CHAPTER 31

"A fascinating solution," a man's voice said.

"Your compliments are worthless to me, but thank you all the same, Professor," a woman's voice replied.

"Oh, come now. Isn't it somewhat rude to criticize me for lacking in *your* personal specialty?" he said.

"I'm not criticizing your lack of knowledge in my personal specialty, *Professor*. I just don't really understand… why you're here, if I'm being honest."

I could hear him gasp.

"This is my assistant professor. Of course I'm going to be here to—"

"Piggyback off her accomplishments. I know. You're a man who is very easy to read."

"No, I am *not* here to piggyback off her accomplishments. How rude. Besides, if it's such an issue for me to be here, what about these other two girls? They're—"

"Her friends."

He sighed. "Then what about this loud red-haired woman who keeps stomping in and out of here, shouting at random people, and nearly knocked me down when I passed her this morning?"

"You mean her other friend?"

"Fine. Perhaps I'm her friend too. Had you considered that?"

The woman chuckled.

"No. That's a good one, Barth. No, I hadn't considered that. I don't think anyone had."

Barth? I tried to open my eyes, and I could feel them flutter. Not quite.

"What is the progress on this girl's treatment?"

An unfamiliar voice.

"Thank you for stopping by, President. The doctors are administering the agent to wake her now. If you can spare a few minutes, I think you'll be able to see it yourself."

The door opened and closed again.

"Is she awake yet, or what?"

A loud woman's voice. No mistaking this one.

"You're still this impatient? You and I developed the treatment to save her brain, or don't you remember? If you hadn't reprogrammed the thing, the permanent damage would've been much worse. Can't you be satisfied that we've turned a multi-year process into one that's only taken three months?"

Three months!

I finally opened my eyes and struggled to speak words. Everyone crowded around me. Elise, Barth, and Frelya. Then Linda and Joyce popped in too. Amazing. They'd been sitting quietly the whole time.

"General Markus…" I said. I should've said something more positive, but it was the only thing on my mind. "Is he…"

"Dead?" the president asked. "No. That suit of his restarted his heart as we arrived, but it gave us the opportunity we needed to immobilize him and remove it. Once it was removed, his implant couldn't override the shadowfalcon's toxin. We applied a device to keep his heart beating."

"W—why?" I choked as Elise handed me some water. I eagerly drank it and felt much better.

"Why did I spare his life? There are no executions here at PanTech, and there are no exceptions to this rule. He's only lost his way. In time, his reeducation will take hold."

"The animals…" I said, still having trouble speaking. It was like learning to speak all over again.

"Yes, the experiments. I learned that he'd intended to use them as expendable soldiers. I don't find that to be a bad idea. However, considering you are the assistant professor overseeing this project, and given the effort you put into saving both myself and this organization, I will respect our philosophical differences and allow you the final decision on what purpose they will serve. For now, they are undergoing training as was originally planned, but you are welcome to end this training at any time. I leave the rest to you. Once you've recovered fully, you may oversee it in person. Oh, and pardon me, Professor. I believe I referred to you incorrectly as an assistant professor."

"Stop the training," I said. "They will be companions from now on. Assistants and friends."

"As you wish," he said, leaning forward on his cane and standing to his feet with an audible grunt. "I have thought of a new division for you to lead. Recover and I will explain the rest later. For now, it isn't important. You may involve the animals too if you wish. I'm very busy, so I'm afraid this is goodbye."

He said nothing else before leaving. After which, I was crowded by everyone. Their voices mostly blended together, but I was so happy that everyone survived.

~~o~o~o~~

Recovery was difficult, but I managed it with the support of my great friends and the genius minds of Frelya and Elise.

Henry took it upon himself to be my personal nurse and was a quick learner from the actual nurses. Though, most of the time they seemed far more preoccupied with laughing with him instead of helping me. Not that I blamed them.

Ghost and I finally talked more, and his personality was fascinating. His monotone speech made it difficult to read his intentions. He remembered our original meeting clearly and thanked me for stopping him from killing himself. He revealed that he'd been studying our language and learning about our behavior for quite some time. Long before he could communicate. Though, he'd very much taken a liking to Frelya, and requested we visit her often.

Frelya was the one person the other commanders expected the president to make the new general. However, in a surprise decision, he declared the post to be removed. There wouldn't be another general. Instead, commanders would be given more independence. They'd submit reports directly to the president's office regularly to be evaluated. She was actually relieved by this because she'd intended to turn it down. Frelya was often interrupting my treatment sessions and shooing the other nurses away. I thought it was annoying at first, but soon looked forward to it.

Linda took over as the new assistant professor of Animal Research. She'd completely gotten over her fear of authority figures, and I was told she challenged him often. Barth, surprisingly, was very welcoming of these challenges. He was now the professor of one of the major divisions and was graced with visits from the president. In person, no less.

Joyce took a surprising liking to Daniel, and the two became a well-known team. Infamous might be a better way to describe it. Though we'd all assumed it was temporary, Joyce officially transferred divisions. Since then, I didn't see her much anymore, though the two of us would talk from time to time. I was happy to hear her talk about her father more and more, too. It was nice to see the two of them making up for lost time.

The differences between the dogs and cats were striking, and sometimes problematic. Most of the dogs were like Henry, with a few exceptions. The cats... well, the cats were the same as they were before the procedure, only smarter. They'd play tricks, start fights, and spar between naps. They didn't like to listen either. However, when you needed a task completed without distraction and without fail, you were probably better off sending a cat. Mostly because of the distraction part.

Most of all, we enjoyed the newfound peace and the feeling of optimism that spread in our group. Even Frelya was calmer and nicer to everyone.

The fight to end PanTech certainly wasn't forgotten, but my mind shifted to long-term strategy, now that the immediate threats were over. It felt good knowing there wasn't anything potentially world-ending to deal with.

At least for now.

EPILOGUE

"PanTech Explorers League, eh?" a petite, dark-skinned girl said.

"Oh, don't say it that way. You sound jealous," answered a man who might have been mistaken for her brother.

"It seems counter-intuitive, don't you think? PanTech stands for Pandemic Technologies. We're not some mountaineering, or settlement establishing cooperative."

"Um, does the term 'Adversity Zone' not ring a bell for you? In some ways, that's exactly what we do," he said, shaking his head.

"Well, regardless of your implication, I am *not* jealous. I'm the professor of the Pandemic Research Division. A core division of this organization."

"You mean one of the most pointless divisions the president keeps around? Come on. A lot of employees have been here for years and barely know we exist. Why does it have to be about status?"

"It isn't about status, Cherun! It's about proper prioritization of divisions. Not just about me. Professor Taylor's PanTech Explorers League is all about looking forward, but the people from my division have an expression about looking both ways before you cross the street. If you simply look forward without looking back, disaster will follow."

"I'm not sure *I* follow, Professor Lexili. So, what if she takes those animals out and explores the forgotten parts of the world a little? Isn't *that* just as much about looking back as looking forward? Besides, I met Professor Taylor yesterday. I like her."

"Oh, I'll bet you do. I'm not talking about the exploring aspect of it. I'm bothered by the single largest problem our Adversity Management is facing right now. The general, traitor as he might've been, at least had a solution in mind that would've worked to solve the problem. Every year, fewer and fewer applicants pass the exam and join us here. Despite that, nearly all of them are expanding in population. No matter what kind of artificial restrictions we place on their populations, they overcome them and continue birthing idiots into the world. In fact, seeing the adversity, the more intelligent couples are choosing more often to have fewer children. Do you not see how this is a problem?"

"What do you mean by that 'I'll bet you do' comment?"

"Weren't you listening to anything else I said just now?" she asked, snapping her fingers in front of his face.

"Yes, I was. Look, you know how much I admire you and your work, but I'm just not sure your solution is the best one."

"Fine. Give me an alternative."

Cherun scratched his head. There was nothing he hated more than debating his professor like this.

"Lower the test score threshold needed to pass. Just a few points would solve the problem, would it not?"

She chuckled, as though this was the single dumbest suggestion made in the history of humanity.

"And degrade everything that PanTech stands for as the pinnacle of humanity and our achievements across all of time? Sure, run that one by the president and see what he has to say about it. Hopefully, you don't kill the old man with laughter."

"Not to be too bold, *Professor*, but didn't he shoot down your suggestion too?"

Professor Lexili raised a finger. "Oh, but my dear friend, that was *before* all of that insanity with the general. Since then, he has reconsidered. My plan has been green lit, and we are to begin our research to that end in earnest."

"But that's too dangerous!" he blurted. "We're not some different species here, you know. We're human too, and we can make too many mistakes. I'm sorry, but I *strongly* disagree, and will tell the president as much."

"You're welcome to, of course, but even you recognize it was a deadly worldwide pandemic that solidified our organization's power. PanTech would not have existed without it, and humanity leaped forward in all forms of industry because of that recovery. PanTech's power grew to where not even governments could compete. It's basic history. Ancient history at this point. If we handled it then, it can easily be handled now."

"But that was a natural occurrence. PanTech fought the virus. They didn't create it."

Lexili grinned. "I wouldn't be too sure of that, considering how everything turned out."

He stared at her, unsure of what else he could say to convince her. She was so self-assured already, and with the president allowing her to move forward, he guessed no one in the world could change her mind.

"So, a virus to eradicate a large portion of every zone's population, regardless of their level of advancement. We are really fine-tuning and releasing such a thing?"

"Oh, my dear friend, of course we are. You're too paranoid. Such a thing is easily controlled if the right precautions are taken. Once we develop the proper virus, and the proper vaccine, it's essentially a fool-proof solution. Much better than the general's cruel plan. You'll at least give me that, right?"

"I'm sorry, but I…" he stopped himself. He wanted to resign. Every fiber in his body screamed at him to. But if he did, then who would take his place? Someone in full support of this insane plan, no doubt. Someone who would say everything she wanted to hear. At least she respected him enough to debate him, no matter how condescending she sounded. Maybe he could change her mind… Maybe he could do something. "I… need some time to think. We'll need to develop stricter safety measures. Better handling procedures."

"I knew you'd come around. You're far too brilliant to think this is something we can't handle. As long as I have your help, this will be a simple feat," she said, patting him on the shoulder and walking away.

I have to do something, he thought. *And I'm going to need help*.

PANTECH CHRONICLES

PANDEMIC

BOOK 3

CHAPTER 1

"Arachnid B-Class unit, incoming and arriving in approximately seven minutes. We can move to engage in four under more favorable environmental conditions," the falcon said in his usual cold, even tone.

"Then I suppose we should get moving!" an anthropomorphic dog declared, his long, fluffy tail wagging with excitement. The canine unit lead—eager for action as always—was more than happy to engage.

"Is it possible to avoid it, Ghost?" the feline unit lead asked. "We'll have to return early if we expend too many resources on this one."

"Oh, would you look at the scaredy-cat!" the dog bellowed. "Kelin just doesn't want to get her claws dirty. Ignore her, Professor."

"What? Big talk coming from you, Harlow. You scored lower than me in virtually every combat assessment. Shut your mouth, mutt, or I'll dirty my claws with your eyes." The cat's ears laid back on her head, nearly flat, and a low growl resonated from her chest.

I could only roll my eyes. Day in and day out. This was exhausting. Or, at least it would be, if I didn't love it so much. Not the bickering, of course. I'd be happy to do without that. The missions, on the other hand, were the most fun I'd had in as long as I could remember. "Okay, you two. That's enough. Harlow, we're all scared of these things, and—"

"Not me!" he protested, looking around at all the blank expressions. Even his dogs were showing doubt now. "Okay… maybe a little."

"And no one's individual combat scores matter here because none of us could take down one of these things alone. It's a team effort. Dogs score higher on team drills, but cats make the better decisions, especially as individuals. We all share the same missions, and you're all my valued team members. Everyone's strengths and weaknesses are better when we act as one."

"No. It isn't possible to avoid it. Its sensors are functional. Engagement in three minutes," Ghost interjected.

Harlow sighed, scratching his ear with his paw. "Fine. I didn't feel like walking down that hill anyway."

Kelin's ears went back again, and she opened her mouth to speak, clenched her jaw, and thought better of it. Instead, she walked back over to her own unit to prepare them for the engagement.

"I swear, the two of you fight like—" I started but was interrupted by Harlow again.

"Like cats and dogs?" he asked, doing his best to smile.

"I was going to say siblings," I said, tightening my headband and checking my sword, Twisted Key.

"Try not to show everyone up too much today, eh Professor?"

Ghost glared at him. He barely showed it, but everyone here had learned to read when Ghost was getting annoyed. He waved his paws in the air, still smiling, and walked toward his own group. "Children…" Ghost said. I felt that if he was capable of it, he'd have spat on the ground when he said it.

It was strange referring to them that way, but he wasn't technically wrong. They'd undergone accelerated aging. Basically lab-grown from start to finish. Genetic modification to allow easier upright mobility, elongated fingers for gripping, and more human-like mouth structure to make speech and expression easier. Long gone were the days of designer pets. I was making the best of repurposing General Markus's disposable insurrectionist super soldiers into something less sinister. They were physically, functionally full-grown adults, but their complete lack of worldly experience would often become obvious. That's what this field work was for.

Some days were better than others.

I really, really hoped today would be one of the better days.

"Counter-EMP deployed. Auditory resonance deactivator deployed," Kelin's voice called out over the communicator.

"Primary attack groups Alpha and Beta in position. Ambush team is cloaked and in position, ready to engage on signal," Harlow announced over the comm, barely giving Kelin time to complete her sentence.

The once-terrifying low hum of the machine's motor filled my ears. The clanking of rusted legs rattling beneath the weight echoed. The squeaking of joints and gears nearly drowned it out. These machines were once nearly silent, but years in the elements without maintenance changed that.

This was the same type of unit I'd once fled from, that nearly killed my friend Linda and me. Now, here I was, hunting them almost for sport. It wasn't even required for the missions, but I felt compelled to dismantle as many of them as possible.

I drew my sword, holding it ready at my side.

"Okay, everyone, I have a visual on the approach, but not the machine. Engagement in ten, nine…"

Trees began falling in different directions, sending birds scattering into the sky.

"Eight, seven, six…"

Red lights beamed through the openings between trees, scanning for its targets.

"Five, four, three…"

With a lunge, it appeared in our camp's large clearing. The dome of its head rotated, locking on to me.

"Two, one…"

This one was equipped with two very problematic tools. One was a very effective EMP, capable of interfering with much of our equipment. The second was a resonance generator that emitted a frequency that would shut down human hearing. It was very painful to the cats and dogs especially, but stopped us from communicating. We'd developed excellent countermeasures for both. It attempted to activate them, and failed.

"Go, Harlow!" I shouted.

"Ambush team!" he responded.

Six shots rang out in perfect unity, so close together they might've been confused for one. High-velocity, small-caliber rounds shattered the protective layer of the machine's head, taking out all six of its main sensors. It would have to rely on auxiliaries now, slowing it down.

"Alpha team, you know what to do," he said.

They certainly did. They'd done it at least a dozen times now.

I joined in now, leaping onto the machine's dome, severing cables and hoses in order of importance. We'd done extensive research on a destroyed unit, and had a good idea now of how everything worked. And, of course, how to make it not work anymore.

Several dogs ran between the legs, tossing a weighted cable over the legs, at the point where they connected with the main body.

One stood directly beneath it with a control box that attached to the other end of the cable. As they tossed it, he would extend it to accommodate the throw, but not far enough for it to tangle.

Ghost hovered above us, watching closely.

The machine lowered a machine gun, struggling to point it at the quickly moving dogs beneath it. Typically, this was something to be ignored, as they'd long since run out of ammunition.

"The gun is hot," Ghost declared, casually.

"What do you mean *it's hot*, Ghost?" Harlow asked. It was a rhetorical question, but he couldn't help it. This had never been the case before.

"Kelin, your unit is in range. Same with the canine Beta team. Take cover!" I shouted.

Reactions were slow. They'd become adept at what had become routine. They'd mastered the expected. This, though? This was one of those moments where the lack of experience showed through all the skill and training.

"Now!" I repeated, screaming this time.

They scrambled to find cover and ran toward the closest thing. Not the smartest thing. The closest thing.

"Not the transport. Gah!" I said, nearly slapping myself in the forehead. Machine gun rounds ripped from the gun's barrel, filling the transport with holes as I struggled to maintain my footing, slowly making my way around and toward the gun.

"Less than a minute until the legs are disabled, Professor," Harlow said, sounding quite proud of himself.

In a minute, our transport would be past-tense.

"Do it faster!" I roared. "Your comrades are pinned behind that transport!"

One of the dogs below me tossed the anchor, but fell short, getting it stuck at the base of the leg. He howled in frustration, and began barking at the dog next to him, who returned the barks with his own.

"It's stuck, Harlow. Improvise," I said, nearly slipping from the vibrating, narrow platform I struggled to scale.

"Can you kick it off?" he asked, his voice shaking.

"I'm busy. Figure something out," I replied, trying to make it the one more step I needed to get in range of the machine gun.

"Let's see… umm… We could… how many legs are wrapped?"

"Most of them," a dog replied.

"Activate it now," Harlow said.

"No, wait! Gah!" I gasped. I was going to fall off this thing and leave a machine gun spraying bullets in every direction.

Before the dogs could react to my words, the wire had already been activated, sending the machine toppling to the side.

As I fell, I sliced at the ammunition feeding belt loaded into the gun, severing it.

Several more bullets sent dirt flying into the air as the gun lost its target and shot wildly in every direction. The last one hit the tree Harlow was standing in, and he let out an instinctive yelp. He was instantly embarrassed by it.

Dodging the two legs still flailing, I weaved my way back to the exposed underside of the unit. Pulling a tool from my belt, I jammed it into the seamless door, and popped it open. I reached in and yanked several small wires, causing the machine to buzz and whir to a complete stop.

Harlow hopped down from the tree, hanging his head. Kelin and her unit emerged from behind the heavily damaged transport, her head hanging even lower.

"I'm sorry, Professor," she said meekly.

Normally, this would be Harlow's moment to rub it in, but he could only echo the sentiment. "Sorry, Professor," he said, clasping his paws tightly in front of him.

I couldn't help but laugh, grabbing them both and hugging them tightly. "Everyone's still alive, right?" I smiled.

"Painful optimism…" Ghost said, landing on my shoulder after I took a step back.

Harlow and Kelin both nodded.

"The last one standing wins when it comes right down to it," I said. "Remember that. Now… Harlow, salvage that machine gun and whatever ammunition is left in case we encounter any of them on the way back. Kelin, repair the transport so we can actually get back."

"Yes, Professor!" both shouted at the same time, nearly trampling one another before turning and running in a different direction.

"What do you think, Ghost? Could've gone worse, right?" I asked, looking up at him.

"Children…" Ghost said, taking to the air.

I spent several moments staring at the transport in front of me, now billowing with smoke.

I sighed.

It's going to be a long walk back…

CHAPTER 2

By the next morning, the cats had our vehicle operating well enough to move. I'd once again underestimated them. They'd scrapped the Arachnid, and miraculously used all the parts and pieces to get it back in working order. If I'd been out here alone, I'd have been walking back by now—leaving valuable machinery alone in the wilderness.

Not that PanTech couldn't produce another in a matter of hours, but the paranoia still remained that somewhere, somehow, citizens could wander out of their adversity zones and stumble upon the tech, somehow know how to fix it, somehow know how to drive it to PanTech headquarters, and actually accomplish... something?

"There was an adversity zone only a few miles away. Why didn't we just go there and do the repairs? They have vehicles in that zone, so I'm sure we could've made something work," Harlow said, looking over the repairs—too proud to simply praise the cats and acknowledge a job well done.

"Arc City? They don't have cars there, Harlow. Besides, they wouldn't be eager to help us anyway. They'd be just as likely to shoot us," Kelin said, nodding as she looked over each patched hole.

"They don't have cars, nor do they have guns. You're assuming that based on the time period theme, but remember that PanTech takes liberties to change things up. These zones aren't historically accurate. Sometimes, they barely even resemble the periods and places they're based upon. They're basically PanTech's experimental little role-play bubbles. They want to see how growing up in these settings affects someone's personality. The mean streets of Arc City, rife with organized crime... just another example of pointless suffering," I said, somehow getting myself off topic.

"I wouldn't say it's pointless," Harlow said, hesitant to argue. "Not if it accomplishes what they say it does."

"Well, it doesn't make any sense to me. Even if they don't have a high enough intelligence to pass PanTech's entry exam, that doesn't mean they can't still be useful. We do have you, after all," Kelin said, happy to argue the entire way if it came to that.

"Hah… you know what? I'll take it. That's probably the closest you've ever come to giving someone an actual compliment. I guess sitting back and letting everyone else do the real work is what makes someone 'intelligent' to you."

Kelin's hair stood up on her neck, and her ears went back. "It only looks like sitting back to you because you couldn't understand it if we wrote a manual for you."

Harlow showed his teeth, taking a step toward Kelin, punching one paw into the pad of the other. "You couldn't write anything unless we were standing there protecting you."

"Enough!" I said, holding my hands in the air and stepping between them. "It's like both of you acknowledge the good traits of the other but can't say so without throwing an insult in with it."

Both were silent, unwilling to apologize to one another. Definitely getting the sibling impression from these two. Ferris and I argued just like this.

"Let's get ready to depart," I said, walking away to take one final look over my maps.

Another productive expedition, despite the hiccup at the end.

I found a rock to sit on, pulled out my navigation sphere, and activated it. A hologram appeared in front of me, and I began touching various areas to move around, using different gestures to leave markers.

It had been nearly two years since the failed insurrection, and nearly as long as that since I was assigned to lead the president's latest division: PanTech Explorers League. It was my chance to take the animals away from the military, or so I'd thought. I was able to get about half of the original thousand, and even *that* was a stretch. I had to rack my brain to find something for five-hundred anthropomorphic dogs and cats to do.

"It's a shame we couldn't have made it over the hill," I said, without looking up at Ghost when he landed beside me.

"Why? That zone is one of the most primitive. Clubs and rocks."

"Haven't you been curious?" I asked, looking up at him with a grin.

"I see. You're wondering why the machine was so close to one of the zones. It's by far the closest one we've encountered to an adversity zone."

I nodded, looking back to the map display. Ghost was always

so perceptive. I was surprised I even needed to tell him. Most of the time, it was almost as though he could read my thoughts. "Do you have a theory?"

"This far out, it was probably ordered there to protect something. It's a no-contact zone anyway. We already have enough problems."

As much as I wanted to disagree, he was right.

Technically, anyway.

The last couple of years had been mostly peaceful, at least inside PanTech itself. I'd kept myself busy, and mostly away on missions to chart new wildlife and scout old territory. I'd tried dating again, but that proved to be fruitless. Zel, the soldier I'd met when the general tried to have me killed in one of the zones, was good-hearted and not at all the womanizer he'd made himself out to be. Not that I ever believed he was. Seeing each other once every few months didn't work for either of us, and so it goes.

"What are you thinking about?" Ghost asked, jarring me from my daydream.

I resumed adding logs to the map. "Do you think we've lost sight of what's important, Ghost? Are we getting too comfortable?"

"You humans are very strange creatures. You're never satisfied with anything, are you?"

I laughed. He certainly had me there. "Ouch. As honest and direct as ever. Maybe you're just an old man. Ever thought of that?"

"I'm not a man."

I snapped my fingers. "Ah, so you admit you're old, then?"

"I have no idea how old my species live," he said.

"According to the labs, they project somewhere around one-hundred and fifty. Speaking of which, I should get that assessment done on the cats and dogs, now that they've matured and are aging naturally."

"That means you and I are likely to spend the next eighty years together? Wonderful."

"I'm going to assume you aren't being sarcastic! I could always leave you with Frelya, you know."

Ghost tilted his head.

"Alright, I'll stop teasing you," I said.

Looking around at the dense forest that surrounded our camp,

I found myself suddenly wishing we hadn't been able to repair the transport. Another week away from PanTech—even if it was spent on a grueling journey on foot—was appealing.

I really was getting too comfortable.

I'd started to forget.

"Frelya should be pleased about the results of the new implant," Ghost said.

I nodded. "Not that I had much of a choice. She insists this one is better, but I think I got a downgrade."

"Passive enhancement that frees up your concentration does not sound like a downgrade. You are still considerably stronger than the unenhanced of your species. Even the males."

I laughed. "Whose side are you on anyway?"

"Yours," he said, flying off.

Ghost was cold, but Frelya was much more scathing when I'd woken up from surgery. Damaged brain tissue had to be repaired. She'd said I couldn't be trusted not to take things too far, so she developed a new version that operated at net zero. It calculated energy input, and matched it in output automatically. No more overdrawing power, overheating… and potentially brain damage. Frelya had said that if I'd been back at my zone with that kind of injury, I'd have been in a coma for the rest of my life.

Frelya had certainly changed… in some ways.

"We're all loaded up. Do you… have a minute, Professor?"

It was Kelin. I'd gotten lost in my thoughts again, and hadn't even noticed her approach. Then again, she was very stealthy without meaning to be. "Sure. What's on your mind?"

"I wanted to apologize for causing the transport to be damaged in the first place. We should've gone into cover somewhere else."

I shook my head, focusing again on the map in front of me. "The transport can be replaced. You can't."

Kelin tilted her head, and seemed to be confused by the statement. "There are just as many of me as there are transports. Probably more."

"That's not true, Kelin. There's only one of you and there'll only ever be one of you, even if we clone you. Even if you have kittens. Understand? This conversation is proof that you're unique. Will any of the other cats remember this conversation we're having right now?"

"Well, no, but—"

"No 'but' necessary, Kelin. Don't let PanTech sell you on that disposable crap. You're no more disposable than the president himself."

Her eyes were wide. "Professor, are you sure you should be saying things like that?"

"Why not? He might even agree with me. To be honest, I almost wish you weren't able to repair it. I look less and less forward to returning every time we finish a mission than the time before.

She leaned in, whispering. "Would you like me to sabotage the repairs?"

I grabbed her around the neck, hugging her tight. "No. It's for the best. If anything, I think you impressed Harlow."

"Do you think so? It didn't seem that way to me."

"You have a lot to learn. Go ahead back, then. Load your people up. I'll be there in a few minutes once I've finished my logs. Ask Harlow to take one more sweep around."

Kelin left, and I went back to my work. So many interruptions. I'd just told myself I wasn't in any hurry to get back, but found myself in a hurry anyway.

I guess I did miss my friends… a little.

"Professor, do you have a moment?" Harlow asked, stomping his way up to me, making up for the noise Kelin didn't make.

I sighed. "Sure. What's on your mind?"

"I just wanted to apologize for our mistake yesterday. It could've been costly. We have no excuse for it. I take responsibility as the unit leader."

I slammed the log closed, and took a step toward him, raising both of my hands into the air. He flinched instinctively, lowering his head.

I grabbed his ears, scratching behind both of them. "Who's a good boy? You're a good boy! Scratch, scratch, scratch!"

"Uh! Knock it off, Professor!" he said, his smile contradicting his words as he jumped back.

"You know, Kelin just bothered me with the same nonsense. If I apologized for every tiny screwup I ever made, I'd spend the next ten years apologizing for the last few years alone."

"That… doesn't even make any sense."

"Harlow…"

"Yes?" he asked, tilting his head. I always loved the head tilts.

"Get on the transport. If you and Kelin are going to apologize to anyone, it should be to each other. Not me."

He grunted, walking away without acknowledging my suggestion.

I did my best impression of Ghost, once he was gone.

"Children…"

CHAPTER 3

It turned out the cats, while amazingly talented and skilled, could not produce miracles. A few miles from headquarters, the transport failed to go even another inch, forcing us to come in on foot. Fortunately, at my request, our division was on ground level, built off the edge of PanTech. Similar to how the Adversity Management Division had been built. This allowed easy entry and departure… and also came in handy from time to time when that entry was particularly embarrassing. Not that anyone even noticed that we didn't have the transport with us. As usual, I was immediately approached by someone. I already knew full well what they were about to say.

"Welcome back, Professor. You have several requests for meetings. Assistant Professor Cherun from the Pandemic Research Division said—"

I sighed, waving my hand. "Just leave the requests on my desk and I'll go through them later. Anything from Frelya?"

The cat stood up straight, adjusting her decorative glasses. "Yes, Professor. She came here three days ago when you were scheduled to return, and has been back every day since. She requested you come to see her immediately over in Adversity Management's science building."

I chuckled. Requested? Yeah, right. "I guess that's where I should go first, then. Anything here that needs my attention first?"

She shrugged. "We managed to keep the entire division in one piece and didn't catch a single thing on fire the entire time you were gone."

"That's what I like about you dogs and cats. You really go above and beyond."

"Thank you?" she asked, tilting her head.

I patted her on the head, then went to inform Harlow and Kelin to enter the new information into our database, and start making sample deliveries to other interested divisions. Animal Research still wanted live samples brought back, despite the fact they were scanned in the field. Typical Barth, assuming no job is truly complete until his hands have touched it.

Thankfully, *former* General Markus wasn't in power anymore or maybe we'd have squirrel soldiers running around too.

After sending them off, I departed too, boarding the transport pod through the vast tubing that networked all of PanTech. I didn't vomit anymore when riding them, at least, though I still felt like it was a close call every time I stepped off.

Taking a moment for several deep breaths after stepping off on the Adversity Management side, I made my way toward the science building. It had been a while since the fight with General Markus and his sympathizers, but I still struggled with the bad memories that came from this place. Just more fuel for the nightmares. Though, as they say, time heals wounds. Not the whole truth. They never heal completely. The scars are there forever, and old wounds are easily reopened.

"I'm here to see Commander Frelya," I said, stepping up to the front desk.

"Thank goodness," she said, pressing a button on her desk. "Commander Frelya, the professor from Explorers League is here to see you."

"Send her through," the familiar, and very, very annoyed voice said from the other side.

The receptionist looked up and smiled. A passive aggressive sort of smile that told me she was happy to see someone else get a bit of what she'd been getting the past few days. "You know where to find her," she said, punctuating it with an even bigger smile.

"Right… thanks," I said, strolling down the halls of the science building. Even though there were much larger facilities throughout PanTech dedicated to specific fields of study, it was clear which division the president favored the most. The science building at Adversity Management, a glorified military division, could hold its own against just about any proper division. When it came to oppressing regular citizens in their adversity zones, nothing was held back. If Adversity Management wanted it, they got it. If someone else had something they needed, they were allowed to take it. Something no other division had the privilege to do.

Yet, despite the overall purpose, and despite the president's urging, I'd learned that the overwhelming majority of zone commanders and personnel here took no pleasure in artificially injecting adversity into people's lives. Despite PanTech's motto, *Strength Through Adversity*, the arbiters of that mission had become lax. It wasn't this outcome that concerned me. It's what

I'd always wanted to push for, and I'd played a role in this myself. I was determined to destroy PanTech in whatever capacity I was capable of achieving. This was a start. It was the consequences that I was afraid of. Some kind of overcorrection that only made things worse.

For now, that hadn't happened, which only made me relax even more. I'd gotten soft, just like everyone else does after they've been here for a while. I wasn't even twenty yet, but I already felt like I'd been here for the majority of my life. Like everything else was a distant memory, growing hazier by the day.

"Just going to keep walking, huh?" a voice said, jarring me from my thoughts.

"Sorry. Guess I was just daydreaming," I said, looking over my shoulder, realizing I'd passed up Frelya's office by several doors. "Good to see you, Frelya."

"Good to see me? Miss me, then? You wouldn't have to if you'd just carry long-range communication with you on your expeditions."

I shrugged. This argument was an old one by now.

"I just don't want to be bothered when I'm out. It's my vacation from… everything PanTech."

She ushered me inside, gesturing for me to sit in an examination chair. "You do see the irony in that, don't you? You're a PanTech professor, one of the youngest ever, and the head of a brand new division that was basically made just for you. You're a living, breathing flesh ball of irony. You realize you've done more to preserve PanTech than probably anyone here? You stopped a rebellion in your own zone, then saved headquarters from the biggest threat it ever faced. You're a model PanTech employee. Like it or not," she said, rambling. She'd barely given me the chance to speak since she spotted me.

"Ah, these tactics don't work on me anymore, Frelya. I know what a sweetheart you are, and that you only tease me because you care about me and worry about me."

She turned on a bright light directly into my eyes without warning. "Sh—shut up! Don't change the subject," she said, her voice cracking. "The fact that I worry about you is *why* I'm saying these things. It's not a tactic. I'm serious. Don't forget, I know you pretty well too. The *real* you. Don't start pushing everyone away again. Your friends still support you."

"Speak for yourself. I rarely see any of my old friends anymore."

"Is that their fault, or yours?" she asked, recovering her blunt tone.

"Ouch… that one cut deep. Mine, of course. Okay… point taken," I said, conceding. "I'll pay a visit to Linda and Joyce after this."

"And you'll start bringing long-range communication with you on your expeditions?" she added, trying to seize the opportunity.

"I'll *think* about it."

She sighed. "And people think *I'm* unreasonable. Anyway, talk to me about the new enhancer. What's your impression so far?"

"It's weaker than the last one," I said, frowning. "It lacks controls."

"No, Taylor. *You* lack control, which is why I developed this new version in the first place. No more frying your own brain inside your skull, or destroying your bones and ligaments. You realize some of that damage was permanent, right? We have technology, not miracles."

"Right for the throat again. I might have to take back that sweetheart comment from earlier."

"I'd prefer it if you did. Any other positive or negative effects you've noticed?"

She switched off the light, and I rubbed my eyes.

"I'm only teasing you. It's brilliant, actually. Far less dangerous than the other one, and being able to focus completely on the task at hand without splitting your attention with needing to control the enhancer is a plus. One that may make up for the lack of concentrated power. I was able to leap onto one of those machines and cut the reinforced hoses and wires without any major damage to myself. Just some soreness."

"That's because the new model also integrates deeper with your brain's core functions, delegating power to things like healing bone and tissue damage when not actively in use. Mainly when you're sleeping."

"That sounds a bit like bragging," I said.

"And so what if it is?"

"You're probably the most capable person in this entire

organization. It's a shame you've been taken out of active duty and put in this science building all day. Not really fair, if you ask me."

"Well, I didn't ask you, and I don't mind anyway. I *thought* that being stuck here meant I'd get to see you more, but clearly that hasn't been the case. While you were gone, the rank of commander was revoked. It's Chief Scientist Frelya now."

"Congratulations," I said. I meant it, no matter how sarcastic it sounded.

"As if this place needs a chief scientist. Everyone is calling me 'boss' now, even though I don't tell anyone to do anything. It's far more annoying than having no title at all."

"I think the fact that you don't like telling people what to do is what makes you perfect, Frelya."

"R—really? Anyway… it's just the way I am."

"Well, I like the way you are. At least now that you have the title, it'll keep someone else from taking it that goes around micromanaging everyone."

She ignored my compliments as usual. "How are the dogs and cats getting along? They're having some challenges with that here."

I sighed, rubbing my eyes again. "I think I'm making progress. I think they'd like each other if they'd just give each other a chance. I guess that's as good of an excuse as any to go and see Linda… and maybe Barth too, not that Barth cares about such trivial things. He's too busy wining and dining the other professors, now that he's the head of a higher level division. Still, I think I'm making some progress. I hope. That's enough about me, though. How are you holding up?"

"Never better," she said. "So how about you take a long-range communicator with you on your next expedition? For me, to help keep my stress levels down. You do care about my mental health, right?"

"Of course I do… Alright, you win. I'll take one, but I'm leaving it turned off unless something happens."

She gestured for me to get out of the chair, glancing over the scans she'd been taking while we were talking. "The enhancer's actually healed damage we thought might be permanent. Your immune system is off the charts, even for an employee. If there are any negative effects, I don't see them."

"I'd expect nothing less from the chief scientist of Adversity

Management," I said, wrapping my arms around her neck in a tight hug.

"Okay, you're getting a little too comfortable. Oh, and bring Ghost with you when you go to Animal Research. Henry would appreciate seeing him."

"That's up to Ghost. Oh, and you better watch your weight sitting around in that chair all day. Can't be good for you."

She shoved me from behind, nearly sending me tripping over myself through the doorway. "I still train every day. I'm in far better condition than you."

"Sheesh. I'm *definitely* taking back the sweetheart thing," I said, turning around and waving.

"Just get out of here," she growled. "And… come back soon, alright?"

"If I didn't know better, I'd say you installed this new implant just to have an excuse to—"

And the door slammed in my face. That's one friend successfully annoyed. Now to see if I could do the same to Linda.

CHAPTER 4

The Animal Research Division continued to transform in ways that I hadn't expected and were, frankly, unsettling. The size and scope had expanded to the point it was hardly recognizable from when I was the assistant professor there. The only silver lining was the fact that the president had become paranoid of anthropomorphic animal experiments and ordered them to be temporarily limited to simulations only. Barth had no protest, of course. His only concern was prestige, and he'd gotten more than enough of that to keep him busy for a while.

It had been a while since I'd seen Linda. At least six months if I had to guess. Reflecting on things, I'd done a lot of lying to myself, and Frelya had helped me to see that. The insurrection and the fallout that followed it had affected me much more than I'd let on, and I'd isolated myself from everyone who had supported me. I'd even refused to communicate with them from afar, which I could have done easily.

I immediately thought better of teasing Linda the way I'd done Frelya. I should probably be more apologetic instead.

Yes, let's go with apologetic…

Gah, you can be so dense sometimes, Taylor.

"Welcome to Animal Research. Can I offer you a tour of the facil—Oh, Professor! Sorry, just routine. I say that same line so many times every day that it just comes out before I even think," the young girl said. She was young. Probably this year's inductee, and it was the first time we'd ever met.

"Oh, no. That's alright. It's changing so much around here that I'd probably need a tour if I waited much longer to visit. I used to work here, actually. Taylor. Pleasure to meet you," I held out my hand.

The girl took it and shook with far too much enthusiasm. And palm sweat. "The pleasure is all mine, Professor. Can I get you anything, or maybe you'd like me to call for a guide to take you to see someone?" she asked, letting go of my hand.

"No. Really, it's fine. I'll just wander over to see Assistant Professor Linda if that's alright."

"Of course. You have free movement, being a professor and all." She beamed.

I smiled my best smile in return, more practiced than genuine at this point, and took my opportunity to slink away before further inquiry could be made.

I did still know my way around, after all. More or less.

As I walked the looping corridors, I came to the realization I was wasting time. I knew full well this was the residential area, and that I wasn't likely to find Linda here. I guess after all this time, I could still get cold feet. Accepting that you're the jerk of the group, after everything your friends have done for you, will do that to a person I suppose.

Walking in circles was making it worse, not better.

Come on Taylor. You've got things to do. You need to see Joyce after this. Joyce... right. The person likely to scold you even harder than Frelya. Did the pep talk work? No?

I took a deep breath, then let out a sigh. Then another deep breath. Alright. Time to turn around and go to the labs, where I'll *actually* find her.

When I turned around, I nearly jumped to the ceiling. A short, upright beagle was standing behind me, panting excitedly. I hadn't even noticed him walk up behind me after I stopped.

"It's you! Taylor, I am so happy to see you. I am so excited you're here. Sorry for scaring you, but I did not want to interrupt your thinking. You were thinking so hard! What were you thinking about? Were you thinking about how happy you would be when you saw us?"

I grabbed up Henry in a big hug, spinning before putting him back on the ground. Henry loved it. He loved everything. Of course, this made not loving Henry basically impossible. "I'm really happy to see you too, Henry. You scared me a little."

"Oh, Taylor. You are silly. The labs and offices are not this way," he said, laughing. When he laughed, his big ears flopped around. The new generation wasn't quite as cute as this. It almost felt like we'd taken a step back—giving them bigger feet, more functional thumbs, and better speaking ability.

"Of course. How could I forget something like that?" I lied. Seeing Henry now, procrastinating and getting nervous felt so silly. Of course he'd be happy to see me, and Linda would be too.

"I don't know. Maybe it is because you were walking here on purpose because you are scared Linda will be upset with you for not visiting in a long time."

I tensed, squeezing my fists together, letting my head hang. "You... got me. Was it that obvious?"

"It was obvious," he said, smiling wide, holding out his paw.

I took it, and he led me toward the labs. He couldn't really hold onto my hand, but just trusted me to know that it's what he wanted. It was good to see that he was still so sweet, even after spending so long at PanTech.

After several minutes of quiet walking, we made it to Linda's office. She dressed a little differently than I remembered. She almost reminded me of... yeah. Professor Elise. A size too small shirt, one too many buttons undone, skirt a little too short for comfort, Professor Elise. I mean... none of those things applied to Linda's clothing, but maybe it was the hair and the glasses that made me think of Elise.

"So nice of you to finally show up, Taylor," she said, cold and even toned. "I'm disappointed."

"Right. It has been too long. I'm sorry for shutting all of you out like that. You're right to be upset," I said, hanging my head again.

Suddenly, Linda's arms were around me, hugging me tight. "Did you think I actually meant that? Come on, Taylor! I'm thrilled to see you. We've all been busy. I'm an assistant professor, so it's not like I couldn't have gone down there any time I wanted to. If there's something that needs blame assigned to it, then we can all share it. Otherwise, I think you know what time it is."

I thought for a moment. I knew exactly what time it was, but I knew that's not what she meant. I thought for a second before the realization finally hit me. I almost sighed instinctively. "It's lunch time..." I said quietly, grinning.

"You got it! Henry, would you mind getting us a few sandwiches from the cafeteria?"

Henry was already halfway to the door before he answered. "I'll go right now!"

I couldn't help myself but laugh again after he left. "I hope Henry never changes. By the way, what's Barth up to these days?"

Linda crossed her arms and shook her head. "As if you don't already know."

"Hey, it's worth asking the questions. I still remember when he would work almost around the clock, emaciated from only consuming nutrition packs." I shrugged, but Linda only narrowed her eyes and tapped her finger on her arm.

"But you *know* why he worked so hard. The end goal has been reached. He's lost his motivation to spend so much time in the lab. In fact, he isn't even here. You'll never guess where he is."

"Where?" I asked, hoping for a quick answer without having to guess.

Linda wasn't having it. Too much fun to be had. "Come on. Guess."

"He's massaging the president's shoulders."

"Close! Well… not really, but equally surprising."

"He's writing a book on modesty and humility," I said, really getting far-fetched now.

Linda chuckled, lowering her glasses to look at me above them. "Serious guesses, please."

"He's… planting a garden? Sorry, I think you'll just have to tell me," I said.

"He's on a *date*, Taylor. A date."

My mouth dropped open.

"A date? Wow, that really is surprising."

"Wait until you hear who the lucky lady is."

"I think I've got this one. Professor Elise, right?"

Linda's hands shot to her hips. "How did you know that?"

"Remember the whole brain density research thing? I had a feeling there was a history there. I just expected it to be more competitive and less romantic."

Linda pointed to one of the chairs across from her desk. "Have a seat. Henry should be back any minute. Oh, and don't assume those two things are mutually exclusive. Have you never met a romantic couple made up of two very competitive people? In my zone, that was the norm."

I thought of answering with my experience in my zone, but before I could, the thought struck me. "Hey, Linda…"

She leaned forward, reacting to the somber tone. "Yeah?"

"Have you ever noticed that we don't really bring up our zones that much anymore? And, that the older employees virtually never do at all? It's almost like the most reliable way of telling how long someone has been here. Almost as reliable as their age itself."

"Growing and changing is normal, Taylor. It doesn't mean you've abandoned your past, or forgotten the people you left behind. It just means that you're creating more history. More things to remember. Like it or not, we're completely different people than we were before we came here."

"Yeah, well I *don't* like it, Linda. That's the problem!" I growled, slamming my fist onto her desk, causing everything on top of it to bounce, some of it falling over. I think it surprised me more than it did her. "Sorry, Linda. I…"

She shook her head. "I'm just glad you stopped by. Have you thought about seeing one of the counselors about your stress levels? You shouldn't neglect your mental health any more than your physical health."

"I know. It's just not something they can help with, in this case. If I'm honest with them, they'll just send me to reeducation."

Linda shuddered. "Point taken. But you can at least start coming by to see myself and Joyce more often. We should try to come see you more often too. Especially me. I have plenty of excuses to go and evaluate your animal team."

The door suddenly flew open, almost making me jump from my seat.

"Lunch is here! Hot sandwiches and soup."

Henry burst through the door, carrying a tray, barely balancing the contents. He was almost bursting with enthusiasm. Linda had clearly rubbed off on him.

"Lunch time!" Linda shouted, clapping her hands.

I smiled. So hard my cheeks hurt.

I had put this off for far too long.

CHAPTER 5

Joyce was the last item on the list before returning to my work. Like Linda, she was also a notorious lover of lunch. Though, by the time I made it over to the Division of Investigation, lunchtime was well and over. She'd probably spent it eating with Daniel anyway. By the way Linda described it, the two were basically inseparable now. More or less joined at the hip. I was happy for her. Something I obviously needed to say, rather than just think.

It had been a long time since I'd walked into the DOI building, and it was just as quiet as ever. No receptionist here. Just that same big sign in the middle that told you what office an investigator was in. I found out later that it's set up this way because the DOI isn't a building just anyone is supposed to visit. They aren't set up to accept visitors, and when they have a job, they go where the job is. As Croshaw, Joyce's father, so aptly put it: "We aren't private investigators."

I was in higher spirits now as I checked the board and followed the helpful area in the direction of Joyce's office. The walk was short, and I didn't drag my feet this time, but once I arrived, the only thing that greeted me was an open door and an empty office.

No problem. I'm sure she's just in Daniel's office instead. I should've checked where that was first so I didn't go all the way back.

Way to think ahead, Taylor.

I took in a deep breath and let it out. Back to the sign.

After checking Daniel's office, I realized the two were straight across from one another. I went all the way back only to find, yet again, an open door and an empty office.

"You again?" an elderly man said, sticking his head out of his office, next to Daniel's.

Elderly? Perhaps ancient. With age-reducing procedures available, it was impossible to tell who was sixty and who was one hundred and sixty.

"Sorry to disturb you. I'm looking for Joyce," I said, bowing slightly.

"Ah, you're the new professor. Those two lovebirds have been out all day. Investigating… well I can't tell you what they're investigating. Only that it's minor. You may be able to find them near the eastern exit."

"Not *that* new, actually. Almost two years now."

He narrowed his eyes. "Well that's new to me. Oh, and since they're friends of yours, maybe ask them to pipe down every once in a while. They shout across the hall at each other all day with their doors open like children."

"That sounds like something you should take up with the chief investigator. Wesley, right?"

"I *am* Chief Investigator Wesley. Besides, I'm just yankin' your chain. Wanted to see if you'd actually do it, and how they'd react. You have any idea how boring this place is?"

I had some idea, but didn't want to say so openly. "I'll play along and see what kind of reaction I get. Anyway, thank you for the information. I'll head out now," I said, pivoting and walking away quickly before he had a chance to respond. Last thing I needed was to be stuck here chatting with this guy all day. I needed to talk to Joyce and get back to my own division. As much as I appreciated the promise of no fires, explosions, or cat versus dog civil wars, I didn't like leaving the place alone this long.

The wall wasn't far from here anyway, so I was there in less than a minute after stepping on the transport again. Maybe I didn't heave every time I got off, but today was really putting that to the test. I looked forward to planting my feet back on firm ground again.

Walking along the wall, I could see a figure waving in the distance. I only knew a couple of people normally this far out who would recognize me. Two, to be exact.

"Farle? Is that you?" I asked, as I drew closer.

This man might've been even more handsome now than the last time I saw him. His long, black hair was tied back in a ponytail, and his dark, narrow eyes gazed at me against the beaming sun. Something I loved about being a mostly outdoor division. Those who lived in the labs didn't understand the magic of the sun.

"Ah, Taylor. You remember me after all this time? It's been nearly two years. You are a professor now." I expected the last part to be a question, but he meant it as a statement.

Had he kept track of me? *No, don't be silly, Taylor. Of course he knows you're a professor. It's a completely new division. Gah...*

"Of course I remember you," I said, brushing the hair out of my face, blown there by an unfortunate gust of wind. "It hasn't been *that* long." I looked at him, waiting for him to respond, but he only smiled. Why was he smiling like that? Oh, right! "Have you seen a couple of members of the DOI out here today? A young woman, black curly hair, and a young man, with red hair."

He nodded, still smiling. "They were here earlier. Asking the kind of prying questions they always do. They were looking for my sister too, a little further down the wall. Perhaps they found her and we can catch up."

"We?" I asked, surprised.

"Walk with me?" he asked, gesturing down the path that followed the wall.

I nodded, returning the smile. "Concerned about your sister and looking for an excuse to check in on her?" I asked as we began walking.

"That's part of it, but Glimmer can take care of herself. I just wanted the excuse to walk with you. I find you to be a fascinating woman. You're—"

I was a bit taken aback by the forwardness, and I'd learned a long time ago that no one is ever really honest at PanTech. "What is it you want from me? Or is it the Explorers League? Are you looking to transfer? You should know that I dislike it when someone pretends to be direct but is the opposite. You're a very attractive man, and you're good with words, but perhaps your flattery would be better suited on another professor."

He stopped briefly, looking down at his feet before resuming our walk. "Many things can be true at the same time, Taylor. There is truth to what you said, but also to what I said. I do find you to be a fascinating woman. I have been to your division to see you several times, but you are never there. You can confirm this with your people. Adversity Management sticks me out here so I'm not causing trouble. If it wasn't for Frelya, they'd have done the same with Linus. My sister volunteered to be stationed out here with me to keep me company."

I nodded, but was quickly getting more and more irritated. "Now that you've used Linus's name, be especially careful what you say after."

He sighed, rubbing the back of his neck. "You're right. Mentioning him wasn't necessary. And yes, I'll avoid keeping anything from you, even if telling you everything makes me sound strange."

"That's wise," I agreed.

"My sister and I already knew who you were. To an extent. I'd hoped to have a chance to talk to you for a while now. Before there was a new division, and before you were a professor."

"Since you know so much about me, let's make it fair. Tell me about yourself. What was your zone like? What kind of life did you have there? What made you decide to join PanTech?" I needed to keep him on the defensive. For better or worse, I just couldn't trust people like this... precisely because of how drawn to them I was.

"I was a killer of men and hunter of beasts. A hunter, trapper... even dabbled in poisons. I sometimes did bad things to bad people... and sometimes good people. I was disliked by everyone and disliked them just as much. Still, I wanted to protect my sister. We didn't have parents. My father was Great Khan... making me a prince. Don't be fooled, though. Being born a prince was often worse than being born a peasant. When my brother killed my father and took the throne, the rest of us were either killed or exiled to villages on the outskirts of the zone."

I nodded, suddenly understanding why he and Linus might have gotten along. Linus had fallen in with a similar lifestyle, though his only motivation for it was freedom. As he put it, freedom to do bad things was sometimes better than being forced to do good things. "Is Glimmer your younger sister, then?"

"Older. Since women couldn't become rulers in our zone, she was mostly left alone to live a normal life. We hunted together, by day, which is how she became a falconer."

"Why tell me all this?"

He raised a brow. "I'm honoring your request of being fully honest. That's all."

"So you decided to become a PanTech employee to continue looking out for your sister, but you're unsuited to the rules and structure here so they sent you to a remote post to keep you out of trouble. You seem to very much dislike PanTech," I said.

If he was going to lie, this would be the time.

"No one in their right mind feels otherwise. When I got here and saw what the world was really like outside of my adversity zone, I cursed them. All that fighting over a throne, control of land and resources, when the world had already eliminated the need for those things hundreds of years ago. You and I have this in common. That resentment."

Perhaps he really was being honest, and saying what was on his mind. Was there really no trickery or ulterior motive?

"You certainly like to jump to conclusions about things you can't possibly know anything about," I said. Even if it was unfiltered honesty, this felt more like a possible trick than anything else he'd said.

"All I ask is that you give me a chance. I long to be in the presence of a kindred spirit, and you have isolated yourself. Make the request with Adversity Management that I accompany you on your next mission. If you value my company in any capacity once it's over, request my transfer. If that happens, my sister will get away from this wall duty and return to the division to be amongst the others."

"You don't want your sister transferred with you if all goes well?"

"That is her choice, but I know that she is not in any danger here. She no longer needs my protection. Now it is her who is protecting me."

I wondered for a moment the extent he meant what he just said. Was she simply protecting him from loneliness, or was there more to it? Still… the proposition intrigued me. Maybe this was just the sort of thing we both needed.

"Alright. I'll do it. Just don't expect to get easy work, and get used to the idea of taking instructions from talking dogs and cats."

He stopped, smiling and turning to me. "I hope this is the beginning of a bond between us that only grows."

His smile caught me off guard a bit.

"Right… we'll see," I said, trying to maintain my tone of authority and failing spectacularly. Instead, I sounded like a girl who just got asked on a date and agreed. Is that what I just did?

He opened his mouth to speak, but a shout from behind us interrupted him.

"Professor Taylor! I've been all over PanTech looking for you. There's something urgent I need to speak to you about!"

CHAPTER 6

He had a long, white coat on, from one of the science divisions—but I'd never met this man before.

"Make an appointment. I'm already on my way to see someone else, and can't you see we were having a private conversation?" I said, already frustrated with the pile of inquiries I knew I had sitting on my desk. All I wanted to do right now was talk to this man, find Joyce, catch up with her, and go back to my division and start going through the logs and entries for analysis. However important this man thought he was, he was mistaken.

"You don't understand. This is a serious matter. I've been running all over the place today looking for you."

Judging by the sweat droplets pooling on his dark skin and dripping from his chin, he seemed to be honest about how much he'd been chasing after me. He had me curious. Farle seemed unbothered, standing quietly, waiting for me to decide what to do. "What is it you needed to talk to me about that's so important?"

"None of the other professors will listen. They won't see reason. It's madness." He doubled over, putting his hands on his knees, trying to catch his breath. He looked up at Farle, and then to me.

I nodded to Farle. "Go ahead without me. If my request is approved, we'll talk more tomorrow. Tell Joyce I'd like to see her soon."

After hesitating a moment, he simply nodded and continued along.

"Thank you. This isn't secret information, but my professor probably won't be happy that I talked to you."

I waved my hand. "I understand. Please tell me what's so urgent."

"I'm the assistant professor at Pandemic Research, Cherun. There's going to be a planned pandemic. The goal is to calibrate a virus to around twenty percent mortality rate, and release it simultaneously across all adversity zones in order to control the population increases that we've been experiencing across the decades. Despite the—"

I held up my hands, and I could feel myself become light-headed. "Wait! Slow down. First of all, why in the name of everything sensible left in the world would they do such a thing?"

Cherun shook his head. "Because they believe we can. Professor Lexili has been proposing the idea for years, as a way of lowering the population without altering adversity ratings to a massive degree. The president has never approved it, but after everything that happened with the general…"

Could the president really approve such a thing? If that's true, then… was everything I did to stop the insurrection all for nothing? We traded military dictatorship for what? A pandemic that would wipe out at least twenty percent of the human race? PanTech really do think of themselves as gods…

I slammed my fist into my palm. "The old man has only gotten more paranoid after being betrayed by Markus. I assume you've tried talking Professor Lexili out of it?"

Cherun threw his arms into the air. "Of course I have! I've done everything I can to convince her it's far too dangerous to unleash such a thing. Adversity Management would need to be exposed to it on an ongoing basis. Then it comes back here. There are too many variables to consider. She even wants to try further programming the targeting so that it gains a higher mortality among the less intelligent. Of course, we'd all need to be fully vaccinated against any effect well in advance of it being deployed. What concerns me is that the virus only needs the slightest of tweaks to become completely lethal, and we have yet to develop a vaccine that's fully effective against it. I've been tasked with safety measures and if something goes wrong, all of this is going to come down on my head."

I rubbed my forehead, holding up my hand again, signaling for him to stop talking. Of course this wouldn't be because the man had a conscious. That he found it unacceptable to murder hundreds of thousands, or more, across every zone, including his own. His quandary was how to pull it off in such a way that posed no threat to PanTech, and to avoid looking bad to his professor.

It was as though every ounce of cynicism I'd cast off was crawling slowly back up my body, burrowing its way into my brain, whispering into my ears like a ghost that refuses to go away. Perhaps it refused to go away because, yet again, it turned out to be justified. This was all the reminder I needed. I hated PanTech. Deeply, and completely, I hated them. From the very bottom of my heart to the darkest depths of my soul. Perhaps I'd chosen the wrong department to sign up for, because maybe I could've performed a few of those tweaks Cherun mentioned and have it target only members of PanTech. Wiping this organization off the face of the planet really would be doing humanity a favor.

No. That's not right. If I did that, it would make me just like them. I had friends here that I cared about. People I loved. Could I really do something to hurt any of them? It was easy to get carried away in the memories and the resentment, but PanTech was still made up of humans. And, the fact was, no matter where humans amass, you will always find some bad and some good. Even in PanTech.

"Your professor obviously believes the virus can be made safe for everyone in PanTech. If she's your professor, she should be at the forefront of your field of study. If everything could be performed exactly the way she specified, would you help her do it?"

He took a deep breath, and his eyes locked with mine. It was as though he hadn't expected the question, and at the same time, knew it was coming and dreaded it. "I… I don't know. It was different all these years when it was all theory and study. I've always been infatuated by pandemics, partly as a historian. This organization was founded on the back of the worst one to ever occur. That they'd want to reproduce it is…"

"Hypocritical?"

He nodded slowly.

"Worse than that. Hubris. Assuming godhood. If even the slightest variable is miscalculated… If we fail to consider even the most minor of details… If we stray even slightly from whatever plan we create… it could be the end of all humanity. Even if it isn't, this sets a terrible precedent. We have never directly engaged in genocide, even when it might have made sense to do so. We've always used adversity management to control population and moral character. To use a virus is no different than digging mass graves, lining up twenty percent of the population, and shooting them dead."

I shuddered. He'd put it even better than I would've. He told his professor all this, and she still pushed for it? "Why is this important to Professor Lexili?" I asked. "Why does she want to do this?"

"Because she's brilliant, and because she can."

I was dumbfounded. And to think, I was annoyed by Barth being this way when I arrived. Now, I was truly understanding the virtue in him admitting to being a glory seeker up front, and still having lines he wasn't willing to cross. Is this all that's left after a while? Does that become the only motivation for all professors once they've been here long enough? "That's…"

He continued. "Pandemic Research is the original division. You could say that we are PanTech itself, and that everything else has grown out of it, like children from their mother's womb. Once a pharmaceutical company, it was PanTech, no, Pandemic Technology's original mission to protect humanity from contagions and ailments of all kinds. There were problems, of course. Actions taken and steered through the motivation of greed first and benevolence second, but still… it accomplished the goal. Now we are to become the opposite? Spreading disease and viruses to humanity? It's an abomination. Since I've been in the division, we've limited our research to data and simulation. More than adequate with such advanced predictive algorithms and processing power. We no longer need active viruses to create and study them on pure theory. We would need to add so many safety measures, completely changing the way we operate and our goals… and for this… stain on the organization?"

He was clearly passionately against this, and surprisingly eloquent for a scientist. I was moved by his words, despite already being on his side. If he'd expressed these concerns to the decision-makers, what exactly was he expecting from me?

"Do you and Professor Lexili get along?"

He sighed, placing his hands behind his back, pausing for a moment, as though this was the heaviest topic of all.

"I have long admired Professor Lexili. More than anyone I've ever met. She dwarfs the scientific minds of anyone who called themselves great in my zone. That includes myself. She has always put science above everything, and as a fellow scientist, I found her approach to be ideal. I would like to believe we're friends. She is always kind to me and gives me the utmost confidence. She appreciates those around her and notices everyone's contributions. It's just that lately… she seems so absorbed in science, she's detached herself from the consequences of pursuing it relentlessly. She has erased all artificial and ethical limits for herself. I've protested this many times, and she always listens to me but… I can't convince her no matter how many times I try."

"Let's call this what it is… we are dealing with two people who have become unhinged, and there's no failsafe in place to stop them. That being the case, what exactly are you expecting me to do about them? I'm not saying I won't help you, but where do I fit into *your* plan."

"No failsafe? You see, that's where you're mistaken. It's little known by those who aren't familiar with PanTech's history, but any of the president's decisions can be overturned by a vote of no confidence by the board. This vote can be initiated by any single member of the board. It takes a while to get going, but it's our best chance."

"And who is on this board?" I asked. I'd certainly never heard of it, and I could see why it was kept under wraps.

"Why, the professors, of course. That includes you. You are so bold and adventurous that I thought you would be the perfect one to approach about this. This is our last by-the-books option available."

"Are you suggesting you're open to less by-the-books approaches if the vote fails?"

He paused, as though to reconsider his words. "Apologies. I misspoke. This vote cannot fail."

"Who else knows?" I asked.

"Only those in my division for the most part, though it's no secret. Talk will eventually spread."

This might be our opening. "I think talk should spread sooner than later. Leak the news to other divisions. Let it spread anonymously. Let's gauge the reactions of everyone to the news, and we'll target the divisions most sympathetic to our positions first. We should build support before initiating the vote."

He scratched his chin and smiled for the first time since we began talking. "That's brilliant. Yes. That's what we will do. Thank you for your time and your wisdom, Professor," he bowed.

I waved my hand. "Please don't be so formal. I can never get used to that. Just call me Taylor… and no more bowing or saluting."

He nodded enthusiastically. "Right… Thank you, Taylor. I'll take my leave now." He turned and jogged away, as quickly as he'd come. I admired his optimism.

In my opinion, we wouldn't get that vote in a million years…

CHAPTER 7

I continued in the direction Farle and I had been walking together, hoping to catch up with him. Even though this was an opportunity to spread the word about this plan to the DOI, it made sense to allow them to get the information later than sooner. If I spread it now, they'd know the source almost certainly. If it spread after filtering through half a dozen other divisions… not so much.

After a few minutes of walking, I saw Joyce and Daniel talking to Glimmer. I'm not sure why, but I expected an aggressive interrogation of some sort. Instead, it looked like three friends chatting. They were laughing, and none of them had noticed me approaching yet. Farle had seemed far more serious than his sister. Had he overblown the whole thing? I wouldn't fault him for it. After all, that's what siblings do. Ferris wasn't any different. I guess I wasn't either.

Glimmer tilted her head out from behind Daniel, throwing her arm into the air and waving at me. "Professor Taylor!" she yelled, prompting Joyce and Daniel to turn toward me, mouths agape. Was I really that elusive?

"Well, if it isn't the elusive superstar professor of PanTech. To what do we owe the rare pleasure of your visit?" Joyce shouted, far too loudly, despite the fact I was close enough to hear her normal voice now.

Apparently I was that elusive. "Hi Joyce. Been a while, huh?"

She nodded. "Mmhmm. Yes indeed it has. You do know we're conducting DOI official business here, right?"

Daniel nodded. "Yep. Interfering with official DOI business is a crime, even if you're a professor."

"Put 'em up, Taylor! Keep those hands where I can see 'em!" Joyce laughed and jumped on me without warning, attempting to wrestle me to the ground.

"Ugh, you haven't changed at all," I easily pried her arms away and reversed her hold on me, hugging her tightly from behind.

"Oh no, looks like you've botched this one, dear," Daniel casually looked over his nails while Joyce struggled.

"Requesting backup," she said, struggling with my tight grip around her waist.

"Denied," he prompted an exaggerated gasp from Joyce.

I laughed, letting her go. "Seems my many months of training in the mountains to become a martial arts master have paid off. You don't stand a chance against me as you are now. Challenge me again in a hundred years!"

"You do have a sense of humor!" Joyce exclaimed. "I know you'd develop one someday, with enough hard work. Miracles really can happen."

I grinned. Glimmer's horrified face through all of this may have been the funniest part of the whole exchange. "I was hoping maybe you'd have grown up a little bit since I saw you last."

"Ouch. Professor Taylor with the deep cuts. You know, it's only been months, not decades. See? Check out my youthful appearance. Am I even old enough to be here?"

"That's a good question," I said. "I missed you, by the way."

"I missed you too," she said, stepping forward and hugging me for real this time.

"Was there… uh…" Glimmer pointed at herself.

"No further questions at this time. Just come see Joyce or me if anything seems strange or out of the ordinary. Day or night. Don't think too much of it. These are routine investigations. Most people get a visit like this eventually," Daniel said, his voice resuming a professional tone.

"I'm going to head back to my post, but bring Ghost by to see me sometime soon, alright? My brother would like that too." Glimmer said, her voice cheery again.

"I met your brother just a few minutes ago, actually. I'm surprised I didn't see him on the way here, since he was heading in this direction when I had to stop and speak to someone else."

She nodded. "He's prone to distractions. I'm sure he took a detour or two on the way here. Maybe two or three."

"I think I'll head back too," Daniel added. "I'm feeling a nap coming on."

I instantly got the feeling this lazy, laid back persona was a cover up tactic to encourage people to let down their guard. This was the same Daniel who, legend says, single-handedly foiled a sophisticated assassination attempt on the president and asked to transfer to the Department of Investigation as a result. I also got the feeling he wasn't being honest with Glimmer. As much as I hated PanTech, even I hadn't gotten one of these visits.

"That'll give Taylor and me a chance to catch up a bit," Joyce put her arm around my shoulder.

"Oh, and Chief Investigator Wesley asked me to tell you guys to shut up every once in a while. He says you're always yelling back and forth."

Daniel and Joyce looked at one another, then shook their heads.

"He tells everyone to tell us that. I think the old guy has a few screws loose," Joyce said, leading me away and further down the path along the wall. We both waved at Glimmer and Daniel behind us, who returned the wave and went about their own ways too.

"I guess that's one thing we have in common," I said.

"Are you kidding me? One thing we all have in common. Courtesy of our 'adversity', most likely. Or a necessary side-effect, as PanTech's maxim would imply."

I was surprised to hear this from Joyce. Normally she kept sentences like that out of her mouth. "I didn't really expect to hear you say that," I put my arm around her too.

"Working in DOI, you get a really firm grasp on what you're allowed to say and what you aren't. We're all paranoid when we first get here, but it turns out the president couldn't really care less how much the average employee criticizes the organization. In fact, it seems to be welcomed to an extent."

I squinted at her, making sure she knew I didn't quite buy that. "Oh? Then what was the reason for Farle and Glimmer's little visit today?"

She snapped her arm away from me, stood straight, left fist behind her back, right fist on her chest in a snappy PanTech salute. "Apologies, Professor. I can't reveal that information. Classified DOI business."

"Oh ha ha ha," I said, in as monotone a voice as I could manage. "I'm sure. DOI has to justify its existence, after all. I get it. I get it." I flicked my wrist at her several times dismissively.

"Exactly! Well, truth is, I don't really know why. We suspect it has something to do with those people being an actual risk to PanTech or a danger to other employees. These names just show up, and an investigator goes out and sees them. Ninety-nine times out of a hundred, it really is nothing. Someone's going through a tough time, or had a little too much to drink, or maybe their mental health isn't being properly cared for. We just put them in touch with the right people and all is well. Occasionally it's something credible, but even that's up for debate."

"What do you think of Farle, then? I'm thinking of having him transferred to the Explorers League," I said, careful not to make eye contact with her when I said it. Not that it would matter.

"I think he's cute! Being around you would probably do him some good… and would probably do you some good too. Have a little fun. Settle down. Have a few kids."

"You're hilarious. You know we can't have kids," I said, my voice a little quieter now.

She nodded. "I guess it's not really all that funny, is it? Why do you suppose they sterilize everyone who comes in here?"

I sighed. Seems I was given the window to go into this topic anyway. I hadn't planned it. "There's the reason on paper, and then there's another I just learned about today. Of course, the proclaimed reason is that everyone must endure adversity. Anyone born here isn't going to experience that."

"Yeah, I know… it was a rhetorical question," she said. "But… you think there's another reason?"

I nodded. Here goes nothing. "It seems there's a population problem, and it's getting harder and harder to deal with. They can't realistically increase adversity any higher without affecting mental stability in a major way. They're considering drastic solutions."

"Spill it," she said, getting impatient with my build up.

I stopped, turning toward her, and putting my hands on her shoulders. "They're going to engineer a virus to kill off a certain percentage of the population. If possible, they plan to program targeting based on intelligence. It's going to every adversity zone beyond the population threshold. Maybe all of them."

Joyce punched me in the shoulder and laughed, turning, about to continue down the path we'd been walking on. "Your sense of humor could use a little work, but I'll give you an 'A' for effort."

I held onto her arm, stopping her. "I'm not joking, Joyce. I just spoke to the assistant professor of the Pandemic Research Division. It's not even a proposal. It's already been green lit by the president. I don't know how soon, but it's going to happen. They have some hurdles to get over because all of their study until now has been simulations, but it's coming."

Joyce stood there, still and quiet. Two things Joyce wasn't known to be. "That's… are you sure?"

"I'm telling you, I'm not lying. I'm not joking."

"But… if the president has already signed off on it, there's nothing we can do. Besides, is it really any worse than all the other things they've done?"

It was a fair question. Was it worse? I'd say yes. Absolutely. *Much* worse. How much worse than say… planned starvation? Structuring some of the adversity zones so that they war within, and making sure it continues year after year, until the dead are piled high as mountains? Worse than releasing a giant, man-eating snake into a small village to hunt and kill until the villagers gave up the rebels hiding inside? They'd done too many horrible things to count, but this was still the worst, and most dangerous.

"Yeah. It is. Even the assistant professor is concerned. The obvious ethical question isn't all there is to it. Playing with viruses like this is like trying to burn down only one room in a straw building. Too many things can go wrong."

Joyce sighed, and shrugged my arm away. "I haven't seen you in all this time, and the first thing you do is rope me into another big end-of-the-world thing."

"If not us, then who?" I asked.

"I'm sorry. I can't help you, Taylor," she said, taking a step before turning back to me. "Be careful how you go about this. I don't want you and I to end up on different sides."

"What's that supposed to mean?" I growled. "This can't happen. Don't you understand that?"

"You were on the list, Taylor. Before all of that with the former general, you were going to be investigated. The only reason it never happened is because the president himself asked that you be removed. You could end up back on there if you cause more trouble. Do you have any idea what reeducation is like, Taylor?

"I'll answer that for you. No one does. I've escorted people to those facilities, and months later, I escorted them back. Most of them aren't the same. Not just different in the way you'd expect, but every way. Right down to their tastes in food and music. It's like they're replaced. It's horrifying. Have you met Markus after he came out? He's deeply fascinated with marine studies. The ocean, Taylor. Do you remember Professor Pinta, the professor tasked with assimilating the new arrivals? She was the person who orchestrated the assassination attempt on the president! That's how she ended up. You don't have to save the world, Taylor. Why can't you just accept the things you can't change and move on? Why are you so stubborn?" She shouted the last line, probably far louder than she meant to.

I didn't know any of this. About what happened to those who had undergone reeducation. About General Markus. About Professor Pinta. That I was a candidate… "Thank you, Joyce… for always looking out for me. Sorry for throwing something like this in your lap again. If it makes you feel any better, I plan on stopping them through completely legal means start to finish."

She turned her back to me, and at first I thought she might not say anything else before leaving. "And if it doesn't work… what then? What if you try every legal means and none of it works? What then?"

I opened my mouth to answer, but stopped myself. No matter how I considered wording it, every honest answer would come out the same. "Take care, Joyce," I said, turning and walking away before she could push the question again. She didn't chase after me. She didn't shout behind me. She didn't cry out or apologize.

Way to go, Taylor. You handled that so, so well…

CHAPTER 8

Back at the Explorers League, I sat at my desk mulling over the mountain of information that had been dumped on me today. I found myself regretting allowing the transport to be fixed. No… all of this would've just been waiting for me whenever I got back.

There were a couple of tempting ways to approach things now. I knew neither of them would work.

I could go speak directly to the president and make my case against using the virus. Out of respect for my role in stopping Markus's insurrection, he'd probably hear me out. Hear me out, then promptly ignore my concerns. The old man was stubborn, and the last time he did something different because someone asked him to, he was probably in diapers. He seemed particularly prone to paranoia. This was exactly why going to him wasn't a real option. The most likely outcome was that he'd become paranoid of me, remember I was on the infamous list, and assume I was out to get him.

The second option was to speak directly to Professor Lexili, which I had to truly consider. Eventually, I would have to, but probably after the word spread around a bit more. Perhaps she'd feel the pressure from the other professors and be willing to change her mind. Hey… a girl can dream.

"It might help if you come up with another solution," Harlow said, interrupting my thoughts.

"Then why not offer one?" Ghost said, cocking his head and staring at Harlow as though he'd committed some kind of grave sin.

"You're right. Sorry. I'm just thinking aloud."

"Try thinking inside your head. That's what it's for," Ghost said, prompting a laugh from Kelin.

"He got you good, Harlow!" she said.

"I wonder if cats taste like squirrels," Ghost mused.

"So much for thinking inside your head, huh? My species likes to eat birds, you know?" Kelin replied, grinning.

"I wonder what dog, cat, and bird stew would taste like!" I shouted, throwing my arms into the air.

Silence filled the room. Of course, I shouldn't have been so short with them. Especially since they were only kidding around…

I think. And, they were actually trying to help. I couldn't say the same for the humans who had families left behind in the zones, who would happily stand by while the people they once cared about die from some lab-made virus. The dogs and cats, and Ghost for that matter, didn't even have anything at stake. Then again, I couldn't be sure of even that. Since they'd been altered, and the basis for that alteration was human DNA, then maybe…

"Apologies, Professor," Harlow said, putting his paws behind his head and leaning back in his chair. "I just wish we could help you come up with a solution."

"There is no solution," Ghost said. "If the human society has reached this point, foiling the current course will only briefly delay the inevitable. We would be better off—"

"Delaying the inevitable is the essence of what it means to be human, Ghost. Every day you choose to live instead of die is a day you've only delayed the inevitable. There's value in that."

Ghost stared at me for a moment, offering no reply. For him, this meant he was actually considering my words. He saw no value in arguing, holding onto erroneous views, or winning.

"We're the Explorers League. Why don't we… you know… expand and establish new zones?"

I tapped my chin, and for a moment ignored the absurdity of a human, a cat, a dog, and a bird sitting in a room together, trying to come up with a plan to save humanity. Or… I tried to, at least. "It's a good idea, but there are problems. Let's say we could make a zone, and populate it with babies and youth from all the various zones across PanTech territory. Let's say we could somehow assimilate them with one another. Let's say PanTech would even approve of a mixed culture zone that didn't match the fictional stereotype frameworks. Let's say we could do all of that, which would be nigh impossible, but let's say we could do it… what's to stop this problem from returning within a generation or two?"

"Sterilization?" Harlow asked.

"Sure, that would solve the problem, and create an even bigger one. The purpose of these zones are to provide PanTech with the next generation of intelligent, hardship-hardened employees to keep our society running. If they all just slowly die off, it's not much different than the virus."

Ghost shook his head. "No. It is different. It's controlled. It's a way of handling the overflow of population in a controlled, you might even say 'humane,' way. The members of this zone can live happy lives, grow old, and die naturally. Far less terrifying than perishing by a dangerous virus at random. It also avoids all the many complications and risks of using a virus."

I rubbed my hands over my face, the exhaustion suddenly catching up with me. He was being extremely cold, analytical, and emotionless with his assessment, but he wasn't exactly wrong. Maybe this was a valid counterproposal if other efforts failed.

Suddenly, a knock came at the door. Given everything happening, my heart skipped a beat.

"Come in," I said.

Linda stepped in and invited herself to sit in one of the chairs. "Mind if I join the big meeting?"

"Does that matter?" Ghost asked.

"What? That I join the meeting, or whether or not you mind if I join?"

"The latter," he said.

Linda grinned. "You're funny, Ghost."

"Where's Henry?" he asked.

"I thought… maybe the weight of the topic might not be to his liking."

I sighed. "So, Joyce sent you?"

"She did, but I'm here for my own reasons. You two are prone to not really hearing the other out sometimes. I'm more concerned with the topic that started it all. Tell me about this virus situation."

After spending the next several minutes catching Linda up on everything, she was finally comfortable adding her own input.

"I think offering to have the Explorers League establish a new adversity zone is a decent alternative. However, with your good intentions, you seem to be forgetting how it'll be interpreted."

I tapped the desk with my fingertips, understanding immediately what she meant.

"Self-promotion. Jumping at an opportunity to undermine Pandemic Research and advance the Explorers League. It's the reason everyone else would do it, after all."

"Let me talk to Barth about that. Maybe he'd be willing to

suggest it on your behalf."

I laughed. "Do you think Barth really cares about how this all plays out? He's the very definition of self-promotion."

"I think he owes you, and he knows it," Linda said. "As for joining with you in a no confidence vote…"

"Yeah, I know. Not a chance. He'd do anything to get closer to the president. If anything, he'd welcome the opportunity to take his side on any issue with no questions asked."

"Don't be so sure. He does have lines he isn't willing to cross. This virus might be one of them. I agree if it's about most things, but even though Barth is a grandstander, there are ethical lines he isn't willing to cross."

I nodded. I hadn't even considered the possibility we'd have his support, and still wouldn't hold my breath for it. "Did Joyce tell you I was on 'the list' when she talked to you?" I asked, curious why she hadn't brought this up yet.

"She did. I was on it too, Taylor. Lots of people get on it and get taken off of it. Reeducation is rare. Rare enough that a lot of people confuse it with being retrained for their division. She's being paranoid. There's no actual reason for you to be on it, regardless of what your philosophy on PanTech is. You're basically a hero here. You've foiled a rebellion in your own zone, and then a massive insurrection here. One that if we hadn't intervened, might have actually worked. They can shove their list. Those of us who just want the organization to go in the right direction aren't the same as someone actively trying to destroy it."

Was that true, though? Was there really a difference? The general certainly felt like he was steering the organization in the right direction. He thought a more military-oriented PanTech was what was best for humanity. In his mind, he was the hero of his own story. Isn't that how it is for everyone who ends up being called a villain? "I don't know, Linda… The president is becoming more and more paranoid as time goes by. That's how the general made his opening in the first place, and after being betrayed by someone he thought was a friend, that's only gotten worse. He'd turned down the virus proposal before, but now he supports it."

Kelin, Harlow, and Ghost all watched the exchange. Quietly, for some reason.

"Maybe you're assuming too much. Reading too much into it. Why don't you just go talk to him?" she asked.

"Because if I go talk to him, it's just going to put a target on my back. According to Joyce, there's already one there anyway."

"Don't you think he'd be more upset that you didn't go and talk to him first?"

I took a deep breath, leaning back in my chair and closing my eyes. What a great point. Wasn't she right? Of course she was, but so was I.

I really, really hated PanTech politics, and all the games that had to be played. So close to just going back out on a mission and seeing how long I can stay gone without a search party coming after me. A month? Two months? I could never be that lucky.

"Alright. I can't argue with that."

Kelin shook her head slowly, looking me in the eyes. "I don't like that… It sounds dangerous."

I shrugged, clasping my hands on the desk in front of me. "Of course it's dangerous. We're dealing with an awful situation, and this time it's authorized from the top," I said.

"Not our problem," Ghost said, repeating his previous sentiments.

"We're a team. Anyone's problem is everyone's problem," Harlow interjected.

"Do you want me to come with you?" Linda asked, not allowing herself to be pulled into the debate going on around her.

"No, that's alright. I think it'll be fine as long as I play everything right. I'm not going anywhere until tomorrow, and there's someone I want to see first anyway. Talk to Barth, and let me know what he thinks about the whole thing. Maybe he'll surprise me after all."

"He has been known to be full of surprises. Not always good ones, but maybe this time."

"Thank you for stopping by. You should bring Henry next time. Ghost likes to see him."

Ghost nodded. "I do like Henry."

"Oh, come on! We should be buddies by now too, Ghost," Harlow said, throwing his paws into the air.

Ghost eyed him for a moment, thinking it over. "Fine," he said, after a minute of serious contemplation.

"Me too, right, Ghost?" Kelin said, raising her paw like a timid student in a classroom.

"I only agree to this because it will reduce Taylor's stress,"

Ghost abruptly flew out the window after finally having enough of the conversation.

At this rate, Ghost would have more friends than me, despite only making them on my account.

Sheesh.

CHAPTER 9

When the morning came, I found myself dreading the detour more than the destination. Not that I didn't have plenty of dread about seeing the president. He'd already agreed to my request to meet, and there was no turning back now. I'd have to follow through. I should've gone straight there, but a morbid curiosity had gripped me ever since Joyce mentioned his name.

"Welcome to Marine Biology," a tall woman said, her voice not at all matching her appearance. She had possibly one of the smallest and cutest voices I'd ever heard. "You're Professor Taylor, right? From the Explorers League?"

I nodded. "That's right. There's someone here I'd like to borrow for a few minutes if you wouldn't mind. Just for a conversation."

"Oh, I see. Are you exploring as far out as the sea? If so, I'm sure several of our experts would love to tag along. You'd have no problem finding volunteers."

I raised my hands, trying to calm her down before the buildup leading to disappointment. "We've not gone out that far just yet, though that's a wonderful suggestion you've made. I'll keep it in mind once we make it that far out. I just want to speak with one of your members. Markus is here, right?"

She grew instantly quiet, and her shoulders sagged. Her expression tightened, and she broke eye contact, suddenly looking ill. "Oh… Markus?"

"Yes. Are… you alright?" I placed a hand on her shoulder, despite the fact I could barely reach it.

"Yes, thank you, Professor. Markus isn't really a member of this division. Just an enthusiast we host. The president asked us to treat him, on account of his previous…" She trailed off. She was really struggling to phrase all this in a way that didn't seem completely insane. Unsurprisingly, she was finding that impossible.

"His previous service as PanTech's head of Adversity Management?" I offered, helping the poor girl as much as I could to get through this conversation.

"Yes."

"So, can I see him?"

"Eh… don't you want to speak to one of our scientists instead? If it's ocean life you're interested in learning about, one of our official scientists would be much better educated and equipped to help you. They also have access to our vast database of records, as well as—"

"I'm not here to learn about fish or anything like that. I'll do that another time. If I can't see him, just say so," I said. The frustration was building. I didn't want to spend the next hour playing word games with this woman, no matter how well-intentioned she was.

Silence again, lasting several seconds.

Finally, she gave in.

"Follow me," she said, almost under her breath.

She brought me to a room, separated from the rest. It reminded me a lot of the recreational simulation rooms back at Animal Research, where you could spend hours on end immersed in a fantasy world. I wondered if that's how they'd done it. Had they trapped him in some kind of fantasy world where he won, and was now the supreme leader of PanTech?

"Wait here," she said, stopping in front of the large door that stood between us and the room's interior.

I nodded, and she held up her hand, triggering the door to open. She stepped inside, and was there for several minutes before returning.

"He'll see you now," she said. "Try not to stay in there too long. It's been a while, but he's still… adjusting."

I swallowed hard, giving away my nerves. "Thank you." I stepped inside the room, and was amazed by what greeted me.

The interior of the room was much smaller than the outside because it was a giant aquarium. The entire room. Ceiling, floor, walls. Everything. All manner of fish and shark swam around the room as a man walked frantically along with one of them, jotting down notes in a book as he did. An actual, physical book. His silver hair was different, but the rest of the giant man was unmistakable.

He turned abruptly, smiling wide.

"Oh, Taylor! Very kind of you to visit. Come have a look at this beautiful hammerhead. Isn't she a thing to marvel at, truly?"

"Um… yes. She is," I tried to say. It came out more like a mumble.

I'd done everything I could to brace myself for this before

arriving, but nothing prepared me for this.

"I'm sorry, dear. The filtration system and the poor acoustics make the room a bit noisy. Come on over here. Let me point her out to you," he said, his smile still not wavering.

I walked slowly, but the floor felt like it wobbled under every step. I wanted to believe the sensation was from the transparent glass below, giving me the sensation of walking on water, but I knew better. It was repressed fear coming to the surface. This man had tried to kill me not all that long ago. Not long ago, he was the most dangerous man at PanTech.

"How have you been, Markus?" I managed, with effort, to speak loud enough for him to hear this time.

"Never better in my life. We haven't had a chance to talk much in the past, but did I ever tell you that I was a boat captain in my adversity zone?" he asked, his tone disarmingly chipper.

"I… no. You never told me that."

"A fisherman, I was, or at least that's what we told everyone. In truth, we were pirates. There were three sizable islands in the territory of my zone—with enough distance between them, our ports weren't visible to one another. There was a small island in the center where supplies would be dropped. Food, medicine, building supplies, you name it. PanTech would break up any kind of monopoly of the island, so we'd wait for the flare gun to fire, signaling when supplies would be dropped."

"That sounds…" I hesitated. How would he react if I said what was on my mind. Should I? Again, curiosity got the better of me. It's why I was here, after all. "Awful. It sounds awful to have to fight like that over resources."

"My dear, it *was* awful! Of course it was. It wouldn't have molded us into strong men and women if it wasn't. Awful is the whole point. I did make a bit of a mistake. A group of merchants pooled together money, hoping to clean up that whole pirate problem and establish a trade agreement between the islands, resulting in peace and profit. As the man with the best fleet at the time, I was the one they approached, and I was a sucker for gold. Let me tell you, a bigger sucker for gold there likely never was."

"You established a navy?"

He nodded, laughing heartily as though I'd told a joke. "It all happened so quickly that we managed to beat every pirate fleet into submission before PanTech's next drop and seal the treaty. When

PanTech arrived, they attacked us immediately. It should've been a bloodbath, but I anticipated their move and set an ambush. We killed quite a few of them by luring them off the island and into the water. The suits at the time weren't easily removed and weren't the best for swimming. About like swimming with a suit of lead."

"What happened after that?"

"Oh, we lost very quickly. You can imagine the technology and firepower difference. I thought we'd all be executed, but the zone commander was so impressed he ordered my whole crew to be captured alive, tested that very day regardless of age, and forced to join PanTech if our scores were high enough."

"And if they weren't?"

He made the throat-slitting gesture, and winked.

"I've never heard of involuntary recruitment," I said, wondering if this story was even true, or if it was something implanted in his mind as part of reeducation.

"Nor have I. Not before, and not since. It was a very unique moment in history, my dear. But all of that's a bit of backstory. The important thing is that's where I developed my love of the sea and all her creatures. Being a part of Adversity Management, I never got to pursue my true love. Thanks to the president, and this kind division for hosting me, I get to indulge in that love every day."

"Markus…" I said, my voice growing quiet again.

He looked at me, narrowing his eyes, but eager to hear my question.

"What do you remember about reeducation?"

His face contorted, and he scratched his chin while he watched a school of fish swim by. "Nothing. I remember going in, and I remember coming out. When I asked about it, they told me that was normal."

"Do you…" I hesitated again. This felt like playing with fire. "Do you feel better off or worse off as a result of the process?"

"Oh, better. Completely. It's not like they took someone else's brain and put it into my body or replaced my memories. I remember everything I did before. I'm just deeply ashamed of it now, as I should be. I'm sure you'd agree. My heart was full of anger and unhappiness before, and I wasn't always like that. The president and I were good friends ever since I was appointed as general, the head of Adversity Management. I don't know what came over me. Maybe a mental illness, or a hubris combined with a bitterness that came with age, or just a sour view of the world as a whole. This division was here the entire time, and I didn't once visit it."

I stared down at my feet. He was the same man, just different. I couldn't shake the feeling that there was something odd about him. But the way he spoke about it, he made it sound as though reeducation was a wonderful experience everyone should try. His happiness didn't seem fake. He loved spending his days here, and I could see he meant it. He wasn't spouting lies for an audience.

"My companion and I almost killed you. Almost, and not for lack of trying. Doesn't that stir anything in you?"

He sighed, letting his smile fade for the first time. "I do feel something. A lot of things. Sadness, for one. Shame. I want to apologize to you for what I put you through. Perverting your experiments, toying with Ghost and implanting him with tech, and sending you to that adversity zone to die. I was deserving of your hatred, and even more. You're young still, so I hope that if enough time goes by, you'll be able to forgive me for the things I've done. I don't expect you to do it right now, here in this room, but maybe someday."

He meant it. He was tearing up as he struggled to force out the words. He deeply, sincerely, meant every word of this apology. And that terrified me more than anything I could have expected. "Thank you for agreeing to meet with me," I said.

"Congratulations on making professor," he said, saluting.

"Thank you," I said, before leaving the room.

I'm not sure I've ever felt so much pity for a person.

CHAPTER 10

Even though I'd met with the president a few times before, this was my first time meeting him in his office. Only a handful of professors were given the honor. Otherwise, they could only wait for him to come and see them. For many, that didn't happen. You have to prove yourself important enough. Barth had been trying for years, after all, and only managed to achieve it after the intelligent animal experiments. Still, I wasn't sure if he'd ever been invited to a meeting here.

Two very imposing guards met me in front of a large metal door. My guess is that these two were fully enhanced. They wore a lighter version of the soldier armor, and carried the same sidearm on their hips. They didn't say a word to me, simply pointing to a round platform in front of them.

"Nothing abnormal," one said to the other.

"Pat her down anyway," he replied.

"Raise your arms," the other said, finally turning his attention to me.

I wasn't thrilled about it, but I also wasn't surprised. The man was paranoid, and growing more paranoid by the day. I was lucky they weren't shackling me in chains.

He patted me down, which was one of the most uncomfortable experiences of my life. The entire time, he didn't say a word. "You guys should really work on your people skills," I said.

"I have the right people skills for the job," he replied.

True, I suppose.

"Into the elevator," the other man said, motioning me inside a square room.

When I stepped inside, the door closed behind me, and I felt the entire room shift and wobble. It was moving.

There was a ding after a brief wait, and the door opened again. There were ten guards in this room, but the elevator's opening was blocked by a layer of thick glass. One man's hand rested on a large button, which I assumed would lift it. One of the other guards stood next to a different button, which he pressed after waving at me.

So, if I'd gotten on this elevator with bad intentions, and somehow got past the two guards by the door, this is where I would've died. Good to know.

Another movement, then another stop. This room was completely dark, but felt larger than the last somehow. I squinted, wishing I had some kind of light on me. Before I could make anything out clearly, the door closed again. Just before it did, I saw something. The shadow of the door closing gave it the faintest shape. Was that... a machine?

The elevator moved again, and I fought back the fear building inside of me. I worried that, on the next stop, there'd be something there that would shoot me if it detected fear. It was a joke I told myself inside my head at first, but it seemed plausible at this point. Just how paranoid could one man be?

The elevator stopped again, and I braced myself for whatever oddity awaited me next. Instead, it opened to reveal a very normal looking office, even if a bit old-fashioned. There were a lot of old-fashioned people at PanTech, so this wasn't at all strange. The only thing that was out of place was the fact it was empty. I stepped inside, looking around.

"Mr. President?" I said, looking all around me.

No answer.

I sat in one of the large, overly-cushioned chairs across from his desk. I was a little early, so maybe he'd be coming behind me. Yet, that seemed strange, given all the security. There was a door at the back of the room I saw when I came in. Perhaps it was a restroom, or maybe he kept more bodyguards hidden away back there, ready to spring out at the first sign of trouble.

"Through the door in the back of the room. I'll be waiting for you there," a voice said, filling the room.

Now I really was regretting my decision to come here. Everything about this felt eerie. It was too late to turn back now. Leaving things like this would only make me look just as paranoid.

I stood up and walked slowly to the back of the room, taking several deep breaths as I went. One final deep breath, then I pushed open the door.

The light filled my vision, like stepping outside into the bright sun after a snowstorm. After a few seconds of adjustment, my mind struggled to process what I was seeing.

The room was massive. As big as the auditorium we introduced Henry in. No, bigger! Giant machines of war lined the walls the whole way around. Fifty or more. Closer to a hundred. Not the rusty, impaired versions we'd been encountering in the wilderness. These were well-maintained, polished, and topped off on ammo. Why in the world were these things here?

"Welcome to my laboratory, Professor. You're now one of fewer than a dozen people currently living who have seen this place. Tell me, what are your first thoughts? Don't hold back. I will know if you're lying."

He'll know if I'm lying?

My eyes moved to the side of the room, where a man stood upright and tall in front of a large work desk. There was an arm in front of him, but it wasn't made of flesh. Instead, it was mechanical, like the giant machines themselves. He picked it up with his right arm, attaching it to his torso. A prosthetic?

"Awe. Confusion. Fear. I'm impressed, but I don't understand what I'm looking at. I don't understand why you're showing me this place. It's a lot to take in all at once."

He laughed, strolling toward me with the zest and bounce of an athletic youth. This man who walked around PanTech with a cane in his hand, his back curved with age… his face was the same, but his body was different.

"All perfectly reasonable reactions," he said. "I'm aware of your research on this organization's history, and your conversations with our former general. I'm even aware of the one you had with him today. Not much goes on in PanTech that I'm not aware of. Though I'm only human, and like all humans, I do have my blind spots. These machines. You recognize them, yes?"

I nodded. "Are these the machines PanTech used to crush the rebellion?"

As if to answer my question, he began to remove his clothing. I instinctively took a step back.

"Bear with me for a moment. It's not what you're probably thinking. You just may not believe me if I don't show you."

He was almost fully machine. Nothing human remained below the neck. As hard as I was trying to put things together, this didn't make any sense.

"The organization bans mechanical augmentation of humans… so why?"

"I was originally a supporter of the rebels, from a society where augmentation was commonplace. A scientific leader among them, you might say. That was set to be a long and brutal conflict. The loss of life, primarily targeting the brightest and most capable humanity had to offer, would have set humanity back to the dark ages. A great man is able to change his position in the face of changing evidence and circumstances, and I did my best to be a great man."

"You… betrayed the rebellion?"

"In a sense, but I saw it as maintaining my loyalty to the advancement of humanity. The previous leader of PanTech came up with the idea of the adversity zones, but that involved capturing and pacifying every remaining territory not under PanTech's control. With our advanced technology, rivaling PanTech's in all the ways that counted in war, we didn't prove so easy to control."

I rubbed my head. This wasn't getting any easier to understand.

"I can see you're struggling, but please be patient a bit longer. This will all fit together for you very soon. I met in secret with PanTech's president at the time, and we came to an agreement, brought about by what you might call a fast friendship. If I would be willing to turn my machines on our own forces, it would essentially be two armies against one. The slaughter would conclude in mere days. At worst, weeks. Humanity could retain its progress. Even learn a few valuable lessons. Certainly, I was eager to make this humanity's final war. Eternal peace through a unified rule. A scientific utopia where humanity maintains all the virtues built through hardship, and all of the advancement built through excess."

"Humans are born to be free…" I said. It was all I could think to say. It was all I could manage to feel in the moment, and also the kindest thing I could think of while suppressing my anger.

"It seems I've really upset you. Your heart rate is rising rapidly, and your breathing has quickened. Your skin's temperature is up. But to your remark, I ask: What is so great about freedom? If you could choose freedom and misery, or servitude and happiness, which would you choose?"

"This is where you're mistaken. You connect freedom and misery as though they can't be separated. What if the third option was free and happy?"

He laughed, shaking his head at me, the way a teacher might pity a struggling student learning the basics of a subject. "For brief moments in time, this is indeed possible. Again, I don't deny evidence. There are many examples. However, they all crumble in mere centuries. Often far sooner. Humanity experiences cycles of extreme hardship, followed by peace and plenty, only to have it repeat again endlessly. Aren't you interested in a solution that ends this cycle?"

"By condensing the cycle into a single lifetime?"

"Our formative years are brief in the context of our lives. The hardships experienced as youth remain with us into adulthood and beyond. We carry them to our graves. Even in my long life, the hard times are burned into my mind like scars into flesh that never fade. I won't minimize the price paid. It's steep. However, isn't what you gain from it well worth it?"

"Except most aren't given the privilege, and they remain in that hardship until the day they die because they scored too low on an exam."

"An unfortunate but necessary sacrifice to guarantee the advancement of humanity."

"According to whom? You? And with the less intelligent left behind while the 'worthy' are brought here and sterilized—the pool of humanity has to grow larger in order to maintain the intake. All the while, the average intelligence decreases more and more within the zones. Larger populations become difficult to manage."

"In addition to the many other things about you, I'm also aware of your reason for coming. You can get straight to the point if you'd like."

"It's wrong to unleash a virus on humanity. On such a massive scale, but even on any scale. We have to stop playing at being gods here. It's dangerous."

"You have a lot in common with Markus it seems. He said the same thing, and kept convincing me to put it off until we could come up with better solutions. As I said, I do have my blind spots. I expect it played a role in why he wished to overthrow me, but he was not quite as benevolent as you. He at least recognized the problem, only wanting a different solution. You don't seem to realize the problem is a problem at all. You even seem to believe that the problem itself is the solution. Abolish the adversity zones, right? Unify humanity and dissolve PanTech?

"How naive. It would be less than a hundred years before the bombs began to fall once again, and factions arm themselves to kill one another over any perceived differences they can use to justify it. The color of your skin. Your religion. A leader scorned. Any excuse. Do you really want humanity to return to that endless cycle of awakening and nightmare?"

"It's not our place to decide what's best for each person."

He sighed, walking back to the table where he'd been working when I arrived.

"I invited you here, to see this room, because I had high hopes for you. You're bold, bright, and care for humanity's future. I thought I could convince you, but it seems your thinking is so fundamentally flawed that even I can't manage it. The virus's study, and the plan's ultimate execution, will continue on the current path. Not simply because I want it to, but because it is essential to maintain humanity's ascension. Our path toward our true potential and greatness. I would advise you strongly against acting rashly. If it makes you feel any better, know that you did everything in your power to stop it. Now go. If you have a change of heart, let me know."

"Mr. President… you don't—"

"Go!" he shouted.

I didn't linger further. I'd already overstayed my welcome, and I knew it.

Coming here was a mistake.

CHAPTER 11

Now that I'd foolishly made the no confidence vote the most dangerous approach, I had to change my plan once again. Everything was moving so quickly, but misstep after misstep upped the stakes and narrowed the window. Even though this virus wasn't likely to manifest inside of a year, my opportunity to stop it was dwindling. If it could be stopped.

No, it had to be stopped. No matter the cost. This was no different than the snake Linus and I had killed. I'd risked my life to stop the snake. Linus ultimately paid that price. This was even worse. It would be an insult to his memory to back down.

I stepped through the doors at Pandemic Research, and was approached by a smiling young man.

"The database says you're Professor Taylor from the Explorers League? It's a pleasure to meet you, Professor. How can we help you here in Pandemic Research?"

"I'd like to have a meeting with Professor Lexili," I said, not in my calmest voice. I was still shaken up from my meeting with the president, and my anxiety was likely coming across as aggression. That was fine, though. Aggression worked too.

"Um… when would you like to schedule the meeting? She doesn't normally accept them, but I'm sure she'll make an exception for another professor."

"I don't want to schedule it. I want to have the meeting right now," I said, this time with the force intentional.

"Professor. With all due respect—"

"Your respect isn't necessary, and the meeting isn't optional. Go and tell her I need to meet with her urgently and it can't wait."

"But… she's currently analyzing a very important—"

I grabbed the young man by the shirt collar, pulling him close. "Look, I'm sorry that I've just stormed in here unannounced and made your day difficult. If it makes you feel any better, I've had a *very* surprise-filled and difficult day myself. So much so that it's led me here, storming in unannounced, demanding a meeting with your professor. I'm not taking no for an answer. I'm not leaving. If you don't arrange the meeting for me, I'm going to walk the halls of this place until I find her myself."

"You can't do that! This isn't your division."

I sighed, letting go of his collar. "Then you'll have to accept my apology after the fact." I turned to leave, but made it just three steps before his hand gripped my wrist.

"Wait! I'll inform her you're here and the meeting is urgent. Please don't cause any trouble. Just wait a moment."

I stopped and turned back around, only nodding in reply.

He pressed his finger to his ear, and spoke. "Professor… yes, I know you're—I'm sorry. Yes… There's someone here who is demanding a meeting with you, saying it is of the utmost urgency. No, Professor. She—Professor Taylor of the Explorers League. Yes, Professor." He looked up to me, his face growing even more pale than before. "Down the hall and to your left. Room 108."

I nodded, making my way down the hall. It was so close to where we were that she'd likely heard me shouting.

I stepped into the room, and a petite, dark-skinned woman pushed up her glasses and crossed her arms. She was small enough that she might have been mistaken for a child, were we not in a place a child couldn't exist. Her small, brown afro bounced when she tilted her head.

"You have the nerve to demand a meeting like you're the president, then stand there as though you're a confused low-level primate? And you're supposed to be the great Professor Taylor? I'd laugh were I not so disappointed."

And the child-like aura was very quickly dispelled.

"Forgive me. I've had an eventful day and I'm gathering my thoughts so I don't waste any more of your time than I have to," I said, sitting in the seat across from her.

"Allow me to surmise. My assistant professor, in his lust-addled stupor, approached you starstruck, spouting all manner of nonsense about saving the world? It's you who is owed an apology that he has caused such a disruption to your day. I'll speak to him for you and ask that he be more aware of his station. He's my close friend by the way, so do stay away from him if you intend to use your wiles to manipulate him to do your bidding. Goodness knows he's quite prone to it, after all."

"What?!" I shouted. "No. That's not it at all. It's obvious that you're only trying to get under my skin so I lower my guard, though I don't know why. It's not like we've met before or I've done anything to you."

"Are you joking? You know exactly what you've done to me,

you little temptress, and I'll not have you disrupt my work. If need be, I'll bring security over here to escort you back to your own division. Perhaps you're used to barging in places and getting your way, but I'll remind you that Pandemic Research is my domain, and I am the queen who sits upon a very old and powerful throne. We are not equals."

What was her deal? Why was she so hostile with me? I might have assumed she would be annoyed with me for the way I barged in, but it went much deeper than that. She already hated me before I showed up today… but why? Another setback I did *not* need…

"I'm very sorry for getting off on the wrong foot with you. I'll stop making excuses for forgetting my manners. I'm not sure what you think I've come here to discuss, but it has nothing to do with your assistant."

"Do you mean to tell me he didn't go and see you recently to complain of my sinister plans to kill off a sizable swathe of the human race?" she asked, tilting her head again, causing her glasses to slide down her nose. "I guess idealists are Cherun's preference after all."

Why did she keep coming back to this?

Oh…

I was starting to understand.

"He asked that I come here, more out of concern for you than for any other reason. He spoke over and over about how much he admired you, and he worried that you'd lost your way. He was afraid that you didn't respect him enough to consider his words. He thought a fellow professor's concerns might carry more weight."

"That idiot…" she mumbled, pushing her glasses back up and turning away from me. "That stupid, dense…"

This woman was a firestorm. She reminded me of Frelya a bit… if Frelya was less than five feet tall but somehow just as scary.

"I could tell just from how he described you that wasn't the case, but he insisted," I said, shrugging.

She sighed, turning back toward me again. Her jaw wasn't clenched now, and her eyes looked as though they might release tears. It worked. She wasn't about to explode anymore, at least. I hoped.

"I *did* hear him out. Of course I respect him. He's the most important person in the world to me. I depend on him for everything. If I didn't have so much faith in him to implement perfect safety measures, I would worry too. You have to understand that there aren't any alternatives to this. They've been explored for years. General Markus was insane, but he held the only alternative. Don't you at least see how his plan was even worse than mine? It's a pity the president gave him so much weight in the organization despite being a military man. Don't misunderstand. I recognize Markus as the genius he was, perhaps still is, but these matters should not be left to a military solution. We are, at our core, an organization built on the back of science. Pandemic Research, if I can be even more specific. There is no other field of study this organization is more experienced in and capable of handling."

"Would you be gracious enough to allow me to propose one? I didn't come up with it, but I wanted to at least offer it to you to get your thoughts on it."

She tilted her head the other way, her glasses sliding to the end of her nose again. She eyed me from above them. "Go on," she said, raising a brow.

"The Explorers League is in the unique position to establish new adversity zones quickly and to rigorous specifications. Through our exploration, we've rediscovered land that had been previously disregarded, much of which would make an excellent home for a run-off population zone."

She grinned, visibly relaxing. "A run-off population zone, you say? I'm listening."

She was actually hearing me out. This might work!

"Yes! A run-off population zone. We could take children born in the zones with the biggest population challenges, and integrate them into this run-off zone. I don't have any ideas on this zone's theme, but I'd love to hear your suggestions. Additionally, a transferee to this zone could be sterilized, just as we are here. In fact, it could function similarly to the way we recruit here, only it would recruit based on population criteria rather than testing scores. Those with lower projected intelligence based on their birth parents could be prioritized. Perhaps we could encourage volunteers based on a reward system. There are many possibilities, and challenges to overcome. There are many flaws to this proposal, I know, but they can be addressed with the effort from great minds.”

She leaned back in her chair, pushing her glasses back up her nose and uncrossing her arms.

“You are actually… I mean, you are genuinely approaching this from the perspective of humanity’s best interests. This isn’t some ploy or power grab? You aren’t trying to undermine me, or steal my assistant?”

“I swear it, on my life, I would never do something like that to another woman.”

She nodded, slowly at first, then with more enthusiasm. “You know… this idea of yours. It could work. I’d be risking a lot by asking the president to withdraw his order for the project, so if you could allow me to formulate a way for my division to be involved with this zone’s theme, then—”

“Absolutely, Professor Lexili! That would not be a problem. I can’t tell you how much it means to me that you… No one else would listen to me. You have the most to lose, but you did. Thank you.”

“Pfft! Stop that. Get your emotions in check. You are a professor, not some fawning fan girl.”

“Right. Sorry.” I took a deep breath, trying to compose myself.

For once, something was going differently than I expected and it was actually in a good way.

“I’ll expect you to come back here tomorrow so we can go over these plans in greater detail. Bring at least one person with you, and I’ll invite Cherun into the meeting as well. A human, if you don’t mind, not that I have anything against your animal assistants. They aren’t technically employees, and that is a requirement. We need to enter data to construct a simulation and begin addressing the most glaring points for potential failure. Just as with my own plans, it may need months or years of refinement before implementation.”

“I look forward to working with you,” I said, saluting after I stood to my feet.

“Oh, not that silly salute. What a waste of energy that is. Goodbye. I’ll see you tomorrow. Now, I really must get back to my work. I need to draft a formal request for the president and now you’re eating into that time. Plus, I need to move the analysis to tomorrow…”

She continued mumbling to herself before looking back up to

me.

"Well? What are you still standing there for?" she asked.

"Right. Tomorrow, then," I said, pivoting and quickly walking away.

It seemed this crisis would be averted after all. Peacefully.

I just couldn't shake the feeling that it was all too good to be true.

CHAPTER 12

The next morning, I slid out of bed feeling refreshed and excited about the day ahead, despite the fact I'd barely slept. Farle's transfer had been approved yesterday morning before I went to visit with the president, and Harlow had already given him a tour.

When I stepped out, I was surprised to find a crowd of cats and dogs concentrated around the center of the lobby. We'd spent very little time on anything extravagant, so the Explorers League was almost the opposite of Adversity Management, with its large buildings and architectural marvels. Our division was set up not so much different from our camps when out on missions. In truth, I gave them this design as something temporary, planning to flesh it out later. Only we got used to it, and the thought never crossed my mind again. I'd planned on spending as little time here as possible anyway.

"Good morning, Professor. Care to come see what all the fuss is about?" Farle shouted from the middle, leaned over a large cauldron billowing smoke.

I walked over, past several dogs and cats holding stone bowls, blowing on spoons of some kind of stew.

"Making yourself right at home, I see," I said, picking up an empty bowl and holding it out in front of him. "What is this stuff?"

"PanTech's artificial meat garbage, with a twist. I have a secret garden outside the wall, using seeds I brought with me from home. Potatoes, carrots, tomatoes and peas. Plus rice I bartered from a soldier a few days ago, along with garlic for flavor."

I nodded several times and whistled, more impressed by the fact he chose to bring seeds with him than anything else. Everyone else brought some kind of family heirloom, expensive furniture, or weapon. For me, it was Ghost—though I was lucky in that I was able to smuggle in my father's smoking pipe and mother's unique dress as well. "You're quite the cook. I wish I'd paid more attention to my mother when she tried to teach me."

He filled my bowl with a generous serving, and dropped in a spoon.

"My father once said that grass is for animals, and meat is for a man. My father also taught me that there is no more vicious an animal in all the world than a man. Our camp is also shared by both carnivores and omnivores, so both should be served."

"Actually, these cats are a bit different. Modified in all the ways you can see, but with some 'upgrades' as well. They're perfectly able to survive on vegetables, unlike their wild counterparts."

Farle laughed, catching me off guard. "Give them meat, and you will see. No one is ever far from their wild roots. Not humans, and I'd wager not cats either."

I guessed that he was probably correct. We found in our studies that certain things are so deeply ingrained in an animal's being that we were never able to identify and alter them. Birds were often born with entire maps imprinted into their minds, as accurate as any of our modern navigation hardware. It's strange how a creature can be born with knowledge that should only be possible to pass down through teaching. Even if their body could sustain itself on vegetables, cats probably did still have a strong craving for meat, even if most of them had never eaten it and didn't know it yet. "We'll go on a hunt soon, and find out."

He smiled. "I'd be honored to accompany you on a hunt."

The more I saw of this man, the more attractive I found him. He was poorly adjusted to life at PanTech, and his mannerisms and behavior were consistent with someone who had never set foot here. Even I'd adjusted better than this. Based on Farle, I could almost imagine his zone and how people interacted there. "I'd like for you to accompany me today actually, though not on a hunt. I was asked to bring another human from my division, and it just so happens you are the newest and only one. We'll be meeting with Professor Lexili of Pandemic Research and her assistant professor to discuss a major project for our division."

"Harlow filled me in on the whole situation with the virus. I'd heard rumors, but I didn't really believe it. Did she accept your new zone proposal?"

"Yes. I was really surprised by that, actually… I met with the president yesterday too, and that didn't go so well."

He stood to his feet. "Wait. You met with the president? I've only seen a glimpse of the man from afar. Virtually no one goes to see him."

"And I wish I hadn't either… but that's a story for another time," I said, taking a bite of the stew in hopes of changing the subject. "Not bad!"

"Everyone should be able to help themselves to breakfast. My sister asked me to pass on a request to meet Ghost, and I… think that may be where he is now. Walk with me there?"

"Instead of riding in a transport pod? Music to my ears. Sure, let's go. Oh, and why did you say you *think* Ghost is with your sister?"

He laughed as he began walking toward the entrance. "I told him, and then he just flew off without saying a word. Didn't even acknowledge I'd spoken to him.

I giggled, shaking my head as I walked beside him. "No, I'd say that's pretty typical Ghost. He's only recently started talking to anyone other than me and a dog name Henry."

"Henry? That dog from the original animal intelligence experiment?"

"That's him. An unlikely friend for Ghost, but the two learned to get along quite well out in the field. Henry differs from Ghost in a way that makes them surprisingly compatible. I'm not sure there's an intelligent creature on the planet that Henry can't make friends with."

"I still remember meeting him. I got that impression, even then."

"Oh, that's right. He was with us when we journeyed outside the wall for the first time. Linda, myself, Ghost, and Henry."

"My sister teased me, if you'll remember. Your beauty left me stunned, even then. I normally have no shortage of words, but I did on that day."

We continued walking along the wall. It was a beautiful day, and I found myself missing the searing rays of the sun. PanTech's weather control field only allowed the light in, without any UV. No wind, rain, or fog either. Nothing but light. It was impossible to tell whether it was chilly, or burning hot from within the walls. I knew it was summer, only because I'd been outside of the walls recently, beyond the barrier. I wanted to ask him if he missed the desert like I did, but I had a more pressing question on my mind.

"Why are you so direct, Farle? Aren't you afraid it'll frighten me away?"

"Frighten you? Do you even know the feeling? You have a burning spirit. I can feel it just walking beside you. Even the Great Khan would tread lightly if he met you. No, the possibility of frightening you has never crossed my mind."

"Not sure about burning spirits, or anything like that. I think you're giving me far too much credit."

"Everyone knows what you did, stopping the general. You rushed into a war zone in your pajamas, if the rumors are true. Are they false?"

I laughed before I could stop myself. "No. That one's true, but I'd say that qualifies more as stupidity than a burning spirit."

He shook his head, pointing out the two figures coming into sight ahead.

"A burning spirit drives us to brave things and stupid things. It drives some men to evil, and some to good. The spirit burns when it rages at the world. It's never satisfied until it gets what it wants. Until justice is served, or revenge is achieved. Not even then. A burning spirit can turn a poet into a warrior, or a warrior into a poet. Burning spirits attract one another, like moths to a flame. Once lit, that flame can never go out. Not completely. All it takes is a whisper in the wind to ignite it again, into an inferno."

I suddenly thought of Linus, and Frelya. Even Joyce and Linda. It was especially true of the first two. Linus believed that freedom mattered more than anything. As he put it, he'd chosen the freedom to do bad things over a life of peaceful servitude. Frelya learned the value of strength far too early, and became obsessed with it. She threw away all parts of the normal girl she'd been meant to be, in order to attain as much power as she could.

And what about me? Was I really any different? I always hated PanTech, but after what they did to Linus all I could think about was destroying them. More than Linus, what they've done to everyone. The feeling isn't as strong as it once was, but it also isn't gone.

"There's truth in what you're saying. But… I do think all flames die out. Eventually."

He looked at me, his expression unreadable.

Before he could respond, Glimmer caught sight of us, and began waving her arms furiously. Her bright smile was visible even from the distance. It was strange how chipper and contagiously happy she was, and how serious Farle was by comparison.

"Hi, lovebirds! Ghost was just giving me some old man wisdom."

"This girl is stranger than her brother. Her obsession with raptors borders on unhealthy," Ghost said, with less bite in his voice than usual.

"Bordering, so not over the line. Which means I'm good!" Glimmer responded.

Ghost had nothing to say in return.

"Forgive Ghost. He doesn't have any kind of filter or any interest in learning etiquette," I said.

"Wasted words to spare the egos of fragile humans," he said.

Wow, Ghost. Tell us how you really feel.

Farle nodded in agreement.

"Are you planning on venturing out soon and finding a falcon to raise?" he asked his sister.

"Do you think it's safe enough now, Taylor?"

I shook my head.

"Absolutely not. I can try to bring one back for you, but it might be easier to just ask around Adversity Management. One of the soldiers could do some bartering for you. Better yet, you could transfer over and have no problem getting one yourself."

"I think I've grown attached to the wall."

Farle sighed. "Why? Don't you love being around people?"

"Maybe I've changed?"

A man approached from the distance, but I'd never seen him before. He was clearly walking toward us, but didn't even look.

As he walked by, he bumped into me.

"Hey!" Glimmer said, taking a step after him. Farle stopped her, looking at me, then nodding to the ground. He'd dropped something. A piece of paper? It was rare for anyone to write anything on paper here.

I picked it up and unfolded it, and read. My veins felt as though they'd been instantly filled with ice.

Do not come.
Lexili

Before I had an opportunity to consider the meaning behind the message, loud stomping sounds came from both directions. Three soldiers appeared, guns drawn, stopping the man behind us who had dropped the note. I turned, seeing another three, pointing their blasters at us.

Farle reached down toward his belt, and in the same moment, Ghost flared out his wings, ready to take flight.

"Stop!" I screamed, grabbing Farle's arm. I looked at Ghost, shaking my head slowly. "Stop…" I repeated.

Farle lowered his arm slowly to his side, and Ghost relaxed his wings.

"Wise choice," one of the soldiers said, taking a step forward and grabbing me by the arm.

"Professor Taylor, you are under arrest."

"On what charge?" I said, taking a step toward the man.

"Sedition. Come quietly," he said, turning his back to me, waiting for me to follow. The other five still had their guns pointed directly at me. Even with my enhancer, six soldiers in power armor wouldn't be a small feat. Even if I managed it, they'd only send more. Commanders next time. There was no fighting this.

"Of course. I have nothing to hide," I said.

CHAPTER 13

Shortly after making it out of sight of the others, I was blindfolded and taken to the transport pod. They took the blindfold off only a minute later once we arrived at our destination. I was taken to a room, though I wasn't sure where. I could've guessed based on the direction of travel and how long it had taken us, but that all went out the window once we boarded the transport pod. We could've been on the moon for all I knew.

"Stanford. I will be representing you during the trial," a man in a suit said as he approached me. He wore round-framed glasses, and sported a thin mustache and goatee. His hair was slicked back. This felt more like a diversity zone than PanTech… was it?

"Taylor…," I introduced myself, "…and I have no idea what's going on. Trial?"

"Yes. Your trial is set to begin in a few minutes. We need to go over your case so we can be prepared for the prosecution's questions."

"We don't have time to do that in a few minutes. We've never even met before," I said, raising my voice as I noticed all the robed figures sitting in a circle around the room. The president sat in a chair elevated slightly above the rest. "Wait… so the president will decide my fate?"

He nodded. "That's correct."

"And he's also the one who brought the charges against me. Is that right?" I asked, clenching my teeth.

"That's correct."

"Do the other 'judges' also get a say, or are they just the audience."

"They all get an equal vote, but it is overridden by the president's judgment."

"That's… a complete joke!" I shouted.

It was nothing more than a bit of theater, so the tyrant could claim fairness. Historically, these are called kangaroo courts. This was a perfect example of one. So much for that big speech on the advancement of humanity and leaving past mistakes behind.

"We're nearly out of time, and I'm afraid your lack of faith in the process is a clear admission of guilt in the eyes of the court."

"How about I just represent myself, then?"

"That's uncalled for, Professor. I'm afraid that simply isn't allowed," he said, turning away from me and looking through a folder in his hands.

I shrugged. It didn't really matter anyway.

Suddenly, a sharp pain pierced my skull. It felt as though my brain was on fire, just like it did when I overused the implant before. Except, I hadn't even used it here. Was it because of stress, or were they doing something to me?

I collapsed to the floor, and woke up a few minutes later sitting in a chair. My lawyer was sitting beside me. He shined a light into my eyes, then nodded to the judges.

"She's ready to proceed now. Sorry for the delay, Mr. President."

I was groggy, and my limbs felt heavy. I wasn't even sure I could speak. I wasn't even sure if they'd have let me even if I could.

"How does your client plead, Stanford?"

"Guilty, Mr. President. Unfortunately, the client wasn't cooperative and that left me with no other choice but to enter a guilty plea."

"I see," the president said. "Very unfortunate."

I opened my mouth, but the words came out so quiet that no one could hear me. Not even Stanford, sitting right next to me.

Of course, the words I said weren't at all befitting of a PanTech employee, and wouldn't have helped matters any.

Another man stepped forward from across the room, dressed similarly to Stanford.

"The prosecution would like to lay out the case for all the justices present, Mr. President."

"Proceed," he said, sounding almost like he cared.

"Thank you. Professor Taylor of the newly founded Explorers League stands accused of sedition. However, the prosecution would assert that she's getting off far too lightly here. Treason would be a more appropriate charge. There is plenty of evidence to back this up."

"Objection, Mr. President," my lawyer said, genuinely surprising me. "The prosecution can't simply trump up charges during the middle of a trial, especially since my client has already pled guilty to the lesser charge."

"I'd like to hear this evidence all the same," the president said, waving for the prosecutor to continue.

"Thank you, Mr. President. We can go back as early as the written note of Commander Frelya, adversity manager for Taylor's zone, where she mentions the girl as a troublemaker. Her reckless actions caused the death of three of our employees, and the massive loss of an animal experiment."

"Mr. President, immediately following this, my client single-handedly ended a rebellion within her zone, potentially saving an equal or possibly greater number of lives."

"So glad you brought that up," the prosecutor said. "Later questioning of the rebels revealed that Taylor was a member. She'd taken part in an operation where food and other essential supplies were stolen from our camp. Including testing kits, which delayed our ability to administer exams. It's more likely Taylor betrayed them in order to gain a stronger foothold in her own admission as an employee. She was allowed many special privileges as a result of this."

"Such as?" the president asked.

"She was allowed to bring several items with her, including a Shadowfalcon. I believe you're familiar with it. She calls it Ghost."

"Mr. President, I fail to see how any of this is relevant. Since coming to PanTech, Taylor foiled one of the most dangerous plots against PanTech since the rebellion over a hundred years ago."

The president nodded. "I'm aware. She was rewarded heavily for it, in anticipation of her continued loyalty."

"To you, or to PanTech?" I said, forcing the words out loud enough for him to hear.

"As its president, we are one and the same. Does the prosecution have anything else to add?"

"Before learning of the insurrection plot, Taylor had already begun undermining PanTech. First, by sneaking Ghost out of our walls without the general's permission. That—"

"Former general!" the president roared, startling several of those in the room. "You must be clear about that."

"R—right, Mr. President. Sorry. At the time, she believed this was brazen disobedience to the former general. It was only her good fortune that the man had been secretly planning to betray us. She was the enemy of our enemy, and that was the *only* reason she was our friend."

"Mr. President, this is all wonderful information, and I'm not doubting it, but I don't see how it's relevant to the current charges."

"It's relevant because I said it's relevant," the president said.

"Of course. Sorry, Mr. President."

The prosecution continued.

"And more recently, Mr. President… just yesterday in fact, Professor Taylor went to your office for a meeting. A rare privilege, I might add, for any PanTech employee. Your time is valuable, and anyone offered that time is receiving a rare gift.

"And what would all of you wager is done with this time given? I'll tell you. Professor Taylor spends it undermining the president's authority, and subverting his great vision for PanTech and the future of humanity. Even when she is given the president's final word, she still goes behind his back to sew discord throughout the divisions. Before this meeting, starting rumors and planning a vote of no confidence. After the meeting, secretly obstructing his plans along with the professor who was trusted to carry it out."

"And does everyone here know the plan they're talking about is to kill off a chunk of humanity with a virus?" I asked.

There were a few gasps around me, but they quickly silenced themselves before the president could lay eyes on them.

"Spoken like a true seditionist. Once a rebel, always a rebel it seems. Can anyone here deny the words from the defendant's own mouth spoken aloud, openly and proudly, for all to hear?"

"I'm tired of listening to the president play judge in a fictional court. Just pass out the sentence already!" I tried to sound as defiant as possible. In truth, I was terrified, to the point I could barely speak. I knew what was coming, and delaying it like this was a kind of torture. I'd rather be dead than have… whatever was done to General Markus, done to me.

The president stood up, wobbling on his cane. "Very well. I will ask that everyone vote with a show of hands. All of those in support of an acquittal?"

No hands were raised.

"All those supporting a guilty verdict?" he asked.

An eruption of jeers filled the air. Every hand went up at once, waving enthusiastically in the air as though they were trying to hold it above their peers next to them. Everyone was jostling to show their loyalty to the president. He'd surrounded himself with sycophants.

"Then I will deliver the sentencing," he prompted everyone to go quiet again and sink into their seats. "Professor Taylor will maintain her position as professor, of course. We don't believe in punishment here at PanTech. Rather, rehabilitation and healing. We want very much for Professor Taylor to be happy and conquer the sickness that plagues her mind. She is sentenced to reeducation, effective immediately, and we ask that everyone forgive her past transgressions and welcome her with open arms as she emerges, a brand new person, reborn, and free of the pain and suffering that brought her to this point. That will be all," he banged a gavel on the small table in front of him.

I stood up, grabbing the chair I'd been sitting on. I took a deep breath and held it. I tried to clear my mind, thinking only of this one single thing. I picked it up, and with all of my strength, hurled it toward the president. He used his cane to parry it easily, sending it flying to the side, striking one of the justices and knocking him to the floor. I ran forward, intending to jump to where he was. I'd rather be dead than live on as a brainwashed husk.

Several soldiers rushed at me from both sides. Commanders, with more than enough speed and strength to overpower me and pin me to the floor.

I screamed as loudly as I could, fighting against them, but I couldn't move.

He looked down at me, shaking his head.

"Take her away."

CHAPTER 14

Three Months Later

My name is Taylor.

I'm a professor at PanTech, heading up the Explorers League. PanTech's newest division that ventures out into the wild and unknown, reclaiming old territory lost to nature, and discovering brand new events that occur spontaneously when the land goes long enough without human touch. Sometimes, this means encountering a machine that has ceased to serve its function and needs to be decommissioned. Sometimes, this means documenting new species. Other times, it's simply a relaxing exploration of nature.

I also oversee the largest anthropomorphic cat and dog crew in PanTech, acclimating them to living their life as close to human as possible. Even though they can never become proper PanTech citizens, they can still become valuable assets to the organization and everyone in it. Every day, they grow and learn. Despite their rebellious nature that has popped up as of late, no one could offer a single complaint. I will help them learn the lesson of loyalty over time. It will come to them.

Every day, I wake up thankful for the wonderful opportunity I have to live a life of service. All thanks to PanTech. All thanks to the president's devotion and hard work toward building an organization dedicated to the betterment of all humanity, for all time.

I look back on my life, and almost pity myself. So much time spent hating and trying to make someone pay for imagined crimes, circumstances that were no one's fault, or things I simply didn't understand. I would think about PanTech, and my skin would boil. I'd look at the adversity in my life, not as the gift it was, but as some sort of punishment. Now, it was like looking back on one's own childhood with the clarity of an adult mind.

That was the old Taylor.

This is the new Taylor.

~~o~o~o~~

Despite being the happiest I've ever been, the headache episodes continued on a daily basis. One episode per day, like clockwork, lasting only a few minutes. They'd leave me exhausted for several minutes after, barely able to move. Now that I had finally completed reeducation, I hoped they'd subside. They hadn't, despite being out for nearly a month.

Farle placed his hand on my shoulder, and I forced a smile.

"Did you have one early today?" he asked.

I nodded, bringing my hand up and squeezing his weakly. "This is good. I just need a few minutes, and now I should be good for the whole day."

"They must have done something to your brain during reeducation. Damaged it somehow."

"This again?" I asked, pulling my hand away. "We've been over this. Whatever they did to my brain, if anything, was a good thing. Aside from these headache episodes, I'm the best I've ever been. Besides, my scans after completion showed everything as normal."

He sighed, sitting down beside me. "I'm sorry. Then perhaps it's time to see Frelya and have your implant examined."

I shook my head, picking his hand up again. "I don't want to see her. I'll be fine. She's part of a history I'd rather put behind me. I'll find a way to resolve these episodes eventually, and I'm sure it can be done without her."

"Why not see her just once? You can limit the visit to only talking about the implant, and then you can never see her again if that's important to you. It would be a small price to pay. At worst, maybe she could even remove the implant for you."

A welcome knock came at the door, interrupting a conversation that was making me more and more uncomfortable as it continued.

"Come in," I said.

Linda stepped in, timid as usual. She'd been acting so strange around me since I completed reeducation. It made no sense. Why was it so difficult for everyone to accept? I explained the benefits over and over to everyone, but they still treated me like I was ill and they felt pity for me.

"How are you feeling?" she asked.

"Other than the episodes, I feel great. You know, you really don't need to keep coming over here and checking on me every day like this. I'm fine, and Farle is here in case anything happens."

"Have you gone to see Frelya yet?" she asked.

Were these two planning these conversations? Why did everyone keep insisting that I go and see Frelya? I mean, of course she's the one who could help if it was related to the implant but… I just didn't want to.

"I don't really want to, Linda. I will eventually."

"Taylor…"

"I don't want to! She makes me feel uneasy. I don't like her. She was part of the former general's secret group, remember? She breaks a lot of PanTech's rules."

"But she really cares about you. You haven't forgotten that, have you? She's risked her life to help you more than once. She would never hurt you, and that's coming from me. Remember that I didn't like her that much at first either, but I think at this point she's your best hope for resolving these episodes. She'll do anything she can. I know it."

"I don't… want… to go!" I said, slamming my fists down on the arms of my chair.

Linda scowled, crossing her arms. "Alright, Taylor. That's it. If you don't go and see her today, I'm going to have Harlow and Kelin tranquilize you and drag you down there in your sleep. Either that, or I'll tranquilize you, and bring Frelya here. You talk about how happy you are, but you're more stubborn than ever! It makes no sense to just sit here and deal with these pains every day when you don't have to. Go and see her!"

"I hate her! She's a snake!"

Linda's jaw dropped, and she looked at me as though I'd sprouted three extra heads before her very eyes. "Taylor! Don't say things like that."

I jumped up from my chair, pushing her toward the door. As gently as I could, but with enough force to move her despite pushing back against me.

"I'll go! Okay? Are you happy? You make me so mad. Why can't you just let me be happy? Why can't all of you just let me be happy! I wouldn't do this to you. Fine, though, I will go see her, and then everyone can stop talking about it."

"I love you, Taylor, like my own sister. Push me all you want, but I'll never stop coming back."

I didn't answer, just kept pushing. No matter how much she

cared, she didn't have the right to do this to me. She and Farle were bullying me, and they were clearly in on it together. Even Kelin and Harlow had mentioned it. Come to think of it, this was a form of insubordination. I needed to make it clear the next time it was brought up. If there was one thing I couldn't tolerate, it was insubordination. I was a professor, after all. They all ranked beneath me.

Still, I'd already agreed to go, so I would go.

~~o~o~o~~

Without saying a word to anyone else, I left for Adversity Management.

Walking by myself, I was free to feel happy again. No nagging. No telling me what to do. Everyone treated me like a child since I got back, except for Farle. I was starting to not like his attitude about PanTech, though, assuming they'd done something harmful to me on purpose. Those two things couldn't be more antithetical.

Stepping through the door of Adversity Management's science building, a sinking feeling arose in my stomach again. I considered turning around and walking out, and just telling everyone I'd gone there. That wouldn't be a lie, after all, right? Before I had the chance, a voice shouted from the front desk.

"It's about time, Taylor. Frelya is finishing up a meeting with some of our scientists. Please have a seat and wait patiently."

I nodded, sitting in one of the empty chairs.

This woman was far too pushy to be a receptionist. I'd decided I didn't really like her either.

Thankfully, I didn't have to wait long. Frelya must have cut the meeting short in order to see me sooner. I braced myself for whatever lies or tricks awaited me.

"Have a seat," she pointed to the exam chair.

Reluctantly, I followed her instruction. "I'm here because I'm having painful episodes. I want you to remove the implant."

"Not going to happen," she replied. She hadn't looked me in the eye once since I came in.

"Why not?" I asked, hoping it wouldn't come out as the growl I'd wanted it to.

"If we remove it now, you'll die. Considering that's the outcome anyway, you're welcome to remove it yourself."

I gasped. "I knew I was right about you."

"What's the matter? I thought those who completed reeducation didn't get angry anymore," she said, putting her hands on her hips. Was she actually happy about me being angry?

"It's these headaches, and the fact I don't believe you're being honest with me."

"Okay, let's try this…" she said, crossing her arms. "I'm the chief scientist at Adversity Management. You do understand who appointed me to this position, correct?"

"The president," I said.

"Do you think the president chooses poorly?"

"No… I… but sometimes we fall short of his expectations anyway."

"Taylor. I'm conducting the research I think will lead to stopping these episodes, but I need you to be a little more patient with me. I found an unexpected lead, and I'm looking into it, but this isn't something I can easily solve. As I said, removing the implant is not an option. It's already been modified as much as possible to put the least strain on your body and mind."

"Can you tell me what's causing them, at the very least?" I asked.

"Mental stress."

"What mental stress?" I shouted. "You're lying to me! I don't have any mental stress. I'm happy!"

"If you're so happy, then why are you screaming about it and spitting at me like a viper?"

"It's because you're antagonizing me!" I said. It felt so obvious.

"By doing what, exactly? Tell me what I'm doing to antagonize you," she said.

She was smiling again! "You're smiling!"

"Maybe I'm smiling because I'm happy too. Or maybe I'm just happy to see you. Are you the only one allowed to smile now? Just know that I'm taking your episodes seriously, and I'm doing everything I can to resolve them. Obviously, I can't go into every single tiny detail. This isn't your area of expertise. I invented the implant. It's *my* area of expertise. Go back to your division, and I'll summon you when I'm closer to a solution."

"I don't know why we were ever friends."

She frowned, finally letting the arrogant facade slip. "Do you really mean that?"

I got out of the chair and stormed out of the office. What a waste of time. I had no idea what the president saw in Frelya.

The woman was nothing but trouble.

CHAPTER 15

The last thing I wanted to do was spend the rest of my day working after that frustrating experience, but Professor Lexili decided this was the best time to summon me back to Pandemic Research to have our follow up meeting. I didn't even understand the purpose. She already had her instructions from the president, didn't she? Why even meet with me?

Still, it was considered rude to refuse a meeting with another professor, so I went straight over there. A silver lining, most likely, since now I wouldn't have to deal with all the prying questions from Harlow, Kelin, Farle, Linda, and whoever else decided they would make my personal life their personal business. Not that I'd be able to avoid them. They'd be asking them anyway as soon as I returned. Maybe this was a better break after all.

"Have a seat," she said, as I entered her office. Even hearing Frelya's words repeated again today was enough to set me off.

"I'm intelligent enough to know how to sit without being told," I said, dusting off my coat as I dropped into the chair.

"Excuse me?" she asked, tilting her head, looking at me above her glasses.

I sighed and pulled in a deep breath, rubbing my face roughly with both hands. "I'm sorry. I've been having daily episodes of pain for the past few months and I think it's starting to get to me."

"I see. Have you determined the cause? It's quite rare for an illness to go that long here at headquarters. The only other cases I'm aware of were all intentional. You aren't holding onto this intentionally, are you?"

"Why would I do that?"

She shrugged. "How should I know? Do I look like a psychiatrist? Anyway, I assume you've seen an expert about the cause. They've been unable to resolve it?"

"I only saw her today. Frelya from Adversity Management. It's related to a physical enhancement implant I have."

Lexili grinned, raising her brow. "An employee who isn't a ranking member of Adversity Management with a physical enhancer? Tell me, how did you sweeten the woman up to give you something like that? Perhaps you'd be too shy to tell me."

"Shut up!" I shouted, nearly rising to my feet. "I don't even like her!”

Lexili raised her hands slowly, narrowing her eyes. “I don’t know who you think you are, coming in here and shouting at me like this, but you’re mistaken if you think it’ll be tolerated. If you’re on such poor terms with the woman, why were you given… Actually, never mind. I don’t really care. It’s not why I asked you here.”

“Sorry. I’m not sure why I keep snapping at you like that. It must be related to these episodes. I’m listening,” I said, trying to compose myself. I was happy. So why was I reacting this way? Why was I getting so angry for seemingly no reason?

“I was hoping to go over your original plan in greater detail. I’m sure by now the old man has had a chance to cool his head about the whole thing and will hear us out.”

“The old man? Are you referring to the president?” I asked.

“Yes, I’m referring to the president. I think he—”

“I don’t think it’s appropriate for you to refer to him that way, Professor Lexili. I doubt he’d approve.”

She chuckled. “Approve? Of what? The name or the plan?”

“None of them,” I said.

“What are you? His mother? I’m pretty sure his ego could survive a tame joke. At any rate, so what if it isn’t his favorite plan? Ethically, I must insist that any alternative solutions to live virus creation and intentional infection be explored thoroughly.”

“He’s made his instructions very clear. He wants the virus to be used to control the growing population. It’s what’s best for humanity.”

Lexili eyed me, staring at me as though the perfectly reasonable things I said were insane. “I think I would like to talk about a completely different topic. We can come back to the population control issue shortly. Let’s discuss the reeducation process. It has always been a curiosity of mine, and you’re the only employee I’ve talked to both before and after.”

“There isn’t much to discuss, really. I was angry and impulsive before reeducation, and now I’m calm and the happiest I’ve ever been,” I insisted, nodding along with my own words as though they needed confirmation.

“Would you call your reaction to my teasing about this Frelya woman something other than angry and impulsive?”

“I… don’t understand it. These episodes are doing something

to me, and I can't help but feel she's responsible. My reactions to her are also involuntary. I hear her name, and I immediately get upset."

"Do you think you were influenced to feel this way toward her during your reeducation, or were you always on bad terms?"

I thought about this, but questions like these ended up being some of the hardest to answer. It's something I'd thought about many times since completing reeducation. I had memories of how I felt about certain people or things before, but I couldn't connect with those feelings. They felt distant. Like they were part of a story that belonged to someone else.

"I don't remember many specifics. I only know that I had one set of feelings before, and a lot of them became different after. I know that I liked Frelya before, just as I did many of my other friends. After reeducation, I came to realize that the things I saw in them that I loved, appreciated, or even admired, were... or at least some were, for the wrong reasons. It was like being brainwashed, and then having that brainwashing dispelled, and seeing the world and the people in it for what they truly are.

"Farle and I have become much closer since he's been by my side. He'd just transferred to my division a day or so prior. I like him just as much now as I did before, but I have to admit something. Most of the things I liked about him were superficial. Surface level. He's incredibly handsome. His voice is deep and attractive. He's unapologetically masculine and doesn't handle me with care. He's brutally honest, and doesn't mind saying things that are on his mind. I think, maybe, those things don't really change. If someone likes a food before, they'll like the same food after. If they dislike cold weather before, they'll dislike it after."

"Curious..." Lexili said, rubbing her chin. "Aren't our attractions toward friends similar to our romantic attractions?"

"I suppose they could be. It probably has more to do with the depth of the relationship. And maybe how long it's lasted. A lot of friendships are formed on deep ideological basis. The same with more established romantic relationships, I suppose."

"Do you despise your other friends now too?"

"I'm distrustful of some of them, especially knowing some of the things we did together. I suppose I just feel more distant from most of them. There seems to be another degree of separation. At times, I do feel like a different person. Like I took over someone's life for them and, while I know everything there is to know about it, I don't feel… like it actually happened to me?"

Lexili leaned back in her chair, crossing her legs. She sat quietly for a moment. "And no matter how hard you try, you aren't able to remember what happened to you *during* reeducation?"

I shook my head. She said it as though it were an earth-shattering revelation. Objectively, I could understand why she might feel that way. However, my personal feelings were that of indifference. The fact I couldn't remember any of it never crossed my mind as an issue. "I think of it a bit like our birth. None of us remember our own birth, but we're here. We know it happened. We acknowledge it and appreciate it. We wouldn't exist without it."

"Pfft! Nonsense. Similar only as a metaphor. We know everything there is to know about the process of childbirth. Plenty have witnessed it. Only those who oversee the reeducation process even know what it is, and it's a very well-kept secret. As things are, how can you be sure you weren't downloaded into a system, uploaded into a new body, had your memories tweaked, then sent out into the world like some kind of fleshy machine?"

"I'm not sure I see the point of hypothesizing about something so abstract. Not very scientific."

Lexili shook her finger at me. "Spoken like a true amateur scientist. Science at the deepest levels is basically philosophy. Of course it is abstract. Especially what we study at Pandemic Research. Viruses are alive, and evolve, just like human thinking. If you're that narrow-minded, perhaps you're better suited to engineering, rather than science."

"You're right, of course. I guess the possibility isn't so farfetched that it's abstract. I just don't know what I could do about it if I did turn out to be a replacement Taylor with all of her memories. Besides, only Frelya and her team can install these physical enhancers. The fact it's still in my head proves I'm the original."

"At least physically. So, are you certain you won't be willing to advocate for the overflow zone plan? I understand you've been through a lot recently, and I'd be willing to take on the brunt of the president's anger. All I'd need you to do is help me flesh out the plan into something rock-solid so he no longer has anything to argue with."

"He's made his position clear," I said. "The virus is what's best for humanity."

Lexili ran her finger along the edge of her desk, looking deep in thought. If she was considering another way of phrasing the same question again, it wasn't going to work. No one cared about PanTech and humanity's future more than the president. I was not too arrogant to believe I knew better than someone who'd lived for hundreds of years.

"Fine," she said, surprising me. "However, you did agree to help me already, and I expect you to honor that agreement in the capacity your newfound moral compass will allow. Cherun is currently looking into the many safety measures needed for implementing a plan like this. If I can convince the president to change his mind, I'm sure you'll support him and be willing to revisit the overflow plan. In the meantime, will you help Cherun? You can even bring the man you mentioned along. Farle, right?"

"Sure, I can do that. I'll join him first thing tomorrow."

Lexili nodded, offering a clearly fake smile.

What was she up to?

CHAPTER 16

The next morning, Farle and I showed up to Pandemic Research. I'd considered the possibility of bringing Ghost along. It had become clear by now that his intelligence was at least on par with, if not above, human. However, I rarely saw him since reeducation. He spent all his time with either Frelya or Glimmer. Mostly Frelya. Sometimes he'd visit Henry, but that was rarer. If I questioned him about why he spent so much time with Frelya, he wouldn't even pretend to answer. Since he'd been spending so much time with her, I'd begun to trust him less too.

"What are you thinking about?" Farle asked, nudging me with his elbow.

"Nothing," I lied. "Just wishing we could get back to our work at the Explorers League, instead of having to honor commitments I made prior to reeducation. It feels like having to keep the promises of a stranger."

Farle looked around as though he was afraid of Cherun and Lexili overhearing the conversation. Luckily, we were alone in this room, still waiting for them to arrive.

"Don't you remember making the commitment?" he asked.

"That isn't the point," I insisted. "The point is I don't care about this anymore. I only got involved originally because I wanted to stop the plan by offering an alternative. Now that my original suggestion was declined in favor of the original plan with the virus, shouldn't things go back to how they were before? With Pandemic Research handling everything without the interference of outsiders."

Farle sighed, taking my hand in his. "You know that I am patient and I support you, even though you've changed, right?"

I nodded. "I know that."

"But do you truly support this plan with the virus? You were so against it before. It's been hard for me to understand. Each day it feels like you'll reveal to me that this was all just an act. That you were only pretending to change your views in order to mislead PanTech. That—"

"Well it's time for you to accept that it won't happen, Farle. So far you're the only one who hasn't pestered me about every little thing. I understood why you wanted me to see Frelya. You were concerned about my health. I do appreciate that. However, it's time for you to accept that the old Taylor is dead."

"I know, but—"

"And she's never coming back, Farle. You either care for me as I am now, or you should move on."

"The old Taylor isn't dead, no matter how much you insist she is. I know these changes are permanent, but you are still the woman I care about, before and after. You are the same woman. I think *you* need to accept *that*," he said, holding his ground.

I looked at him, trying to decide how exactly I felt about what he'd said. I didn't necessarily disagree, but the more people brought up the way I used to be, the more I felt like this person they knew was dead. In my heart, I still felt like me. Only I felt… better. Like I'd been cured of a mental disease. I did still feel like the same person.

"Good morning, Taylor. Farle," Cherun said as he opened the door after knocking once. "We didn't expect you so early. I was still preparing the containment area. We obviously have to be much more careful, dealing with live viruses now."

I nodded. "Just tell us what you need us to do, and we'll be happy to help."

"Lexili has requested Farle come and help her with setting up a new room, while you and I run a routine check on the virus. It has been one month since the virus was checked last, and we need to monitor for any spontaneous, though unlikely, changes."

Farle let go of my hand and squeezed my shoulder firmly. "I'll see you soon."

I nodded, following Cherun to another room just down the hall. "Don't I need to suit up or something?" I asked, a bit alarmed that we were walking into the room with a supposedly deadly virus wearing just our normal clothing.

"At some point, of course," he said, waving his hand. "Right now, the virus is contained with specimens designed to rapidly progress the life cycle. The specimens from last month have been passed on to another team already, as with the month before that. They've been safely transported to Animal Research where long-term health changes will be studied and logged into reports we'll review before releasing the virus."

"Will reinfection rates be studied?" I asked.

"Ah, I'm glad you're paying attention. Do you see how this is no more possible now than it was before? I was so relieved when Lexili was willing to see reason and give your plan a try. Now, we're right back to where we started. Sure, we can check reinfection rates, but only within simulated, condensed periods of time. However, we're dealing with a live virus now. One can't simply program it into a simulation and expect fully accurate outcomes. Things like reinfection should be studied in real time, for years. The president is completely committed to seeing this virus deployed in three months."

I shrugged. "If the president believes it's possible, then it's possible. I'm sure it'll be fine. Let's just look at the mortality rate for the current specimens. I can't believe we're still using rats all these years later. Seems dated."

Cherun looked at the rat colony within the contained area, shaking his head. "I can already see that we're experiencing a solid twenty percent mortality. We aren't 'still using rats' either. Not in the way you implied it. These rats are genetically indistinguishable from humans as far as the virus is concerned. We don't make guesses based on how things translate to humans anymore. In more sane times, we wouldn't even use animals at all. Just simulations."

"Good. Let's go visit Animal Research and put your mind at ease. Then we can move on to other safety measures."

He nodded. "Nothing's going to put my mind at ease, but alright. It'll be better to see the specimens for myself in case there are any unexpected long-term effects."

Stepping onto the transport, I immediately regretted my suggestion of going in person. Even if we were only a few seconds away on the transport, we could've just gotten a verbal report over the communicator and been just as well off. Still, I'd known Cherun just long enough to know how much he worries about everything. If he doesn't see the rats in person, he'll worry that the reports were logged incorrectly. Even though the virus had already run its course. That didn't matter. I could see why Lexili trusted him with safety measures.

"Assistant Professor Cherun. Professor Taylor. I'm glad you're here. We were going to come see you first thing tomorrow.

There are problems with the rats you sent over," a blond man said, recognizing us as we stepped off the transport.

Cherun held up his hand. "Slow down. What kind of problem are you talking about?"

"They're all dead," the man said, almost as though we should've expected it.

"What?" Cherun asked, narrowing his eyes. "That's not possible. Did you make a mistake in the handling?"

"This is Animal Research, Assistant Professor. I don't think we made a mistake. Please, come see them for yourself. That last one died just a few hours ago," he said, starting to walk away.

"From the first group we sent?" Cherun asked, his voice desperately hopeful.

"No. All of them. We wanted to prepare a complete report, but with you here it's all the better. We can examine them together."

"I don't understand. That isn't possible, unless you handled them improperly. All the specimens we sent over had already made a complete recovery. There was no trace of the virus left in their system. None. What's your name?"

"Aisic, Assistant Professor. Again, I can assure you, we did not make any mistakes in handling. Please be patient. We're almost to the lab," he said, continuing to face ahead.

He wasn't nervous at all. His confidence told me he truly believed there was no issue with handling. I knew Barth and Linda well enough to know that they were both perfectionists. But if they weren't mishandled... then how could this have happened?

"Here we are," he said, leading us into a room.

"Should we wear protective equipment?" I asked.

Both men shook their head at the same time.

"The virus had already left their system before they were sent over. They were quarantined until that happened."

Aisic nodded in agreement. "We tested them again using the same programming as you. There is no trace of the virus in their system."

He pulled out a tray, revealing a drawer filled with dead rats.

Cherun immediately picked one up, scanning it with a device in his shirt pocket.

"Cardiac arrest," he said, turning the rat over before placing it back in the slot and picking up another.

"Cardiac arrest?" I asked. "Perhaps it causes long-term

complications with the heart you weren't aware of."

He ignored me, scanning the next rat. "Blood clot," he said, putting it down and picking up the next. "Aneurysm. Stroke. Kidney failure. Pneumonia…" he continued, picking up and scanning one after another. He put the last rat back into its slot, then took a step back, looking at Aisic. "Tell me… they all have random causes of death like this?"

Aisic nodded. "Not exactly random, but a variety of inconsistent complications. Some of them had behavioral episodes before experiencing a fatal symptom, attacking other rats. But even when we separated them individually, they still all died."

"You checked to see if the acceleration was still present?" Cherun asked, hopeful it was he who'd made the mistake.

"It was present. I suspect these deaths would occur within three years for humans, but… one hundred percent mortality," Aisic confirmed.

"One hundred percent… mortality. And in such an unusual way. That means the virus embedded itself into the brain and initiated these failures in different areas of the body. In a way that wasn't detectable. Even though it was already gone from the body. The programming is left behind. This virus can never be released. It's out of the question. The schedule will have to be altered, or the president will have to accept an alternative plan."

I gasped. "That can't happen. He gave very specific instructions that your division was expected to meet. If you weren't capable of achieving it, he'd never have asked. You can't just override the president like that!"

He grabbed me by the arm, pulling me toward the drawer of rats, pointing to them. "Did reeducation fry your brain? Look! It isn't mere speculation. This virus will kill everyone if it's ever released. It has to be carefully discarded, and we'll need to start over. This has to be reported to Professor Lexili and the president immediately."

I yanked my arm away, nearly causing him to fall. "First of all, don't ever grab me like that. Second of all, I'm sure we can keep this outcome to ourselves and work on vaccinations that create the same outcome we originally wanted. In the end, it's all the same, right?"

Cherun stared at me, stunned. "Do you hear yourself? I'm going to report this to Professor Lexili this instant. She'll bring it to the president's attention, and he'll have no choice."

He stormed off, not waiting for me to follow. I couldn't believe he was so willing to disappoint the president like this. It was unfathomable to me. I couldn't comprehend it.

No matter what happened now, he wouldn't be happy.

CHAPTER 17

Everything was quiet for the next few days as I waited to hear back from Cherun and Lexili. Considering how upset the president had been over my alternative plan being proposed before, I doubted this would go over any better. I didn't understand their insistence on opposing the president anyway. If this is the path forward he was confident in, it was clearly the right plan. All they needed to do was believe in it, and I was sure they could achieve it just as he'd envisioned.

"More stew?" Farle asked, gesturing to my bowl. Glimmer smiled next to him as if to reassure me it was good.

Right. We'd been reduced to sitting around and eating stew and other pointless tasks while we waited for Pandemic Research to get its act together. Of course we couldn't leave HQ in the meantime.

"No offense, Farle, but I'd much rather we be eating this on an expedition. Ever since Cherun and I made a spectacle out of the whole virus thing, now everyone's eyes are all over everything. It's impossible to get anything done around here without someone having a problem with it."

Ghost landed next to me as if on my signal. "Something is happening. Something big. Adversity Management is gathering many people and escorting them to the auditorium. The same one where Henry was unveiled."

I narrowed my eyes. "Well, I knew it was bad, but I didn't think it was that bad. Hopefully we'll be getting an announcement putting all of this to rest, and finally complying with the president's request."

Several soldiers walked into the camp. They had their helmets on. I would've loved to have seen their faces, given the circumstances. I hated those helmets.

"Professor Taylor. PanTech is holding an emergency meeting and your presence is required. You may bring a few of your members with you, but please keep it to a minimum so there's adequate space. All departments will be present." I nodded, then looked to Farle and Ghost.

"Not interested," Ghost said, shooting me down before I could even ask.

"I'll join you. Of course," Farle said.

"Me too," Glimmer said, raising her fist. "I don't think anything like this has happened since I've been here."

The soldier closest to her shook his head. "Something like this hasn't happened in a very long time. There's been a call for a vote of no-confidence against the president."

Farle and Glimmer looked at me, almost hopeful. I hated to disappoint them.

"Are you kidding?" I said. "You think it was me? Well, it wasn't."

"Of course it wasn't," Farle said, rising to his feet. "But it's a strange coincidence, right? You have to at least admit that."

I nodded. "Yeah, it is. The fact that I intended to do this before means I probably gave one of the other professors the idea."

Glimmer put her hand on my shoulder. "Oh, I wouldn't worry so much about that. It's knowledge that's available to everyone. I knew about it before, as did many of the other professors. Long before you were considering it as an option."

I sucked in a deep breath. I knew she was probably right, but I was still afraid of getting into trouble. Even more important than that, I was worried I would disappoint the president. What if he thought I had something to do with this?

"If it's just the three of you, let's get going," the soldier said. "Many of the professors will already be there waiting."

I shrugged, then gestured toward the exit. Now I just wanted to get this over with. Obviously, I would vote in support of the president, no matter what. This situation may even work out in my favor, if it means proving to the president that I'm loyal now. Of course, the fact that I'd completed reeducation should already prove that. I had complete confidence in him as a leader.

When we arrived, I couldn't help but feel sick with anxiety. I knew what was happening, and I knew how I would cast my vote, but I couldn't shake the feeling that something was about to go wrong.

"Hello, Taylor. How have things been?" a familiar voice called out to me. I could see his hand waving above the crowd.

Despite his slim stature, he was extremely tall, even if he looked a bit less so with Linda standing next to him. A giantess in her own right.

"Professor Barth. It's good to see you, though I wish it could be under better circumstances," I said, crossing my arms.

He nodded. "Agreed. I heard about your visit to my division the other day, and what you discovered. Troubling."

"Not really," I said. "If the president is confident the problem can be cleared up in just a few months, then I'm sure he's correct. The man has lived a long time, and has been a devotee of science longer than anyone else here has even been alive. To question him is absurd."

Barth stared at me blankly. "Taylor… you know I'm a staunch supporter of the president. I've been trying to win that support ever since I joined PanTech. It was all I dreamed of. But…"

"But what?" I growled.

He wasn't intimidated. In fact, he seemed encouraged by my hostility. "One can't simply manifest success by wishing it were so. You of all people should understand that. If it were so, everyone would be here at PanTech with us. There'd be no need for adversity zones. We could wish everyone to be qualified, and our wishes would be magically granted."

I took a step toward Barth. "I'm not the one talking about magic, Barth. The experience and qualifications of a scientist should garner an equivalent level of confidence. Yet, ever since this whole debacle with the virus, suddenly everyone knows better than our president and the professor of Pandemic Research. Between the two of them, who could possibly understand that plan better?"

Barth laughed, pointing his finger into my face. "A debacle *you* caused if you'll recall. You, and the assistant professor of the very division you're praising as the authority. And, for the record, I *agree* with that skepticism. Even if we support our leader, we are all men and women of science first and foremost. Our devotion to science should come before everything else. Our homes, our families, and yes… even our president."

"Did you initiate the vote?" I asked, taking another step forward, having to look up at him now.

"What? How preposterous. It isn't my place to do such a thing. You are *way* out of line, Professor. I suggest you cease your peacocking. You're still a child compared to most of the other professors. If you keep acting like a bully, even if it's on behalf of the president, you'll only embarrass yourself in the end."

"A bully? Me? You wouldn't be where you are if it wasn't for me. It would serve you well to remember—"

"That's enough, Taylor! What has happened to you? You've never acted this way as long as I've known you," Linda said, stepping between us. "Barth is right. This is an embarrassing way to treat friends and coworkers. We're on the same team. We've literally been on the same team, actually."

"Of course you'd stand up for your professor, Linda. Have your eye on his position yourself, I assume."

Linda's eyes welled with tears, and she slowly shook her head. "I don't even know you anymore…"

"Well, maybe—"

Farle firmly placed his hand on my shoulder, stopping me from finishing the sentence.

I turned to look at him, but he only shook his head, trying to dissuade me from saying anything else. Was he protecting them, or me? Either way, I'd said my piece. There was nothing left to say anyway.

A surge of pain shot through my skull, causing me to collapse to my knees and cradle my head in my hands. Farle caught me before I collapsed completely. I had the urge to shove him away, but the pain was unbearable. This was the worst episode yet.

"Taylor, are you alright?" he asked, putting a hand on each shoulder to steady me.

"I'm alright. Just… give me a minute."

Linda bent down in front of me, grabbing my hands. "Is there anything I can get for you? Do you need something to drink?"

I tried to shake my head, which ended up being me shaking my whole body as I held a tight grip with both hands. "It'll be over in a minute or two. Really, I'm alright."

I hoped that was true. All of the other episodes were just a couple of minutes long, but this one was more painful than the others. I could feel so much anger boiling inside of me all of a sudden, but I had no one to direct it toward. The emotions that would come with the episodes were one of the most confusing parts, especially when they came from nowhere.

When I looked up and opened my eyes, I spotted Frelya a short distance away, just watching me. Of course, she'd made no effort to help or see if I was alright. She probably hoped this would kill me. Clearly, she knew more than she let on.

I jumped to my feet, grabbing her by the collar of her coat, pulling her close to me. I was sweating now and breathing heavily. I must've looked deranged, but of course Frelya would never be afraid of anyone, or even intimidated. "You're causing this, aren't you? Answer me!" I said, shaking her.

She smiled, ever so slightly, and patted me gently on the head. "I told you I was working on it. That was the truth. I think I'll be able to put a stop to these episodes very soon. I know they're uncomfortable, but please bear with it just a little longer."

"Just bear with it? They're getting worse! You're lying to me. I just know it. I hate you. I'm so angry I could break your neck right here in front of everyone. After you fix this implant, I hope I never have to see you again." I felt sick as the words escaped my lips, but I didn't understand why. I meant everything I said, but felt as though I might faint after saying it.

Frelya's stoic expression gave way a little, and she lowered her head. She clutched her hands together in front of her. "You don't mean that…" she said, her voice becoming barely a whisper. "I know you don't mean it."

I shoved her, releasing her coat as I did. "I… I don't know what I mean. I don't know what's happening to me. I just know you make me so angry. Just get away from me," I said, turning and facing the stage as several loud claps directed everyone's attention ahead.

"Attention, everyone! A vote of no confidence has been called by a professor. As is the rule, we will hear their concerns and take a vote."

It was the president. He didn't even look at me.

I was relieved that he didn't suspect I was the one responsible for this. If he did, he didn't show it.

Sitting down slowly in a chair on the stage, he raised his hand, asking for silence. "Would the concerned professor please step forward and make your case to everyone present?"

A silence washed over the crowd, and heads rotated and bobbed about like we were in the middle of a silent earthquake. Everyone wanted to know who it was, bold enough to force such a gathering.

Professor Lexili stepped up on the stage and stood in front of the podium. She nodded first to the professor, and then to the others.

"I'm Professor Lexili of Pandemic Research, and I am the one who has called this vote."

CHAPTER 18

Gasps and incoherent chattering washed over the crowd like a wave. Even though it was the most logical source, given current events, it was still difficult to imagine Professor Lexili doing something like this. She was the champion for this plan, against all resistance, from the very start. The only caveat to her devotion to seeing it through was that it should only be used if there was no alternative. I'd made the mistake of giving her an alternative, and now she was no longer focused on seeing it through.

"I've asked everyone here because I've been left with no choice. The virus that we were tasked with designing to solve the population problem facing PanTech territories has mutated, behaving in a way we've never seen a virus behave before. I petitioned the president to give us more time. To let us destroy this virus and start over. To consider viable alternatives that have been proposed. All of this has fallen on deaf ears. We've been instructed to proceed as though there isn't a problem at all. Make no mistake… the consequences of doing this could lead to the most catastrophic event humanity has ever experienced."

The president waved his hand, offering a rebuttal. It felt good seeing the man defend himself. "First of all, I firmly believe none of this would have happened if it wasn't for the softening work ethic of Pandemic Research and their insistence on using simulations over live specimens. I realize we should always be advancing science, but certain parts of the old ways should not be sidelined. Otherwise, we get outcomes created by laziness, as we're seeing here. Everything I've ever done, I've done for the betterment of humanity. This is no exception. If the population problem isn't remedied, it won't be long before we feel the effects here. Not immediately, but we can't just kick the can down the road for future generations to deal with. I've been alive long enough to know what that looks like. There are no alternatives."

Lexili waited patiently for him to finish his statement before countering. "Pandemic Research has been at the forefront of safety for all of PanTech. We utilized simulations, and improved upon that system, in ways even the original creator hadn't anticipated. The president's criticism of our use of that system comes from a place of misunderstanding and outdated knowledge. It's also irrelevant, and he is misleading you by acting as though it is. There are alternatives, and I only agreed to pursue the development of this virus as long as there weren't. Professor Taylor of the Explorers League came up with a very viable one, involving runoff zones with sterilization for the inductees. These inductees could also be selected based off lower intelligence scores, solving both of the president's concerns in one swoop. Population adjustment, controlled for the advancement of humanity."

My stomach turned at the mention of my name. The last thing I wanted was to be dragged into this any further, even though I knew that was inevitable.

"Just as I and many others once thought augmentation was a possible solution. Humans can be modified like machines to produce almost any outcome. They can essentially become machines. The consequences of those beliefs have been forgotten by nearly everyone, but I lived through them."

Those present seemed torn, though I couldn't understand why. The president had the wisdom and experience, and deserved our trust. Even if what he asked for seemed dangerous, or outright illogical, he'd kept humanity on the best possible path for more than a century.

Professor Lexili was undeterred. She should have given up already. She had a lot of nerve keeping this up!

"Professor Taylor, do you support this challenge? If so, please come up here and make the case next to Professor Lexili for your zone idea."

"Of course not!" I shouted. "I had nothing to do with this!"

Everyone who knew me seemed to turn and face me with a single movement. The shock on their faces was unmistakable, but why? Did no one around me want me to be happy? Did they not understand that going against the president was the same as going against humanity itself?

Glimmer, who I'd forgotten about until just now, grabbed my arm and whispered to me. "What are you doing? Go up there. This might be your last chance."

Farle stepped between us, gently pulling her hand away.

"Glimmer… you don't understand. She can't. Not after what they did to her. Pushing her is only going to make it worse."

"What they did to me? What they did to me? What they 'did to me' was fix me, take away all my misguided anger, and make me happy. Something everyone around me is trying to take from me. Those who are supposed to love me. Supposed to be my friends."

Farle tried to reach for my hand, but I slapped it away.

"Well, it seems you don't have the support you thought you did, Professor Lexili. Are you sure you don't want to withdraw the vote?" the president asked, smiling.

Lexili was still unwavering, the tiny woman showing no signs of fear.

"Of course I won't withdraw the vote. I haven't even gotten to the important details yet. We just discovered mere days ago that this virus has an indirect one hundred percent mortality rate. Every specimen infected throughout the several months of testing has since died, if not directly during their infection, then in the months following through seemingly unrelated circumstance. I don't think I need to spell it out to all of you here, men and women of science."

The president was noticeably frustrated, gripping his cane tighter than before. His left eye twitched. "And I told you that three months is more than enough time to sort something like this out. More than enough. You are just digging your heels in and insisting on being disobedient. It's only by my kindness that you aren't being arrested for treason."

A hand shot up from the crowd. It was Barth. What in the world was he doing?

"I'm sorry, Mr. President, but I have to support Professor Lexili's claim. I examined these specimens myself. Her conclusion that the virus should be destroyed was partly based on my recommendation. We can't identify the mechanism by which it triggers delayed fatalities, so it is far too dangerous to proceed with the same virus. We should delay the project, and start over with a new specimen. The population problem isn't going to change much in the next few years."

The president sighed, picking his cane up and slamming it down on the floor. "I'm disappointed in you, Professor Barth. And you showed so much promise over the past few years."

Lexili continued on with her new momentum. "The president is becoming obsessed with loyalty, and that's the wrong way to view these circumstances. It isn't out of disloyalty that we make these recommendations, but because we are equally devoted to the advancement of humanity. It is *because* we are loyal."

"Enough!" the president shouted, slamming his cane down again. "We'll get this vote out of the way, and I think everyone here fully understands how they should cast that vote. When this is over, Professor Lexili, you'll return to your division and solve the problem as I instructed you to. Stop wasting precious time you could be using to diagnose the mechanism and fix it."

Another man stepped onto the stage, holding some kind of device in his right hand.

"Everyone, we are calling the matter to vote. Only professors may vote, and they'll do so by show of hands. A hand raised in the support of 'aye' will support the vote of no confidence. A hand raised in support of 'nay' will support the president's original instruction, defeating the motion. If you understand, please raise your hand."

I raised my hand along with everyone else. Finally. We could get this whole thing out of the way and return to our duties.

"Votes for aye," he said, looking over the crowd.

An alarming number of hands shot up. I was in disbelief. Barth was one of them. I couldn't believe that he would betray the president.

"Votes for nay."

I didn't count the previous show of hands quick enough, but it was close.

I held up my hand, as enthusiastically as I could. I wanted the president to see that I was loyal. That I had learned from my mistakes. I had become better. I wanted him to be proud of me.

The man taking count seemed to freeze in place, not wanting to speak or move.

"I… the vote is twenty-four yays and twenty-three nays," the man said, as though he'd confessed to a crime.

The president stood, pointing his cane at Professor Lexili. We'd all assumed he was about to lecture her. Give her one final chance to withdraw the motion. To change her vote.

That's not what happened.

Without a single sound or a shred of evidence that his cane was used as a weapon, Lexili fell to the ground, clutching at her chest. Only there was no blood. She was stunned into silence, whatever had happened. She pointed at him, and her hand fell to her side. She was lifeless. Dead.

Surely he did it for a reason. Had he even done anything?

Surely he had his reasons. He had to. He was the president. He wouldn't do something like this unless there was a very good reason. No way. Everyone here was probably thinking differently. They lacked faith. Loyalty. Faith? Why did I think of faith? Loyalty? Of course it was loyalty!

Anyone who doubted him was sorely lacking in loyalty.

"I believe that makes the vote a tie, and the motion fails. Unless someone cares to change their vote?"

He looked over the crowd of professors. Most had not seen violence since they'd left their zones. For many, it was so long ago they likely didn't remember. The only response anyone had to offer was silence.

Glimmer grabbed my arm, shaking me.

"Taylor, you have to change your vote!"

He pointed his cane at her, and it was like time stood still. My thoughts seized in my mind, like a machine dry of oil. I'd seen things like this before. I'd known this kind of horror, and all too many times. I should've been able to react in an instant, but I couldn't. My thoughts, and my body, refused to budge.

She fell to her knees, and I could feel her grip tighten, then loosen on my arm. Farle cried out, reaching for her and catching her before she fell completely.

"Glimmer!" he shouted, holding her tight to his chest. She was already gone. Whatever this weapon was, it was unlike anything I'd seen. Not even a visible wound. Truly spectacular technology. No surprise, and likely designed by the president himself. What a great man. What an impressive mind.

Why was I thinking this? Two people just died. One was right next to me. But the president wouldn't have done it if he didn't have a good reason. They deserved it. Maybe he didn't even do it. If he did, they deserved it.

Didn't they?

They must have.

Right?

Surely they deserved it.

They deserved it.

I looked down at Glimmer, with her empty eyes. She'd been so kind to me. Farle's gasping cries dug into my skull, like a nightmare. His sister. What would I have felt if this was Ferris? Like a fire set inside the bone cage of my brain, the pain erupted again. Twice in one day. A first. More intense than any other that had come before.

I vomited. The pain was paralyzing. I couldn't even reach for my head. I dropped to my knees. Linda grabbed my shoulders.

"Taylor, are you hurt?"

"My head… it's on fire…" is all I could manage.

Linda looked around. Panic had finally set in, and she saw it as her opportunity.

She picked me up and hoisted me over her shoulder. An easy feat for her.

"We're going to see Frelya," she said as she slipped away, leaving the room before anyone had noticed.

"But I don't—"

"We're going to see her right now, Taylor. Don't say another word."

I couldn't have even if I wanted to. I passed out a few seconds later.

CHAPTER 19

I sat alone in a thunderstorm, watching the lightning bounce from the earth and back to the sky. Only there was no sky. The earth existed both above and below. Not like a cave, but like a mirror pointed down. The upside down trees above me dripped water from their leaves, adding their own drips to the downpour that was enveloping me. Despite the fact lightning fell all around me and sprang up from the ground, there were no sounds. Only pain. Instead of hearing the boom, I felt it resonating within my skull. I could only hear the rain. A single roar, but if I listened closely, I could pick out the breaks in the sound. Every once in a while.

The individual impacts against my skin helped me keep track. Kept me from going numb. Though, even that wasn't easy. With all the pouring rain, it was a feeling not too dissimilar from being submerged in a river. Wait, how would I know that feeling? It's not like I'd ever been submerged in a river. A bath, then. Like sinking into a bath… except that wasn't right either. The water was too tame in a bath. Too still. This was…

"How is my girl doing? Getting nice and clean?" a voice said from above me.

The lid of the world was peeled back, revealing a giant man's face against the newly revealed sky. It was the president!

"I'm doing great, Mr. President. All of my sins are being washed away. See?" I replied, smiling.

"Filthy. Disgusting. You're all covered in mud. I thought I told you to get cleaned up. You're really disappointing me, Taylor."

I looked down, seeing the mud that had splashed up on my lower body from sitting on the ground. I leaped to my feet, rubbing my legs down with rainwater.

"I'm getting it. See? It's gone."

"You make me sick," he replied. "You let mud get all over you again. What are you doing?" he said, shaking his head.

I looked down. Mud covered me from the neck down. I washed and scrubbed as hard as I could, until it was gone again. "I did it. Look at me. You're proud of me?"

"It's going to take more than this," he said, holding a light above me, shining it down. It was so bright, I thought I might be blinded.

"More?" I said, feeling the strain on my lips. I could barely speak.

~~o~o~o~~

"Awake, are we?" a different voice asked.

It was Frelya, shining a light into my eyes. Linda stood next to her, crossing her arms and biting her lip.

"What do you mean it's going to take more?" Linda asked.

"I meant what I said. I'm surprised too. Go back. Things are going to get ugly around here soon, and I'm going to lose my chance. You need to take care of your own division."

"Stuff it, Frelya. I'm not going anywhere. Taylor's my friend too. Everything's already ugly. He killed two people, right in front of everyone. I saw it myself. There wasn't any blood."

"No blood. You're certain?" Frelya asked, her voice nearly a whisper.

"I'd know blood if I saw it. He killed them just by pointing his cane at them," Linda said, lowering her own voice to mirror Frelya's.

Frelya switched off the light in my eyes. "Thank you. That could prove useful. If something like this happens again, don't let him point it at you. I can think of some possible explanations, but I'd need to examine the cane itself. That's beside the point, anyway. He'll get away with it. You know it as well as I do. All he has to do is give the order, and the adversity management morphs into our police. In fact, I'd say that order is coming soon. We need to move quickly."

"He had his reasons, Frelya. Idiot!" I shouted, reaching for her. Only my arm barely moved. My grab was barely a touch.

"It's for the pain," she said.

"Liar! What's happening to me?"

"It wasn't enough," Linda said.

"I told you it wasn't enough! We need to go. Now. Can you carry her?"

"Of course I can carry her," Linda said. "I could carry both of you."

"Why would I go anywhere with either of you? People like you are the cause of everything that happened today. You pushed him to take action. He has to enforce his leadership and decisions. He can't just let everyone run wild and have their way."

Frelya sighed, ignoring everything I said, leaning above me on the table I was strapped to. "You say he had a reason? I actually agree with you. Would you let me show you what that reason is? I think you'll feel better, knowing the reason."

"I had two episodes today. I've only had one before. This one was awful. It felt like my brain was being smashed to pieces and put back together. Fix it! Now!"

I grabbed for her again, but my hands slid harmlessly off her lab coat. Frelya caught one of them before it fell, squeezing it tightly.

"We need to get your mental state in check first, and I believe I found something that will end the episodes once and for all. You just have to trust me. Only once. Please?"

"No!" I said, using all my strength to slip my hand away from her.

"I trust her, Taylor. You did too. We foiled an insurrection together, remember? Do you think we're traitors? We've done more for PanTech than anyone else here. I'm begging you to, okay? Trust us just this once, and let Frelya fix your episodes. After that, you never have to see either of us again. We'll leave you alone forever. Right, Frelya?"

Frelya's expression darkened as she looked down at the floor. I could see her jaw clench, and she tightened both of her hands into a balled fist.

"I promise. I'll fix it today, no matter what, and you'll never have a need to see me again."

I looked between both of them. It felt like blackmail. I didn't trust either of them anymore, but… these episodes. They'd only get worse without Frelya's help. Once. I knew they'd at least keep their word, or at least I had no choice but to believe that. I was at their mercy. "I'll go with you," I said, defeated. "Let's just get it over with."

Linda and Frelya looked at one another as though they were having second thoughts.

"Hold on tight to my neck, Taylor. Frelya's going to unstrap you from the table and put you on my back."

I nodded, and Frelya did just that. I could barely keep my arms around Linda's shoulders, but we were stable enough. Linda was plenty strong enough to keep me upright and steady. Her size made me feel like I was riding a desert camel. For a moment, the thought gave me comfort.

We left the room through a back door I hadn't noticed before, with Frelya checking the door.

"As expected, everyone's left their stations because of the commotion," she said.

"I'm not stupid. I see it just as well as you do. Now let's just go," Linda said, sliding her foot into Frelya's.

We continued on, slowly and carefully, for some reason, until we reached a door in the very back of the facility.

"I don't understand. You said you were going to show me his reason for doing what he did today. Here?" I asked.

Frelya held up a device to the door. "If I'm right… if what I think is in this room… Yes. You'll understand everything perfectly."

The door rattled, and eventually gave way.

"That's now how these doors are supposed to open?" Linda tilted her head and stared at the device in Frelya's hand.

"That's how this one opens," she growled.

We stepped inside. I couldn't see anything clearly at first. The room was dark. There was the gentle hum that almost vibrated in the air.

I could see Frelya fiddling with the device in her hand again, and the door behind us shut, leaving us in complete darkness again.

"One moment… almost," she said before the lights turned on.

The room was filled with tanks, holding humans inside them. Floating upright, and lifeless.

"The president has always ordered us to bring back bodies, no matter the condition, of any soldier killed in the line of duty. I always thought it was strange… maybe a way of honoring them. It's an old military tradition, after all. No matter how often it was pressed, we were told that the bodies were disposed of with dignity. They'd be taken into this room, and only a few people were ever allowed in or out. I created a device that would let me break in because I picked up readings from this room. I've been investigating for a while," Frelya said. Her voice had gone cold. Like she was peeling away my sanity with each word. Thoughts flooded into my mind. I was putting it together. I didn't want to. I didn't want to.

I did.

"No. Frelya…"

"Taylor. It's experimenting, with actual specimens, just as the president prefers. No simulations. The real thing. Look, I recognize this man. You could fit your whole hand into the hole that was in his neck. Look!"

She pointed at him, and the wound she mentioned simply wasn't there.

"So he's alive?" I asked.

"No. He's dead. You can't bring the dead back, no matter what. I found the research, and what they were attempting. No one is supposed to know, but I found it. He wants to reverse aging completely, Taylor. He wants to become immortal. He knows that even if he lives another hundred years, his life is finite. Eventually age will take him. Over here. Take her over here," Frelya said, pointing further into the room.

Linda shook her head, turning away. "There has to be another way. There has to be. Don't do this to her," she said, slipping me off her back and onto the floor. She dropped to her knees and hugged me tightly.

Frelya grabbed her, throwing her at least ten feet toward the entrance of the room. She grabbed me by the hair, dragging me.

"I told you I'd show you, so I'll show you. Look! Look at this one. Recognize him?"

I put my hands over my mouth, and tears erupted from my eyes. I screamed.

"No. No no no no no. Liar."

"Look at him, Taylor! It's Linus. You remember Linus, don't you? Or do you hate him too? He was a rule-breaker, after all."

I looked away, collapsing to the floor, covering my eyes.

"I don't want to see. Don't make me… please."

Frelya grabbed my arms, ripping my hands away from my face and forcing me to turn toward him. He looked almost like he would wake up any moment, even though I knew he wouldn't. The horrible wound in his side was gone. His chest expanded and released breath, no doubt assisted by the machine attached to his face and the many cables running out of his limbs. It was unmistakably him. It was Linus!

A pain shot through my head. White hot. As though a volcano erupted, filled with ravenous birds pecking away at my brain, devouring it as I could only do nothing. The agony was unfathomable, even as I felt it, I couldn't understand it. I screamed, and I felt Linda's arms around me.

"That's enough, Frelya! It's going to kill her!"

"If this doesn't work, she's already dead."

Frelya grabbed Linda, and pried her arms away from me, throwing her again. I felt another pain in my neck, looking up to see Frelya emptying the contents of a syringe into me.

The pain was gone. Gone as quickly as it had come.

"Tell me what you think of PanTech. What do you think of the president now, Taylor? Do you still love him?"

"I..." I started to speak, but was distracted by my own trembling hands.

"Say it!" Frelya dropped to her knees and grabbed both of my hands to steady them. Was she crying?

"I hate him. For what he did to Glimmer, and to Lexili... and Linus! For what he did to me! He turned me into a slave. I wish he'd have just killed me."

Frelya released my hands. "I did it... I can't believe it. No one has ever reversed the effects of reeducation. I don't even know how they do it... but I did it. I reversed it."

I grabbed her hands before she could pull them away, and squeezed them as tightly as I could.

"Thank you," I said, barely able to form the words through my tears. "Thank you for not giving up on me."

She wrapped her arms around me and pulled me close. "I could never give up on you. Never," she said, nearly whispering.

Linda came over to us, and dropped to her knees, wrapping her arms around me too.

"Welcome back, Taylor."

CHAPTER 20

Back in Frelya's office, she did her best to explain everything to me.

I did my best to understand it, but it was hard to think about anything other than Linus. I couldn't wash his image from my mind. Frelya assured me he was long gone, that there was no reviving the dead. But… seeing his body in front of me. His chest rising and falling. I couldn't bear it.

"I beat that cocky old idiot at his own game. I'm sorry. I know how hard this has been for you, Taylor. But I actually did it. No one's ever done it, and I did it. I reversed the reeducation process, without even knowing how it works."

"Could you be a little more sympathetic? My goodness… Think about everything Taylor has been through."

Forcing myself back into reality, I held up my hand. "No, Linda, she deserves the credit. I wouldn't be me if it wasn't for her. I can't even begin to describe how horrifying it was feeling like I was trapped inside my own body, forced to think thoughts that weren't mine. I could feel myself, just below the surface, but I couldn't acknowledge it. I was just out of sight. Nothing more than an odd feeling now and then."

Frelya put her hand on my forearm, smiling. "But that's all over now."

I nodded, returning her smile. "How *did* you do it? How did you know what would work?"

She was all too happy to explain. Seeing her pride with scientific achievement was so strange, since most of my time knowing her was admiring what an impressive warrior she was. So brave and capable. And beautiful. And a genius. What didn't she excel at?

"I bet everything on the new processing capabilities of this enhancer. Let's just say I included some technology that wasn't exactly approved. Because you nearly died when your last enhancer almost cooked your brain, it wasn't a problem convincing them that you would die if I removed it. They didn't even question it. You probably experienced a headache shortly after they arrested you. That one was downloading your brain map onto the enhancer. A snapshot of your identity and everything that makes you… you."

I rubbed my head, trying to process what she just said. "So does that mean I'm some kind of backup copy of myself right now?"

Frelya huffed, as though the implication itself was insulting.

"It's not possible to fully rewrite the brain. You can just mold it a little. Tease it into being what you want. Make small changes that lead to big differences in thought. I'm not sure how they alter the brain in reeducation—I can't figure out how to alter it to even one percent of that. Yet, target the right areas, and stimulate unalterable memories with an intense emotional experience…"

"And you've primed the brain to pull in the correct information. It wasn't enough to see two people murdered right in front of me. It took… Linus, but… what are we going to do about Linus?" I asked, finding it impossible to talk about anything else for very long.

"For now, nothing. There's nothing we can do. Just going into that room was risking our lives. I had to fake or disable so much security and monitoring just for the few minutes in there that there's almost no chance I'll be able to do it again once the vulnerabilities are fixed. I'll be lucky if they don't trace it back to me anyway, but with all the distractions today and chaos happening as a result, we had this one precious window. Nothing is recorded in the room, for obvious reasons. The president is always afraid of things like this coming to light. There's nothing he fears more than a rebellion. Judging by the animosity they put in your mind toward me, I'm already suspected. I will have to keep a low profile for a long time. And for that matter, so will you."

Linda sighed, understanding right away.

I nodded. "So I need to continue acting like a blind loyal pet of the president, and keep saying hurtful things to my friends. That's not going to be easy."

Frelya shook her head, breaking eye contact with me. "Even worse. You may have to hurt people, or watch people be hurt or worse. You can't break character no matter what. Understand? Even if you have to kill someone because he asked you to, you may have to do it. Even if it's me."

I stood to my feet, clenching my fists. "No way! I'd rather die in your place, so don't say that!"

Frelya looked at me, her eyes wide. Was she blushing? Shock?

What had she expected me to say? Then, she laughed, which surprised me even more.

"What? What's so funny?" I asked.

"It's just that there was a time when I think you would've jumped at the chance to kill me. Yet now you're offering to die in my place. I thought being forced to be only a scientist here and losing my position as a commander was one of the worst things to happen, but I was only able to save you because of it. Sometimes things happen that are unexpected. You should go see the president to offer your help, or he will suspect you. After what happened today, a true loyalist would step forward and offer to help. That's what you should do."

I nodded, reluctantly agreeing. She was right, but I wasn't sure I could. If I didn't, though, that would also put Frelya in extreme danger. If they suspected her already, they'd immediately suspect her if I suddenly reverted back to my old self. If they didn't just go ahead and arrest her outright. Or… thinking back on the events of today, maybe even worse.

"I should go then. The longer I'm here, the closer they'll look at the two of you. It'll be best if we don't meet again for a while."

"I'd like to stay behind and talk to Frelya for a bit, Taylor. Good luck out there."

I nodded, leaving to find the president.

The entire way back to the auditorium, I wondered if I had the acting skills to pull this off. I reminded myself repeatedly that my friends' lives were on the line if I messed it up. That would have to be motivation enough. I wished I could tell Ghost, or Farle, especially with what Farle must be going through. The thought of telling him that the president must have had his reasons for killing his sister sickened me, but that's what I would have to say. What an awful situation.

He was still sitting on the stage, with a few professors standing around him that I hadn't met before, along with a whole unit of adversity management soldiers.

I approached cautiously, but quickly corrected it to something I hoped looked like confidence and eagerness.

"Mr. President. I'm sorry I had to leave earlier. My episodes were acting up again. Are you alright?"

He only noticed me after I spoke, waving away the professor he was speaking to previously.

"Professor Taylor. I'm sorry to hear you're having problems again. Yes, I'm fine. Just a little shaken up after everything that happened. We don't see death here very often, and to have two people drop dead in front of my very eyes... well... it's an adjustment even for an old man like me who has seen it all."

Dropped dead? That's really what he's going with? He's going to try to deny responsibility. You'd have to be brainwashed to believe that explanation over your own eyes. Unfortunately, brainwashed was what I had to pretend to be.

"I can't believe there are employees, professors even, who believe you would do such a thing. I'm sad about what happened to Glimmer and Lexili, but it was clearly the stress of the situation. If it wasn't for the panic and overreaction, maybe we could have saved them."

"Too true, Professor. I regret it deeply that we couldn't save them."

Another lie, of course. The general's heart had stopped too, and had been stopped for several minutes. They were able to save him anyway, even if his suit did help. It should have been no problem to revive them if they'd acted quickly.

Brainwashed, Taylor. Come on. You believe everything he's saying. You have to.

"Is there anything I can do to help?"

He rubbed his chin, considering for a moment. "Yes, actually. With the tragic loss of Professor Lexili, I have promoted her assistant professor to Pandemic Research's new professor and instructed him to continue in her stead. You've already been working with him, so would you mind going and keeping an eye on him for me? Help him, where possible. He has a lot to do in a very short amount of time. And with the misunderstandings and rumors that are already circulating, I wouldn't want him to reach the wrong conclusions and do anything... rash. Help him to understand that situation if he's still confused. It's the least we can do for the poor man."

So, he suspected Cherun already. Is there anyone in all of PanTech he doesn't suspect? Perhaps. I suppose only myself and others who have undergone reeducation enjoy that privilege at the moment. I had to be careful.

"Great idea. He will need my help anyway. I'll make sure he understands what really happened and that you weren't at fault. I'm sure he'll see reason and focus on the important task at hand."

"I'm glad I can still count on professors like you, Taylor. You are thorough and don't jump to conclusions without all of the facts. I will remember your loyalty through these trying times."

I snapped my left hand behind my back, right fist over my chest in the traditional PanTech salute. "It's my honor, Mr. President. Thank you for trusting me to help bring about a brighter future for all of PanTech. No, all of humanity. It's the greatest privilege any of us could ever hope for."

He nodded. I would get better, but for now it seemed I was giving a good enough performance that he hadn't seen through it. That I'd noticed. I hoped.

"You're too kind. Now, go on and catch up with him. No doubt he's already returned to Pandemic Research, and if he's allowed to spread this misinformation before someone he trusts corrects him, there's no telling the damage that'll be done as a result. And, what I'll have to do to remedy that damage."

An ominous statement. No doubt he was already considering what to do next. Cherun couldn't be the only dissenter he's worried about.

"Understood, Mr. President. I'll go right away."

I turned on my heel and strode away quickly, with purpose. I had hoped this would be the request. Now I could remain close to Cherun and make sure no one interfered with whatever he had planned.

We were running out of time.

CHAPTER 21

Considering what had happened to Glimmer, I was afraid to leave Farle alone. I knew the kind of things that went through a sane person's head when they witnessed someone close to them killed that way. Thoughts that were now crossing my own mind.

If only I didn't have to keep it secret.

Arriving at Pandemic Research, there was no one to greet us. It looked as though it had been abandoned. Walking through the common areas of PanTech were even worse. The headquarters, basically a city, looked like a ghost city. The silence was almost unbearable. Every footstep I took felt like it echoed through some kind of amplification. A sense of dread and fear weighed heavy, almost clinging to the air itself.

"Hello?" I said, standing in front of the receptionist's desk.

I stretched my head around, peeking over it, then looking down both hallways. All empty.

I stepped around, knowing there were only two places Cherun could possibly be. Farle followed close beside me, but did nothing to change the atmosphere. As we passed residences, I walked close to the doors, hoping to hear someone talking. I might have, but everyone's door was locked up tight. No one was out chatting.

They'd have to leave eventually. We had access to limitless resources, but there was only so much you could fit into a small living space.

Cherun was exactly where I thought he'd most likely be. Professor Lexili's office. He was sitting in her chair, moving side-to-side slowly, staring ahead as though he'd expected me.

"Come to get me too?" he said, still looking down at the desk. He wouldn't even meet my gaze. "I loved her. Did you know that? I think she knew it. I think she even felt the same way. But I never told her. We both put our work first. She… the way she'd tilt her head at me, from this very chair, if I ever said something amusing. It was meant to be condescending, but it was infectious. The way her glasses slid down her nose every time. You noticed it too, right?"

I nodded. "Yes…"

That's all I could say. Just that one word. I understood how he was feeling. I wanted to tell him that, but I couldn't.

"I understand how you feel. The other woman who died… she was my sister," Farle said, as though he'd read my intentions.

Cherun choked on whatever word he was about to say, and it came out only as a sad grunt.

I placed my hand on Farle's shoulder, and did my best to comfort him without speaking.

"Her name was Glimmer. She just shared your professor's perspective on the virus. Like a lot of others there, she'd convinced her. She tried to convince Taylor… No, never mind. It's not Taylor's fault."

"Isn't it, at least in part?" Cherun said, looking up at me for the first time. In his mind, he'd placed some of the blame on me, and I couldn't fault him for doing it. So did I.

"No," Farle said calmly. "Taylor is just another one of his victims, but I'm also not going to talk about her like she isn't here. You understand why we've come here, right?"

"It's not to finish the job?" Cherun asked.

"Don't play coy," Farle said. He never raised his voice, or was confrontational. He was always calm. Calculating. Even after I underwent reeducation, he stuck around, stayed calm, and bit his tongue. Even without talking to my friends, he instinctively seemed to know certain things. It was painful to see him like this.

"I'm not being coy. Surely the president knows I'm no supporter of his anymore."

I spoke up, hoping to continue the act when it wouldn't be quite as hurtful.

"The president is counting on you to continue Lexili's legacy. He knows you're the most capable person to carry on in her stead. There's so much to do in so little time. He wants to place his trust in you to see it done, and he's carrying over his belief in Professor Lexili to you."

Was that really any better?

"How kind of him, Professor Taylor. What would he have me do? Divine a miracle from the gods? Nothing short of that will accomplish what we need. Is that—"

He paused, looking to Farle, then to me.

"What is it?" Farle asked.

"If I have this kind of leverage, then maybe there is something I can do. I'm going to change the approach. Instead of modifying the virus itself, I'm going to focus purely on vaccines that can effectively stop it."

"And what if nothing we come up with can?" Farle asked.

Cherun shrugged. "You're asking me? I don't know what that man will do next. Will he call off the release of the virus? Will he demand we release it anyway, leading to a containment issue bigger than even PanTech can address? I have no idea. That's the trouble dealing with a mad man. They have no reason, and no purpose."

"He has his reasons," I said. It was the truth after all. An evil, selfish purpose.

I didn't know what role the virus played in that purpose, if any, but there was a good chance it played one. I still questioned whether or not he was sane. Perhaps he was.

"Right," Cherun said, punctuated with a sigh of frustration. "You may well be right."

"You realize I don't know anything about vaccine research," Farle said. "I can only be an assistant."

Cherun nodded. "I had hoped since Taylor brought you here, you had some experience. However, an assistant may be needed too. Normally no one can be compelled to work on a project they don't want to work on. At least… that's how it's supposed to be. Until recently that applied to professors too."

"Okay… but maybe we should have a proper funeral for Professor Lexili before we get started with all of that. Do you know how her culture cared for the bodies of the dead?" I asked, hoping to offer some kind of comfort.

"What do you care? They already collected the bodies anyway!" he shouted, before taking in a deep breath and letting it out. "But… Lexili was a professor for a reason. The best way to honor her would be to pick up where she left off and honor her memory by doing our best to match her skill and knowledge." He put his hands on his face, and for a moment I thought he might scream. He took another breath, exhaling slowly. "Lexili was a genius with no peer. She said it was impossible for her, so how could I ever do it?"

"She believed in you, Cherun. More than anyone else in the world. If she believed in you, I do too. So does Farle. Everyone does. Even the president. Let's do as you said, and focus on the vaccines rather than altering the virus. Do you think that will work?" I asked.

"Do I think it will work? Of course it won't work, but what else can I do? Sit on my hands and do nothing while the president wipes out most or all of the adversity zones, leaving us sterile 'superior' beings here to slowly perish from old age? We have to do something, even if we know it won't work. We have to try. My goodness, what a horrible situation. What is he trying to accomplish? What would have been the harm in delaying the project for another year? Such pointless loss of life."

I sighed. I wanted so desperately to speak my true thoughts, but I wasn't sure how much surveillance was being monitored in this room, or how Farle and Cherun might handle that information. "I'm sure the president… regrets the loss of life too. Do you mind if I take a sample of the virus to Animal Research and work on things there a while? We developed vaccines there too, even if it was in a much more limited capacity. Maybe we can make use of a different perspective and bring all of the different information together soon."

Cherun scratched his chin and shook his head. "There are only so many ways one can go about creating a vaccine, even with our advanced technology, methods, knowledge, and resources compared to when they were first created all those centuries ago. Still, there's some merit. It's not like it can cause any harm. Just *be careful* with your sample! We've yet to determine the transmission rate, and it may very well be one-hundred percent. You'll kill us all if you do something stupid and let the thing out. At this point, it may well be a Pandora's Box, something that can never be put back in."

"Don't worry. The way we secure the sample is not something any scientist would have an accident with. If someone lets it out, it'll have to be on purpose."

A loud knock came at the door, but the one who knocked didn't wait for an answer. They barged inside, weapons in the ready position. At least they weren't pointed at us. Three soldiers.

"Professor Taylor, state your reason for being here," the first one in said.

"I'm here because the president requested I come! Why are you here?" I snapped. A mistake, but likely one the soldier wouldn't pick up on.

The soldier looked back at the two others, who nodded, then returned his attention to us.

"The president has declared martial law. Only professors may come and go as they please, as usual, but professors will need prior approval in order to venture out. Only for the approved reasons, and only to the approved places."

"And how am I supposed to get anything done like that, huh? Do you suggest I learn every mastery under PanTech's umbrella in only a few months?!" Cherun shouted, rising to his feet.

"You will be the one exception to this, Professor Cherun. That's the other thing we came to inform you about. We'll need you to submit a list of everyone who will be directly assisting you. We can grant them free movement, but I'll warn you that the president has stated that their necessity will be verified," the soldier said.

How could he just calmly carry out orders like these? So much for the president's pride in human advancement. Many of the terrible stains on human history happened only because everyone obeyed when they should've refused. One well-placed shot at close range to the old man's head should do the trick no matter how geared up he is on machinery. Then again… it seemed he saved the most advanced technology for himself. Everything he forbade Frelya and others from building, he'd been using.

No question, this was a long time coming. Maybe he really was going insane, but he never was anything better than a tyrant all along.

"Go ahead and put Taylor and Farle on that list. I'll consider others. You're wasting my precious time coming in here and waving your stupid guns around. Now leave!" Cherun growled, slamming his fists on his desk as he returned to his seat.

To my surprise, they listened. Maybe they even pitied Cherun. I certainly did.

Things were about to get a lot harder for him. For all of us.

CHAPTER 22

I couldn't shake the feeling that the president declaring martial law already could be a good thing. If he was taking such drastic measures this quickly, it likely meant that there was suspicion that dissent would continue growing. Not that anyone could be a threat to him. I wasn't even sure if it mattered. One thing about someone who is paranoid… it was almost impossible to catch them off guard.

The only card I had available to me was the secret recovery from reeducation. Assuming he wasn't already onto me. Then again, if no one had ever managed to reverse the process, maybe not. He's arrogant. Maybe he thinks it's impossible.

One thing at a time, Taylor. Keep your eye out for an opening. For now, focus on the vaccine.

No receptionist available at Animal Research either. Instead, I found a pacing Barth, who approached me the moment I appeared. "You're not welcome here anymore, Taylor," he said, putting his hands on my shoulders and attempting to turn me back toward the door. "You need to leave."

Despite the fact he towered over me, and had a man's strength, my enhancer made this feel like nothing more than a gentle nudge.

"Sorry, Professor. I've been asked by Professor Cherun of Pandemic Research to come here, and for good reason. I can't honor your request to leave," I said, taking hold of his wrists and forcing his hands away from me. "Besides, Animal Research has been given an opportunity to impress all of PanTech again. Are you sure you want to turn it down?"

I knew Barth well. Well enough, I hoped.

He sighed, relaxing his arms. He looked me in the eyes for a moment, no doubt weighing his options. "Come to my office. Let's talk, then," he said, lowering his voice, as though uttering these words were a crime against humanity.

I followed behind him, and no one came out to greet us. I knew many of the people here at Animal Research, but none of them wanted to see me. I couldn't say I blamed them.

We stepped into his office, and he gestured to the chair in front of his desk. I followed his lead, sitting as he did. This would be difficult, as I had nothing to offer him, and he had no real way of stopping me from being here. He could get in my way, but the first threat from an armed soldier would likely break his resolve. As it would any reasonable person's.

I couldn't offer him attention and respect from the president. He no longer wanted it. He couldn't offer me permission to use Animal Research's resources. I no longer needed it.

"What's on your mind?" I asked.

He shifted in his chair, sighing as he did. Barth was never one to have a shortage of words. "Do you really believe the things you're saying now about the president? Be honest with me."

If only I could. "Of course I do. Reeducation cured me of my rebellious thoughts completely. I was always so angry at the world, and myself. I blamed it on other people, like the president. Now I'm happy, and—"

"Even after today? You're still happy, even after today? You still believe the president has the best interest of humanity at heart, even after today? You're going to just blindly do his bidding, even after today?"

"And just what are you going to do, Barth? Go in there and beat up hundreds of super-soldiers, many of them in suits, many of them with enhancers? Are you going to organize an uprising, locked up in Animal Research, using your army of unarmed and scared scientists and technicians?"

To my surprise, there was no quick-witted retort. No scathing rebuttal to fly into my face without missing a beat. There was only… silence. He leaned back into his chair, looked up at the ceiling and interlocked his fingers over his stomach. He looked like a lost child.

"Do you think we're doomed, Taylor? This isn't the PanTech I joined anymore. An institution of science and progress, free of violence and even needs. No one was afraid, cold, or hungry anymore. No one desired food, shelter, or safety of any kind. But it went beyond that. Even wants were eradicated. With unlimited resources and technology beyond any of our wildest dreams, there was no desire a human being held that couldn't be met. Even the most unattainable thoughts could be obtained in simulations indistinguishable from reality. PanTech is… was… a true utopia. But at what cost?

"We placed our full trust in the leadership. Everyone is disarmed. We're watched everywhere we go, and everywhere we are. Even this conversation is probably being monitored by someone, but I no longer feel compelled to care. I voted against the president today… the *president*. After seeing what happened afterward, I'll never feel safe again. In our adversity zones, there is a goal. A place to reach, where you can put the pain and hardships behind you. Now? Here at PanTech? There's nothing else. This is it. There's not a third place where we can put PanTech behind us. This is where all paths lead. The pinnacle. The greatest height humanity will ever reach… only to be toppled over by the ambitions of a single man."

What was I supposed to say to that? My heart ached. Even if I didn't agree that PanTech was ever anything other than a dystopian dictatorship, how could I not agree with the rest of it?

"Don't get distracted. There's still something we can do. Something that everyone wants, including the president, to potentially salvage this situation. We need to mitigate this virus, and Professor Cherun believes vaccinations are now the best bet to make this happen within the timeline we have. Whatever the… important reason the president has for insisting this virus be released in a form that puts all of humanity at risk, we can still make sure that we reduce the loss of life to a level that…"

"Look at you. You can't even say it anymore. Do you even believe the things you're saying? I'm not sure even reeducation is enough to keep you convinced anymore."

This wasn't good. I needed to step it up a notch. If Barth could notice gaps in the performance, the president surely would too. That couldn't happen. I'd lose any opportunity I might ever have to escape his attention, or catch him off guard. My friends would be in danger. Since Frelya helped me, he might… She might… I couldn't finish the thought. I couldn't accept it.

I stood from my chair, leaning on the edge of his desk. I forced every bit of imitation outrage I could onto my face. I clenched my teeth. My arms shook. My eyes were wide. My breathing became heavier. This had to work. This had to be convincing.

"I won't sit here and listen to you say things like this about PanTech's leadership anymore. I've heard enough. Either you are on humanity's side, or you're against it. The president has placed his faith in Professor Cherun, and that's what I've done too. He's asked him to finish Professor Lexili's essential work on the virus project. I'm helping him achieve that. Are you going to help us achieve our goals, or do I need to bring your… insubordination… to the president's attention? Don't push me, *Professor*, because we may have the same rank but we are not equal. One word from me, and you'll be locked up and unable to do anything anyway. Or perhaps you prefer reeducation?"

He slammed his fist down on the desk, looking me in the eye. He had more guts than I remembered, but it was working. He went from questioning whether I believed what I was saying, to looking at me like the lapdog I needed to appear to be.

"What choice do I have, then? Do as you please. Tell me what you want from me, and naturally I'll comply. I don't want to end up on one of your lists, after all. Or worse, like your supposed friend and Professor Lexili. Oh wait, they were both your friends, weren't they? Or so they thought. Whatever kind of brainwashing they used on you, it's unbreakable and permanent. There's no talking sense into you. The Taylor I knew is dead. You're barely even human anymore. You're an organic machine, programmed to repeat the words fed into it."

I laughed, relaxing back into my chair. "Are you finished? Do you feel better now, getting that off your chest? I'm glad you understand your place now, at least. Insult me until you're satisfied, because that's all you can do. You have no power anymore, and be thankful the president tolerates your tongue, or even that might change."

"Get to the point, then. What is it you need? Be specific."

"I need Linda's assistance from now until further notice, and I need unhindered access to Animal Research. Let everyone know that they're to assist me with whatever I ask of them as though I were you."

Barth shrugged. "Well, I suppose I should thank you for having the manners left to at least pretend to ask for my compliance. Perhaps you don't hate me after all."

"Of course I don't hate you. The president and I value your contributions to PanTech."

"The way he valued Professor Lexili's contributions? At any rate, go ahead. I'll let Linda know you're coming. I've already been warned about martial law before you arrived. There's plenty of research I can focus on… or maybe I'll just catch up on some reading. Elise gave me some of those old paper books like a lot of us had back in our zones. I'm overdue for some time off. As long as I don't get in your way, right? You don't mind, do you?"

"Unless I ask for your help specifically, read as much as you want. Developing a vaccine for the virus takes priority over every other function of PanTech, and that obviously applies to Animal Research."

"Very good. Thank you for laying it all out so clearly, Professor Taylor. I'm looking forward to working with you. For all our sake, I hope Professor Cherun develops a vaccine as quickly as possible."

I stood and bowed. "Thank you, Professor Barth. I'll be leaving now."

"Tell the president I said hello, will you?" he said as I was leaving.

I stopped short of the door, turning partway back around. "Of course," I said, before leaving the room and making my way toward Linda's office.

Barth and I really did feel the same way about that situation. I wished there was a way I could've told him.

I stepped into Linda's office, finding her leaning over a half-eaten meal of PanTech's signature nutrition slop. She didn't look surprised when she saw me. More like relieved. Henry was sitting in the chair next to her. Naturally, nothing would deter him from finishing a meal. If I'd shown up a few seconds later, I'm sure he would've taken care of Linda's uneaten portion as well.

"Taylor!" Henry said, running to give me a hug.

I patted him on the head. "How are you doing, Henry?"

"I'm scared. Soldiers showed up and told us we couldn't go anywhere. Even with Linda being an assistant professor. What are we going to do?"

I glanced up at Linda. Both of us understood what the glance meant, but neither of us could acknowledge it. I didn't want to say anything too extreme and scare Henry. Thankfully, Linda wouldn't force me. "I don't know what we'll do about the soldiers, Henry, but how would you like a little vacation?"

He shook his head, and his ears slapped the back of his head and his face in succession. "They won't even let us leave the division, Taylor. I'm not sure how we'll take a vacation."

Linda dropped the spoon she'd been holding into her bowl, giving me her full attention. "I'm also intrigued, Taylor. Tell us how you plan to pull off this vacation in the middle of martial law."

"Simple," I said, smiling at Henry, who returned the smile to the best of his limited ability without hesitation. "I'm a professor. Not just any professor, but a professor assigned to helping Professor Cherun develop a vaccine for the virus they've created. Anyone assisting him is immune from the enforcement of martial law. We can come and go as we please. I can also have Cherun add anyone to the list. PanTech's policy already excludes non-humans as employees, and so they're already excluded from the rule."

"I'm not sure now is the time to pull something like this…" Linda said.

"Aren't you curious why I'm here?" I asked.

Linda sighed, picking up her spoon and playing with her food. "Well I was hoping it was to have lunch with me."

"I'm sure Barth warned you in advance that I was coming, and I'm sure lunch wasn't mentioned," I said.

Linda nodded. "Oh, he said a lot of words. Shouted most of them. A few of them I'd rather not repeat. Now that you mention it, I don't think the word 'lunch' was mentioned once."

"Professor Cherun wants me to work with Animal Research to see what they're able to contribute to a vaccine, since they've been made here. But I've been thinking. Why not go a step further? Now that the virus is a live specimen, not just a simulation, we should go the old-fashioned route too. There are new species outside these very walls that have never been studied. We can collect samples and see what kind of reaction they have to the virus. At this point, luck is just as viable of a pursuit as anything else. We have three months to come up with something, and Cherun believes it's impossible. We'd need some kind of miracle. So, why not try our hand at raw luck instead? I prefer it over hoping for miracles."

Linda nodded. Henry mirrored her nods, only more enthusiastically.

"Alright," Linda said. "Who is coming along on this expedition, and how long will it take?"

"You, Henry, and Ghost at least."

"Not Farle?"

"I considered it, but I think it's best he stays and helps Cherun here for now."

"How long has it been since you've seen Ghost, Taylor?"

I frowned, trying not to think too much about the question. "I see him sometimes, but not often. He spends a lot of time observing things, and rarely speaks to anyone. Just this morning I saw him flying above. I'm sure we can get his attention somehow. If he notices us leaving, he will probably come along without being asked. He has a way of knowing things without being told. Know what I mean?"

Linda nodded. "I think I know exactly what you mean. Alright. Well... if that's your order, I'll meet you over at the Explorers League first thing in the morning. I'll prepare containment cages for our samples, and everything else we may need for collecting different samples. I'll leave the rest to you."

I reached down and gave Henry a pat on the head. He was still holding onto my leg.

"See you tomorrow, Henry."

~~o~o~o~~

I left, and made my way back to the Explorers League. Soldiers stared menacingly in front of the transport pod, despite the fact they knew who I was and were informed not to impede my movement under any circumstances. They shifted quickly into their new role of police force, and without hesitation. They no longer had another leader to filter their orders through. They answered directly to the president. Perhaps all of this had been planned since the general was removed.

"Taylor!" Harlow shouted as I stepped off the pod.

"Back off!" a soldier shouted as he approached, raising his sidearm.

I grabbed his hand, forcing it back down to his side.

"Don't make trouble in my division, or you'll have the president to answer to!" I said, standing in front of him.

Even with the suit, I was able to overpower him with some effort. Stupid helmets. I would've liked to have seen the look on his face. Instead, all I could see was him glancing down at my hand, and back up to my face, which he repeated several times.

"Sorry, Professor Taylor," he said.

"The dogs and cats here are part of my division, just like those still at Adversity Management. Even if they aren't employees, I'll expect you to treat them that way while you're here."

"Right, Professor," he said.

A second soldier nodded when I turned to look at him.

Harlow didn't miss a beat. "Taylor! Glad you're back. I need to talk to you in your office as soon as possible," he said, turning and motioning for me to follow.

I nodded, following behind him. I had a few guesses. I hoped at least most of them were wrong.

When we entered my office, Kelin glared at me from her chair. "Oh, so now you show up."

Her tone was sarcastic, but I doubted that it was all sarcasm. Her arm was bandaged from the elbow to the shoulder, but she seemed otherwise unharmed.

"I'm so sorry, Kelin. What happened?"

"I'll let Harlow explain. He handled things much better than I did."

She picked up a cup of tea sitting on a table in front of her, taking a sip. At least she was milking out all the special treatment she could from whatever injury she had.

"Right… I guess that's a matter of opinion. I almost got Kelin killed. I don't know what would've happened after that."

"After what?" I asked. "You're going to have to start from the beginning. I've been a little busy."

Kelin huffed loudly. "I'll say."

"I'm sure she means it, Kelin. Anyway… when all of that insanity happened at the party with all the other professors, we got a little visit shortly after. I suppose they'd expected all the other professors to have returned to their division to prepare everyone. Not the case for you. So we have soldiers hopping out of the transport with weapons ready, yelling, pointing. No calm. No effort to be diplomatic. I overreacted…"

"I'll say…" Kelin repeated.

"Kelin, do you want to tell the story? Is there a problem with the way I'm telling it? Am I not admitting fault here?"

"Fine." Kelin sighed, waving for Harlow to continue while taking another sip of tea.

"I gave the order for Kelin to take down the first two off the transport, which she did… very impressively."

"Is that how she got hurt?" I asked.

"No…" Kelin said.

"Ghost did that to her," Harlow said.

"What? Ghost did that?" I asked, raising my voice.

"He saved her life is what he did. He'd been watching. He knew what was coming directly behind them. Kelin disarmed one of them and was about to blast the other. Ghost dove in, wrapped his talons around her arm, and made her miss. He threw her to the ground and made her drop the sidearm at the exact moment a dozen others hopped off. When they saw Kelin on the ground and unarmed, they didn't fire."

Reinforcements? That quickly? Of course… it's entirely possible. The Explorers League is the closest division to Adversity Management. With soldiers already mobilized in front of the transport… sure, they could respond in seconds.

"I'm sorry to both of you. I should've been here. I won't make any excuses."

"You don't have to. Ghost knew you couldn't make it, and

told us as much. He didn't say where you were. Only that you couldn't be here and to follow his instructions carefully."

Kelin raised her cup. "Which you better believe we did."

I nodded. Thank goodness for Ghost. "I'm relieved. It could've turned out a lot worse. Kelin, are you fit for duty?"

Kelin's ears twitched, and she tilted her head. "Ready any time."

I nodded. "Harlow, how soon can you prepare a transport vehicle? It needs to hold a very small team. You, Kelin, myself, and a few others. It needs to be able to safely transport captured samples too, so nothing very rocky."

Harlow tapped his cheek with his paw. "Couple of days at most. We can start first thing in the morning and probably have it ready by the end of the day. Just need to make a small adjustment to one of the vehicles in the garage right now and it should be perfect."

"Any chance you could have it by the morning?"

Harlow nodded. "I'll put a night shift on it, and pull in a few of Kelin's cats to speed up the fine tuning."

"Woah," I said, grinning. "It almost sounds like you two have learned to respect one another since the last expedition."

Kelin hacked, like she was about to cough up a hairball. "Right. Practically best friends at this point. Sure, I'll send a few of my cats over. Are you sure you don't just want us to do it? We could probably have it ready by midnight."

"Oh, no you could not…" Harlow said, with a hint of a laugh. "Your cats could never match our coordination for the bigger work."

Kelin frowned, but didn't disagree.

"Alright. Make sure it's ready in the morning."

"Do we really have to come back once we leave?" Kelin asked.

"Yes, Kelin. We have to come back. We're just collecting a few samples, and that's it. We'll only be gone for a day, then I unfortunately have to leave again to spend some time with Animal Research and Pandemic Research. I'll have to ask you to keep this place together yourselves just a little bit longer."

If only I could say what I actually meant.

Leaving and never coming back was the very thing I wished I could do.

CHAPTER 24

The feeling nagged at me throughout the night, and made it difficult to sleep. My relationship with Farle seemed superficial, but I wondered how much of that was me. He'd been sincere, and even stuck by me after reeducation. I remembered everything I said after that. It must have been awful, being around me. The people I'd been through so much with, like Linda and Frelya… it at least made more sense for them to stick around and at least try to help me. Maybe not as long as they did, but Farle didn't have any real history with me.

In the morning, when I woke up, I communicated with Cherun about what I'd planned to do and asked that he send Farle over to help since he was part of the Explorers League. Happy to get both of us out of his hair for now, he was all too eager to grant the request. Linda might not be happy about it, but she'd understand.

Just as promised, Harlow delivered the vehicle to the specifications I'd asked for. Even more, apparently. "What's all this extra equipment?" I asked, pointing all around the inside as he was giving me the tour.

"Requested by Linda. Green lit by Cherun. Fabricated by Engineering." he said, shrugging. "If you feel like it's too much, let me know and I'll start tearing it out. It does limit the specimen transport space."

"Requested by Linda? When did she request it?"

"While you were still snoring a few hours ago," Linda said, making me nearly jump out of my skin when she appeared from behind one of the taller units.

"You scared me… but why the whole lab? This is like a portable facility. We could even make a vaccine in here, albeit in very limited quantities. Genius design and… actually, how did you get everything custom made and sent over here so quickly?"

"Thank Cherun for that. I told him what we wanted, put him in touch with Harlow, then he put Harlow in communication with Engineering. They took the order and churned the stuff out within a few hours."

"That quickly? Normally, Engineering takes weeks, or months, to do a custom job like this. They don't use prediction software on these types of jobs. It's all configured on the machine by hand."

"Anything Cherun asks for is put at the front of the line, even if it's a coffee mug."

"This is going to be fun," Kelin said, stepping into the back of the vehicle. "Where are we going to put all our guns?"

"Sorry, Kelin, this is a portable lab, not a rolling barracks. I'm just as disappointed about it as you are," Harlow said, patting her on the back.

"Taylor and I will be the only humans aboard, so there should be plenty of room to spare," Linda said.

"Where's Henry?" I asked.

"Barth offered him a job delivering food to the employees too scared to leave their rooms. Anyone would open their door for Henry, so he agreed to it. Despite how much he was looking forward to the trip. Guess you could've brought an extra along if we had enough notice, but I didn't find out until we were ready to leave this morning."

"Yeah, about that…" I said.

Just as I was about to explain, Farle stepped aboard with a pack slung over his shoulder. "Do you think we can fit the cooking supplies in here, Harlow?"

"The sort of equipment you've been cooking with here? No. It does have a basic kitchen though, stocked with all of PanTech's finest nutritional blends with near-infinite shelf life. There's beef flavor. Chicken—"

"Harlow, have you ever even seen a cow or a chicken?" Farle grinned.

"No…?" Harlow asked, narrowing his eyes. "They didn't send us anything human flavored."

Kelin burst into laughter, slapping Farle on the back. "We may have to find out what they taste like the old-fashioned way."

"I was *going* to suggest that Linda might be able to help us source one through Adversity Management once everything goes back to normal, but since you went there…"

"It's a nice thought," Harlow admitted, "if I shared your optimism that things were ever going to turn back to normal."

"Why is Farle here?" Linda asked, directing the question squarely at me.

"I requested that he come, and got Cherun's permission," I replied.

"That's not what I meant," she said, narrowing her eyes. "That's the how, not the why."

Farle cleared his throat. "Kelin, can you come with me to find some halfway decent cooking supplies?"

"Why? Don't you know where—"

Harlow cleared his throat, and Kelin took the hint.

"Oh, right. Sure. I'll show you where we keep the good stuff," Kelin said, hopping out of the back and waving her paw for Farle to follow.

"Guess I'll join them," Harlow took a step toward the back.

"Wait," I said, looking around to make sure no one else had shown up. "I have a question first."

Harlow perked his ears up and tilted his head.

"You do have surveillance installed, right? So we can be monitored by headquarters after we leave?"

Harlow laughed. "Do you honestly think Kelin would allow anything like that to be in here. She already checked every square inch of this thing. Do you want me to add it?"

"No," I said.

"No?" he repeated, clearly confused by my recent behavior. I wasn't sure yet if I should tell him the truth, or if I would, but he definitely found my answer odd.

"No," I repeated. "We don't have enough time, unfortunately. We'll add it later."

Harlow nodded, then hopped out of the back.

"Are you crazy? You barely know the man," Linda said.

"You'll have to trust me. I don't want to hear anything else about it. I personally requested for him to be transferred to the Explorers League, so I think he's capable of handling a small expedition like this."

Linda and I both knew this wasn't what she meant, but she seemed to understand that it was an answer to her true question nonetheless. She let it go, even though she wasn't happy about it.

"I just hope you know what you're doing. He seems to be handling his sister's death a little too well. Don't you think?"

"And how should he handle it exactly? How would you handle it? I'm sure inside he's screaming. There's no right way to grieve the loss of a sibling. Or anyone. Farle hasn't been…"

Sensing I was about to say too much, I held my tongue.

"Is that… smoke?" Linda asked. "It smells like a fire."

"I have a feeling I know what it is. Come on. Let's head out and have a look."

I pointed at the center of the common area.

"Is he… cooking?" Linda asked.

"He likes to do that for the dogs and cats, so they can have a proper meal from time to time. He's actually a great cook with these camp-style dishes. Something he learned in his zone. Come on. Let's go take a look."

As we walked over, he began pouring in ingredients. Kelin was chopping furiously next to him, treating it like a competition rather than a cooperative effort.

"I've finished the potatoes," she said proudly as she poured them into the cauldron.

"You're fast, Kelin. You're going to lose a paw if you don't slow down," Farle scolded, slowly slicing the ham. A stark contrast.

"You underestimate a cat's finesse. Even with these paws, I can still slice rings around you."

"Oh yeah?" Farle raised a brow, grinning at Kelin. "How about a wager then?"

"What's on the line?" Kelin asked, flipping the knife into her paw several times, catching the handle cleanly with each toss.

"Everybody here gets one slice. Winner gets an extra slice of ham all to themselves."

"No punishment for the loser?"

"Well, that's going to be you, and I assume the embarrassment will be punishment enough."

Kelin squawked with laughter, running a claw down the length of her whiskers.

"You're in for a surprise. Get our ham ready. Sorry in advance for embarrassing you in front of your girlfriend. Just remember, you're the one who suggested this."

Farle smiled, separating out two large chunks.

"Half an inch cubes. If you're not at least close to that, you're disqualified. First one to finish slicing is the winner. Ready?"

Kelin nodded, gripping the knife in her paw and letting it rest against the chunk of ham. "Ready."

"Count us down, Harlow. For three. On go."

Harlow sighed, holding up his paw. "Three… two… one… go!"

He swung his arm down, and the two began slicing.

At first, I got caught up in the excitement. Both of them ripped through the ham with amazing speed and accuracy, leaving squares almost exactly half an inch behind, quickly piling them up. Farle dumped his already sliced chunks into a bowl beside him, clearing up room in his plate to slice easier. Kelin looked to her side, finding no bowl there. Harlow read her intentions before she even settled her eyes on the spot she hoped the bowl would be. He used his foot to kick one over to her. She quickly dumped her extra pieces into the bowl, then resumed slicing. Only a few moments later, Kelin finished, tossing all of her pieces into the bowl and looking up at Farle with a huge smile.

Only Farle had already finished, leaning over with his elbows on his knees.

"What took you so long?" he said, tapping on the empty plate with the handle of his knife.

Harlow huffed. "Don't let him pull your leg, Kelin. He beat you by two or three seconds. Tops."

A round of applause echoed around us, distracting enough for the two soldiers stationed near the transport to take a few steps toward us for a better look.

Seeing them coming close, Farle held a bowl into the air.

"You must be hungry. Join us for breakfast?"

One of them took a step toward us, but the other soldier grabbed his arm, shaking his head when he looked back to see why he'd stopped him. Both returned to their posts.

"It was kind of you to offer," I said.

"Yeah, maybe they'll forget the fact Kelin almost killed one of them if we're nice enough," Harlow added with a laugh.

"You *told* me to!" Kelin shouted indignantly.

All the dogs and cats around us burst into laughter.

Then, I finally saw a hint of it. The sadness in his eyes. The face of a brother who'd just lost his sister, but still found the space in his heart to be strong for everyone else. And in that moment, I was glad I'd decided to bring him along.

After all this time, and everything we'd been through, I still found it so difficult to open up to anyone, and allow others to help me.

This time, as with the others, I was going to need every bit of the help I could get.

CHAPTER 25

"No sign of Ghost yet?" I asked, frowning as the gate closed behind us, signaling the beginning of our journey.

"That doesn't necessarily mean anything. The weather field doesn't prevent Ghost from flying through, so he can show up whenever he wants," Kelin said from the driver's seat.

"I was just hoping he could be here when I talked with all of you. His input would have been valuable. We need to discuss what's happening at PanTech."

Everyone shifted uncomfortably. There was plenty of room to move through the lab with other people, but with bringing up this conversation, it suddenly felt stuffy and small.

"It's not something you have to discuss, Taylor. But I won't stop you."

At this point it felt more dangerous not to tell them than it did telling them.

Farle didn't look at me. Instead, he looked out the windows.

"I'm taking a big risk by telling you anything, but let's start by taking a weight off everyone's mind. My reeducation has been… reversed. I don't want to get into the details, but know that I'm myself again. I'm not going to be giving you any long, annoying speeches about how great the president is and how much I love him. Obviously, no one can find out. I'll have to keep pretending back at headquarters, and you'll have to go along with it."

"Is it true?" Farle asked, standing up straight and facing me.

"It's true," I said. "…And I'm sorry. It was after what happened to Glimmer. I wish I could've done something to…"

"Save her? I was standing there too. There's nothing we could have done to save her. We can't blame ourselves."

I ran over and hugged him tightly. A wave of relief washed over me. I was glad that he didn't blame me for what happened to her. Even if I couldn't do the same for myself.

"What? Harlow told me it was irreversible and that we were just going to have to get used to it," Kelin said.

"Why would you rely on my word, Kelin? I just go by what I'm told, same as you. I assumed Frelya would know."

I squeezed Farle's shoulders and took a step back. I knew

everyone would have questions.

"As far as I know, it's the first time it's ever been done. That's why it can't ever be mentioned beyond this trip where we can't be sure there's no surveillance."

Linda nodded. "And as important as all of this is, everyone still needs to remember that the virus isn't going away just because we have Taylor back."

"Yes, but it changes a few things," I said. "My goal is to reach full immunity with whatever vaccine we happen to create. Not eighty percent, not tied to intelligence, but one hundred percent. If we can spread a vaccine ahead of the virus, in a way that can reach everyone, no one has to die."

"And when the president sees that no one is dying, what then?" Linda asked.

"Then gives us more time than now," I said. "Right now we're sitting on three months to do something that would probably take years. If a deadly virus was this easy to deal with, there wouldn't be a PanTech in the first place. Conquering a virus that nearly wiped out humanity is a great feat, but it's not wise to tempt fate twice. That's what the president's doing now. Taking this virus and daring it to try again."

"Have you considered the fact that it may be easier to handle the president than the virus?" Kelin asked.

Farle nodded in agreement.

Linda was wide-eyed and clearly didn't agree.

I was somewhere in the middle.

"I have considered that, Kelin… but I'm not sure if that's true. I went to see the president shortly before being dragged off to reeducation, and saw his office and the area beyond. The old, half-broken machines we fight that were abandoned in the wilderness? He has a giant room filled with them, lining every inch of the outer wall. Shiny and new, fully armed, stocked on ammo, and ready to attack at any moment."

"What?" Kelin, Harlow, and Farle shouted nearly at once. Linda's mouth hung open, like she wanted to speak, but couldn't.

"Why does he have those?" Harlow asked.

"He was originally a leader of the rebellion, but betrayed the others in exchange for his new position and power. He's also completely fitted with machine parts, something that's strictly forbidden for every employee at PanTech. From what I can tell, everything from the neck down. Minimum. It's safe to say he has other machine upgrades too. Eyes, maybe ears, and so on. Based on what we know about the humans that used these parts on their bodies, he's probably many times more capable than someone with a physical enhancer. Like me, or the other commanders. Add in the machines…"

"But if he's still organic…" Farle paused, tapping on his chin. "That means he's still vulnerable to the virus, so what's his angle there? Surely he must be afraid it'll get to him too."

"He wants to become immortal," I said.

Harlow laughed, leaning on a cabinet next to him. "Come on. Be serious. You can't really mean that. He'd risk the future of humanity to become immortal? How's a virus that kills humans supposed to help with that anyway?"

"I haven't figured that part out yet, but considering his obsession with making this virus a reality, it must play in somehow. He's pushing too hard, and risking too much. Maybe he thinks he's running out of time. He is the oldest human to ever live, as far as I know. His time could be closing in."

"It sounds like a cliché," Linda said.

"Until it starts to seem attainable," Farle said. "If you find a way to become immortal, then what's the reason for humanity to continue producing heirs? Kill off, sterilize, become a society of hand-picked humans living and learning endlessly? No need for recruiting. No need for exams. So what if it kills off half the human race? Or even more?"

I hadn't considered that angle. I'd assumed he wanted to learn the secrets of immortality all for himself, but Farle was probably right. It was probably to create an elite society of immortal geniuses. The best humanity could offer. Instead of a revolving door of men and women who learned a bit more than those before them, died, and then left slightly more for those who came after, these elites could progress endlessly. They could build knowledge and experience never before imagined.

Linda shook her head. "But how is this any different from the rebel society's fascination with replacing themselves with machinery?"

"I'm not sure it is," I admitted. "He was a part of that society, after all."

Kelin spoke up from the driver's seat. "So, we gather samples, try to make a vaccine—let's say none of it works, the president still doesn't stop… take him out?"

"Then what?" I asked. "What comes after? What kind of precedent does that set? No, I'd rather avoid that outcome if possible."

Instinctively, I placed my hand on the strap that ran across my chest. The strap that held Twisted Key securely to my back. Would I need to use it again?

"We should all want to avoid that outcome," Linda said.

Harlow nodded.

Farle looked blank and distant, as though he was considering another option altogether. Just not one he was willing to share.

Harlow raised his paw. "Kelin is probably going to drive us to the moon if no one tells her where to go."

"Going to keep moving until you tell me to stop," Kelin confirmed. "Going to roll right through the middle of Arc City. Always been curious about the adversity zones anyway."

"Stop in the meadow ahead," I said. "We can start collecting there."

"Do you actually think these animals can offer anything helpful, or did you mostly bring us out here so we could talk?" Linda asked.

"I think it's possible, but yeah, there are very few opportunities for us to talk at headquarters. We might also need to flee at some point if things get bad enough."

Farle shook his head. "Do you honestly think PanTech would ever let you escape? Even if it was the last thing they ever did, they'd catch you. No one has ever escaped, and there's no chance any of us would be allowed to be the first."

"You think we don't all know that, Farle? You think Taylor doesn't?" Linda said.

He sighed, and nodded.

"I didn't really mean us anyway," Taylor said. "Our dogs and cats aren't official employees, remember? An employee escaping is one thing… but a bunch of experiments getting loose? If other, more important things are going on, will they really prioritize lost pets?"

Linda interrupted my point with one of her own. "Has it ever occurred to you that the president was awfully enthusiastic about these modification experiments with animals in the first place, particularly considering the intelligence-increasing aspect of it? Brain density. Couldn't this also be performed on humans?"

That might've made sense if it wasn't for something Elise told us. It still might…

"He denied it when Elise proposed it originally, but I'm not sure. I'm not really sure about anything anymore. Despite everything we've learned, there are still a lot of unknowns in his plans. We've only recently been made aware of a few components of it, and we're able to speculate a bit on the rest, but how much of that puzzle are we missing?"

The movement stopped, and Kelin looked over her shoulder. "Passengers, we have arrived at our destination. A field in the middle of nowhere. Please don't leave trash behind and exit in an orderly fashion."

"You read the book I sent over to you!" Harlow said.

"I did. You actually remind me a lot of the guy who loses the race in the third chapter," Kelin said, grinning as she opened the side door, taking a step off while still looking at Harlow.

"Aw, come on. Why do you have to do that to me? That guy was horrible," Harlow said, frowning.

"Why do you think he reminded me of y—Ah! Sheesh!" Kelin squeaked, nearly jumping out of her fur when she turned to step off the transport. "Ghost… you almost scared me to death!"

CHAPTER 26

I ran out ahead of Kelin, nearly knocking her over.

"Ghost!" I shouted. "I have so much to tell you. I wish you were on the transport with us. I'll have to catch you up."

"No need," he said.

"No need?" I repeated.

"I already know you're back to normal. I've talked to others about your behavior, and I've been watching. I know what's been going on around PanTech. Maybe more than anyone else."

I stared at him, unsure whether I should be irritated or impressed.

"Why didn't you come see me before?"

"You couldn't be helped, or so I thought. You are lucky to have such impressive friends," Ghost said.

Ghost was every bit as difficult to read as those soldiers wearing their helmets. He had no facial features, and very little in the way of tone.

"You're one of them, you know?"

Although he didn't answer the comment directly, I got the impression that he agreed.

"Are you out here to collect samples? I can either help you collect them quickly if you plan to return soon, or I can go back and monitor what's going on at headquarters if you'll be here for a while."

I looked at the others, who had filed out behind me. It would be irresponsible to stay too long, even if I wanted to. We were taking a risk by simply making the trip and discussing the topic we did on the way here. If any kind of monitoring device was hidden that Kelin didn't find, it would be all over for us the moment we returned. We all had to trust one another.

"Help us collect them quickly. I don't want to raise too many suspicions at headquarters if I can help it."

Ghost nodded, then flew away. I hadn't even described to him what kind of samples I was looking for, but that was Ghost. He didn't like wasting words on things he considered obvious. I guessed that most employees of PanTech forgot he could even talk. Not that many of them had ever spoken to him in the first place.

"With Ghost collecting samples, will there be much point in

the rest of us trapping any?" Farle asked.

Linda answered for me. "Absolutely not. You'll just interfere with his collection and end up getting doubles. Just let him gather the samples on his own."

"You know what that means," Farle said, looking to Kelin, who nodded as though she indeed knew what that meant.

"Lunch time!" Kelin said, rubbing her paws together.

"What? Already?" Harlow said, shaking his head. "You two have your snack break. I'm going to find a tree to watch from and take a rifle up, since we're not needed for samples."

"Oh, lighten up, canine. Ghost will be keeping a watch. He'll let us know if he sees anything unusual," Kelin teased.

"Ghost is busy. He might not notice. Besides, I'd prefer at least one other be at a strategic attacking point in case we run into any machines."

Kelin laughed. "We wiped out all the machines in this area ages ago. Besides—"

"Besides nothing. Maybe I just like the view. What's it to you?"

"Ah, now that's the hard-nosed dog I know. I feel safer already."

"Are you trying to start a fight with me, Kelin?" Harlow said, leaning in, showing Kelin his teeth.

"Are you trying to start one with me?" Kelin asked, following it up with a low, rumbling growl.

So much for being friends now. Maybe this would be how they always were. Maybe this was even a part of how they showed their affection for one another as friends. I wasn't about to put up with a brawl two minutes into arriving at our destinations, well-intended or not.

"I'm going to have Ghost paralyze both of you if you don't shut up," I said.

They both continued to stare down one another for another few seconds, before simultaneously turning away.

Kelin followed Farle into the kitchen corner to gather supplies, but returned out a moment later chasing after Harlow.

"Don't forget about this, mutt," Kelin said, tossing the rifle to Harlow, who turned just in time to catch it.

"Thanks, hairball," he said, before spotting a tree and heading toward it.

Linda and I took the opportunity to set up the cages for Ghost to drop the specimens into. With his help, we might not even have to go anywhere else. He could fly around the area to catch them and spot them from much further than we ever could.

Ghost reappeared, dropping a squirrel into each of two cages and kicked the doors closed behind him as he took flight again. Somehow, he managed not to injure them with his razor-sharp talons. Though, his paralyzing toxin certainly helped.

"Hey! Next time Ghost comes back, have him check about a mile northeast! I think I saw something!" Harlow shouted from the top of his tree above us.

"Don't you have a short-range communicator?!" Linda shouted back at him.

"Blame the cat! She's too paranoid, so she ditched them! Anyway, let him know!"

"Could it be another one of those machines?" Linda asked.

"I doubt it," I said. "We've destroyed several in this area and sightings are rare now. Things aren't like they were when you, Henry, and I were out here seeing one for the first time. We've learned about them. Most of these spider units are identical. Ghost can sense them coming too. I wouldn't worry."

Linda nodded, but didn't appear convinced.

Neither did I, I'm sure, despite what I was saying.

Harlow was rarely wrong. Maybe a tree fell?

As Ghost flew back with more samples, I waved for his attention. "Harlow said he spotted something moving about a mile northeast. Could you go check it out?"

Ghost didn't answer. Only dropped the paralyzed specimens in the cages and flew in that direction. I crossed my fingers.

"Ham and potatoes again?" Kelin complained as she and Farle exited the transport. "I don't like the potatoes."

"Then don't eat them. Harlow likes them. I'm sure he'd be happy to take your share," Farle said, placing the smaller cauldron on the ground between all of us.

"I'm sure it's nothing, but we should be on standby until Ghost gives us the signal that everything's clear," I said, reaching out and touching Farle's arm.

Before they could comment, Ghost reappeared and landed on the ground next to us.

"What is it, Ghost? What did you see?"

"I don't know," he said. "But it's coming this way. A machine, but not a spider."

He flew away, joining Harlow in the tree where he could offer better support.

We waited for several minutes, though it felt like hours. Everything was quiet. Fortunately, you could hear the slightest sound. There were very few trees in the meadow, so little cover for a large machine. If nothing else, even though we were out in the open, it would be almost impossible to ambush us.

After several more minutes, Harlow lost his patience.

"Unless it's a slug machine, I think it would've made it here by now," he said.

"Is it possible that both of you were mistaken?" Kelin asked.

Ghost didn't answer, eyes still darting around and focused.

"Maybe. It can get windy over there, so maybe that's why the trees were—"

Ghost reacted instantly to the hand that came around the tree. It clutched at his neck, but was only able to grab his leg as he propelled himself away. Harlow's reaction speed was only a hair slower. He leaned back, raised his rifle to the arm—placing the barrel against the wrist—and fired. At point-blank range, that rifle could have pierced anything I've ever encountered aside from General Markus's armor.

Ghost ripped the damaged mechanical hand away from its owner, though it didn't immediately release. He struggled to fly, wobbling in a fruitless attempt to correct himself before landing roughly below.

Harlow lost his footing from the force of firing such a powerful weapon up close. Had it only been the recoil, he would have held on. He'd done it many times. But add the additional force of the impact being so close.

"Harlow!" Kelin shouted, running toward him as quickly as she could.

He landed with a thud, and grabbed his leg, badly broken.

"Stay back!" Ghost said, trying to kick away the hand squeezing his leg. "Quick, Harlow!"

Harlow understood Ghost, somehow, though it was a good thing. He grabbed the hand, prying with all his strength. With a growl, he finally succeeded in opening the grip just enough for Ghost to pull his leg out. He hurled it up into the tree, and it exploded, sending the mechanical humanoid falling to the ground. It landed with a hard thud, sinking its legs deep into the soft earth.

Kelin took advantage of the opportunity, ignoring Ghost's warning from the start, and closing in quickly. She leaped through the air, swinging her blade in a perfect line before her feet touched the ground. Though Kelin didn't have an enhancer, there was no other way to describe her reflexes other than cat-like. Though it should have been obvious.

Despite this, the way this thing moved made her look more like an elderly human woman. The dodge was almost imperceptible. Kelin switched her grip in the follow-up strike, looking to plunge her knife into the thing's neck. With a swat, her paw was deflected at the wrist, and the knife continued along a harmless path. It freed one of its legs, then the other, kicking her in the chest and sending her flying onto her back.

"Wh… what is that?!" Linda screamed.

Farle grabbed her wrist, and placed his sidearm into her hand.

"Stay calm. I've heard you're good with these. Wait for your moment."

He smiled, and it made me feel uneasy. How could Farle be so confident and relaxed against something so terrifying and unexpected. Then again, losing the person you love most in your life will numb you to everything else. It was entirely possible his fear of living and dying was completely dormant.

I couldn't say the same for myself. I'd stayed calm on the outside, observing, and holding myself back from rushing in hastily. On the inside, I felt fear unlike anything I'd felt in a long time. Maybe this thing wasn't any stronger than the spider machines we'd fought so many times before, but it was different and unknown. Seemingly sensing this, Farle put his hand on my shoulder.

"I won't let anything happen to you, Taylor. I promise."

A sweet sentiment, but I was the one with the enhancer, and even the three animals with us had abilities well beyond what a human was capable of. All three were already out of the fight. Unfortunately, the protecting would be left up to me.

Kelin struggled to her feet, managing to make it to her knees while clutching her ribs. She hadn't pulled in enough air yet to do anything besides gasp. Her rib was absolutely broken. I hoped it was nothing more than that.

It took a step toward her, intending to finish the threat.

"Distract it. Fire!" I said, turning back to Linda, drawing Twisted Key from my back.

It would charge us next. Now or never.

Perfect shooting from Linda—striking precisely where its eyes appeared to be. I hoped, at least. It was clearly modeled after a human.

As expected, it turned. No doubt it had redundant visual sensors, because its path was direct. I charged forward, bringing down Twisted Key in an effort to end the fight quickly. I wanted my strike to have the power to end the fight if it landed. If we turned this into a fight of trading blows, I would lose quickly.

It deflected the blade, stepping quickly to the side with amazing dexterity. This was martial arts.

I was wide open.

I made a mistake.

Faster than I could possibly react to when I was already overextended this far, its fist flew toward my chest. Every muscle in my body tensed.

Just before the fist made impact, Farle's hand caught it, twisting it behind the creature.

It stepped away, carefully attempting to reverse the hold, but Farle anticipated that, and stepped in. As he did, not only could it not escape his grip, but he was able to slash a deep groove into its neck. Following through in that same slicing motion, Farle curled his arm around and moved into a headlock. With a grunt, he pressed hard against the weakened, sliced area of the neck, spreading it open further and further. With a sudden twist, he yanked the head off, sending it bouncing across the ground, the body collapsing in a straight line with it.

"Farle?" I whispered, finally beginning to gather my composure after avoiding what should've been certain death.

"There are a few things I should tell you, now that you're yourself again, Taylor."

"Kelin, if you're done staring, go get the vial of bone repairing agent from the vehicle. It's locked up in the first cabinet of the lab," Harlow said, still holding his leg. "Open it and use some on yourself first."

Kelin snapped back to reality, running into the vehicle. A moment later, she shouted back out.

"This orange sealed vial, right? I tried it, but it doesn't seem to be working. Isn't this stuff supposed to be instant?"

Linda's face went pale, and she looked like she might faint.

"Kelin, seal the transport! Don't move!" she screamed, far more panicked than she was at the sight of the machine.

It finally hit me.

Oh no…

CHAPTER 27

Kelin reacted quickly. She sealed the rear door of the transport and enabled the pass-through communication with the outside. "Somebody mind telling me what's in this? It's not the bone repair cocktail. I know that much," she said.

"There's a suit in the cabinet directly behind you. You'll know what it is. It's a containment suit for working on active contaminants in the lab, but it works both ways. Put it on after you inject the bone repair, and make sure it's completely sealed," Linda said, dodging Kelin's question.

"Oh, so this was a sample of the super killer virus with one-hundred percent mortality rate? That's fantastic. Why was it in here in the first place?" Kelin asked with a hiss.

"In the cabinet next to the sample you opened, you'll find the bone repair solution you were looking for. It's an injection, not ingested orally. Inject it into your arm before you seal up the suit. Let me know when the suit is sealed."

As Linda continued to dodge questions, I found myself wanting to know the answer as well. Though I could assume some of them. Linda most likely wanted the lab to be fully functioning. Not just to transport samples, but to study them, and actually apply the information to a potential vaccine. A true portable lab.

"It's sealed. Now what? Decontamination set for half an hour?" Kelin asked.

"No. We're going double on this one, just to be absolutely sure," Linda said, turning to Harlow. "Sorry, Harlow. You'll have to wait an hour on that bone repair injection."

"I'm fine. Is Kelin…" he started, choking on the words. He took a deep breath, but his voice still came out strained. He looked at me, his eyes glistening with the tears forming in them. "Is she going to die?"

I walked over to him and knelt beside him, wrapping my arms around his shoulders.

"I'm sorry. I don't know if there's anything we can do to save her. I'll try, but…"

Farle knelt behind both of us, putting a hand on each shoulder, but said nothing.

"Don't talk about me like I'm not here," Kelin snapped. "In

the old world, humans had a saying that cats had nine lives. I only need two. Even if nothing else has survived, there has to be a first. I'll be the first."

Everyone was silent. It was hard to fault Kelin for her optimism. After all, all of us wanted her to pull through it. But all of us, including Kelin, knew that was all but impossible.

Ghost, as usual, couldn't be read. "The mortality rate in Kelin's unique species is completely unknown."

And in those few words, in that one sentence, I felt a surge of optimism. Ghost was right. This virus was made to kill humans. The rats used to test it were programmed to be affected exactly as a human would be, with perfect accuracy. Kelin's infection is organic, and Kelin's feline species is completely unique to the world. It's never existed before, and isn't designed to mimic humanity with precision. Only some of the traits. Even though there was a significant genetic overlap.

Linda seemed to sense my shift in perspective. "Taylor... in all practical likelihood, the chance of her making it are... essentially zero. I'm sorry. This is all my fault. I didn't anticipate a need to rush into the lab to grab something so close to it. I'd planned on going over the capabilities of the lab with you, and then the machine... I'm sorry. Everyone. I'm so sorry, Kelin."

Linda sat on the ground, hugging her knees to her chest, and began to cry like the rest of us.

"Let's talk about this machine," Kelin said, more than eager to change the subject.

"Theories?" Ghost asked, backing her up.

I shook my head. "I've never seen one of these before. It looked almost human. We've seen different models, mostly based on spiders. This isn't the first unique sighting. We did see the one that looked like a wolf. A quadruped. This is the first biped."

Harlow shifted his broken leg, and took a deep breath, trying to find a comfortable position to sit in.

"The question is... why make it like that? It was dangerous, but nothing like the large arachnid units when it comes right down to it. At least, not in raw combat ability. That sneak attack was pretty impressive, but the arachnid units have a ton of mounted deadly hardware and utility. EMP capability and heavy guns that exceed our current issue rifles but with rapid fire of previous generation projectiles. Not energy. Sound neutralizers too, and communication jammers. Mass, and weight, and even their speed is more impressive over longer distances. Yet, that humanoid machine was clearly more complex. The programming and processing made it react faster."

Farle nodded in agreement. "It fought like an actual, trained human. That seems advanced, even for the society that was responsible for making them. Suspiciously advanced."

"Do you think it was made recently, then?" Linda asked, wiping her nose on her sleeve and sniffing.

"I don't remember seeing a model like that in the area behind the president's office. They were all arachnids," I said. "But... I suppose I probably didn't see everything. But that would create a new question. Why was the thing out here?"

Kelin cleared her throat. "Maintenance model. What if its role was to go around and do maintenance on the larger machines? They're too large to perform delicate repairs on themselves. They also couldn't restock their own ammunition."

We all sat silent. Even Ghost. That could have been it. Except...

"So why hasn't it been doing its job?" I asked. "Most of the machines we've encountered have been barely holding together, or show long-term scars from battles over a hundred years ago. We haven't seen any evidence of recent repairs on any of them, and consider how many broken down units we've encountered that weren't even operational."

"Pilot for larger units somewhere? Some kind of human experiment?" Ghost asked, throwing out the two theories simultaneously.

I remembered seeing the president's machine body up close. It was definitely similar to the machine we just encountered.

"I suppose either is possible. The president has a body that's pretty similar. Fully machine from the neck down."

Farle sighed. "If they were that good over a hundred years ago, imagine what his body must be able to do."

"I'd rather not," I said, feeling like we already had more than plenty on our plate at the moment.

"Should we take it back with us?" Linda asked.

"Too risky. You saw what the hand did. We don't have anything to contain explosives with us and if that thing springs back to life inside the transport, we're all dead. As much as I hate to leave it, we're going to have to. We'll save the location information and send a recovery team with proper equipment out to retrieve it later."

Farle nodded. "As valuable as it is, there's no argument to be made. It's too dangerous to do anything besides leave it here. We already have the deadliest virus humanity's ever known to contend with. We can't add an unstable bomb to that."

Kelin cleared her throat again. "Agreed. I'd rather not be infected and blown up in the same day."

Ghost looked at all of us. "If you're afraid of it blowing up, why are we all sitting here?"

I sighed, holding up my hands in defeat. "Right. Right… Sorry. I guess we all got caught up in all the things going on. Kelin, move the transport to the other end of this meadow. We'll follow on foot. I'll carry—"

"I'll carry him," Farle interrupted. "I'm much bigger than you, so I won't have to contort him as much."

Another mystery to be solved.

"I don't need anyone to carry me. Just support my right side and I'll hop along. I just need to endure it for another hour, right? Even I can handle that," Harlow said, trying to preserve as much of his dignity as possible. Just as I was about to scold him, Farle quickly backed him up.

"Apologies. You're a warrior, like me. I'll give you an arm. But we need to go. Now."

Linda took in a deep breath, wiping her nose again. She stood and walked ahead of us, following the vehicle as Kelin drove it slowly across the field.

I walked side-by-side with Farle and Harlow as Ghost flew above. Thankfully he wasn't among the injured. I suppose the mechanical hand couldn't get a tight enough grip on his small leg.

"Farle, I need you to be honest with me. Former commander?"

He nodded. "There really isn't anything spectacular about the story. I was a commander. I disobeyed General Markus. I was sent to wall guard duty and forgotten about. Glimmer… requested to be transferred there. Being in her company every day… why would I bother to remind them that I was ready to return to Adversity Management duty? I had no desire to return, and they had no desire for me to return. That's all."

"Not everyone becomes a commander. I feel like there's more

to it, but I won't pry if you don't want to talk about it."

He simply nodded. I'd hoped he'd take that as an invitation to talk more, and accept that invitation, but alas… the man barely talked more than Ghost. Still, he saved me today, and risked his own safety in doing it. Maybe I was a sucker for a man like that, but…

Ah, I'm hopeless.

I wrapped my arms around his left arm, and looked up at him. He turned his head, his eyes meeting mine, and he smiled softly.

Harlow stretched his head around, noticing. "Oh, come on, Taylor! Why do you have to do this to me?" he complained.

"What? Do what to you?" I asked, confused.

"We're both holding on to his arms now. You're making it weird!" Harlow said, lowering his voice so the others couldn't hear.

Farle and I looked at one another, and laughed.

The world was falling apart around us, and this was only a moment of time. Even if we never laughed again, at least we shared this one moment together before the weight of our circumstances came down upon us once again, crushing our ability to feel joy.

It's going to be okay, I said to myself. For a moment, I believed it. But only a moment.

It's going to be okay, I lied.

CHAPTER 28

Two Months Later

"We need to talk about Kelin, Taylor," Cherun said, pulling up a hologram spreading so much data around the room it felt like I might drown in it.

"I know. I can't believe it either. Maybe cats really do have nine lives," I said, shrugging.

If he was hoping I'd impart some kind of deep understanding, he was mistaken. I was just as confused as he was.

"Two months without a single symptom. Not one," he said.

"Nothing?" Farle asked, sitting in the chair next to mine.

"I said nothing, and I mean nothing. Not even a little sniffle. Kelin has been remarkably resilient to this virus, beyond any expectation. Yet, we haven't been able to isolate what particular part of her is responsible. We requested typical felines as samples from Adversity Management, but they've all died. The anthropomorphic cats we have here have only those two genetic influences. Human, and cat. Both died with one-hundred percent mortality when separated."

"Are we sure it isn't just Kelin? Something unique about her?" I asked.

Cherun shook his head, pointing to one of the data points on the hologram, gesturing with his fingers to expand that particular set. "See that? That's a dog named Melo from Adversity Management. One of the hybrids. He volunteered shortly after Kelin's infection. See for yourself how that has gone."

I scanned over the data, and the results were nothing short of amazing. "He survived too, with no symptoms. But… these results here… how can this be?"

"I don't understand how that's possible," Farle echoed. "They're still testing positive? How?"

"Yes, I wondered about that as well. Continue to wonder about it, obviously. How can all those other subjects, particularly the ones that die of secondary symptoms so much later, test negative for the virus only a couple of weeks after becoming infected? Even when they die anyway. Yet, Kelin and Melo continue to test positive. The virus has somehow acclimated to them as an especially suitable medium. A temporary host to infect others, perhaps. They will have to remain in quarantine indefinitely I'm afraid, though we have worked hard to improve their accommodations so they aren't left wanting for anything."

"And how's that working out for Kelin?" Farle asked. A rhetorical question, to be sure.

"I can tell by the way you asked the question that you know the answer. She's restless. She wants to leave and resume her duties, and she's growing tired of cooperating with us. If we're able to derive a cure from her unique circumstances, we can then move to exterminate the virus from her body. Though I can't guarantee that doing so would… you understand the risks, don't you, Taylor?"

"Kelin didn't ask for this, Professor. We owe it to her to be sure. By then, hopefully she can be. For the time being, you should continue doing the best you can with her. If there's nothing else, I should get going," I said.

"I see. You didn't notice…" he said, sliding Melo's data aside and opening Kelin's again. "There is one thing that seems to be unique to Kelin. I randomly sampled other cat hybrids, but couldn't replicate it. Have a look at the behavior of her cells," he said.

I perused through the data, for what seemed like an eternity. There was nothing out of the ordinary. At least, as far as a humanoid feline was concerned. Whatever Cherun thought he…

No. This wasn't possible.

"Is this what I think it is?" I asked, not even sure I was actually seeing what was right before my eyes.

"You played a key role in this project as the assistant professor of Animal Studies. Even if it was already established before you joined PanTech, I was hoping you could enlighten me. Many things in science happen accidentally. Like a chef creating a new dish in the kitchen. This… this does not happen accidentally. This was intentional, and I want to know if you knew about it. Tell me the truth."

"I didn't know anything like this was built into the research. We should keep this quiet. All of it. Don't let it leave this room," I said.

"Mind enlightening the layman in the room?" Farle asked.

Despite Cherun's subtle head shake urging me not to

elaborate, I thought Farle deserved to be included.

"Look at her measured metabolism. Look at the rate her cells break down and replicate. It's not something that would be picked up in a routine physical, but Cherun's investigation into Kelin's biology has been especially thorough because of the virus."

Farle strained his eyes, browsing over the data again. A few minutes later, he sighed, seeming a bit embarrassed. "I still don't see it. Explain it to me like I'm five."

Cherun sighed, pointing to the data again. "She's barely going to age. At all. It's not exactly the same, but this is essentially immortality. If nothing happens to her, she could theoretically live hundreds, potentially even thousands of years. You're almost certain to be killed by something in that length of time, but this is the most extraordinary thing I've ever seen. There is something in this related to these animals, possibly related to their resilience against the virus. Or... far worse, a potential value in its host the virus sees, which is why it chooses to spare them and only use them to spread further. This is all very troubling."

Farle's eyes bulged. He looked to me, then to Cherun again. "Are you... well of course you're sure. But... Alright. I need to wrap my head around this."

Cherun nodded to me. "It doesn't leave this room."

"I'll talk to Barth about it, if he'll listen to me. If anyone would know, it would be him."

Cherun tapped his finger on his chin and sighed. "I'm not sure if the potential gain would be worth the risk at the moment. The last thing I want to do is distract from the more important task at hand. I'm not against it. Obviously, it isn't even my call. This was your research, and a result of that research. As a courtesy to a fellow scientist, could you wait until we've resolved the virus issue? Assuming we resolve it. If he discovers the information on his own first, that's a different story. You'll have no choice then."

I nodded. "Of course. I'm not eager to approach Barth about it anyway."

"Alright. Thank you for stopping by. Both of you. We'll continue our own separate vaccine research and of course, I'll continue sharing all of my findings with you and Animal Research, asking that you continue doing the same."

I nodded, and stood to my feet. Every day, it became harder and harder to remember to shoehorn in my faux appreciation for the president.

"I'm sure the president would be proud of your dedication to making sure we get through this, Cherun."

He rolled his eyes, shooing us out with a wave of his hands.

The truth is I didn't need to approach Barth about this at all. Why had the president suddenly decided to approve the project back then? Was it only because General Markus suggested it? Of course not. Somehow, and I have no idea how, he inserted research goals of his own into the project. Without anyone noticing? So it would seem. The man was a genius, but that was expected for someone so old. How often in history did someone transfer themselves so seamlessly into the leadership position of their enemy's organization? Just how much of a threat were these people, for PanTech to allow such a thing to happen? I was beginning to wonder if PanTech was the overwhelmingly overpowering force they claimed they were.

As we walked back to the Explorers League, Farle poked my shoulder, interrupting the several minutes of silence we'd enjoyed thus far. "Harlow said Frelya's diagnostic should be complete on the machine core we sent back today. Excited?"

"Not as much as you, apparently. Kelin and Ghost have that bet going too. I'm inclined to agree with Cherun. We have more important things to worry about at the moment."

Farle pointed ahead of us, bringing my attention to a Harlow jumping up and down, waving.

"You two should just take the transport here. I was about to shake my tail off waiting for you guys!" Harlow said.

"Are the results that exciting?" Farle asked.

Harlow gasped, as if the question itself was a great insult. "Like we're going to open them without you guys!" he said, running back through the entrance and into my office.

Farle and I followed. Ghost was perched on my desk, waiting patiently. The opposite of Harlow, who opened up the data the moment we stepped inside.

I cleared my throat and read Frelya's note aloud.

"In regards to the maintenance versus pilot theory, residual data suggests both are correct. Or rather, can be correct. There are no programmed actions for this unit. Only a repository of information that remains locally accessible via the unit's vast memory. Even by our best standards at Adversity Management, we are unable to achieve this. Despite this, material degradation as well as corrosion would indicate this machine is well over a hundred years old. Perhaps hundreds."

"Unable to achieve it?" Harlow asked.

"Take a deep breath, Harlow. Let her finish," Farle said.

I sucked in a deep breath of my own. During this interruption, I'd accidentally read ahead on my own. This only made things worse…

"She… says that it is theoretically unachievable, because this memory core is an exact replica of information copied from a human brain. The human is unknown, but I don't believe this to be a robot with data built from scratch. Too much irrelevant information for possible tasks and/or duties. Despite holding all of the information one would expect to extract from a human brain, it did not appear to have awareness or a human-like consciousness. It seems to have reverted to some sort of sleepwalking-like state. I will continue to study it."

"That thing was human?" Harlow asked, far less excited now.

"No, it wasn't human," I said.

"It was a human experiment, from the machine-worshiping society of centuries past. Who would have thought they were capable of such a thing?" Farle said.

The more important question wasn't what that society was capable of, but what the president was capable of, now knowing all this. It was all self-serving all along. Secretly inserting immortality research into our animal intelligence project. These machines, showing us that they were attempting to transfer human consciousness over a hundred years ago. Well before the rebellion. It was all coming together.

And the picture it was painting was not a pleasant one.

CHAPTER 29

The past few days had turned a slight shift in the direction of optimism. The first such shift since all of this began. It seemed that, despite the fact all of this seemed impossible, there was a slim possibility we might be able to pull it off. With the new developments around Kelin and Melo, the progress Barth and Linda were making at Animal Research was proof alone that things were looking up. Of course, that's speaking very relatively. There was still a long way to go, and a short time to get there.

If there's one thing I've learned in my short life, it's that optimism often has a short lifespan, and it's most active predator is reality.

"Taylor. Wake up!"

I sat up straight in my bed, trying to clear the fog from my mind. I wasn't awake enough yet to really process anything happening. I could only tell it was Harlow.

"What time is it? What's going on?" I asked.

"Cherun sent a written letter by one of his scientists. Hand-written. I've never seen such a thing. The lady said it was an emergency and to waste no time, but ran off before I could ask her anything. I came straight here to deliver it to you." He handed it to me, and I read it aloud.

"It got out. I don't know how. It shouldn't be possible, but it did. Adversity Management guards immediately reported it to the president and have switched to protective gear. His plans were leaked back to me. By who, I don't know, but they've saved many lives. The president plans to lock us in and execute everyone in Pandemic Research, including our held subjects. They intend to transfer Kelin soon. I think he knows. This will probably be the last communication I will be able to send, and I'm not sure I'll be an exception to be spared. By the time you read this, I may already be dead. Lots of people here are sick and dying. Don't try to save us. This isn't a plea for help, but a warning. As a thank you for everything you did to help us all along. I don't blame you for anything. None of it was your fault. Lexili would have agreed. Thank you."

Harlow paced back and forth, rubbing his paw across the top of his head. Just as we thought things were about to get better, they come crashing down. Quarantining and executing an entire division? Even for PanTech, this was a stunning level of madness. Is the population problem that bad that they really don't care to lose a whole division? Do they really think those people can just be replaced? Like meaningless numbers? Evil. The president was the most evil man I'd ever known, and now I was certain of it. This was monstrous.

"Why are they transferring out Kelin? Why would they do that?" Harlow mumbled to himself as he paced.

"Harlow, listen. I think you and the others were secretly part of some kind of immortality research. Kelin is the only subject that is showing the desired results. She's essentially ageless beyond the artificial aging we did in the beginning. She doesn't age naturally."

"What?" he said, stopping and staring at me. He was trying to be understanding, but I could sense the anger on his face. "When were you going to tell me? How long have you known this?"

"I'm sorry, Harlow. Since yesterday. We just found out. We were trying to keep it quiet so the president wouldn't find out, but somehow he did anyway. We can't outwit him or stay ahead of him at all it seems. All those people…"

"I'm saving Kelin!" he said, heading toward the door.

"No! You can't. They'll kill you. Harlow, you need to listen to me."

"I'm done listening. We're not your servants, or your slaves. We have our own thoughts and feelings. PanTech may not consider us real employees, but Kelin is my friend. I won't let them play science with her like a piece of cheap meat."

"I've *never* thought of you, or Kelin, or any of the dogs and cats here as servants or slaves. You're all my friends. Kelin is my friend too. We just have to be careful. They're killing humans over there, or will be soon. They won't spare anyone. If we can just find out where they plan to transfer—"

"An imperfect plan executed in time is better than a perfect plan executed too late, Taylor. I'm asking Ghost for help. I was going to ask Farle too, but he's gone. He picked a fine time to slip away without telling anyone. Do you know where he is?"

"I don't. Let's see if we can find him. I have a feeling I may know who leaked the transfer information. They'll know where they're taking Kelin."

"That will be too late! Knowing isn't enough. She's in a

holding cell being guarded by, at the most, a couple of Adversity Management grunts. They'll prepare for the transfer, and it won't matter what we know. It has to be done *now*."

I stood up, and hugged Harlow tightly. "I… you're right. Good luck, Harlow. Tell Ghost I sent you to ask. Tell him not to worry about me, and to come to me as soon as you've gotten her out."

"We'll bring her back," he said, hugging me in return.

"I know you will. Go on. Do what you have to do. Just be careful."

Without another word, Harlow ran out.

I sat in bed, trying my best to formulate a plan quickly. It was going to be too late to save all those people in Pandemic Research. Probably too late to save Kelin.

"Taylor!" a cat rushed in, shouting. "Professor Barth and Assistant Professor Linda request your presence at Animal Research immediately. They said it's an emergency."

"Tell them I'm on my way," I said. I jumped from my bed and got dressed as quickly as I could manage, grabbing Twisted Key and running to the transport. The guards stationed here were either exceptionally calm given the circumstances, or they had no idea what was about to happen. I suspected the latter, as they gave me no trouble.

I hopped off the other side and sprinted through the halls of Animal Research.

The last thing I expected to see was a jumping and waving Linda, a big smile on her face. "Taylor! Come here. We did it!"

I ran to her, wrapping my arms around her so tight I nearly tackled her to the floor. "I love you, Linda. I'm so glad you're okay."

She laughed, patting me on the shoulders. "I love you too, Taylor, but it's just a prototype. There are still major… Wait, did something happen? Are you alright?" She pushed me away from her, looking me in the eyes.

"The virus was released in Pandemic Research somehow. They're quarantining the whole division, and the president plans to kill everyone there."

"What?" Barth said, stepping into the hall. "This isn't some trick the president asked you to use to test us, is it?"

"Barth, you have to listen to me. I'm back to normal. I'm

myself again. It was... a good friend of mine who found a way. This isn't a trick. This prototype. Let's see it, quickly."

Barth scoffed, standing up straight and running his fingers through his long, blond hair.

"It's barely a prototype, Taylor. The material we'd need to make more of these is organic and has to be grown. It can't be produced instantly. It's difficult and takes time. We have three doses that we can test on volunteers, but one needs to be preserved for redundancy. In case a formula needs to be reverse engineered."

"Is it effective?" I asked.

"Instantly, and completely. However, it permanently sterilizes human subjects in every simulation we ran it through. All of them, with every tweak we tried. We even gave the AI a shot at it with the same results. We thought at first it was because we're altering human genetics by mimicking the unique cat and dog species we created, and that it might make them compatible once a group was all vaccinated. That didn't happen."

I sighed, leaning on the wall and putting my face in my hands. "The future of humanity can't be saved with this. We'll go extinct."

"I disagree," Barth said. "It gives us a lifetime to find a solution. With that kind of time bought, we can surely find a way to restore reproductive ability to the humans in zones. Within a year, we should be able to produce enough vaccines for everyone, assuming we focus our resources."

"I... don't know if things will be stable enough for that here, Barth. The president has a complete disregard for others. He isn't listening to anyone, and the worst part is that I don't think he's crazy. I think it's according to plan. In fact, there's something I need to ask you."

"Yes? What's that?" he asked.

"Did you know the president included immortality research with our new dog and cat species experiments when he approved them?"

His eyes widened, looking between Linda and me. "He said they were some formulations he'd come up with related to aging, and that it wouldn't interfere with any of the other outcomes. He asked me to keep it a secret, and I was too starstruck by him at the time to even question it... Part of this is my fault, then."

Linda shook her head, putting a hand on his arm. "You can't

blame yourself for any of this. There's much more to it than just the animal research. We also discovered a machine that the rebels used more than a hundred years ago in a failed attempt to transfer human consciousness. The man has been self-serving from the very start. He never cared about PanTech or the future of humanity. It's possible his goal was to destroy it all along."

Why hadn't that thought occurred to me before? He was part of the rebellion, after all. What she just said is entirely possible. I knew the man was evil, but I hadn't considered that it could go that far.

"Inject me with one of the doses," I said.

"Are you crazy?" Barth asked, knocking on the top of my head with his knuckles. "Is anyone home in there? We just created it. We don't even know what all the potential long-term side effects could be. It should be tested, but we aren't there yet. It needs more time."

When I turned around, Linda was already filling a syringe. She stepped around Barth, and I raised my sleeve. She wiped my arm with disinfectant, then plunged the needle in.

"She's right, Barth, and she knows the risks."

Barth growled, spinning around and grabbing the other two vials, placing them in a small bag. "Take the other two. I know you're going to run off and do something incredibly stupid. You may need help from someone you meet along the way. I have the formula and already have every system in this room producing additional doses. I'll have more within the hour, so don't worry."

"If you use just one dose in the lab vehicle at the Explorers League, it will generate the formula, as well as the regions where ingredients can be found. If not found, how they can be grown," Linda said.

"Are you suggesting she leave? That's suicide. No one has ever escaped PanTech. They'll never let her go, Linda," Barth said.

"Stop trying to be reasonable. Just tell her goodbye. If things keep falling apart like this, you may never see her again," Linda scolded.

Barth took a deep breath, and struggled to speak. "Good luck, and thank you for everything."

"Take care of Elise if you can," I said, hugging him.

I hugged Linda again, and turned to leave. I knew who I needed to see now.

"Oh, and Taylor…"

I stopped, turning to face her.

"If you think hard about who has been leaking the information and helping us, I think you can figure it out."

I smiled. I didn't need to think all that hard about it to know. *Good work, Joyce.*

"Thanks for telling me. Please take care."

"You too," she said.

I ran for the transport. I needed to see Frelya before everything started completely locking down.

CHAPTER 30

The moment I exited the building, I was stopped by two guards. Either word was spreading, or the official orders were finally being handed down.

"Professor Taylor. Due to a developing situation, you are no longer permitted to travel freely. Return to the Explorers League and await instructions."

"Okay, I understand. I'll head there now," I lied.

Both guards moved out of my way, and I continued in the same direction. Toward the Explorers League, but also my true destination, Adversity Management. Ferris was on a long deployment, which was likely for the best. I wished I could see him now, more than ever, but he would be safer in whichever zone he was in.

I needed to see Frelya, and I needed to see her fast. However, it's one thing to convince a guard to allow me to leave. I can get away with that once by lying about heading back to my own division. It's another to allow me to enter one I clearly don't belong to after they've been locked down. Still, I'd have to find a way.

I was so focused on finding a way that I didn't notice Ghost swoop down right in front of me, breathing heavily. "Harlow got Kelin out with a team of dogs and cats."

I couldn't believe it. Almost as unbelievable as the fact he extracted her successfully, was the fact a unified team of cats and dogs followed his orders. Ghost too, apparently.

Good going, Harlow.

"Is everyone okay?"

"Harlow is badly wounded. They've evaded reinforcements and I left to avoid becoming a liability. I've also found where Farle went. He convinced at least a hundred dogs and cats over at Adversity Management to leave PanTech and warn zones to prepare for the impending virus. He should be at the Explorers League doing the same thing now. He told me animals were immune to the virus and couldn't carry it."

I couldn't have heard that right.

"Ghost. Are you positive? That's not true. Dogs and cats can get it too. They're just immune to the effects. They carry the live virus long-term. That would doom everyone if any of them have been exposed."

Ghost looked at me and tilted his head. "You should stay away from there. Leave the city, now. I can't expose myself either, or I'll expose you."

"I'm vaccinated against it, Ghost. I don't know if there will be any negative side-effects, but there wasn't time to find out. It's immediately effective." I placed my hand on the pouch. "Ghost... I could vaccinate you. I'll have one dose remaining to analyze, but I know I'm going to need your help. I don't know how the virus will affect you, because you're one-of-a-kind. I don't know how this vaccine will affect you either. You have to be the one to choose."

He answered without hesitation. "Do it quickly."

I filled a syringe, and gave it to him. I watched him for just a moment.

"Do you feel off in any way?" I asked.

"We don't have time for this, Taylor."

"You're right. Go warn Frelya. Tell her what's happening. I need to confront Farle."

"Alone?" he asked.

"Alone," I repeated. "As you said, we don't have time for this. Go... and be careful, Ghost. I'll see you soon."

He nodded, and flew away. I placed my hand on the pouch. Only one left, and I'm supposed to save this one. I barely made it out of Animal Research and already used one of the two...

But it was the right choice. I needed Ghost more than anyone.

Shaking the thought from my head, I ran to the Explorers League. The guards stood aside. This was it. They wouldn't let me out after this. Not without a fight, and there would probably be more than two.

Walking through, my stomach sank, along with my heart. There was no one here. All the dogs and cats were gone. Farle stood in the center of the camp, stirring a pot of stew.

"Sorry. All that's left is scraps, really. Some potatoes. You like potatoes, right?" he said, pretending nothing had happened.

I sat across from him, picking up and holding out a bowl for him to fill. I was fighting back tears in spite of the confusion. Was it all a misunderstanding?

"Farle, I—"

"She was my whole life, Taylor... Glimmer held the last piece of me left in my soul that cared if anyone lived or died. Myself included. The part of me that thought humanity might still have value. That it was worth continuing. That it hadn't completely lost its way. Lost its meaning."

He dipped the ladle into the stew, and dropped a few small potatoes into my bowl and handed me a fork. I picked one up, and stuffed it into my mouth. There was no fighting back the tears now. I was already beginning to piece together what he'd done, and why he'd done it.

"What about Kelin, and Harlow? What about Ghost? What about… me? How could you doom all of humanity when you love even one? Glimmer wouldn't have wanted you to—"

"There's no dissuading me, Taylor, and I'll save you the time of asking the other questions on your mind. Yes, I set the virus loose at Pandemic Research. Cherun was so trusting of me, a stranger he barely knew. It was all too easy. After finding out about the dogs and cats being immune from symptoms, but carrying the active virus indefinitely, the next thing to do was obvious. I infected myself, and have been infecting the dogs and cats ever since. I sent them away, and told them there wasn't time to prepare the proper gear or ready long-range communicators. Just in case, I've already destroyed the relay system tied to those specific communicators while I was there. I have a few more plans I'll be leaving to carry out soon. Surprised?"

I sat my bowl down on the ground, and slowly stood to my feet. I couldn't believe it. I had been developing stronger and stronger feelings for this man. I might have even loved him. He used me, and everyone else who trusted him.

I gripped the hilt of Twisted Key, and drew it from its resting place. "Not surprised. Heartbroken. Heartbroken about what you've done, and heartbroken that you've left me with no choice but to stop you."

He stood, drawing two knives from his belt. "It wasn't all a lie, Taylor. I really did care about you. I still do. We don't have to fight. You can help me end the real virus once and for all. Humanity."

"There are still people I love here, and it's for their sake… that…"

I took a step forward, bringing down my sword with intent.

Farle side-stepped, as though he'd been attacked by an

amateur. He brought down one of the knives, and with that one attack, also made it clear that he did not intend to spare my life.

I removed one hand from Twisted Key, blocking the knife with the guard and catching the knife in the palm of my other hand. The blade emerged from the back of my hand, and I screamed out in pain. I couldn't stop. I couldn't leave any openings, or have any mercy. I couldn't let the pain slow me down.

Wrapping my hand around his fist, I kept him from pulling it away. He was so much quicker than me, and skilled, that I could barely keep up with his offense and defense alike.

Twisting my sword, bringing it toward his neck in the same motion, he somehow found the time to bury the knife nearly an inch into my shoulder before withdrawing it to parry the sword before reaching his neck.

My enhancer might be better for long-term health, but his manually activated older model was clearly superior for short-term effectiveness. I was outmatched. Human reflexes couldn't match something like this.

I slammed my head into his face, causing him to take a step back. I followed up with the fastest technique I was capable of. A double-armed thrust, hoping to catch him before he fully regained his composure and his footing.

Instead, he rolled his hand across the blade, pushing it with the back of his hand, redirecting it to his side. It sliced him, but the wound created was only superficial. At first, I thought he'd dropped the knife because of the attack, but soon realized it was intentional.

He gripped my arm, pivoted, and flung me over his shoulder. The impact expelled all the air from my lungs, leaving me unable to even gasp. I could only groan. This was it. He'd won. I failed everyone…

"I wish I could spare you, Taylor. I really do, but you've left me with no choice."

He knelt above me, and I grasped in futility for the sword I'd dropped next to me. I couldn't find it, but I'd never be able to create an attack strong enough anyway.

He held the knife above his head, and as he was about to plunge it, a blur slammed into him, sending him rolling across the ground.

"Farle!" she screamed.

It was Kelin!

Farle steadied himself to one knee, but was slow.

"That was a hard hit. Someone's given you a present. Frelya's handing these out to everyone these days."

"A new version. This one's removable by the user, and can be installed into someone else. The weakest one she's ever made, but it'll be more than enough."

"I'll bet if I add it to the one I already have, I might even be strong enough to take on Frelya. Maybe even the president. I don't suppose you'll offer it to me voluntarily."

"Come and get it," Kelin hissed, pulling out the two knives on her belt.

I only just now realized that Kelin only started using them after she met Farle. She looked up to him. As tough as she was trying to be at the moment, this couldn't be easy for her either.

"I've wasted enough time here. I won't waste any more on you," Farle said, charging at Kelin with his remaining blade.

Kelin jumped through the air, flipping behind Farle. He turned, attempting to slice where Kelin should have been when she landed. Instead, she continued dropping, down to a low crouch, slicing horizontal. Then, as Farle attempted to counter, she leaped back, leaving only air for his blade to pass through.

He took a step toward her before freezing. He hadn't even noticed it at first, but Kelin had sliced through his femoral artery. I wanted to scream to tell them to stop, but I couldn't. Even if I could, I knew I shouldn't. I knew it wouldn't work. It was wishful thinking. I could only watch on helplessly, still fighting for air in my lungs, unable to even speak or crawl to my knees.

Farle knew full well the capabilities of the enhancer, redirecting function to staunch the bleeding. The problem he faced, is that he had to redirect too much, in too short a time, in order to prevent bleeding out. It was clear in his eyes. He'd already lost, and he knew it. Kelin had won with only one move.

To claim cat-like reflexes wasn't a compliment for Kelin, nor was it a special feat. Catlike reflexes were natural to her. All her reflexes were simply reflexes. Not catlike, but truly the reflexes of a cat. A human simply fell short, even with enhancement. Even without Kelin's new enhancer, I'm not sure anything would have changed.

Kelin did not allow him time to recover, charging him while

he focused on two things at once, draining the advantage of his enhancer.

He sliced forward, but Kelin delayed her charge almost imperceptibly, halting just short of the blade. With a strike as powerful as it was swift, her claws slashed across the side of his neck. She'd dropped her blade, making four slices instead of one. It was too much to stop.

"Nice one, Kelin," he choked, attempting to laugh but failing.

He fell to the ground, dead. I wanted to scream, but thought of Kelin. I sucked in, and fought hard to hold it in.

"I had to. I'm sorry, Taylor," she said, nearly a whisper. Tears were streaming down her face. "I didn't want to. I had to…"

"I'm sorry too, Kelin. You did the right thing, and you saved me. You may have saved many others too. But… I still have to ask more of you. Will you help me?"

Kelin nodded. "Just say it. I'll make sure it's done."

"There are probably cats and dogs just outside the walls, ready to depart because Farle lied to them. Stop as many as you can, and have them wait for me just outside. If I don't make it, you're in charge."

"I understand. We'll wait for you no matter how long it takes. I don't want to be in charge."

I struggled to my feet, placing both my hands on Kelin's shoulders. "I have such stubborn friends. Fine. I'll see you soon. I promise. Wait for me."

Kelin saluted, then ran toward the outside.

I picked up my sword, and sheathed it. I couldn't wait a second longer. I had to find Frelya.

Closing in on Adversity Management, I could hear shots booming like thunder. This wasn't a small encounter. It was a skirmish with multiple soldiers on each side. Had there been a split in the forces? Did the president decide to take his personal guard and attack Adversity Management? There's no way. Too many soldiers, and too well equipped. Even his elite guards wouldn't stand a chance.

As I pondered the potential scenario, the question soon answered itself. The wall surrounding Adversity Management was tall. It was meant to be a bastion in times past, in case PanTech was attacked. Now, there were arachnid model machines crawling all over it. As they emerged from the top, a barrage of rifle fire slammed into them, all while they emptied their machine guns down on the soldiers below.

Instead of a bastion, it had become an enclosure for killing. They'd been herded in like cattle, and were slaughtered no differently. The broken machines and parts lying all over the ground outside was a testament to the fight they were putting up. They weren't going to go down easy. But machines were replaceable. People weren't.

One spotted me, and I drew my sword. Encountering broken down units in the wild was completely different from a new unit fully stocked. As it ran down the wall, several soldiers emerged from within, firing their rifles. Frelya was with them.

"What's happening?" I asked. "Where's Ghost?"

Frelya grabbed me by the hand, and pulled me through the opening in the wall. She continued walking, saying nothing. The respirator over her mouth probably made it difficult to speak.

"There's a vaccine, but there's a catch. I'm immune, so don't worry about catching it from me," I said.

She turned her head half around, holding her finger to her lips.

We continued, as the soldiers fought behind us, into the science building.

Reaching her lab, she pulled the respirator from her face.

"I miscalculated. These don't seem to be working anyway. Soldiers are getting sick already."

"Frelya, I have one more. I'm supposed to save it, in case I need to reverse engineer the formula. Barth is working hard on making more. I can always catch up to him later and collect more."

"I have something for you too," she said. "See this black bodysuit I'm wearing? It's going to look great on you."

"You're joking around, at a time like this?" I asked, taking out the last vial and syringe from my pouch.

I was taking such a huge risk by doing this, but seeing her now, looking her in the eyes… I could not bear to lose her. She'd risked everything for me, more than once.

She snatched them from my hand. "Take your clothes off and put on the bodysuit. You probably already guessed, but the point of it isn't to flatter your figure. That's just a bonus. Oh, and I can't stand being injected by someone else. I'll inject myself while you change. You can change on the other side of that desk… or right here. Up to you."

I sighed, slipping off my outerwear and dropping the empty pouch, then stepping to the other side of the desk. "The full vial. Understand?"

"I understand. The suit is based on the principles of the power suit, in compact, mostly self-maintaining form. It converts and filters sweat back through the skin to keep you hydrated, for example. It will stimulate sore muscles, and provide slight support for the amount of strain any enhancer places on the body. It's stab, cut, and somewhat bulletproof. The elasticity of the material means the bullet won't go through you, but could still kill you if it's powerful enough. Barely any protection against energy rounds. Understand?"

"Do you ever get tired of being a genius?" I asked, stepping out from behind the desk.

She eyed me briefly, then quickly turned her back. "No. Oh, and you asked me about Ghost. The vaccine you gave him did a number on his nervous system. He made it here and couldn't fly again. I'm fixing that, by the way. You saw the enhancer I gave Kelin? I also gave one to him. If he loses it, he may lose his mobility again, though he may regain it naturally over time. I don't know what this vaccine's done to him, but he's stable now. He'll be up and going like new within an hour or two." She cleared her throat. "Do you have the rest of your clothes on yet?"

"All dressed. This thing is surprisingly comfortable."

She stepped toward me, her emerald, green eyes bright with

excitement, grabbing my hands and leaning in close to my face. So close our noses nearly touched.

"Want to go on an adventure with me?"

I'd mostly adjusted to her instability and unpredictability, but in serious times like this, it was still so jarring.

"What? What kind of… are you serious?"

"The president is ordering his machines to attack and kill anyone infected. That's how I realized our standard suit respirators aren't working. There's a secret path to his office through the back of his lab of horrors. It's how he'd been using it without others realizing. What do you say we pay him a visit and ask him nicely to stop killing everyone?"

She touched her forehead to mine, then suddenly let go, wrapping a belt around her waist holding two sidearms. She picked a rifle up and flung it over her shoulder.

Nicely. Right.

But she was right. It was exactly what I had in mind. I just wasn't sure how to get there. Now that I knew a way, it's where I would have gone regardless. The man had to be stopped, or there would be no one left to save. Here, or anywhere else. The way she asked, it almost sounded like a dying wish. Even if it seemed impossible, we had to survive.

"Take me on an adventure. There will be time to cry another day."

She smiled, offering me a rifle, which I took from her. Then, she placed both her hands on my face. Without warning, she stuck her fingers into my ears, making me jump. "Sound compressors. Raises the quiet, lowers the loud. If we fire our rifles in a small room, say goodbye to your hearing forever if you aren't wearing these. It's going to tenderize your organs a bit too, so you may be sore for a few days. Might get a concussion too, but I don't want to scare you too much."

I checked my rifle before slinging it on my back. "I'm not worried. I know we'll win, because you're with me. Let's go."

She grinned. A wild grin, like I remembered the first few times I met her. It was painful to see. She should have been a normal girl, not some crimson-haired, jade-eyed genius berserker. I made up my mind. Once we dealt with the president, I would ask her to come with me. There's no way I'd make it to anyone else, but I'm not sure I'd rather it be someone else anyway.

Arriving at the lab door, she unlocked it using the same method as before. It was a relief, but it also made me feel uneasy. It should have been more difficult than that.

I looked down at the floor. I knew what was in here, but didn't have the stomach to look. Frelya seemed to understand that, guiding me by the hand to the back, where she pulled down a hidden compartment and opened a secret door using the same device.

"I've never been further than this, but according to what I've found, this will bypass the main elevator and take us straight into the room behind his office."

"Full of the machines that have been attacking everyone. I'm sure there are still some there, so we have to be careful stepping out," I said.

We stepped onto a small platform, activated by a button on the rail near the wall. We quickly shot forward, changing direction slightly and curving to the left. Then rose up a narrow hallway at a sharp incline.

The door at the top opened, and we stepped out, unslinging our rifles as we did.

We'd come out in the large room, which no doubt had many other secret tunnels leading to and from other divisions.

The president stood in front of a large control panel, his hands clasped casually behind his back, watching events unfold all across PanTech.

"It looks much worse than it is," he said, without turning to look at us. "Once all the infected are neutralized, things will go back to normal quickly. This was always a possible, and acceptable outcome. We can recruit more talented individuals from the adversity zones, essentially putting a big dent in the overpopulation problem at the same time. Clever, no?"

"You've clearly lived for too long," Frelya said, raising her rifle.

He laughed, turning and looking at me.

"Taylor. Kill her."

I stood rigid, and for a moment, a fear gripped me that I would actually follow the order. But, it seemed whatever Frelya did to reverse the reeducation process also disabled whatever had been etched into my mind to make me follow these orders.

"Oops. Maybe you should try speaking up," Frelya said.

"Why are you just standing there? I gave you the order to kill her. Shoot her. Now!"

I raised my rifle, pointing it at him.

"Oh, you really are clever. I don't know how you've done it, but clearly I was right not to trust you. I wanted Taylor to hate you more than anything, but it seems you found a way to save her anyway. It's endearing, really. Did you know I originally immersed myself in robotics in order to save the woman I loved? I failed, of course. It was impossible then, but now…"

"What use is technology to bring back the people you love, if everyone you love is dead?" I asked.

"You're so young, Taylor. If a human lives long enough, they mature beyond small concepts like love and hate, and gain immense insight into the unseen world. The practical. The logical. I don't even need new recruits to fill PanTech. I don't even need other humans. I can fill it with… well… me."

"Not even you can survive two consecutive rifle blasts from this distance. Since you care about yourself so much, disable the machines, and surrender. I'd have killed you by now, but I know it has to be you who disables them. I have ways of making you do it voluntarily, you know. I won't hold back, either," Frelya said. A heavy threat, coming from her. I believed it, and no doubt he did as well.

He laughed, a full belly laugh, taking a sidearm that was lying on the panel and holding it in the air.

"This isn't going to go the way you think it is, Frelya. You play chess like a grandmaster, but I'm afraid it's checkmate already. It's been that way long before you arrived. And now, I'll show you…"

He held the blaster to his head, and fired, stunning both of us. We looked at one another, our eyes wide.

"…what a true genius is capable of," the voice continued his original sentence, but from a large machine stepping out of the shadows. Humanoid, but massive.

Frelya grabbed me by the arm. Her hands were trembling, and she guided me around the room. I saw where she was going. An escape pod!

"Good call. We need to get out of here," I said, standing inside the door of the pod as she opened it with the same device we'd used to make it this far.

When I turned, she shoved the pouch I'd been using to carry the vaccines into my chest, and shoved me hard into the pod. I fell back hard, sitting up just in time to see her using the device to shut the door behind her.

"I will never let her escape, no matter what you do. Your efforts are wasted!" the machine roared.

"Taylor… I'm sorry. I'm sending you straight to the wall where your friends will be. Fight! Fight the pursuers with everything you've got, and live to see tomorrow. I'll handle this thing," Frelya said through the transparent door.

"No!" I looked in the pouch. She never took the vaccine. She never intended to. "No. No. No! Not without you! Frelya, open this door right now. I can't do this without you!" I choked on my words through the flow of tears. My heart felt as though it would burst.

"You can't do this without me, and that's why I have to stay. Do what you do best, Taylor. Help people. Thank you. For everything."

She hit the panel again, and I screamed, reaching out for her.

The pod shot from its platform, and into the main tube system, in overdrive. It flew so hard that it broke through the stopping mechanism, through the doors, and broke into pieces on the hard ground several yards beyond. I rolled and flipped, getting struck by materials from the pod, and scraping across the surface. No doubt I'd have been ripped to shreds without this body suit. Even the rifle was in pieces.

I turned, looking back toward the president's tower, and was met with a sea of glowing red eyes. Arachnid units swarmed down the wall, fixated on me as they crawled. More than I'd ever seen. Fifty, at least.

I could barely stand, but I had to. I fought to balance myself. I was alive, but riddled with injuries. Somehow I found it within me to make it to my feet and stumble toward the gate. As I got close, it flung open, and Kelin ran toward me, catching me before I fell again.

"Taylor, are you alright?" she asked.

"Kelin…" I squeaked. "Look…"

Kelin tilted her head. "What is it?"

"Up…" I finally managed to say, with effort.

Kelin looked up, and her eyes dilated into saucers. She hissed. "Harlow, massive incoming! Fifty plus arachnids, top class!

Prepare for combat on the run!" She picked me up, and ran through the gate.

Frelya...

Why?

CHAPTER 32

I raised my head, looking at what was left. Hundreds of dogs and cats remained, hesitant to follow Farle's instructions. Unlike the hundreds from Adversity Management who followed orders without hesitation, probably already arriving at adversity zones to unknowingly spread the virus, believing they are helping. The very thought made me sick. Yet another monster created by PanTech, but this time the monster eats the creator.

"Is she conscious?" Harlow asked.

"Take her to the lab. She's going to need it. You lead the vanguard. I'll lead the rear guard."

Impossible. There were at least fifty of those arachnid units closing in. We didn't stand a chance.

Kelin handed me off to Harlow, and he ran to the new lab vehicle.

"Harlow, are you still hurt?" I asked weakly.

"Yep. But I have something way more interesting to tell you," he said. "Just need to get you into the bed first."

"No… the passenger seat. We're in this together. I'm hurt. You're hurt. We all fight together."

Harlow smiled, placing me gently in the seat. "There's a cocktail next to you, waiting. We prepared. More than you know. We stand a chance, Taylor. This isn't an impossible battle. It's an uphill one, but we can win."

I remembered the vaccine, and quickly checked my pouch. By some miracle, it remained undamaged. I sighed with relief, picking up the medic cocktail and stabbing it into my neck.

"What have you and your arch nemesis come up with now?"

"Best friend," he corrected. "Kelin and I have decided that we're best friends now."

"Wow, that's… quite a twist from your old relationship," I said, trying to make light of a situation I still believed was impending, certain death. At least I wouldn't be alone.

"Well, for starters…" He pressed a button on the dash. "Everyone, follow my lead. We deploy at maximum speed. Rear guard, you are under Kelin's orders. Trust her with your life."

"Impressive. You did that in no time at all," I said as Harlow laid on the accelerator a bit too enthusiastically. I tried to keep what was left in my stomach where it was.

"No. We did this yesterday. Kelin and I share in a bit of paranoia. Well… her paranoia has grown on me. What's wrong with being prepared? So we set up short-range, encrypted communication between all our vehicles."

"I understand installing the system, but I'm surprised the two of you could make it."

"Make it? No… that was Frelya. She's helped quite a bit in secret. Especially when you were… not yourself."

I buried my face into my hands, and couldn't hold back the tears anymore.

Harlow placed his paw on my back.

"I know… I'm sorry, Taylor. I saw what was happening when you shot out of the tower. We know she stayed behind."

"Did you see what happened after?" I asked, sniffling and trying to hold everything in again.

"They started fighting, but moved out of view. Sorry. I don't know what happened."

"She's going to win. We'll see her again," I said.

Harlow nodded enthusiastically before we were interrupted.

"First units making contact. Rear guard engaging," Kelin's voice said.

I could hear the gunfire being exchanged.

"Good luck, Kelin. Update us as often as possible." He looked over at me. "Music?"

"What?" I asked.

"I've got all kinds of tunes. You know I like to listen while I work. Biggest hits from the last thousand years on here. You know, I'm even thinking of making a radio station when all of this is over. They used to do that to deliver news and play music."

He was definitely nervous. His body betrayed his words as his paws trembled and his leg shook.

"Sounds good. You pick," I said.

Harlow flipped a switch and ran his paw across a screen. The gentle hum of a cello filled the space around us. It was oddly comforting, but not what I thought he'd pick. I was expecting some kind of Harlow-heavy-battle music.

"The human who played this died in prison. He opposed the mechanization of humanity, but never hurt anyone. Copper Clementine was his name. There are hundreds of thousands of more like him, specks of dust on the old table of history."

"That's surprisingly profound, coming from you," I pressed on my sore spots, relieved that the cocktail was beginning to work.

"Hey, what's that supposed—"

"We've destroyed eight units. Lost two vehicles and about ten cats and dogs so far," Kelin said. "They're… behaving strangely. They're not staggering their approach anymore. I think… I think they're grouping up for a unified attack, Harlow."

"I hear you," Harlow said, sighing, then turning to me. "We have a little surprise for them if they do that. Don't worry. We still have a chance."

"It's a central command. These arachnid drones aren't smart enough to come up with that strategy on their own."

Harlow nodded. "I know…"

"Cluster incoming. All of them at once. Hit the brakes Joker unit. Harlow, activate it on my word," Kelin said.

"English?" I asked.

Harlow grinned. "Unmanned vehicle in the center of the escape group. Okay, I can't keep it a surprise any longer. Kelin and I made the biggest EMP you've ever heard of. We used the EMPs from the machines, collected them, and wired up a kind of massive EMP cluster bomb. This isn't your grandmother's EMP."

"My grandmother didn't have an EMP. That's dangerous, Harlow. How do you know the thing won't explode and kill all of us?"

"Perfect situation to test it in, don't you think? Certain death versus almost certain death."

I nodded. "You have a point."

Kelin's voice came in. "Harlow, they're doing something strange again. I think they're moving beside us to try to… No, now they're… What? Now! Hit it now!"

Harlow nodded at me. "Kelin. Taylor. Everyone. It's been an honor," Harlow slammed his paw on a button above him.

We waited a moment. Nothing.

"Did it work?" I asked.

"Save the speech, Harlow. Hit it, now! We're getting slaughtered!" Kelin screamed.

"I did!" Harlow yelped, hitting it again.

Kelin hissed. "Oh no… Harlow, keep going. Everyone else, stay behind with me. We have to stop and fight. They've almost surrounded us. Harlow, break through and don't look back."

Harlow trembled, looking between the button and me, breathing heavily.

"I…"

"I'm not going to give you an order. Neither can Kelin. Do what's in your heart, Harlow," I said.

If I knew the right choice to make, maybe I would've given the order. But we'd run out of right choices. A long time ago. We were grasping at smoke in the darkness.

Harlow stopped the vehicle.

"What are you doing? If you don't keep going, I'll never forgive you!" Kelin screamed.

"I'm sorry, Kelin," he said, opening the transport door and turning to me. "I'm going to detonate it manually. Cover me," he said, tossing me a rifle as I stepped out. "Only Kelin and I know how, and she's a bit busy at the moment."

I nodded and stepped fully into the carnage. The landscape we'd visited many times, once so green and beautiful, now littered with blood and metal. We'd lost so many. There were dead dogs and cats everywhere. Even if we survived, no one would ever be the same after this…

"Try to keep up. Our target is that antenna on top of that vehicle in the center. Come with me, but stay back a few hundred yards. You'll need to be accurate with your rifle within that distance. Think you can do it?"

"I can do whatever you need me to do, Harlow. Lead on!"

We ran through the carnage, dodging bullets and shrapnel, explosions, cats and dogs running from one target to another. Until finally, we arrived at the center.

"Stay here! When I start climbing, it'll draw attention. Take it off me."

He continued running, climbing up the vehicle that housed the antenna. At the base of the antenna was a series of devices, connected neatly by wires. This must be the EMP device he mentioned.

Immediately, one targeted him, rotating its gun toward him. I shot it, causing it to target me instead. I had to run for cover.

As I did, another targeted him. I took a hit in the side. The suit saved me, but my ribs were certainly broken. Worse, it flung me to the ground, causing me to drop my rifle. Through the pain, I picked it back up. I fired at the other, bringing its attention to me as well. Harlow had taken a shot and was bleeding, but kept climbing. He reached the top, and grabbed a lever. Too many were targeting him now. I couldn't shoot them all. I used my enhancer, switching targets as quickly as possible, but the gun overheated as I put it through more stress than a normal human likely ever would.

He gripped the lever, and pulled it hard, taking several more shots as he did. I threw the gun to the ground and drew Twisted Key. I'd run between them if I had to.

I ran up the closest one, slicing every weak point I'd memorized, severing the control box from the body when I reached the top, severing the optics just in case. I turned to move to the next one, when I saw Harlow flip the lever from the corner of my eye. He looked at me, smiled, and offered a weak salute.

The device activated, knocking me off the machine and onto the ground.

My head felt like my brain had been turned to soup. I was seeing double, and could barely decipher what direction I was facing or moving.

Kelin's voice snapped me back to reality.

"You have about one minute! Disable every remaining unit, but mind the scrap!"

Cats and dogs swarmed the slouched machines, severing all their vital connections as I just had. I fought to my feet, and joined them, sprinting and leaping as quickly as my legs would carry me. I cut, and cut, and cut. Until that was all that occupied my mind. One minute. It would never be enough time, but… it would be close.

I saw Kelin only once, like a blur, focusing all her attention on units as they began to reactivate.

Fluid sprayed from every machine, until it misted over the battlefield like sickening rain, covering up the blood and tears.

I collapsed to my knees, exhausted, spent beyond my limit.

I saw Kelin standing atop one of the machines, looking around desperately. This continued, until she'd scanned every direction dozens of times.

Eventually, she raised her paw into the air.

"Victory!" she screamed. Wails and barks followed, almost deafening. We'd lost so many, but more than half had survived. It was nothing short of a miracle. We should all be dead by now, but here we were. Alive.

"Harlow!" I said, fanning through the smoke. "You did it! It worked. We won. Harlow!"

Kelin jumped down from the machine, and ran toward the center, slowing to a walk. She looked at me, then fell to her knees. Was she hurt?

I ran to see what was the matter, and saw Harlow. He was covered in blood, lying on the ground. Dead.

I gasped, covering my mouth.

Kelin scooped him up into her arms and hugged him tightly.

The remaining cats and dogs gathered around us, draping their arms around one another, forming a circle.

At first, the howling started, then the wailing from the cats joined in. It gave me chills.

I was inside the circle, but could barely bring myself to look at those around me.

I approached Kelin, and put my hand on her shoulder. "He was a great friend. And a hero in the end, wasn't he? We only made it because of him. Oh, Harlow…"

She touched her head to his, and cried.

"He was a hero. I look around us and all I can think is that it must be some kind of miracle we survived, but it's not. It's friends like Harlow… and Frelya, Lexili, Cherun, Linda, even Joyce… and so many others. And you, Kelin, and all the other heroes who are still alive, and even more those who aren't. Everyone here. All of you gave everything. You could have ran before the machines came, but you didn't. I'd be dead so many times by now if it wasn't for everyone who helped. Thank you. All of you. Every one of you."

I finally forced my head up, looking at each of them.

Every one of them saluted.

"Spoken like a true leader," Kelin said, gently lowering Harlow to the ground before standing and saluting herself. "Leader! Your orders?"

Ghost swooped down, landing next to me, covered in the viscous fluid from the machines. I was so happy he'd made it. He didn't say anything, but he didn't need to. All of us here were thinking and feeling the same thing.

I took a deep breath, and gave my first orders.

EPILOGUE

One Week Later

"I'm afraid this is all we managed to make it out with," Linda said, "But we continue to lose more because of the virus. Those who weren't already infected before the vaccine have been fine, but it's still running its course. We're vaccinating everyone just in case."

"Of those who made it out, how many do you think will make it?" I asked.

Linda shrugged, looking at the wounded and sick all around her. "I don't know. A hundred. Maybe. We plan to try getting more out, but the machines have the city locked down. For some reason, they're replenishing very slowly. Something severely hampered them, otherwise we'd be swarming with hundreds by now. As it is, the dogs and cats are doing a great job dispatching them shortly after they leave the wall. Once we've gotten all we can, we're thinking of integrating into nearby adversity zones and helping there. Once we're sufficiently quarantined as a group."

I nodded. "Soon, the dogs and cats will be able to make contact with you, but they'll never be able to go to the zones unless we can vaccinate everyone. It's going to take a while since my lab is our only way of producing it."

"You need to go soon, and liberate every zone you can."

"I just… wanted to see if she made it. If any of my other friends made it."

Linda frowned, squeezing my arm.

"I'm sorry."

I shook my head.

"The only person who has anything to be sorry for is the president. At least some part of him made it, since the machines are still coming. Frelya must've done a number on his little factory too. I know I probably won't ever see her again, but… I just wish… No. There's no going back, and no one to grant our wishes. She's gone, and I have to accept that. Are you sure you'll be okay without me?"

"Now that we've made enough vaccines for everyone, it's alright. We'll figure something out. PanTech is lost, and the dogs and cats from Adversity Management have probably made contact with nearly every zone by now. I think you've probably realized it…"

"Yeah… humanity is going to go extinct in a generation. But that doesn't mean we can't leave a better legacy for those who will come after. The dogs and cats have seen true human selfishness and evil, but also our heroism and compassion, and love. We need to keep showing them what made humanity worthwhile. Even if we can't save it, we can give a better life to those who are left and their children, before they grow old and die too. When the last human takes their last breath, I want the world we leave behind to be a better one than men like the president would have given them."

Linda nodded, giving me a hug. "We're all proud of you, Taylor. I know I probably won't ever see you again, but I want you to know—"

Henry ran up and wrapped his arms around my leg.

"Don't leave without telling me goodbye, Taylor. I'll cry!"

I smiled, patting Henry on the head. "I'd never do that, Henry. Of course I was going to tell you goodbye first."

"Are you sure you don't want me to come, Taylor?" he asked, looking up at me.

"They need you here. Only you and Ghost could be vaccinated before getting infected. Ghost will be coming with me to keep me company since the other dogs and cats can't, and you can keep the surviving humans company. I can't think anyone better for the job."

He wiped his eyes with his paw. "I will do it."

"Do you think your dogs and cats will be able to catch up with the others, and bring all of them together? They can't fight the machines forever. They're organic."

"Organic, but capable of having children, unlike the human employees at PanTech. They're allocating some of the population to live in communities, to raise children, who will one day join them fighting the machines."

Linda frowned. "That's no kind of life, Taylor."

"I know. One day, when they win, I hope there's still room in their hearts for a peaceful world. I know I may not live to see it, but one day, one of those animals is going to walk into PanTech for the final time, and disable whatever is creating those machines. I feel it in my bones."

I placed a helmet on my head, adjusting the straps, and hopped on the seat of my land cycle.

"Between that thing and the lab vehicle, you should have plenty of mobility and everything you need to survive. Don't hesitate to return if you ever need anything from us."

I smiled. "I know it sounds insane, looking at the world around us… but live a good life, Linda."

"Live a good life, Taylor," she said, smiling and waving.

I rode out toward the lab vehicle, where I'd revert this bike to its compacted form and drive to who knows where. If I'm going to visit all of them, I may as well start with the closest.

It was time to save what was left of humanity from a terrible death from the virus, and let them live out their lives free of PanTech's tyranny for the first time.

First stop… Arc City.

NEW BOOK RELEASES

Thank you for reading the *PanTech Trilogy*! If you'd like for us to write more in this series, let us know in your review! We'd be thrilled to continue!

Sign up for our newsletter for updates on new releases at:

twistedkeypublishing.com

mrbrogath.com

You may also follow the authors on Amazon and Goodreads for updates on works-in-progress and Goodreads giveaways.

DETECTIVE TRIGGER SERIES

If you enjoyed reading about the world of *PanTech*, you may enjoy M.A. Owens *Detective Trigger* series, set in the future. Get *Mister Big* for free at mrbrogath.com/free